THE BLACKWELL PAGES

THE BLACKWELL PAGES
BOOK 1

K. L. ARMSTRONG
MELISSA MARR

Little, Brown and Company
New York Boston

Text copyright © 2013 by Kelley Armstrong and Melissa Marr
Interior illustrations copyright © 2013 by Vivienne To
Text in excerpt from *Odin's Ravens* copyright © 2014 by K.L.A. Fricke, Inc. and Melissa Marr
Illustrations in excerpt from *Odin's Ravens* copyright © 2014 by Vivienne To
Shield and logo by Eamon O'Donoghue based on the work of Lisseth Kay

Little, Brown and Company

Hachette Book Group
1290 Avenue of the Americas, New York, NY 10104
Visit our website at lb-kids.com

Little, Brown and Company is a division of Hachette Book Group, Inc.
The Little, Brown name and logo are trademarks of Hachette Book Group, Inc.

The publisher is not responsible for websites
(or their content) that are not owned by the publisher.

First Paperback Edition: April 2014
First published in hardcover in May 2013 by Little, Brown and Company

Library of Congress Cataloging-in-Publication Data

Armstrong, K. L. (Kelley Lorene), 1968–
  Loki's wolves / by K. L. Armstrong and M. A. Marr.—1st ed.
     p. cm.—(The Blackwell pages ; 1)
  Summary: "Matt Thorsen is a direct descendent of the order-keeping god Thor, and his classmates Fen and Laurie Brekke are descendents of the trickster god Loki. When Ragnarok—the apocalypse—threatens, the human descendents of the gods must fight monsters to stop the end of the world."—Provided by publisher
     ISBN 978-0-316-20496-5 (hc) — ISBN 978-0-316-20497-2 (pb)
   [1. Adventure and adventurers—Fiction. 2. Supernatural—Fiction. 3. Shapeshifting—Fiction.
4. Gods—Fiction. 5. Monsters—Fiction. 6. Mythology, Norse—Fiction.] I. Marr, M. A.
(Melissa A.), 1972– II. Title.
  PZ7.A76638Lok 2013
  [Fic]—dc23

                                                                                    2012029851

14

LSC-C

Printed in the United States of America

Melissa: To Dylan—
This one is for you and because of you
(also, yes, there will be goats).

K. L.: To Alex and Marcus—
Whatever parental horrors I may inflict on
you guys as you move into teenhood, I will never
make you fight a giant serpent. I promise.

ONE

MATT

"CONFRONTATION"

Matt walked through the center of Blackwell, gym bag in hand, jacket thrown over his shoulder. It was dark now, with an icy wind from the north, but the cold felt good blowing back his sweat-soaked hair. After two hours of boxing practice, he'd been tempted to take a detour and jump in the Norrström River, even if he had noticed ice on it that morning. Ice in September. Weird. Even in South Dakota, winter never came *this* early.

A muscle spasmed in his leg, and he winced as he stopped to rub it. The upcoming tournament might be for charity—raising money to help tsunami victims in Hawaii—but Coach

Forde still made Matt work as hard as he would before a title match.

Matt started walking again, limping slightly. As much as he wished he could call for a ride, he knew better. He'd made that mistake last winter, when Coach had said a blizzard was coming. He'd gotten his ride—and a lecture on how his brothers had never needed one, even when it *was* storming. He couldn't catch a lift with his friends, either—that was worse because it set a bad example. If Sheriff Thorsen's boys weren't safe walking through Blackwell at night, who was?

Matt was reaching down to rub his leg again when something moved in the town square. His head shot up, eyes narrowing. Outside the rec center, two kids climbed onto the weathered Viking longship. Shields lined both sides as if invisible warriors rowed the old wooden boat, protection always within reach. A carved dragon arched from the hull.

The kids were probably setting up a prank, trying to beat the one Matt had done with his friend Cody at Sigrblot, the spring festival. The parade had arrived at the longship to find it covered in a tarp...and making honking noises. Underneath the tarp, they'd discovered a flock of geese wearing little Viking helmets.

Best prank ever, that's what everyone said. Unfortunately, Matt had to pretend he didn't have anything to do with it. If his parents had found out...well, they wouldn't ground him or anything. He'd just get "the talk." How disappointed they were. How embarrassed they were. How much more responsible his brothers were. Personally, he'd rather be grounded.

In a few more steps, he saw that one of the kids was a guy with shaggy brown hair that needed cutting and clothes that needed washing. With him was a girl. Her clothes weren't in such rough shape, but her blond hair needed a trim just as badly.

Fen and Laurie Brekke. Great. The cousins were always getting into trouble. Still, Matt told himself they really might just be pulling a prank... until he saw Fen wrench at one of the shields.

There were a lot of things Fen could do and Matt would just look away, tell himself it was none of his business. That wasn't always easy. Being the sheriff's kid meant he'd had lectures about vandalism since he was old enough to carve his name into a park bench. But this wasn't a park bench. It was an actual longship—something the people in Blackwell were really proud of. And there was Fen, yanking on it and kicking at it.

As Matt's temper flared, his amulet flared with it. He reached for the silver pendant. It was in the shape of an upside-down hammer and almost as old as the longship. Thor's Hammer. Everyone in Matt's family had one. Thorsen wasn't just their name. They really *were* descendants of the Norse god.

As Matt looked at Fen and Laurie again, his amulet

burned hotter. He was about to yell at them, then he stopped and took deep breaths, sucking in cold air.

He could hear his mother's voice. *You need to learn to control it, Matty. I don't know why you have so much trouble with that. No other Thorsen has this problem. Your brothers could handle theirs even when they were younger than you.*

Controlling his temper—and Thor's Hammer—seemed especially hard around the Brekkes. It was like the Hammer knew they were related to the trickster god Loki. The cousins didn't know that, but Matt did, and he could feel it when he looked at them.

Matt took another deep breath. Yes, he needed to stop Fen and Laurie, but he had to be cool about it. Maybe he could just walk past, pretend he didn't notice them, and they'd see *him* and take off before they were caught.

Fen spotted him. Matt continued walking, giving them a chance to sneak off. Being fair. His dad would be proud—

Fen turned back to the longship and yanked on the shield again.

"Hey!" Matt called.

He didn't say it too loud, and he tried not to sound too angry. Just letting them know he saw them, giving them time to run...

"Yeah?" Fen turned and stared straight at him, chin up, shoulders back. He was shorter than Matt. Skinnier, too. The only "big" thing about Fen was his attitude, which was always getting him into fights with larger guys...not that he seemed to mind.

Laurie stepped beside her cousin. Matt couldn't see her expression, but he was sure it matched Fen's. They weren't going to walk away. He'd been stupid to think they would.

"You shouldn't be doing that." Even as Matt said the words, he wanted to smack himself. It was exactly the kind of thing everyone expected the sheriff's kid to say. By tomorrow, everyone at school would have heard Fen and Laurie repeat it with a twist of their lips and a roll of their eyes.

Matt cleared his throat. "It's an artifact, and it's really important to the town." Yeah, like *that* sounded better.

"Really important to *your* town," Fen said. "Thorsen-town."

"Just...don't do it, okay?"

"But I want to. And if you want to stop me..." Fen stepped forward, giving a grin that was all teeth, and for a second, Matt thought he saw—

Matt shook it off. "Look, I'm just asking—"

"The answer's no." Fen jumped out of the ship with a leap that would make an Olympic athlete proud. "So what are you gonna do about that, Thorsen?"

Matt's amulet heated again. He took a deep breath. *Cool it. Just cool it.*

He remembered something Coach Forde had said during practice. He'd been trying to teach Matt how to intimidate an opponent. *You're a big guy,* he'd said. *Use that.*

It was hard for Matt to remember how big he was. At home, he only came up to his brothers' shoulders. But he *was* the tallest kid in eighth grade.

"What am I going to do?" Matt squared his shoulders, flexed, and stepped forward. "Stop you."

Something flashed in Fen's eyes, something cold and hard that made Matt hesitate, but only for a second. He finished his step, stopped in front of Fen, and pulled himself up to his full height.

Laurie climbed out of the ship and moved up beside her cousin. She leaned in and whispered something. Egging him on, Matt was sure.

Fen waved her off. When she hesitated, he said something so low it was almost a growl. Laurie looked at Matt, then backed into the shadows of the longship.

Fen moved forward. "You think you can fight, just because you've won a few in the ring? That's not *real* fighting. I bet you've never thrown a punch without gloves on."

"Then your memory sucks, because I'm pretty sure I beat the snot out of you and Hunter when you two ganged up on Cody."

Fen gave a short bark of a laugh. "That was what? First grade? I've learned a few things since then, Thorsen."

Matt took another step. He was sure Fen would back down. He had to. Taking on Matt was crazy. He hadn't just "won a few in the ring." He'd made it all the way to the state championship.

But Fen just planted his feet far enough apart to keep steady if he got hit. He wanted to fight. Really fight. Matt should have known that. Mom always said this is what got him into trouble—he never thought things through.

If he got into it with Fen, his dad would…Matt inhaled sharply. He didn't even want to think what his dad would do.

The power of respect. The power of authority. That's what let Thorsens walk through Blackwell at night. *Not* the power of violence. If he fought Fen Brekke, his dad would haul him in front of the council and let them handle it. The humiliation would be worse than any punishment they'd order.

"You really want to do this?" Matt asked.

Fen cracked his neck, tilting it side to side, and said, "Yeah, I do."

"Well, too bad. I've got a big match coming, and I need to save my strength for a real opponent."

Matt started to turn. As he did, he heard a growl like a dog's, and he saw Fen lunge, eyes glinting yellow, teeth bared. Matt wheeled. The heat of the amulet flared in a wave of fury that turned his world red.

He felt the power surge down his arm. Heard the crackle. Saw his hand light up and tried to pull the power back.

Too late.

The white-hot ball shot from his hand and exploded with a boom and a blast of wind that sent Matt tripping backward. Fen flew right off his feet. He hit the longship hard, his head whipping back, striking the side with a thud. Then he crumpled to the ground.

Laurie yelled something, but Matt couldn't hear the words. She raced to her cousin. Matt did the same. Laurie dropped beside Fen, took him by the shoulder, and shook him. Fen groaned, his eyelids fluttering.

"Is he okay?" Matt said, crouching beside her.

She stood up, lifted her bag like she was about to slug him with it. "You knocked him *out*."

"I didn't mean to. I'm sorry. I—"

"I don't know what kind of trick that was. Throwing that light thing to blind him before you hit him? You call that fair?" She scowled. "Exactly what I'd expect from a Thorsen."

"I didn't—"

"Whatever. Just go. Fen's not swiping anything tonight." She looked at him. "Or do you want to call your dad to lock us up?"

"Of course not. I just—" Matt swallowed. "We should get him to the doctor."

"You think he can afford a doctor?"

"I can. I'll—"

"We don't need anything from *you*. Just go away," Laurie snapped.

"But if he's—"

"Go. Get out of here."

He pushed to his feet and hesitated, but she was still glaring at him, and Fen was coming to. Matt probably didn't want to be around when Fen woke up. So he mumbled another apology, backed away, and left them alone.

TWO

LAURIE

"CHANGES"

Laurie helped Fen up from the ground. Her cousin wasn't ever good at accepting help, and being knocked on his butt by Matt Thorsen of all people wasn't helping matters. The two of them had a natural dislike of one another that she didn't always understand, but *this* time, she got it. Matt was a jerk.

"I'm going to kill him," Fen snapped for the third time in as many minutes. "He thinks he's so special, but he's just a spoiled rich kid."

"I know."

"I could take him." Fen climbed back over the side of the ship.

She didn't tell Fen he was wrong. She wasn't going to be disloyal, but they both knew Matt was a better fighter. Matt was like a Rottweiler to Fen's back-alley mutt: the mutt might try its best, but the bigger, stronger dog was the one likely to win.

All she said was, "We need to get out of here before he tells his dad and we get arrested."

He ignored her and continued ranting, "We'll see who's smart when I find him alone after school."

"Getting arrested *or* getting detention isn't going to make you seem very smart," she said, as calmly as she could.

"Maybe I won't get caught." Fen stared down at her. He had the bag in one hand, and the other hand rested on the shield he'd been prying loose when they'd gotten to the park.

Laurie dropped her gaze to the weathered ship that stood outside the Thorsen Community and Recreation Center. "What were you thinking? We could've ducked. I know you saw him."

"I'm not afraid of him." Fen stood aboard the ship and stared out at the town.

Laurie shivered. It wasn't hard to think of Fen as a Viking Raider. She wasn't shaking as badly as she'd been when she'd told Matt to shove off, but she still felt all twitchy, like the time she'd grabbed a frayed electrical cord in Uncle Eddy's garage. She stared up at Fen. "His dad is the *sheriff*. He could send you away . . . or tell the mayor. You know Mayor Thorsen hates our family."

"I'm not afraid of any Thorsens." Fen straightened his shoulders and gave her a look that reminded her of Fen's dad, her uncle Eddy, which wasn't a good thing. Uncle Eddy never backed down from a challenge. She might not know exactly what he'd done to end up in prison, but she'd bet it had started with a challenge.

He tugged on the shield. "I can't get it loose."

"Just leave the shield alone!" She rubbed her hands again.

"Fine." He hopped over the side of the ship and came to stand beside her.

Laurie didn't always understand her cousin, but she knew that he had a stubborn streak that led him—and often her—into trouble. That wasn't what they needed. "Matt's not worth the hassle."

With a soft snort, Fen said, "You got that right."

"So you'll stay away from him *and* the shield? I don't want you to get into anything." She looked at him, hoping for a promise that didn't come, and when he stayed stone-silent, she gently bumped her head into his shoulder and immediately felt silly.

But then Fen butted her head with his and said, "I'm okay."

She paused. That's what she'd meant, some combination of *I'm worried, you fool. Are you okay?* and *Talk to me.* Fen got it. Her dad's side of the family always seemed better at communicating without words. Her dad did, too—when he was around, at least, which these days wasn't very often.

"Come on," he said. "You need to get home anyhow."

They started toward her apartment building. She wouldn't have time to walk Fen home, but even if she did, he wouldn't let her. He was the older brother she didn't have, determined to protect her even as he drove her crazy. Most of the Brekke side of the family treated her like she was something to be shielded. Even though she didn't see them, she knew they watched out for her. No one at school ever gave her grief, and she was pretty sure that Fen had let it be known that he'd pummel anyone who started anything with her.

"I miss seeing everyone," Laurie said quietly. Aside from Fen, she only really got to see her dad's family when she passed them in town. Fen was in her class, so they saw each other at school, but there were no family barbecues, no parties, no even stopping by for a chat. Her mother stayed clear of the Brekkes, and since her dad was off on one of his neverending trips, Laurie wasn't able to be around the family, either.

"Everyone misses you, too...and Uncle Stig." Fen didn't mention her half brother, Jordie, or her mom, of course. The Brekkes hadn't quite rejected Jordie, but he wasn't *family* to them. He was proof that her mother and father had separated, that her mother had tried to move on, but that hadn't worked out. Now, her mom let her dad move back in every time he came to town. *He* treated Jordie like a son, not as much as he did with Fen, but still he accepted Laurie's brother. The rest of the Brekkes weren't that cool.

"Has Uncle Stig called lately?" Fen asked. There was so much hope in his voice that Laurie wished, not for the first time, that her dad would try to remember to call Fen, too. Of course, he didn't remember to call her most of the time, so expecting him to do much else was silly.

"A few weeks ago. He's coming to see me soon. That was what he said, at least." Laurie ducked her head.

Fen nudged her with his shoulder. "He'll come."

"Unless he doesn't," Laurie added. Both were equally likely. Her father came and went as the mood struck him; he called or sent presents if he thought of it.

"Maybe he'll stay for a while," Fen suggested.

And Laurie knew the part he didn't say, *and then I can stay with you.* Fen had no real home. Uncle Eddy had been locked up the past few years for some crime no one would talk about in front of either of them, and Aunt Lillian had packed her bags years ago. Fen moved between the relatives like a bag of hand-me-down clothes. When Laurie's father was around for a while, he was likely to invite Fen to live with them. Once he left, Fen moved out. Laurie's mother never *said* he had to go, but Fen always did—and her mother never stopped him.

"Can you just try not to fight with Matt? Or anyone?" she blurted.

Fen stopped, gave her a look, and then resumed walking.

"It'll be easier if you don't fight with him." She grabbed Fen's forearm. "Mom worries about your influence on Jordie, and if Dad does stay, it'd be nice if you came home, too."

They rounded the corner and were almost at her apartment building. The drab beige building sat like a squat stone giant from one of the stories that they all had to learn in sixth-grade English class. Fire escapes that the landlord insisted were scenic balconies clung to the side of the building. The red and blue swaths of spray-painted graffiti were the only colors to be seen.

Fen gave her a quick hug, a sure sign that he was feeling guilty, before he said, "I'll try to keep out of trouble, but I'm not going to sissy out."

That was the best she could hope for. Fen didn't really look for trouble, but it found him—and her—more often than not. Or maybe they simply didn't resist trouble very well. That was what her mom thought. *I can stay out of trouble, though.* She'd had a few visits to Principal Phelps and that one little misunderstanding at the lockers, but mostly, she'd stayed out of trouble lately, which would totally change if she started spending more time with Fen.

He didn't have many friends, so she always felt bad when she didn't hang out with him, but she felt just as bad when she was grounded all the time. He didn't get into half as much trouble when she was around him, but she got into twice as much. Like tonight, all she knew for sure was that he'd said he needed her with him, and she'd come along. She wasn't sure if he was trying to break the shield or take it. With Vetrarblot—the big festival for the start of winter—coming, either one would be a problem.

Laurie ran up the stairs to her apartment. Her mother was working nights at the hospital, so one of the neighbors, Mrs. Weaver, stayed with them after school, but she didn't really enforce the whole get-home-right-away thing. She did, however, insist that Laurie be in the apartment before Jordie went to bed. Laurie took a couple more deep breaths as she ran up the rest of the steps to their fourth-floor apartment. It wasn't quite high enough to have an elevator, but it was enough steps to complain about, as far as she was concerned. If they ever got hit by a tornado—which was a risk in South Dakota—she was pretty sure they'd all die. The apartments all had storage units in the basement, and her mother swore they could get downstairs fast enough if the time came, but that was five floors' worth of stairs. They'd waited a couple storms out in the storage unit, but mostly they stayed upstairs in the apartment, waiting and listening, and planned to run down all those steps if necessary. It was a bad plan.

She thought about that as she reached her floor, unlocked the door, and went inside. The lights were off, and the flicker of the television cast strange flashes of light into the room. Even though Mrs. Weaver would be leaving soon, Laurie still locked the door.

"You're late," Mrs. Weaver said as Laurie walked into the living room.

"Is Jordie asleep?"

Mrs. Weaver shook her head. "Unless he's started snoring in the sounds of explosions and spaceships, no, he's not asleep."

"Then I'm not late," Laurie pointed out. "Curfew is before Jordie's asleep, so—"

"Nice try, missy." Mrs. Weaver's mouth was trying not to curl into a smile, though.

Laurie opened the door to her little brother's room. Piles of books and toys were everywhere, but Mom wouldn't yell at him. Jordie was her "little angel," the baby who didn't worry her. If his school called, it was to say what a great job he did or what award he was getting. *He should've been a Thorsen.*

"Good night," she said. "Stop blowing things up."

"A volcano blew up for real!" Jordie squirmed in his bed, flopping over so he could see her.

"A what?"

"Volcano." Jordie made another explosion noise. "The whole top blew off like a rocket. Isn't that cool? Lava and smoke and—"

"Mom doesn't like you watching the news." Laurie sighed.

"And she doesn't like you being out this late. I won't tell if you don't," Jordie said, with the sort of bargaining powers that had kept him in gummy bears for months.

She rolled her eyes, but she still said, "Deal."

After she'd pulled the door shut, she went back out to the living room. Mrs. Weaver had gathered up her knitting needles and was slipping on her shoes. They said their goodnights, and Laurie curled up on the sofa with her math homework.

The sound of the lock turning woke her. Sort of. Sleepily, she let her mom direct her to bed. It wasn't like Laurie usually worried, but the whole episode with Fen tonight had freaked her out a lot. If Matt would've stayed out of it, she could've talked Fen into leaving the shield alone. *Maybe.* Either way, though, Matt didn't need to throw that light thing or whatever it was he did.

"Saw Fen," she told her mother.

"Laurie..." The tone that her mom always had when she talked about Fen was already there; even half-asleep, Laurie heard it. It meant *Fen's bad news, stay away from him.*

"He's family," Laurie murmured as she crawled into her bed.

Her mother pulled a cover over her. "One of these times he's going to get you into the sort of trouble you aren't ready for. Then what will you do?"

"Handle it." Laurie snuggled into her bed. "I can handle it."

A few hours later, Laurie woke with the vague sense of suffocation, which wasn't entirely unexpected because she had woken up as a...*fish*—a salmon, to be precise.

I am a fish.

She'd gone to sleep as a perfectly average thirteen-year-old girl and woken up as a fish, and as much as she'd like to try to figure out how that had happened, she had a more pressing concern: air. Salmon needed water to get that, and since she was a girl when she'd crawled into her bed, she was now a fish nowhere near water.

Her fishy eyes spied a sports bottle, and she felt a flicker of hope, but the lack of thumbs and the inability to put a salmon in a bottle made that useless as far as solutions go.

She flopped around on her bed, torn between trying to figure out how not to be a fish and trying to decide if she could flop her way to water—and trying to wake up for real because the odds of this being a bad dream seemed pretty high...except she felt awake.

I can't be a fish. It's a dream. No. I'm really a salmon.

The only water nearby was the toilet, and flopping her way into that germy thing sounded gross...but the need for air outweighed the sheer nastiness of trying to swim in a toilet.

With a burst of energetic wiggling, she managed to launch herself from her bed. She hit the floor, her fall cushioned by the piles of clothes strewn all through the room. She wriggled her way across the clothes, books, and accumulated junk on her floor—and hit the closed door.

I need help. I need Fen.

If fish could cry, Laurie would be weeping. The thought of dying as a fish, of her mother finding a stinky dead fish on the floor, was far from good.

Where is Fen?

Her cousin should be here; he should help her. That's how it worked: they helped each other, but he wasn't here, and she was going to die. Her gills opened and closed rapidly as she panicked, too exhausted to even try to figure out how a salmon could open a door.

The door opened, and Laurie stared up at her rescuer. *Not Mom. Not Dad. Not Fen.* Her little brother stood in her doorway. "Why are you on the floor?"

"Because I'm a fish," she said.

Jordie stared at her. He opened his mouth, apparently thought better of whatever he was going to say, and closed it. He shrugged.

"Can you open the bathroom door and put me in the tub? My fins—"

"You're kind of weird." He turned away.

"Is she awake?" Her mother called.

"Yeah, but she says she's a fish," Jordie yelled back to their mother.

Laurie took a deep breath . . . and realized that she had no gills. "I can breathe!" She looked around her room. The bedcovers were tangled, and she was on the floor. It had been a dream—a vivid dream, but not real. Girls don't turn into fish. She went over and sat on the bed—and was still sitting there half-dazed when her mother walked into her room.

"Honey? Are you okay?" Her mother leaned down and kissed her forehead, checking for fever. "Jordie said you had a bad dream."

"I was a fish," Laurie said, looking up at her mother. "Fen wasn't here, and I was going to die because Fen wasn't helping me."

Her mother sighed and sat next to her. Silently, she pulled Laurie into a hug and rested her cheek against Laurie's head. After a minute, she said, "You can't count on boys, especially your cousin Fen. I know you care for him, but Fen's trouble. He has no one teaching him right and wrong, and the way he's been raised . . ."

"We could let him live here," Laurie suggested.

Her mother's pause held the things her mother wouldn't

say—that she disliked Fen, that that side of the family made her uncomfortable, that the only reason she let any of them into the house was because she still loved Dad. Finally, what she did say was, "I need to think of what's best for my kids, and having Fen around Jordie isn't what's best. I'm sorry."

Laurie pulled away, got dressed, and walked out of the room. She didn't argue with her mother. That was something she tried not to do. She felt like she started enough trouble without meaning to, so causing problems on purpose was a bad idea. She stayed quiet. She wanted to tell her mother about the dream, but she felt silly. She'd wait and talk to Fen. He was her best friend, her almost-brother, and the only person who wouldn't think she was crazy for worrying over fish dreams.

Maybe.

THREE

FEN

"DUES"

Fen spent the next day expecting the sheriff to come grab him and the evening hiding in the damp of the park looking for a chance to get the shield. Even though Thorsen apparently hadn't specifically ratted him out, he obviously had said something because there were patrols around the longship all night. Fen had tried to get the job done, but he'd failed.

And he wasn't much looking forward to telling Kris, but when he trudged home from the park and saw the rusty pickup truck, he knew he had no choice. His cousin was home from wherever he had been the past few days.

Fen didn't ask too many questions about where Kris

went. Lesson number one in the Brekke family: what you don't know, you can't spill. It wasn't a matter of trust, really, just common sense. Brekkes looked out for themselves first. They might do a good turn for someone—or not—but they weren't foolish enough to go sharing things that could land them in hot water.

He crossed the pitted gravel drive and stood in the doorway to the garage.

"Fen? That you?" The voice called out from under the shell of an old car. Kris had been working on it for the better part of the year. Music blared from an old stereo. Like everything in Kris' place, it hadn't been in good condition for years.

"Yeah."

"Grab me a beer." From under the car, one greasy hand pointed in the general direction of the rust-covered refrigerator in the back corner of the garage.

Fen dropped his bag on the floor. He shoved it to the side with the toe of his boot and went over to the fridge. The door creaked, and the old metal handle clacked as he opened it. He pulled out a can of beer and popped the top. He didn't understand why anyone drank it. Kris gave him some one day, but it was gross. Beer tasted like how he suspected dog urine would taste, but everyone in his family drank the stuff.

"I heard that top pop, boy. It better be full when you hand it to me," Kris said.

Fen walked over and held the can out. "It is."

"Good pup." Kris slid out from under the car. He lay stretched on the creeper, grime, oil, and grease covering him from boots to bandanna. He was in his twenties, but now that Fen was in middle school, one of the aunts had decided Kris was old enough to keep Fen this year. It was a lot better than the year he'd spent with Cousin Mandy. She was older than dirt and had some crazy ideas about how many chores he should have. Kris, on the other hand, was young enough to remember hating chores. He gave Fen things to do, but they weren't exactly chores most of the time.

Kris sat up, grabbed the can, and took a long drink. He wiped his mouth with a grubby hand. "So did you get it?"

"No."

Kris frowned. "It was a simple task, boy. Go steal a shield. Easy stuff."

"Thorsen... Sheriff Thorsen's son Matt was there yesterday, and today there were patrols all day." Fen squatted down so he was eye to eye with Kris.

"The last thing I need is Mayor Thorsen or the sheriff to come around here asking questions. You need to stay clear of that kid."

"I know, and I did. Last night was the only time Laurie could be there, though, and I need her to be a part of the job," Fen added. "What was I supposed to do?"

"You were supposed to get the job done. You better figure

that out fast, boy." Kris finished his beer and crumpled the can. "If you don't pay your dues to the *wulfenkind*, there won't be anything anyone can do to help you."

"I heard you the first three times you told me," Fen snapped.

"Don't be smart." Kris stood and walked back to get another beer. "Bet there aren't as many patrols during the day."

"I have school," Fen started.

Kris opened the second beer. "You think the *wulfenkind* are going to care that you had school?"

"I could try again tonight," Fen suggested. "But what about Laurie?"

Kris nodded. "She *did* help, so that term is met. Go get it on your own, and if you can't get it tonight, you miss school tomorrow."

"Right," Fen said.

"If you don't get the job done, Laurie will have to meet them," Kris threatened.

Years of protecting his cousin made his answer obvious. He said, "I'll get it. Promise."

Fen heard the alarm go off in the middle of the night, far too few hours after he'd set it. It was one of those horrible clocks that ticked, and the alarm was a little hammer that smashed back and forth between two bells. *Like Thorsen's little Hammer*

trick. Fen threw the alarm at the wall. *Like I could throw him.* Even as he thought it, though, Fen scowled. The sad truth was that Fen couldn't toss Matt at a wall. Thorsens were unnaturally strong, and even though every Brekke had a few extra skills of their own, they also knew not to tangle with Thorsens. Well, not *every* Brekke knew it. Laurie was still clueless. Fen had only known what was up for a few years, and he'd done his best to play dumb.

Like the Thorsens think we all are.

After Kris snarled about the alarm—and the *thunk* of the alarm hitting the wall—Fen figured he'd better make as little noise as possible. He carried his boots to the front door. When he stepped outside, he held the screen door rather than let it slap closed. A rush of relief hit him when he turned to face the darkness. He could pretend it was just because he'd avoided Kris' temper, but the truth was that Fen always felt a bit of stress vanish when he stepped outside. Wolves, even those in human skin, weren't meant to be inside. This time of night was the best. Most people were in their beds in their homes, and the world was his.

He sat on the stoop, shoved his feet into his boots, grabbed the sack and crowbar Kris had left out for him, and started off toward Sarek Park. If Fen didn't take care of what he owed the Raiders, there would be consequences. The Raiders—*wulfenkind* packs—lived a life of thievery and scavenging, roaming from camp to camp, barely a minute ahead of the law. They could join packs once they shifted, but from birth they owed dues. Usually their parents paid. If not, the pack held a running tally of dues. Fen, like every Brekke, had to either pay dues to the local pack of his age group, join it, or—once he was old enough—go lone-wolf. For now, he'd opted to pay dues—his *and* Laurie's. He wasn't going to offer obedience to anyone simply because they were the best fighter.

Laurie didn't even know a lot about the ways things worked. She didn't know what he was or what she might be—because she didn't know about their ancestor Loki. So she had no idea that Fen was sometimes a wolf. Unless Laurie changed, they didn't need to tell her.

Her dad, Fen's uncle Stig, didn't think she'd change. Her mother wasn't *wulfenkind*, so she might turn out to be just a regular person. If she didn't change, she didn't need to know. Fen wished he could tell her, wished she would be a wolf, too…almost as much as he hoped, for her sake, that she wouldn't be one. For now, he agreed to pay her dues to the *wulfenkind* during the transition window. Usually *wulfenkind* parents did that, but Uncle Stig was a lone wolf, so Fen had taken on the responsibility. It's what he'd have done if Laurie were *really* his sister, not just his cousin. It meant double payments, but he could handle it. Once they knew if she'd change, she'd take over her own payments, join a pack, or go lone-wolf like Uncle Stig. Laurie was even less likely than Fen to join, so if she changed, Fen figured he'd either help her with payments or they'd go lone-wolf together. The problem with being a lone wolf was that you couldn't stay in any one territory too long. He couldn't imagine going lone-wolf without her, and he certainly wasn't joining the Raiders.

For now, that left him with dues, and for reasons he didn't want to know, the Raiders said the old shield was payment enough for both of them. The only weird thing was that the wolf in charge of their age pack, Skull, had said Laurie had to be involved at least a little—and she had been. Now Fen just had to finish the job.

His feet hurt from too many trips between Kris' trailer and the park, but there were rules about running around Blackwell as a wolf, so he went as he was. Of course, even if he was allowed to shift to wolf, it would cause other problems. *What would I do? Bite it free?* He smiled a little at that image, and he ran the rest of the way to Sarek Park.

This late—*or early, really*—the patrol cars weren't passing by as often. He took the crowbar Kris had given him and applied it to the side of the ship with as much force as he could. The shield was already loose. It had to be that specific one, the third shield from the front with the weird designs on it. Viking symbols, Fen guessed. He didn't know why it had to be that shield; he didn't really care. He just put his strength into prying it free.

Fifteen minutes and several splinters later, Fen was starting to really worry. "Come on; come on." He gave another good tug, and the final bolt popped free. The shield dropped to the ground with a loud crash.

Fen jumped over the side of the longship, landing in a crouch with one hand flat on the ground, and grabbed the shield.

As he did so, a big gray wolf padded into the park. He was as large as a full-grown wolf, but even before he shook off his fur and stood on two feet, Fen knew who it was.

Skull grinned at him and said, "Not bad."

Skull was only a few years older than Fen, but he was a lot scarier than any of the guys at school. He had scars on his arms, and right now, he also had a red scrape on his cheek that kept company with a number of purple and yellow bruises. He wasn't skinny, but he didn't have any fat on him. Skull was nothing but muscle, scars, and attitude.

"Where's Laurie?"

"Not here." Fen shoved the shield into the bag he'd brought with him and held it out to Skull. "She helped the first time I tried to get it, but she doesn't need to meet *you*."

Skull didn't take the bag Fen held out. "You can carry it."

He turned his back and walked away without seeing if Fen had obeyed. Of course, they both knew that he could follow or fight Skull—and that fighting would either result in being hurt pretty bad or being in charge of this pack of *wulfenkind*. Winning a fight with the lead wolf meant replacing him. As much as Fen disliked Skull, he didn't know that he could beat the older wolf, and even if he could, he didn't want it badly enough to risk getting saddled with the responsibility of a pack.

They walked at least five miles, so on top of the lack of sleep, Fen was dead on his feet by the time they reached the camp. Small groups of *wulfenkind* looked up with interest.

Skull's twin sister, Hattie, walked over and held out a chunk of some sort of meat on a stick, probably elk from the smell. "Want a bite?" She took a bite out of it, chewed, and swallowed. "It's safe."

He accepted it with a nod. He wasn't as constantly ravenous as the older *wulfenkind* got, because he didn't change forms as much yet, but he was starting to notice a change.

Skull nodded at Hattie, and she put her fingers to her lips and whistled. Once everyone looked at her, she signaled different people and then different directions. "Check the perimeter."

Of the almost two dozen boys and girls there, half—in two groups of six—left. Fen watched with appreciation. They were a well-organized, obedient pack. The camp was impressive, too. Gear was in small piles, firewood was stacked tidily, and sleeping bags were rolled and stowed. Camp could break and depart in moments.

"You could stay with us," Hattie offered. Her attention had both flattered and frightened him for years. She was one

33

of the strongest *wulfenkind* he'd met, but she was also weird and kind of mean. When they were ten, he'd watched her kill several squirrels by biting their throats. If she'd been in wolf form at the time, he might not have found it so gross. She hadn't been, though.

"Here." He pulled the shield out of the sack and tossed it to her. He didn't expect it to hit her, but he might have hoped a little. Unlike fighting Skull, there were no downsides to fighting Hattie.

She caught the shield in midair. "You brought me a present?"

Skull laughed.

Fen shifted his feet and said, "No. It's the dues for me *and* Laurie."

Skull clamped a hand on his shoulder and squeezed, but he told his sister, "Leave Fen alone. You're scaring him."

Although he was trying not to get into too much trouble with Skull, Fen couldn't ignore the insult. "I'm not sc—"

"You belong with us, Fen," Skull interrupted. "You know something big is coming. We need it to come. We'll make it come."

Hattie laid the shield down on a piece of animal hide that one of the younger wolves had dragged over to her. She squatted beside it and looked over her shoulder at Fen. "This wood was from the bog. This will be used in the final fight."

"The *what*?"

"Ragnarök," Skull said reverently.

"Ragnarök?" Fen repeated. He shook his head. It was one thing to remember the old stories, to know where they came from, but it was another to think that the end of the world was coming.

"The prophecy is true," Skull said. "The final battle will change everything. It will be the sons—"

"And *daughters*," Hattie interjected with a growl.

Skull continued, without even glancing at his sister, "The children of Loki will rise up; the monsters will wake. We'll rule the world, and everyone will tithe to us. We'll reign over the world like kings."

And as much as Fen thought they were a little crazy before, right then he knew that they were far beyond simply crazy. The whole there-used-to-be-gods bit was true, but the gods were stupid. They were all dead. If the gods were dead, how could there be a final battle? It didn't make any sense. Of course, that didn't mean Fen felt like getting into it with Skull and Hattie. He tried to sound a little less disdainful than he felt as he said, "Right. Gods and monsters will fight, and a new world will be born. You'll be in charge. Sure thing."

Hattie stood and instantly arranged her body for a fight. "You doubt it?"

Ignoring her, Fen tossed the stick with the rest of the meat toward the fire and pointed at the shield. "I stole the shield. I carried it to your camp. We're square. My dues and Laurie's are paid. Whatever you do with it now is your business."

"We just need one more thing," Hattie started.

Fen looked from Skull to Hattie and back again. It was one thing not to start trouble with them; it was another thing to be their errand boy. "I *paid*," Fen said. "Those are the rules. I paid, and now I'm done."

Skull punched him.

Fen staggered. The whole side of his face hurt, and he knew he'd have a black eye for school. *Great. Just great.* He stepped backward.

Hattie walked over to stand beside Skull. Behind her, Fen could see other members of the pack watching. There would be no help here. They followed orders. They protected their pack and worked toward the goals of the pack.

"The final fight is coming. That changes things," Hattie added.

The temper Fen was trying to keep in check flared. "Rules are rules, so—"

"*You* can help, or we can go to Laurie, and *she* can help," Skull said. "The monsters will come, and they will fight alongside our champion. We need to be ready."

There was no way Fen was letting them near Laurie, especially after the things they'd just said. He lowered his gaze as meekly as he could. "What do you want?"

"A Thorsen. The youngest one," Skull said.

Every Brekke knew there were things the Raiders did, things that were better not asked about. That didn't mean that Fen liked the idea of helping them get at anyone he knew—even someone he disliked. Turning a person over to them was wrong.

"Why?" Fen asked, hoping that they would say something that didn't involve hurting Thorsen.

Hattie sighed. "Because he's *their* champion in the final fight."

"Right," Fen drawled. "You need to stop a kid from fighting in Ragnarök. What are you going to do, really?"

Skull and Hattie exchanged a look, and then Skull stepped forward and slung an arm around Fen. "The boss said to deliver the kid. We aren't dumb enough to ask what for, but"—he paused and grinned—"if you want to ask, we can deliver you and Laurie, too."

"No," Fen said carefully. "I'll get him."

Skull squeezed Fen's shoulder tighter, painfully so, and said, "Good pup."

FOUR

✦

MATT

"PREMONITION"

Matt lay in bed. It'd been a day since he'd unleashed Thor's Hammer. Fen hadn't said anything to anyone. Laurie hadn't, either. Matt wanted to believe that meant they were going to forget it, but he couldn't help thinking they were only waiting for the right moment. Then they'd tell everyone how he'd used something like a flash-bang and knocked Fen right off his feet, and Matt's parents—and every other Thorsen in town— would know exactly what had happened. Matt had broken the rules: he'd used Thor's Hammer.

Thor's Hammer was the only magical power the Thorsens still had. Sure, they were usually bigger than other people, and stronger, too, but that wasn't magic. The old books said there used to be other powers, like control over weather, but that was long gone. They were left with the Hammer, which for everyone else was like an invisible punch that they could throw whenever they wanted. Only Matt got the special-effects package—the flash and the bang. And only Matt wasn't able to control when it went off.

His grandfather had tried giving him different amulets, but it didn't fix anything. His parents were right: it wasn't the amulet messing up—it was him. The power was in the descendants of Thor themselves—the amulet was just a…Matt struggled for the word his family used. Conduit. That was it. The necklace was a conduit that allowed the power to work. Which should mean the solution was easy: take off the necklace. Except a Thorsen couldn't do that for long before he got sick. Matt could remove his in the boxing ring, luckily, but that was it.

He should just tell his parents what happened. He'd started to last night, then chickened out and told Dad he'd seen some kids messing around at the longship, and Dad said he'd have his men patrol for a while. He'd lectured Matt, too, about taking more responsibility for their town, how he should have done something about it, not come home and tattled to his parents. That stung, especially when Matt *had* done something. He already felt bad about it. He should have been able to handle Fen without setting off the Hammer.

Don't think about that. Focus on something else. Think of your science fair project.

Oh, yeah. That helped. Let's focus on *another* example of how badly you can mess up, Matty.

He'd totally blown his science project, and he needed to do a new one before tomorrow night's fair. He'd overcomplicated things, as usual. He'd been trying extra hard because his family always won the eighth-grade science fair. First his dad. Then his brothers, Jake and Josh. If it were any other subject, Matt would be fine. But, as usual, if his family was good at it, he wasn't.

Maybe if he slept on it. He got some of his best ideas at night, when he could relax and stop worrying.

When he finally fell asleep, he did dream about his science project...all the ways he could mess it up again and embarrass his family. He kept dreaming about building the best project ever, only to accidentally unleash Thor's Hammer and blow it to smithereens in front of the entire school. Then his brain seemed to get tired of that and plunked down in the middle of a field.

It was daytime. He was standing there, staring up at the sky. He wasn't alone; he could sense someone behind him. But he didn't turn to see who it was. He was busy staring at the sun—and at the wolf chasing it.

The wolf was a huge, black shadow, all gleaming red eyes

41

and glistening fangs. The sun was a glowing chariot pulled by three white horses.

"It's Sköll and Sól," Matt murmured.

"Huh?" said a girl's voice behind him. He felt like he should know the voice, and in the dream, he seemed to, but his sleeping self couldn't place it.

"A Norse myth. The sun circles the earth because she's trying to escape the wolf Sköll. And the moon—" He squinted against the bright sun. Behind Sól's chariot, he could make out a paler version, chased by another shadow wolf. "There he is. Behind her. Máni, chased by Hati."

"Looks like the wolves are catching up."

Matt shook his head. "That won't happen until Ragnarök."

"Ragnarök?"

"The end of the world. It's supposed to begin when Loki kills Balder. Then Sköll catches Sól, and Hati catches Máni, and the world is plunged into endless night and winter. But that's not going to—"

The wolves leaped and closed the gap. The chariot riders whipped their horses, and they pulled ahead.

Matt exhaled. "Okay, it's just—"

The wolves lunged again. They caught the chariots in their powerful teeth and wrenched. The chariots toppled backward, horses flying. The sun and moon tumbled out. The wolves dove after them, opened their jaws, and . . .

Darkness.

Matt bolted up in bed, his heart thudding so hard he swore he could hear it.

Ragnarök.

The end of the world.

He blinked hard. Then he shook his head. Yes, his family did believe in Ragnarök, and the Seer was always looking for signs, but they'd been looking since before the old gods had died. Because the gods had been...well, *stupid*, they'd all managed to get themselves killed long ago. According to the Seer, that meant that when Ragnarök did come, some of the descendants would have to stand in for the original gods in the final battle. They'd be filled with the gods' powers and would fight the monsters as it had been foretold. Luckily, Ragnarök wasn't coming in his lifetime. What *was* coming was the science fair. Not exactly apocalyptic, but it sure felt like it.

He rubbed his face and yawned. Every time he closed his eyes, though, he saw the wolves chasing the sun and the moon.

He shook his head. That wasn't going to help his science...

Or could it?

Matt smiled, stretched out again, and fell asleep.

"Rakfisk!" Josh yelled, thumping open Matt's door. "Hey, Mini-Matt. Don't you smell that? Mom's making rakfisk."

Matt lifted his head, inhaling in spite of himself. He groaned and clenched his teeth to keep from barfing into the pillow. Nothing smells as bad as raw fish. Unless it's raw fish that's been left to rot for months, then served on toast. For breakfast.

Jake grabbed Josh's shoulder. "Don't wake the baby. More for us."

Josh was seventeen and Jake a year younger, but they were both so big that Josh practically filled the doorway by himself, and all Matt could see of Jake was a shock of red hair over his brother's shoulder.

They took off, thudding down the hall. Matt lifted his head, nose plugged. He tried breathing through his mouth, but that didn't help, because then he could *taste* the rakfisk. If there was one thing that totally ruined Norse holidays, it was the food. Ancient Viking traditions, his mom would say. Traditions the Vikings should have kept to themselves, he thought.

He found his mom in the kitchen, working at the counter while his brothers sat at the table and devoured plates of rakfisk on toast. He opened the fridge and found two milk containers. The first was filled with a thin, bluish-white liquid. Whey—the stuff that's left over after you curdle milk for cheese. He groaned and shoved it back in.

"Whey's full of protein, Matty," his mother said. "You won't get any bigger drinking pop."

"Oh, he won't get any bigger no matter what he drinks," Jake said. "Or no matter how many weights he lifts. Josh and I were both bigger than Matt at his age."

Josh shrugged. "Not by much. There's still time. Maybe if he'd join the football team..."

"I like boxing."

His mother tried not to make a face. She didn't like boxing. Or wrestling, which Matt also did, although he wasn't as good at it. She said she worried he'd get himself hurt, but he knew she just didn't get it. Football was the only real sport in the Thorsen house. Or in all of Blackwell.

"Oh," she said. "Your granddad asked about you last night. You haven't had any more..." She gestured to his amulet. "Outbursts?"

Matt struggled to keep his expression blank. "No, not since the last time." Which, technically, was true. Just not the "last time" she knew about.

His mom exhaled in relief. "Good," she said. "Now, let me get you some rakfisk for breakfast."

Science fair night. There were about a hundred people milling about the gym, pretending to be interested in the projects.

Hunter stood beside Matt's table. "I don't get it."

"That's 'cause you're too lazy to read." Cody waved at the explanation Matt had posted. "Which isn't a surprise, since you're too lazy to even do your own project. Did you think no one would notice you borrowed your brother's?"

Hunter's project was supposed to be a volcano, but after three years in storage, the "lava" kept running out through the holes mice had chewed.

Matt heard a snort. He glanced over to see Fen, who sported a fresh black eye. He was there with Laurie, keeping his head ducked down like he was trying to hide his shiner.

As Laurie approached Matt's table, Fen scowled. Laurie just gave him a look, and then asked Matt, "What's it supposed to be?"

Matt started to explain, but then noticed his granddad and two of the Thorsen Elders heading over, so he switched to his grown-up lecture.

"It's from a Norse myth," he said. "The wolves, Sköll and Hati, chase the sun, Sól, and the moon, Máni."

He waved to the board, where shadow wolves were supposed to be chasing two glowing balls on a modified railroad track. It hadn't quite worked, though, and they weren't actually moving. Biting off more than he could chew, his dad had said. Still, it looked okay. Granddad and the others had stopped now for a better look.

"In the story, they finally do catch them." Matt leaned over to push the wolves around the track, and they picked up speed until they moved over the balls, and the toy globe in the middle went dark. "That marks the beginning of

Ragnarök. The battle of the gods. From a scientific point of view, we can see this as an explanation for eclipses. Many cultures had a myth to explain why the sun would disappear and how to get it back."

He motioned to a second board, covered in eclipse pictures and graphs and descriptions. It was a rush job, and it looked like it, but it wasn't as bad as some…or so he kept telling himself.

"That's very interesting, Matty," his grandfather said, putting a hand on his shoulder. "Where did you come up with an idea like that?"

Matt shrugged. "It just came to me."

"Did it?"

Granddad's blue eyes caught Matt's, and under his stare, Matt felt his knees wobble. His grandfather studied him for another minute, his lips pursed behind his graying red beard. Then he clapped Matt on the back, murmured something to the Elders, and they moved on.

Matt got a B, which was great for a rushed project that didn't actually work right. His teachers seemed happy. His parents weren't. They'd headed out as he packed up his project, and he'd taken it apart carefully, slowly, hoping they'd get tired of waiting and leave.

"So it just came to you," said a voice behind him.

It was Granddad. The gym was empty now, the last kids and parents streaming out.

Matt nodded. "I'm sorry I didn't win."

His grandfather put his arm around Matt's shoulders. "Science isn't your strongest subject. You got a B. I think that's great." His grandfather pointed to the honorable mention ribbon on Matt's table. "And that's better than great."

Of the thirty projects at the fair, five got an honorable mention. Plus there were the first-, second-, and third-place winners. So it wasn't really much of an accomplishment, but Matt mumbled a thanks and started stacking his pages.

"So, Matty, now that it's just us, tell me, how *did* it come to you?"

Matt shrugged. "I had a dream."

"About what?"

"The wolves devouring the sun and moon. The start of the Great Winter."

"Fimbulwinter."

Matt nodded, and it took a moment for him to realize his grandfather had gone still. When he saw the old man's expression, his heart did a double-thump. He should be more careful. With the Elders, you couldn't casually talk about dreams like that. Especially not dreams of Ragnarök.

"I was worried about my project," Matt said. "It was just a dumb dream. You know, the kind where if you fail your project, the world ends." He rolled his eyes. "Dumb."

"What exactly did you see?"

Sweat beaded along Matt's forehead. As he swiped at it, his hands trembled.

Granddad whispered, "It's okay, Matty. I'm just curious. Tell me about it."

Matt did. He didn't have a choice. This wasn't just his granddad talking—it was the mayor of Blackwell and the lawspeaker of the town.

When he finished, his grandfather nodded, as if...*pleased*. He looked pleased.

"It—it was only a dream," Matt blurted. "I know you guys believe in that stuff, but it wasn't like that. I didn't mean to—"

Granddad cut him off by bending down, hands on Matt's shoulders. "You didn't do anything wrong. I was just curious. It's always interesting to hear where inspiration comes from. I'm very proud of you. Always have been."

Matt shifted, uncomfortable. "Mom and Dad are waiting...."

"Of course they are." After another quick hug, Granddad said, "I've always known you were special, Matty. Soon everyone else will know it, too."

He pulled back, thumped Matt on the back, and handed him the box. "You carry this, and I'll take your papers. It's windy out there. We don't want them blowing away."

Matt started across the gym, Granddad beside him. "I saw ice on the Norrström a few days ago. Is that why we're having Vetrarblot so soon? Winter's coming early?"

"Yes," Granddad said. "I believe it is."

FIVE

MATT

"CHOSEN"

After the science fair, Granddad came to the house and took Matt's parents for a walk. By the time they came back, Matt was heading off to bed—early wrestling practice—but they called him out to the living room and gave him a long speech about how proud they were of him for getting a B and an honorable mention. As a reward, they'd chip in the forty bucks he still needed to add to his lawn-cutting money so he could buy an iPod touch.

He knew they weren't really proud of him. He'd still messed up. But his parents always did what Granddad said. Most people in Blackwell did. Anyway, he wouldn't argue about the money. Now he could start saving for a dirt bike, and maybe if he managed to win the state boxing finals, Granddad would guilt his parents into chipping in for that, too. Not likely—his mom hated dirt bikes almost as much as she hated boxing—but a guy could dream.

Vetrarblot. It wasn't as cool as Sigrblot—because Sigrblot meant summer was coming, which meant school was ending—but it was a big deal. A really big deal this year, for Matt. He'd just turned thirteen, which meant he'd now be initiated into the *Thing*.

The *Thing*. What a dumb name. Sure, that's what it had been called back in Viking days—the word *thing* meant assembly—but you'd think one of Blackwell's founding fathers would have come up with a new name so the town meetings wouldn't sound so stupid. They hadn't.

In Viking times, the *Thing* was an assembly made up of all the adult men who weren't thralls—what the Vikings called slaves. In Blackwell, women were members, too. And by all "adults," they meant all Thorsens past their thirteenth birthday.

As for what exactly the assembly did, well, that was the not-so-exciting part. It was politics. They'd decide stuff. Then the town council—which was mostly Thorsens—would make it happen.

They discussed community issues, too—ones you couldn't bring up in a town council, like "That Brekke kid is getting into trouble again" or, he imagined, "Matt Thorsen still can't control his powers." Which was why he'd rather not be sitting there listening.

And during Vetrarblot, he'd really rather not be there. They held the meeting just as the fair was starting. Cody and the rest of Matt's friends had a nine-o'clock curfew, which meant he wasn't even sure he'd get out of the *Thing* in time to join them. Which was totally unfair, but his parents wouldn't be too happy if he began his journey into adulthood by whining about not getting to play milk-bottle games.

He'd already gotten a long talk from them that morning about how he was supposed to behave. Matt was pretty sure they were worried it would be a repeat of the disaster at Jolablot. That was the winter festival where they retold all the old stories, and Granddad had asked Matt to tell the one about Thor and Loki in the land of the giants, just like Josh and Jake had when they were twelve. His parents hadn't wanted him to do it, but Matt insisted. He knew the myths better than his brothers did. A lot better. He'd make them proud of him. He'd really tried to—memorizing his piece and practicing in front of his friends. Then he got up on the stage and looked out at everyone and froze. Just froze. Granddad had to come to his rescue, and his parents weren't ever going to let him forget it. This festival, he'd just keep quiet, keep his head down and out of the spotlight, and do as he was told.

Between the parade and the *Thing*, there was food. Real food, not corn dogs and cotton candy. At that time, everyone who wasn't a Thorsen went home or filled the local restaurants or carried picnic baskets to Sarek Park. The Thorsens took over the rec center. That's when the feasting began. There was rakfisk, of course, and roast boar and elk and pancakes with lingonberries. Mead, too, but Matt didn't get any of that.

Inside the rec center, there were a bunch of smaller rooms plus the main hall, which was where the feast took place. The hall would have looked like a gym, except for the mosaics on every wall. Matt's granddad said they were nearly five hundred years old, brought over from some castle in Norway.

The mosaics showed scenes of Thor. Fight scenes mostly— when it came to myths about Thor, that's what you got. Thor fought this giant, and then this giant, and then this giant. Oh, yeah, and a few dwarves, but they were really mean dwarves.

Back when Matt had signed up for boxing and wrestling, he'd pointed this out to his parents. Sure, people loved and respected Thor because he was a great guy, but more than a little of that came because he sent monsters packing. And he didn't send them packing by asking nicely.

His parents hadn't bought it. Physical strength was all very good—they certainly wouldn't want a bookworm for a son—but the Thorsens weren't like Thor. They had each other, so it was a team effort, and those skills were better developed through football.

Still, those mosaics were what Matt grew up with. Thor fighting Hrungnir. Thor fighting Geirrod. Thor fighting Thyrm. Thor fighting Hymir. And, finally, in a mosaic that took up the entire back wall, Thor's greatest battle with his greatest enemy: the Midgard Serpent.

According to legend, Thor had defeated the serpent once but hadn't killed it. He'd fished it out of the sea and thrown his hammer, Mjölnir, at it, leaving it slinking off, dazed but alive. According to the myth, when Ragnarök came, the serpent would return for vengeance. The mosaic on the wall showed how the epic battle would play out, ending with Thor delivering the killing blow. As Thor turned his back, though, the dying serpent managed one last strike: it poisoned Thor. And the god staggered away to die.

Matt kept looking at the Midgard Serpent scene as he sat with his family at the head table. The hall was filled with wooden folding chairs and long tables set up for family-style feasting. A small stage stretched across the front of the room.

The Seer was already up there with her assistant. At first look, he always thought the Seer could be a grandmother, but when he'd look again, he'd think she barely looked old enough to be a mother. She had that kind of face. For the festivals, the Seer and her assistant both dressed like women from Viking times, in long, plain white dresses with apronlike blue dresses overtop. White cloth covered their blond hair. Otherwise, they looked like a lot of women in Blackwell, and he was sure he passed them all the time on the streets and never even recognized them without their Viking dresses.

As the feasting went on, the Seer stood on her platform, throwing her runes and mumbling under her breath, making pronouncements that her assistant furiously jotted down. Matt noticed some of the younger members of the *Thing* had taken seats near her. They were hoping to hear something important. They weren't allowed to talk to her. No one could. And they really, really weren't allowed to ask her anything.

Divining the future through runes was a very serious matter, not to be confused with fortune-telling, a lesson Matt had learned when he'd bought a set of fake ones and charged kids two bucks to get their futures told. That scheme got him hauled in front of the *Thing*, and he'd had to miss the next festival. He should have known better. Okay, he *did* know better. But it was like pulling pranks—he knew he should just behave and make his parents proud, but he couldn't seem to help himself. It was hard, doing the right thing all the time, trying to live up to his brothers when he knew he never could—not really—and sometimes, he just got tired of trying.

As dinner wound down, more people moved to sit cross-legged around the Seer. Others shifted to the Tafl tables set up along the sides of the room. When Granddad asked Matt to play a match against him, it was no big deal—Matt played Tafl with his grandfather all the time. Maybe not at the festivals, but only because Granddad was usually too busy. As they walked to a table, though, Matt could hear a buzz snake around the room, people whispering and turning to look, some making their way over to watch.

Tafl—also known as Hnefatafl, but no one could pronounce *that*—was a Norse game of strategy, even older than chess. It was called the Viking game because that's where it came from, and it was based on the idea of a raid, with each player getting two sets of pieces as his "ship" and the king and his defenders in the middle.

Matt wasn't worried about people watching his match with Granddad. Tafl was like boxing: he knew he was good at it. Not good enough to win every time, but good enough that he wouldn't embarrass his family.

He didn't win that match. Didn't lose, either. The game had to be called on account of time—kids were itching to get out to the fair before dark, and it was Granddad's job to officially end the feast. As Granddad did that and the kids took off to the fair, Mom led Matt over to the chairs that had been set up as the tables were cleared.

When Granddad stepped onto the stage, everyone went silent. Someone carried a podium up and set it in front of him. He nodded his thanks, cleared his throat, and looked out at the group.

"As some of you know," he began, "this will be very different from our usual assemblies. No new business will be brought forward tonight. Instead, we will be discussing a matter that is of unparalleled importance to all of us."

Some people shifted in their chairs. Were they worried about what Granddad was going to say? Or did they know something Matt didn't, namely that *important* meant "you're going to be stuck in those chairs for a very long time"?

Granddad continued, "As you know, our world has been plagued by natural disasters for years now, but recently the rate of these disasters has increased to the point where we barely have time to deal with one before we are hit with another."

That was the truth. It seemed like every day there was a new school fund-raiser for a newly disaster-torn country. So far, Matt had helped out with two dances, a dunk tank, a bake sale, and now the charity boxing match...and it wasn't even the end of September yet.

Was that what this was about? Raising money for disaster

relief? Or maybe looking at the town's emergency plan? His parents had totally redone theirs after all those tornadoes went through in the spring.

Granddad was still talking. "Last week, a volcano erupted that scientists had sworn was dormant. Today, they closed down Yellowstone Park because the hot springs and cauldrons are boiling over, releasing deadly amounts of poisonous gas into the atmosphere." His grandfather paced across the tiny stage. "Dragon's Mouth is one of those. The Black Dragon's Cauldron is another. Aptly named, as our history tells us, because what keeps those cauldrons bubbling—and what makes fire spew from the mouths of mountains—is the great dragon, Nidhogg, the corpse eater. For centuries, his destruction has been kept to a minimum because he is otherwise occupied with his task of gnawing at the roots of the world tree. But now he no longer seems distracted. We know what that means."

Matt felt icy fingers creep up his back.

This was his fault. He had the dream, and it was just a dream, but now his grandfather believed it, was using it to explain the bad things that were happening in the world.

"Nidhogg has almost bitten through the roots of the world tree. One of the first signs of Ragnarök."

Matt gripped the sides of his chair to keep from flying up there and saying Granddad was wrong. He'd misunderstood.

He'd trusted some stupid dream that was only a dream; Matt was only a kid, not a prophet, not a Seer.

"And we understand, too, the meaning of the tsunamis and tidal waves that have devastated coastal cities around the world. Not only has Nidhogg almost gnawed through the world tree, but the Midgard Serpent has broken free from its bonds. The seas roil as the serpent rises to the surface. To the final battle. To Ragnarök."

Matt sucked in air, but it didn't seem to do any good. He started to gasp. Mom reached over and squeezed his hand. On his other side, Dad eased his chair closer, his arm going around Matt's shoulders as he whispered, "It's okay, bud." Josh leaned around Dad and gave a wry smile.

On Mom's other side, Jake snorted and rolled his eyes. Scorn for the baby who was freaking out because bad things were coming and he couldn't handle it, which was how it would look to everyone else.

Matt disentangled his hand from his mother's and shrugged off his father's arm. Then he pulled himself up straight, gaze fixed on his grandfather, who was saying something about nations in Europe breaking their promises on an environmental treaty and rumblings of conflict. All signs of Ragnarök. Oaths broken. Brother turning against brother. War coming.

"In that final battle, we have a role." Granddad looked over at the mosaic, and everyone's gaze followed to the epic confrontation against the Midgard Serpent. "For centuries, the Thorsens have worked together, stayed together, fought together. But this battle is different. This job is for one and only one. The Champion of Thor, who must win the battle, defeat the serpent, and save the world from destruction."

Dad's hand went to Matt's leg and squeezed. When Matt looked over, his father's face was tight and unreadable as he stared straight ahead.

"We have waited for the signs that point us to our champion," Granddad said. "We had seen some, but we were still unsure. Now, though, the prophecy has been fulfilled and the runes..."

He moved back, and the Seer shuffled forward. She didn't step up to the microphone, so her reedy voice barely carried past the front rows. Matt had to strain to listen.

"The runes have spoken," she said. "I have cast them again and again, and the answer remains the same. We have chosen correctly. We have our champion."

Matt glanced at his father. Tentatively, his father slid his hand around Matt's and held it so tightly that Matt had to fight not to pull away.

On the stage, the Seer's voice rose, so all could hear. "Our champion is Matthew Thorsen, son of Paul and Patricia Thorsen."

Matt froze.

There was a moment of stunned silence. Then whispers slid past. *Did he really say the Thorsen boy? He's just a kid. No, that can't be right. We heard wrong. We must have.*

Granddad's voice came back on the speakers. "I know this may come as a surprise to some of you. Matt is, after all, only thirteen. But in Viking times, he would have been on the brink of manhood. The runes have chosen Matt as our champion, as the closest embodiment of Thor. His living representative. And they have chosen others, too, all the living embodiments of their god ancestors, all children born at the turn of the millennium. Young men and women like Matt. The descendants of Frey and Freya, Balder, and the great god Odin. They will come, and they will fight alongside our champion. And…" He pointed at the mosaic of Thor's death. "That will not happen, because they will win and they will live."

Another moment of silence, like they were processing it. Then someone clapped. Someone else joined in. Finally, a cheer went up. It didn't matter if they thought Matt was too young—the runes called him the champion, so that's what he was. However ridiculous it seemed.

Matt looked around. People were turning and smiling, and his mother was pulling him into a hug, whispering how proud she was. Josh shot him a grin and a thumbs-up. Jake's glower said Matt didn't deserve the honor and he'd better not mess this up.

So Ragnarök was coming? And he was the Champion of Thor? The chosen one? The superspecial kid?

I'm dreaming. I must be.

Once he figured that out, he recovered from the shock and hugged his mother and let his dad embrace him and returned Josh's thumbs-up; then he smiled and nodded at all the congratulations. He might as well enjoy the fantasy. Too bad it wasn't real, because if he did defeat the Midgard Serpent, he was pretty sure he could get a dirt bike out of the deal. He laughed to himself as he settled back into his seat. Yeah, if he fought and killed a monstrous snake, Mom really couldn't argue that a dirt bike was too dangerous.

He looked around as everyone continued congratulating him.

It had to be a dream. Anything else was just…crazy. Sure, Matt believed in Ragnarök, sort of. He'd never thought much about it. That's just how he was raised, like some kids were raised to believe an old guy named Noah put two of every animal on one boat. You didn't think much about it—it just *was*. So Ragnarök must be real, even if it sounded…

He looked around. No, everyone else believed it, so it must be true.

Maybe it wasn't an actual serpent. Maybe it was a… what did they call it? A metaphor. That's it. Not an actual snake, but some snake-like guy who had to be killed or he'd unleash nuclear war or something.

Except that wasn't what Granddad was talking about. He meant the Midgard Serpent. Like in the picture. An actual serpent.

That's the story, Matt. Don't you believe it? You've always believed it.

His head began to throb, and he squeezed his eyes shut.

Let Granddad handle it. Just do what you need to do.

Do what? Be their champion? No. He'd make a mess of it. He always did.

The *Thing* ended, and every Thorsen lined up to shake Matt's hand. He *was* awake, and he was the chosen one— and he was going to fight the Midgard Serpent and save the world. First, though, he was going to throw up.

Every time someone shook his hand, he felt his stomach quiver, too, and he thought, *I'm going to do it. I'm going to barf. Right on their shoes.* The only way he could stop it was to clamp his jaw shut and keep nodding and smiling his fake smile and hope that the next person who pounded him on the back didn't knock dinner right out of him.

After the others left, his grandfather talked to him. It wasn't a long discussion, which was good, because Matt barely heard any of it. All he could think was *They've made a mistake. They've made a really, really big mistake.* He even tried to say that, but his grandfather just kept talking about how Matt shouldn't worry, everything would be fine—the runes wouldn't choose him if he wasn't the champion.

Check again. That's what he wanted to say. *If a kid has to fight this... whatever, it should be Jake, or even Josh. Not me.*

Granddad said they'd talk more later, then he slipped off with the Elders into a private meeting, and Matt was left alone with his parents. They told him a few more times that everything would be fine. Then Dad thumped him on the back and said Matt should go enjoy the fair, not worry about curfew, they'd pick him up whenever he was ready.

"Here's a little extra," Dad said, pulling out his wallet. "It's a big night for you, bud, and you deserve to celebrate."

When he held out a bill, Matt stared. It was a hundred.

"Uh, that's—" Matt began.

"Oh. Sorry." His dad put the hundred back, counted out five twenties instead, and put them in Matt's hand. "Carnies won't appreciate having to cash a hundred, will they?" Another slap on Matt's back. "Now go and have fun."

Matt wandered through the fair, sneakers kicking up sawdust. He didn't see the flashing lights. Didn't hear the carnies hustling him over. Didn't smell the hot dogs and caramel corn. He told himself he was looking for his friends, but he wasn't really. His mind was still back in the rec hall, his gaze still fixed on that mosaic, his ears still ringing with the Seer's words.

Our champion is Matthew Thorsen.

Champion. Really? No, really? I'm not even in high school yet, and they expect me to fight some giant serpent and save the world?

This isn't just some boxing tournament. It's the world.

Matt didn't quite get how that worked. Kill the serpent; save the world. That's how it was supposed to go. In the myth of Ragnarök, the gods faced off against the monsters. If they defeated the monsters, the world would continue as it was. If the monsters won, they'd take over. If both sides died—as they did in the myths predicting Ragnarök—the world would be plunged into an ice age.

What if the stories weren't real?

But if the stories aren't real, then Thor isn't real. That amulet around your neck isn't real. Your power isn't real.

Except it obviously *was*. Which meant . . .

Even thinking about that made Matt's stomach churn and his head hurt and his feet ache to run home. Just race home and jump in bed and pull up the covers and hide. Puke and hide: the strategy of champions.

Matt thought of his parents catching him, and his heart pounded as he struggled to breathe. They expected him to do this, just like they expected him to walk home after practice and make his own science fair project. They expected him to be a Thorsen.

Something tickled his chest, and he reached to swat off a bug. Only it wasn't a bug. It was his amulet. Vibrating.

Um, no, that would be your heart, racing like a runaway train.

The tickling continued, and he swiped the amulet aside as he scratched the spot. Only it wasn't his heart—it really was the pendant. When he held it between his fingers, he could feel the vibrations.

Weird. It had never done that before.

"You are looking for Odin," said a voice behind him.

Matt wheeled. There was no one there.

"You are looking for Odin," the voice said again, and he followed it down to a girl, no more than seven. She had pale blond braids and bright blue eyes. She wore a blue sundress and no shoes. In this weather? She must be freezing. Where were her parents?

"Hey," he said, smiling as he crouched. "Do you need help? I can help, but we should probably find your parents first."

The girl shook her head, braids swinging. "I do not need your help, Matthew Thorsen. You need mine."

Strange way for a kid to talk. Formal, like someone out of an old movie. And the way she was looking at him, so calmly. He didn't recognize her, but in Blackwell, there were so many little blond kids that it was impossible to keep them all straight.

"Okay, then," he said. "You can help me find your parents."

"No, you must find Odin. He will help."

"Help what?"

She frowned, confused. "I do not know. That is to come. That is not now. I know only what is now, and *now* you must hear."

"Hear what?"

She took off into the crowd.

Matt bolted upright. "Wait!"

The girl turned. She looked at him, her blue eyes steady. Then she mouthed something, and he understood her, like she was standing right there, whispering in his ear: *You must hear.*

She turned and ran again. Matt hesitated, but only for a second. As safe as Blackwell was, no kid her age should be wandering around alone.

He raced after her.

SIX

LAURIE

"OWEN"

At the parade, Laurie had seen that the shield was missing, and she'd known that Fen must have gone back for it. She wasn't sure if that's where he got the black eye, and he wouldn't tell her what had happened. All she got out of him was that he was "handling it," but he looked like whatever it was had handled him.

Her temper wasn't often horrible, but as she waded through the carnival games and crowds of people standing in lines to buy food or tickets to the rides, she was shaking mad. Even the smells of popcorn, funnel cake, and cotton candy didn't distract her. Admittedly, she still kept looking at all the games of chance that were set up to convince people to spend all their money on games with pretty lame prizes. She won at those. She had a weird luck with carnival games and had toted home enough stuffed bunnies and creepy dolls over the past few years that her mother had taken a trunkful to the kids at the hospital. Maybe if Laurie wasn't so mad she could stop and play just one, but she *was* mad. If Fen got caught with the shield, he would put them both at risk. If her mom weren't so adamant that Fen wasn't welcome, or if her dad was around, or if Matt weren't the sheriff's kid, or if…well, if Fen weren't being so stupid, things would be better, but none of the *if*s were truths. The worst possibility was that Matt told the sheriff and she and Fen were both arrested. The best case was that Fen would get in trouble—and she'd lose him. So, even the best case was horrible.

Unless Matt doesn't tell.

Even before this, Laurie had needed to talk to Fen about the weird fish dream, but she hadn't been able to get him alone since the other night at the longship. Even at the science fair, he wasn't available. He'd actually invited his friend Hunter to join them. She wasn't going to be ignored any longer. She'd talk to him whether he wanted to hear it or not. Maybe if they turned the shield in, Matt would keep their secret.

As she walked around the festival, she kept a lookout for Fen. She stopped at the Ferris wheel, the Tilt-A-Whirl, and the teacup ride. No Fen. She wandered through the petting-zoo area. No Fen.

"Where are you?" she muttered. She'd call him, but he didn't have a cell phone.

"Hello." A boy a few years older than her stepped up beside her. "I wondered where you were."

"What?" She paused.

He looked like he belonged . . . well, anywhere but Black-well. He wore a pair of black-and-blue tennis shoes, black trousers that hung low, a blue shirt that looked silky, and slightly longish hair that was dyed blue. Odder still, the boy had on jewelry that was almost girly: a pair of tiny black bird earrings in one ear and a twisted metal ring on his finger.

"Are you looking for me yet?" he asked.

"No." She scowled. "I don't know you. Why would I look for you?"

"I'm Odin."

"Uh-huh. Odin." She did laugh then. Anyone who grew up in Blackwell knew the basics of their mythology. Between school, parents, plays, a well-stocked myth section in the library, and some pretty terrible videos in every grade, it was impossible to completely avoid myth in Blackwell. That didn't mean it was real.

"So, *Odin*, I guess there's another play this year?" She hadn't picked up any activities listing for the fair, but even if she had, she wasn't so much up for watching another play on some battle or other. Some people in Blackwell took their Scandinavian heritage far too seriously.

"Would you like to play a game?" Odin looked around for a moment and then pointed to a booth where some sort of gambling game was set up. "You'd be good at that one."

It was supposed to be a game of luck, but she'd been banned from it the year before when she won every time. The man running it insisted she was cheating somehow; she hadn't been. This year, she was staying out of trouble—no games of luck for her. This boy obviously had heard about the ugly scene last year when she'd had to give up every dollar she'd won *and* the money she'd paid to play.

"Very funny," she said.

Odin gave her a weird little smile, but didn't reply. He just stood there waiting. It seemed odd, but she didn't have the time or interest to waste on some blue-haired boy. She shook her head and turned away.

"You're leaving already?" he asked.

"I need to find someone."

"Not me?" He sounded sad.

She looked back at him. "No."

"Oh. I must be early then." The boy calling himself Odin frowned. "They won't like me, unfortunately."

Laurie stepped a little farther away from him. He was starting to make her nervous, and she wasn't used to talking to boys without Fen showing up to snarl at them anyhow.

Her whole family was overprotective in one way or another, and talking to Odin made her think maybe they were right. "I think I'm going to go now. Good luck with your play or whatever."

"It's real, you know," Odin said. "That's why you're good at those games. I know. You don't cheat, but you win."

At that, Laurie didn't know what to say, so she gave up. "I'm not allowed to play gambling games. My cousin will probably be a jerk to you if he sees you talking to me, and even if he doesn't, I'm not looking for you, so please just go away."

He studied her for a moment. "I expected you to be less of a rule follower, but I guess we're still becoming."

"Becoming *what*? What does that even mean?" She looked around for Fen—or even Hunter at this point. All she could see was the crush of people milling around the sawdust-covered paths of the festival. Blackwell itself wasn't that big, but the festival always drew in people from outside the area. It made sense, she supposed. The fair might celebrate Scandinavian heritage, but it still had the trappings of a lot of festivals. There were wooden booths where volunteers manned games of chance and skill; there were all kinds of good foods, and usually there were bands and fireworks and whatever else the committee felt would add to the overall excitement and appeal.

As Laurie looked, she saw a few of the odd acrobats who

were running through the festival, doing tricks that made her think of the extreme sports games Fen liked to watch. They didn't have bikes or skateboards, but they did handstands, weird half jumps, and crazy flips as they ran.

"Becoming more than we are," Odin said.

"Okaaaay, *Odin*, I'm not in your play or whatever, so I'm going to go now," she said.

"You can call me Owen, if you'd feel better," he offered. "I'd rather you call me my true name, but you're not ready. Maybe next time I see you."

She stared at him and said, "I don't need to call you Owen or Odin or whatever other name you want to use. I won't be talking to you. Now *or* later. Go away before my friends show up."

"They *would* misunderstand." The boy nodded to himself. "I just wanted to see you. You're the one who will understand me. I hoped... I hoped you'd be ready. Soon, though, we can talk as we are meant to."

He turned and disappeared into the crowd.

She watched him go; his blue hair made him stand out enough that it was easy. The acrobat kids seemed to be following him, but not with him. It was weird. They trailed him, and he walked as if he were alone. For a moment, she had a flash of worry for him. *What if they aren't with him? What if he's in trouble?* But they didn't seem to be trying to hurt him, and he didn't act like he was worried. *And it's not*

my problem. Still, she watched them as they headed toward the exit.

Owen was barely out of view when another, more important person caught her eye. "Fen!"

She pushed through the crowd, not caring that she was drawing attention or being rude. She shoved between him and the ever-present Hunter and grabbed Fen's wrist. "I need to talk to you alone...." Her words died. Fen had flinched from her touch. She let go of his arm and said softly, "Please, Fen?"

He looked directly at her.

And she said the magic words, the words that they'd both used over the years: "I need your help with something."

Her cousin opened his mouth, but before he could ask, she spoke. "I need to talk to Fen alone. If you could—"

"Go away, Hunter," Fen finished for her. Then, he started through the crowd away from Hunter. He was pulling her with him as he had on who-knew-how-many adventures over the years, and she felt such relief that she almost hugged him. Everything would be okay now. She had Fen at her side again.

By the time they'd reached the edge of the festival, behind a row of booths where the tangled wires for the strands of temporary lights were stretched, Laurie was bursting with the words she'd been waiting to say. The music over the loudspeakers made it impossible for anyone in the booths to hear them, but that didn't mean they wanted witnesses.

They both knew that if the other one said "I need your help" that meant they also needed privacy.

After he confirmed that no one was watching, Fen let go of her and tucked his hands in the pockets of the torn jacket he was wearing. He looked around to make sure no one was nearby. "What happened?"

She didn't want to start by accusing him—that never went well—so she started with her other worry. "I thought I was a fish," she blurted.

"Okay." Fen nodded, and then he paused, blinked, and said, "*What?*"

"A fish," she whispered.

He stepped closer to her and said, "Say that again."

"I woke up in the middle of the night, and I was a fish and I couldn't breathe and you weren't there." She sounded crazy even to herself. "I know it was just a dream, but it was so real, and all I could think about was telling you."

Fen stared at her.

"Say something," she half begged.

"Maybe you should keep a bucket of water by your bed, because Aunt Janey isn't going to let me stay with you unless Uncle Stig is around." Fen folded his arms over his chest.

Laurie stared at him.

The music on the loudspeaker was interrupted by some sort of squeal that caused them both to jump. After a minute, Fen said, "What I mean is maybe you really were a fish."

"It was a dream; it had to be," Laurie said.

"Maybe. Maybe not." Fen shrugged. "There's weirder stuff out there."

"Like what?"

"The Raider Scouts," he said.

"Who?" Laurie couldn't always follow the way his mind jumped around, but she knew he usually got to his point. "I don't get it."

"Those weird people who just camp and stuff all the time," Fen said.

Laurie shook her head. "You think turning into a fish is *less* weird than camping?"

Fen shrugged. "They say they're wolves, you know."

Laurie laughed. "Right. Well, maybe they are, and I'm a fish. Do you think I ought to join them? Can you imagine Mom's face? I dreamed I'd turned into a fish, and Fen says maybe I'll be a real fish, so I'm going to drop out of school and camp with these kids who say they're wolves."

"No, you shouldn't join them, but..." The way Fen looked at her seemed off, but maybe that was just because his face was so bruised. He smiled, but it didn't look quite right. "What if the Raiders really *are* wolves, Laurie? What if you really are a fish, or your dream means you will be?"

For a moment, she stared at him, and then she burst out laughing. "You don't know a guy named Owen, do you?"

Now it was Fen who looked confused. "No. Why?"

"Everyone seems crazy tonight. He was a stranger who acted like he knew me, got into his role for the play too seriously. It was weird. Now, you're telling me that there are kids who might be wolves, and...well, I'm telling you I am freaked out by a dream about being a fish. Crazy. Everything just seems crazy."

"Some of the cousins joined them."

"The Raiders?" she asked.

"Yeah." Fen folded his arms over his chest. "Dad was one, you know."

"So Uncle Eddy is a wolf? That makes you one, too."

"Maybe," Fen hedged.

"Okay, so I'm a fish; you and Uncle Eddy are wolves." She shook her head. "I know it's silly, but I feel better for having told you. I've never had such a realistic dream."

For a moment, Fen said nothing. He stared at her as if he would, but then he grinned. "Come on. I stole some tickets earlier for the rides."

She paused. Fen was relaxed enough for her to ask him about the other thing, but that didn't mean he'd like it. She put a hand on his forearm. "You still need to tell me what happened." She pointed at his swollen and blackened eye. "And about the shield. If Thorsen tells the sheriff, we're going to get in so much trouble."

Fen ignored her, as he always did when he didn't feel like answering.

"Seriously, Fen! If they go to your house and find it, we're going to—"

"It's not at the house," Fen interrupted. "I don't have it, and *if* I knew anything, that's not enough to get me—or you—in trouble."

She rolled her eyes.

"Trust me. I won't ever let anything happen to you. You know that, don't you? You're my sister even though we don't have the same parents." Then he head-butted her. It almost hid his blush. He was embarrassed every time he admitted to having feelings.

For a moment, Laurie didn't react. She knew he'd stolen it, but she also knew he looked out for her.

The look on his face was nervous, and he pulled his arm away from her—but he still tried to sound like he wasn't hurt when he said, "Come on, fish. Or are you afraid you'll slip off the Ferris wheel?"

"Jerk." She shoved him carefully. Hugs weirded him out, but a gentle shove, punch, or head-butt he was okay with. "I'm not afraid of anything…as long as you're not."

SEVEN

❧

MATT

"PAST, PRESENT, AND FUTURE"

When Matt saw the little girl racing into the rec center, he yelled at her to stop, but she kept running, bare feet slapping on the pavement, blond braids streaming behind. He flew through the entrance—only to see her running for the closed door into the private meeting his grandfather was having with the Elders.

Great. They choose me to stop Ragnarök, and what's the first thing I do? Prove I can't even stop a little girl from bursting into their meeting.

He could just turn around and walk away. Pretend he hadn't seen where she was going. Or pretend he never met her in the first place. The easy way out, which meant he'd never take it, even if he wished he could.

He raced across the main room as fast as he could. But the girl had stopped at the meeting-room door and was just standing there, waiting patiently as she watched him with those weirdly grown-up blue eyes.

"Now you hear," she whispered. She pointed at the door. "Listen."

He started to tell her they had to leave when he caught the word *Ragnarök*. Then his name.

He leaned toward the door. Yes, he shouldn't eavesdrop. Totally disrespectful. But the conversation was about him, which kind of made it his business. If he was caught, well, he'd just chased this little girl inside so he could return her to her parents. *That's champion-worthy behavior, isn't it?*

"... no need to tell the others yet. What I told them at the *Thing* is enough for now," his grandfather was saying. "Those who need to know the truth already do. For the rest, it will come as a shock, and we must ease them into it."

Was he talking about Matt being chosen as champion? That they had to tell the Thorsens who didn't live in Black-well? In Matt's opinion, it was the ones who did live there—and *knew* him—who'd be the most shocked, and they'd already heard.

"We must begin a quiet campaign to convince them that Ragnarök is not the end of the world. It is a change. A cleansing. Ultimately, it is an event that will benefit our people, present and future."

He leaned closer.

"Ragnarök, as it is foretold in the myths, will not end the world. We must remind them of that. It will be a time of great turmoil and upheaval and a tragic loss of life, but the world will emerge the better for it. America is corrupt, from Wall Street to Washington, and it is the same in every country around the world. No politician or advocacy group can change that. Our world needs cleansing. Our world needs Ragnarök."

The other Elders chimed in their agreement.

What? No. I'm hearing wrong. The champion is supposed to stop Ragnarök.

"We know how this must work. Matt must fight the serpent. Matt must defeat the serpent ... but he must be defeated in turn. The champions of the gods must die, and the monsters must die, as the prophecy says, so the world can be reborn."

Matt had stopped breathing.

They don't want me to win.

His grandfather continued. "I do not take this lightly. I will be honest in saying that when I first realized Matt was the champion, I prayed that the runes would tell me I was mistaken. But I have come to realize that this is right. The boy is strong and he is good, and he is deserving of this honor. That is how I must see this. My grandson is being honored in the highest fashion, and he will do us proud, and he will take his place in the halls of Valhalla as a champion with the long-dead gods. As a hero. Our hero."

Matt stumbled away from the door.

They expect me to die. They want the ice age to come, the world to end. I'm not their champion. I'm their sacrifice.

Of course I am. That's why they chose me. Because I'm guaranteed to screw this up.

He'd been planning to tell Granddad exactly that: *You made a mistake.* But there'd been a little bit of him that hoped he really was the champion, that he'd finally show his family and everyone else—

The little girl took his hand and tugged him across the room, and he was so dazed, he just followed. When they were at the door, she whispered, "You seek Odin."

Odin? Why would I...?

Because Odin was the leader of the gods. The most powerful of them all. The father of Thor.

He stared at the little girl. Who was she? *What* was she? Not just a little girl—he was sure of that now.

"Odin will tell me how to fix this, right?" Matt said. "He'll tell me how to defeat the Midgard Serpent and survive."

Again, she looked confused. "I do not know. That is to come. That is not now. I know only—"

"You only know what is now. Yeah, I got that the first..." His gaze shifted to the mosaic on his left. A scene of Thor asking the Norns for advice.

The Norns. Three women who knew the destiny of gods and humans. In a lot of the old stories, Future was the youngest. But their tradition—and the mosaic—followed one from the old sagas. The oldest was Past. Then came Future. And finally, the youngest Norn—Present.

He turned to the little girl, and his heart started thumping again. By this point, he was pretty sure it was never going to beat at a normal rate again.

"Who are you?" he asked as the hairs on his neck prickled.

"You know."

"One of the Norns. Present."

She nodded. "I said you know."

"And *you* don't know anything except what's happening now. Or what should be happening now. So where do I get the rest?"

"From Future. She waits."

"Where will I find her?"

"I do not know. That is to come—"

"All right, all right. Where is she *now*?"

The little girl pointed. "Out there. She waits."

Matt followed her finger to the door. "Where exactly out there?"

No answer. He turned. The girl was gone.

This time when Matt walked into the fair, he still didn't notice the smells, the sights, the sounds, but only because he was focused on his task. Find the Norn.

Find the Norn? Are you crazy? A Norn? Like in the stories? That's all they are, you know. Stories.

Earlier, when he'd thought of fighting the serpent, he'd tried not to focus on what he believed. It was easy when they were old stories, like Noah's Ark. You could say, "Sure, that could happen." But then you thought about it, really thought about it, and said, "Seriously? One boat with two of every animal on Earth? How does that work?" It was easier to just not think about it. Accept it. That's what he'd done his whole life.

That's what he had to do now. Accept it. Believe it. He was looking for a Norn.

Which would be a lot easier if he had any clue what she looked like. The mosaic wasn't much help. In it, the youngest Norn had been about his age, and the only thing she had in common with the little girl who had actually appeared was her blond hair. Blond hair in Blackwell was as rare as fleas on a homeless mutt.

He weaved through the crowds. Normally, that would be easy. While people knew who he was, they wouldn't do more than nod or smile. Now Thorsens would stop mid-carnival-game to say something, and of course he had to be polite and respond.

With so many Thorsens talking to him, others noticed, and they said hi, too. Any other time, that would have been great. The center of attention. Can't argue with that, especially when you're usually only there if you've done something wrong. But right now, when he was on a mission, it was kind of inconvenient.

Finally, he spotted her. The Norn on the mosaic had been about his mom's age, but this girl didn't look older than Jake. She was dressed differently from the other girls at the fair, too. She wore a skirt of rough cloth, and her hair was piled up on top of her head in a heap of tiny braids. She sat on a bench, legs swinging as she watched kids on the merry-go-round.

So how did he know it was her? Because his amulet started vibrating. The same way it had right before he'd met the first Norn.

Still, he had to be sure. So he walked up as casually as he could and said, "Hey," but she only smiled and said, "Hello."

"Are you waiting for me?" he said.

She got that look of confusion, a mirror image of the little girl's. "I do not know. That is—"

"The present. You only know the future. Got it." And got the right girl, apparently. "Kind of feels like it should be Christmas, don't you think?"

She tilted her head, frowning.

"Scrooge? The ghosts of Christmas past, present, and future?" He shook his head when she continued to frown. "Never mind. Okay, so I should be looking for Odin, because he's going to tell me...what exactly?"

"How to defeat the Midgard Serpent."

Matt exhaled as relief fluttered through him. "And stop Ragnarök? So things don't need to happen the way they do in the myth, with all of us dying and the world ending?"

"Some parts cannot be changed. Some can. You must discover which is which."

"But you can foresee the future, right?"

"There are many futures. I cannot tell which will come to pass. You will try to change what the myth foretells. You will succeed in some parts and fail in others."

"Right. Except the whole die-defeating-the-serpent thing. I can definitely survive, despite what the myth says?"

"Yes," she said.

"And if I do, the world doesn't end?"

"It does not *end*, even if you fail," she said carefully. "However, almost all life on it will perish."

"Same thing. But if I defeat the serpent and survive, that doesn't happen, right?"

"Correct."

"Good. Now, where do I find him?" He paused again. "Is

it really Odin? I mean, the gods died, didn't they? Did Odin survive?"

She smiled. "No, the gods are dead. The one you seek is like yourself: a descendant. He is Odin as you are Thor. Yet he is not Odin, as you are not Thor."

Which made perfect sense.

"So he's a kid then. Where is he?" Matt asked.

"I do not know. Where Odin is, that is present. I know only what is to come."

Matt exhaled. They really weren't making this easy. "I *will* find Odin, though. That's a guarantee, which means I don't need to look for him."

"You may find him, or you may not." She had a faraway look in her eyes as she spoke. "There is more than one future."

Great.

Before he could try another tactic, the Norn said, "This is the best future. This is the one we wish for you: that you will find Odin, and you will find the others; that you will fight, and you will win."

"The others? But they'll come here, right? The *Thing* is going to gather them up."

"They will gather possible champions, but they will not gather the right champions. That is your task."

"And, let me guess, you have no idea where I'll find anyone."

"That is how. I do not know how. Only—"

"That I will or won't," he interrupted. "Do you know how completely useless that is? I'm thirteen. I can't just hop in my car and let my magical god-descendant-finding GPS guide me."

She looked at Matt blankly.

"Can I get one clue?" he said. "A bread crumb to start me on the trail? An e-mail address, maybe?"

"E-mail...?"

"Anything. I'll do what you tell me, because while saving the world and all would be great, I'm not keen on the dying part, either. I'd like to live long enough to get out of middle school."

She nodded. "That would be wise."

"So, the other descendants. It'd be nice if I could find them all in Blackwell, but it's only Thor and Loki here, isn't it?"

"You will not find the others here. *Around* here, yes, but not here."

Matt tried to be patient as he asked, "Around here...? In the county? The state? The country? The continent?"

"In the place known as South Dakota."

At least she hadn't said "continent."

The air beside her shimmered, and the little girl took form again.

"I know where Loki is," the little girl said.

"Okay, that's great, but I don't need Loki. Sure, he's to be at Ragnarök, but he leads the other side."

"That is not the present," said the girl Norn.

"Okay so..." He turned to the older Norn. "Am I right that Loki—or his descendant—will lead the monsters?"

"Loki may, or he may not. That is up to you," she said.

"Meaning he could help us, which would sway the battle our way, so I need to get him on our side. Got it." He turned to the youngest. "Where is he?"

"Loki is there." She gestured.

Matt followed her hand to see Laurie and Fen standing in line for the Tilt-A-Whirl. *Fen? No way.*

"Right *there*. Now?" He pivoted to watch Fen and Laurie as they climbed into one of the red cars. "But you said there were other champions. Maybe you can find another one for Loki, because Fen is not ever, in a million years..."

He turned back and found he was talking to himself. The Norns had vanished.

"...going to help me with anything," he muttered.

EIGHT

❖

MATT

"ALLIANCE"

Right after the Norns vanished, Cody and the others found him. While the last thing on Matt's mind was hanging out at the fair, right now, being part of a group might be the best thing. No one would bug him if he stayed with his friends, who also wouldn't really notice if he was quiet. He wasn't exactly loud at the best of times. He could just retreat into his thoughts. And he had a lot of thoughts to retreat into.

He had no idea what to do next. Apparently, he was supposed to buddy up with Fen. Which was not happening. Fen wanted nothing to do with any Thorsens, and Matt's family was worst of all—his dad had been responsible for putting Fen's father behind bars.

Speaking of his parents, what did they think of all this? He remembered his grandfather's words. *Those who need to know the truth already do.* His dad and mom would need to know, obviously. So they must. That's why they'd been so nice to him. That's why Dad had given him a hundred bucks for the fair.

Enjoy yourself, son . . . while you still can.

The Norns had said that he didn't have to die fighting the Midgard Serpent, but Granddad believed the prophecy was fated to come true. That meant he couldn't go to his grand-father or his family for help. He needed to do this on his own. Gather up the other kids and find Odin. Train. Fight. Win. There was no other way. If they failed, the world as they knew it would end. Which was kind of a big deal.

He was supposed to start with Fen. And then what? He had no idea. He only hoped something would come to him.

He was waiting for Cody and their friends to get off the Avalanche—his stomach sure couldn't handle that tonight— when he saw Fen trudge past without Laurie, his gaze on the ground, boots scuffing the sawdust as he headed for the exit, looking like he'd had a really bad day.

Matt figured Fen had a lot of bad days, with his parents gone, being passed from relative to relative. Even if Dad said that's because Fen was too wild for anyone to handle, maybe all the moving around *made* him a little wild. And those cuts and bruises on his face... Matt had heard Fen was staying with his cousin Kris, and everyone knew Kris was quick with his fists.

Thinking about that put Matt in the right state of mind to talk to Fen. Not to tell him about Ragnarök and the Midgard Serpent, of course. That'd be crazy. If Matt had any chance of winning Fen over, he had to take it slow. He'd just happen to be leaving the fair at the same time and bump into Fen and offer him some...

Matt looked around. Corn dogs. Sure, that might work.

He told Cody he wasn't feeling great and was catching a ride home. Then he grabbed a couple of corn dogs. By that time, Fen was leaving. Matt jogged to catch up, but one aunt and two cousins stopped him on the way.

When he reached the exit, Fen had veered right, passing the parking lot and heading into the field. The sun was almost down, but the sky was oddly bright with a faint tinge of yellow. The wind seemed to be picking up, promising another cold night.

Fimbulwinter was coming.

Matt shivered and walked as fast as he could toward Fen, who'd disappeared around some trees. Matt broke into a run then, slowing only when he'd passed the trees, and saw Fen just ahead, trudging along.

"Hey," Matt called. "Fen? Hold up!"

Fen glanced over his shoulder. Then he turned back and kept walking.

"Fen!"

"Shove off, Thorsen."

Matt jogged in front of Fen and held out the tray of corn dogs. "I was just leaving, too, and I thought you might want these. I bought them, but I'm stuffed."

"And I look like I'd want your leftovers?"

"They're not leftovers," Matt exclaimed. "I never touched them. Even the ketchup's still in the packets. See?"

"You don't want them?" Fen asked.

"No, I thought I did, but I ate so much at the feast...."

"Fine." Fen took each by the stick and whipped them into the field. "The crows can have them. They're scavengers. Not me."

Fen walked around Matt and kept going. Matt looked out at the corn dogs, yellow blobs on the dark field, and felt his amulet warm. Maybe offering Fen food hadn't been a good idea, but he didn't need to do that. He—

Loki may, or he may not. That is up to you.

Whether Fen led the monsters into the final battle depended on Matt. He took a deep breath, broke into a jog, and called to Fen, but a sudden gust of wind whipped his words away and nearly knocked him off his feet. He recovered and caught up to Fen again, this time walking beside him.

"I noticed your face looks kind of messed—" Matt began. "I mean, you have some bruises."

"Do I? Huh. Hadn't noticed."

"About that..." Matt cleared his throat. "If you're having problems—with Kris or anyone else—you should talk to the counselor at school. No one should do that to you. You've got rights."

Fen stopped and turned. A gust of wind whipped past, and Fen's hair fell over his eyes. "Excuse me?"

"If someone's hitting you, you should talk to Ms. Early at school. She can help. It's against the law for a grown-up to hit a kid. You don't need to take that."

"No one knocks me around, Thorsen, unless I'm knocking them back. I got into it with someone, okay? Someone who fought back. Someone with more guts than you." Fen didn't shove Matt, but he looked like he was considering it.

"More guts than me? Um, you know what I said last week, about your memory? It really does suck, because I'm pretty sure I *did* fight back. You jumped me, and you didn't land a single hit before I knocked you flat on your butt. Which is where you stayed."

Fen lunged. Matt ducked, swung around, and nailed Fen with a right hook that sent him stumbling. As Matt watched Fen recover, he reflected that this might not be the best way to make friends.

Matt clenched his fists at his sides and held himself still. "I don't want to do this, Fen."

"Really? Because it sure looks like you do."

Fen charged. Matt told himself he wouldn't hit him back. Defensive moves only. Except, as Coach Forde always said, he really wasn't good at the defensive stuff. So when Fen charged into Matt, they both went down.

Fen went to grab Matt by the hair, but Matt caught his arm and tried to hold it—just hold it—but Fen started thrashing and kicking, teeth bared, growling, and the only way Matt could stop him was another right hook that sent him skidding across the grass.

Then a blast of wind hit, so strong that it knocked Matt to his knees. He struggled up, blind, his eyes watering. When they cleared, he could make out figures. At least four. Surrounding them. The one in the middle towered over him.

Grown-ups. Someone at the fair had seen the fight and come over, and now Matt had been caught fighting Fen, and his dad was going to kill him before the Midgard Serpent even had a chance—

He blinked as the figures came clear. Not grown-ups. Kids. Six of them. Wild-looking kids, some in well-worn military surplus, others in ripped jeans and T-shirts. *Raider Scouts.* A weird Boy-Scouts-gone-bad kind of group. His dad and his deputies ran them off every time they found their campsite. Raiders didn't get their name because they thought it was cool: they really were like old-fashioned Viking Raiders, swooping into town, stealing everything that wasn't nailed down before disappearing into the woods again.

The biggest one looked about sixteen. He wore shredded jeans, hiking boots, and a skintight sleeveless shirt that showed scars on both arms. The group leader. Had to be. As Matt tensed, he kept his gaze on him. First sign of trouble, that was his target.

The leader reached down and picked up Fen by the scruff of his neck. He leaned over to whisper something before tossing him aside. Fen hit the ground, and Matt took a step toward him. It didn't matter that Fen had been trying to beat the snot out of him; Matt wasn't going to stand there and let outsiders treat a Blackwell kid like that.

But as soon as Matt stepped forward, the boy to his right lunged. Matt wheeled and nailed him with a left. There was a satisfying *thwack* and a grunt of surprise as the kid staggered back. Matt started toward him, but another kid leaped onto his back.

Matt yanked the kid over his shoulder, thinking as he did that the kid seemed awfully light. When Matt threw him down, he found himself standing over a boy no more than ten. Matt froze then, his gut clenching, an apology on his lips. The boy grabbed Matt's leg. Matt tried to kick him off, but halfheartedly. When you grow up bigger than other guys, you learn really fast that if you so much as shove a little kid you'll get hauled down to the office for a lecture on bullying and a call home.

The kid sunk his teeth into Matt's shin. Matt yelped and tried to yank back, but another kid jumped him. He wheeled to swing, but this one was a girl, and seeing her face, even twisted into a snarl, made his hand stop midpunch. Hit a little kid? Or a girl? He knew better than that.

The wind howled past, stinging his eyes again, and he dimly saw the girl go flying. For a second, Matt thought he'd accidentally hit her, but when he blinked, he saw Fen slamming his fist into her gut. Then he turned on Matt.

"I need to rescue you from a little kid and a girl? Really?" Fen grabbed for the boy, still snarling on Matt's leg, but another kid jumped him from behind. As Fen hit him, he yelled back at Matt. "Fight, Thorsen!"

Matt shook his leg, trying to disengage the boy. Behind him, another one snickered, taking in the spectacle as he waited his turn.

"Thorsen!" Fen snarled.

"But he's just a—"

"He's a *Raider*!" Fen yelled.

The boy lunged to bite again, and Matt grabbed him by the arm and threw him to the side. Then he looked up to see the leader smirking. The boy was twisting, scrambling to his feet, and to Matt's left, another was getting ready to take a run at him—a kid closer to his age, but scrawny, half a foot shorter. Matt glanced back at the leader, just standing there, arms crossed.

Matt charged. He heard Fen shout "No!" but Matt didn't stop. At tournaments, Coach Forde always tried to arrange it so Matt took on his toughest opponent first. Take care of the biggest threat while you're fresh. If you win the round, you're left with weaker guys who've just seen you knock out their best fighter.

As Matt rushed the Raider leader, he saw surprise flash across the Raider's face. Matt barreled into the guy and sent him staggering. It was only a stagger, though, and the guy came back swinging. Matt managed to duck the first blow, but he took the second to the side of his face, his neck wrenching.

Matt swung. He landed three blows in quick succession, the last one hitting so hard the guy went flying.

As the Raider leader fell, the wind whipped up again. This time it sent Matt stumbling. His ankle twisted, and he went down on one knee. He started to rise again and—

A low growl sounded behind him.

Matt lifted his head to see a wolf standing there. A giant wolf with gray fur and inch-long fangs. The guy he'd thrown to the ground was gone.

Matt could tell himself that the wolf had somehow run in without him noticing, and the Raider leader had taken off, but one look in the beast's eyes and he knew better. This *was* the Raider leader. The guy had turned into a wolf. Now it was hunkering down, teeth bared, ready to leap and—

Someone screamed. A long, drawn-out wail of a scream that made the wolf stop, muzzle shooting up, ears swiveling to track the sound.

Not a scream. A siren. The tornado siren.

Matt looked up and saw that the sky had turned yellow. Distant shouts and cries came from the fair as people scrambled for cover. Then, far to the left, a dark shape appeared against the yellow sky. A twister. It hadn't touched down, but the gathering clouds seemed to drop with every passing second.

A howl snapped Matt's attention back to the wolf. It wasn't the beast howling; it was the wind, shrieking past, as loud and piercing as the siren. The wolf's eyes slitted against the wind as it sliced through his fur, and he turned away from the blast.

Matt charged. He caught the wolf with a right hook to the head. The beast staggered, but only a step, better balanced on four legs than two. Then it lunged, teeth flashing. Matt caught it with an uppercut. A yelp, but the wolf barely stumbled this time, and its next lunge knocked Matt down, with the wolf on his chest. He grabbed its muzzle, struggling to keep those jaws away from his throat as the beast growled and snarled. Matt tried to kick it in the stomach, but his foot wouldn't connect.

Someone hit the wolf's side and sent it flying off Matt. Matt scrambled up and tackled the wolf. His rescuer did the same, both of them grabbing the beast and trying to wrestle it down. It was only then that Matt saw that it was Fen who'd come to his aid.

"Attacking a *wolf*?" Fen grunted as they struggled. "You're one crazy—" The wind whipped the last word away.

Matt looked across the field. The tornado had touched down. They needed to end this and get to safety. Now.

With a sudden burst of energy, the wolf bucked. Matt lost his grip and slid off. Fen stayed draped over the beast's back.

"Use your thing!" Fen shouted.

"What?"

"Your—" Fen's face screwed up in frustration as he struggled to stay on the wolf's back. "Your power thing. What you hit me with."

How did Fen—? Not important.

Matt clenched his amulet. It had barely even warmed since the fight had begun, and now it just lay in his hand, cold metal. When he closed his eyes to concentrate, something struck his back. A chunk of wood hit the ground. A sheet of newspaper sailed past, wrapping around his arm. The next thing that flew at him wasn't debris—it was one of the Raiders. Matt slammed his fist into the kid, then turned back just in time to see the wolf throw Fen off.

The wolf looked at Matt. Their eyes met. The wolf's lip curled, and it growled. Even as the sirens drowned out the sound, Matt swore he could feel it vibrating through the air. Matt locked his gaze with the wolf's. It didn't like that, snarling and snapping now, but Matt held its gaze, and as the beast hunkered down, Matt pulled back his fist, ready to—

A black shadow leaped on the wolf's back. Matt barely caught a flash of it before the two went down, rolling across the grass. Then all he could see was fur—gray fur and brown fur.

Two wolves. The big gray one and a smaller brown one. Matt looked over to where the wolf had thrown Fen, but he wasn't there.

Loki. The trickster god. The shape-shifter god.

Fen was a wolf. These kids all were—which wasn't possible. The Thorsens all said that the Brekkes didn't know about their powers. You can't use powers if you don't know about them.

He looked at the wolves again.

Apparently, everyone was wrong.

Matt ran at the leader wolf. Another Raider jumped into his path. It was the little kid from earlier, but Matt was beyond worrying about fighting fair. He hit the boy with a blow to the stomach, followed by an uppercut to the jaw, and then shoved him aside.

Now the big wolf had Fen pinned, jaws slashing toward

his throat. Matt jumped on the beast's back. It reared up. Matt grabbed two handfuls of fur, but that was really all he could do. He didn't have claws or fangs, and he wasn't in any decent position to land a punch. Just get the thing off Fen. That was his goal. Just—

He saw something sailing toward them as fast as a rocket. A branch or—

"Duck!" he shouted to Fen as he leaped off the wolf's back.

He hit the ground hard. He heard a yelp and rolled just in time to see the wolf staggering, a piece of pipe hitting the grass beside him. The beast snarled and tried to charge, but it stumbled and toppled, blood trickling from its ear. It hit the ground, unconscious.

Fen leaped up and they turned to face the other Raiders, who'd been standing back, letting their leader fight. Half of them were wolves now, and they were closing in, growling and snarling, eyes glittering.

A figure jumped one of the human Raiders. It was Laurie. The Raider grabbed her and threw her aside. Two of the wolves jumped Fen. The biggest ran at Matt, but he veered aside and raced toward Laurie. He caught her attacker in the side and knocked him away.

He put out a hand to help Laurie up.

She waved off the help and glowered at him. "I could have handled it."

"I was just—"

"I'm here to help you two. Not to be rescued," she said.

Before he could answer, the bigger Raider was on him, and Laurie's attacker was back on his feet. Matt managed to take down his, and Laurie seemed to be doing okay with hers, but when he went to help her, a hand grabbed his shoulder.

Matt turned, fist raised. It was Fen, now back in human form. He pointed to the east, and Matt saw the twister coming. The dark shape was stirring up a debris cloud, making it seem even bigger than it was.

"We gotta run," Fen said.

"What? No. We're—" He slammed his fist into a charging attacker. "We're fine. That twister—"

"Not the twister," Fen said as he ducked a blow. He jabbed his finger east again, and Matt made out a group of figures racing across the field. Coming their way. More Raiders. He faintly caught a groan to his left and glanced over to see the big wolf rising.

"We need to *run*." Fen gave Matt a shove in the right direction and went after Laurie.

Matt turned to help, but Laurie had thrown off her attacker. Fen grabbed her by the arm, and they started to race toward the fair. Matt took one last look around—at the twister, the Raiders, the giant wolf.

At this rate, I'll be lucky if I make it to Ragnarök, he thought, and tore off after Fen and Laurie.

NINE

LAURIE

"TORNADO TOSSED"

Laurie shook off Fen's arm. Hailstones pelted them as they ran. Everyone knew not to run from tornadoes, but tornadoes *and* wolves? That changed things, but maybe not everything.

"I don't want to get separated," Fen yelled over the wind. He grabbed her hand and twined his fingers with hers.

She yanked away from him again. She was hurt and angry that Fen had kept such a huge secret from her.

"Then hold Matt's hand," she yelled back and got a mouthful of the sawdust that was lifting and swirling in the air.

He was family, her best friend—and he'd lied to her. *He's*

a wolf. How could he not tell me! She felt tears sting her eyes as the wind slapped her face.

She wasn't sure which of the shrieks and howls in the air were wolves and which were from the tornado sirens and the storm itself. She wasn't going to look back for either threat. If she'd been at home, she'd have gone into the basement of the building. Here, she wasn't sure what to do, but Matt seemed to have a plan. She'd never expected to be following a Thorsen, especially after the fight Matt and Fen had had the other day, but right now they were all on the same side: the three of them versus the wolves.

"Over here." Matt gestured toward the longship.

Climbing up seemed crazy, but the ship would protect them from the hail, flying things, and maybe even the wolves. It wouldn't protect them from the tornado. The roar of it was awful, and being higher up seemed like a great way to fall farther.

"We can get inside it." He scrambled up the side of the ship. Matt tapped in a code on a lockbox mounted on the wall. It popped open, and he grabbed a key. "Come on."

Would Fen go with him? She wasn't sure, and her loyalties were divided. She might be mad at Fen, but he was still Fen—and Matt was the kid who had thrown Fen at the longship. *Was that magic, too?* She felt like an idiot. They both knew things. Matt wasn't freaked out about the wolf thing, either. She wasn't sure what was going on, but right now, the two people who had answers were both staring at her. A new burst of hurt and anger filled her.

She ignored the hand Matt held out to help her over the side of the ship, and she didn't say a word as Fen climbed over after her. They crawled across the deck of the ship on their stomachs, keeping themselves as low as possible; the sides of the longship protected them from the worst of the wind and kept them hidden from the wolves.

Matt fumbled at the lock, taking far too long for her liking.

The wind ripped at their clothes and hair; rain and hail pelted them. She opened her mouth to say "Hurry," and the air took her breath away. She snapped her lips closed.

Behind her, she felt Fen move closer. He had put his body behind her to shelter her from flying branches and hailstones. Because he was blocking her from the storm, his mouth was directly beside her ear. "I wanted to tell you," he said. "Wasn't allowed."

She didn't answer. Later, they would have to talk—or yell, more likely—but right now, she couldn't say anything. If she did, she might start crying, and she wasn't going to look all wussy in front of the two of them.

Matt looked back and said something, but all she caught was "Fen, pull."

Fen yelled, "What?"

"Pull," she shouted, turning to him as she did so.

Fen glanced behind him, and then he nodded, apparently satisfied with what he saw—or with what he didn't see.

As her cousin reached past her, she looked back, too, and realized that no one had followed them onto the ship. She wasn't sure where the wolves had gone, but they weren't here now. Maybe they'd had the sense to seek shelter, too. Being caught in a tornado could be deadly for a wolf, just as it could for a person.

Together, Matt and Fen tugged the door open. Matt's arms were tight as he held on to the door, and Fen had to brace a foot on the wall, but they had the door open. Fen gestured with his head, and even though she couldn't hear what he was saying, she knew it was some version of *You go first.*

She scrambled inside, fumbling in the dark, and felt someone bump into her almost immediately.

"Sorry," Matt muttered as he steadied her. "Steps. Be careful."

The door crashed shut, taking away any light. She'd already seen that there were steps. They were all standing on a small landing, and another foot in front of her steps descended into the still deeper darkness of the ship. "How many steps?" she asked Matt.

"Maybe twelve. Just follow me."

"You can't see any better than I can." She rolled her eyes, even though neither of them could see. Boys had some pretty

ridiculous ideas about what girls could do. She might not be able to wrestle—or turn into a wolf—but she was just as capable of climbing down the steps as they were. Unless...
"Can either of you see?"

Fen snorted. "My vision is better than regular people's, but when it's this dark, I'd need to be a wolf to see."

"Right," she murmured. She started to laugh at the strangeness of... well, *everything* today, but stopped herself. Fen was prickly on the best of days, and he was as likely to think she was laughing at him as not. The sound that started as a laugh ended like a cry.

"Are you hurt?" Fen sounded less worried than he would have if Matt weren't there, but she knew him well enough to know that he was alarmed.

"I'm fine." She sighed. It was hard to stay mad at him sometimes; he'd made it his personal goal in life to look out for her, to be there whenever she needed anything. He was a combination of her best friend and brother. She tried to push the hurt further away and said, "Bruises, but that's all. I think. You two?"

Matt shrugged. "Like going a few rounds in the ring. No big deal."

Fen snorted. "Yeah, right."

Matt ignored him and said, "Just feel with your foot. We're right behind you."

"Let me pass," Fen demanded. "I can go first in case—"

"I got it," she cut him off, and eased her foot forward. The only way he was going to stop trying to shelter her from everything was for her to push him more.

Between the darkness of the storm and the lack of lights inside the ship, she had only her sense of touch to guide her. She made her way down the steps, counting as she went.

"Twelve," she said when she reached the bottom.

She heard and felt them reach the bottom, too. They stood there in the dark, not speaking. Behind them and above them, she could hear the *ping*ing and *thump*ing of things hitting the wood, and the roar of the storm outside. She wasn't sure if the boys were scared, but now that they were out of the storm and away from the wolves, the fear of what could have happened hit her, and she shuddered. *We're fine*, she reminded herself. *Right now, we're just fine.*

She felt around with her hands, but she wasn't sure what would be down here. Was it storage? Things she'd knock over? And even if it wasn't, did she want to fumble around in the dark and then have to fumble back to the steps when the storm ended? She ended up standing still.

She hated waiting in the dark while a storm tore around outside. Twisters were scary in a way that blizzards weren't. They had those in South Dakota, too, but those mostly just meant school was canceled or delayed. Sometimes, there were whiteouts, where the wind blew the snow, and every-thing was a white blur outside. That was the thing, though:

it was outside, and she was safe inside. Tornados were different. Inside wasn't the same sort of protection from a storm that destroyed buildings. She shivered.

Immediately, Fen's arm went around her. "It'll be okay. We'll get out of here."

She nodded even though he couldn't see it and then whispered, "I'm mad at you."

He growled, and now that she knew he was a wolf sometimes, it sounded somehow more like a real growl. "There are rules. I couldn't tell you unless you changed, too."

Quietly, she asked, "Does the whole family change?"

Fen was quiet for a minute. "No, only some of us." He butted his head into hers, and for the first time, she realized that the gesture was one an animal would make. She'd known it was an odd thing that the Brekkes all did, but she hadn't made the connection before now. Their version of affection was because they were part animal.

When she didn't respond, Fen added, "Don't be mad. Please?"

Matt's voice saved her from answering. "We can sit over here."

There was no way to tell how long they would have to wait. They were all wet and cold, and once the storm left, they still had to deal with werewolves—*Were they werewolves? Or were they just wolves?* She wasn't sure the term even mattered. "So are you a Raider, too, then? That's what they all are, right? The Raiders are all wolves."

"I'm not one of them," Fen spat. "I follow my *own* rules, not theirs. They're *wulfenkind*, too, but I'm not joining them. I pay my dues... and yours, so I don't have to join them."

"*My* dues?"

She felt him shrug next to her, but all he said was, "No big thing. Once we figure out if you're going to change, you'll either pay, join, or go lone-wolf—like Uncle Stig."

"*Dad* is... that's why he's always gone?" Laurie felt like everything she'd known was suddenly different. Maybe it wouldn't have made things easier, but so much made sense now that she knew the family secret. "He could pay them and stay here? Why doesn't—" She stopped herself. They had other things than her father to deal with right now, but she couldn't help adding, "I'm not joining them. I can tell you that... and neither are you, Fen Brekke. You think I'm mad now? If you join them, I'll show you mad."

He didn't answer, but he gave her a brief one-armed hug. She'd told him she cared about him. That was all Fen ever really needed when he was worried: to know she cared.

A click in the dark was followed by a flash of fire. In Fen's hand was a lighter. It wasn't exactly him saying *Let's change the subject*, but it did the trick all the same.

"How long have you had *that*?" Matt asked.

Fen shrugged.

The light it cast was scant, but she could see stacks of boxes and more than a few cobwebs. Nothing particularly interesting, and then the light went out.

"Did you see any candles?" Matt asked. "Or a lantern?"

"We could burn one of the boxes," Fen suggested.

"Don't even think about it," Matt said. "Give me the lighter, and I'll look for—"

"Yeah, right. I don't think so, Thorsen."

"If we're going to work together—"

"I don't remember agreeing to that," Fen interrupted. "I saved your butt with the Raiders, but that doesn't mean—"

"You saved me? Were we at the same fight?"

"Stop. Just *stop*," Laurie interrupted. "You're both better than the other one. Now, we can stay here and wait for the monsters to—"

"Wolves," Fen muttered. "Not monsters."

"Well, since you didn't even tell me, how would I know that? And they weren't being friendly, were they? How would I know what you act like as a wolf, since you hid it from me?" She poked him repeatedly as she spoke.

Fen flicked the lighter again and looked at her.

"You lied to me." Laurie folded her arms over her chest.

"Um, planning?" Matt reminded them quietly before her glare-fest with Fen could turn into an ugly argument. "Laurie's right. We need a plan." He took a breath. "I know this is going to sound crazy, but we need to work together. Quick version: Ragnarök is coming. We have to find the rest of the gods' descendants. We have two already—I'm the stand-in for Thor, and Fen is for Loki. That's what the Norns told me tonight."

"The Norns?" Laurie interjected.

"They're the ladies in charge of everyone's fate," Matt said. "I talked to them, and that's how I knew I needed to talk to Fen." He stopped, took a breath, and added, "Look, I know Loki and Thor weren't always friends in the myths, but they could work together." He paused and turned to Fen. "I'm guessing you know the Brekkes are descended from Loki."

The lighter clicked off, so they couldn't see each other again. Laurie was glad they couldn't see the shock on her face. *Loki? The god Loki? From the myths?* She pinched her arm to make sure this wasn't like her weird fish dream. It hurt, but she was definitely awake—and apparently the only one surprised that their ancestors were real gods.

"Yeah, and that Thorsens don't think we know." Fen sounded smug. "Guess you didn't know some of us kept Loki's skill in shape-shifting, either. We might have only kept the wolf, but it's a lot more useful than most of Loki's shapes."

Matt let it drop. "So we need to find the other descendants and stop Ragnarök. If we don't do something, the world will end. They're not here in Blackwell, so we need to go find them. Are you in?"

Laurie tried to not freak out over the things they were talking about. It was bad enough that Fen had hidden that he was a wolf, but then Matt said the god thing and the whole world-is-ending thing. She'd thought the worst trouble they had to face was theft of a shield. These were much bigger problems. When she could finally speak, she asked, "Why were the wolves after us?"

Neither boy said anything for a moment. Then Matt said, "Maybe they know we're the god stand-ins."

"Or they're just out starting trouble," Fen added. "You're a *Thorsen*, and that means you're the enemy to *wulfenkind*."

"I'm not your enemy, Fen."

At that, Fen flicked the lighter on again. "Why should I believe you about any of it?"

"I don't lie," Matt said simply.

"Fen, I think we can trust him," Laurie started.

The lighter went out.

Laurie knew that Matt was telling the truth. Somehow, it just made sense to her. Believing it was as easy as believing that she and Fen were descendants of the long-dead god Loki. She wasn't sure why she was so sure, but she was. The question was how she could convince her stubborn cousin.

Before Laurie could say anything else, though, Fen said,

"Fine. If it's a choice between working with you or the world ending, I can put up with you for a while."

Although Laurie knew Fen was trying to sound like he didn't really care, she knew him. That was the voice he always had before he was about to go and do something colossally stupid. It meant that he expected something crazy or dangerous to happen. Proof positive that he expected true trouble if he joined up with Matt came in Fen's very next sentence: "We need to get Laurie home first and—"

"Are you *joking*?" All of her anger and frustration came roaring back. She shoved him so hard he fell sideways.

Fen flicked the lighter on and glared at her.

"No," she snapped. "Don't even start! You can't expect me to stay here."

He sat up, lighter still flickering with its small flame, and began his list of objections. "Come on, Laurie. You're not the one who has to do this. It's dangerous, and you don't have a way to protect yourself." He jabbed Matt in the arm. "Thorsen has his knockout thing. I have teeth and claws. You're just a girl, and Uncle Stig will kill me if you get hurt."

"You're not going anywhere without me," Laurie insisted. Fen might think he was keeping her safe by leaving her behind, but she *knew* that he wasn't safe without her. Between his temper and his recklessness, there was no way he could avoid trouble when he was here in Blackwell. Once he was on the road running from other wolves and who knows what—or who—else, he'd be in trouble she couldn't even begin to imagine.

The lighter died again.

"Why would I risk you getting hurt?" Fen asked. She heard the fear in his voice that he always thought he hid, and she understood, but it didn't matter. She wasn't letting fear—his or hers—stop her. He needed her.

Laurie tried to think of an argument. She felt like she was missing something obvious, and then it hit her. "I met Odin," she blurted. "Oh. Wow. I thought he was just a weirdo, but I met *Odin*. Remember? I told you I met a stranger who acted like he knew me." She filled them in on her whole conversation with Odin and was surprised by how quiet Fen still was when she was done. "Fen?"

Fen flicked the lighter on one more time.

"I'm coming with you, Fen," she said. "I know what Odin looks like, and he said I'd see him again, so I'm *supposed* to come."

Fen opened his mouth to say something, no doubt an objection, but she folded her arms over her chest and used the one thing she knew he couldn't ignore: "What if the Raiders come back, and I'm here alone? They know who I am, and I'm not a wolf. How am I supposed to fight them on my own?"

"I don't have a problem with it," Matt said. "We can take care of her."

"Take care of me?" Laurie sputtered.

"Yeah," Fen snarled. "If you're coming, next time there's a fight you stay out of it. If they're up there right now, you let Thorsen and me handle it. Or you can stay here, where it's safer."

"Safer?" Laurie echoed. "Did you listen to *anything* I said?"

"About as well as you did to what I said," Fen muttered.

They sat in tense silence for a few moments until Matt pointed out, "Sounds like the storm's ended. Let's get out of here."

Cautiously, they started up the stairs. Matt was in front, and Fen was behind her.

When they stepped outside, they stopped and looked at the destruction all around. A lot of the shields on the side of the ship were thrashed. Trees were uprooted. A car was overturned. The stop sign at the intersection had been flung halfway down the block.

Laurie didn't see any wolves, but people were already appearing, and she wasn't sure which ones were the ones who became wolves. Fen hadn't technically agreed to her coming, but she wasn't going to wait for him to stop being difficult. She looked at him and said, "We need to get out of here before the wolves find us. We'll stop at home, grab some clothes and whatever money we have, and then figure out where to go." She glanced at Matt, who was now squirming. "Look, if you'd rather tell your dad, we can—"

"No," he interrupted. "It's just...I can't go home."

Laurie and Fen exchanged a look.

"You're a Thorsen. Just walk in, get your stuff, and pretend like you're going to the gym or something." Fen shook his head. "I know you've probably never told a lie in your perfect life, but I can talk you through it. Easy as falling off a pedestal."

Laurie hid her sigh of relief. If Fen was focused on Matt, he'd stop being a pain about her going with them. She felt a little bad for Matt, but better Matt having to put up with Fen's teasing than her needing to fight about being left behind in Blackwell.

"I'm okay with lying, Fen," Matt was saying. "It's just... My family..." He took a deep breath. "They don't expect me to kill the Midgard Serpent. They expect me to die. And, apparently, they're okay with that."

For a moment, no one spoke. Fen's characteristic rudeness vanished, and Laurie wasn't at all sure what to say. The Thorsens were perfect; Matt had a family, a big family, who treated him like he could do no wrong. Carefully, she repeated, "They're okay with you dying."

"They told me I was going to be the one to stop Ragnarök, but I overheard my grandfather"—he paused, and then he spoke really quickly, all his words running together, as he looked at them both—"when I was with one of the Norns. My grandfather and the town council *want* Ragnarök to happen. Granddad wants me to fight the Midgard Serpent. He wants me to defeat it—so the monsters don't take over the world—but he expects me to die trying, just like in the myth. Then an ice age will come, and the world will be reborn, fresh and new."

"After almost everyone dies. That's messed up." Fen shook his head. Then he looked at Laurie and said, "We'll go to your place first. It's closest. He and I will stay outside. Aunt Janey won't let you go anywhere with me. Then we'll stop by the garage for my stuff."

They didn't have to worry: her mom wasn't home, so Laurie left a note and they headed to Kris' place. Leaving Blackwell seemed scary, but the other descendants weren't here—and the Raiders were. Plus, there was the whole Matt's-family-wanting-the-end-of-the-world problem. Leaving home was necessary.

But she was still nervous, and she was sure the boys were, too.

Once they had backpacks and a couple of sleeping bags they'd borrowed from Kris' garage, she turned to the boys and asked, "Okay, where to?"

The boys exchanged a look. Neither spoke. Day one and

they were already lacking any sort of plan. They had no idea what to do. They were kids and supposed to figure this all out...because Matt said his family and some women claimed he and Fen were to defeat monsters. It was crazy. No one was saying it out loud, but she suspected they were all thinking it.

Fen turns into a wolf.

There was that one detail, proof that the crazy was real, that kept her from thinking it was all a great big joke. The rest of her "proof" was just her instincts and a conversation with a blue-haired boy. It wasn't much. The wolf thing was real, though. She'd seen it.

After a few moments, Matt said, "I can do this."

"Riiiight." Fen drew out the word. "Didn't we already decide that?"

"Not *that*," Matt said. "Maybe I can..." He stood straighter. "I'll talk to my brothers. They'll know about this. They're smart. They can help."

"Are you sure?" Laurie asked.

Matt nodded, but she didn't believe him, and from the look on Fen's face, neither did he.

"I'll go with you," Fen suggested. "You"—he looked pointedly at Laurie—"need to stay out of sight in case the Raiders come back."

She wanted to argue, but she was pretty sure that Fen

wouldn't need much of an excuse to decide to leave her behind. She nodded as meekly as she was able. "Fine."

This time, she added in her head. *I'll hide and wait* this *time.*

Fen and Matt both looked tense, but she knew they were trying to hide it. They had a start of a plan of sorts. For now, that would have to be enough.

This is going to be a disaster. The world is going to end because we don't know what to do.

TEN

MATT

"NIGHT FRIGHT"

Matt stood on the corner, looking at his house. For the first time in his life, he realized how much it looked like every other house on the block. Each was painted a different color, but otherwise, they were identical—split-level houses with single-car garages and exactly the same size lawns, sometimes even the same flowers now dying in the same size gardens.

"Come on," Fen whispered. "We don't have all night."

Matt tried to hurry, but his feet felt like they were made of lead. Shame burned through him. Some champion he was, too frightened to even face his family. That was nothing new, but—like looking down this street—it felt different now. Maybe it was because Fen was here, and he was seeing things like Fen would, just a bunch of nice houses, all in a row. Just an ordinary family living in the third one down. Nothing special. Nothing to be afraid of. Not for a kid who was destined to fight a giant serpent.

Matt took a deep breath and imagined Jake standing there. *Man up*, he'd say, like he always did, with that look on his face, like he couldn't believe they were actually related.

Man up. Matt wasn't sure what that meant exactly, but he was pretty sure Fen would say the same thing. *Stop dragging your feet like a baby and start acting like a man.*

Matt straightened and started forward before Fen noticed him hesitating.

"Wait," Fen said. He was even more prickly now that Laurie wasn't with them.

Matt ignored him. He wasn't trying to be rude; he needed to keep moving or it'd be morning and he'd still be on this street corner.

"I said *wait*," Fen snapped, and moved in front of Matt. He looked left and right, head swinging. *Like a wolf*, Matt thought. *Watching for trouble.*

"Back," Fen said.

"What?"

Fen shot him a glare and motioned him back around the corner, behind the Carlsens' garage.

"Raiders," he said.

"What?" Matt repeated, and then caught himself before he sounded like a total idiot. He took his voice down a notch like Jake did sometimes. "The Raiders are there?"

"Watching the house. We gotta go back."

Which was, Matt admitted to himself, exactly what he wanted. Forget grabbing stuff from his house. He'd happily stay in the same shirt and jeans for a week if it meant he didn't need to face his family.

Coward.

He peered out.

"I said—" Fen began.

"Just taking a look."

"Because you don't believe me?"

"No, I just—"

"Who's the guy who can see better at night?" Fen asked in a voice that sounded a lot like a warning growl.

"I know, I just—"

"Look at the house on the other side of yours. By the garage."

Matt peeked out and saw a young Raider hiding in the shadows.

"Three of them," Fen said. "Maybe more. Skull's not with them this time."

"Skull?"

"The leader. He was at the field."

"Right." Matt remembered the big Raider and was glad

at least he wasn't here, but still, three Raiders were three too many. "We need to draw them off."

"Um, no, we need to get out of here before they see—"

"You go," Matt said. "They're looking for me. If they don't see me come home, they'll think I snuck in later. They might go after my family."

"So?"

Matt looked at him.

"Isn't this the family that was going to sacrifice you to a dragon?" Fen asked.

"Serpent. Well, it's kind of like—never mind. My brothers don't know. They can't."

"Are you sure?"

He was certain Josh didn't know. But could he help? He was only sixteen. No. He had to do what Jake would. Man up. Protect his family. Prove to them that he could do this.

"I'm drawing the Raiders off," he said. "They need to know I never went home. That'll keep my family safe."

Fen snorted.

He thinks I'm an idiot. I shouldn't care. But I do. Matt shook his head. *Doesn't matter. I'm still a Thorsen. Family comes first.*

"You go on," Matt said. "I'll—"

"Walk," Fen said.

"What?"

Fen made a move, as if to shove him. "Go. Move. Pretend you're walking home."

Matt stepped out and started down the sidewalk. It took a moment to realize Fen was beside him. When he did, he started to protest, but a look from Fen shut him up.

"So, um, how's..." Matt struggled—and failed—to think of any sports or clubs Fen was in. "School. How's school?"

Fen looked at him like he'd asked how he liked ballet lessons.

"Mr. Fosse is being a real jerk this year, isn't he?" Matt continued.

"What the—?" Fen began.

"I'm making conversation."

"Seriously? We're on the lam together, Thorsen. Not buddying up."

"I'm doing it for them." Matt jerked his chin at the Raiders. "So it looks normal."

"Us talking does *not* look normal," Fen pointed out.

They continued in silence. It took a minute before the Raiders noticed them. Matt kept going, like he hadn't seen the figures sliding from behind the neighbor's garage.

"I'll just grab some clothes and a toothbrush," Matt said, as loudly as he dared. "Then we'll run away together. I mean—"

"Shut it, Thorsen," Fen hissed. "Just shut it."

There were five Raiders. They'd all come out now. Matt looked straight at them.

"Uh, Fen?" he said. "Aren't those the—?"

"Go." Fen wheeled and ran, Matt racing after him, the Raiders giving chase.

They managed to ditch the Raiders before they got back to Laurie. Then, as they were heading out of town, they saw them again. It didn't seem as if the Raiders noticed them, but they weren't taking a chance. They ran from Blackwell and didn't look back.

Late that night, Matt awoke smelling the sharp tang of wet grass. A distant coyote yipped. Beside him, someone groaned in sleep. *Camping*, he thought. *I'm camping.*

He started to drift off again, then he felt the wet grass, dampness seeping through his sleeves, and he bolted upright, remembering his father yelling at him for leaning his knapsack against the tent.

Anything touching the tent lets in the rain. You're not a child, Matthew. It's time you stopped acting like one.

Matt scrambled up, trying to see what he'd left against the tent. But there was no tent. He was looking up at shards of night sky through the treetops. He blinked hard as he struggled to focus. Then he looked over, saw Laurie and Fen, and it all came back.

He heard the Seer's voice: *Our champion is Matthew Thorsen.*

Then Granddad: *My grandson is being honored in the highest fashion, and he will do us proud, and he will take his place in the halls of Valhalla as a champion with the long-dead gods. As a hero. Our hero.*

Matt's stomach lurched. His foot slid on the wet grass, and he went down on his knees, his stomach tumbling with him. He fell onto all fours, retching.

Mistake. It's gotta be a mistake. They wouldn't do that. Not Mom. Not Dad. Especially not Granddad.

But even as he denied it, his stomach kept heaving, a thin trickle dripping as he coughed.

"Matt?"

He pushed up fast, his hand swiping the dribble from his mouth. Laurie sat blinking at him.

"You okay?" she asked quietly. After a moment's pause, she added, "Or is that a dumb question?"

"I'm fine." He wiped his mouth harder and straightened, letting his voice drop an octave. "Sorry about that. Just . . . fair food. Corn dogs taste great, then you wake up in the middle of the night, feeling like they were made from real dogs."

She didn't smile, just kept peering at his face in the darkness. He tried to straighten more. He couldn't let her see he was scared. She was a girl. She had to be protected. That's what Dad always said.

"Everything's fine," he said.

"Um, no. It's not," she said. "You and Fen nearly got killed by Raiders. We all nearly got killed by a tornado. And now we're sleeping in the woods, resting up so we can fight to stop the end of the world. Things are *not* fine."

"But it will be. Everything is under control."

No, it's not, you idiot. You have no idea what you're doing. No idea where you're going. Morning's going to come soon, and they're going to find out you don't have a good plan. You don't have any plan at all.

"Everything is under control." *Say it often enough, and I might even start to believe it.* "Just go back to—"

"Shhh!"

Matt looked over at her. "Huh?"

Laurie opened her mouth to say something, but another *Shhh!* came from beside her as Fen sat up, scowling. His head cocked. He motioned around them.

When Matt frowned, Fen's scowl deepened. "Are you deaf, Thorsen? Stop yammering and listen."

Matt did and heard the faint rustle of grass. He was about to say it was just the wind, but Fen already thought he was a clueless rich kid. When he listened more closely, he heard a *thud*, like...

He wasn't sure what it sounded like. Not the wind. Not a scurrying rabbit, either. It *was* familiar, but only vaguely, some memory locked deep in his brain.

Then another noise: a *click-click*, like dice knocking together.

"I'm going to take a look," he whispered.

Fen shrugged. "Whatever."

When Laurie gave Fen a look, he said, "What? He offered."

Laurie began getting up. "I'll come—"

Fen caught her arm. "The more of us go, the more noise we make. Thorsen can handle it."

Matt squared his shoulders and gave what he hoped was a confident nod. Then he slipped to a patch of bushes, crouched, and made his way along. He'd gone only a few steps when he heard the clicking again. Then a snort. A bump. All three sounds came from different directions. He tried to take another step, but his body wouldn't listen, frozen in place.

His amulet had started to vibrate again, like it had with the Norns, only it felt different. It felt like trouble.

A whisper sounded behind him. Matt looked back to see Laurie leaning toward her cousin, her gaze on Matt as she whispered something. He couldn't hear the words, but he could imagine them. *Thorsen can't do it. He's scared.*

He wasn't usually so jumpy—he'd been camping plenty of times. But after last night, he couldn't be sure it was just a wild animal out there. It might be…well, there were lots of things it might be. Norse myths were full of monsters.

He gritted his teeth and resumed walking, straining to see in the dark, leaning forward until he almost tripped. Then he glimpsed a huge pale form just beyond the forest. It had to be at least seven feet high and almost as long.

That's not possible. Nothing's that big.

Nothing natural.

But there was nothing natural about giant serpents and kids who turned into wolves.

Something had tracked them down. Some monster. His mind whipped through his mythology books. Trolls. Frost giants. Berserkers.

Another snort to his left. When he turned, he could make out a second huge pale shape. And a third behind it. And a fourth...

He swallowed.

They were surrounded. These things had found them, and now—

"I come for Thor's son. Send him out!" It was a woman's voice. But not like any woman's voice he'd ever heard. There was no softness to it. It was as harsh as the caw of a crow.

He took a slow step back.

"You!" The pale beast moved to the forest edge. "I see you, boy. You cannot be the one I seek. The son of Thor does not cower in shadows."

Anger darted through him, and he almost barreled out to confront her. He stopped himself, but after that first jolt of *Are you nuts?* he thought maybe that wasn't so crazy after all.

Fen must be able to hear the woman. He'd know they were in danger and that Matt was the target. He'd take his cousin and run. And that, Matt reasoned, was probably their only chance.

Matt strode from the forest. "I am a son of..."

As he stepped into the moonlight, he found himself staring up at a white horse bigger than any he'd ever seen. On its back was a woman. But not like any woman he'd ever seen, either. She had bright red hair that rippled and snarled around her pale face. Her cheeks were stained with what looked like handprints. The horse was painted with them, too, handprints and lines and swirls that shone blue in the moonlight.

The horse snorted and shifted, and when it did, he heard that clicking noise and looked over. The horse's bridle. It was...it was made of bones. Finger bones strung together. More bones hung from the saddle, which almost looked as if it was made of...nope. He wasn't thinking of that. It was leather. Just regular leather.

"Are you Matthew, son of Thor?" the woman asked.

He looked up at her. He had to. Even if his heart was pounding so hard he could barely breathe.

He noticed then how young she was. Not much older than the elder Norn. Pretty, too. His stomach twisted as he thought it. He didn't want to think it. She shouldn't be pretty with that wild hair and blue-stained face. She should be terrible—and she was. But as she sat there, perfectly straight, blue eyes flashing, shield over one shoulder, sword gripped in her free hand, he didn't see a monster, he saw...

He swallowed as he realized what he saw. What she was. They had mosaics of her, too—her kind—in the rec center. Only they didn't look like this. The women in those pictures were tall and beautiful with long blond braids and horned hats and breastplates that didn't totally cover...well, he remembered how much his friends liked that picture. And maybe he'd kind of liked it, too.

The only thing this woman had in common with them was her sword and shield, but Matt remembered an older painting in a dusty book his granddad kept in his private library. In that painting, the women were wild-haired and painted, riding great winged steeds through the battlefields, stripping trophies from the enemy dead.

"Valkyries," Matt whispered.

"Huh?" said a voice behind him.

Matt spun to see two women on foot leading Fen and Laurie around the forest patch, as if they'd tried to escape out the other side. Laurie was struggling and snarling. Fen just walked, as if he'd realized he couldn't fight.

"They're Valkyries," Matt whispered as he stepped back beside Fen.

ELEVEN

FEN

"READING MOUNT RUSHMORE"

Valkyries?" Fen echoed. That explained how the women had managed to sneak up on them. He looked back at the woman who held him. She was blond, but otherwise looked like the red-haired rider, right down to the blue war paint.

"The son of Thor is correct," the red-haired Valkyrie said in her rough voice. "The son of Loki knows too little of his heritage." She turned to Laurie. "And the daughter?"

Laurie pulled herself straight. "I'll learn."

"The descendants of Thor are taught their heritage." Fen pulled away from the Valkyrie holding his shoulder. "Not all of Loki's descendants are taught—because of the sons of Thor."

He sent a glare Matt's way.

"You must learn," the Valkyrie said. "I am Hildar of the Valkyrie. We are pleased to see you have accepted the challenge. We have come to offer assistance."

Fen looked around as a half-dozen horses and riders drifted in from the shadows. His gaze went not from face to face but sword to sword. He smiled. This was the kind of help they needed. The *wulfenkind* would be in for a surprise next time they came sniffing around. "So, how does this work?"

The Valkyrie gave Fen an amused look.

Laurie cleared her throat; Fen pretended not to hear. "Do we lead—"

Matt interrupted. "I know we need to find Odin. That's what the Norns said."

"One cannot rely on the Norns to set the order of battle plans—they jump forward and back and do not see the proper path," Hildar said. "Odin is not your concern yet; your priority is finding the other descendants of the North. We will help you."

Matt exhaled. "Thank you. I was wondering how we'd—" He stopped and glanced at Fen and Laurie. "I mean, I had a few ideas of how to do that, but I appreciate any help you, um, ladies can offer."

"Yeah. Me, too." Fen felt a guilty rush of relief. So far the entire plan had been to run and hide and stumble around in the dark without a clue. They'd avoided the Raiders for now, and they would have to keep doing so because he was pretty sure that Skull was going to deliver them all to his boss if they were caught. Fen had told Skull he'd deliver Thorsen, but instead he'd fought Raiders to *help* him. He wasn't entirely sure why he'd done that—other than the obvious fact that he didn't want to work for the Raiders—but it had been a sort of last-minute decision. Still, last-minute or not, it would have consequences if Skull caught up with them.

So we need to be far enough ahead that they can't catch us.

Fen stepped forward. "Do you have extra horses, or do we share with you?"

"It is not our place to take you to the descendants. You must find them yourselves," Hildar said.

"So you'll tell us where they are?" Matt prompted.

The Valkyrie frowned. "No. We will tell you where you can go to learn where they are."

"Uh-huh." Fen's hopes of real help were quickly vanishing, but maybe it was a case of the Valkyries just not understanding. "Could you make it a little less complicated? We're talking about the end of the world here."

The look she shot him made him step backward, but all she did was say, "First, you must be tested."

"I haven't studied," Matt said.

Fen stifled a laugh, but either Hildar didn't get the joke or didn't think it was funny.

"It is not that kind of test," she said. "You must win a war."

"I get that," Matt said. "But I'm pretty good at fighting already. Can you just skip the scavenger hunt and do this the old-fashioned way? Mano a mano. I take on a challenger."

The other Valkyries murmured among themselves in a language Fen didn't know, and Hildar shook her head. "You are indeed a son of Thor: you think you can overcome any obstacle with a hammer in one hand and a stein of mead in the other."

"I don't think they'll let me have mead, but I wouldn't mind the *real* hammer." Matt fingered his amulet.

All the Valkyries just stared, stone-faced. Fen felt just as frustrated as they looked. Sure, Thorsen didn't know what Fen had risked or what trouble awaited if the Raiders caught up with them, but here they were with an offer of help that was being dashed as quickly as it had arrived. He didn't feel like arguing the matter, either, but Matt was persistent. Fen had to give him credit for that. He was ready to walk away, but Thorsen was obviously still clinging to the hope that the Valkyries could be convinced to offer genuine aid.

Matt sighed. "Come on. It's a war. The Midgard Serpent isn't going to let us settle this over a game of Tafl." He paused. "Unless that's a possibility, 'cause I'm pretty good at that, too. Would save a lot of trouble. Lot less messy, too. So, what do you think?"

"I think you are not taking this seriously enough," Hildar said.

She seemed to think that Thorsen was being flip with her, but she'd already said it wasn't a fight. It only made sense to come up with other possible types of challenges. Fen didn't figure pointing that out would earn them any favors, though, so he kept his mouth shut and waited.

"The fate of the world is in your hands," one of the other Valkyries said.

Laurie stepped forward, drawing everyone's gaze to her. "Then *help* us."

Fen felt a flash of worry and eased closer to her. She was where his loyalty should be—and would be. Hildar saw his movement and smiled.

"You're the descendants of gods," Hildar said, almost kindly. "They died, and it's up to you now to fulfill the roles in the great fight. Ragnarök comes. This is your duty. We can't assume your duty for you."

"I didn't sign up for this. None of us did," Fen objected. It was like the world had spun backward a thousand years and they were now old enough to leave home and get married, old enough to fight, old enough to die. They were being asked to risk death because somewhere forever ago they had relatives who were gods. Worse still, those gods had died and left them a mess to handle.

"Did you not?" Hildar asked.

And Fen wondered briefly how much she knew. He *had* made a choice. When the Raiders came at Thorsen, Fen had chosen. When they were on the longship and Fen had heard Thorsen talk about Ragnarök just like Skull had talked about it, Fen had chosen. He'd decided to throw in on the side of the gods, the side that the prophecy said would lose. There was a part of him that wanted to be better than the god who was his long-gone ancestor, be a hero instead of a troublemaker, and maybe in doing so keep the monsters from winning. Being *wulfenkind* didn't make Skull or anyone else a monster, but wanting to destroy the world certainly did.

"What are we supposed to do?" Matt asked.

"We would prefer you to win," Hildar replied, not quite answering the more practical question Fen suspected Matt was asking. The Valkyrie continued, "If you are to win, you must be ready. You must not be children, waiting for things to be handed to you. You must find the others. In time, you must find Odin. You must collect Mjölnir, a feather from each of Odin's ravens, and the shield. These things will help you fight the serpent."

"Mjölnir? You mean...*the* Mjölnir? Thor's hammer?" Matt looked like someone had offered him a great big prize, which, Fen supposed, she kind of had. A god's hammer would be pretty handy in a fight with monsters. It was a shame that no one was offering him a superweapon, too.

After another of those glances that made Fen think Hildar knew more than he'd like, she looked back at Matt and her lips twitched with the faintest sign of a smile. "That is what you wanted, is it not, son of Thor?"

"I was kidding," Matt said in a half-shocked voice. He took a deep breath. "So Mjölnir, feathers, and some shield. And the other kids. And Odin."

"You'll give us a clue, though, right?" Fen interjected. "That's what you said: you'd help."

Hildar nodded. "Indeed." She looked at them each in turn and then said, "Seek the twins first. To find them, go see the presidents. Their faces hold the answer."

Then she lifted her hand, and all the Valkyries turned away.

The riders swung onto their horses' backs. In an instant, hooves pounded; the horses and their riders were a blur, and then they were gone.

"Seriously?" Fen said, spinning around to face Laurie and Matt. "Seriously? Answers on the faces of the presidents? What kind of riddle is that?"

"It's not a riddle," Laurie said evenly. "It's Mount Rushmore."

"Yes!" Matt already looked calm again, and Fen wished briefly that he were that sure of himself—not always or anything, but sometimes.

Matt continued, "They mean we'll find the answer at

Mount Rushmore. That's got to be it. Something there will lead us to the twins."

"What twins?" Laurie had a nervous look on her face. "Sorry. My mom was anti–Blackwell history because my dad gets so into it. I had no idea it would ever matter."

Fen felt another flash of guilt. He hadn't had a choice about keeping secrets, but he also hadn't tried to convince her to pay attention to the myths, even though he knew she might turn into a wolf like him. Now she was caught up in a dangerous situation with a lot less information than she needed to have.

Uncle Stig is going to kill me . . . unless the Raiders do it first.

While Fen was stressing out, Matt seemed perfectly calm now that Laurie had asked a question he could answer. He launched into explaining the myths: "The twins are Frey and Freya. In the old stories, Freya is the goddess of love and beauty. Frey is the god of weather and fertility. We need to find their descendants, who are apparently also twins." Matt paused. "Two for one. That'll make it easier."

Fen scowled at him. "I don't think any of this is going to be easy."

"And that's the point," Laurie murmured.

"Okay, then," Matt said. "I guess we visit the presidents."

Blackwell wasn't too far away from Mount Rushmore, but it was a long enough walk that Fen wished he could change into a wolf and run. He wasn't about to leave his cousin behind, though. He'd promised Uncle Stig that he'd keep an eye on her, especially around boys. The idea of telling any of the family that he had left her alone with a Thorsen made his stomach twist inside him. He glanced at Matt and Laurie talking animatedly while they walked toward Mount Rushmore. It seemed like just friendship, but even that would anger the family.

And they'd blame me.

Fen was all on board with the stop-the-end-of-the-world part, and he hoped his family would be, too. They were mostly lone wolves or tithed. That had to mean his dad and Uncle Stig wouldn't side with the crazy let-the-world-end plan, right? Fen wasn't entirely sure about some of his family. What he did know, however, was that the Raiders definitely wouldn't be forgiving of any *wulfenkind*'s decision to side with a Thorsen.

And Thorsen won't be forgiving if he finds out I was supposed to capture him and deliver him to them.

His whole family would be angry if they found out he was running across the state with a Thorsen. They might not all like the Raiders, but *wulfenkind* didn't help Thorsens. That part was just the way it was, the way it always had been. Matt didn't seem like most Thorsens, though. They'd fought side by side against the Raiders, and they'd stood side by side in the face of warrior women. Both times, Matt seemed to want to win more than be a show-off. It reminded Fen of what packs were supposed to be like, what families were supposed to be like. It wasn't what Fen would expect from a descendant of Thor. Surprisingly, Matt seemed like he was kind of an okay guy. Fen wasn't about to tell him that, but he really didn't want Matt or Laurie to know that he'd considered helping the Raiders capture Matt. Matt would hate him—and Laurie would probably be mad, too.

He hadn't wanted to deliver Matt to them, and he'd been trying to think of a solution. Throwing in against his own kind wasn't the one he'd meant to pick, but it had seemed like a good idea at the time. Still, if Laurie and Matt learned that Fen had given them the shield and that he was supposed to deliver Thorsen to the Raiders, they wouldn't understand. He knew it.

So they can't find out.

He knew how to keep a secret. He'd been dealing with knowing he was Loki's descendant for years, turning into a wolf the past year, paying tithe to the Raiders, keeping secrets from Laurie, and alternately hoping and not hoping that she'd be a wolf like him.

"Are you still with us?" Laurie looked over her shoulder at him.

"Sure." He thought about telling her the truth, or at least some of it, but Thorsen was watching, and Fen wasn't about to tell him. Fen would just continue to keep an eye out for

Raiders, and they'd deal with any trouble if it came. What he could tell them was, "I know where the shield is."

"The shield the Valkyries said we need?"

A car passed, with music blaring, and Fen almost growled at how close it came to Laurie. He moved to walk beside her, and she stepped onto the gravel along the road. He nodded. "The Raiders have it. It's the one I was trying to get."

"Why didn't you tell me that's why you were trying to steal it?" Matt asked.

Laurie hugged him. "You could've at least told *me* you were trying to keep it out of their hands."

Gratefulness shot through him: their misunderstanding of his role in the shield's theft was the perfect cover.

"I never wanted you to know anything about the Raiders," he told her. That part was true. The part where he was trying to *protect* it from the Raiders, not that he stole it and delivered it to them, wasn't exactly true, of course.

He looked from Matt to Laurie and then added, "I don't know how we're going to get it from them, but at least we know where it is."

"And we know that Odin says we'll talk again, and even I know that Odin is supposed to be all-seeing in the stories. I'm guessing he'll be able to get us the feathers from his ravens." Laurie laughed. "Is it weird how easy it is to believe that all of this is real?"

"Don't know," Fen hedged. "I've always known some of it. Thorsen probably has, too."

Matt nodded.

"Well, I haven't, and I still think we can do this," Laurie said. She stared at the giant carved presidents in the distance and smiled.

After a friendly smile at her that made Fen want to snarl protectively, Matt said, "Let's go find our clue."

Fen shook his head. They'd barely survived a fight with the Raiders, and he didn't expect a tornado to pop up and save them the next time. He knew the Raiders, knew how well patrolled their camps were, knew that the way Hattie and Skull were about the shield meant that it would be well guarded. He couldn't tell Laurie and Matt any of that without admitting how well he knew the Raiders, and he wasn't willing to do that. He'd figure out a way around the shield problem later, but for now, he kept his mouth shut and followed Laurie and Matt through the visitors' entrance to Mount Rushmore.

They walked past the tall gray columns. On one side was a wall with names carved on it, and on the other was a statue of the guy who was behind creating the monument.

There were more stone columns, with state flags on top of them, and at the end was a big open space where people stood staring at the presidents' faces. Fen wasn't really much into school stuff, but they'd come here on a field trip, and he'd been impressed by the idea of making such an enormous sculpture. These were the sort of giant carvings that meant explosions and giant power tools were needed. Far cooler than sitting there with a tiny blob of clay, trying to make a sculpture, which is what they'd had to do in art class. He smiled at the idea of getting to use explosives in art class. *That* would be cool.

The three of them stood there with the people, all staring up at Washington, Jefferson, Teddy Roosevelt, and Lincoln. He felt like one of them should have a camera so they'd blend in, but no one was staring at them like they were doing anything wrong. And they weren't...yet.

They had to wait for a while until they were able to get closer to the faces—where the Valkyrie had said the clue was—so they killed time until the park closed, watching the movie in the visitors' center two times, and then buying something to eat using money that they'd all brought. No one asked where he'd gotten his, and he didn't tell them he'd taken it from Kris' stash. Laurie had hers and some jewelry she said they could sell if they needed to. Matt had used a cash machine to add to the money he still had from his dad.

"We'll hide and wait," Matt said.

They crept into the woods and settled in for a few hours. This part of their quest was far from exciting. Fen was a lot more at ease fighting Raiders than sitting in silence. He wasn't great at staying still in general, but from the looks of it, neither was Matt. He fidgeted almost as much as Laurie and Fen did. They exchanged an almost-friendly nod.

Eventually, the statues were lit up, and then people started leaving. But the guard didn't leave. So they kept waiting.

Unfortunately, the waiting part was a lot harder than the hiding. They had a number of places to hide over in the wooded area, but that guard not only watched the visitors' area but also the monument itself. Plus, there were cameras aimed at the monument and around the area.

Earlier that day he had overheard someone talking about some sort of environmental protest a few years ago that had resulted in new security. Fen was all for taking care of the environment, especially since he was a wolf part of the time, but he wished they'd staged their protest elsewhere because the extra security meant getting close to the presidents' faces was seeming pretty impossible. There was no way they were going to be able to climb up there with a guard watching and who knows how many *more* scanning the security feed from wherever the cameras sent their signal.

A couple of hours passed, and they were no closer to progress than when they'd arrived. The guard stayed alert, and the cameras weren't going to vanish. It was ridiculous.

"I could get up there," Fen said in a low voice.

Matt shot Fen a warning glare.

"No one's going to stop a wolf." He turned to his cousin. "I wish you could change, too."

Then he turned his back on them and became a wolf.

It would be so much better if she was a wolf, too. He'd hoped in a weird sort of girly way that if she changed, too, Uncle Stig would take them with him. Then they could all three live together like a normal family. Laurie wasn't happy with her mom and brother, and Fen wasn't happy moving from house to house, and Uncle Stig surely wasn't happy alone. Laurie hadn't turned into a wolf, though, and he didn't know if she would. He felt sad, which made him want to howl.

She was already crouched down, so they were face-to-face. "Be careful," she whispered. "Don't do anything too stupid."

He butted his head against her shoulder, and then he was off. He walked right up to the guard, who looked at him with the sort of respect that he saw more often from the American Indians in South Dakota. Ranchers weren't usually keen on wolves, but the Sioux were more likely to respect nature—which included wolves.

The guard watched him warily, and then looked around as if he were seeking shelter. Fen didn't like that he had frightened him, so he smiled, which he always forgot never looked very friendly when he was a wolf, and the guard took a step backward. Fen felt a little guilty about scaring the

guard, but he had no intention of hurting the man. He kept the man's attention, hoping that Matt and Laurie were moving farther into cover.

Then he leaped over a low wall and started toward the monument. He knew the guard was watching him. The weight of the man's attention felt good, almost as good as stretching his muscles after hours of sitting and doing nothing. He grinned. Getting close enough to see whatever clue was on the presidents' faces was going to be easy.

He left the tourist section of the monument—and the guard—well behind him as he made his way up closer to the mountain, enjoying the feel of the ground under his paws, and was almost there when movement caught his eye. He stopped and looked. Rocks were raining down from the faces.

He waited, torn between natural caution and rushing forward to look for the clue before an earthquake or avalanche hid it even more. Several more rocks fell. Then, it looked like a giant part of the rock face was about to come crashing down. He was glad the guard was well out of range, but when he looked back, he couldn't see where Laurie was.

Whether it was an earthquake or avalanche, he didn't know. What he did know was that if there was a disaster of any sort starting, he needed to be with Laurie to keep her safe. He turned his back to the mountain and started to race back toward Laurie. He could hear a rumble behind him as he picked up speed.

TWELVE

❖

MATT

"TROLL CONDO"

When Thomas Jefferson's nose dropped off, Matt's first thought was: avalanche. He'd never actually experienced one, but he'd seen plenty in movies, and if pieces start falling off the faces at Mount Rushmore, that'd be the only natural and logical explanation. Then, when George Washington's nose dropped, he thought *It's an earthquake*, immediately followed by *It's Ragnarök*. More natural disasters. More signs—as if he needed them after being visited by Norns and Valkyries—that the world was indeed sliding into Fimbulwinter.

His first reaction, he was ashamed to admit, was to look around and see who was handling this. Who was in charge.

Who'd tell them to get to safety. Then he realized that was him.

He was turning to warn Fen and Laurie when Teddy Roosevelt's mustache got up and stretched. There was a second where Matt just stared, sure he was seeing wrong. The gray lump on the lip of the twenty-sixth president of the United States could not be stretching. It must be rolling or something, breaking loose.

Except it wasn't. It was *stretching*. And Abraham Lincoln's beard was dangling from what looked like thick gray arms. Then it started going up and down, like it was doing chin-ups. Using Lincoln's chin.

They'd gotten as close as they could, but the faces were still so far away you'd need binoculars to really see them. Those lumps *were* definitely moving, though, and the more they moved, the less they looked like hunks of stone. The one that had been Roosevelt's mustache now crouched on the president's lip, long, apelike gray arms dangling. Then the arms swung, and it leaped down to the rocks below.

"Trolls," Matt whispered.

"Right," Fen said. "Mount Rushmore is really a giant troll condo. Makes perfect sense."

Laurie looked at Matt. "The trolls must have the answer. That's what the Valkyrie meant, don't you think?"

"They didn't say the answers were written on the faces. Just that the answers were on the faces." Matt looked at the

squat stone figure lumbering over the piles of broken rock, and he realized what he had to do.

"We need to get ourselves a troll," he said.

As they picked their way across the forested mountainside, Matt kept waiting for Fen or Laurie to argue. He'd just told them he planned to capture and question a troll. Fen should say it was a dumb idea, or Laurie should say it was too dangerous. At the very least, Fen should say *Go for it, Thorsen,* and walk away. But there he was, right beside Matt, peering through the dark forest, head tilting to listen, nostrils flaring to . . . to sniff the air? Could Fen smell things, like a wolf? Matt thought of asking but figured it was safer to keep his mouth shut. Just because they weren't trying to hit each other anymore didn't make them friends.

Laurie was right there, too, on Fen's other side, looking and listening. The night forest was a scary thing at any time— hooting owls and creaking branches and patches of darkness so complete you had to walk with your hands out, feeling your way. Add trolls, and his own heart pounded in time with his footsteps. He was sure Laurie had to be terrified. She didn't look afraid, though. Just cautious, like them. Maybe she didn't really believe there were trolls. Maybe she was humoring him—maybe they both were. Playing along, waiting to laugh at him when his trolls turned out to be piles of rock.

Almost as embarrassing was the fact that he was kinda hoping he *was* wrong. Otherwise, he had to carry through and actually catch a troll, and he had no idea how to do that.

This time, he was the one who heard something first. His arm shot out to stop Fen, who plowed into it, then turned on him, snarling. Matt lifted his hand to motion for silence.

Off to their left, a twig cracked. Matt pointed.

Fen rolled his eyes. "We're looking for a walking pile of rock," he whispered. "It's gonna make more noise than that."

True, if a troll was in the forest, they should all hear it, crashing through the undergrowth like a boulder rolling downhill. Maybe it was the guard? But there weren't any paths here, and they'd seen no sign of guards since they'd come into the forest. Matt guessed that if the trolls came to life at night, they were careful to do it when the guards wouldn't be watching.

Matt felt his amulet heat. It didn't get red-hot, like before a Hammer flare, but it was getting warmer. He touched his cold fingers to it.

"There's a troll coming," he said, before he could even think it.

"What?" Fen waved at the amulet. "Now it's a monster detector?"

"Giants," Laurie whispered. "You must pay even less attention in class than I do. Trolls are a kind of giant. Thor was known as the giant-killer."

"Right." Fen sized up Matt. "We'd better hope they're very *small* giants."

Matt plucked at the shirt he was wearing. It was Fen's— Laurie had made her cousin grab extras for him. The tee rode at the top of Matt's jeans and stretched across his chest and biceps. When he'd come out wearing it, Laurie had giggled, which had made Fen scowl and say it was an old one that he'd outgrown, and she couldn't expect him to let Matt wear his good stuff. Now Matt didn't respond to Fen's crack. He just tugged at the shirt. Fen's scowl returned, and he opened his mouth before his cousin cut him off.

"Do I need to separate you two?" she muttered.

Laurie was stepping between them when the ground vibrated under Matt's feet. He tensed and looked around.

"What now?" Fen said.

"Didn't you feel that?"

Matt didn't wait for an answer. He dropped to his knees and pressed his hands to the ground. It was vibrating. So was his amulet. He closed his eyes, one hand on the necklace, the other on the ground. Fen snickered and said something about troll-whispering, but Laurie shushed him. Fen was right, though, it looked stupid. It *was* stupid. Matt let go of the necklace, opened his eyes, and started to rise, but Laurie crouched in front of him.

"What do you feel?" she asked.

He shook his head. "Nothing. I just thought—"

"Try again," she said.

He paused. *Fen won't ever follow you if he thinks you're an idiot.*

"Try again," she said, more firmly this time. She met his gaze. "We're descended from gods, so we've all got some sort of god powers, right? We just need to figure out how they work."

"It might not be—"

"But it might be. If you're wrong, no one's going to laugh at you." She shot a warning look at Fen.

They've been following me so far, haven't they? They don't know me well enough to realize I don't know what I'm doing. I can worry that they'll find out I'm a fraud, or I can try to prove that I'm not. Try to be something different, someone different.

Matt shut his eyes and stretched his fingers against the ground. The vibrations were getting stronger now, and even if he couldn't hear so much as another twig cracking—which made no sense if a troll was nearby—he *knew* it was nearby. He could feel it walking across the earth.

"Which way?" Laurie whispered.

He started to hesitate, then stopped himself and pointed. Almost as soon as he did, another *crack* came, this one close enough that they all heard it.

"Okay," Matt whispered as he stood. "They're going to be big, so we need to make sure it's just one. If this guy has friends, we have to find another troll."

Fen pressed his lips together, and Matt knew he didn't like the idea of running from a fight to search for an easier one. Maybe he even thought Matt was being a coward.

Am I? No. That has to be part of leading. Knowing when something is too risky.

At least Laurie seemed to agree, as she nodded and waved for Matt to lead the way.

"You stay here," he said. "Fen and I—"

"Stop," Laurie interrupted.

"I'm just suggesting—"

"Suggestion noted. And rejected. I'm going with you, and the more times you do that, Thorsen, the more ticked off I'm going to get." She glanced at Fen. "Same goes for you."

"But you're—" Matt began.

"Don't you dare say 'a girl.'" She made a grumbling noise and then waved into the darkness. "Go."

Matt hesitated and glanced at Fen—who only shrugged.

When Matt didn't move, Laurie gave him a shove and muttered, "You know what you need, Thorsen? A sister." She gave him another shove, harder this time, and they headed into the deep forest.

Matt crouched behind an evergreen stump and peeked out at the troll. If he didn't know better, he'd think it was a big pile of rock. The troll was hunkered down next to a stream, staring at something in its hands. It turned it over, grumbling, the sound like stones clattering together. Then it reached out a long arm into the stream and scooped up a handful of rock and silt. It jiggled its hand over the water to let the silt rain down. Then it clenched its fist, dipped it into the water, and shook it.

Panning for gold. Or some kind of treasure. Maybe even just sparkly rocks. The old stories said trolls loved anything shiny. Matt didn't care much what it was doing; he was too busy staring at that hand. The troll itself wasn't a real giant—crouching, it wasn't taller than him. That hand, though, was huge. Bigger than his head. With claws as long as steak knives and probably just as sharp.

The troll opened its massive hand and poked at the rocks on its palm. Its grumbles grew louder when it found nothing of interest.

"What if we can't communicate with it?" Laurie whispered, coming up behind him.

Matt looked over at her.

"That doesn't sound like a real voice," she said. "It's just making noises. If we can't talk to it, how are we going to find out—"

The troll's head swung their way, and Laurie stopped. As the troll peered into the darkness, Matt got his first real look at the thing. It had a gray, misshapen, bald head with beady, sunken eyes and a nose that hooked down over a lipless mouth. The nose twitched, as if the troll was sniffing the air. Then the mouth opened, revealing rows of jagged teeth.

The troll rose to its full height. It would tower over Matt now. At least eight feet tall and half as wide, standing on squat legs, its long arms dangling, claws scraping the ground. It kept looking in their direction but just stood there, head bobbing and swaying, nostrils flaring. Then it charged.

There was no warning. One second it was standing there, and the next it was barreling toward them so quickly and so quietly that for a second, Matt thought he was seeing things. Then Laurie grabbed his arm, and Fen shouted, "Run!"

Matt lunged from behind the stump, breaking free from Laurie's grasp, and then he did run—straight at the troll. There wasn't a choice. It was coming too fast for them to escape. So Matt ran toward it, yelling.

The troll skidded to a stop. Its beady eyes went as wide as they could, its stone jaw dropping.

Matt kept running. As he did, his fears and worries seemed to fall behind. This was the part he understood, the part he'd always understood. This was when he really felt like a son of Thor.

That's why he loved boxing and wrestling. When he got into the ring, he didn't feel like a loser, like a screwup. His family was never there, watching and waiting for him to make a mistake. They didn't care. Win or lose, they didn't care, and if that kind of hurt, it also felt good in a weird way. It felt like freedom.

He ran at the troll, and he didn't think *I can't do this*. He didn't think *I* can *do this*, either. He just thought what he always did in the ring: *I'm going to give it my best shot.*

He concentrated on Thor's Hammer and imagined throwing it at the troll. Nothing happened. So he kept going. When he was a few feet away, he pitched forward, dropping and grabbing it by the leg. It was a good wrestling move, one Coach Forde had taught him for dealing with a bigger opponent.

The bigger they are, the harder they fall. In theory. A theory that, apparently, didn't apply to trolls, and when Matt grabbed it by the leg, it barely stumbled. Then it pulled back its thick, short leg, kicked, and sent Matt sailing into the undergrowth.

Matt hit the ground in a roll and bounced up. He wheeled to see the troll charging. Matt feinted to the side. He heard a *clunk* and saw a fist-sized rock bounce off the back of the troll's head. The troll staggered, its charge broken. As it turned, snorting, Matt saw Fen lifting another rock.

"What is it with you and attacking things that can kill you, Thorsen?" Fen yelled. "Next time, I'm not saving you."

Matt could point out that he hadn't needed saving. Not yet, anyway. But the troll was now charging Fen. So he ran at the monster. His first impulse was to jump on its back. One quick look at that solid stone slab told him he wouldn't get a handhold. So he dove again, this time landing in the troll's path. It ran into him, its feet hitting his side like twin sledgehammers.

The troll tripped. As it went down, Matt flew to his feet and jumped on the monster. It was like body-slamming a bed of rock. He was scrabbling for a hold when the troll leaped up.

Matt rolled off. He bounded to his feet and faced off against the thing.

"Now what?" Fen said from behind the troll. "It's a pile of rock, Thorsen. You can't fight that."

Matt ignored him and kept his gaze fixed on the troll's. They circled. The troll was grumbling and muttering.

The troll swung one long arm. Matt managed to back away enough that it should have only been a glancing blow. And it was—a glancing blow with a sledgehammer. It caught him in the stomach and sent him whipping into a tree and slumping at the base, doubled over, wheezing and gasping.

Out of the corner of his eye, he saw the troll coming at him. He leaped up and lunged. Except it was more of a stumble-up-and-stagger. It got him out of the way, but barely in time. His foot caught a vine. As he slid, he saw that massive stone hand heading straight for him—

"Hey!" a voice called as stones rained down on the troll. "Hey, ugly, over here!"

It was Laurie. The troll spun, and Matt launched himself at the thing's back, only to slide off. He saw Laurie holding up something that glinted in the moonlight. A coin. She threw it. The troll dove for the treasure. Matt clenched his amulet in one hand and concentrated on launching the Hammer. Nothing happened.

Why wasn't it working? Not now and not with the Raiders. But it had worked when he'd fought Fen at the longship. What was different?

At the longship, Fen had come at him, and he'd reacted without thinking. He'd reacted in anger. That was the difference. He hadn't been angry at the Raiders, and he wasn't angry with the troll. Sure, he was scared, but he also felt... good. In a weird way, even as he panted, stomach aching, what rushed through his veins wasn't anger. It was fear and excitement.

The troll scooped up the coin and turned on Laurie. Matt instinctively started to charge but stopped himself. Fen rushed forward, yelling and waving. Matt planted his feet, and he thought of what would happen if the troll got to Laurie. If the troll hurt her. If it hurt Fen. Matt would be angry *then*. Angry with the troll and angry with himself for dragging them into this, and if he couldn't even fight a single troll, how could he ever hope to—

The amulet's heat shot through him and now he ran forward, flinging out his hand, feeling the energy course down it, seeing it leap from his fingertips like a bolt of electricity.

It knocked the troll off its feet. Sending the thing flying across the clearing would have been even more satisfying, but it did go down. And it didn't get up. It lifted its head and looked at Matt, gaping and blinking as he stood there, fingers still sparking, amulet glowing through his shirt.

"Hammer," the troll said in a deep rumble. "You have god Hammer."

"Thor's Hammer," Matt said, and he pulled it out, the metal glowing bright blue. "I'm a descendant of Thor, and I demand—"

"Want Hammer." The troll used its long arms to push to its feet, like an ape rising. "Leaf want Hammer."

Again, it charged so fast that it caught Matt off guard. This time, he stumbled back, hand going to his amulet, other fingers shooting out to . . .

To do nothing.

Panic pounded through him, and he stepped back. Then he stopped himself.

Don't give in to the fear. Use it. This troll wants your Hammer. It'll take your amulet, and then what? You'll lose your only power in your first giant-fight? Against one troll? Oh, yeah, you were tested, Matty. And you failed on the first question.

The energy shot out and hit the troll. This time the thing

did sail off its feet, hitting the ground so hard the earth shook.

Laurie stumbled as if her knees had almost given way.

Matt advanced on the fallen troll. "You want the Hammer? *That's* the Hammer. You go after any of us again, and I'll give you a bigger taste of it. Now, I have questions, and you're going to answer, or you'll *get* the Hammer."

The troll said nothing, just stared at the amulet as if transfixed.

"We are looking for…" He remembered the term Hildar used. "The descendants of the North. Specifically, a pair of twins. From the gods Frey and Freya. They're about our age. Do you know where they are?"

Even before the troll answered, Matt could tell by its reaction that it did.

Finally the troll said, "Leaf knows." Then it narrowed its eyes. "Leaf could tell son of Thor. *Will* tell son of Thor. For Hammer." It pointed at the still-glowing amulet. "Give to Leaf, and Leaf will tell."

Matt tucked the amulet under his shirt again. "The only Hammer you're getting is the one I just gave you. Now answer the question."

"No."

Matt launched the Hammer again. It was easier now— he was honestly getting angry—and when the troll refused, he got madder, which made him launch it a second time, almost without meaning to. But the troll just sat there, absorbing the blows and refusing to talk.

Before he could try again, Laurie came up behind him and whispered, "I have an idea."

He was about to say no, he could handle it, but she stepped forward and announced, "There *is* a way you can have Thor's Hammer, Leaf."

THIRTEEN

LAURIE

"SLEIGHT OF HAND"

Laurie was unexpectedly calm as she smiled up at the troll. She took three steps toward him. "You're right: we *can* make a deal. We can trade with you."

Matt started to object, but she shot him a look over her shoulder, and he quelled. Fen was back in wolf shape, but the gaze he leveled on her made it pretty clear that he wasn't particularly in favor of her approaching the troll, either.

"You give god Hammer," Leaf demanded.

"Maybe," she said.

Both Matt and Fen had followed her. From the corner of her eye, she could see them standing on either side, but slightly behind her. She glanced quickly at them, hoping they wouldn't mess this up. Fen's expression was impossible to read, since he was a wolf, and Matt was definitely tense. "We need to find the two descendants of the North. The Valkyrie Hildar sent us to you. Do you know where they are?"

The troll glared down at her from its unsettling rocklike face. "Yes."

"And you will tell us where they are if we give you the god Hammer?"

The deep gravel voice said, "Yes! Want it."

Laurie nodded. A small flash of guilt filled her. She'd promised her mother that she wouldn't trick people like her dad's family did—*like the descendants of Loki did*—but this was a pretty extreme set of circumstances. Ragnarök was coming. That *had* to change the rules.

She turned to face Matt, who reached up to cover the Hammer with one hand.

"Trust me," she said.

Warily, he removed his hand.

Laurie stepped behind Matt and undid the knot of the cord. "Stay still," she said loudly. She moved closer to Matt, angling her body so the troll couldn't see her lips, and whispered, "It's just the Hammer, right? The cord doesn't matter?"

"Right," Matt said.

"What?" the troll grumbled at them.

"I was saying she's right. I need to stay still." Matt managed a smile. "See? I'm staying still now."

The mammoth creature frowned. It might not know what it had missed, but it was obviously not sure about trusting them, either.

Excitedly, Laurie removed the necklace from around Matt's neck and held it up so the troll could see the Hammer dangling from the black cord. The troll's attention left Matt and zeroed in on the Hammer.

"So, if I give you this, you'll tell us?"

"Leaf wants," the troll rumbled.

"I know." Laurie switched the necklace to her right hand and slid the cord free of the pendant itself. As she stepped from behind Matt, she slipped the Hammer into his hand; at the same time, she held up her left hand. The black cord dangled from her closed fist.

She stepped in front of Matt.

"I'll give you this. You have to bend down, and I can tie it on you." Laurie shook the hand holding the cord, making Leaf look at her hand again. With her right hand she reached into her pocket, where she had the necklaces she'd brought to sell. She nimbly slipped a pendant off one.

"Now," Leaf demanded. He bent forward.

"Just hold still, and I'll tie it on you." She slid the pendant, a tiny silver unicorn, onto the cord while Leaf's gaze was on the ground. As she approached him, she let the metal of the pendant flash briefly into his line of sight and then quickly palmed it again.

She peered at his neck, all the while trying not to inhale through her nose. Trolls, or at least this troll, did not smell good at all. She smothered a gag. "I don't think it will fit around your neck."

"Twins near," the troll cajoled. "Leaf made deal!"

Laurie tilted her head and stared at Leaf. "I suppose I could put it on your ear." She brushed her own hair back. "I wear things there."

The troll nodded and bent down again. Thankfully, this meant his fetid breath was no longer blowing at her.

She put one hand on his large, slick ear and then paused. "Where are the twins, Leaf?"

"Dead Tree," Leaf said.

"They're in a dead tree?" she repeated skeptically. "People don't usually live in trees."

Leaf made a loud, grating noise. He slapped the ground with one massive hand, and spit flew from his mouth.

Matt and Fen both surged toward her, and she backed away from the troll in fear. "I wasn't trying to insult—"

"God girl funny. Place called Dead Tree," Leaf rumbled.

That horrible noise had been *laughter*. She shook her head. A troll laughing was not funny. She slowly walked back toward him. As she did so, she saw that Fen stayed right beside her.

"Deadwood," Matt said. "They're in Deadwood."

"Leaf say that." The troll turned his gaze on Laurie. "Give Hammer now."

"Right." She looped the cord around a big wart on the troll's ear and tied it into a knot. The tiny silver unicorn looked funny on the creature, but it was hanging where the troll couldn't see that it wasn't really the Hammer, and that was the goal. They had their information, Matt had his Hammer, and the troll had an earring.

The troll straightened. It smiled, exposing teeth in serious need of scrubbing and flossing, possibly even sandblasting. Oral hygiene clearly wasn't a priority with trolls. After seeing that, she made a mental note to buy a toothbrush for her cousin, who undoubtedly had not packed one.

Cautiously, she walked over to Matt. Fen was tight to her side. Her wolfy cousin kept looking back at the troll, who was staring at them, but not saying anything.

"Laurie," Matt said quietly. He was looking past her, and she looked over her shoulder at the almost-lightening woods. Morning was coming, thankfully, and they had what they needed. She didn't see anything but trees, and all that was left was to walk away.

"What?"

Fen growled. His fur stood up.

"Family come." The troll grinned. "Show family god Hammer."

"Crud," Laurie muttered. Four more trolls were coming toward them. Two of the trolls were even bigger than Leaf.

"Run," Matt urged as soon as Leaf turned to see his family.

She heard Leaf grumble, "God Hammer on ear."

And she tried to run faster. Matt was in front of her, and Fen was behind her. They were running as fast as they could, but the trolls would still be able to catch them in minutes. Trolls weren't fast thinkers, but they certainly could *move* quickly.

She heard the weird sound of trolls laughing, and then the ground shook as the trolls came toward them.

They were almost at the edge of the woods. *Maybe they can't leave the woods.* She hoped that was the case. *Please let them be unable to follow us.*

Frantically, she looked for a place to hide, as if there were a place secure enough to be trollproof. She didn't see anything. Matt suddenly grabbed her arm and half pulled her forward.

Before she could ask him why, she heard a deep growl. *Fen.* She turned to look back just as she saw her fool cousin standing with his paws firmly planted, growling at the five trolls.

Matt shoved her behind him and yelled, "Run!"

The troll in the front had almost reached Fen when Matt used the Hammer and sent the troll sailing backward. He threw another and another thunder of energy at the trolls, and all the while Fen darted out of their reach, trying to keep them too distracted to chase Laurie.

"*Run!*" Matt yelled at her again.

She wanted to, but she couldn't leave them. She looked around desperately for something to use as a weapon. The nearest things were a trash bin and some rocks. She ran toward the bin and tried to tug it free.

Then she heard a sharp *yip*.

"Fen!" She whirled to see Fen being lifted into the air. "No!" she screamed. "Matt! *Help!*"

A massive clawed troll hand was wrapped around Fen's throat. He hung limp in the troll's grip.

"Do something!" she yelled at Matt. Tears slipped out of her eyes, and she started to race toward the trolls.

"Wait." Matt grabbed her arm as she ran past him. "Look."

As the sun rose, the trolls all turned to stone. They looked like a cross between massive sculptures and rock piles. If she hadn't seen them moving, she might've thought they were oddly shaped rocks—well, that and the fact that a wolf hung limply from what was basically a stone noose.

She ran over to Fen. He wasn't moving, and his muzzle hung open like he was gasping for air. His eyes were closed, and she thought for a second that he was dead.

"He's still breathing," Matt said. He was right beside her now.

"Not for long. He'll choke." Then she spun to face Matt. "Blast it."

"Blast it," he repeated.

"Break the stone with your energy thing, or Fen's going to die." She hated the thought of breaking the troll's hand, even though it had chased them and probably would've killed them, but she hated the thought of Fen dying even more.

Matt frowned, but he obviously couldn't see any other solution, either. The circle of stone that was the troll's hand had to be cracked to remove Fen. Their only other choice was to wait till nightfall, when it would wake back up—and then probably finish choking Fen anyhow.

The energy blast cracked the stone around Fen's throat, and he dropped to the ground with an awful *thump*. He didn't move.

Laurie pulled the motionless wolf into her lap. "Fen! Fen, wake up!"

As she did so, she petted his face. *What do you do when your cousin who is a wolf gets choked by a troll who is part of a mountain?* These weren't the sorts of things ever covered in health class.

"I'll carry him out of here and..." Matt's words faded as Fen shifted from wolf to boy.

Blearily, Fen blinked up at Laurie. "Did we win or die?"

She patted the top of his head like he was still a wolf. "Won."

"Oh, good," Fen murmured. Then he rolled over and went to sleep.

After Matt carried Fen into the woods to sleep, Laurie and Matt took turns napping. They were pretty sure that Fen was okay. He'd woken up a few times, asked a question, and then gone back to sleep. She wished that they had their tent and sleeping bags with them, but they'd stowed them near the Mount Rushmore parking lot because they were pretty sure that walking into the monument area with camping equipment would attract attention they didn't want. So now they had only the cold ground to sleep on, and their backpacks to use for any kind of pillows.

In one of his brief awake periods, Fen told her that going back and forth between wolf and human took a lot of food, and he was just exhausted—and also healing from injuries. She was leaning against a tree then, and Fen scooted over and laid his head in her lap. It was warmer with him cuddled against her, but it meant she couldn't move.

When Matt woke, he offered her his sweatshirt, so she slipped it on and, with Matt's help, moved so she wasn't Fen's pillow. Then she stretched out on the ground next to her cousin for a short nap.

By afternoon, during one of Matt's shifts, Fen woke, and

they'd woken her up, too. Her cousin seemed fine—tired, but okay.

They filled him in, and then they went to buy something to eat and figure out how to get to Deadwood. They were finishing their breakfast-lunch when Fen inclined his head toward a group of kids about their age, who were starting to board two buses with big DEADWOOD TOURS signs painted on the sides. A woman with a clipboard stood outside the bus, checking names off a list as kids boarded.

"We could go with them," he suggested. Now that he'd had food, he was a lot more alert.

"They *are* headed to Deadwood," Laurie mused.

Matt didn't say anything for a moment. He looked at the crowd, and then he stood. "Better than walking or trying to hitch a ride."

Fen grinned. "Excellent."

All of her father's side of the family had the uncanny ability to persuade people to do things. It made sense now that she knew that Loki was a relative, but it still made her uncomfortable, even though it was clear they'd have to use those skills to get on the bus without being noticed. Fen was obviously a lot like their ancestor, though: he had that trouble-ahead bounce to his step that always worried Laurie, but after seeing him almost killed by trolls, she didn't have the heart to say anything. Maybe a little bit of Brekke skills were justified after cases of near-death by trolls.

Fen looked over at her and noticed her expression. Quietly, he said, "You can do this." Then he glanced at Matt and said, "When we distract her, just get on the bus like you belong. Clear back. Head down."

Matt nodded.

Then Fen said very softly to Laurie, "You're a Brekke. It's in our blood."

"Right," she breathed. "I can do this."

As they approached the bus, Fen started poking at her and said loudly, "I get the window seat."

"You had it earlier." Laurie shoved him. "Jerk."

"You know it." Fen flashed his teeth at her, looking so wolfy that she wondered how she'd never noticed.

"Enough." The woman with the clipboard scowled at them. "Where are your badges?"

"He lost them," Laurie whined. "I told him, but—"

"You told me after I lost them. What kind of help is that?" Fen looked at the woman. "I don't want to sit with her on the way back."

Matt boarded the bus.

"Well, maybe I'll sit on the other bus." Laurie shoved his shoulder, and then she turned to walk away.

"Get on the bus." The woman sighed wearily.

Fen folded his arms. "Fine. *You* get on this, and I'll—"

"*Both of you*, on the bus." The woman looked at the line of kids waiting. "Now."

They went to the back, where Matt was seated. He nodded at them, but they said nothing else. Laurie might not be experienced at this like Fen was, but she *was* a Brekke. She knew instinctively that they'd used a distraction to get on the bus, but now they needed to avoid attention to *stay* on the bus.

They took the seat directly in front of Matt's.

A few kids looked at them, but this wasn't a school group. *Thankfully.* Blending into a school group would be harder. There, the kids mostly all knew each other. This was a group, but probably for something like a community center or church or youth group.

A girl sat down beside Matt. "Who are you?"

"Matt," he answered.

Beside Laurie, Fen smothered a sigh. They exchanged a worried look. Matt just wasn't used to trickery. Even though she tried not to use it, she still knew Tricks 101: don't use your real name. Laurie opened her mouth to intervene before he said something crazy like *We're runaways from Blackwell.*

But before she could, she heard Matt say, "Didn't we meet earlier?"

Fen looked at her and raised both eyebrows in surprise. Matt was taking the act-like-you-belong thing to a new level. In the seat behind them, they could hear Matt and the girl chattering away about the monument. It wasn't a strategy she would've used, but it seemed to be working. The kids in the seat across from Matt were talking, too.

"Laurie might know," Matt said, suddenly drawing her into the conversation.

"Know what?"

"How far to Deadwood?" the girl beside Matt said. She was smiling, but Laurie didn't think it was particularly friendly.

"Ummm, I don't know. Maybe an hour?" Laurie had a rough guess from trips she'd taken before, but that wasn't the sort of thing she usually paid much attention to.

"Which school do you go to?" the girl asked. "I don't think I've met any of you before."

"We were on the other bus," Fen said. He leaned his head back on the seat and closed his eyes before adding, "Do you mind not talking? I have a headache."

"Sorry, I forgot." Laurie was silently thankful for Fen's surliness, but she looked at the girl and mouthed, "Sorry."

The girl said, "Whatever."

Matt nodded.

Once they'd looked away, Fen leaned in and whispered, "Knew you could do it."

Laurie tried not to feel too excited by their success so far. They had a huge list of impossible things in front of them . . . but they'd already overcome trolls, wolves, and chaperones. They really weren't off to a bad start.

FOURTEEN

MATT

"ALL-POINTS BULLETIN"

On the bus trip, Matt relaxed for the first time since his grandfather had named him champion. He'd done well so far. Really well. They'd found the trolls, and they'd gotten the information they needed. His idea hadn't exactly gone as planned, but Laurie had figured out a solution, and they'd all worked together to escape. That's what it was about—working together. He wasn't a perfect leader, but maybe he wasn't totally faking it, either. Maybe he really could become the leader they needed.

When the bus stopped, they were in Lead, making an educational pit stop to visit the Black Hills Mining Museum.

Matt thought of just staying on the bus, but everyone was getting off.

"The chaperone said it's only three miles to Deadwood," Fen whispered as they filed out. "We're walking."

As they stepped off the bus, a tour guide was trilling, "And don't forget, if you decide to try the gold panning, you are guaranteed to find gold!" The older kids jostled past her, some mimicking her and rolling their eyes. The younger kids just trudged along, casting pained looks at the museum and the prospect of an hour of sheer boredom.

The museum didn't look like much. It was mostly a single-story building with a flat roof. Near the front, though, a weirdly shaped silo jutted out. A model of a mining shaft, Matt guessed. He was following along, gaze fixed on that silo, thinking maybe this could be interesting, when Fen stopped him.

"Did I say this is where we get off?" Fen whispered.

"Right, but—"

"But what? We're in the middle of saving the world, and you want to take a museum tour? You really are a geek, aren't you, Thorsen?"

Matt could see Laurie tense, and he struggled to keep his voice calm. "No, but we're only three miles from Deadwood. I don't see the point in bailing now."

"Right. We're *only* three miles, so I don't see the point in *not* bailing. Getting back on the bus again is risky."

"Fen has a point," Laurie murmured.

When Matt opened his mouth to argue, she directed his attention to his seat partner from the bus. The girl stood over at the side, talking to the adult leader as she pointed at them.

"Okay, we'll bail," Matt said.

"Glad we have your permission," Fen said. "Follow me."

Now it was Matt's turn to stop him. They were in the middle of a parking lot, with a single stream of kids flowing to the museum doors. If they broke from that stream, they'd be spotted. He pointed that out, then said, "We'll go inside and circle back. Just stick with me."

He continued on toward the museum. Laurie stayed beside him. When he realized Fen wasn't with them, he looked back. Fen stood there, staring at Laurie, looking shocked and maybe a little hurt. She waved him forward. He turned a scowl on Matt and fell in line with the other kids, making no effort to catch up.

Fen finally did catch up, right inside the doors, which was as far as he'd go. Laurie convinced him to chill out long enough for them to get into the museum's re-creation of an actual mine—a long, semidark "underground" passage. Once they were in there, Matt pretended to be fascinated by the next exhibit, and he and Laurie talked about it while the other kids and the grown-ups all passed. Then they backed out.

There were a guy and a girl on duty near the front, but they were too busy talking to each other to notice anyone else. Matt ushered Fen and Laurie past and out the doors.

Once they were outside, they didn't need to walk more than a block before they saw signs for the highway. That would be the easiest route to Deadwood, Matt explained. The Black Hills towered all around them, and that thick, mountainous forest was a really bad place to wander. Besides, it was less than an hour's walk. If they picked up the pace, they'd be in Deadwood before the bus even left the museum.

Lead wasn't exactly crowded, but it was busy enough, so they didn't have a problem blending in as they moved along. Matt kept one eye on the road, though, just in case.

"Side road!" Fen said suddenly. "Now!"

Matt glanced around, frowning.

Fen gave him a look like he was standing in the path of that tornado. Then he muttered under his breath and started steering Laurie quickly to the next side road. Laurie looked back at Matt and whispered, "Cop!"

Matt peered down the road. A police car was creeping along. Matt had seen it turn the corner, but to him, it was about as alarming as seeing a delivery truck. Unlike other kids, he didn't see a police car and immediately think, *Am I doing something wrong?*

No, that wasn't true. He did. But that question was

quickly followed by *Is it my Dad?* If the answer to both was *yes*, he was in trouble. Otherwise, if Blackwell officers saw him doing something he shouldn't, they'd just roll up and say hi, and Matt got the message.

So he'd seen the car, and since he was just walking and this wasn't his father, he hadn't reacted. Except they weren't in Blackwell. This wasn't some officer he'd known since he was a baby.

He broke into a jog and followed Fen and Laurie down the side road.

"You think the lady on the bus called it in?" he asked.

Fen shrugged and kept bustling them along. They turned another corner, getting into a residential area lined with row houses and pickups, both in need of fresh paint. Two kids on rusted bicycles watched them. Then the kids looked up sharply, pushed off, and rode fast, legs pumping, bikes zooming around the corner.

Matt glanced over his shoulder to see the police cruiser gliding along the side street they'd just left, slowing as it approached the corner.

"If it turns, we run," Fen said.

"Where?" Matt gestured at the road. The next side road was a quarter mile away, and he couldn't see a break in the row houses. "Just be cool. I've got this."

He kept his gaze forward as he strolled along the sidewalk. He heard the rumble of the engine as the car turned the corner and rolled toward them. Moving slowly, which meant the officer was checking them out.

"Be cool," he whispered. "Just be cool."

They were on the left side of the road. The police car crossed over, ignoring an oncoming truck as it slowed by the sidewalk. Matt pretended not to notice. He heard the window slide down. Then he looked over. He smiled at the officer, a heavyset guy in his twenties.

"Afternoon, sir," he said.

"Afternoon." The officer stopped the car and put it in park. "Where you kids heading?"

"Just stretching our legs. Our folks took my little brother to the mining museum. It didn't seem like our kind of thing, so we begged off." Matt peered down the street. "Someone said there was an ice-cream place down here, but I think we made a wrong turn."

"You did. Easy mistake, though. It's off the strip. Why don't you kids hop in, and I'll give you a lift."

"Thanks, but we've been in our minivan forever," he said. "We need the exercise. We'll just head back downtown and find it."

The officer swung open the door. "No, I really think you should let me give you a lift"—he unfolded himself from the car—"Matt."

Matt turned to run, but the officer grabbed his wrist. He

saw Fen take off, Laurie following. The officer whipped Matt around to face him.

"Do you have any idea how much grief you've caused, son?" he said. "As a sheriff's boy, you should know better."

"I—"

"Exactly how far did you think you'd get? Your dad put out a statewide APB on you. Any kid goes missing, we pay attention. Sheriff's boy? We *really* pay attention." He gave Matt a yank toward the car and opened the back door. "Get in there. If you behave yourself, I'll let you come up front. For now, you're going to be treated like any other runaway."

Matt looked over to see Laurie standing about twenty feet away. She was frozen there, as if torn between running and coming back. He waved for her to go. The officer saw him and glanced over at Laurie. Fen was behind her, jogging back to get her.

"Is that Laurie Brekke?" the officer said. "We have a report on her, too. Your dad said it wasn't connected to you. Should have known better." He called to Laurie, "Don't you try running, missy."

He put his hand on Matt's shoulder to prod him into the car. As he did, his fingers loosened on Matt's wrist, and Matt tensed, waiting until he felt that grip relax, the one on his shoulder still loose enough to—

Matt flung himself to the side, wrenching from the

officer's grip. Then he ran. Instinctively, he ran toward Laurie and Fen. When he realized what he was doing, he veered across the road. He had to head in the other direction and let the Brekkes get away. Which would have been a perfectly fine plan, if Laurie hadn't run after him. Fen shouted for her to come back, but she'd already almost caught up to Matt.

Matt looked back at the officer. The guy was in his cruiser, on the radio, as his car lurched out of park.

Matt raced up the curb and onto the lawns. Laurie followed. Fen was following, too, cursing Matt with every step. Fen was right: Matt had messed up. Really messed up. And he couldn't believe he'd been so stupid. He'd run away from home, and he hadn't known his dad would put out an APB? His only excuse was that, as crazy as it sounded, it wasn't until this moment that he really realized he *had* run away from home.

His family wanted to sacrifice him to a giant serpent. His only chance of survival was to hit the road and find help to fight the serpent. It wasn't exactly your typical *my-parents-are-mean-and-totally-unfair-so-I'm-running-away* situation. But to the rest of the world, that's exactly what he'd done.

The police car roared up alongside them as they raced across the lawn. The officer put the window down.

"Get over here now, Matthew Thorsen!" the officer snapped. "You're a sheriff's son. You're supposed to set an example. Do you have any idea how much you've embarrassed your father?"

Behind Matt, Fen snorted and muttered, "Well, if you put it that way..." his voice thick with sarcasm. Except that Matt did stumble a little. The officer's words made his heart slam against his ribs, a voice in his head screaming that he was right. Matt couldn't be irresponsible. He couldn't embarrass his family.

It was only a quick stumble, though, before Matt realized that the old rules didn't apply. Being responsible now meant saving the world, even if it meant disobeying a police officer. Even if it meant embarrassing his family. It also meant...

"There!" he shouted, waving at a gap between two row houses. "Go! I've got this."

Fen gave him a shove toward the gap. "No, Thorsen, *I've* got this. You've done enough."

Matt tried to argue, but Fen only shoved him, harder, and all three of them raced through the gap between the row houses. Then Fen ran into the lead. He took them through the yard and over the fence. Through another yard, this one on a street of detached homes. They raced across the yard, over the front fence, and down the driveway.

The police car was nowhere in sight...yet.

Fen looked around. Matt was about to make a suggestion when Fen waved toward a pickup across the road.

"In there," he said. "Take Laurie. Lie down and stay down."

They ran across and hopped over the tailgate while Fen stood guard. Matt saw the police car turn the corner. He ducked as he called a warning to Fen.

"Lie down. Stay down. Stay quiet," Fen hissed. "Can you do that, Thorsen?"

Matt was about to answer, but Laurie silenced him with a look. He listened as Fen's sneakers slapped the ground. He seemed to be jogging toward the oncoming cruiser. The car stopped, engine rumbling.

"Hey," Fen said.

Matt heard the officer grunt a return greeting. "Where are your friends, boy?"

Fen lowered his voice. "That's what I'm here to tell you. But we gotta make a deal."

Silence.

Fen continued. "I'm from Blackwell, too. Laurie's my cousin. She ran off with Thorsen after the fair. Got some crazy idea they'd go on an adventure together. Dumb, huh?"

Matt listened as Fen snorted a laugh and the officer responded with a chuckle, as if relaxing now.

"Anyway, I caught up with them this morning. Only my cousin won't listen to me. So I want you to catch her and take her home. Can you do that?"

"Sure can. Your folks will be proud of you, son, looking after your cousin like that."

"It's the right thing to do," Fen said.

"All right, then. Just hop on in."

"See, that's the problem," Fen said. "My cousin and me, we're kinda friends, and if I turn her in, she's not going to be happy with me. Could you pick them up first? Then I'll walk to the next street over, and you can pretend to corner me there?"

The officer agreed. Matt realized that Fen wasn't even surprised that there wasn't an APB on him. Matt strained to listen as Fen told him that Matt and Laurie had raced along the row of lawns, intending to circle back downtown and hide out in the shops. Fen was explaining that he wasn't sure exactly which shop, but "Thorsen's not hard to find, with that red hair." The officer thanked him and promised to meet up with him as soon as he could.

After Fen's trick, they got away easily. They did stay off the roads, though, walking just inside the forest, keeping an eye on the ribbon of blacktop so they didn't get lost.

"I'm really sorry," Matt said as he held back a branch for Fen and Laurie. "I screwed up. I didn't—"

"—see it coming," Fen interrupted. "*None* of us saw it coming, but we should've. You're the sheriff's kid. Of course the cops are looking for you. For both of you." Fen paused, and with more patience than Matt had expected, he added,

"We've had other things on our minds, though. Tornadoes, Raiders, Valkyries, and trolls. We'll just add cops to the list, right?"

"Right." Laurie nodded, and then she bumped her head against Fen's shoulder and laughed. "We just hadn't stopped to think of regular problems. Like the fact we're all runaways."

"We can't forget it again," Matt said. "We need to be extra-careful now. No more hitching rides or anything."

"Exactly," Fen murmured. He shot a look at Matt and then at Laurie and smiled.

And no one commented on the fact that only two of them had APBs out on them.

FIFTEEN

❖

LAURIE

"DEADWOOD"

Laurie was surprised that they'd had a reasonably calm walk, but they'd realized that once again they had no more than a vague plan: "go to Deadwood, find the twins." It wasn't all bad to get a few hours' peace. Neither boy admitted that they were becoming friends, but they obviously were. Between the cops and the creatures out of myths, their world was turned completely upside down, but they were working together as a team. After a few hours, though, Matt seemed worried, and Fen was fussing over food.

"Let's go up here first." Laurie motioned to Mount Moriah, the cemetery on the hill above Deadwood. She wasn't sure why, but it made perfect sense to her.

"Sure," Matt agreed. His eyes lit up in the same way they had at the museum.

"Whatever," Fen said, but he trudged up the hill in front of her.

Both boys obviously were scanning the area for threats as they had during the several-mile walk, but Laurie couldn't fault them for that. She could fault them for thinking she hadn't noticed, but she didn't feel like bringing it up just then.

Just inside Mount Moriah, Laurie saw them: two kids, a boy and a girl who were unmistakably siblings, doing gravestone rubbings. There were other people inside the cemetery, and there had been plenty of people in town, but her feet had led her here. She wasn't sure how she knew they were the ones she needed to reach, but as soon as her gaze fell on them, she knew they were the descendants. She looked closer and confirmed that these two weren't just siblings: they were twins. *Like Frey and Freya. They are the ones we need.* The question was how to tell two strangers that they ought to join up with three kids they'd never met and plot to kill a big reptile to save the world. It sounded crazy any way she tried to phrase it.

"That's them," she whispered. "The twins."

The one holding the paper on the stone watched them approach; the one kneeling on the ground rubbing the chalk over the paper looked back at them briefly and then resumed rubbing. They didn't smile, say hello, or seem at all sociable. At school, she would've been a bit nervous approaching them.

But this wasn't school.

And after trolls...well, a couple of kids who were trying to be unfriendly didn't seem nearly as scary. She'd seen scary, and the bored, you're-not-worth-my-time looks she was getting weren't scary. She smiled, and they continued to ignore her. The one standing up said something to the one on the ground, who laughed.

"Are you sure?" Fen asked.

Laurie nodded, but she didn't take her attention off the twins. She had the sudden fear that they'd run. *They can't. We need them.* The problem was that she didn't know how to convince them to join the team.

She wasn't sure why, but she had sort of expected them to be like Matt or like Fen, but they weren't. From here, they seemed tall, and she thought they might be almost as tall as Matt. They both had shoulder-length, straight, pale blond hair. She wasn't entirely sure which of the twins was the girl and which was the boy because they were dressed almost identically in black pants with straps and zippers, big black boots, and jewelry flashing in their ears and on their fingers.

"Do we have a plan?" Fen asked.

Matt said nothing, but he shifted his path to walk toward the twins.

The twins, however, seemed completely unconcerned with the attention that they were getting. Maybe they were used to being watched, because they weren't uncomfortable about it. Then again, they hadn't faced wolves, Valkyries, or trolls. Laurie reminded herself that she probably ought not to mention any of those details just yet. The twins continued their studious not-paying-attention while Laurie and the boys continued walking through the hilly cemetery toward them.

She wanted to hurry. The cemetery bothered her more than she'd expected; as they passed graves of people long dead, she shivered. Maybe it was just the cold, or it was that she just now realized that they could die. Fen almost did die—and according to the mythology, Matt would die. The thought of either of them dying made her feel sick. She hadn't known Matt that well before the tornado, and what she thought she knew about him wasn't entirely accurate. After facing a few monsters at his side, they were becoming friends. *They can't die. They won't.* She was going to do everything possible to keep that from happening.

And that started with convincing the twins to cooperate. She walked faster.

Matt sped up to keep pace with her. His voice was a low whisper as he asked, "What are you doing?"

"Talking to them," she said resolutely.

"You're just going to go up and tell them they need to

help us fight a big snake and stop the end of the world?" Matt asked incredulously. He wasn't whispering this time, but he was still too quiet for the twins to hear. "This isn't Blackwell. They might not even know who Thor and Loki are."

"So we ask what they do know," Laurie said.

Matt looked at Fen for help, but Fen just shrugged. Her cousin might not like her plan, but she knew he'd side with her. Fen always took her side. Okay, *almost* always. He would side with Matt if he thought it would keep her safe. She knew that. She also knew he'd pound anyone who was rude to her. He'd made that pretty obvious as far back as kindergarten. And maybe it made her a little braver knowing that, she admitted.

In another few moments, they reached the gravestone where the twins were and stopped. This close, Laurie could see that they both had short black fingernails and both wore black eyeliner. The twins still acted like Laurie and the boys weren't there. They didn't even glance at any of the three of them.

"Hi," Laurie said.

Neither twin replied.

"My cousin is talking to you," Fen said.

"And my brother and I aren't interested in talking to her...or you," said the standing twin, who, now that she'd spoken, Laurie could tell was the sister.

Fen growled.

The twin on the ground stood and moved so he was shoulder-to-shoulder with his sister. He said nothing, just glanced at her, a little uncertain.

"Look," the girl continued. "We don't know you, don't want to know you, and really don't care about whatever you want. Ray and I are busy." She turned her back on them and flicked her hand at her side as if to shoo them away. "Now go away."

Fen growled again.

"Fen," Matt started.

"I got strangled by a *troll* to find Goth Ken and Barbie here, so I'm not going to 'go away' so they can play with chalk or go do each other's makeup." Fen's eyes actually flashed yellow, and Laurie wondered briefly if he'd hidden a lot more of himself from her than she'd realized or if he was just exhausted.

"Excuse me?" the girl said in a tone that made it sound more like a challenge than a question.

"Reyna..." her brother said under his breath.

She ignored him and turned back around to face Fen. "Don't think our eyeliner means we can't kick your scrawny butt. Ask anyone in town. And trolls? Seriously. Go back to your video games."

"Whoa! Both of you, stop. We're not here to fight." Matt stepped between Ray and Fen. "We just want to talk to you.

We're tired, and some of us"—he glanced at Fen—"have had a rough trip. We don't care about the, ummm, makeup."

"Really? He's wearing nail polish and *guyliner*," Fen grumbled.

"Stop it, Fen." Laurie put her hand flat on Fen's chest, and then she looked at Reyna and Ray. "Please? Just let us explain."

They all stood in an awkward standoff for several moments until Reyna said, "Fine. Say whatever you need to say and then leave." She linked her arm through her twin's at the elbow.

A strange tickle crept over Laurie, as if she had pins and needles all over. Whatever god powers these two had, they were stronger when they were connected. Apparently, Matt could feel monsters, and she could sense descendants? *And what? Trouble? Threats?* She wasn't sure, but there was something going on here and it increased when the twins touched.

"Right," Laurie started. "Do you want to sit down or walk or—"

"No. We don't," Reyna said. Apparently, she spoke for both of them. Ray stood silently at her side, more like an extension of her than an actual person.

"Fine." Laurie took a deep breath, but she didn't know how to start. She looked at Matt. "Ummm?"

He stepped in and said, "The end of the world is coming. We need your help to stop it."

Reyna took a step backward, pulling Ray with her.

Matt hurried on. "There's more, of course. That's the short version. I can tell you the rest if you just give us a few—"

"Come on, Ray." Reyna crouched down and started gathering up their stuff with one hand. Her other hand was still holding Ray's elbow. Ray stood staring at Matt.

"There's something different about you, something you can do that most people can't," Laurie blurted out. "It's because you're like us."

"We're nothing like you." Reyna released her hold on her brother and folded her arms over her chest. "We're—"

"Descendants of the Norse gods. You have some sort of power. I know you do," Matt said evenly.

"Or you will soon," Laurie added.

The twins exchanged a look, and then Ray murmured, "We don't know what you're talking about."

In the next minute, the twins had scooped up their art supplies and they all but ran away from the three of them. They were walking so quickly that if they went a single step faster, they would be jogging.

"That went well," Fen deadpanned.

After the walk to Deadwood from Lead and then up the hill to the cemetery—and after their failure with the twins—the walk into downtown Deadwood felt like punishment. It had been an awfully long couple of days, and Laurie was tired. She wanted a bath, her own bed, and to curl up on her own living room sofa with a book—or maybe to watch a movie with Fen and Matt. What she didn't want was to try to figure out how to convince the twins, who were obviously hiding something, to join them in a fight to save the world. In all honestly, she didn't want to sign up to save the world, either, but it didn't seem right to know that there was something that important at stake and not help out. Sure, she wasn't one of the people destined to be in the fight, but her cousin was and her friend was, and she was helping them get there. She *had* tricked the troll, and she *knew* she was right about the twins—at least that's what she told herself.

"What if I was wrong about them?" she asked.

Matt stopped and looked directly into her eyes. "Do you think you were?"

"No. Maybe. I don't know." She jumped as she heard a man yell something about "calling the law."

Suddenly, as they stood there on the sidewalk along the streets of Deadwood, two men were yelling at each other and aiming guns. For a brief moment, Laurie wanted to get involved, to protect...one of them. In that split second, she wasn't sure which one to help, but she was trying to figure it out. One of them was dressed in a suit and tall hat, and the other wore a brown fringed leather jacket, dirty trousers,

and a battered cowboy hat. A blink later, she realized that this was a sort of theater. These were actors, reenacting some of Deadwood's Wild West history.

"Wild Bill wasn't killed in the street," Matt muttered.

"What?" Fen asked.

"I don't think that guy's supposed to be Wild Bill. He might be the most famous person here, but he wasn't the only gunslinger," Laurie said.

She and Matt had both stepped forward to watch the show.

"Seriously? We're going to stand here? I'm bored." Fen stepped between her and Matt.

Laurie stepped closer to her cousin. He had always been a little bit of a jerk when she paid attention to anyone other than him. Her mom had told her that she only encouraged him to do it more by giving in, but someone had to encourage Fen, and in her family, the only two people who had in years were her and her dad. "Come on, Fen. I think it would've been cool to live here then. You don't?" she teased. "I thought you were a Brekke."

He was quiet for a minute while they watched the two men face off in their pretend fight. "Maybe a little cool, but these are just people pretending."

It was hard to tell which one they should be cheering for. She watched as the man in the suit drew his gun and the man in the cowboy hat drew his and twirled it around so fast it looked like a magic trick. She hadn't been paying attention to what they were saying, so she still had no idea which one was the one they were to cheer for. It would be easier—in plays and real life—if things were as simple as good guys and bad guys, heroes and villains, but right and wrong weren't always clear. She glanced up at Fen. What was clear was that her cousin was going to be a hero. She'd been right about him.

"Bet there were Brekkes here then, and"—Fen glanced at Matt—"Thorsens arresting them for every little thing."

Matt shrugged.

"Be nice," Laurie chastised Fen. "Not all Thorsens are the same, just like not all Brekkes are. Matt was running from the cops with us, and you jumped in to fight with him."

Both boys shrugged, and both looked uncomfortable.

Matt's interest in the pretend gunslingers seemed to vanish. "We should eat, and then figure out how to convince the twins to join us," he said.

"And find somewhere to sleep tonight," Fen added. "We don't have sleeping bags, and unless you want to break into a hotel room, we don't have rooms anywhere."

They started walking down Main Street, looking for a place to eat. To be safe, they stopped in a tourist shop and bought a hat, which Matt wore pulled down low. After their run-in with the police in Lead, a little extra precaution was in order. With their police situation and their age, getting anywhere comfortable to sleep wasn't likely. Trying to steal some sleeping bags wasn't a great idea, either. They'd left theirs hidden back at Mount Rushmore, first in order not to attract attention at the monument, and then they couldn't bring them on the bus. Laurie sighed. The thought of sleeping on the cold ground again was far from appealing, but she knew hotels didn't rent rooms to kids, and she wasn't sure they should spend their little bit of money on a hotel room even if they could get someone to rent it for them.

Her family members usually had pretty good luck with cons; she felt strangely proud now that she knew about her ancestry: her family's con and luck skills were because of Loki. In a way, her mom was right: she was just like her dad. But maybe that wasn't a bad thing, despite the way it sounded when her mom said it. Admittedly, her mom said it after there had been a call from the principal's office, but sometimes Laurie thought that her mother forgot the good things about her father. Being lucky—or clever—wasn't all bad.

"Maybe the twins would let us stay at their house," Laurie suggested, thinking about the possibility of convincing them through a mix of luck and tricks.

Fen laughed. "They don't even want to talk to us, and you think they're going to invite us to their house?"

"Maybe," she hedged. If it was just Fen, she'd tell him why she thought so, but she suspected that even though they were all friends of a sort, Matt still wasn't going to be too much in favor of trickery.

"I hate to agree with Fen, but he's right on this one. They ran off pretty fast." Matt paused. "When we brought up gifts, they spooked."

"Are we sure that they're on *our* side?" Fen asked. He rubbed his hands on his face like he was trying to wake up, and his words all sort of started to tumble out. "I mean, how much of the myth stuff is supposed to be what happens? If I could switch, they could, too. Could they be on the snake's side? And also, aren't people going to notice a big monster snake and do something about it? I get that in whenever it was, big snakes were probably hard to kill so call in the gods, but today, there are tanks, bombs, and all sorts of stuff."

Laurie didn't say anything beyond, "Fen has a point... or points, or whatever. He's right. We don't know what we're doing or where to go." She paused and then said, "And I'm tired and hungry."

Fen's burst of frustration seemed to vanish. "We'll eat. We'll figure it out."

He gently bumped his shoulder into hers.

Matt was silent as they walked. He stayed that way while they ate at a little diner. Then, as they left the diner, he looked at Laurie and casually asked, "Which way are the twins?"

Without thinking, she pointed to the left.

Fen and Matt both grinned at her, and once she realized what she'd done, she smiled, too. "I *can* find them," she said. "It is them, and I can find them."

"We can do this," Matt said. "The three of us, and then we'll convince the others. We're a good team."

Laurie half expected Fen to flinch away at Matt's words, but he just looked at her and said, "Lead on."

They walked away from the tourist-filled, casino-filled heart of Deadwood to the streets they'd skirted on the way from Mount Moriah to downtown. She didn't speak and neither did the boys as she followed the instinct that told her where the twins were—until she realized that they were headed back to the cemetery. That was weird.

Matt must've figured out the same thing, because he was frowning.

"Wait, maybe I'm wrong." She glanced at the boys. "I was so sure this feeling was leading us to them."

"Maybe the people we needed are still in the cemetery, and we just missed them," Matt suggested helpfully.

The frustration and fear that she was leading them on another long, pointless walk made her let out a small scream of frustration.

Fen squeezed her hand. "It's cool."

"Not really." She closed her eyes and tried to concentrate.

The same sensation was there, urging her, telling her which way to go. She turned away from the cemetery, but the directions remained unchanged.

She shook her head. "I don't know. Maybe they went back there, or maybe it is someone else we're supposed to be looking for."

With the boys behind her, she continued walking, but the trail ended a few moments later—not at Mount Moriah, but on Madison Street. She felt the end so strongly that it was as if she could see a trail dead-ending on the ground. The house in front of her was a sprawling mess. It looked like the owners had bought several houses on the street, demolished them all, and constructed one of those garish oversized houses that screamed "more money than we need." Laurie gestured toward the house and said, "I think they're inside there."

"Well, then." Fen snorted. "Looks like Goth Barbie and Ken are loaded, too."

Matt shook his head. "We walk in there and they get nervous again, we'll end up needing to deal with police. I'm guessing if they're looking for me in Lead, they'll be looking here, too."

Fen gave Matt an appraising look. "Not a bad point, Thorsen. So now what?"

With surprise, Laurie realized that Fen was still looking to her to lead them. "I don't know."

After a moment, Fen suggested, "We need to move away before someone reports us for loitering."

The house was near the cemetery, and the twins were obviously fond of it, so the three of them decided that the best thing to do was tuck in there and wait. Either the twins would come back, or when they went somewhere else in Deadwood, Laurie could find them. It didn't help with the convince-them-to-join-the-fight part, but convincing them meant finding them first.

SIXTEEN

MATT

"UNMARKED GRAVES"

When they got back to the cemetery, Matt couldn't resist the chance to take a look around, so he said they should walk through and make sure the twins weren't already there. Fen grumbled that the twins had been right up front last time and Laurie's hound-dogging had led to their house, but Matt insisted. Finally, Fen bought it and followed him inside.

They passed through the black gate. Matt walked into the cemetery proper, moving at a decent speed, but after the fourth time Matt stopped to read a sign, Fen growled.

"What?" Fen said. "Are you prepping for a history paper, Thorsen? Those twins aren't hiding in that sign."

"There are almost four thousand marked graves in here," Matt said, reading. "And that's only a third of them. Lots more are unmarked."

"They're not hiding in one of those, either," Fen drawled.

"I'm just saying it's interesting."

"Interesting?" Fen scowled. "It's a cemetery."

"In *Deadwood*." Matt swept a hand across the hills, dotted with graves. "Think how many of these guys died in gunfights at high noon. Isn't that cool?"

Laurie laughed softly. "I don't think it'd be too cool if you were the one dying."

"You know what I mean," Matt said. "It's a cemetery from the Wild West. *That's* cool."

He looked down the hill toward the town of Deadwood at the base. Trees blocked enough of it that if Matt squinted he could picture it the way it should be, with saloons instead of coffee shops and gambling dens instead of casinos. He was relaxing now, for the first time since leaving Lead. He'd messed up there. Really messed up, and he'd been sure Fen and Laurie would figure out he wasn't the leader they needed. But they'd just carried on. So now he was relaxing, feeling more like himself. Even kind of feeling like he was around friends.

"Deadwood was the last frontier," he said. "I remember reading letters on it for a project, and someone said they didn't fear going to hell because they'd been to Deadwood."

"Why was it the last frontier?" Laurie asked as they resumed walking. Fen rolled his eyes, but she gave him a look and said, "I'm interested, okay? As long as we're here, might as well get the unofficial tour."

Matt smiled. "I can do that. Never been here—my parents don't approve of Deadwood, past or present—but I know all the stories. They called Deadwood the last frontier because the town itself wasn't even legal. The land was supposed to belong to the Native Americans, but General Custer found gold here and that started a gold rush, which started the town of Deadwood. Because it was illegal, though, there wasn't a whole lotta law and order, not until Seth Bullock— a Canadian guy who became the first sheriff—came along."

Matt continued with the tour as Fen trailed along behind, shaking his head.

As they walked, Matt managed to find all the famous graves— Wild Bill, Calamity Jane, Seth Bullock, Preacher Smith, and Potato Creek Johnny—but they didn't find the twins. And they took so long getting to the back of the cemetery that they then had to search on the way out, in case the twins had come in during the meantime. Fen complained about that...and about the fact that Matt continued to stop for things he'd missed the first time, including Potter's Field. He explained to Laurie that was where most of the unmarked graves were.

"I'm going to put *you* in an unmarked grave if you say one more sentence with the word *dead* in it," Fen muttered.

"Does that include *Deadwood*?" Matt said, grinning.

"Yes."

Matt laughed, but Fen had a point. They really should get back to the front of the cemetery and watch for the twins.

They found a place to hide behind a monument and waited. An hour passed. Then another. Dark began to fall. Matt was out stretching his legs when he heard something cracking and snapping. He looked up to see a flag whipping in the wind.

"See something?" Laurie whispered as she crept out from behind the monument.

Matt shook his head. "Just the flag." He squinted up at it in the twilight. "It's weird. They don't lower it at sunset like most places. I read that they leave it up twenty-four hours a day and—"

"Are you at it again?" Fen said. "I swear I'll find you a nice empty grave if you keep it up."

"I'm not too worried," Matt said. "Cemetery's full." He thought of stopping there, but really, it was fun to push Fen's buttons sometimes. Especially when there wasn't much else to do for entertainment. "You know, though, there actually might be some empty graves. Back in frontier days, they'd bury prospectors here, and then sometimes their families would find out and want the bodies sent home. Except, of course, by that point, the person had been dead awhile, so digging them up and mailing them would be pretty gross. They'd just send back the bones, which meant they had to boil—"

"Hey!" Fen jabbed a finger at Laurie. "You think she really needs to hear this?"

"Actually..." Laurie began.

"No." Fen swung his scowl on Matt. "Shut it, Thorsen. Or I'll shut it for you."

"Before or after you put me in the empty grave?"

Fen growled. Matt grinned back.

Laurie stepped between them. "He's baiting you, Fen." She turned to Matt. "Stop that." Then to Fen. "You stop it, too."

"But he started—"

Her look silenced Fen, and she stalked back behind the monument. Matt and Fen followed. As Matt stepped behind the monument, though, he thought he heard something. He looked around. When he didn't see anything and turned away to ignore it, he felt a...brain twitch. That was the only way he could describe it. Like the weird sense of someone watching you, except it wasn't the hairs rising on his neck, it was a *ping* in his brain that said *Pay attention*.

Then he really felt the ping as his amulet jumped and began to heat up. He opened his mouth to say something, but wasn't sure what exactly to say and leaned out from the monument instead, peering into the growing darkness. That's when he saw two figures making their way toward the cemetery.

Norns? Valkyries? Trolls? His amulet had reacted to all three. As the figures drew closer, though, he saw that it was the twins—Ray and Reyna. So he could detect descendants, too? That hadn't happened before. Maybe it was a new power.

He tapped Laurie on the shoulder and pointed. She saw the twins and murmured that they should wait until they got closer. Fen shuffled impatiently, but he didn't argue.

Matt wasn't sure what to make of the twins. They weren't the kind of kids you saw in Blackwell or Lead or even Deadwood. Not that there was anything wrong with being different. He just...he didn't know what to make of them. That meant he didn't know how to talk to them or how to convince them to join the fight.

But that's your job, isn't it? That's the test the Valkyries gave you. Find the others and get them to join up.

The fighting part was so much easier.

He sized up the twins. The answer seemed to be to ignore the weird clothes and the makeup and just talk to them. But Laurie had already tried that.

The heat of his amulet flared, as if to remind him that he could *make* the twins join up. Scare them into it. The very thought made him queasy. That wasn't how a leader acted. It wasn't how Thor had acted, either. Sometimes people thought he had, but in the old stories, he always used his strength for good. To help others, not hurt them.

Matt watched the twins, now close enough for him to see their faces, set in that same the-world-bores-me look they'd had earlier. And he realized he had no idea what they could do now that they hadn't done earlier, and Fen and Laurie were expecting him to do more, to find the right words, except he didn't know them and now they'd gone through all this for nothing and—

He took a deep breath. He'd talk to them. He'd be reasonable. Use logic.

Logic? They were telling these kids that they had to help them save the world. Fight a giant serpent before wolves ate the sun and moon and plunged Earth into eternal winter. Logic didn't even—

His amulet began to vibrate now. He tugged the new cord and flicked it outside his shirt so he could concentrate. Only even as he was moving it, he felt the vibration, and it wasn't coming from his warm amulet. He dropped quickly and pressed his fingers to the ground. *It* was vibrating. Which meant it wasn't the twins making his necklace react.

Matt leaped up. "Tro—!"

He didn't even finish the word before two headstones sprang to life. They vaulted over the wall before Matt could get out from behind the monument. The twins turned and gaped.

The trolls scooped them up and swung them over their shoulders. The boy—Ray—froze. Reyna pounded at her captor's back and shouted. Matt raced from the monument, Fen and Laurie behind him, but the trolls moved lightning-fast, swinging back over the wall. As the trolls ran, another headstone jumped up and followed, and the three tore through the cemetery. All the while, Reyna was howling and struggling.

Matt raced after them, but by the time he reached the spot where they'd jumped the wall, they'd vanished into the dark cemetery. He ran in the direction they'd gone. There was no sign of them, though, and he slowed, squinting as he kept jogging forward. Finally, he saw something move over by the monument to Wild Bill Hickok.

He stopped Fen and Laurie and pointed. The troll who'd been playing backup for the kidnappers had stopped at the fence surrounding Wild Bill's grave. He was trying to shove his hand through the chain-link fence to grab at something.

"The coins," Matt whispered, remembering Laurie throwing one to the troll at Mount Rushmore.

As he moved from headstone to headstone, he could see he was right. Earlier, they'd noticed that people had reached through the fence to leave "offerings" on Wild Bill's grave. There were a couple bottles of whiskey, a flower, a set of aces, and coins. It was the last that had caught the troll's attention.

As Matt watched the troll struggling to get the money,

he had to stifle the urge to laugh. It was kinda funny, like watching a six-hundred-pound tiger stop chasing a gazelle to bat at a butterfly. The other trolls were long gone.

"I'll circle around," Fen whispered. "When I give the signal, we'll both run out and jump him. Make him tell us where they took the twins."

A day ago, Matt would have thought this was a perfectly brilliant plan. But he'd fought the last troll. He knew that, as silly as this one looked, grunting and grumbling and straining for pocket change, it was still a living pile of rock...with a sledgehammer punch. Forcing Leaf to reveal the twins' whereabouts hadn't worked so well. So he motioned for Fen to hold off and just watch.

The troll spent about five minutes trying to get its oversized arm through the wire before it realized that the fence barely came up to its chest. Then it took a few more minutes to figure out how to climb over.

"Not too bright, are they?" Laurie said with a soft laugh.

That was an understatement. And something Matt needed to remember if they had to take this guy on. They didn't, though. It got the money, climbed back over the fence, and loped off. Matt motioned for them to follow.

With the other two trolls long gone, this one didn't seem to be in as much of a rush, and they were able to keep up. The troll continued over the hills, occasionally disappearing behind clumps of trees or melding with gray headstones then emerging a moment later, still on the move. Finally, nearly at the far side of the cemetery, Matt heard the twins.

"Do you really think we're stupid?" Reyna was saying. "You're working with those kids. They tell us stories about gods and trolls, and you guys show up wearing troll costumes. *Lame* troll costumes. I can see the zipper in the back, you know."

"I don't see a zipper," Ray's whispered voice drifted over on the breeze.

"Well, there must be," his sister said. "They've put on costumes to kidnap us for ransom. That's what you want, isn't it? Ransom?"

"Treasure," one of the trolls rumbled. "Aerik want treasure."

"See?" Reyna said.

Matt darted along the headstones until he could see the trolls. The third one had joined its companions, and all three crouched around the twins, who sat, bound back-to-back. Ray looked terrified; Reyna looked furious.

Now that they were closer, Matt recognized one of the two trolls who'd taken the kids. He'd know the crags of that ugly face anywhere. Leaf.

It was Leaf who spoke next, turning to the one who'd been delayed and saying, "Where Sun go?"

The troll—whose skin was veined with dark red, like rusty iron—opened his hand, revealing the coins.

"More?" Leaf asked.

Sun shook his head.

Leaf grunted and turned to the twins. "You have treasure."

"Money?" Ray said. "Sure, our parents have money. Our dad runs one of the casinos."

"Don't—" Reyna began.

He shot her a look that silenced her, then he turned back to the trolls. "Our dad will pay. I can give you his cell phone number. Or . . ." He looked them up and down. "I can call on mine."

The trolls stared blankly at him. Then Aerik said, "Treasure. Aerik want treasure. Leaf say girl daughter Freya. Boy son Frey. God kids want. Frey and Freya have treasure."

Laurie leaned over and whispered, "They know the twins are valuable because we wanted to find them so badly."

Matt nodded. "And to them, valuable means treasure."

They listened for a few more minutes, as the two sides tried—without much success—to understand each other.

"They'll be at this for a while." Laurie turned to Matt and asked, "Should we wait until they turn to stone?"

Matt looked up at the sky. The stars had just appeared about an hour ago. It was a long way from dawn. He glanced over at the trolls. One they could handle. Two might be okay if they could free Ray to help. Three? Not happening.

Matt nodded. "We have to."

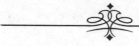

A half hour later, the twins finally started to get what the trolls meant. Kind of.

"No paper money?" Reyna said. "How do you get a ransom without paper money? Bonds or something?"

"Gold," Ray whispered to his sister. "They said shiny treasure, so I think they mean gold."

"Then why don't they say gold?"

Ray looked at the trolls, and Matt could see by the way he studied them that he'd figured out they weren't guys in costumes. But when he glanced at his sister, he seemed to decide this wasn't the time to argue with her about it.

Ray wriggled in his bonds and pulled off a ring. Then he held it out as best he could, pinched between his fingers. "Is this what you want? More of this? Treasure?"

Aerik made a move to snatch the ring, and Ray quickly tossed it onto the grass. All three trolls dove for it. Leaf came up victorious, chortling in that scraping-rocks way that made Matt's teeth clench.

"That's what you want then?" Ray said. "That's treasure?"

"Yes," Aerik said, bouncing. "Treasure. More treasure. Aerik want treasure."

"Give them your ring," Ray whispered to his sister.

"What? I am not—"

"Reyna!"

Reyna grumbled, but managed to yank it off and tossed it. Again, it was like a football tackle as all three went for it. Leaf got this one, too, but Aerik snatched it away, and they argued in wordless rumbles before Leaf gave in.

"There," Reyna said. "Now, if you can untie us..."

"More treasure," Sun said, rolling forward to crouch in front of her. "Want more."

"We don't have more with us," Ray said.

Reyna wriggled her fingers. "See? No more rings. That's it."

Now Leaf sidled forward, rocking from side to side, knuckles dragging. "More treasure."

"We don't have—"

"More treasure!" Aerik roared as he shot forward and grabbed Ray by the throat.

Aerik swung Ray up, Reyna dangling behind him by her bound hands. He lifted Ray overhead and started to squeeze. Ray gasped and kicked. Reyna shouted and tried to twist around.

"Treasure!" Aerik shouted. "Give treasure or Aerik break son Frey. Break his bones. Grind his bones. Do now!"

Matt yanked off his amulet and lunged from his hiding place. "Did someone say treasure?"

Aerik turned, the other two turning with him, and Matt found himself facing off with three trolls. He swallowed and found his voice.

"Remember me?" Matt said.

"Son Thor." Leaf held up an injured hand. "Cracked Leaf fingers."

"Right. And the son of Thor has a very special treasure, doesn't he?" Matt unclenched his fist and let the amulet fall. "You remember this, too?"

"Hammer," Sun said. "God Hammer."

"And the god Hammer is a very special treasure, isn't it? Better than a whole mountain of rings and coins. It has power. Thor's power. Giant-killing power."

He swung the amulet. All three pairs of beady eyes tracked it, back and forth.

"You want this?" Matt asked.

Three ugly heads nodded.

"Then put those kids down."

Aerik dropped them, Ray landing on Reyna, who let out an *oomph.*

"Good. Now, I know all three of you want it, so we have to make this a race. I'll throw it. First one who gets it wins the power of Thor. Is that fair?"

They nodded again. Leaf inched forward. Aerik shot out a long arm to stop him, and they grumbled at each other for a moment before Leaf moved back in line.

"Everyone ready?" Matt said. "On the count of three. One." He pulled his hand back. "Two." He flexed his arm.

"Three!" He pretended to whip the necklace, instead tossing it up, hidden, in his fist.

None of the trolls moved. Matt lowered his fist to his side and waved with his other hand. "It's out there. Go get it."

"Is in hand," Sun said.

"What?" Matt held out the hand he'd waved. "No, it's empty. See?"

"Other hand."

Aerik took a long stride forward. "Son Thor think Aerik stupid. Aerik not stupid. Hammer in hand."

Matt opened his other hand and faked surprise at seeing the necklace there. "Huh. It must have gotten caught on my finger. Sorry about that. Let's try again."

He waved Aerik back in line between the other two. Behind them, Ray and Reyna were working furiously to get free. Reyna had one hand out and was pulling at the knot. Matt tried to stall, but the trolls started grumbling and rocking back and forth, as if ready to attack.

"Okay, okay," he said. "Here we go. I'll throw it this time. Everyone ready?"

The trolls nodded. As Matt had been stalling, hoping the twins would get free, he'd tugged the amulet off the cord. Now he gripped the cord, letting it dangle, but held the amulet firmly between his thumb and palm. He counted down and then whipped the cord as hard as he could.

Again the trolls just stood there.

"Didn't you see it?" he said, waving with one hand as he slid the amulet into his pocket. "I threw it this time."

"I saw it!" Ray piped up. "I can still see it, on the base of that grave over there."

"Is black strap," Aerik said. "Thor son threw black strap. Not want black strap."

Why isn't it working? Laurie tricked them easily. Panic swirled in his gut.

Laurie moved forward. "But the black strap is what holds the Hammer on his neck. It's over there. Just like Frey's son said. See it?"

"Is trap," Aerik said. "Hammer in pocket."

"What?" Matt said, patting his pockets, hoping his hands weren't shaking. "How would it get in there? I threw it. It's—"

Aerik charged.

Matt shoved Laurie out of the way and hit Aerik with a Hammer blast. A perfect hit, almost instantaneous, and he couldn't help grinning as the troll sailed to the ground. Unfortunately, there were two others with him, and they were charging now. Matt dove to the other side, away from Laurie, hitting the ground and rolling.

"Hey!" Fen shouted. "Ugly number two! Over here!"

As Matt got to his feet, he started motioning for Laurie to get to safety, then stopped himself: they needed to get the twins untied. She was a step ahead of him and already racing toward them as her cousin baited the trolls.

Matt hit Sun with the Hammer as Fen dodged Leaf's charge.

Fen ran up beside Matt as Aerik lumbered to his feet. "Word of advice, Thorsen? Stick to fighting. You have no future as a magician."

"Yeah, yeah."

Aerik rushed them. Matt sent him flying with the Hammer, but by then, Sun was on his feet and Leaf had wheeled, and they were both running at Matt and Fen. They dove opposite ways, and the trolls went after them.

As Sun lunged, Matt launched the Hammer. Or he tried to. Nothing happened. He rolled as Sun's fist came down, hitting the ground with a boom. He tried the Hammer again, focusing harder, getting madder. Sparks fizzled and drifted to the grass, barely even making it smolder.

Matt saw that massive fist coming at him again and tried to scramble up, but he was too late. It caught him in the shoulder, and he crashed into the nearest grave, his head striking it hard enough that he blacked out for a split second. When he came to, he was hanging three feet off the ground, staring into Sun's face as the troll held him by the collar.

Matt clenched his fist and called on the Hammer. His hand barely glowed.

"You're out of juice!" Fen yelled. "Think of something else."

Matt started to yell back that he could use a little help, but Fen was facing off with Leaf. The twins were free and now with Laurie. The three of them were dancing around Aerik, trying to keep him distracted.

Sun shook Matt. "Give Hammer. Give Hammer now."

"Wish I could," Matt muttered. "But I seem to be running on empty."

"Sun break Thor son. Break him—"

Matt swung at Sun and hit him square in the jaw. A knockout blow...that barely made Sun flinch and sent white-hot pain stabbing through Matt's arm, like he'd punched a brick wall.

That's what he is. A brick wall. Like Fen said. They're monsters made of stone. You can't fight—

"Give Hammer!" Sun roared. "Give now!"

He shook Matt so hard his teeth rattled and his stomach lurched and all he could see was the blur of Sun's beady eyes and open mouth and—

Yes!

Matt clenched his teeth and waited for Sun to stop shaking him. Then he pulled back his fist and punched the troll in the eye. Sun let out a grating howl. Matt hit him in the other eye.

Sun dropped him, and Matt hit the ground as Sun staggered back, yowling a nails-down-chalkboard yowl.

"Sun no see! No see! Sun blind!"

"Thorsen!" Fen yelled.

Matt struggled up and wheeled to see Laurie in the grip of Aerik. The twins batted at the monster, who ignored them. Fen was twenty feet away, facing off with Leaf, who stood between him and his cousin.

"Thorsen!" Fen shouted again.

"Got it!"

Matt ran and launched himself at Aerik. As he did, he remembered why he hadn't done this the first time—because it was like leaping onto a smooth rock face. There was nothing to grab. No, wait, maybe...

As he jumped, he managed to hook one arm around the troll's neck and hold on. He reached around to grind his palm into the troll's eye.

Aerik roared and dropped Laurie. He whacked at Matt, his claws catching Matt's T-shirt. Matt lost his grip and fell off before he was hooked.

The troll spun as Matt jumped. He landed with Laurie, Ray, and Reyna. When Matt realized that, he tensed to run, to draw attention away from them, but Sun had recovered from his temporary blinding and blocked Matt's path. He turned again, looking for a way out. Fen ran at them, Leaf right behind them, and then noticed that he was running straight for Sun and stopped.

The five of them stood together, three trolls circling around them, gnashing their teeth and rumbling with rage and frustration.

They were trapped.

SEVENTEEN

LAURIE

"A DOOR OPENS"

L aurie's heart was racing, and her lungs felt like someone was trying to suck the air out of them. They were
surrounded by trolls, and they hadn't fared well the
last time they'd tangled with trolls. There *were* more of
them, but Ray and Reyna were huddled together, Matt was
low on energy, and Fen's other form wasn't too much use
against creatures made of stone.

As the trolls' circle grew tighter and closer to them, the
pressure in Laurie's chest intensified until she thought she
was going to fall or throw up. She saw Fen and Matt both
reach out to steady her, and she lifted both of her hands to
signal them to keep back. As she did so, the air in front of

her started to ripple. She widened her hands, staring at the oddly colored space in front of her. It was as if the space between her hands was taking on the colors of an opal.

"Laurie?" Fen stepped closer, but didn't touch her. "What are you doing?"

"I don't know." She felt light-headed as the space grew, and she wondered abstractly how long had passed because she felt disconnected from her skin as she stared at the flashes of color in front of her and tried not to puke.

Beyond the light, she knew trolls waited. They had stopped and were staring at the portal that had appeared between her hands. Behind her were the twins. And in front of her, on the other side of the doorway she'd somehow created, was a room filled with plants. "Go on," she said.

Ray said, "Where?"

"Who cares, as long as it's somewhere without trolls," Reyna muttered. She grabbed Ray's hand and dove into the doorway, tugging him with her.

It hurt. Laurie's body felt like she was being squeezed, and she thought for a moment that the trolls had grabbed her. They were all staring at her, the trolls and the boys.

"Go *now*," she demanded.

Matt exchanged a look with Fen, but he said nothing as he went through the doorway. Then Laurie shoved Fen through the door and jumped in after him, leaving Deadwood and the stupefied trolls behind.

They weren't inside the doorway long, but it felt like space was folding in on her. The pressure of letting others through the doorway was completely different from the sensation of going through it herself. It was as if she were being folded inside out, and the temptation to close her eyes was almost overwhelming. Fen's hand held tightly to hers, and she tried to concentrate on that.

In either a moment or maybe a piece of forever, they stumbled forward into a giant open room filled with tropical plants and brightly colored birds. Overhead was a dome window, and through it, she could see trees outside. Around her in the room were orchids, and something scaled with a long, thin tail vanished under a plant she couldn't identify. They were in a greenhouse or something; they were alive; and she was not, in fact, inside out.

There were also no trolls here. That alone was enough to make her want to sit down and relax for a minute. However, Matt and Fen stood on either side of her, looking around for dangers. Fen still had hold of her hand, and the twins were behind them. As Laurie looked around at their little group, she realized that everyone looked like they expected trolls or some other monster to jump out at any second, and considering where they had been mere minutes ago, that wasn't an altogether unrealistic fear. They also, she admitted to herself, were darting looks at her like she was something peculiar.

"I'm going to puke," she whispered to Fen.

As Laurie slumped to the ground, Fen said, "Put your head between your knees."

"It's all real," Reyna said quietly. "There weren't any zippers, were there?"

Without seeing him, Laurie knew Fen rolled his eyes or scowled at them.

"Slow much?" he said.

"Be nice," Laurie whispered, not because she was trying not to be heard but because speaking any louder seemed impossible right now.

"Don't puke on my feet," Fen said just as quietly.

"I'm okay," she lied to him—and herself. There was nothing okay about how she felt. She had the horrible feeling that her insides had been turned wrong side out by whatever she'd just done. They were safe from trolls, but she wasn't sure what had happened. Maybe the Norns or Valkyries or whatever else was out there had given her a weird gift. Right now, though, she wasn't so sure it was a *gift* and not a curse.

"That was unexpected," a boy said. "I've never seen a portal open before."

Laurie looked up to see a boy who looked about their age watching them. She hadn't noticed him at first when they'd arrived, but the whole making-a-gateway thing was dizzying. The others were staring at the boy, too, so maybe even going through the portal was unsettling for everyone.

"Where did you come f—"

"Around the corner as you portaled in." The boy pointed at the walkway, which had, in fact, curved just out of their line of sight.

The boy himself was taller than her and Fen, but not quite as tall as Matt and the twins. He was almost as big as Matt, bigger than either Fen or Ray. Sand-colored hair, somewhere between light brown and blond, flopped in his face. Freckles dotted his cheeks, and brown eyes stared at them with open curiosity. He had on a T-shirt with what looked like an advertisement for a skateboard.

When he took a step closer to them, Fen growled.

"I got it." Matt stepped in front of Fen and Laurie. "There's nothing here to see, so—"

"He's the person we're looking for," Laurie interrupted. The pins-and-needles feeling was back, and she suspected now that it meant that she'd found a descendant of the North. She smiled at the boy.

"You're like a homing pigeon, aren't you?" Reyna said from behind her.

Laurie looked over her shoulder, but said nothing. The sudden movement made her dizzier, and Fen was starting to look like a dog straining on a leash, ready to attack everyone. He leaned away from the twins and toward the new boy.

As she stood, she reached out for his hand as much for her stability as to keep him restrained.

"Come on." Reyna pulled her twin farther away from them.

Fen and Matt stayed beside Laurie, but they kept an eye on the twins. Laurie noticed—with a not-insignificant amount of pride—that the twins didn't move so far away that they couldn't see the rest of the group. She and the boys had saved them from trolls, and while the twins might not entirely like the situation, they had enough common sense to know that keeping the girl with gate-opening skills and the two warriors in sight was a good idea. *That's what they are,* she thought with a smile. *Warriors.* They might be kids, but they were going to do something amazing.

"Are you sure about this?" Fen prompted her.

She nodded. "I am."

It felt good that they were all working together, and now that they had found this boy, they were even closer to having the whole monster-fighting team assembled. Everything was working out.

"I'm Laurie. That's Fen, Matt, Reyna, and Ray." She pointed at them as she said their names.

"Baldwin." The boy smiled again. Unlike the twins, he seemed thrilled to see them, more so as he started talking. "This is so cool. I've never met anyone with weird powers like me before. I knew there had to be others. It's like knowing inside that there's something different about you, and then realizing you can't be the only one. I mean, my parents took me to doctors, but I just knew that it wasn't sickness. I just don't ever feel pain or get injured. What are your powers? Are we like superheroes? I don't read a lot, but I like comics."

Everyone stared at him. Even the twins stopped whatever quiet conversation they had been having to look at him. Baldwin was excited, accepting the oddity of their situation with a happiness that was different from any of their reactions.

"Weird powers?" Fen echoed.

Baldwin nodded. "Well, most people can't open portals...or *can* you? Can all of you do that? I bet I could get some epic air on my board if I could go through a portal."

Laurie laughed. "This is *so* much easier than the twins." She winced and looked over her shoulder. "Sorry."

Reyna pursed her lips like she was trying not to say anything.

Laurie turned back to Baldwin. "I open portals. They do...other stuff."

"Cool." Baldwin kept smiling. "Like what?"

Laurie was half afraid that Fen was going to snarl at Baldwin. Cheery people got on his nerves, but before she could reply to stop Fen from being mean, her cousin said, "We'll get to that later, but first—"

A noise nearby made Baldwin say, "Hide."

The descendants, by habit or common sense, all stayed silent until Baldwin popped up from behind a giant fern.

"Sorry. I thought it might be a guard. I can usually smile at them and they'll be cool, but I'm not sure how it would be if there are other people here. I'd hate to get them or you in trouble."

"A guard? We need to get out of here." Matt looked around. "Wherever *here* is."

"Reptile Gardens, Rapid City, South Dakota." Baldwin swept his arms out. "I love it here. I keep hoping they'll let me see the venomous snakes up close, but every time I get near someone freaks out." He paused, and for the first time, his cheeriness faded. Then his grin was back. "I thought maybe at night, though, since it's just a couple of guards here…"

"The snakes aren't on display?" Laurie frowned. She wasn't exactly a snake fan, especially right now, when she kept thinking about the Midgard Serpent, but it seemed odd for a place calling itself a "reptile garden" to not have venomous ones on exhibit.

"Oh, no, the snakes are on exhibit, but I want to *touch* them, so I stayed after hours tonight." Baldwin looked at them as if his explanation made sense—which it didn't.

"Great," Fen muttered. "He might be nicer than the makeup sisters here"—Fen pointed over his shoulder—"but he's mental."

Baldwin laughed. "No. Not at all. I just wanted to experiment with the snakes, but now you're here. The snakes will wait."

"It's like the myth," Matt said.

They all looked at him, and Matt continued, "He's *Balder*. The god couldn't be hurt by anything except mistletoe... and he was really nice. Always happy."

"Huh?" Ray and his grumpy twin sister rejoined them.

"You mean he's impervious to injury?" Reyna pointed at Baldwin. "From everything?"

"Except mistletoe," Matt repeated.

"I'm a god? Cool...Huh. I've never seen real mistletoe." Baldwin looked dangerously interested. "So, if I poked myself with it, it would hurt?"

They stared at him. Fen's mouth opened to say something, but then he closed it and shook his head. After a moment, he walked away. The twins followed him.

"No, really," Baldwin said as he caught up to Fen. "Do you snowboard? Skate? I have a ramp." His words never seemed to end, but instead of Fen growling, he had slowed down so Baldwin could keep pace with him.

Matt looked at Laurie questioningly, and she shrugged. She could find the descendants of the North well enough, but that didn't mean they were going to make a lot of sense to her. The twins were still keeping some sort of secret; she was sure of it. Baldwin apparently wanted to poke himself with a stick to experience pain. All she really wanted was to hide away somewhere, get a shower, and maybe put on some clean clothes—or at least wash hers.

After they left Reptile Gardens, they walked to Baldwin's house. Along the way, Matt filled him in on the coming of Ragnarök and what it meant that Baldwin was a descendant of the god Balder. Maybe it was because of his inability to feel pain, like Fen's wolf thing and Matt's Hammer power, but he had already known there was something special about himself, so he accepted their explanation with the good-natured ease that Laurie suspected was his response to most everything. If anything, he was too eager. He wanted to fight, loved the idea that his invulnerability was because of an upcoming battle, and—perversely, in Laurie's opinion—was crazy excited at getting to see a giant snake.

"It's even better than the little ones at the Reptile Gardens," Baldwin was saying as he opened his house door. "And unless the snake is made out of mistletoe—which would be weird, right?—it'll be just like everything else. No pain. No injury. This is just too epic."

As they followed him inside, Laurie was secretly glad it wasn't like the oversized place where the twins lived. She was pretty sure that neither she nor Fen would be comfortable somewhere like that. This was just a regular-sized place surrounded by other normal houses.

Fen flopped down on the sofa. The twins sank gracefully to the floor in movements that mirrored each other. Matt paced the room, looking out windows and locating exits.

"You could all stay here if you want tonight. My parents

are away for the weekend. I'm supposed to sleep at the neighbors' house, but they don't ever make me. People are always weird like that, letting me have what I want. Is that a descendant thing too? Do you all get treated like that?" Baldwin went into the kitchen as he was speaking, his words all hyperfast. "You're probably hungry, too."

"No, but yes, hungry," Fen said, but Baldwin was already gone. Fen rubbed his face and then called out to Matt, "Thorsen? What's the myth on him?"

"Aside from the can't-be-hurt-by-anything-but-mistletoe part, everyone likes him because he's just so nice. I bet that's why he gets what he wants. People just want to make him happy." Matt looked away from the window at them. "In the myth, all the gods liked him. They made a sport of throwing weapons at him, but it wasn't to *hurt* him, though."

Baldwin poked his head around the doorway. "Maybe we could do that."

"No," Fen and Matt said at once.

"Okay. Maybe later." Baldwin shrugged. "I don't know much about myths, so who are you?"

Matt pointed at Fen, "Fen's a descendant of Loki, trickster and troublemaker. Laurie is, too."

Laurie smiled at Baldwin.

Then Matt gestured at the twins. "They're Frey and Freya. She was goddess of love and beauty; he was weather

and fertility. And I'm, uh, a descendant of Thor. I'll...
umm...fight the Midgard Serpent."

"Thor smash," Reyna interjected.

"That's the Hulk, not Thor," Matt started to explain.

"Whatever," Reyan muttered.

Ray laughed, but then Fen said, "At least Matt's powers
are useful—unlike the power of eyeliner and baby-making."

For a moment, Matt's expression was of total shock
at Fen's stepping in to defend him, but he wiped it away
before Fen could notice—not that he would've. Fen was
already headed toward Baldwin, asking, "What do you have
to eat?"

Laurie wasn't sure she'd ever seen Fen quite so friendly
with a stranger, but Baldwin was really likable. The whole
extreme sports thing would appeal to Fen, too. He wasn't
exactly bookish. She glanced at Matt, who was beckoning
her. They went into the foyer.

Matt stared directly at her and said, "In the myths, Loki
kills him."

When she didn't reply, Matt continued, "Loki gave Balder's blind brother a spear of mistletoe, and that spear killed
him. That's the main version. There are others. They also say
that the gods tried to get Balder back from Hel—the lady in
charge of the afterlife—because everyone was so upset. Hel
said that if everyone mourned Balder, he could go back to

life, but Loki wouldn't cry at all, so Hel wouldn't let Balder go. Loki was responsible for Balder's death and his staying dead. But that's the real Loki. It doesn't mean anything for *us*." He looked toward the kitchen, where they could hear Fen and Baldwin laughing. When he continued, he sounded almost angry, as if she had argued with him. "The Seer and my family say the myths are true. After everything we've seen, I believe some of it is, but we're ourselves, not god clones. The Norns say we aren't destined to lose, so that means the rest doesn't have to happen like it does in the myths, either."

Laurie weighed the details out in her mind. She wasn't entirely sure what to think of a lot of things, but she was certain that they could win. What would be the point in doing all the stuff they were if she thought they were going to be trapped by what the myth said happened? That was just a story; this was *real*. She called, "Do you have any brothers, Baldwin?"

"No." Baldwin came into the foyer, swiping at his floppy hair as he did so. "Do you want to borrow some clothes? I can throw yours in the washing machine."

They both smiled at him. He really was the nicest person she'd ever met. She liked him, but it was sort of the way she liked Matt—with the sense that he could be a brother, that he was important to her the way Fen was. She didn't feel that way about Reyna or Ray, though, and that made her nervous…more so because Reyna was the only other girl. She'd mostly had boys for friends, because of Fen, but still, she *wanted* to have girls as friends, too.

As she followed Baldwin, he chattered about the pictures on the wall as they went upstairs, the first time he'd jumped out of the second-floor window, and something about trying to order a sword on eBay, which had gotten him grounded.

Upstairs, he grabbed a T-shirt and jeans to lend her— and a belt to keep them from falling off. At the door to the bathroom, he pointed at the towels. "I'm going to see how many pizzas Mom left in the freezer. Probably better than going anywhere, right?"

"Yes, please." She yawned. "It's been a long few days."

"Right." He walked away humming.

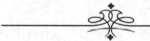

It was a blurry couple of hours of everyone getting food and claiming spots to sleep. Matt had tried to talk about the next part of the plan, but Fen had threatened to bite him if he didn't give them a few hours of peace. The twins appeared to be in a daze over everything, and Baldwin peppered Fen and Matt with questions. As the boys relayed mostly accurate stories of Mount Rushmore, tornadoes, trolls, Valkyries, and all the rest, Laurie dozed—until the doorbell rang.

At first, Laurie was confused. She was in a strange house, sleeping on an unfamiliar sofa, wearing someone else's clothes.

The ringing was followed by a knocking, and then Baldwin was standing beside her. Seeing him made her remember where she was.

"Trolls don't ring the bell, right?" he said.

"I don't think so." She got to her feet and went with him to the door. They both took turns looking through the peephole in the door.

A girl stood on the porch. She had short dark hair that was dyed pink at the tips and was wearing the sort of clothes that screamed "not from here": a funky cropped jacket with a fur collar, a skirt that looked like it was sewn together from all sorts of different materials, and a pair of tall pink boots.

"Is she with you?" Baldwin asked.

Laurie shook her head.

"Huh." Baldwin opened the door. "Hello."

The girl beamed at them and said, "Hi, I'm Astrid. I hear you're looking for my boyfriend."

EIGHTEEN

MATT

"WAKING NIGHTMARE"

After talking to Baldwin for a while, Matt had drifted off. Now he was dreaming that he was back at home, before Vetrarblot, his mother making rakfisk in the kitchen.

"I'm quitting boxing," he said to his mother as he took milk from the fridge. "Wrestling, too."

His mother looked over, knife raised, frowning. Josh and Jake stopped eating. All three stared at him.

"I'm thinking I'll join the football team," he said. "Be a team player." He put the milk back. "I'm not very good at fighting anyway."

"Of course you are," his mother said. "You're the best in middle school."

"You'll be the best in high school, too," Josh said, shooting him a thumbs-up. "You're a natural, Mini-Matt."

Matt slammed the fridge door. "No. No, I'm not. I'm a lousy fighter. You need to find someone else."

"Find someone else for what, dear?" his mom asked.

"Matt?" his dad called from the hall.

"In here!" his mom called back.

Dad walked in holding a box with holes punched in the top. "Got you something today. I know we've always said you can't have a pet, but I think you're finally ready."

"Finally responsible," his mom said.

"*Finally* responsible," his brothers echoed.

Dad handed him the box. Matt opened it to see a small snake curled up in the bottom. It lifted its tiny head, red eyes flashing as it hissed at him.

Matt dropped the box onto the counter. It toppled, snake spilling out as he backed away. The snake uncurled, and when it did, it was half as long as the counter, its head as big as the box it had come in.

"Matt!" his mom said. "You'll hurt the poor thing."

"It—it's a serpent."

Dad scooped up the snake, draping it over his arm. "It's a very special serpent, Matt. It's *your* serpent. You need to take care of it."

The doorbell rang. Everyone ignored it and just watched Matt, shaking their heads in disappointment as he recoiled from the box. The serpent stretched until its head touched the floor, then it swung over and wrapped around his father's legs.

"Dad!" Matt shouted.

He tried to leap forward, but he couldn't move. The serpent wound its way up his father's body, wrapping around and around like a python, green scales glittering, red eyes gleaming.

The doorbell rang again.

"Aren't you going to take your serpent, Matt?" his mom said. "You won't make your father look after it, will you? That isn't very responsible."

The serpent's coils now enveloped his father's entire body, its head poised over his father's. Its jaws opened, fangs flashing. It looked at Matt, who couldn't move, couldn't even shout now, but was frozen there, watching the serpent's giant jaws hover over his father's head.

"You really should take care of it," his father said . . . right before the serpent devoured him.

Matt's eyes snapped open, and he found himself staring up at a white ceiling with a weight on his chest, pushing him down, pressing the air from his lungs. He struggled to breathe, but he couldn't open his mouth. He couldn't move. It was like he was still in the dream, paralyzed. He couldn't

even blink. His eyes stung, and his chest was on fire, and he couldn't breathe.

Somewhere he heard Laurie's voice and Baldwin's and he tried to yell for them, but he couldn't get words out. He was trapped there, on the floor in Baldwin's living room, suffocating.

"You need to take care of it," a voice said behind him. His mother's voice.

She leaned over him, and her face was gray and pale.

"Are you going to take care of your serpent, Matty?" she asked. She leaned down farther, until he could smell her breath, stinking like rotted fish. "You really need to take care of it."

She kept bending, her mouth opening, eyes glowing red dots now, skin green scales, teeth sharpening to fangs, forked tongue flicking out.

Matt bolted upright like a slingshot. He bent over, coughing and sputtering as he caught his breath. Then, slowly, he turned. The serpent was gone. He blinked and rubbed his eyes and looked around.

He was in Baldwin's living room, on the floor. Fen was fast asleep, curled up in the recliner. The couch where Laurie had been was empty now, her blanket draped over the side, and he could hear her talking to Baldwin at the front of the house. Just like in his dream.

So it wasn't a dream?

No, it must have been. Some weird kind of waking nightmare.

He blinked again and rolled his shoulders, then squinted at the blue numerals on the DVD player. Past midnight. Why was Laurie up and talking to Baldwin?

He gave a soft laugh as he thought it. Dumb question. He'd seen Reyna sneaking looks at Baldwin earlier. He supposed if a girl *that* pretty was checking Baldwin out, the guy must be good-looking.

Matt yawned and rubbed down the last goose bumps on his arms as the wisps of the nightmare finally floated away. He was stretching out again when he heard another voice— a girl's. *Reyna?* It didn't sound like her. As he sat up he dimly remembered the doorbell in his dream—the one no one else had seemed to hear.

Matt got up and padded barefoot toward the front hall. The girl's voice came clearer now, saying something about Odin. Baldwin asked her to come inside, and the voices retreated to the dining room. Matt followed. When he drew close, he could see the girl through the doorway.

She had...pink hair. He blinked and rubbed his eyes. Okay, it wasn't completely pink, but the ends definitely were. She wore pink boots, too, ones that went right up to her knees. Weird, but cool-weird.

She looked up. When she saw him, she smiled, a smile so bright and wide that it made her whole face light up. Laurie was saying something, but the girl started toward Matt, as if she didn't hear Laurie. If it was possible for her smile to widen, it did. Matt felt his cheeks heat.

"You must be Matt," she said. She looked him over, and he was sure his face went as red as his hair. "Wow. You really are Thor's son, aren't you?"

"N-no. Just a descendant. A distant descendant."

She smiled. "You know what I mean."

"Matt?" Laurie said. "This is Astrid. She's Odin's *girlfriend*."

Laurie emphasized the last word, and Matt yanked his gaze away, cheeks flaming now. Had he been checking Astrid out? He hoped it hadn't looked like that. He wasn't. Or, at least, he didn't think he'd been.

"Odin's girlfriend," he said quickly. "Cool." He walked in and leaned against the wall, as casually as he could. "So what's going on?"

"Odin sent her," Laurie said. "He's busy doing stuff to get ready for Ragnarök, so he sent Astrid here to help us."

"Cool."

"Is it?" Astrid sighed in relief. "Good. Odin said you'd be okay with it, but I wasn't sure. It's your call, right? You're the guy in charge." She was looking right at Matt.

Matt managed a laugh. "I wouldn't say that."

She shot him a small, secret smile, as if they knew better.

Matt cleared his throat. "So, how exactly can you—?"

Something drifted past the window, wispy, like a puff of smoke. He instinctively reached for his amulet. When his fingers touched bare skin, his eyes widened.

"Matt?" Laurie said.

"My Hammer. It's—" He stopped and patted his pocket. Then he paused again, thinking back. "Right. I left it on the end table so I wouldn't lose it."

"Because we need to get a new cord again," Laurie said. "I'm starting to think we should buy them in bulk."

"Yeah, yeah." His gaze rose to the window again. It was empty.

"Did you see something?" Laurie said.

"Just fog, I think." He gave a short laugh. "Getting jumpy. Too many trolls."

"No kidding, huh?" Laurie pulled out a chair. "Okay, so—"

"Did you say fog?" Astrid cut in. She looked at Laurie. "Sorry. I didn't mean to interrupt. But..." Her gaze shot to Matt. "Fog?"

"Or something," he muttered. "Maybe nothing." He pulled out a chair.

"No, it could be something." Astrid walked to the window and tugged the curtains back more, her hands clenching the fabric, voice going tight. "What exactly did it look like?"

"I dunno. Fog. Smoke." He walked over and peered out into the night. "It's gone now."

Astrid turned. "Was everyone sleeping okay?"

"I just heard the doorbell," Laurie said. "I wasn't sound asleep, but that's it."

"Everything was fine with me," Baldwin said.

They all turned to Matt.

"Um, sure," he said. "All good. Just sleeping."

Astrid's eyes bore into his. "Really? This is important, Matt. Was anything going on when you woke up? Were you dreaming anything?"

He flinched. "Sure, I guess. Kind of a bad dream, but I don't see—"

"A nightmare?" she asked. "And then when you woke up? Did you feel anything?"

He looked from one face to another.

"Matt," Laurie murmured. "She said it's important. Don't play tough guy."

"Yeah, I was having a nightmare," Matt admitted. "I thought I woke up, but I didn't really. Not completely, anyway. I couldn't move, and I was seeing things, and I couldn't breathe."

"Because it felt like something pressing down on your chest?"

"Yeah," he said. "How'd you—?"

"Mara." Astrid yanked the curtain closed. She spun. "I thought I'd gotten rid of them."

"Gotten rid of what?" Laurie said. "What's a mara?"

She looked at Matt for the answer, but his brain just

spun, whipping through all the old stories and finding nothing.

Astrid strode into the hall and looked around, tense, as if braced for attack. "Odin warned me, but I thought I'd lost them. I am so sorry. If I knew they'd followed me, I would never have come here."

"What's a mara?" Matt asked, as she strode to the window and peered out.

"Mara. Mares," Astrid muttered.

"Horses?" Baldwin said.

Matt shook his head as he pulled the answer from some half-forgotten saga buried deep in his brain. "Spirits of confusion. That's where the word *nightmare* comes from. *Mares*, or *mara*."

"Okay," Laurie said. "But are they outside?" She cast a slow look around. "Or in here?"

"I-I don't know," Matt said. "I don't know anything about them, really. It's minor stuff in the stories. Just a mention or two in the sagas. Astrid?"

He glanced toward the front hall, but she was gone. He jogged into the hall and found her at the front door, hand on the knob.

"I need to go," Astrid said when he walked up to her. "I brought them here. If I leave, they'll follow me."

"What are they after?" Matt asked.

She frowned up at him.

"What are the mara after?" He repeated.

"The same thing all the monsters are after. You guys. The descendants of the North."

"Right. Me, Laurie, Fen, Baldwin, the twins . . . they followed you here to get to us. Your leaving isn't going to help," Matt pointed out.

"Right. Of course. I'm so sorry. This is—" She took a deep breath. "I'll handle it. Get everyone in the basement."

"What? No. We've fought trolls and Raiders. We can do this. If you want to get in the basement—"

Her chin shot up. "I don't hide. Especially not when I'm responsible."

"Okay," Laurie said, walking into the hall, Baldwin trailing behind. "So how do we fight these things? What exactly are they?"

"Spirits, right?" Matt said. "Like ghosts. That's what I saw outside."

Astrid nodded.

"But they're inside, too," he said. "Or they can get inside us somehow. In our brains. Mess us up. You said you thought you'd gotten rid of them. What did you do?"

"It won't work for you," Astrid said. "That's why you guys should go down—"

"We're staying," Matt interrupted. "Just explain."

"Quickly, please," Laurie said, glancing out the side window.

"I'm descended from Queen Gunnhild of Norway, who was believed to be a witch. She was—and I have her powers. Dispelling the mara takes magic. Special magic. I'll handle that part. You guys just...do what you can."

"Laurie, can you wake Fen?" Matt said. "I'm liable to get my hand bitten off if I try."

"Like Tyr," Astrid said, struggling for a smile.

Something crashed in the living room. They all ran in, Matt pushing into the lead.

It was Fen. He'd fallen off the chair and lay on the floor, still sleeping.

Matt laughed under his breath. "Have fun trying to wake him up, Laurie. He's dead to—"

Matt saw Fen's eyes then, wide and staring, and he ran over, dropping beside him. Fen lay there, frozen, eyes filled with terror, mouth open, too, chest heaving as if gasping for breath.

"Sleep paralysis," Astrid said. "Like you had."

Matt shook Fen's shoulder.

"Don't!" Astrid said, leaping forward. "You'll only make it worse. You have to let him snap out of it naturally."

Matt turned to say something to Laurie. But she wasn't there. He turned and saw her across the room, staring into nothing, and he thought she was frozen, too. Then her lips parted, and she whispered, "Jordie?"

Jordie? Who was—? Her little brother.

"She's hallucinating." Matt leaped up. "Laurie? It's not—"

"Jordie!" she shouted and ran from the room, as if chasing her invisible brother.

Matt looked back at Fen, still frozen and wide-eyed on the ground.

"We've got this," Astrid said. "Baldwin and I will be here when Fen snaps out of it. You go get her."

Matt ran after Laurie. He could hear her, her voice choked with sobs, saying, "I'm sorry, Jordie. I had to leave. I had to."

Matt followed her voice to the kitchen. She was standing in the middle of it, looking toward the counter, tears streaming down her face as she begged her brother for forgiveness.

"I didn't know," she said. "I thought I was protecting you. I didn't know."

"Laurie?" When she didn't turn, he said, louder, "Laurie? It's not him. It's not Jordie. Whatever he's saying happened, it didn't. It's a mara, remember?"

"No," she said, shaking her head. "No!"

Matt thought she was talking to him, until she said, "I would never do that. I was trying to stop Ragnarök. Protect you."

"Laurie!"

Matt strode over and stood between her and the counter. He was right in front of her, but she couldn't seem to see him. Trapped in a waking nightmare, like the one he'd had.

"No!" she screamed. "Jordie, no!"

She rushed forward and plowed right into Matt. When he tried to hold her back, she clawed and kicked, and finally, he moved out of her way and she dropped to the floor, sobbing and reaching out, as if there were someone there, lying on the floor.

"Laurie." Matt took her shoulder and shook her. "Laurie!" When she didn't respond, he grabbed her under the arms, heaved her to her feet, and said, as sharply as he could, "You're dreaming. Jordie's fine. He's miles away. You know that. You *know* that."

She started to struggle, but weakly, as if she could hear him. He said it again, even sharper, then he gave her a shake and pulled her away from her brother's imaginary body.

"Wh-what?" she said, looking up at him. "Where—?" She looked up at him and shoved him away. "Thorsen!"

"You were hallucinating. I think you thought Jordie died and it was your fault."

"Jordie...?" She swallowed and swayed, as if it was coming back, but when Matt reached for her again, she pushed him away and straightened, then took a deep breath.

"Everything's fine," Matt said.

"Is it?" said a voice behind him.

Matt turned slowly. There stood his father, his hair and clothes soaking wet, his face almost...melted.

"Do *I* look fine?" Dad said, stepping forward. "You let

your snake swallow me, Matt. You let it *eat* me, and you did nothing to stop it."

"I couldn't. I—"

Matt stopped himself and squeezed his eyes shut. Hallucinating. He was just hallucinating. He knew that, but it felt real. That was the magic, like with Laurie. She knew Jordie couldn't be there, but it *felt* real.

"Matt?"

He heard Laurie's voice, but dimly, as if she were across the house. *She's right there. Focus on her. Pull yourself back.*

He kept his eyes shut as he turned back toward Laurie's voice.

"Keep talking," he said.

"Talking about what?" It was Jake now. "What's there to talk about, Matt? You messed up. I knew you would. You always do."

"Laurie? Talk. Please."

He could hear her saying something, but her voice was drowned out by another—Josh.

"Why'd you let this happen, Matt?" Josh asked. "I thought you could do it. Even when Jake said you couldn't. Even when Dad thought you couldn't. I believed in you."

"Laurie? Louder."

He felt her fingers wrap around his arm. "Snap out of it, Thorsen. Get a grip. You know it's not real. Fight it!"

His eyes snapped open, and he saw her standing there, glowering up at him.

"I'm back," he said.

"*Stay* back."

"Yes, ma'am." He looked around, blinking away the last of the vision. "Okay, we need to get to—"

A scream from upstairs.

"The twins." Matt pushed Laurie toward the door. "You check on Fen. I'll go help them."

As they ran for the door, something hissed to Matt's left, and he looked to see a serpent's head coming through the window, red eyes glowing.

"It's not there," he muttered under his breath. "Nothing's there."

Laurie shrieked, hands flying up to cover her head as she ducked from some unseen monster.

"It's not—" Matt began.

"I know," she said, already uncovering her head. She cast an angry look around the room. "Not real. You hear me? You're not real."

"You got it." Matt put his hands on her shoulders and steered her, in front of him, toward the doorway.

When a puff of smoke appeared in the doorway, swirling, he instinctively stopped and pulled Laurie back. The smoke took the shape of a woman—so thin she looked like a skeleton with skin stretched over her bones. Long white hair swirled around her. Her eyes were empty pits. When she opened her mouth, it was filled with rotting stumps of teeth.

"You're not there," Matt said, pushing Laurie forward. "You're a figment of my imagination."

The apparition hissed and reached out a long, bony finger.

Laurie dug in her heels. "Uh, Matt? Are you seeing a really ugly woman pointing at us?"

"Yeah..."

"Then she's actually there, because I see her, too."

"A mara," he said. "That must be what they look like." He stepped in front of Laurie and squared his shoulders. "But it's still just a spirit. It can't hurt you. Remember that. Close your eyes and hold my shirt, and we'll walk right through—"

Something shot from the hag's finger and hit Matt like a jolt of electricity, knocking him to the floor and stunning him.

Laurie pulled him up. "Your theory is wrong."

"No kidding."

The mara pointed again, this time at Laurie. Matt pushed Laurie to the side and dove after her. The bolt hit the wall, leaving a sizzling hole in the plaster.

"Other door!" Matt shouted.

He pushed Laurie and ran behind her. When he heard a sizzle, he shouted a warning and dodged. The bolt whizzed past into the wall again. They raced out the other door and found themselves at the foot of the stairs.

From above, they could hear Reyna shouting and Ray gibbering.

"Guess I'm going up with you," Laurie said.

They raced up the stairs, the mara in pursuit, seeming in no hurry, as if just herding them along, cackling and throwing her bolts. When a figure appeared on the steps, Matt almost fell backward. It was his mother—her face gray and dead, like it'd been in his dream.

"I believed in you," his mother said. "I told them you could save us."

His father appeared at the top of the stairs. "You let her down, Matt. You let us all down."

"Not real," Matt whispered. "Not real."

Laurie shrieked, seeing some apparition of her own, and she turned as if to run back down the stairs, but Matt pushed her up, his voice getting louder as he chanted, "Not real. Not real!"

The more he fought the nightmares, the harder the mara tried. His parents came first, then his brother, then his grandfather, then friends at school. All dead. Devoured by serpents and rotting in graves. All dead. All blaming him.

But Laurie was getting it just as bad. He could tell by her yells and cries, but all he could do was keep pushing her forward and deal with banishing his own nightmares. When they finally reached the top, the apparitions fell in behind with the mara chasing them.

Laurie ran to a closed door and yanked it open. Inside,

Matt saw Baldwin's parents' room, and he almost stopped her, ready to say they shouldn't go in there. But now wasn't really the time to worry about being rude. So when she pulled him in and slammed the door, he let her.

On the other side, he could hear his family, shouting at him. A bolt from the mara went right through the wood and burned his shoulder. As he stumbled back, Laurie spun and raced into the room. She ran to the balcony door and yanked it open.

"Wait!" Matt yelled.

"We have to get outside. They won't follow us there."

She raced through. Matt ran after her. The balcony was long and narrow, with a wooden railing that overlooked the backyard. Laurie climbed onto the railing.

"No!" Matt shouted, lurching forward.

"We need to get over the fence," she said. Her eyes were blank again, and he knew she was dreaming.

He ran for her. "That's not a—!"

She dropped over the side. Matt let out a cry and raced for the railing. He looked down to see Laurie lying on the ground. He scrambled over the railing, stood on the edge of the balcony, crouched, grabbing the edge, then dropped.

He hit the ground hard enough to let out a gasp, pain shooting through his legs. Then he scrambled over to Laurie. She was sitting now, cradling her arm. It was bent at a weird angle. Broken.

"Are you okay?" he said. "Other than your arm, are you—?"

"There you are," said a voice from the house.

They both looked up as Fen barreled out the patio door, his face twisted with rage. "Did you really think I'd let you take my cousin away?"

NINETEEN

FEN

"TROUBLE IN PINK BOOTS"

en saw the two of them and realized they were trying to ditch him. His cousin, his almost-sister, was leaving him because he wasn't as strong as Matt. He'd known it could happen, but he'd believed in her. She was the only one who'd ever stuck by him.

"So what, you creep out while I'm sleeping? Leave me here while you go save the world?" Fen advanced on them, growling deep in his throat like he wasn't on two legs anymore.

"It's a dream, Fen." Matt had his arm around Laurie, and she was leaning on him.

"You and Thorsen?" Fen reached for her, but she flinched away. "You're going to be heroes and leave me behind?"

"No." Laurie pushed away from Matt. "This is a *dream*, and we're all having nightmares about the things we fear."

"They're called mara. They're attacking us with nightmares." Matt stepped closer to them and pointed up to the second floor. "Laurie jumped from there thinking it was a fence."

Fen looked at Laurie, and she nodded and then looked pointedly at the arm she was holding tight to her chest. "I broke it. *That's* why I pulled away."

He started to answer, but then Kris walked out of the shadows and stood behind Laurie. "You believe this trash? You always were dumber than the rest of the family, boy. You know they offered to pay me to take you in? And I still said no." Kris laughed and then tossed a half-empty beer at Fen. "I lost the betting pool, though, and now I'm stuck with you."

Fen ducked to avoid the can.

"Fen." Laurie stepped up to him. "Whatever you're seeing, it's not real. Focus on me. Please. I need you to help me."

He shook his head, and Kris vanished. "How do we fight illusions?"

"Focus on what's real." Matt looked back toward the house. "The bony women inside aren't illusions, though, and my Hammer is in there. If we're going to fight them..."

"Let's go get it, then." Fen marched up to the door and went back inside. His dad was on the floor in the kitchen, being kicked in the sides and stomach by Skull and Hattie. They grinned at him.

"You're next," Hattie said. "Wait till I tell your little friends about how we got the shield and how you're going to help us get Matt, too. Bet we won't have to hurt you then. They'll do it for us."

Beside him, he heard Laurie repeating, "Not real. Not real. Not real."

Fen squared his shoulders and looked away from the Raiders in the kitchen. They needed to find the mara and get rid of them. Baldwin ran toward them. "There are monsters in my house." He held out a hand to Matt; cupped in his open palm was the Hammer amulet. "Here. You left this in the living room."

"Thank you!" Matt folded the tiny Hammer in his hand so tightly that Fen thought it might cut the skin. Baldwin really was a good guy: he'd brought them what they needed without even being told.

"Where are the twins?" Laurie asked.

"They're shooting something at the mara. I can't *see* it, but every time they hold hands, the air ripples, and the illusions near them vanish." Baldwin shook his head. "The bone people don't, though. They're not going away."

"And Astrid?" Matt asked. "Is she okay?"

"Who?" Fen asked.

"New girl. With us when you woke," Baldwin said, and

then he looked at Matt and shook his head. "She's somewhere in the house, said something about magic."

Fen, Laurie, and Matt made their way up the stairs and to the guest room, where the twins were to be sleeping. They stood arm-in-arm, staring out the door. Between the twins and them were five bony, ugly old women. The women couldn't get in the room, but they weren't retreating, either.

Reyna and Ray looked tired, but they kept flinging their free hands as if they were throwing things. The mara flinched, but they weren't destroyed. Laurie had been right that the twins had a secret. They were witches of some sort.

A girl—presumably Astrid—opened another door and peered out at them. "Matt!" She grabbed Matt's arm. "I couldn't get in to the twins."

With a sudden smile, Baldwin started to walk up to the mara. The mara didn't look their way, even as Baldwin tried tugging them back from the doorway.

Then Fen heard the growls. He looked over his shoulder and saw at least three wolves coming up the steps. "Wolves! Get into the other room!" He started trying to herd them into the bedroom across from the twins' room.

"Not real," Laurie murmured. "Fen. Not real. Jordie's not here. Mom's not here. The wolves aren't here." She was too pale, and he knew she was going to pass out. The break in her arm meant they needed to go to a hospital, but he couldn't leave Baldwin out there alone.

"Come on." Fen shoved Matt aside, pushing him closer to Astrid and helping Laurie over to sit on the bed. "Need a plan, Thorsen. The twins and Baldwin are buying time, but we need a plan."

"Let me see," Astrid offered.

Fen snarled at her. He wasn't going to let a stranger near Laurie when she was hurt.

"Plan, Thorsen," he half snarled, half spoke.

Through the open door, Fen could see Baldwin clinging to the back of one of the mara like a cheerful monkey; the mara ignored him. The twins were making no progress, and Fen wasn't keen on leaving Laurie's side.

"Trying, Brekke," Matt said. He was staring past Fen at something only he saw.

One of the mara turned and advanced toward the door.

"Not real," Matt muttered.

Astrid came to Matt's side and slammed the door, like a thin piece of wood would keep out a monster.

"They're on their own out there, Thorsen. Either you go or I go. One of us has to stay in here to protect Laurie." Fen gestured at her, and for the first time since they'd faced the Raiders in Blackwell, Laurie didn't argue. That alone meant she was in real pain.

Matt must've noticed, too. He grabbed Astrid's wrist. "Whatever you did before, you need to try it again."

"I don't know if it will work, but"—she put her hand on

top of Matt's hand, who quickly yanked away from her—"I can try."

"Now!" Fen demanded.

"Fen's right." Matt was at the door, ready to yank it open. "If you can't do it, he and I need to go out there."

"I'll try," Astrid said.

Matt yanked the door open. Astrid shot Fen a grin before she followed Matt into the hallway and started saying something unintelligible. The mara shrieked, horrible shrill noises that made Fen cringe, and then they vanished.

Astrid collapsed, swaying into Matt, who caught her and helped her sit on the floor. He stayed crouched beside her.

The twins left their room, stepped around Matt and Astrid, and came to the bedroom where he and Laurie were.

"Who is she?" Reyna asked.

"Astrid. Witch or something," Baldwin sang out as he came bouncing past them into the room. "Did you see? She just zapped them away. I told you we were like superheroes. Bring on the next villain!"

Despite everything, Fen couldn't help smiling at Baldwin's attitude. "He's as bad as us, Laurie," he said.

When she didn't even smile, a cold spike of panic rushed through him. "Laurie?"

She gave him the least convincing smile he'd ever seen. "Sorry. Maybe there's aspirin or something here. Baldwin?"

"Sure, but we should call a doctor," Baldwin said. "That's

what people do when they get hurt, isn't it? I never have, but there are kids at school and..." His words dwindled. "I'll get aspirin and the phone."

"No phone," Laurie objected. "Aspirin. Then we can wrap my arm or something. If we go to a hospital, they'll call the cops, and we just can't."

"We'll fix it." Ray stepped closer to the bed.

Fen put himself in front of Laurie and bared his teeth. The only thing keeping him on two legs was the realization that he couldn't speak if he became a wolf.

"It's okay, Fen," Laurie said. When he didn't reply, she snapped, "*Fen!*"

He glanced over his shoulder at her. He whimpered before he could stop himself.

"We've got this one, puppy." Reyna walked over to stand beside her brother. "No hospital needed. Honest."

"Let them pass," Laurie said gently.

And Fen wanted to say something rude, but the truth was that if they could take that too-pale look away from Laurie's face, he would owe them. He did, however, look at Matt—who had now left Astrid to stand with Fen beside the bed.

Matt looked as worried as Fen felt. That, at least, made Fen feel a little better. If there was trouble, he wouldn't be alone in dealing with it.

"Don't touch her while we do this," Ray cautioned.

And then the twins stood on either side of the bed where Laurie lay. They clasped hands, right-to-left, so they were a circle of two over her. Then they lowered one set of clasped hands to her oddly angled arm and began whispering words in a rising-falling-rising way that made Fen's skin prickle.

Baldwin came to stand with him, and Astrid walked over and leaned on Matt. He awkwardly put an arm around her waist to steady her, and Fen had a prickle of unease. Matt, despite Fen's years of disliking him, had turned out to be a really good guy. Like Laurie and Baldwin, though, he was too trusting. That left Fen with several people to protect. He wasn't sure what he thought of the twins, but he knew he didn't like Astrid.

"Thank you," Laurie whispered, drawing his attention. Her arm was looking straight again.

The twins stood in one movement, as if their very muscles somehow communicated and had to move as perfect mirrors.

"You saved us from the trolls; we fixed you. We're even now," Reyna said.

"You'll need to sleep, but it's healed," added Ray.

"I knew you had a secret," Laurie murmured drowsily.

As Fen stepped closer to her, both twins backed away. Ray held up his hands disarmingly, but Reyna snorted. Fen wasn't entirely sure how much magic any of the three witches had, but he didn't care just then. They all needed to step away from Laurie.

"Thanks." He remembered to say that part first, and then he added the important words, "Now leave." A small growl slipped out, and he was pretty sure his eyes weren't all the way normal, either. Laurie being hurt had scared him enough that he wasn't feeling very in control. He'd learned that when he felt like this, he shouldn't be around people. They *had* helped her, though, so he tried to sound a little nicer. "She needs to sleep."

Matt said, "If you need us . . ."

Fen only nodded because he wasn't quite sure he could talk. Too many strangers were in the room near Laurie, and Fen's instinct to protect his cousin was making everything else unimportant. He trusted Matt and Baldwin, but the other three were threats until they'd proven otherwise. One battle didn't make them allies.

Threats should be removed.

Baldwin stayed at the door, standing like a sentinel awaiting orders. Matt led the twins and Astrid away. As they left, Matt said to the twins, "Thanks for healing Laurie. What else can you do? Does the magic work for offense, too, like Astrid's?"

There was a part of Fen that wanted to know, but mostly he was glad that they were gone. He and Matt weren't friends, but they'd gone to school together long enough that Matt knew Fen was overprotective. The only thing new there was that Matt knew now that they could be tangling with a grumpy wolf if Fen got too angry. Matt had done exactly what Laurie would've: taken the people away so Fen didn't have to try to be nice.

He felt like something heavy fell off his shoulders as he walked to the doorway, where Baldwin waited. "Thank you," he said again, and then he closed the door and lay down on the floor. The only way to get near Laurie was to get past him, and even as tired as he was, he'd wake if anyone came in.

TWENTY

❖

LAURIE

"WITCHING AND WHINING"

When Laurie and Fen came downstairs at almost lunchtime the next day, she felt more rested than she had in days. Her arm felt a little tender, but it seemed to be healed. The twins had definitely had a secret: they were witches. From what Fen had said had happened with the mara, so was Astrid.

That should mean that Laurie was happier. Having three witches along seemed like it should be an asset in stopping Ragnarök, except it didn't feel like that. Laurie hated admitting it, but she was nervous. They'd gone from a group of three to seven in a single day, and they hadn't had any time to stop and recover from the craziness before they were attacked again. It felt like they were getting battered at every turn, and if Astrid hadn't arrived, they would have had no idea how to defeat the mara. Laurie was grateful to the new girl, but she also realized that they couldn't keep counting on surprises to save them.

As they walked into the living room, Fen ordered, "Sit."

"I'm fine, Fen. Honest! It's just a little sore, but not broken." She held out her arm. "I can—"

Fen growled and pointed at the sofa.

"You're being silly," she objected, but she still sat. She was tired, and she was sore, and they both knew it. He'd spent almost an hour trying to convince her to go home. Even if her mom couldn't keep her safe, he was sure that Kris and a few other wolves would protect her from the Raiders. Fen's biggest objection to her coming along was that it was dangerous, and here she was, already injured— not that he hadn't been as well. Strangulation by troll had to have been pretty painful. The problem with arguing with Fen, though, was that he didn't see injury to *himself* as a big issue.

So Laurie sat on the sofa while Fen wandered off to get her something to eat. It would make Fen feel better to look after her, and it didn't hurt her to let him. She could hear him talking to Baldwin, and she smiled. That was good for him, too. Whether it was because of the other boy's god powers of likability or something else, Fen obviously really liked Baldwin. Matt and Astrid were talking as they walked in the room, and the twins were absentee. Laurie felt oddly alone.

Then Matt headed to the kitchen, and Astrid walked toward her.

Laurie tried for a cheerful voice as she said, "Hi."

"Hello." Astrid sat down beside Laurie.

"Thanks for the save last night," Laurie said.

Astrid laughed. "They followed me here, so it's not actually a *save*, right?"

At that, Laurie relaxed. "Well, you defeated them, so that's the important part."

The smile Astrid gave her was as friendly as one of Baldwin's. It made Laurie feel less alone. Astrid was like her, too: not really one of the important descendants, but still a part of it all. Maybe that's why Reyna and Ray weren't as friendly as Astrid—maybe they didn't think she should be here. Fen and Matt certainly thought Laurie ought to go home. It was only Odin who had seemed to believe that she should be there. *Kinda like Astrid. We're both here because of him.*

"I met Odin. He seemed...nice," Laurie told Astrid. "You must miss him."

Astrid laughed. "Nice? Odin? He's a freak, but it's not all his fault. I mean, we are who we are because of some story that was written forever ago."

"I hope not!" Laurie shook her head. "He was a little different, but like Fen and Matt and...everyone"—she gestured toward the kitchen and upstairs—"he's got a huge responsibility. We're lucky that we don't have to do what they're going to. I mean, we'll help, but it's not the same."

Fen had come back while she was talking. He handed Laurie a plate and then glared down at Astrid like she was a bug he didn't know whether to squash or eat.

Astrid seemed oblivious. She smiled at him and said, "Hi." But she didn't move to a chair so Fen could have her seat.

Laurie didn't say anything. They could figure it out; she was going to eat. As she chewed her sandwich, she wondered briefly if his protectiveness was a result of his wolfyness. Now that she knew that he was *wulfenkind*, so many of his behaviors seemed logical to her. He had declared himself her protector when they were little, but he'd gotten worse when her dad left. Fen—and her father—both knew that there were seriously scary things out there because they were aware of the shape-shifting thing. Knowing there were big bad wolves out there *and* being wolves had to make them more worried about the family members like her who weren't wolves.

But none of that meant that he should be so snarly to a girl who had done nothing but save them last night. He still hadn't moved, and now Astrid was staring up at him.

"Can you scoot over?" Laurie asked. "He's still acting like I'm hurt."

"Sure," Astrid said. She slid to the other end of the sofa, and Fen flopped down between them.

He sat there silently, and conversation suddenly seemed impossible as a result.

After a few moments of tense silence, Astrid said, "So you and Laurie are Loki's great-great-whatever kids?"

Fen looked at her, but all he said was, "Yeah."

Laurie smiled gratefully at Astrid. This was a topic they could discuss, one that would lure Fen out of his silence. "We are. That's why Fen does the wolf thing. I'm not a shape-shifter, though. Fen's going to fight with Matt against the serpent." She smiled at Fen. "I'm not going to fight, but I'm not too bad at tricking trolls."

"Or you could go home," Fen suggested.

Instead of arguing with him in front of Astrid, Laurie took another bite of her sandwich. She was sick of everyone trying to get rid of her. Just because she didn't need to be present to fight the serpent didn't mean she couldn't help.

Matt walked toward them. He looked so much more confident than Laurie ever felt. Maybe that's what it was like to be a champion. She had moments of feeling sure, but those were when she was doing something worthwhile, not when Fen was acting like a crazy guard wolf.

"At Ragnarök, Loki led the monsters." Astrid glanced at Matt. "But like Matt says, we don't have to follow the stories, so you shouldn't worry about that."

"Okay..." Laurie said. That seemed like an odd thing to say. Of course Fen wasn't going to lead the enemies! Astrid was probably trying to be reassuring, but she had sounded a little suspicious.

Instead of sitting, Matt stood behind the chair with his hands on the back of it. "We're all awake now, so let's plan. We can't sit around waiting for monsters to keep attacking us." He raised his voice and called, "Ray? Reyna? Baldwin? Conference time."

Baldwin came in and flopped down on the floor beside Fen. The twins strolled lazily down the stairs and into the living room. They stayed back a bit, but they were technically present.

Matt stood beside the empty chair and looked at all of them. "We have our team, so now we need our stuff."

"What *stuff*?" Reyna asked.

"Feathers, hammer, shield," Matt recited. He turned to Astrid. "Can you reach Odin?"

"I wish," she said with a sigh. "He's wandering around as usual. That's why he sent me here. He'll show up eventually, but until then you're stuck with me. But I do know where we should start. Mjölnir. Our champion needs his hammer."

Matt blushed and shook his head. "We're a *team*, Astrid."

"Oh, I know. But the serpent is the big baddie in this fight, and you need to defeat it alone." She gave a little laugh. "You're the lead singer in this band, Matt. We're the backup. Hopefully, really good backup, but still backup."

Matt looked uncomfortable and opened his mouth to answer, but before he could say anything, Fen spoke up, "Pinkie here has a point. Might as well get Thorsen's hammer next." He slouched back into the sofa then and folded his arms. "I'm ready when you are."

"Excuse me?" Reyna said. "If this is your idea of planning, it's a wonder you survived a minute."

"What?" Fen drawled. "You and Ken have a better plan?"

"Who's Ken?" Baldwin whispered.

"Hold on," Matt said. "Reyna, are you objecting to going after the hammer? Or are you objecting to focusing on me? Because I never said I was special or—"

"Chill, Thorsen." Fen shook his head. "I was serious. You need the real hammer. Your little whatsit is only good so long."

"But do we know where Mjölnir is?" Laurie asked. "We do know where the shield is, so I say we get that first." She looked at Astrid. "Unless you know where the hammer is, since you suggested getting it…"

"I was hoping you guys did." Astrid looked at Matt. "Did the Valkyries give you any clues? The Norns maybe?"

He shook his head.

"Can you contact them? Ask?"

"I can ask if and when they show up. Until then, we're stuck...." Matt straightened. "No, we aren't stuck. Laurie's right. We know where the shield is."

"Great, but we need the hammer more," Astrid said.

Fen growled loudly enough that Reyna and Ray exchanged a look, and Laurie hoped that she wasn't going to have to step between them. His temper was never good, but today it was worse than usual because he was worried about her.

"Being Odin's girlfriend doesn't make you a part of this," Fen said.

Astrid jumped up, glared at him, and ran out of the room.

Casually, Fen looked at Matt. "So how do we find the hammer?"

No one said a word. Matt glared at Fen, and then he walked out. Laurie wasn't sure what to do. The twins fled back upstairs, and Baldwin looked from the doorway to Fen to her. He didn't say anything or follow Matt and Astrid.

"Fen..." Laurie started, but she wasn't sure what to say.

Fen stood. "Tell me when there's a plan," he called as he left the room.

He was being a jerk, but Astrid was going to need to be less sensitive if she was going to be around them. If she was going to run away every time Fen said something rude, she might as well never sit down. Laurie liked her, and she liked

the idea of having another girl around in addition to Reyna—
who hadn't warmed up to Laurie...or anyone else, either.
However, Laurie was going to have to talk to her. No one
had run away when Astrid pointed out that Laurie and Fen
were descendants of the god who fought on the other side—
or when trolls, Norns, Valkyries, or mara appeared.

TWENTY-ONE

MATT

"RAIDING THE RAIDERS"

Matt needed to make Astrid feel better. It was like being on the boxing or wrestling team. You might fight the other guys at practice, but at a tournament, you had to support each other. Help each other. Cheer each other on. Whenever there was a problem—like one guy razzing another—Coach Forde would send Matt in to cool them down. He supposed that meant he was good at it. Now it was up to him to make things right. Bring the team back together.

But what if Astrid took it the wrong way? What if she thought he liked her? He did like her, as a person. But the way she kept looking at him and talking about him...his cheeks heated just thinking about it. She probably didn't mean it like that. She had a boyfriend. She was just being super-nice to him because he was being nice to her. Like at school sometimes, when he was nice to new kids and all of a sudden they were sitting beside him at lunch and walking home from school with him.

But what if, by chasing her, she thought he meant something else. He'd have to tell her it wasn't like that. Or, worse, she'd tell *him* it wasn't like that for *her*—*You're a great guy, Matt, but I have a boyfriend.* He'd probably burn up with embarrassment.

So he followed her for a bit. Then he imagined her looking back and seeing him *following* her and how much worse that would be.

"Hey, Astrid," he called, as calmly as he could. "Wait up."

She turned and when she saw him, her whole face lit up in this smile that made him stumble over his feet.

"I'm sorry about that," he said, pointing to the house. "Fen didn't mean to snap at you. Everyone's just really tired and freaked out. You're right about Mjölnir."

She walked toward him. "Thank you. You're the brains *and* the brawn of this operation, aren't you?"

"No, we all are. It's a team effort. Fen has a point. We don't know where Mjölnir is. But we do know where to find the shield."

Her shoulders slumped, and she let out a deep sigh.

"Sure, I can't wait to get Mjölnir," he said. "But the Valkyries say the shield is just as important."

"But if you know where it is, you can get it anytime." Her fingers touched his arm. "You need Mjölnir."

He brushed back his hair, "accidentally" dropping her fingers from his arm.

"There must be someone you can ask," she continued. "The Norns. The Valkyries. I bet you could call them. Ask them for help finding Mjölnir."

Matt shook his head. "I need to find it myself. It's part of the test."

"Test?" She gave a scornful laugh. "If they're testing you, they don't know you very well. Anyone can see that you're ready. And who are they to test the mighty Thor? You're the important one. You always have been. Even these days, everyone knows the name of Thor. Can they name a Norn? A Valkyrie? Most don't even know what they are."

Except he wasn't Thor. He was only the god's representative, which meant he had to prove himself worthy of the honor. He wasn't ready to meet the serpent. It was nice that Astrid thought so, but she was wrong.

She moved closer again, lowering her voice as if they might be overheard. "I suppose you've heard that Odin was king of the gods."

"He was."

"True...but he wasn't the most popular one. He wasn't

the most-worshipped one. Look it up. Odin was the god of the nobility. Thor was the god of the common man. He was the most popular. The most worshipped. The most beloved. It's not Odin who got to be a comic-book hero, is it? There's a reason for that. It's all about Thor. It's always been Thor." She met his gaze again. "And that's you. You are Thor and you need Mjölnir, and if your friends are saying you don't, it's because they're jealous. You're Thor. They're... someone else."

"If you're upset about what Fen said, that you're not really a part—"

"I don't care about that. I care about getting that hammer for you, Matt."

That seemed a weird thing to be concerned about, and Matt suspected she really was hurt over what Fen had said, but he decided not to push it.

"No one's saying I don't need the hammer. I know you're trying to help, but we should get the shield first." Now it was his turn to meet her eyes. "I understand if you don't want to help with that, but it would be great if you could."

Did he imagine it, or did *she* blush now?

"Of course I'll help, Matt."

The others had gathered in the kitchen. Matt walked in, Astrid trailing after him.

"Fen? You know where the Raider camp is, right?" Matt asked.

"Uh, I did. If your dad and his posse haven't rousted them," Fen said.

Matt turned to Laurie. "If Fen knows where it is, can you open a door?"

"I can *try*, but I'm not entirely sure how I did it the first time." She paused and smiled. "You're going after the shield. We'll have one of the weapons then."

"*If* we get it."

"You want Laurie to open a door into the Raider camp?" Fen said. His voice wasn't a full-out growl, but it was pretty close. "Seriously?"

"Not into the actual camp," Matt said. "We'll touch down a little ways from it and walk."

"All of us?" Fen paused, and then he shook his head. "I'll handle this, Thorsen. Laurie opens the door, and I'll go through and get your shield."

Even Laurie looked over sharply, as if shocked. Matt was a bit surprised, but it was nice to see Fen finally becoming a team player.

"I appreciate the offer," Matt said. "But I've fought them with you. You'll need backup. Lots of it. We're all going in."

"All?" Reyna repeated.

"Yes." Matt fixed her with a look. "All of us."

Fen locked gazes with Matt. "Not Laurie. She was *just* hurt. She's not going in there, and she doesn't have fighting skills like everyone else." He glanced at his cousin and snapped, "Don't argue."

Laurie folded her arms over her chest and glared at him, but Matt was just glad she was mad at Fen, not him.

After a few failed attempts, Laurie opened one of her portals. She was shaking by the time she did it, and Fen looked ready to bite someone. Matt didn't want to step between them, and he wasn't sure who he'd side with anyway. Laurie was right that they needed her help, but Fen was right that she looked like she was going to be sick.

They stepped through a door that brought them out in a forest. After a quick look around, Fen declared the Raiders camp was about a quarter mile away. Blackwell was nearby, too. Matt thought about that—how close he was to home. He could be there in a half hour. But he couldn't. Not now. Maybe not ever again.

At this moment, all that was important was that they were far enough from both Blackwell and the Raider camp that no one would stumble on them as they plotted. As evening fell, the forest shadows lengthening, Matt explained his idea.

"I don't get it," Baldwin said. "You said you needed us for a fight."

Matt shook his head. "I said we needed everyone for backup. That's *in case* of a fight. This is more than a couple of dumb trolls. These guys outnumber us, and they're *all* good fighters. Plus, some can change into wolves. Big wolves."

"So . . . there's no fight?" Baldwin said.

"Thorsen's right," Fen said, probably because he was still angling to keep Laurie out of danger. "We don't want a battle if we don't need one. Better to sneak in and grab it while the rest of us watch for trouble."

"Actually, I was going to ask you to come along," Matt said. "You know the camp."

"Just what I've told you already. I have no idea where they're keeping the shield."

Fen looked at Matt with a strange expression, half challenge and half pleading, and Matt realized that Fen must have been *really* shaken up by Laurie getting hurt. It made sense, considering how close they were.

"I think it's better for everyone if I stay here," Fen continued. "I'll change to a wolf so I can listen for trouble, and I'll run in if I hear anything."

"I guess that's okay." Matt looked at the others, ignoring Laurie, who was staring suspiciously at Fen as he studied his feet. "So who wants to come with me?"

Baldwin and Matt peered out from behind a bush, having left the others back in the forest grove. Matt started sneaking around it when Baldwin motioned for him to wait.

"Before we go, I just want to say thanks for picking me."

Matt shrugged. "No problem."

He didn't want to add that no one else had exactly jumped at the chance. Laurie had offered, but Fen gave Matt a look to say he'd better not pick her... or else. Ray volunteered, which earned Matt the same kind of look from Reyna. Astrid offered, but Matt didn't know enough about her skills—her powers or her ability to defend herself. He probably would have picked Baldwin anyway. He couldn't get hurt, and he'd promised not to try to cause a fight.

"I just wanted to say thanks," Baldwin said. "I'm usually not the guy anyone picks."

Matt peered at him. "Why not? Everyone likes you."

"Oh, I'm never left until the end or anything. But I'm never the *first*. If it's math teams or spelling bees, I do okay, but lots of kids do better. Same with sports. Art. Music. Whatever. I'm never first." Baldwin gave a small laugh, a little sad.

"I know what that's like."

"But we were definitely someone's first pick now, huh?"

Baldwin grinned over at him. "Those Norns or Valkyries or whoever. Someone picked us first."

Matt smiled. "Yeah, I guess so."

"They did. Anyway, we should get going. I just wanted to say thanks and that I won't make you regret it. Not you. Not the gods. Whatever I need to do, I'll do it, and I'll do it well."

Fen had warned Matt to sneak in downwind so none of the *wulfenkind* smelled them. There wasn't much of a wind that evening, so Matt had to keep stopping and checking. When they were close enough to see the camp, he motioned that they'd stop behind another bush.

While Baldwin waited patiently, Matt pushed aside branches and peered out. He always thought of Raiders as Boy Scouts gone bad. Now, seeing their camp, he realized that wasn't far off. He'd spent a year in Scouts himself, and part of the reason he'd taken up boxing and wrestling was to have an excuse to quit. His leader used to be in the army and ran his troop like they were cadets. Especially when they went camping. Everything had to be just right. A pile of logs beside the fire pit at all times, with the logs just the right size, piled just the right way. No garbage anywhere, which made sense, but the rule applied to anything you weren't using at the time. Put down a mug and leave on a hike and you'd get fifty push-ups. Even though they stayed at the same campsite all week, they had to roll their sleeping bags and pack their gear every morning. In case, you know, the enemy swooped in and they had to evacuate. Crazy.

Now Matt was wondering if his Scout leader had been a Raider, too. The camp looked the same, with only the tents left up. Even those tents were arranged in a perfect circle around the fire pit.

"Looks like nobody's here," Baldwin whispered. "They must all be off on a raid." He paused. "Was Fen serious about that? They really raid towns? Like the Vikings?"

"More like vultures. They break into empty homes and steal anything that's not nailed down. I'm sure they've left a guard here, though. We need to find him before we go in."

Baldwin didn't ask how Matt planned to go in. He just seemed to accept that Matt knew what he was doing. He was wrong. Matt looked at the camp and felt a weird sinking sensation in his stomach. There were at least a dozen tents that all faced the campfire in the middle, so how would he sneak into one without being spotted? And which was the right tent? Fen said it would probably be in Skull's or Hattie's—they were the leaders. But Fen also said that their tents looked just like all the rest. Supremely unhelpful.

"Oh!" Baldwin whispered, pointing. "Something moved over there. Did you see it?"

Matt hadn't, but as he squinted, he spotted a glowing red dot, hovering in the air. Then he saw a dark figure holding out the dot to another, who took it and lifted it to his lips. Two guys sharing a cigarette.

The two guards were on the far side of the camp, downhill a little, by a stream. When Matt hunkered down, he couldn't see that red dot anymore. Meaning they couldn't see him. He smiled.

He whispered for Baldwin to stick behind him and stay quiet. He didn't really need the warning—that's what Baldwin had been doing the whole time. The perfect team member. Maybe the others could take lessons.

As they drew closer to the ring of tents, Matt's amulet began to tingle. It didn't exactly warm up, and it didn't exactly vibrate, either. He wasn't sure how to describe it, except as a tingle. Like it was reminding him it was there.

Was it reacting to the shield? But it was the shield from the longship, and he'd been around it lots of times and his amulet had done nothing. But it had done nothing around the Raiders before. So . . .

Follow the weird feeling. That's what his gut said. So that's what he did. They circled around the outside of the tent ring. The amulet tingled more with each step, until it started tingling less. Matt backed up and found the tent that seemed to produce the most tingle . . . which sounded completely ridiculous, and he sure wasn't saying it to Baldwin. Again, he didn't need to. Baldwin didn't ask. He just trusted that Matt knew what he was doing.

Matt knew he couldn't just sneak into the tent and expect Baldwin to *know* he should stand guard. Fen would; Laurie would. Baldwin had to be told, but once he was—in a brief, whispered exchange—he got it, and Matt had no doubt he *would* watch his back.

Matt crept around the tent with Baldwin. Then he undid the ties on the flap, lifted one, and slipped in while Baldwin stayed outside. The only thing inside the tent was a pile of blankets. As Matt walked over, he swore his amulet was practically jumping with excitement. Sure enough, under that stack of blankets, he found the shield. He smiled, clutched his still-twitching amulet. Another power, then. Something that must have "turned on" after Hildar had told him what he needed. It would be nice if she'd explained. But, he had to admit, it did feel good, figuring this stuff out for himself.

He pulled out the shield. It was definitely the one from the longship. It was lighter than he expected, the wood smoother, too, as if polished by years of handling. He imagined it in the hands of a real Viking warrior, setting off to battle—

A nice fantasy, but this really wasn't the time for it. He hefted the shield and, without even thinking, swung it over his shoulder, arm through the strap, letting it rest on his back. It felt good there. Comfortable. Protective, too, like he had someone at his back. Now all he needed was Mjölnir, and he'd be set. He grinned to himself and headed from the tent.

Baldwin was right there, waiting, on guard like a pointer,

scanning the horizon for trouble. When Matt whispered, "Got it," Baldwin stumbled, nearly tripping over his feet.

He saw Matt and looked almost disappointed for a second, like he'd been hoping for a real threat to fight off. Then he saw the shield and his eyes rounded.

"Is that…?" Baldwin said. "Wow. That is so cool." He grinned. "Looks good on you."

"Thanks. No sign of trouble?"

"Nah. Cancer boys arc still down by the steam, sharing a smoke." Baldwin paused. "I didn't think kids smoked anymore."

"Only the evil ones," Matt murmured.

Baldwin started to laugh, then swallowed it and settled for a grin. "That's so we can recognize them, right?"

Matt smiled. "Right. Now let's head out. Mission…"

A figure stepped from behind a tent across the circle. Then another and another. Matt wheeled. More were behind him. A Raider stood in every gap between two tents. In every escape route. He turned fast, evaluating the least threat, ready to barrel through—

A familiar figure strolled between two tents. Skull—the biggest of the Raiders, the one Matt fought outside the fair. Matt looked over his shoulder to see a girl about Skull's age. She was even taller than Reyna, with wide shoulders and blond braids. That must be Hattie—Fen had mentioned her. A half dozen of the biggest Raiders followed them.

TWENTY-TWO

MATT

"BATTLEGROUND"

Y   ou wouldn't be stealing from me, would you?" Skull
         said. "Not Matt Thorsen, son of Blackwell's finest."
         "You're the one who stole it!" Baldwin said,
jumping in front of Matt. "You swiped it from that
longship."

Skull laughed, Hattie echoing him. "Is that what Fen
said?" He leaned around Baldwin to look at Matt. "Ask Fen
again, Thorsen. Ask who really stole the shield. Better yet,
ask why he sent *you* to get it."

"It doesn't matter," Baldwin said.

Skull's laugh rippled through all the Raiders. "Really?
Huh. Fen delivered the shield...and now he's delivered the

champion." He looked at Baldwin. "You can go. Tell Fen he's all paid up."

Matt replayed Skull's words. He'd misunderstood. He must have. He could believe Fen stole the shield—this whole thing had started when he'd caught Fen trying to swipe it—but delivering the champion? Matt couldn't believe that. It must be a trick.

It's not. That's why he agreed with Astrid about getting your stuff. That's why he didn't want to come into camp with you. He wasn't helping get the shield; he was turning you over to the Raiders.

Baldwin stepped forward. "If you want him, you have to go through me first."

Matt heard a noise behind him. He turned, but too late. A half dozen of the Raiders were running at him. He took out the first with a left hook as Baldwin raced in, fists flying.

"Ignore blondie!" Skull called. "You can't hurt him, so don't bother trying."

Matt hit another Raider and sent him flying, but as he did, at least four others tackled him from behind. They swarmed over him, forcing him to the ground as he kicked and punched. Baldwin tried to pry the Raiders off Matt, but they'd just backhand him or elbow him away, which only made him madder, fighting like a whirlwind, yelling, "What about me? Hey, you, zit-face, come on! I thought you guys were Viking warriors! Fight me!"

When one finally swung around, as if ready to take Baldwin up on that, Skull shouted, "I said ignore blondie. He's Balder. Can't be hurt unless you have some mistletoe handy. Just keep swatting him off like the annoying little fly he is."

That made Baldwin furious, and he fought so hard that Skull finally ordered a few of the Raiders to grab him and pin him down. Matt was already pinned. Lying on his back, spread-eagle, a Raider holding down every limb, a fifth one sitting on his chest. He'd struggled at first, but realized they had him and stopped, conserving his energy and waiting for his chance.

"Get him up," Skull ordered.

The Raiders obeyed. They dragged Matt to his feet, two holding each arm. Matt felt his amulet, red-hot against his chest, and knew it was charged up, ready to go. But for what? He could take out one guy. That wouldn't stop the other dozen standing around. He needed a better plan. A smarter plan.

"Now, where's my shield?" Skull said.

A Raider had taken it from Matt's back before they'd pinned him. The kid held it up.

"Put it in my tent."

The Raider did as he was told. When he'd disappeared into the tent, Skull strolled toward Matt.

"There's someone you need to meet," he said. "But first I think you need a lesson about stealing."

Skull's gaze dropped to Matt's stomach, and Matt knew what was coming. A blow to the solar plexus against a defenseless target. Except Matt wasn't defenseless. He readied his Hammer as he watched Skull, ready to launch it as soon as he pulled back for—

Someone hit Matt from behind. A hard, fast hit to the kidney that sent pain jolting through him. He twisted to see the girl—Hattie—grinning. Then another blow, this one from the front, the hit he'd been waiting for. Straight to the solar plexus. The air flew from Matt's lungs, and he doubled over, wheezing and hacking.

"Hey, Skull!" Baldwin shouted, struggling against the Raiders holding him. "What kind of name is that, anyway. Do you think it makes you seem tough? It better work with these guys, because you need all the help you can get, loser."

Skull slowly turned on Baldwin.

"Yeah, I'm talking to you!" Baldwin shouted. "The loser who won't even take a swing at Thor's kid unless four guys are holding him down. You call yourself a Viking Raider? The Vikings wouldn't have let you clean their toilets. You won't even fight Matt without help from your girlfriend there. I can see where she comes in handy, though. One look from that ugly face and guys probably run before you *need* to hit them, right?"

Hattie advanced on Baldwin.

"I said to ignore him," Skull said. "You can't hurt him."

Hattie punched Baldwin in the stomach, making him cough. "Maybe not, but it makes me feel better."

"Truth hurts, doesn't it?" Baldwin said as he caught his breath and bounced back, grinning. "Do you turn into a wolf, too? I bet you don't. You don't need to. You're already a dog."

Hattie hit him. Matt winced and wanted to tell Baldwin to stop, but reminded himself that Baldwin couldn't feel it, couldn't be hurt. If Baldwin could draw off Hattie and Skull with insults...

"Enough!" Skull roared. "You want to hit someone? Get back here and hit Thorsen. I bet blondie will feel *that*."

Skull advanced on Matt again. When he pulled back his fist, Matt launched his Hammer. It knocked Skull to the ground, flat on his back. He scrambled up, face twisted in rage.

"You little brat," he said, charging Matt. "I'll teach you not to—"

Fog swirled between them, so thick Matt couldn't see Skull, could only hear him cursing as he fought his way through it. Matt stared at the fog. Had he done that? He did get a few wisps with his Hammer, but this was like smoke from a raging bonfire, spreading over the camp so fast—

Don't just stare at it. Use it!

Matt realized the holds on his arms had slackened, and when he looked over, he saw that the Raiders holding them

were gaping into the fog themselves. He yanked one arm free easily, then swung and plowed his fist into the jaw of one guy holding the other. The guy flew back and knocked over the Raider next to him, the two falling like bowling pins.

Matt dove into the fog, the gray wrapping around him, everything else disappearing. He heard a grunt to his left and turned to see a Raider girl charging him, knife raised. Something hit her from behind, and she fell face-first, Fen on her back. Fen plucked the switchblade from her hand, folded it into his pocket, and leaped up.

"Come on, Thorsen," Fen said.

Matt didn't move.

"I'm rescuing you," Fen said. "Again. Don't make me regret it. Come on."

Matt backed away.

"What the—?" Fen began.

A Raider leaped through the fog. Just a kid. Matt took him down. Then Fen grabbed his sleeve.

"We need to go," Fen urged. "The twins can't hold the fog forever."

Matt paused. "That's them?"

"No, it's natural. Just does that out here." Fen sighed in that annoying way of his before adding, "Yeah, it's them."

Matt hesitated. His brain said he shouldn't trust Fen, but he did. He just *did*.

He took a deep breath. "Okay. Is Laurie safe?"

Fen's face darkened, and Matt felt a stab of annoyance. Fen seemed to hate it when Matt worried about her. Did he think Matt had a thing for Laurie? He'd set him straight on that later. Maybe Fen's world was different, but in Matt's, you could have a girl as a friend without thinking of her as a girlfriend.

"'Course she's okay," Fen snapped. "I take care of her."

And so do I, Matt wanted to say. But he knew better.

"Okay, we need to get Baldwin and—"

"Got him," said a voice. Laurie appeared with Baldwin beside her.

Fen scowled. "I thought I told you to stay—"

"Yeah." Laurie rolled her eyes. "And someday you'll learn that I don't always—"

Two Raiders lunged from the fog. Matt took out one. Baldwin and Fen nearly knocked heads going for the other. A right hook from Fen sent the Raider back into the fog with Matt's.

A growl sounded somewhere in the fog, another joining it.

"I need to get the shield," Matt said.

"What?" Fen said. "All this and you don't have it?"

"They took it back," Baldwin said.

"I'll grab it," Matt said. "Laurie, open a door. Take the others through. I'll follow."

Laurie said nothing, and Matt peered through the thin curtain of fog between them. "Laurie?"

"That's what I've been trying to do," she said. "Open a door. I can't."

"Okay." Matt took a deep breath. "Um, I'll get the shield. You guys just...go back to where you were hiding before."

"Can I go with you?" Baldwin asked Matt.

"Fen?" Laurie said. "I want you to go with Matt."

"No. I'm making sure you get back—"

"Go with Matt. *Please.* If they're changing to wolves, you need to do that and stay with Matt." She stared directly at her cousin. "I'm going to catch my breath and open a door for us. Baldwin will be with me."

Fen seemed to realize there wasn't time for arguing. He nodded and gruffly told Baldwin to watch out for Laurie. Baldwin promised he would, and they slipped off into the fog. Fen went away, too, leaving Matt to fend off a Raider before returning in wolf form and quickly dispatching another.

They made their way to Skull's tent. Matt had no idea where to even find it in the fog, but Fen must have been able to smell it. Matt wondered if the Raider would have put the shield somewhere else, but as he followed Fen, he could feel his amulet's tingle, telling him they weren't quite that bright. The shield was still in Skull's tent.

Matt emerged from the gray to see the tent...and two hulking Raiders standing guard.

The bigger one grinned. "Skull said you wouldn't leave without getting what you came for." He raised his voice. "Hey, Sk—"

Before he finished the word, Matt hit him with the same blow Skull had used on him—straight to the solar plexus. Never anything he'd use in a fair fight, but this wasn't fair. And it shut the guy up fast. Before the second one could raise the alarm, Fen burst from the fog and took him down. Then he snapped at Matt, and Matt didn't need a canine translator to tell him what Fen had said. *Get your butt in that tent and grab the shield.*

Matt found the shield right where it had been the last time—under the blankets. He didn't heft it over his shoulder; he held it the way it should be held, protecting his body as he stepped out. He was just letting the flap fall behind him when a small Raider came charging from the fog. As if instinctively, Matt raised the shield...and the kid plowed into it headfirst and staggered back, dazed.

Matt motioned for Fen to follow him into the fog, but Fen motioned back, jerking his muzzle from the shield to the kid. Telling Matt to bash the guy again. Matt looked at the kid— maybe eleven—holding his head and blinking hard, and when he thought of hitting him again, he felt a little sick. He might have come a long way in a few days—he had no problem hitting a little kid or a girl if he had to—but that was too much.

He shook his head. When Fen started to lunge at the

dazed kid, Matt grabbed him by the scruff of the neck. Fen snarled and snapped, then snorted, yanked free from Matt's grip, and ran into the fog. Matt followed.

They'd barely gone three steps before the kid shouted, "They're here! By Skull's tent! They have the shield!"

Fen growled back at Matt, as if to say *That's what I was afraid of,* but didn't slow down. It was okay anyway. They were deep in the fog, and as long as they kept running *away* from the camp...

Matt caught a glimpse of a dark shape to his right. He turned to hit his attacker, only to realize the guy was about twenty feet away, running in the other direction. There were more shapes around him, some in human form, some in wolf. The fog was lifting.

Of course it was. It wasn't smart to split up any more than they had already, so Ray and Reyna would have gone back through the doorway with Laurie. There wasn't anyone casting the spell.

At least the Raiders were running in the opposite—

"There!" a girl shouted.

Matt and Fen sped up. As they did, Matt mentally calculated how many he'd seen. Four Raiders and two wolves, he thought. None were bigger than him. Maybe they could fight before others joined—

He glanced back to see at least nine shapes, two more appearing from the left. Okay, *not* stopping to fight, then.

"Fen!" It was Laurie's voice from somewhere ahead. "Matt! I've got it. The door is open!"

"Go through!" Matt shouted back. "We're coming!"

"I'll get the others through and hold it open!" Laurie called.

"No! We've got Raiders!" Matt glanced back at the growing mob behind him. Two wolves were leading the pack, closing the gap. "And wolves! Get through!"

Silence. Was she going to listen? Or would she think he was exaggerating? Wanting her out of harm's way because she was a girl? A week ago, he'd have done that, but he'd come to realize Laurie was pretty good at taking care of herself. She might not be big, and she might not be able to turn into a wolf or launch Thor's Hammer, but she was smart.

The problem was that he'd given her the *You're a girl—we must protect you* line so many times that when there was real danger, like now, she might not believe him. It was like the little boy who cried wolf—he glanced back to see the two big canines almost at his heels now—or wolves.

Go through the door, Laurie. Please just go through the door.

Ahead he could see the clearing. And in the middle of it, a shimmering circle of color—the door. There was someone standing outside of it. A figure barely distinguishable through the last veil of fog.

"Laurie!" Matt shouted. "Jump through—"

"It's me!" Baldwin called. "I stayed to help fight in case

this thing closes—" He looked behind them, and his eyes rounded. "Whoa!"

Matt couldn't help chuckling as he ran. "Go through. We're right behind you."

Baldwin waited until they were there. Then, with Fen, they dove through together. They hit the other side, tumbling together, Matt catching a claw scrape across his arm, Fen letting out a grunt as Baldwin's foot connected with his stomach. They lay there for a second, catching their breath, until Matt heard Laurie say, "Um, guys…" He looked up to see the door gone. And in its place? Two very confused wolves were sitting in Baldwin's backyard.

"How do you like *that* trick?" Laurie said to the wolves. "Maybe I can't change into a big, hairy monster, but you have to admit, that is cool. And useful."

The wolves started, as if just realizing they weren't alone. They looked from face to face. One bolted, racing across the yard and vaulting the back fence. The other growled, fur rising, head down. But after another sweep of the seven faces in front of him, he turned tail, too.

"Grab him!" Matt shouted as he launched himself onto the wolf's back.

Baldwin let out a whoop and grabbed the wolf by the tail. The wolf spun and dislodged Matt, but he grabbed a handful of fur with one hand. Then Matt twisted and clocked the wolf on the top of the muzzle. It was a trick his dad taught him for dealing with strays or coyotes. The wolf let out a yelp of pain. With both hands holding on now, Matt dropped over the wolf's side and yanked the beast down. It didn't stay down, but after some wrestling—with help from Baldwin—Matt got the wolf pinned. Then Baldwin sat on it, grinning like a big-game hunter. Astrid laughed. Even Ray and Reyna smiled at the sight.

Fen walked from behind the shed. He was in human form and shaking his head.

"Yes, I know," Matt said. "I keep attacking things that can kill me. It is kinda fun, though."

Baldwin grinned. "See, I'm not crazy."

"Yeah, you are," Fen said. "Thorsen's just the same kind of crazy. I guess we should be happy you two didn't try taking on the whole Raider camp yourselves."

"We were working on it," Baldwin said. "But you totally ruined our fun. Spoilsport."

Fen rolled his eyes. Then he pointed at the wolf. "What's with the captive?"

Matt looked at the captive Raider, and when he did, he felt like letting out a whoop of his own. He didn't, of course. That wasn't very leaderlike. But he still felt that whoop deep in his gut. The sweet thrill of success.

We did it. We got the shield. We got the descendants. We're

*close to getting Odin, and he'll help us with the rest. We did it,
and I led the charge, and I didn't screw things up. I made mistakes, but I learned from them.*

I can do this. I really can do this.

"Hey, Thorsen," Fen said. "I asked you a question. What's
with the captive?"

Matt smiled. "I want to question him."

"Question him? What are you? A cop? Oh, wait…" He
gave a disgusted snort and walked over to the wolf. "What
do you expect him to tell you?"

"Everything he can. What the Raiders' plans are. Why
they wanted the shield. Why they wanted me. Why they
want Ragnarök to happen." Matt paused and stared at Fen.
"Most of all, who they're taking orders from."

"Orders?" Fen said. "The Raiders don't take orders from
anyone."

"I think they are. Skull said something about taking me
to meet someone."

Fen shrugged. "Other Raiders, I guess. There are more of
them. Packs."

Astrid stepped forward. "I think Fen's right. From what
Odin told me, the Raiders are on their own here. They're
representing Loki in the final battle. Loki was in charge of
the monsters. No one *made* him do anything."

"On second thought," Fen said, "Thorsen might have a

point. Skull's a good Raider leader. But leader of all the monsters going into Ragnarök? No way."

Astrid turned on him. "You can't give it up, can you? I say something, and you disagree. I agree with you, and you change your mind. I could say the sky was blue, and you'd insist it was purple."

"No, it's not." Fen pointed up at the night. "It's black."

Astrid went to stalk away, and Matt started leaping off the wolf to go after her, but Laurie motioned for him to stop.

She grabbed Astrid's arm. "We need to work together. I agree that we should question the Raider. I have no idea if there's some big, bad puppet master pulling the strings, but even if there isn't, this guy can tell us something useful. I'm sure he can."

Baldwin nodded. "I agree. So how are we going to do this?"

TWENTY-THREE

"THINGS FALL APART"

The Raider, Paul, had turned back into a human shape, and Matt had dragged him over to Baldwin's shed. Fen and Matt stood staring down at the Raider. Behind the prisoner, Baldwin dug around in a big cardboard box, muttering as he did so.

Matt asked a bunch of questions—all of which Paul completely refused to answer—while Fen assumed the job of enforcer: he knocked Paul back to the ground every time he tried to get up and escape.

Although he'd been raised around fights and harsh discipline, Fen felt horrible all the same. At least Laurie wasn't at the shed to see him like this. He hadn't even hurt Paul, just kept him from escaping, but Fen knew that Matt was too much of good guy to beat answers out of anyone. Not that Fen was *bad*. He just wasn't as good as Matt. Plus, there was a pack order here; whether anyone admitted it or not, Fen knew that Matt was in charge. So Fen stood silently and waited for Matt to decide what they needed to do.

"Aha!" Baldwin blurted.

Fen glanced at him and shook his head. At least Baldwin wasn't freaked out by the whole capture-the-enemy thing. He'd tugged out a dingy shirt with straps on it and was untangling it from a string of Christmas lights.

"It's a straitjacket," Baldwin said in reply to Fen's glance.

All the while, Matt kept talking, asking about the Raiders' plans, their travels, where Mjölnir was, and why the Raiders wanted the shield. It was a waste of time; Raiders didn't betray their packs. Fen knew that, and he respected it. If the situation had been reversed, if it had been Matt or Fen taken captive, Fen was positive they wouldn't talk, either.

"He's not going to talk," Fen said quietly. "Skull and Hattie will kill him if he does."

"We won't let them," Matt insisted. He turned to Paul and added, "You tell us, and we'll protect you."

Paul snorted and made a rude gesture.

"Here." Baldwin held up the straitjacket thing in one hand. He looked utterly unabashed as he announced, "I went through a Houdini phase. This is an escape-proof jacket." In his other hand he had a roll of duct tape. "And this will keep him from yelling. My parents aren't back till tomorrow, but if the neighbors heard yelling out here, they might call my mom."

"I'm...not sure..." Matt began.

"Let him sit out here and think about it," Fen suggested. "We can go in, eat, and try to reason with him later."

"I could eat," Baldwin interjected.

After a moment, Matt said, "Okay."

With relief, Fen slapped a piece of tape over Paul's mouth, and then he and Matt wrestled him into the jacket.

"Go ahead in," Fen suggested to Matt. "Let me give him some wolf-to-wolf advice."

"Okay, but then I want to talk to you," Matt said very quietly.

With as little emotion as he could, Fen said, "Sure."

Then Matt nodded, and he and Baldwin left.

Fen stared at Paul, trying to force the younger *wulfenkind* into submission, and said, "Think about it, Paul. Whether you tell us or not, Skull will beat you to find out if you did tell. You could stay here. Don't be stupid."

Paul snorted through his gag and rolled his eyes.

"You're making a mistake," Fen said, and then he stepped out of the shed and pulled the door closed behind him.

There weren't a lot of times in Fen's life that he'd ever felt like he belonged. Sure, with Laurie, he had, but even there, he'd had to keep a lot of secrets. Being part of a team, being one of the descendants of the North, being destined to do something real and important felt awesome—and Fen had a sinking feeling that it was also about to end. The way Matt had looked at him when he said he'd wanted to talk made it pretty clear that one of the Raiders had told Matt about Fen.

As he walked toward Baldwin's house, Fen admitted to himself that he should've told Matt and Laurie about the Raiders and the deal with delivering Matt, but he couldn't. Now, he wasn't sure what to say *or* what Matt knew. He liked Matt well enough, all things considered, and even if he didn't, he respected him. That didn't mean he wanted to have their little talk in front of everyone. A trickle of fear crept over him at the thought of not only being kicked out, but of everyone hating him.

What if Matt thinks I'm a traitor? I didn't do it, at least not the worst part.

Fen wasn't sure what Laurie would do. She'd been the most important person in his life for as long as he could remember, his partner in trouble, but it wasn't just the two of them anymore. She trusted Matt now. Fen paced across the porch and back into the yard, thinking about the situation. Baldwin was cool. He'd be decent no matter what. The twins were unpredictable; they were growing on him, but they were still pretty apart from the group. Astrid gave him a bad feeling; he didn't care what she thought of him, but the others seemed to like her. If the Raiders said something that Matt believed, if the others listened to the Raiders, things could easily turn against him, and although he wasn't going to admit it aloud, he didn't want to be kicked out. He needed to talk to Laurie and Matt.

He had his hand out to grab the doorknob to go into the house when the door opened. Laurie stood there, scowling, and the trickle of fear exploded. "What?"

"I'm tired of this," she started. She closed the door behind her and walked over to Fen.

"Of what?"

"You acting like I'm unable to take care of myself at all!" she exclaimed. "You can't keep doing that."

Every worry about being asked to leave intensified. If he left, he was taking Laurie with him. There was no way he could leave her here without him. Uncle Stig, Kris, the whole family really, they'd all hate him if Laurie got hurt— or worse.

"Yeah? Well you could've been hurt," Fen growled.

Laurie poked him in the chest. "So could you, or Matt, or Baldwin—"

"Actually, I couldn't," Baldwin interrupted.

Fen looked around in confusion.

"Up here," Baldwin said. He was leaning out of an upstairs

window, staring down at them. "Matt could've been hurt, and both of you. The wolves really seemed to hate you, Fen. They said you were on their side and you gave them the shield."

Fen and Laurie turned to stare at Baldwin at the same time.

"If we have time, like later or something, could you open a door so I can see some mistletoe?" Baldwin asked.

Without looking at his cousin, Fen knew she had the exact same incredulous expression on her face.

"No," Fen said levelly.

Baldwin held up both hands in a placating gesture. "Just a thought!"

"A dumb one," Fen snapped, but then felt instantly guilty when Baldwin looked crushed. Of all the descendants, Baldwin was the only one who didn't actually irritate him. It was some strange result of who he was—*everyone* liked Balder in the myths—but knowing that there was probably weird god stuff in the mix didn't make it less real.

"I'm going to order pizzas," Baldwin blurted. "That's what I came to ask. Do you want anything special?"

"Whatever you want," Fen said, as nicely as he could. He felt embarrassed because Laurie was watching, but it wasn't Baldwin's fault he was weird any more than it was Laurie's fault she opened doors or Fen's fault he turned into a wolf. Fen glanced up at Baldwin. "I'm sorry."

Baldwin grinned. "It's fine." And then he wandered off, calling out questions about pepperoni and olives.

Once he was gone, Fen and Laurie were left alone on the porch. It was hard being around Laurie now that she knew his secrets, hard being around all these people, and hard trying to be himself without upsetting any of them. He braced himself for her to yell at him about the Raiders.

But instead of jumping on the things Baldwin had just said, Laurie continued on with the rant she'd started when she'd come outside: "You need to trust me, Fen. I don't want to die, and I don't want any of you to, either, but if we don't stop Ragnarök, we all will. So, if we are going to stop this, we all have to do the things we can do. I'm part of this, and you need to deal with it."

"I just want to keep you safe. Thorsen does, too," Fen muttered.

"Matt's coming around. Maybe you could try to do the same thing," she suggested.

Fen grunted. "Maybe you could stay where it's safe. I'm the descendant who *has* to fight, not you."

She stood up and glared down at him. "Fine! You fight, but don't you even try to act like I'm not helping, too. I opened that door that got us the shield that *you* gave the Raiders."

Fen glared right back. She had heard what Baldwin had said; he'd thought for a moment that she'd missed it. He shook his head. "Your skill is to open doors, to *escape*. How are you going to protect yourself from the monsters that keep coming?"

She blinked away the tears he could see forming in her eyes. "We're a team. We rescue each other and fight together. That's what teams do. That's how we'll stop Ragnarök. You're a wolf. Think of it like a pack."

Thinking about packs was the problem. For most of his life, the most important person in his life was Laurie; he'd always figured they'd be a pack of two once she transformed— or that he'd hide what he was to keep her safe if she didn't become a wolf. He might not have parents, but he did have a sorta sister in her. If he was going to be a good packmate, a good almost-brother, he'd have to keep her safe, so if she wasn't going to let him protect her, maybe it was best to go home, leave the world-saving to Thorsen. "Well, maybe I don't want to be part of this pack! Maybe we ought to both go home, where it's safe."

"You're such an idiot! There is no *safe* anymore. The world is ending." She went inside, slamming the door and leaving him outside. He was alone, and he told himself that it was what he wanted, that he didn't want to be part of any team— except that the moment she left, he had to admit to himself that it wasn't what he really wanted at all. He just didn't want Laurie to get hurt—or to find out what he'd done and hate him.

Fen rubbed his hand over his face. He was sore, bruised, tired, and, if he was totally honest, he was scared. It was one thing to deal with the Raiders, but it was another to think that if he failed—if *any* of them failed—the world would end. That was a lot worse than getting smacked around a little. At first, he'd thought Skull and Hattie were crazy, talking about the end of the world, but now that he was in the middle of a fight against them to stop the end of the world, it felt so . . . *big*. What if Matt asked him to leave? What if he didn't, but they failed? What if the serpent killed Matt? What if they went up against trolls or mara or who knew what else and Laurie got hurt? What if Baldwin died, like in the myths? What if he or Laurie somehow turned evil or whatever because they were Loki's descendants? *How do you even know if you're turning evil?* He closed his eyes and tried not to think about any of the questions he couldn't answer, especially the last one. He wasn't sure how long he sat there before the door opened. He expected it to be Laurie or Baldwin, but when he turned his head to look, he saw Matt.

"Did you think I wouldn't find out you stole the shield?" Matt asked. "You could have told me. Then you could have come into the camp with me."

"I *was* in the camp. I saved your butt, Thorsen. Again. I'm not sure what you mean, but—"

"Don't," Matt interrupted. "I get it now. You offered to get the shield back alone. Then you didn't want to come into camp. You didn't want me to know you were involved with the Raiders."

"Wolves pay dues," Fen said. "That was mine and

Laurie's. I didn't know the shield mattered, just that I needed to get it."

"And the part about delivering *me*?" Matt asked.

Fen froze. He'd known it was a bad idea to go after the shield, but he hadn't thought Skull would actually tell Matt. *What? Did he stop midfight for a heart-to-heart?* Fen growled low in his throat. "I didn't, though! I fought at your side against *Raiders*. I tramped all over with you and fought monsters at your side. I mighta agreed to deliver you, but I didn't do it."

They faced off. Fen's heart was racing like they were fighting, even though all they were doing was staring at each other.

Finally, Matt rolled his shoulders and nodded. "Okay. I believe you. But no more secrets. We've gotta be a team now, trust each other, watch each other's backs so no one gets hurt."

Fen wanted to say something smart, to pretend he hadn't been wrong, but he couldn't. He would feel horrible if someone got hurt because of him, and he did want to save the world. He lifted a shoulder in a small shrug, but he stayed silent.

"At Ragnarök, Loki was Thor's enemy," Matt said. "But in other stories, they were friends. They traveled together. They fought side by side. We need to be that version. Friends."

And Fen didn't know what to say, so he settled on, "Whatever."

Matt turned and left, and Fen half expected Ray, Reyna, and Astrid to all come out to lecture him about something else. It felt like everyone wanted to tell him what he had done wrong or, worse yet, what he would do wrong.

Twenty minutes later, when the pizza arrived and Baldwin came out to pay for it, Fen took one of the two boxes and followed Baldwin into the kitchen. Astrid was already in there.

"I got everything out," she said. She pointed at the counter where plates, napkins, glasses, salt, pepper, Parmesan cheese, and red-pepper flakes were all lined up neatly.

"Thank you," Baldwin said.

Astrid beamed at him. "You did everything. This part was easy."

"Suck-up," Fen muttered.

Instead of snapping back at him, Astrid turned her supercharged smile at him. "Oh, and thank you, too, Fen, for being *you!*"

He snapped his teeth at her, and she left the kitchen.

After Astrid had left, Fen said, "I don't trust her."

"You don't trust anyone," Baldwin said.

"Not true." Fen picked up a slice of pizza and took a bite. "I trust Laurie, Thorsen . . . and you."

Baldwin shrugged. "Sure, but everyone trusts me. It's

like the not-getting-hurt thing. I don't think I count. Matt's our leader. You might not like Astrid, but she was right about that. He's the one who's going to lead us into the big battle, right? You kind of *have* to trust him, or you wouldn't be here."

Fen knew Baldwin was right, but he still didn't like Astrid or the twins. *Maybe wolves don't like witches?* He chomped the pizza while he thought about it. He'd ask Matt about that later. Right now, he just wanted some downtime. Baldwin was cool about the talking thing, too. He wasn't pushy, like Laurie and Matt were.

"Food?" Reyna—or maybe Ray—said as the twins came in. They were more of a single entity than made sense to Fen.

Everyone else followed. Laurie, Matt, and Astrid were laughing at something, and Baldwin stood there grinning in that way of his that made Fen want to get along with the witch kids. Maybe he was just being difficult.

"Do you want to pick a movie with me?" Baldwin gestured toward the door with a slice of pizza.

Fen nodded and grabbed another slice.

They abandoned the kitchen to the others and headed to the living room to figure out what to watch. They had a better chance of avoiding some girly nonsense if they picked it while all three girls were in the kitchen. It was nice to have someone on his side, too. Laurie seemed so mad at him, and Matt wasn't exactly *mad*, but Fen thought that was only because he'd decided not to be. He'd looked pretty hurt over the whole Raiders thing.

I'd like to pound Skull.

"Fen?"

He looked at Baldwin, who was pulling movies out of a cabinet.

"You're growling again," Baldwin said. "It's a little weird." Then he held up both hands so Fen could see the options. *Star Wars* was in one hand; in the other was a movie with an explosion on the cover and another with a cowboy on it. "Space or Earth? Monsters or humans?"

"Any of them. Just nothing about dances or anything"— Fen made air quotes with his fingers—"heartwarming."

They got the movie set up just as everyone was coming into the living room. Astrid flopped down on the floor. Ray and Reyna were on the sofa with Laurie. That left two chairs. Matt, being Matt, offered one to Astrid—who laughed and told him, "You take it. I'm happier on the floor."

Fen opened his mouth to make a remark, but Baldwin spoke hurriedly, "Come on. They didn't bring out the red-pepper flakes or cheese."

After they both snatched pieces out of one of the boxes, Fen offered, "I can grab it."

"Okay," Baldwin agreed—but he still headed to the kitchen.

They found the jar of red-pepper flakes sitting on the counter right where it had been.

"I love this stuff," Fen said.

"Me, too! Mom doesn't, but I go through jars of it." Baldwin held out his slice of pizza, and Fen shook pepper flakes onto it.

As they walked back into the living room, Baldwin took a bite of pizza and immediately started coughing.

"Baldwin, are you okay?" Matt asked.

Baldwin clutched at his throat.

Laurie grabbed her water and held it out. "Here, wash it down."

But Baldwin lunged toward Fen, grasping his arm so hard that he all but knocked Fen to the ground.

"Maybe he swallowed wrong." Fen pounded Baldwin's back.

Fen took Laurie's glass of water and tried to help Baldwin drink.

That wasn't helping either, so Fen switched to trying to do that Heimlich maneuver they talked about in health class. Matt understood and pushed everyone else back. As Baldwin flailed his arms around, the glass of water fell and shattered on the floor. Baldwin was clawing at his throat with one hand and grabbing Fen with the other.

And then he...stopped.

He stopped grabbing Fen, stopped moving, and stopped breathing. He just stopped.

Fen felt Baldwin's body droop and lowered him to the

floor. He tried to feel for a pulse and didn't find it. Frantically, he pounded on Baldwin's chest like he'd seen in TV shows. In movies, that worked. People pushed on the chest and *what*...? Fen thought for a moment. They blew air in the person's mouth. Fen put his hands into a fist and pushed hard in the middle of Baldwin's chest. Nothing happened.

While he was doing that, Matt reached out and felt for a pulse.

As Fen leaned over to blow air into Baldwin's mouth, Matt caught hold of Fen's shoulder. "He's dead."

"No, no, no! He can't die. He can't even feel pain. No," Fen said.

Matt met Fen's eyes, and then he shook his head. "Fen..."

"No," Fen snarled. "He's fine. You, witches, *do* something."

Reyna said, "Magic can't change death."

Astrid started sobbing. She collapsed on top of Matt, who put his arm around her to steady her.

"It's like the myth! Balder is dead!" Astrid pointed a finger at Fen. "What did you *do*?"

As Fen kneeled there beside Baldwin's motionless body, no one spoke up to say Astrid was wrong, that it wasn't Fen's fault. Matt held Astrid, who was sobbing. Reyna and Ray looked at Fen with wide-eyed shock. Laurie stood motionless. She didn't say anything, didn't do anything. She only stared at Baldwin.

"Help me," Fen said.

It was Ray who came over and helped lift Baldwin.

Silently, Fen and Ray carried Baldwin up to his bedroom.

"I've got him. Pull back the covers." Fen shifted so he held the whole weight of Baldwin's body.

Once Ray did so, Fen lowered Baldwin to the mattress. Without looking back at Ray, he said, "Get out."

"It's not your fault. You tried to save him," Ray said quietly.

"Get out *now*," Fen growled.

And then he sat on the floor beside Baldwin. "I don't understand." Tears started falling. "Stupid freaking myths. How could you *choke* to death?" Fen arranged Baldwin's body so it looked like he was sleeping, and then he pulled the sheet up over his face.

The myth had come true: Baldwin had died...which meant that it was somehow because of Loki's actions, because of *his* actions.

TWENTY-FOUR

MATT

"GRIEF-STRICKEN"

Matt wandered through the house, unable to stop moving, not going anywhere, not looking for anyone, just moving.

Baldwin was dead.

Dead. Really dead. Not sleeping upstairs in his bed. Not knocked unconscious. He was dead.

Just like in the myth.

This was Matt's fault. He'd known the myth, and still he'd brought Baldwin into it. He'd told himself that it wouldn't turn out like that. It couldn't. That's what they were here for—stopping the old stories from coming true.

In the myth, Loki was responsible for Balder's death. He

hadn't killed the god himself, but he'd set it up. Matt had been sure that wasn't what happened here. Fen liked Baldwin. Really, honestly liked him, in a way Fen didn't like anyone except his cousin.

Even if it had been someone Fen didn't like—Astrid maybe—Matt would never think Fen might have killed her. The thought wouldn't cross his mind.

No one had killed Baldwin. It had to be an accident. But how could it be an accident? The only thing that could hurt Baldwin was mistletoe. There was no way that the pizza just happened to have mistletoe on it.

So if it wasn't an accident...

Someone had put mistletoe on the pizza. Shaved the wood to look like a spice and served it to Baldwin.

Wait—Baldwin had gone in to the kitchen for red-pepper flakes. The shavings could have been in them. But who'd put out the pepper flakes? Fen and Baldwin were the ones who'd set up—

No, Astrid had begun setting the table. Then she left, and when she left, the pepper flakes were out.

Matt shook his head. That was crazy. He wouldn't believe it. Couldn't.

Whatever the situation, he needed to talk to Astrid. He couldn't go around making accusations like that. No matter what you thought of a person, you didn't accuse them of murder.

Matt stopped wandering aimlessly and set out with a purpose now. Find Astrid. He went through all the upstairs bedrooms first, even Baldwin's, though he only glanced in fast, trying not to look at the body on the bed.

The body. Not Baldwin. Not the guy who'd been talking to him, laughing with him, fighting beside him only a few hours ago.

Matt took a deep breath and started to close the door. Then he stopped. Something was missing. His shield. He'd put it there, propped up against his bag earlier. Now there was just his backpack.

Matt strode into the hall and almost bumped into Laurie. When he opened his mouth, he was ready to ask where Fen was, but instead what came out was, "Have you seen Astrid?" And once he'd said it, he didn't correct himself. He knew what he was asking, and he knew, in his gut, that it was the right question.

"Um, I don't know. I heard the back door close, and I thought Reyna said it was Astrid, but..."

Matt took off at a jog.

By the time Matt got outside, Astrid was hopping down from the fence. Across her shoulder was an oversized gym bag, the fabric stretched by some large object within.

Some large object? No, it was his shield. Matt knew that even before he started across the yard and felt his amulet tingle.

He waited until he was on the fence before calling, "Hey! Astrid!"

She was in the neighbor's yard, partly hidden behind a rose garden. Matt saw the bag strap fall from her shoulder as she lowered her burden to the ground. Then she stepped from behind the roses without it.

"Hey," she said. She gave him a sad twist of a smile, her gaze downcast, swiping her fingers under her eyes as if she'd been crying.

"Where are you going?" he asked, as casually as he could.

"I just…" Another swipe of her dry eyes. "I just needed a few minutes to myself."

"Oh. Okay. I thought…well, it looked like you were leaving. For good."

She paused. Then she walked back to him and looked up. A deep breath, then she spoke carefully, as if the words pained her. "I think I *am* leaving. I'm sorry, Matt, but this isn't working out. Fen…he scares me. I'm sure he killed Baldwin. I don't know how, but…" She shuddered. "He's a monster. I know you don't see that now, but you will. Just…" She laid her fingers on his arm. "Be careful. I don't want him to hurt you."

"He won't. I just…I can't figure out why he killed Baldwin." He tried to say it like he thought it was true.

"Because it's in the myth. He was destined to. You know that." She tightened her fingers around his arm. "You have a traitor in your midst, and I just pray to the gods that you'll figure it out before it's too late. But in case you don't, I'm going to find Odin and tell him and let him warn you. In the meantime, forget what I said about getting your hammer. Fen will only steal it. Protect the shield, too. He'll go after that, if he hasn't already."

"I'm not worried about that. I know exactly where the shield is," Matt said.

"Are you sure? I really think you need to check and hide it."

"It's already hidden. Right over here." Matt broke from her grip and walked over to the rosebushes.

Astrid raced after him and grabbed his arm, but he shook her off. When he reached down to grab the bag, she jumped on his back, grabbing his shirt and wrenching it so hard that the collar tightened around his throat. He started to choke and spun, fist out. It hit her and when it did, his amulet seemed to ignite, blazing so hot he gasped.

She ran at him, her face twisted into something so ugly that it stopped him in his tracks. She jumped on him, and he fell back with her on top of him. The amulet blazed again, scorching his skin.

Why couldn't you have done that sooner? A little warning would have been nice.

Matt hit Astrid with a fast jab, followed by a second. As he pushed up, she started falling off him, then grabbed him again, both hands wrapped in his shirt. She hissed, and he caught a flash of her white teeth heading straight for his neck. He managed to push her away before she could bite him. One good heave and she went flying to the ground. When she tried to scramble up, Matt knocked her down again.

She seemed ready to bounce up. Then she stopped. Her shoulders folded in, and her hands flew to her face. She started to sob.

"It's not my fault," she said. "He made me do it. He said he'd kill my family if I didn't."

"*Who* made you do it?" Matt asked.

"H-him," she sobbed. "He made me do it, and if I don't come back, he'll kill my family." She lifted her face to his and her eyes seemed genuinely red now. "Please, Matt. Let me go, and I'll tell him you're heading to North Dakota. You'll be safe."

She reached out and wrapped her fingers around his arm, and when she did, the amulet's heat scorched again.

Matt shook his head. "You're going to answer a few questions. Then, if I think you've told me the truth, I'll let you go."

She looked up, and the red shot right through her eyes,

through the whites and through the irises and even the pupils.

"You just don't know when to give up, do you?" She lunged to her feet and gave him a shove.

He'd been crouched on his toes, and the push knocked him off balance. When he saw her going for the bag, he shouted, "No!"

His hand shot out, Hammer launching, but she veered at the last second before grabbing it, and was heading across the yard, for another neighboring yard.

Matt hesitated for a second. He looked at the bag. Then he raced to it, grabbed it, and went after Astrid. He pursued her over three fences, but she was a faster runner, and with each one, he fell farther behind, until he climbed the fourth, looked out, and saw no sign of her.

"You!" a voice boomed.

Matt followed it to a second-story window, where a man glowered down at him.

"Get out of my yard now, or I'll come down there and—"

Matt didn't hear the rest. He was already running for the gate.

Matt spent twenty minutes searching for Astrid. There was no sign of her. He'd have to go back to the house and see if Fen could track her. In the meantime, at least they had the shield. And they still had Paul. Whatever Astrid knew, Matt bet the Raiders did, too.

Matt walked to the shed. He opened the door, looked in, and saw a pile of cords and discarded duct tape. Paul was gone.

TWENTY-FIVE

LAURIE

"LET'S GO TO HEL"

W hen Matt had gone upstairs to Baldwin's room to talk to Fen, Laurie had followed him. They didn't talk, but she knew as well as Matt did that Fen had tried to save Baldwin. She wanted to tell all of that to Fen, but he was gone. She walked over to the window—which was still open—but she couldn't see her cousin outside anywhere. Matt had taken off after Fen had, but Laurie wasn't really sure if Matt could say or do anything to bring Fen back to them.

Laurie had been to funerals, so it wasn't the first time she'd been in the room with a dead person. It was different with Baldwin. He'd just been alive, laughing, and being his goofy self. Staying in the room with Baldwin now that he was gone wasn't like being at a viewing at the funeral home with her dad. This was her friend, one of the descendants, and he was dead.

The whole thing felt unreal, more than trolls or mara. Monsters were one thing, but a dead friend was another. Laurie felt like she was in a haze, too shocked to even cry, though tears kept falling from her eyes. She'd gone downstairs to wait. By then, Fen, Matt, and Astrid were all missing. She was alone in the house with the twins, who retreated to another room. On the heels of their victory in getting the shield, they'd lost in a way no one could have seen coming.

Who dies eating pizza? It was insane. It should be impossible. They weren't even at a battle.

Laurie half sat, half flopped down on the sofa, thinking about how quickly everything changed. It was wrong to be here in Baldwin's house now that Baldwin was gone. She imagined his parents coming home and finding him. The boy who was impervious to injury had died—which didn't make *any* sense.

The only thing that could kill or injure Baldwin was mistletoe. Pizza wasn't made with any sort of mistletoe. It simply didn't make sense.

A door opened, and she scrambled up to see who it was.

Fen walked into the kitchen.

"I'm sorry," Laurie murmured. She started to go to him, to grab him and hug him, but he looked so angry that she stopped.

Fen looked at her, and she knew he wanted to tell her it was okay, but it *wasn't*. If someone had blamed her for anything, Fen would've jumped to her defense—even if she'd done it. She didn't think he had done anything wrong, and she hadn't thought it when Astrid had implied he'd caused it. She'd been shocked, scared, and crying. By the time she'd thought to speak, Fen was already gone.

"I didn't think you did anything wrong," she swore. "I just...I didn't have time to tell you. I would've. It was just that Baldwin was just here, and then he was..." Her words trailed off, and she swatted at the tears that were on her face again.

"Dead," Fen finished.

He grabbed the jar of red-pepper flakes and unscrewed the top. Silently, he poured it into one hand and poked at the flakes with his finger.

"It's not all pepper," Fen said flatly.

Her gaze flickered between his upraised hand and his red, swollen eyes. He might not be crying right now, but she could tell that he had been.

"Mistletoe?" she asked.

"It has to be. Someone put mistletoe in there and left it on the counter for him to...Astrid." Fen looked at Laurie

with fury in his expression. "She said it was easy. She *thanked* me. She thanked *him*."

He slammed his hand down.

"She poisoned him, and she knew I couldn't stop it." Fen looked like he was going to snap, and his voice sounded increasingly like an animal's growls were twisted around his words. "She watched him die. She *killed* him."

Laurie could hear the anger seething in Fen's voice, but she couldn't bring herself to speak. Astrid had poisoned Baldwin. She'd put mistletoe in the pepper shaker, and Fen had put the poison on Baldwin's pizza without knowing he was killing him.

"I couldn't save him," Fen whispered.

Laurie grabbed Fen and pulled him to her. "It's not your fault."

Although Fen didn't pull away, he didn't hug her back, either. "It's just like the myth. I had a part in killing him."

Laurie squeezed her cousin, as much to let her buy time as to let him calm down. She wasn't entirely convinced that Fen could contain himself if he saw Astrid. *What if she comes back?* The reality of it was that one of their group had been murdered by another. She didn't know if she could handle Fen doing the same thing—or if *Fen* could.

They were still standing there when Matt walked into the room. He looked as devastated as Laurie felt. Fen pulled away from her and squared his shoulders, bracing himself for a fight.

"Astrid's gone," Matt said.

At the same time, Fen said, "Astrid poisoned Baldwin."

There was a long moment of silence as the boys looked at one another. Then Matt took a deep breath. "You were right," he said. "About not trusting her. I should have listened."

Fen shrugged. "I didn't have any proof."

Matt met Fen's gaze. "I still should have listened."

Fen nodded and shifted uncomfortably. Laurie cleared her throat and rescued him by asking Matt, "What happens in the myth? After Balder died, what did the gods do?"

Matt paused, and then, slowly, he smiled. "They went after him."

"Went where?"

"To Hel, the land of the dead." Matt looked from Laurie to Fen and back again. "Do you think you can open a doorway there?"

Laurie took a deep breath before she could answer. This wasn't some little thing they were considering. Go to *Hel*? Could they even do that? What kind of monsters were there? All sorts of fears swirled through her, but in the middle of the fear was hope. If they could do this, they could bring Baldwin back. She nodded. "I *do* find descendants of the North."

The horrible look of sadness slipped from the boys' faces, and Laurie felt herself smiling, too. They didn't need to discuss what would happen next. They *knew* what to do.

The twins walked into the kitchen. "We should probably take off before Baldwin's parents get home," Ray suggested.

"We are," Laurie said, and then she turned to Matt. "Did the gods succeed?"

"No," Matt said slowly. "The myth says Hel wouldn't give him up because Loki didn't mourn." He clapped Fen on the shoulder. "But you *are* mourning."

Fen grinned. "Well, then it looks like we need to go to Hel."

ACKNOWLEDGMENTS

We want to thank the following people for making this book possible:

- Sarah Rees Brennan, for suggesting one sleepy morning over an airport breakfast of donuts that we needed to write a "Kellissa book";

- Meghan Lewis, Breanna Lewis, and Dylan Marr, for coming up with titles for the books;

- our agents, Sarah Heller and Merrilee Heifetz, for believing in the project (and us);

- film agent Sally Wilcox, and foreign rights agent Cecilia de la Campa, for enthusiastic support;

- Megan Tingley, Kate Sullivan, Samantha Smith, and the rest of the team at Little, Brown and Atom, for taking a chance on us;

- Xaviere Daumarie, for creating gorgeous art; Deena Warner, for building a great website; and Azoulas Yurashunas, for constructing traditional Viking shields;

- and our kids (Marcus, Alex, Julia, Dylan, and Asia), Kelley's assistant (Alison Armstrong), and our friends (Jennifer Lynn Barnes, Ally Condie, and Margaret Stohl), for feedback on the book at various stages.

THE LEGENDARY ADVENTURE
CONTINUES IN THE LARGER-THAN-LIFE
SECOND INSTALLMENT OF
K. L. ARMSTRONG AND MELISSA MARR'S
THE BLACKWELL PAGES TRILOGY.

Turn the page for a sneak peek of *Odin's Ravens*,
available **May 2014** however books are sold.

"WELCOME TO HEL"

If there was one thing worse than seeing a giant's head rise from the ground, it was seeing *two* giant heads. Belching fire. Still, if they killed Matt, his soul wouldn't have far to travel...considering he was already in the afterlife.

"At least it's only *one* giant," Matt said as they crouched behind a rock.

Fen gave him a look.

"What? It's true. A single two-headed giant is better than two one-headed giants."

And this, Matt realized, was what their world had come to. A week ago, his biggest worry was failing his science fair project. Now he was taking comfort in the thought that he faced only *one* fifty-foot-tall, fire-breathing giant.

It was a Jotunn from Norse mythology. The most famous were the frost giants, but *they* lived in a world of ice, and there was no ice in this smoke-shrouded wasteland, just rock and more rock, as far as the eye could see.

The Jotunn looked like a two-headed WWE wrestler on nuclear-powered steroids, insanely muscle-bound, with reddish-orange skin that gleamed as if it were on fire. The giant stood in a crevasse up to its thighs, but even so, Matt still had to crane his neck to look up at the heads.

Matt touched the amulet on his chest. It was vibrating, warning him that something dangerous was near, just in case he couldn't, you know, *see* a fifty-foot flaming giant. The amulet was Thor's Hammer, worn by all the Thorsens of Blackwell, South Dakota, because they really were "Thor's sons"—distant descendants of the Norse god...which is what got Matt into this predicament in the first place.

Matt dimly heard Laurie say that they would have to pass the Jotunn—answering something Fen had said. He looked over at Fen and Laurie—the Brekke cousins, also from Blackwell, descendants of the trickster god Loki. Matt was about to speak when a distant roar made him jump.

"It's okay," Laurie whispered. "The giant is still talking to itself. That was something else."

Of course it was. He laughed a little at how calmly she

had said it. She was right, though. The Jotunn hadn't noticed them yet.

"It's distracted," he murmured. "Good." Matt pointed at a line of jagged rocks to their left. "Get over there. Behind the rocks. Fast!"

"Shouldn't we—?" Fen began, but Matt waved him forward, and Laurie nudged him along.

As they raced for the rocks, Matt kept his gaze fixed on the giant. He herded the cousins behind the biggest boulders and motioned for them to hunker down. He did the same. Then he took another look.

"Shouldn't we have run that way?" Fen pointed in the other direction. "We could have ducked behind those rocks."

Matt shook his head. "That would lead us right to the giant."

"Um, yeah. Kinda the idea, Thorsen. How are we going to get the jump on it from over here? These rocks lead *away* from the freaking fire monster."

"Yes, because that's where we're going. Away from it."

"But Baldwin is that way," Laurie said, pointing past the giant.

They'd discovered that one of Laurie's powers was the ability to locate other descendants of the gods of the North. In this case, she was homing in on their friend Baldwin, who was stuck in the afterlife.

"Laurie's right," Fen said. "This is no short detour, and

we don't know what we'll find along it. Maybe more giants. We should just fight this one."

"Do you see how big that thing is?" Matt said. "It could swallow a troll."

"But we fought *three* trolls."

"And barely escaped with our lives," Laurie said. "Matt's right. We should try to avoid this guy."

"Great. Side with Thorsen *again*," Fen muttered.

Matt could tell Fen thought he was wimping out. A few days ago, that would have stung enough to make Matt reconsider. But he'd learned a few things since then. Sometimes being a leader *meant* wimping out of a fight. They weren't playing around here. They could die. Their friend Baldwin *had* died, and that's why they were trekking through the underworld, to bring him back to the land of the living. Even then, there was no guarantee they could.

Fen agreed to the long route. There wasn't much else he could do, being outnumbered, but he kept grumbling that they'd probably run into *two* fire giants now. Finally, Matt had to ask him, nicely, to pipe down before the giant overheard. Fen didn't like that, either.

Matt adjusted his shield over his shoulder and led the way along the row of jagged rocks. Sometimes they could walk upright. Sometimes they had to creep along bent over. Now and then they needed to dart between rocks. The closer they got to the Jotunn, the worse the smell got. Sulfur. Matt recognized it now, from chemistry. Soon, he couldn't just smell the fire—he could hear it crackling, deep in the canyon, and he could feel it, waves that made sweat roll down his face. The air shimmered with the heat, and he had to keep blinking to focus.

Laurie glanced over, but Matt waved for her to keep going. They were alongside the Jotunn now, the stink and the heat unbearable. Still, the giant was busy talking to...well, talking to itself apparently, its two heads deep in conversation. Matt could hear the voices, crackling and snapping and roaring, the words indecipherable, the sound like fire itself.

It doesn't matter what they're saying. They're too busy to notice—

One of the heads stopped talking. And turned their way...just as Matt was stepping from behind a rock. He stumbled back, arms shooting out to keep the others from doing the same.

"One's looking," he whispered.

Behind him, Laurie crept to the other side of the rock to peek out that way. Matt resisted the urge to pull her back. He could barely see from his direction—the angle was wrong. It seemed as if the heads were both turned toward them. One said something to the other, and the giant shrugged. As the heads talked, Laurie snuck back to him.

"I think they're trying to figure out what to do," she whispered. "If we want to make a run for it, now's the time."

Matt nodded. The heads did seem to be debating their next move. The left one obviously wanted to check out whatever it had seen. The right head wasn't interested. Then the massive left arm grabbed the edge of the canyon as if to pull the giant out. The right head shook and sputtered something, but the left half started pulling itself out of the canyon in a weird, lopsided climb. Finally, the right head gave in, hissing smoke, and the other huge, muscled arm reached up....

"*Now* can we run?" Laurie said.

Matt hunched over and ushered them to the next rock and then the next. When the ground shook, Matt thought it was just his amulet quivering. Then Fen swore under his breath, and Matt knew he felt it, too. He prairie-dogged up and saw—

A fire giant. Which was, of course, what he knew he'd see, but there was a difference between watching it from a couple hundred feet away and seeing it right there. Okay, maybe not "right there," but close enough. *More* than close enough. It was no more than twenty feet away, so near that Matt could smell fire.

When one head spoke to the other, wisps of smoke wafted out. Sparks flew as the other head replied. Matt could see flames inside their mouths. Did they *spit* fire? That wasn't anything he'd read in the myths, but they were learning not everything was the way it was in the old stories.

"A sword?" Fen whispered. "Seriously? It needs a sword, too?"

Matt's gaze dropped to the monster's belt. "No, it needs two swords, apparently. Flaming swords."

"Of course," Fen muttered.

"You still want to fight it?" Matt said. "'Cause now's your chance."

Fen scowled.

"Hey, you might distract it," Matt said, grinning. "Take one for the team."

"I thought that was *your* job, Thorsen."

"Stop it," Laurie whispered. When they did, she said, "Do you think we should run?"

Matt peeked over the rock again and then shook his head. "It doesn't know where we are. It's still just looking around. Follow me."

He set out, hunched over behind the rocks. When he dared peer out, the Jotunn was still moving, but slowly, looking from side to side. They reached a spot where the rocks were little more than boulders, and they had to almost crawl then, creeping along as they tried not to inhale dust and sand from the rocky ground. That wasn't easy, especially for Matt, with an ancient Viking shield on his back. He had to stay far enough from the rocks to keep from scraping the shield against them. His amulet wasn't helping, either. Now it was vibrating so hard that Matt swore he could hear it.

When they saw a row of taller rocks, Matt let out a sigh

of relief…until he drew close enough to notice the ten-foot gap between their row and that one.

"It's not too bad," Laurie whispered. "We just need to time it."

Matt nodded. "I'll watch the giant. You get in front of me. When I tap your back, run. Fen—"

"Follow. Yeah, I get it." Did he look annoyed? Matt couldn't tell, and this wasn't the time to worry about it.

Laurie inched forward and got into position, crouched as low as she could get, ready to run on his signal. Matt peeked over the rocks. The Jotunn had stopped. Each head looked a different way—neither their way. Matt tapped Laurie. She sprinted, with Fen right behind her.

Matt let them get halfway across the gap, then took one step out, his gaze fixed on the fire giant. A second step. A third…

Blue light flashed. That's all he saw, a flash so bright it was like a stun grenade. He staggered back. Laurie let out half a yelp before stifling it.

Both Laurie and Fen were staring at him. At his chest. He looked down to see his amulet sparking a brilliant blue. His hands flew to cover it. A roar boomed through the air—a crackling, unearthly roar. Matt swung around and saw the Jotunn coming straight for them. No, coming straight for *him*.

He glanced at the cousins. "Run!"

As Matt turned to the Jotunn and raced toward it, Fen

shouted, "Wrong direction! I really wish you'd stop running *toward* danger, Thorsen!"

As Matt ran, the amulet vibrated, but there was none of the usual heat. It was almost cold. The burn of ice. The amulet glowed so bright now that it cut through the swirling smoke and lit the dim wastelands like the midday sun.

The Jotunn had stopped running. It stood there, both heads tilted, looking at him in confusion. Matt pulled the shield from his shoulder and slung it over his arm. All four eyes of the Jotunn widened.

"*Vingthor*," one of the heads rumbled.

Vingthor. Battle Thor.

Not exactly…but Matt still smiled. Adrenaline tore through him, sparking and sizzling like the amulet, and when his hand shot out, it wasn't even a conscious action. He just did it, as naturally as breathing. There was a deafening crack as ice shot from his fingertips. Yes, ice. A blast of white that froze into a shard of solid ice as it flew. It hit the Jotunn in the stomach and sent the giant crashing to the ground so hard the vibration nearly knocked Matt onto *his* butt.

Matt stood there, grinning.

I can do this. I can really do…

The Jotunn sprang up. It didn't struggle up, dazed, like the trolls had—it leaped to its feet like a gymnast and barreled toward Matt. His hand shot out to launch another ice bolt. And it worked—the ice flew from his fingers and whipped straight at the Jotunn. But the giant's massive fist swung, hit the ice bolt, and shattered it into a thousand harmless slivers.

"Matt! Come *on!*" Laurie shouted.

Matt turned and ran. Ran as fast as he could, the ground shaking under his feet. The Jotunn roared, and the heat of its roar scorched Matt's back.

"Run!" he yelled to Fen and Laurie. "Go!"

They took off behind the row of rocks. Matt veered to the left before he reached them. He was heading for another row of rocks, farther down, to keep the Jotunn away from the cousins. Then he saw the fissure—a crack in the rocks, maybe three feet across. If he could get down in there, the Jotunn couldn't reach him. He ran over and raced alongside the crack, getting a look down. It tapered off past the opening. The lowest point he could see was maybe ten feet down. Too far to jump. He should—

The Jotunn roared with a gust of heat that made Matt gasp. Sparks blasted him, burning his skin, singeing holes in his shirt. He spun, and the giant was right there, a flaming sword in each hand. One blade headed straight for him. Matt swung his shield up, but even as he did, he realized his mistake. Flaming sword. Wooden shield.

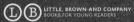

Study Guide for

Maternity and Pediatric Nursing

THIRD EDITION

 Wolters Kluwer

Philadelphia · Baltimore · New York · London
Buenos Aires · Hong Kong · Sydney · Tokyo

Acquisitions Editor: Natasha McIntyre
Director of Product Development: Jennifer Forestieri
Development Editor: Annette Ferran
Editorial Coordinator: Emily Buccieri
Editorial Assistant: Dan Reilly
Design Coordinator: Holly McLaughlin
Production Project Manager: Marian Bellus
Manufacturing Coordinator: Karin Duffield
Prepress Vendor: Aptara, Inc.

Third Edition

Copyright © 2017 Wolters Kluwer Health

9 8 7 6 5 4

Printed in the United States

ISBN 978-1-4511-9401-2

Care has been taken to confirm the accuracy of the information presented and to describe generally accepted practices. However, the authors, editors, and publisher are not responsible for errors or omissions or for any consequences from application of the information in this book and make no warranty, expressed or implied, with respect to the currency, completeness, or accuracy of the contents of the publication. Application of this information in a particular situation remains the professional responsibility of the practitioner; the clinical treatments described and recommended may not be considered absolute and universal recommendations.

The authors, editors, and publisher have exerted every effort to ensure that drug selection and dosage set forth in this text are in accordance with the current recommendations and practice at the time of publication. However, in view of ongoing research, changes in government regulations, and the constant flow of information relating to drug therapy and drug reactions, the reader is urged to check the package insert for each drug for any change in indications and dosage and for added warnings and precautions. This is particularly important when the recommended agent is a new or infrequently employed drug.

Some drugs and medical devices presented in this publication have Food and Drug Administration (FDA) clearance for limited use in restricted research settings. It is the responsibility of the health care provider to ascertain the FDA status of each drug or device planned for use in his or her clinical practice.

LWW.com

Preface

This Study Guide was developed to accompany *Maternity and Pediatric Nursing* by Susan Scott Ricci, Terri Kyle, and Susan Carman. The Study Guide is designed to help you practice and retain the knowledge you have gained from the textbook, and it is structured to integrate that knowledge and give you a basis for applying it in your nursing practice. The following types of exercises are provided in each chapter of the Study Guide.

SECTION I: ASSESSING YOUR UNDERSTANDING

The first section of each Study Guide chapter concentrates on the basic information of the textbook chapter and helps you to remember key concepts, vocabulary, and principles.

- *Fill in the blanks*—Fill in the blank exercises test important chapter information, encouraging you to recall key points.
- *Labeling*—Labeling exercises are used where you need to remember certain visual representations of the concepts presented in the textbook.
- *Matching*—Matching questions test your knowledge of the definition of key terms.
- *Sequencing*—Sequencing exercises ask you to remember particular sequences or orders, for instance testing processes and prioritizing nursing actions.
- *Short answers*—Short answer questions will cover facts, concepts, procedures, and principles of the chapter. These questions ask you to recall information as well as demonstrate your comprehension of the information.

SECTION II: APPLYING YOUR KNOWLEDGE

The second section of each Study Guide chapter consists of case study–based exercises that ask you to begin to apply the knowledge you have gained from the textbook chapter and reinforced in the first section of the Study Guide chapter. A case study scenario based on the chapter's content is presented, and then you are asked to answer some questions, in writing, related to the case study. The questions cover the following areas:

- Assessment
- Planning nursing care
- Communication
- Reflection

SECTION III: PRACTICING FOR NCLEX

The third and final section of the Study Guide helps you practice NCLEX-style questions while further reinforcing the knowledge you have been gaining and testing for yourself through the textbook chapter and the first two sections of the study guide chapter. In keeping with the NCLEX, the questions presented are multiple choice and scenario based, asking you to reflect, consider, and apply what you know and to choose the best answer out of those offered.

ANSWER KEYS

The answers for all of the exercises and questions in the Study Guide are provided at the back of the book, so you can assess your own learning as you complete each chapter.

We hope you will find this Study Guide to be helpful and enjoyable, and we wish you every success in your studies toward becoming a nurse.

The Publishers

Contents

Perspectives on Maternal and Child Health Care

Learning Objectives

Upon completion of the chapter, you will be able to:

- Analyze the key milestones in the history of maternal, newborn, and child health and health care.
- Outline the evolution of maternal, newborn, and pediatric nursing.
- Compare the past definitions of health and illness to the current definitions, as well as the measurements used to assess health and illness in children.
- Assess the factors that affect maternal and child health.
- Differentiate the structures, roles, and functions of the family and how they affect the health of women and children.
- Evaluate how society and culture can influence the health of women, children, and families.
- Appraise the health care barriers affecting women, children, and families.
- Research the ethical and legal issues that may arise when caring for women, children, and families.

SECTION I: ASSESSING YOUR UNDERSTANDING

Activity A FILL IN THE BLANKS

1. A _____ is a nonmedical birth companion who provides quality emotional, physical, and educational support to the woman and family during childbirth and the postpartum period.

2. The _____ is considered the basic social unit.

3. Under certain conditions, a minor can be considered _____ and can make health care decisions independently of parents.

4. The ability to apply knowledge about a client's culture to adapt his or her health care accordingly is known as cultural _____.

5. _____ is the measure of prevalence of a specific illness in a population at a particular time.

6. More children and adolescents die from _____ injuries than from any other cause.

7. Children's medical records are only shared with legal parents, _____, or others, with written authorization by the parents.

8. The resiliency model of family stress and family adjustment and the adaptation response model identify the element of risk and _____ factors that aid a family in achieving positive outcomes.

9. _____ refers to a basic human quality involving the belief in something greater than oneself and a faith that affirms life positively.

10. Children's temperament is categorized into three major groups: _____, difficult, and slow to warm up.

Activity B MATCHING

Match the cultural group in Column A with the characteristic in Column B.

Column A

_____ 1. Asian Americans

_____ 2. African Americans

_____ 3. Native Americans

_____ 4. Hispanics

Column B

a. Childbirth is viewed as a normal, natural process; entire family may be present during birth

b. Bed rest maintained for the first 3 days postpartum

c. Breastfeeding withheld for the first 2 to 3 days after birth

d. Quiet stoic appearance of woman during labor

Activity C SEQUENCING

1. Using the boxes provided below, put the following characteristic approaches in the evolution of maternal and newborn nursing in the proper chronologic order.

   a. The assistance of certified nurse midwives and doulas grew in popularity as a choice in childbirth.

   b. "Granny midwives" handled the normal birthing process for most women; infant and maternal mortality rates were high.

   c. "Natural childbirth" practices advocating birth without medication and focusing on relaxation techniques were introduced.

d. Physicians attended about half the births, with midwives caring for women who could not afford a doctor.

$$\square \rightarrow \square \rightarrow \square \rightarrow \square$$

2. Using the boxes provided below, place the letter of each of the following stages of Duvall's developmental theory into their proper sequence.

   a. Family with school-aged children

   b. Marriage

   c. Family with adolescents

   d. Childbearing stage

   e. Middle-aged parents

   f. Family with preschool children

   g. Family in later years

   h. Family with young adults

Activity D SHORT ANSWERS

Briefly answer the following.

1. How do the risk factors for cardiovascular disease differ between men and women?

_____

_____

_____

2. What are considered the major risk factors for developing breast cancer?

_____

_____

_____

3. What is meant by maternal mortality rate?

_____

_____

_____

4. What are the predictors of infant mortality?

_____

_____

_____

5. How has the Women, Infants, Children program supported the health of women and children?

_____

_____

_____

6. When using positive reinforcement discipline strategies, what three characteristics of feedback are pivotal for success?

_____

_____

_____

SECTION II: APPLYING YOUR KNOWLEDGE

Activity E CASE STUDY

Consider this scenario and answer the questions.

Isabella Gonzales is a 6-year-old female with a history of cerebral palsy. She was born at 28 weeks and is currently admitted to the hospital due to difficulty breathing secondary to pneumonia. Her parents, Jose and Angelina, are very active in her care. Isabella lives at home with her parents and two brothers, Sergio and Tito.

1. Discuss the barriers to health care that the Gonzales may encounter.

_____

_____

_____

2. What cultural aspects would you need to keep in mind when providing care for this family?

_____

_____

_____

SECTION III: PRACTICING FOR NCLEX

Activity F NCLEX-STYLE QUESTIONS

Answer the following questions.

1. A client who has just given birth is concerned about the high rate of infant mortality in the United States. She is anxious about the health of her child and wants to know ways to keep her baby healthy. Which recommendation would **best** meet this goal?

a. Place the infant on his or her back to sleep

b. Breastfeed the infant

c. Begin feeding of solids by age 4 months

d. Give the infant liquid vitamins daily

2. A nurse is caring for a client who wishes to undergo an abortion. The nurse has concerns because abortion is against her personal convictions, and this is interfering with her professional duty. Which action should the nurse take to follow American Nurses Association's (ANA) code of ethics for nurses?

a. Provide emotional support to the client while caring for her

b. Not allow her personal convictions to interfere with her profession

c. Involve the client's family in convincing the client against an abortion

d. Make arrangements for alternate care providers

3. A client who has recently given birth arrives in a health care facility wanting to know ways to prevent sudden infant death syndrome (SIDS) in her infant. Which instructions should the nurse provide to address the concern?

a. Place the infant in warm clothes

b. Feed the infant only breast milk

c. Provide very soft bedding for the crib

d. Place the infant on his or her back to sleep

4. A group of nurses are discussing the most recent statistics on death due to prematurity in the United States. Which action, if implemented, would have the **greatest** impact on improving outcomes?

   a. Track the incidence of violent crime against pregnant women
   b. Examine health disparities between ethnic groups
   c. Improve women's access to receiving prenatal care
   d. Identify specific national health goals related to maternal and infant health

5. The nurse is caring for a pregnant Arab American woman. Which statement **most** accurately describes the client's potential health care beliefs?

   a. Folk remedies are commonly used in women's health care.
   b. The woman will participate in birthing classes as long as her husband accompanies her.
   c. The husband makes all the healthcare decisions for the wife.
   d. Birth control is considered an acceptable method for natality limitations.

6. The nurse is caring for a client with end-stage breast cancer. When the nurse takes chemotherapy medication into the client's room, the client states, "I'm too tired to fight any more. I don't want any more medication that may prolong my life." The client's husband is at the bedside and states, "No! You have to give my wife her medication. I can't let her go." What action by the nurse is **most** appropriate?

   a. Give the medication as prescribed and make a referral to pastoral services
   b. Explain to the husband that his wife has the right to refuse medication and care
   c. Encourage the client to heed her husband's wishes
   d. State that the nurse has to give the medication unless the health care provider prescribes that the medication be stopped

7. A client tells the nurse that she is getting divorced and wants to be sure that her soon-to-be ex-husband cannot have access to her medical information. Which response would be the **most** accurate for the nurse to give the client?

   a. "Don't worry about things like that, you have too much else to worry about right now."
   b. "Husbands always have access to their wife's health records."
   c. "We have to give him access to your records in case they impact your divorce proceedings."
   d. "You have the right to say who can access your health records and who cannot."

8. A nurse is caring for a 31-year-old pregnant client who is subjected to abuse by her partner. The client has developed a feeling of hopelessness and does not feel confident in dealing with the situation at home, which makes her feel suicidal. Which nursing intervention should the nurse offer to help the client deal with her situation?

   a. Counsel the client's partner to refrain from subjecting his partner to abuse
   b. Help the client understand the legal impact of her situation to help protect her
   c. Provide emotional support to empower the client to help herself
   d. Introduce the client to a women's rights group

9. A recently licensed nurse is orienting to a pediatric unit in an acute care facility. The nurse is discussing causes of infant mortality with her preceptor. Which statement by the preceptor **most** accurately addresses this problem?

   a. "Most infants that die during infancy are victims of abuse and neglect."
   b. "The most common cause of infant deaths is chromosomal abnormalities and congenital anomalies, which we have no control over."
   c. Most of the infant deaths I have seen are related to Sudden infant death syndrome (SIDS).
   d. "Infant death rates combine deaths from birth through the first year of life. That is why the numbers are so high."

10. A group of women are attending a community presentation regarding the leading health concerns of women. Which interventions should the nurse recommend to have the greatest impact on the leading cause of death?

    a. Yearly gynecologic exams

    b. Prompt attention to respiratory tract infections

    c. Weight control and being knowledgeable about family history of cardiovascular disease

    d. Regular neurologic exams to note any cognitive or behavioral changes early

11. The nursing instructor is discussing culture with a group of nursing students. Which aspects should be included in the discussion of this topic? Select all that apply.

    a. A sense of personal space

    b. A person's race

    c. Primary language spoken by the family

    d. Level of education

    e. Religious beliefs of the individuals

12. A pregnant client comes to the local health clinic for her scheduled prenatal visit. On her chart, the nurse notices that the client indicated that she resides in an extended family situation. Which arrangement would validate this information?

    a. She lives with her mother, step-father, and his two sons.

    b. She lives with her best friend and her three children.

    c. She lives with her husband and her daughter and son of whom she has joint custody.

    d. She lives with her grandmother, her uncle, her mother, and her younger sister.

13. The nurse is caring for a Hispanic client who is in labor. The client appears to closely follow traditional cultural behaviors. Which behavior would **most** likely to be noted by the nurse?

    a. The woman is stoic during intense contractions, showing little emotion.

    b. The woman reports a desire to have her extended family present during the labor and delivery.

    c. The woman defers to her husband during interactions.

    d. The woman wishes to labor unclothed.

14. The nurse is caring for a 14-year-old boy with a debilitating illness who wants to attend school. Which intervention addresses the child's physical health but not his quality of life?

    a. Helping the child modify trendy clothing to his needs

    b. Consulting with the school nurse at the child's school

    c. Assessing the child's daily oxygen supplement needs

    d. Adapting technologies for use outside of the home

15. The nurse is updating the records of a 10-year-old girl who had her appendix removed. Which action could jeopardize the privacy of the child's medical records?

    a. Changing identification and passwords monthly

    b. Letting another nurse use the nurse's log-in session

    c. Closing files before stepping away from computer

    d. Printing out confidential information for transmittal

16. The nurse is assessing a 9-year-old boy during a back-to-school check-up. Which finding is a factor for childhood injury?

    a. Records show child weighed 2,450 g at birth.

    b. Mother reports she has abused alcohol and drugs.

    c. The parents adopted the boy from Guatemala.

    d. Mother reports the child is hostile to other children.

17. The school nurse is caring for several children who witnessed an 8-year-old girl get hit by car on the way to school. Which intervention is least important to the nursing plan of care for these children?

    a. Determining that the children were traumatized by what they saw

    b. Arranging for counseling for the children who saw the accident

    c. Including friends of the injured child to receive counseling too

    d. Making phone calls to the parents of the children counseled

18. The nursery nurse is preparing a consent form for the circumcision of a newborn. The mother of the child is 16 years of age. The baby's father is not participating in the care. When planning to complete the surgical consent, which action by the nurse is **most** appropriate?

    a. Ask the grandmother of the newborn to sign the surgical consent

    b. Determine if the baby's father is older than 18 years, and if so ask for him to sign

    c. Recommend that the court appoint a guardian for the baby

    d. Ask the baby's mother to sign the surgical consent

19. The parents of a 12-year-old child preparing to undergo surgery explain to the nurse that their religious beliefs do not allow for blood transfusions. What initial action by the nurse is **most** appropriate?

    a. Explain to the parents that the surgeon will make the final decision in the event a blood transfusion is needed by the child.

    b. Ask the child what their preference will be.

    c. Contact the hospital attorney.

    d. Document the parents' requests.

20. Which nursing activity requires the pediatric nurse to implement the ethical principle of nonmaleficence?

    a. Encouraging an adolescent client to take ownership of her health status independent of her parents

    b. Weighing the potential harm caused by a child's chemotherapy with its potential benefits

    c. Mediating between a father, who wants his infant circumcised, and the mother who is opposed

    d. Providing empathic, holistic care to a family who has just learned that their child's prognosis is poor

CHAPTER 2

Family-Centered Community-Based Care

Learning Objectives

Upon completion of the chapter, you will be able to:

- Identify the core concepts associated with the nursing management of women, children, and families.
- Examine the major components and key elements of family-centered care.
- Explain the different levels of prevention in nursing, providing examples of each.
- Give examples of cultural issues that may be faced when providing nursing care.
- Provide culturally competent care to women, children, and families.
- Outline the various roles and functions assumed by the nurse working with women, children, and families.
- Demonstrate the ability to use excellent therapeutic communication skills when interacting with women, children, and families.
- Explain the process of health teaching as it relates to women, children, and families.
- Examine the importance of discharge planning and case management in providing nursing care.
- Explain the reasons for the increased emphasis on community-based care.
- Differentiate community-based nursing from nursing in acute care settings.
- Identify the variety of settings where community-based care can be provided to women, children, and families.

SECTION I: ASSESSING YOUR UNDERSTANDING

Activity A FILL IN THE BLANKS

1. The collaborative process of assessment, planning, application, coordination, follow-up, and evaluation of the options needed to meet an individual's needs is referred to as _____.

2. _____ communication, also referred to as body language, includes attending to others and active listening.

3. _____ may be defined as a "specific group of people, often living in a defined geographical area, who share a common culture, values, and norms."

4. _____ prevention involves avoiding the disease or condition before it occurs through health promotion activities, environmental protection, and specific protection against disease or injury.

5. Cultural _____ involve participating in cross-cultural interactions with people from culturally diverse backgrounds.

6. _____ literacy is the ability to read, understand, and use health care information.

Activity B MATCHING

Match the health care facility in Column A with the service provided in Column B.

Column A

____ **1.** Counseling centers

____ **2.** Wellness centers

____ **3.** Wholeness healing centers

____ **4.** Educational centers

Column B

a. Provide health lecture instruction on breast self-examination and computers for research

b. Provide acupuncture, aromatherapy, and herbal remedies

c. Offer stress reduction techniques

d. Offer various support groups

Activity C SEQUENCING

Using the boxes below, place the steps used to provide education to clients and families in the correct sequence.

1. Intervening to enhance learning

2. Planning education

3. Evaluating learning

4. Documenting teaching and learning

5. Assessing teaching and learning needs

☐ → ☐ → ☐ → ☐ → ☐

Activity D SHORT ANSWERS

Briefly answer the following.

1. What are the three levels of care provided by maternal and pediatric nurses?

_____

_____

_____

2. Describe the components of case management.

_____

_____

3. What techniques can the nurse use to enhance learning?

_____

_____

_____

4. What are the four main purposes of documenting childcare and education?

_____

_____

_____

5. What do discharge planning and case management contribute to in the community setting?

_____

_____

_____

6. What is the focus of community health nursing?

_____

_____

7. What is a birthing center?

_____

_____

_____

SECTION II: APPLYING YOUR KNOWLEDGE

Activity E CASE STUDY

Consider this scenario and answer the questions.

A couple in their late 20s is expecting their first child. They are touring the labor and delivery suite at the hospital they have chosen for the birth. The nurse who is conducting the tour refers to giving "family-centered care" and using "evidence-based nursing" on their unit.

1. During the question and answer period, the couple asks what "family-centered care" is. How would the nurse respond to this couple's question?

   _____

   _____

   _____

2. The couple then asks what the nurse means by "evidence-based nursing" and how that affects the two of them and their newborn. What is the nurse's best response?

   _____

   _____

   _____

SECTION III: PRACTICING FOR NCLEX

Activity F NCLEX-STYLE QUESTIONS

Answer the following questions.

1. A nurse is working in a community setting and is involved in case management. In which activity would the nurse **most** likely be involved?
   a. Help a grandmother to learn a procedure
   b. Assess the sanitary conditions of the home
   c. Establish eligibility for a Medicaid waiver
   d. Schedule speech and respiratory therapy services

2. What is a key element when providing family-centered care?
   a. Communicate specific health information
   b. Be in control of the way care is given
   c. Give only the health information that is necessary while providing care
   d. Avoid cultural issues by providing care in a standardized fashion

3. Nurses play important roles in a variety of community settings. Which nursing goal is common to all types of community settings?
   a. Remove or minimize health barriers to learning
   b. Promote the health of a specific group of clients
   c. Determine the type of care a client needs initially at a visit
   d. Ensure that the health and well-being of women and their families is achieved

4. A pregnant client arrives at the maternity clinic for a routine check-up. The client has been reading books on pregnancy and wants to know ways to prevent the incidence of neural tube defects (NTDs) in her fetus. Which recommendation should the nurse offer the client to reduce the risk of NTDs for this fetus?
   a. Take vitamin E supplements 3 times per week
   b. Take folic acid supplements each day
   c. Increase consumption of legumes such as beans and peas
   d. Consume citrus fruits every day to increase intake of vitamin C

5. A nurse is addressing a group of women on the issue of women's health during their reproductive years. Which reason does the nurse provide regarding the need for comprehensive, community-centered care to women during this time period?
   a. Women have more health problems during their reproductive years.
   b. Increased stress causes more health problems during their reproductive years.
   c. A women's immune system weakens immediately after birth.
   d. Women's health care needs change with their reproductive goals.

6. The nurse has to prepare a discharge plan as a part of her postpartum care of a client, whom she is caring for in a home-based setting. Which aspect of care should the nurse include in her postpartum plan in this environment?

   a. Provide the client with self-help books about infant care

   b. Monitor the physical and emotional well-being of family members

   c. Recognize infant needs in the discharge plan

   d. Identify developing complications in the infant

7. A nurse is caring for a Turkish American client. The nurse understands that there could be major cultural differences between her and her client. The nurse contemplates assigning this client to a staff member who is of the same culture as the client. What is a potential consequence?

   a. Lead to stereotyping of the client

   b. Ensure better care and understanding

   c. Help in assessing client's culture

   d. Help build better nurse–client relationship

8. While interviewing a woman who has come to the clinic for a check-up, the woman tells the nurse that she places objects in her environment so that they are in harmony with chi. The nurse interprets this as which of the following?

   a. Reflexology

   b. Feng Shui

   c. Therapeutic touch

   d. Aromatherapy

9. The nurse is educating the family of a 2-day-old Chinese American boy with myelomeningocele about the disorder and its treatment. Which action involving an interpreter could jeopardize the family's trust in the health care providers?

   a. Allowing too little time for the translation of health care terms

   b. Using a person who is not a professional interpreter

   c. Asking the interpreter questions not meant for the family

   d. Using a relative to communicate with the parents

10. The nurse is striving to form a partnership with the family of a medically fragile child being cared for at home. Which actions on the part of the nurse would **best** support family-centered home care for this family?

    a. Recognizing and utilizing unique family strengths

    b. Ensuring a safe, nurturing environment is maintained

    c. Maintaining all the high tech equipment used by the child is in excellent working condition

    d. Correcting inadequate coping methods to aid the family in dealing with a difficult situation

11. A 4-year-old child is brought to the clinic by his parents for evaluation of a cough. Which action by the nurse would be *least* appropriate in promoting atraumatic care for the child?

    a. Having the parents stay with the child during the examination

    b. Allowing the child to touch the stethoscope before listening to his heart

    c. Informing the child that the stethoscope might feel a bit cold but not hurt

    d. Wrapping the child tightly in a blanket to prevent him from moving around

12. A nurse is working with a family to ensure effective therapeutic communication. The development of which would be least important?

    a. Trust

    b. Respect

    c. Empathy

    d. Literacy

13. A nurse is conducting a teaching session with a child and his family. Which techniques would help to facilitate their learning? Select all that apply.

    a. Use medical terminology emphasizes the importance of the information

    b. Limit each teaching session to about 10 to 15 minutes

    c. Focus on the "need-to-know" information first

    d. Repeat the information about 4 to 5 times

    e. Use videos to help those having difficulty grasping information

14. A community health nurse is engaged in primary prevention activities. Which activities are applicable? Select all that apply.

    a. Drug education program for schools

    b. Smoking cessation programs

    c. Poison prevention education

    d. Cholesterol monitoring

    e. Fecal occult blood testing

15. The nurse is working with an interpreter to gather information from a family. Which action would be **most** important?

    a. Positioning the interpreter between the nurse and the family

    b. Assuming the interpreter is the content expert

    c. Allowing additional time to compensate for the translation

    d. Talking directly to the interpreter

16. A nurse is working on developing cultural competence. Which action would the nurse do **first**?

    a. Become sensitive to the values, beliefs, and customs of one's own culture

    b. Obtain knowledge about various world-views of different cultures

    c. Assess each client's unique cultural values, beliefs, and practices

    d. Engage in cross-cultural interactions with people from diverse cultural groups

Anatomy and Physiology of the Reproductive System

Learning Objectives

Upon completion of the chapter, you will be able to:

- Define the key terms used in this chapter.
- Contrast the structure and function of the major external and internal female genital organs.
- Outline the phases of the menstrual cycle, the dominant hormones involved, and the changes taking place in each phase.
- Classify external and internal male reproductive structures and the function of each in hormonal regulation.

SECTION I: ASSESSING YOUR UNDERSTANDING

Activity A FILL IN THE BLANKS

1. The vagina is a tubular, fibromuscular organ lined with a mucous membrane that lies in a series of transverse folds called _____.

2. _____ stimulates the production of milk within a few days after childbirth.

3. The _____, which lies against the testes, is a coiled tube almost 20 ft long that collects sperm from the testes and provides the space and environment for sperm to mature.

4. In the male, the _____ is the terminal duct of the reproductive and urinary systems, serving as a passageway for semen and urine.

5. The _____ is the mucosal layer that lines the uterine cavity in nonpregnant women.

6. _____ glands, located on either side of the female urethral opening, secrete a small amount of mucus to keep the opening moist and lubricated for the passage of urine.

7. The incision made into the perineal tissue to provide more space for the presenting part of the delivering fetus is called an _____.

8. In the male, the _____ gland lies just under the bladder in the pelvis and surrounds the middle portion of the urethra.

9. The _____ is a pear-shaped muscular organ at the top of the vagina.

10. The _____ is the thin-skinned sac that surrounds and protects the testes.

Activity B MATCHING

Match the hormones in Column A with their functions in Column B.

Column A

____ **1.** Gonadotropin-releasing hormone (GnRH)

____ **2.** Follicle-stimulating hormone (FSH)

____ **3.** Luteinizing hormone (LH)

____ **4.** Estrogen

____ **5.** Progesterone

Column B

a. It maintains the uterine decidual lining and reduces uterine contractions, allowing pregnancy to be maintained

b. It is required for the final maturation of preovulatory follicles and luteinization of the ruptured follicle

c. It is primarily responsible for the maturation of the ovarian follicle

d. It inhibits FSH production and stimulates LH production

e. It induces the release of FSH and LH to assist with ovulation

Activity C SEQUENCING

1. Given below, in random order, are steps occurring during the endometrial cycle. Arrange them in the correct sequence in the boxes provided.

a. The endometrium becomes thickened and more vascular and glandular.

b. Cervical mucus becomes thin, clear, stretchy, and more alkaline.

c. The spiral arteries rupture, releasing blood into the uterus.

d. The ischemia leads to shedding of the endometrium down to the basal layer.

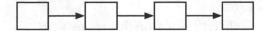

2. Given below, in random order, are pubertal events. Arrange them in the correct sequence in the boxes provided.

a. Growth spurt

b. Appearance of pubic and then axillary hair

c. Development of breast buds

d. Onset of menstruation

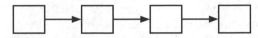

Activity D SHORT ANSWERS

Briefly answer the following.

1. What is vulva?

_____

_____

_____

2. What is colostrum?

_____

_____

_____

3. What are the physical changes observed in women during their perimenopausal years?

_____

_____

_____

4. What is the role of the nurse when caring for menopausal women?

_____

_____

_____

5. What is the function of the testes?

_____

_____

_____

6. What is the function of the bulbourethral, or Cowper, glands?

_____

_____

_____

SECTION II: APPLYING YOUR KNOWLEDGE

Activity E CASE STUDY

Consider this scenario and answer the questions.

Susan is a 14-year-old high school student who came to the school nurse's office after beginning her first menstrual period. She has received health education information in class, but has many questions she asks the school nurse.

1. Describe what a nurse should teach Susan about menstruation.

   _____

   _____

   _____

2. Describe the nurse's response when Susan asks how long her cycles will last.

   _____

   _____

   _____

3. Susan reports that most of her close friends have not yet started their periods. What information can be provided about factors that influence the onset of menstruation?

   _____

   _____

   _____

SECTION III: PRACTICING FOR NCLEX

Activity F NCLEX-STYLE QUESTIONS

Answer the following questions.

1. A client is trying to have a baby and wants to know the best time to have intercourse to increase the chances of pregnancy. Which time for intercourse is **ideal**, to help her chances of conceiving?
   a. A week after ovulation
   b. One or 2 days before ovulation
   c. Any time after ovulation
   d. Anytime during the week before ovulation

2. A nurse is caring for a client who has given birth. The client reports that her breast milk is dark yellow. Which information should the nurse give to the client regarding the situation?
   a. Modify diet to reduce excess fat intake.
   b. The yellow fluid is colostrum and is rich in maternal antibodies.
   c. Breastfeeding should be avoided until the breast milk becomes normal.
   d. Completely stop breastfeeding and use formula instead.

3. A client reports pain on one side of the abdomen. On further questioning, the nurse discovers that the pain occurs routinely around 2 weeks before menstruation. The client has not missed a period, and she exercises regularly. Which cause is **most** likely?
   a. Early signs of pregnancy
   b. Irregular menstruation cycle
   c. Pain during ovulation
   d. Regularly exercise

4. A woman has been assessing her basal body temperature for 4 months. Upon reviewing her temperature history log, the nurse notes no change in her daily temperatures. Which should the nurse expect the health care provider to order **first**?
   a. Clomiphene
   b. Serum progesterone level
   c. Endometrial biopsy
   d. Vaginal discharge culture

5. A nurse is assessing a 45-year-old client. The client asks for information regarding the changes that are most likely to occur with menopause. Which should the nurse tell the client?
   a. Uterus tilts backward
   b. Uterus shrinks and gradually atrophies
   c. Cervical muscle content increases
   d. Outer layer of the cervix becomes rough

6. Which hormone is called the hormone of pregnancy because it reduces uterine contractions during pregnancy?
   a. Luteinizing hormone (LH)
   b. Estrogen
   c. Follicle-stimulating hormone (FSH)
   d. Progesterone

7. During cold conditions, how does the body react to maintain scrotal temperature?
   a. Cremaster muscles relax
   b. Frequency of urination increases
   c. Scrotum is pulled closer to the body
   d. Increase in blood flow to genital area

8. A nurse is explaining the menstrual cycle to a 12-year-old client who has experienced menarche. Which should the nurse tell the client?
   a. An average cycle length is about 15 to 20 days.
   b. Ovary contains 400,000 follicles at birth.
   c. Duration of the flow is about 3 to 7 days.
   d. Blood loss averages 120 to 150 mL.

9. A nurse is providing information regarding ovulation to a couple who want to have a baby. Which should the nurse tell the clients?
   a. Ovulation takes place 10 days before menstruation.
   b. The lifespan of the ovum is only about 48 hours.
   c. At ovulation, a mature follicle ruptures, releasing an ovum.
   d. When ovulation occurs, there is a rise in estrogen.

10. Which hormone is secreted from the hypothalamus in a pulsatile manner throughout the reproductive cycle?
    a. Follicle-stimulating hormone (FSH)
    b. Gonadotropin-releasing hormone (GnRH)
    c. Luteinizing hormone (LH)
    d. Estrogen

11. Which statement **best** expresses the role of the corpus luteum?
    a. The corpus luteum promotes the increased production of estrogen before ovulation.
    b. The corpus luteum secretes progesterone to promote the preparation of the endometrium for implantation.
    c. During the luteal phase, the corpus luteum secretes glycogen.
    d. Increasing amounts of cervical mucus are produced as a result of the luteinizing hormone produced by the corpus luteum.

12. Which client should the nurse assess **first**?
    a. A nonpregnant client with a cervical mucus pH level of 3.8.
    b. A 1-day postdelivery client with dark yellow nipple secretions.
    c. A nonpregnant client with a vaginal mucus pH level of 4.5.
    d. A 6-month postdelivery client whose cervix os has a transverse slit.

13. A client asks the nurse about cervical mucus changes that occur during the menstrual cycle. Which statement should the nurse expect to include in the client's teaching plan?
    a. Cervical mucus disappears immediately after ovulation, resuming with menses.
    b. About midway through the menstrual cycle, cervical mucus is clear and sticky.
    c. During ovulation, the cervix remains dry with scant mucus secretion.
    d. As ovulation approaches, cervical mucus is abundant and stretchable.

14. Which client should the nurse flag for the health care provider to assess **first**?
    a. The female client with an inverted, pear-shaped uterus
    b. The male client with three palpable masses in the testes
    c. The female client with a soft, doughnut-shaped cervix
    d. The male client whose scrotum is covered with hair

15. A nurse is explaining to a client about monthly hormonal changes. Starting with day 1 of the menstrual cycle, place the following hormones in the chronological order in which they elevate during the menstrual cycle.
    1. Follicle-stimulating hormone (FSH)
    2. Progesterone
    3. Gonadotropin-releasing hormone (GnHR)
    4. Luteinizing hormone (LH)
    5. Estrogen

Common Reproductive Issues

Learning Objectives

Upon completion of the chapter, you will be able to:

- Define the key terms used in this chapter.
- Examine common reproductive concerns in terms of symptoms, diagnostic tests, and appropriate interventions.
- Identify risk factors and outline appropriate client education needed in common reproductive disorders.
- Compare and contrast the various contraceptive methods available and their overall effectiveness.
- Analyze the physiologic and psychological aspects of menopausal transition.
- Delineate the nursing management needed for women experiencing common reproductive disorders.

SECTION I: ASSESSING YOUR UNDERSTANDING

Activity A FILL IN THE BLANKS

1. _____ involves the ingrowth of the endometrium into the uterine musculature.

2. Primary dysmenorrhea is caused by increased _____ production by the endometrium in an ovulatory cycle.

3. _____ is the direct visualization of the internal organs with a lighted instrument inserted through an abdominal incision.

4. During _____, the ovary begins to falter, producing irregular and missed periods and an occasional hot flash.

5. Male sterilization is accomplished with a surgical procedure known as a _____.

6. In a _____ abortion, the woman takes certain medications to induce a miscarriage to remove the products of conception.

7. _____ is a condition in which bone mass declines to such an extent that fractures occur with minimal trauma.

8. At the onset of ovulation, cervical mucus that is more abundant, clear, slippery, and smooth is known as _____ mucus.

9. The _____ body temperature refers to the lowest body temperature and is reached upon awakening.

10. Oral contraceptives (OCs), called _____, contain only progestin and work primarily by thickening the cervical mucus to prevent penetration of the sperm and make the endometrium unfavorable for implantation.

Activity B MATCHING

Match the terms in Column A with the correct descriptions in Column B.

Column A

____ **1.** Amenorrhea

____ **2.** Dysmenorrhea

____ **3.** Metrorrhagia

____ **4.** Menometrorrhagia

____ **5.** Oligomenorrhea

Column B

a. Bleeding between periods

b. Bleeding occurring at intervals of more than 35 days

c. Absence of menses during the reproductive years

d. Difficult, painful, or abnormal menstruation

e. Heavy bleeding occurring at irregular intervals with flow lasting more than 7 days

Activity C SEQUENCING

1. Given below, in random order, are steps occurring during diaphragm insertion. Put the steps in correct sequence by writing the letters in the boxes provided.

a. Hold the diaphragm between the thumb and fingers and compress it to form a "figure-eight" shape.

b. Place a tablespoon of spermicidal jelly or cream in the dome and around the rim of the diaphragm.

c. Select the position that is most comfortable for insertion.

d. Tuck the front rim of the diaphragm behind the pubic bone so that the rubber hugs the front wall of the vagina.

e. Insert the diaphragm into the vagina, directing it downward as far as it will go.

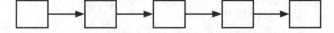

2. Given below, in random order, are steps occurring during cervical cap insertion. Put the steps in correct sequence by writing the letters in the boxes provided.

a. Pinch the sides of the cervical cap together.

b. Use one finger to feel around the entire circumference to make sure there are no gaps between the cap rim and the cervix.

c. Pinch the cap dome and tug gently to check for evidence of suction.

d. Insert the cervical cap into the vagina and place over the cervix.

e. Compress the cervical cap dome.

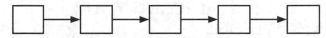

Activity D SHORT ANSWERS

Briefly answer the following.

1. What are the common laboratory tests ordered to determine the cause of amenorrhea?

_____

_____

_____

2. What is menopause?

_____

_____

3. What are the risk factors associated with endometriosis?

_____

_____

_____

4. Compare and contrast primary and secondary infertility.

_____

_____

_____

5. What is the Two-Day Method for contraception?

_____

_____

_____

6. What are intrauterine systems?

_____

_____

_____

SECTION II: APPLYING YOUR KNOWLEDGE

Activity E **CASE STUDY**

Consider this scenario and answer the questions.

Alexa is a 14-year-old lacrosse player who has been training vigorously for selection on her high school team. Alexa comes to the health care provider's office to have her health forms for school completed. The office nurse takes her history, and the client describes that she has been experiencing amenorrhea.

1. How should the nurse describe "primary amenorrhea" to Alexa?

_____

_____

_____

2. State the causes of "primary amenorrhea" that may be related to Alexa.

_____

_____

_____

3. What treatments may be considered for Alexa?

_____

_____

_____

4. What counseling and education should the nurse provide for Alexa at this visit?

_____

_____

_____

SECTION III: PRACTICING FOR NCLEX

Activity F **NCLEX-STYLE QUESTIONS**

Answer the following questions.

1. A couple is being assessed for infertility. The male partner is required to collect a semen sample for analysis. What instruction should the nurse give him?

   a. Abstain from sexual activity for 10 hours before collecting the sample.

   b. Avoid strenuous activity for 24 hours before collecting the sample.

   c. Collect a specimen by ejaculating into a condom or plastic bag.

   d. Deliver sample for analysis within 1 to 2 hours after ejaculation.

2. The nurse is assessing a client for amenorrhea. During the assessment, the nurse notes facial hair and acne. The nurse knows this could be related to:

   a. anorexia nervosa.

   b. enlarged thyroid gland.

   c. excessive prostaglandin production.

   d. an androgen excess secondary to a tumor.

3. A nurse is teaching a female client about fertility awareness as a method of contraception. Which should the nurse mention as an assumption for this method?

   a. Sperm can live up to 24 hours after intercourse.

   b. The "unsafe period" is approximately 6 days.

   c. The exact time of ovulation can be determined.

   d. The "safe period" is 3 days after ovulation.

4. The nurse is instructing a client with dysmenorrhea on how to manage her symptoms. Which should the nurse include in the teaching plan? Select all that apply.

   a. Increase intake of salty foods

   b. Increase water consumption

   c. Avoid keeping legs elevated while lying down

   d. Use heating pads or take warm baths

   e. Increase exercise and physical activity

5. A client is to be examined for the presence and extent of endometriosis. For which test should the nurse prepare the client?

a. Tissue biopsy

b. Hysterosalpingogram

c. Clomiphene citrate challenge test

d. Laparoscopy

6. A client needs additional information about the cervical mucus ovulation method after having read about it in a magazine. She asks the nurse about cervical changes during ovulation. About which should the nurse inform the client?

a. Cervical os is slightly closed

b. Cervical mucus is dry and thick

c. Cervix is high or deep in the vagina

d. Cervical mucus breaks when stretched

7. A client has been following the conventional 28-day regimen for contraception. She is now considering switching to an extended oral contraceptive (OC) regimen. She is seeking information about specific safety precautions. Which is true for the extended OC regimen?

a. It is not as effective as the conventional regimen.

b. It prevents pregnancy for 3 months at a time.

c. It carries the same safety profile as the 28-day regimen.

d. It does not ensure restoration of fertility if discontinued.

8. A 30-year-old client would like to try using basal body temperature (BBT) as a fertility awareness method. Which instruction should the nurse provide the client?

a. Avoid unprotected intercourse until BBT has been elevated for 6 days.

b. Avoid using other fertility awareness methods along with BBT.

c. Use the axillary method of taking the temperature.

d. Take temperature before rising and record it on a chart.

9. The nurse is caring for a client at the ambulatory care clinic who questions the nurse for information about contraception. The client reports that she is not comfortable about using any barrier methods and would like the option of regaining fertility after a couple of years. Which method should the nurse suggest to this client?

a. Basal body temperature (BBT)

b. Coitus interruptus

c. Lactational amenorrhea method

d. CycleBeads or medroxyprogesterone injection

10. A client would like some information about the use of a cervical cap. Which information should the nurse include in the teaching plan of this client? Select all that apply.

a. Inspect the cervical cap before insertion.

b. Apply spermicide to the rim of the cervical cap.

c. Wait for 30 minutes after insertion before engaging in intercourse.

d. Remove the cervical cap immediately after intercourse.

e. Do not use the cervical cap during menses.

11. A healthy 28-year-old female client who has a sedentary lifestyle and is a chain smoker is seeking information about contraception. The nurse informs this client of the various options available and the benefits and the risks of each. Which should the nurse recognize as contraindicated in the case of this client?

a. The medroxyprogesterone injection

b. Combination oral contraceptives

c. A copper intrauterine device

d. Implantable contraceptives

12. A client in her second trimester of pregnancy asks the nurse for information regarding certain oral medications to induce a miscarriage. What information should this client be given about such medications?

a. They are available only in the form of suppositories.

b. They can be taken only in the first trimester.

c. They present a high risk of respiratory failure.

d. They are considered a permanent end to fertility.

13. A client reports that she has multiple sex partners and has a lengthy history of various pelvic infections. She would like to know if there is any temporary contraceptive method that would suit her condition. Which should the nurse suggest for this client?

 a. Intrauterine device (IUD)

 b. Condoms

 c. Oral contraceptives (OCs)

 d. Tubal ligation

14. When caring for a client with reproductive issues, the nurse is required to clear up misconceptions. This enables new learning to take hold and a better client response to whichever methods are explored and ultimately selected. Which misconceptions will the nurse need to clear up? Select all that apply.

 a. Breastfeeding does not protect against pregnancy.

 b. Taking birth control pills protects against sexually transmitted infections (STIs).

 c. Douching after sex will prevent pregnancy.

 d. Pregnancy can occur during menses.

 e. Irregular menstruation prevents pregnancy.

15. A client has opted to use an intrauterine device (IUD) for contraception. About which effect of the device on monthly periods should the nurse inform the client?

 a. Periods become lighter

 b. Periods become more painful

 c. Periods become longer

 d. Periods reduce in number

16. A 30-year-old client tells the nurse that she would like to use a contraceptive sponge but does not know enough about its use and whether it will protect her against sexually transmitted infections (STIs). Which information should the nurse provide the client about using a contraceptive sponge? Select all that apply.

 a. Keep the sponge for more than 30 hours to prevent STIs.

 b. Wet the sponge with water before inserting it.

 c. Insert the sponge 24 hours before intercourse.

 d. Leave the sponge in place for at least 6 hours following intercourse.

 e. Replace sponge every 2 hours for the method to be effective.

17. A 52-year-old client is seeking treatment for menopause. She is not very active and has a history of cardiac problems. Which therapy option should the nurse recognize as contra-indicated for this client?

 a. Long-term hormone replacement therapy

 b. Selective estrogen receptor modulators

 c. Lipid-lowering agents

 d. Bisphosphonates

18. A 49-year-old client who is in the perimeno-pausal phase of life reports to the nurse a loss of lubrication during intercourse, which she feels is hampering her sex life. Which response by the nurse is appropriate?

 a. "Don't worry! This is a normal process of aging."

 b. "Have you considered contacting a support group for women your age?"

 c. "You can manage the condition by using over-the-counter (OTC) moisturizers or lubricants."

 d. "All you need is a positive outlook and a supportive partner."

CHAPTER 5

Sexually Transmitted Infections

Learning Objectives

Upon completion of the chapter, you will be able to:

- Evaluate the spread and control of sexually transmitted infections.
- Identify risk factors and outline appropriate client education needed in common sexually transmitted infections.
- Describe how contraceptives can play a role in the prevention of sexually transmitted infections.
- Analyze the physiologic and psychological aspects of sexually transmitted infections.
- Outline the nursing management needed for women with sexually transmitted infections.

SECTION I: ASSESSING YOUR UNDERSTANDING

Activity A FILL IN THE BLANKS

1. _____ is a common vaginal infection characterized by a heavy yellow, green, or gray frothy discharge.

2. The _____ stage of syphilis is characterized by diseases affecting the heart, eyes, brain, central nervous system, and/or skin.

3. _____ are a common cause of skin rash and pruritus throughout the world.

4. _____ is an intense pruritic dermatitis caused by a mite.

5. Vulvovaginal candidiasis, if not treated effectively during pregnancy, can cause the newborn to contract an oral infection known as _____ during the birth process.

6. _____ is a complex, curable bacterial infection caused by the spirochete Treponema pallidum.

7. Hepatitis B virus (HBV) can result in serious, permanent damage to the _____.

8. Cervicitis, acute urethral syndrome, salpingitis, pelvic inflammatory disease (PID), and infertility are conditions associated with _____ infection.

9. A person is said to be in the last stage of AIDS when the _____ T-cell count is less than or equal to 200.

10. Any woman suspected of having gonorrhea should be tested for _____ also, because coinfection (45%) is extremely common.

Activity B LABELING

Consider the following figures.

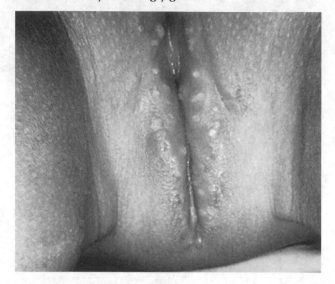

1. a. Identify this disease.

_____

_____

b. What are the risk factors of this disease?

_____

_____

c. What treatments are available to manage this disease?

_____

_____

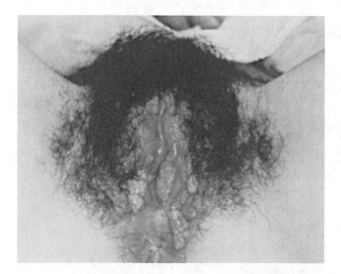

2. a. Identify this disease.

_____

_____

b. What are the clinical manifestations of this disease?

_____

_____

c. What medications may be prescribed to manage this condition?

_____

_____

Activity C MATCHING

Match the STIs in Column A with their related descriptions in Column B.

Column A

____ **1.** HIV

____ **2.** Vaginitis

____ **3.** Hepatitis

____ **4.** Gonorrhea

____ **5.** Genital herpes

____ **6.** Human papillomavirus (HPV)

Column B

a. Inflammation and infection of the vagina

b. Acute, systemic viral infection that can be transmitted sexually

c. Retrovirus causes breakdown in immune function, leading to AIDS

d. A recurrent, lifelong viral infection

e. Cause of essentially all cases of cervical cancer

f. Very severe bacterial infection in the columnar epithelium of the endocervix

Activity D SEQUENCING

Given below, in random order, are the manifestations of syphilis in its various stages. Arrange the stages in their correct order.

1. Flu-like symptoms; rash on trunk, palms, and soles

2. Life-threatening heart disease and neurologic disease that slowly destroys the heart, the eyes, the brain, the central nervous system, and the skin

3. Painless ulcer at site of bacterial entry that disappears in 1 to 6 weeks

4. No clinical manifestations even though serology is positive

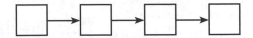

Activity E SHORT ANSWER

Briefly answer the following.

1. What are the predisposing factors for the occurrence of vulvovaginal candidiasis?

   _____

   _____

   _____

2. What are the symptoms of hepatitis A?

   _____

   _____

   _____

3. How is HIV transmitted?

   _____

   _____

   _____

4. What is AIDS?

   _____

   _____

   _____

5. What are the causes of vaginitis?

   _____

   _____

   _____

6. What are clinical manifestations of chlamydia?

   _____

   _____

   _____

SECTION II: APPLYING YOUR KNOWLEDGE

Activity F CASE STUDY

Consider this scenario and answer the questions.

A nurse is caring for a 22-year-old pregnant client who has been diagnosed with gonorrhea. The client seems to be very apprehensive about seeking treatment and wants to know if her newborn would be at risk for the infection.

1. What information should the nurse provide the client regarding the transmission of the infection to the newborn?

   _____

   _____

   _____

2. What factors should a nurse be aware of when caring for the client with gonorrhea or any other STI?

   _____

   _____

   _____

3. Which groups of clients are at a higher risk for developing gonorrhea?

   _____

   _____

   _____

SECTION III: PRACTICING FOR NCLEX

Activity G NCLEX-STYLE QUESTIONS

Answer the following questions.

1. A nurse is caring for a female client who has a history of recurring vulvovaginal candidiasis. Which of the following instructions should the nurse include in the teaching session with the client?

   a. Use superabsorbent tampons.

   b. Douche the affected area regularly.

   c. Wear white, 100% cotton underpants.

   d. Increase intake of carbonated drinks.

2. An HIV-positive client who is on antiretroviral therapy complains of anorexia, nausea, and vomiting. Which of the following suggestions should the nurse offer the client to cope with this condition?

   a. Use high-protein supplements.

   b. Eat dry crackers after meals.

   c. Limit number of meals to three a day.

   d. Constantly drink fluids while eating.

3. A client complaining of genital warts has been diagnosed with HPV. The genital warts have been treated, and they have disappeared. Which of the following should the nurse include in the teaching plan when educating the client about the condition?

   a. Applying steroid creams in affected area promotes comfort.

   b. Even after warts are removed, HPV still remains.

   c. All women above the age of 30 should get themselves vaccinated against HPV.

   d. Use of latex condoms is associated with increased risk of cervical cancer.

4. A female client is prescribed metronidazole for the treatment of trichomoniasis. Which of the following instructions should the nurse give the client undergoing treatment?

   a. Avoid extremes of temperature to the genital area.

   b. Use condoms during sex.

   c. Increase fluid intake.

   d. Avoid alcohol.

5. A nurse is required to assess a client complaining of unusual vaginal discharge for bacterial vaginosis. Which of the following is a classic manifestation of this condition that the nurse should assess for?

   a. Characteristic "stale fish" odor

   b. Heavy yellow discharge

   c. Dysfunctional uterine bleeding

   d. Erythema in the vulvovaginal area

6. A nurse needs to assess a female client for primary stage herpes simplex virus (HSV)

infection. Which of the following symptoms related to this condition should the nurse assess for?

   a. Rashes on the face

   b. Yellow-green vaginal discharge

   c. Loss of hair or alopecia

   d. Genital vesicular lesions

7. A nurse working in a community health education program is assigned to educate community members about STIs. Which of the following nursing strategies should be adopted to prevent the spread of STIs in the community?

   a. Promote use of oral contraceptives.

   b. Emphasize the importance of good body hygiene.

   c. Discuss limiting the number of sex partners.

   d. Emphasize not sharing personal items with others.

8. A nurse who is conducting sessions on preventing the spread of STIs in a particular community discovers that there is a very high incidence of hepatitis B in the community. Which of the following measures should she take to ensure the prevention of the disease?

   a. Ensure that the drinking water is disease free.

   b. Instruct people to get vaccinated for hepatitis B.

   c. Educate about risks of injecting drugs.

   d. Educate teenagers to delay onset of sexual activity.

9. A nurse is caring for a client undergoing treatment for bacterial vaginosis. Which of the following instructions should the nurse give the client to prevent recurrence of bacterial vaginosis? Select all that apply.

   a. Practice monogamy

   b. Use oral contraceptives

   c. Avoid smoking

   d. Undergo colposcopy tests frequently

   e. Avoid foods containing excessive sugar

10. A pregnant client arrives at the community clinic complaining of fever blisters and cold sores on the lips, eyes, and face. The primary health care provider has diagnosed it as the primary episode of genital herpes simplex, for which antiviral therapy is recommended. Which of the following information should the nurse offer the client when educating her about managing the infection?

    a. Antiviral drug therapy cures the infection completely.

    b. Kissing during the primary episode does not transmit the virus.

    c. Safety of antiviral therapy during pregnancy has not been established.

    d. Recurrent HSV infection episodes are longer and more severe.

11. A 19-year-old female client has been diagnosed with pelvic inflammatory disease due to untreated gonorrhea. Which of the following instructions should the nurse offer when caring for the client? Select all that apply.

    a. Use an intrauterine device (IUD).

    b. Avoid douching vaginal area.

    c. Complete the antibiotic therapy.

    d. Increase fluid intake.

    e. Limit the number of sex partners.

12. A client complaining of genital ulcers has been diagnosed with syphilis. Which of the following nursing interventions should the nurse implement when caring for the client? Select all that apply.

    a. Have the client urinate in water if urination is painful.

    b. Suggest the client apply ice packs to the genital area for comfort.

    c. Instruct the client to wash her hands with soap and water after touching lesions.

    d. Instruct the client to wear nonconstricting, comfortable clothes.

    e. Instruct the client to abstain from sex during the latency period.

13. A nurse is conducting an AIDS awareness program for women. Which of the following instructions should the nurse include in the teaching plan to empower women to develop control over their lives in a practical manner so that they can prevent becoming infected with HIV? Select the most appropriate responses.

    a. Give opportunities to practice negotiation techniques.

    b. Encourage women to develop refusal skills.

    c. Encourage women to use female condoms.

    d. Support youth-development activities to reduce sexual risk-taking.

    e. Encourage women to lead a healthy lifestyle.

14. A nurse is caring for an HIV-positive client who is on triple-combination highly active antiretroviral therapy (HAART). Which of the following should the nurse include in the teaching plan when educating the client about the treatment? Select all that apply.

    a. Exposure of fetus to antiretroviral agents is completely safe.

    b. Successful antiretroviral therapy may prevent AIDS.

    c. Unpleasant side effects such as nausea and diarrhea are common.

    d. Provide written materials describing diet, exercise, and medications.

    e. Ensure that the client understands the dosing regimen and schedule.

15. A nurse is caring for a female client who is undergoing treatment for genital warts due to HPV. Which of the following information should the nurse include when educating the client about the risk of cervical cancer? Select all that apply.

    a. Use of broad-spectrum antibiotics increases risk of cervical cancer.

    b. Obtaining Pap smears regularly helps early detection of cervical cancer.

    c. Abnormal vaginal discharge is a sign of cervical cancer.

    d. Recurrence of genital warts increases risk of cervical cancer.

    e. Use of latex condoms is associated with a lower rate of cervical cancer.

16. A nurse is caring for a client who has just delivered a baby. Which of the following information should the nurse give the client regarding hepatitis B vaccination for the baby?

   a. Vaccine may not be safe for underweight or premature babies.

   b. Vaccine consists of a series of three injections given within 6 months.

   c. Vaccine is administered only after the infant is at least 6 months old.

   d. Vaccine is required only if mother is identified as high risk for hepatitis B.

17. A pregnant client has been diagnosed with gonorrhea. Which of the following nursing interventions should be performed to prevent gonococcal ophthalmia neonatorum in the baby?

   a. Administer cephalosporins to mother during pregnancy.

   b. Instill a prophylactic agent in the eyes of the newborn.

   c. Perform a cesarean operation to prevent infection.

   d. Administer an antiretroviral syrup to the newborn.

18. A pregnant client is diagnosed with AIDS. Which of the following interventions should the nurse undertake to minimize the risk of transmission of AIDS to the infant?

   a. Ensure that the baby is delivered via cesarean.

   b. Begin triple-combination HAART for the newborn.

   c. Ensure that the baby is breastfed instead of being given formula.

   d. Administer antiretroviral syrup to the infant within 12 hours after birth.

Disorders of the Breasts

Learning Objectives

Upon completion of the chapter, you will be able to:

■ Define the key terms used in this chapter.
■ Identify the incidence, risk factors, screening methods, and treatment modalities for benign breast conditions.
■ Outline preventive strategies for breast cancer through lifestyle changes and health screening.
■ Analyze the incidence, risk factors, treatment modalities, and nursing considerations related to breast cancer.
■ Develop an educational plan to teach breast self-examination to a group of high-risk women.

SECTION I: ASSESSING YOUR UNDERSTANDING

Activity A FILL IN THE BLANKS

1. _____ is a useful adjunct to mammography that produces images of the breasts by sending sound waves through a conductive gel applied to the breasts.

2. _____, an alternative to radiation therapy, involves the use of a catheter to implant radioactive seeds into the breast after a tumor has been removed surgically.

3. Hormone therapy is used to block or counter the effect of the hormone _____ while treating breast cancer.

4. _____ is contraindicated for women whose active connective tissue conditions make them especially sensitive to the side effects of radiation.

5. _____ involves taking x-ray pictures of the breasts while they are compressed between two plastic plates.

6. _____, a type of therapy for breast cancer, leads to side effects such as hair loss, weight loss, and fatigue.

7. The removal of all breast tissue, the nipple, and the areola for breast cancer treatment is known as _____.

8. When diagnosing a woman with intraductal papilloma, a _____ card is used to evaluate nipple discharge for the presence of occult blood.

9. _____ is used as an adjunct therapy for breast cancer to help stimulate the body's natural defenses to recognize and attack cancer cells.

10. _____ are common benign solid breast tumors that occur in about 10% of all women and account for up to half of all breast biopsies.

Activity B MATCHING

Match the benign breast disorders in Column A with their related descriptions in Column B.

Column A

___ **1.** Fibrocystic breast changes

___ **2.** Fibroadenomas

___ **3.** Intraductal papilloma

___ **4.** Mammary duct ectasia

___ **5.** Mastitis

Column B

a. An infection of the connective tissue in the breast, occurring primarily in lactating women

b. Dilation and inflammation of the ducts behind the nipple

c. Benign, wart-like growths found in the mammary ducts, usually near the nipple

d. Firm, rubbery, well-circumscribed, freely mobile nodules that might or might not be tender when palpated

e. Lumpy, tender breasts; multiple, smooth, tiny "pebbles" or lumpy "oatmeal" under the skin in later stages

Activity C SEQUENCING

Listed below in random order are steps taken to diagnose a breast mass. Arrange the steps in order of typical occurrence.

1. Core needle biopsy

2. Clinical manual breast examination

3. Imaging studies

4. Advanced Breast Biopsy Instrument biopsy

Activity D SHORT ANSWERS

Briefly answer the following.

1. What are benign breast disorders?

_____

_____

_____

2. What are the three aspects on which breast cancers are classified?

_____

_____

_____

3. What is breast-conserving surgery?

_____

_____

_____

4. What is adjunct therapy?

_____

_____

_____

5. What are the side effects of chemotherapy?

_____

_____

_____

6. Why is the status of the axillary lymph nodes important in the diagnosis of breast cancer?

_____

_____

_____

SECTION II: APPLYING YOUR KNOWLEDGE

Activity E CASE STUDY

Consider this scenario and answer the questions.

Mrs. Taylor, age 54, presents to the women's health community clinic, where a nurse assesses her. She is very upset and crying. She tells the nurse that she found one large lump in her left breast and she knows that "it's cancer and I will die." When the nurse asks about her problem, she states that she does not routinely check her breasts and she hasn't had a mammogram for years because "they're too expensive." She also describes the intermittent pain she experiences in her breast.

1. What specific questions should the nurse include in her assessment of Mrs. Taylor?

_____

_____

_____

2. What education does Mrs. Taylor need regarding breast health?

_____

_____

_____

3. Explain what treatment modalities are available if Mrs. Taylor does have a malignancy.

_____

_____

_____

4. What community referrals are needed to meet Mrs. Taylor's future needs?

_____

_____

_____

SECTION III: PRACTICING FOR NCLEX

Activity F NCLEX-STYLE QUESTIONS

Answer the following questions.

1. A client reports lumpy, tender breasts, particularly during the week before menses. She reports pain that often dissipates after the onset of menses. The nurse suspects the client has fibrocystic breast changes. Which should the nurse do **next**?
   a. Determine if the client has had a mammography
   b. Have the client follow up in 1 week
   c. Perform a breast examination
   d. Schedule the client for cryoablation

2. A client arrives at the health care facility reporting a lump that she felt during her breast self-examination. Upon diagnosis, the physician suspects fibroadenomas. Which question should the nurse ask when assessing the client?
   a. "Do you consume foods high in fat?"
   b. "Are you lactating?"
   c. "Are you taking oral contraceptives?"
   d. "Do you smoke regularly?"

3. A female client who has a 2-month-old infant arrives at a health care facility reporting flu-like symptoms with fever and chills. When examining the breast, the nurse observes an increase in warmth. Which instruction should the nurse provide the client to help her cope with the condition?
   a. Increase fluid intake
   b. Avoid breastfeeding for 1 month
   c. Avoid changing positions while nursing
   d. Apply cold compresses to the affected breast

4. Mammography is recommended for a client diagnosed with intraductal papilloma. Which factor should the nurse ensure when preparing the client for a mammography?

   a. Client has not consumed fluids 1 hour before testing.

   b. Client has not applied deodorant on the day of testing.

   c. Client is just going to start her menses.

   d. Client has taken an aspirin before the testing.

5. A female client with a malignant tumor of the breast has to undergo chemotherapy for a period of 6 months. For which side effect should the nurse monitor when caring for this client?

   a. Vaginal discharge

   b. Headache

   c. Chills

   d. Constipation

6. A client diagnosed with fibroadenoma is worried about the chances of developing breast cancer. She also asks the nurse about various breast disorders and their risks. Which benign breast disorder should the nurse include as having the greatest risk for the development of breast cancer?

   a. Fibrodenomas

   b. Mastitis

   c. Mammary duct ectasia

   d. Intraductal papilloma

7. It is recommended that a 48-year-old female client with breast cancer undergo a sentinel lymph node biopsy before a lumpectomy. The client asks the nurse the reason for removing the sentinel lymph node. Which statement will the nurse make?

   a. "It will prevent lymphedema, which is a common side effect."

   b. "It will reveal the hormone receptor status of the cancer."

   c. "It will lessen the aggressiveness of the subsequent chemotherapy."

   d. "It will decrease the amount of treatment you need."

8. A client has undergone a mastectomy for breast cancer. Which instruction should the nurse include in the postsurgery client-teaching plan?

   a. Breathe rapidly for an hour

   b. Elevate the affected arm on a pillow

   c. Avoid moving the affected arm in any way

   d. Restrict intake of medication

9. A 62-year-old female client arrives at a health care facility reporting skin redness in the breast area, along with skin edema. The physician suspects inflammatory breast cancer. For which symptom of inflammatory breast cancer should the nurse assess?

   a. Palpable mobile cysts

   b. Palpable papilloma

   c. Increased warmth of the breast

   d. Induced nipple discharge

10. A 41-year-old female client arrives at a health care setting reporting dull nipple pain with a burning sensation, accompanied by pruritus around the nipple. The physician suspects mammary duct ectasia. Which order should the nurse question?

    a. Penicillin orally for 10 days

    b. Acetaminophen as needed for discomfort

    c. Monitor temperature

    d. Cool compresses to the affected area

11. A 52-year-old female client with an estrogen receptors positive (ER+) breast cancer is undergoing hormonal therapy. While taking a selective estrogen receptor modulator (SERM), the client begins to experience hot flashes. What should the nurse do next?

    a. Notify the client's health care provider

    b. Instruct the client to stop taking the SERM

    c. Document the hot flash in the client's chart

    d. Assess the client's blood pressure

12. A nurse is assigned to educate a group of women on cancer awareness. Which risk factors for breast cancer are modifiable? Select all that apply.

    a. Failing to breastfeed for up to a year after pregnancy

    b. Early menarche or late menopause

    c. Postmenopausal use of estrogen and progestins

    d. Not having children until after age 30

    e. Previous abnormal breast biopsy

13. A nurse is educating a client on the technique for performing breast self-examination. Which instruction should the nurse include in the teaching plan with regard to the different degrees of pressure that need to be applied on the breast?
    a. Light pressure midway into the tissue
    b. Medium pressure around the areolar area
    c. Medium pressure on the skin throughout
    d. Hard pressure applied down to the ribs

14. A female client with metastatic breast disease is receiving trastuzumab as part of her immunotherapy. The client has nausea, fatigue, and diarrhea, appears jaundiced, and has a distended abdomen. What would the nurse do **next**?
    a. Notify the health care provider
    b. Decrease the trastuzumab infusion rate
    c. Assess the client's white blood cell count
    d. Continue to monitor the client

15. A nurse is caring for a female client undergoing radiation therapy after her breast surgery. The client is refusing to eat and states she does not have a desire to eat at this time. Which action should the nurse take **first**?
    a. Continue to monitor the client
    b. Notify the health care provider
    c. Begin parenteral nutrition
    d. Assess the client's BMI

16. A nurse is caring for a client who has just had her intraductal papilloma removed through a surgical procedure. What instructions should the nurse give this client as part of her care?
    a. Apply warm compresses to the affected breast
    b. Continue monthly breast self-examinations
    c. Wear a supportive bra 24 hours per day
    d. Refrain from consuming salt in diet

17. Lumpectomy is a treatment option for clients diagnosed with breast cancer with tumors smaller than 5 cm. For which clients is lumpectomy contraindicated? Select all that apply.
    a. Client who has had an early menarche or late onset of menopause
    b. Client who has had previous radiation to the affected breast
    c. Client who has failed to breastfeed for up to 1 year after pregnancy
    d. Client whose connective tissue is reported to be sensitive to radiation
    e. Client whose surgery will not result in a clean margin of tissue

18. A 38-year-old female client has to undergo lymph node surgery in conjunction with mastectomy. The client is likely to experience lymphedema due to the surgery. Postsurgery, which factors will make the client more susceptible to lymphedema? Select all that apply.
    a. Using the affected arm for drawing blood or measuring blood pressure
    b. Engaging in activities like gardening without using gloves
    c. Not consuming foods that are rich in phytochemicals
    d. Not wearing a well-fitted compression sleeve
    e. Not consuming a diet high in fiber and protein

19. A 33-year-old female client reports yellow nipple discharge and a pain in her breasts a week before menses that dissipates on the onset of menses. Diagnosis reveals that the client is experiencing fibrocystic breast changes. Which instructions should the nurse offer the client to help alleviate the condition? Select all that apply.
    a. Increase fluid intake steadily
    b. Avoid caffeine
    c. Practice good hand-washing techniques
    d. Maintain a low-fat diet
    e. Take diuretics as recommended

20. A nurse is educating a 43-year-old female client about required lifestyle changes to help avoid breast cancer. Which instructions regarding diet and food habits should the nurse include in the teaching plan? Select all that apply.
    a. Restrict intake of salted foods
    b. Limit intake of processed foods
    c. Consume seven or more portions of complex carbohydrates daily
    d. Increase liquid intake to 3 L daily
    e. Consume at least five servings of proteins daily

Benign Disorders of the Female Reproductive Tract

Learning Objectives

Upon completion of the chapter, you will be able to:

- Define the key terms.
- Identify the major pelvic relaxation disorders in terms of etiology, management, and nursing interventions.
- Outline the nursing management needed for the most common benign reproductive disorders in women.
- Evaluate urinary incontinence in terms of pathology, clinical manifestations, treatment options, and effect on quality of life.
- Compare the various benign growths in terms of their symptoms and management.
- Analyze the emotional impact of polycystic ovarian syndrome and the nurse's role as a counselor, educator, and advocate.

SECTION I: ASSESSING YOUR UNDERSTANDING

Activity A FILL IN THE BLANKS

1. _____ occurs when the posterior bladder wall protrudes downward through the anterior vaginal wall.

2. Uterine _____ occurs when the uterus descends through the pelvic floor and into the vaginal canal.

3. A _____ is a silicone or plastic device that is placed into the vagina to support the uterus, bladder, and rectum as a space-filling device.

4. _____ are small benign growths that may be associated with chronic inflammation, an abnormal local response to increased levels of estrogen, or local congestion of the cervical vasculature.

5. Uterine fibroids, or _____, are benign proliferations composed of smooth muscle and fibrous connective tissue in the uterus.

6. _____ exercises strengthen the pelvic floor muscles to support the inner organs and prevent further prolapse.

7. Rectocele occurs when the _____ relaxes and pushes against or into the posterior vaginal wall.

8. Weakened pelvic floor musculature also prevents complete closure of the _____, resulting in urine leakage during moments of physical activity.

9. _____, or irregular, acyclic uterine bleeding, is the most frequent clinical manifestation of women with endometrial polyps.

10. _____ ultrasound is used to distinguish fluid-filled ovarian cysts from a solid mass.

Activity B MATCHING

Match the benign disorders of the female reproductive tract in Column A with their correct definitions in Column B.

Column A

_____ **1.** Pelvic organ prolapsed

_____ **2.** Stress incontinence

_____ **3.** Uterine fibroids

_____ **4.** Polycystic ovarian syndrome

_____ **5.** Urge incontinence

Column B

a. Abnormal descent or herniation of the pelvic organs from their original attachment sites or their normal positions in the pelvis

b. Benign tumors composed of muscular and fibrous tissue in the uterus

c. Presence of multiple inactive follicle cysts within the ovary that interfere with ovarian function

d. Precipitous loss of urine, preceded by a strong urge to void, with increased bladder pressure and detrusor contraction

e. Accidental leakage of urine that occurs with increased pressure on the bladder from coughing, sneezing, laughing, or physical exertion

Activity C SHORT ANSWERS

Briefly answer the following.

1. What are the causes of pelvic organ prolapse?

_____

_____

_____

2. What are Kegel exercises?

_____

_____

_____

3. What are the causes of urinary incontinence?

_____

_____

_____

4. What is the Colpexin sphere?

_____

_____

_____

5. What is uterine artery embolization (UAE)?

_____

_____

_____

6. What are Bartholin cysts?

_____

_____

_____

SECTION II: APPLYING YOUR KNOWLEDGE

Activity D CASE STUDY

Consider this scenario and answer the questions.

Mrs. Scott, age 57, comes in for a gynecologic examination and reports to the nurse that she "feels like something is coming down in her vagina." She has chronic smoker's cough. Upon completion of a pelvic exam, uterine prolapse is diagnosed.

1. What factors may contribute to the development of this disorder?

_____

_____

_____

2. What are the symptoms of uterine prolapse that may affect Mrs. Scott's daily activities?

_____

_____

_____

3. What are the nonsurgical and surgical interventions available to Mrs. Scott?

_____

_____

_____

SECTION III: PRACTICING FOR NCLEX

Activity E NCLEX-STYLE QUESTIONS

Answer the following questions.

1. A 40-year-old client arrives at the community health center experiencing a strange dragging feeling in the vagina. She stated that "at times it feels as if there is a lump" there as well. Which condition may be an indication of these symptoms?

   a. Urinary incontinence

   b. Endocervical polyps

   c. Pelvic organ prolapse

   d. Uterine fibroids

2. A nurse is caring for a client for whom estrogen replacement therapy has been recommended for pelvic organ prolapse. Which nursing intervention is the **most** appropriate for the nurse to implement before the start of the therapy?

   a. Discuss the effective dose of estrogen required to treat the client

   b. Evaluate the client to validate her risk for complications

   c. Discuss the dietary modifications following therapy

   d. Discuss the cost of estrogen replacement therapy

3. A nurse is caring for a female client with symptoms of first-degree pelvic organ prolapse. Which instruction related to dietary and lifestyle modifications should the nurse provide to the client to help prevent pelvic relaxation and chronic problems later in life?

   a. Increase dietary fiber

   b. Avoid caffeine products

   c. Avoid excess intake of fluids

   d. Increase high-impact aerobics

4. Myomectomy is recommended to a client for removal of uterine fibroids. The client is concerned about the surgery and wants to know if there are any associated disadvantages. Which is a disadvantage of myomectomy?

   a. Fertility is jeopardized.

   b. Uterus is scarred and adhesions may form.

   c. Uterine walls are weakened.

   d. Fibroids may grow back.

5. Kegel exercises are recommended for a client with pelvic organ prolapse. Which should the nurse inform the client about the exercises?

   a. They should be performed after food intake.

   b. They alleviate mild prolapse symptoms.

   c. They are not recommended after surgery.

   d. They increase blood pressure.

6. A nurse is assessing a 45-year-old client for uterine fibroids. Which are the predisposing factors for uterine fibroids? Select all that apply.

   a. Age

   b. Nulliparity

   c. Smoking

   d. Obesity

   e. Hyperinsulinemia

7. A nurse is caring for a client who has been prescribed gonadotropin-releasing hormone (GnRH) medication for uterine fibroids. For which side effect of GnRH medications should the nurse monitor the client?

   a. Increased vaginal discharge

   b. Vaginal dryness

   c. Urinary tract infections

   d. Vaginitis

8. A nurse is caring for a 32-year-old client for whom pessary usage is recommended for uterine prolapse. Which instructions should the nurse include in the teaching plan for the client concerning the pessary?

   a. Avoid jogging and jumping

   b. Wear a girdle or abdominal support

   c. Report any discomfort with urination and defecation

   d. Avoid lifting heavy objects

9. A nurse is caring for a 45-year-old client using a pessary to help decrease leakage of urine and support a prolapsed vagina. Which recommendation is **most** commonly provided to a client regarding pessary care?

   a. Douche vaginal area with diluted vinegar or hydrogen peroxide

   b. Remove the pessary twice weekly, and clean it with soap and water

   c. Use estrogen cream to make the vaginal mucosa more resistant to erosion

   d. Remove the pessary before sleeping or intercourse

10. A client with abnormal uterine bleeding is diagnosed with small ovarian cysts. The nurse has to educate the client on the importance of routine checkups. Which assessment is **most** appropriate for this client's condition?

    a. Monitor gonadotropin level every month

    b. Monitor blood sugar level every 15 days

    c. Schedule periodic Pap smears

    d. Schedule ultrasound every 3 to 6 months

11. A client with large uterine fibroids is scheduled to undergo a hysterectomy. Which intervention should the nurse perform as a part of the preoperative care for the client?

    a. Teach turning, deep breathing, and coughing

    b. Instruct the client to reduce activity level

    c. Educate the client on the need for pelvic rest

    d. Instruct the client to avoid a high-fat diet

12. A 40-year-old client reports low back pain after standing for a long time. The primary care provider has diagnosed the client with pelvic organ prolapse. The nurse correctly recognizes which clients are likely not candidates for corrective surgery for pelvic organ prolapse. Select all that apply.

    a. Client with low back pain and pelvic pressure

    b. Client at high risk of recurrent prolapse after surgery

    c. Client who is morbidly obese before surgery

    d. Client who has severe pelvic organ prolapse

    e. Client who has chronic obstructive pulmonary disease

13. A nurse is caring for a female client with urinary incontinence. Which instructions should the nurse include in the client's teaching plan to reduce the incidence or severity of incontinence? Select all that apply.

    a. Continue pelvic floor exercises

    b. Increase fiber in the diet

    c. Increase intake of orange juice

    d. Control blood glucose levels

    e. Wipe from back to front

14. A client has undergone an abdominal hysterectomy to remove uterine fibroids. Which interventions should a nurse perform as a part of the postoperative care for the client? Select all that apply.

    a. Administer analgesics promptly and use a patient-controlled analgesia (PCA) pump

    b. Avoid pillows and changing positions frequently

    c. Avoid intake of excess carbonated beverages in the diet

    d. Frequent ambulation

    e. Administer antiemetics to control nausea and vomiting

15. A client who reported changes in her normal voiding patterns and altered bowel habits is diagnosed with polycystic ovarian syndrome. Which instruction is **most** appropriate for the nurse to provide the client to help alleviate her condition?

    a. Adhere to follow-up care

    b. Increase intake of fiber-rich foods

    c. Increase fluid intake

    d. Perform Kegel exercises

CHAPTER 8

Cancers of the Female Reproductive Tract

Learning Objectives

Upon completion of the chapter, you will be able to:

- Define the key terms in the chapter.
- Evaluate the major modifiable risk factors for reproductive tract cancers.
- Analyze the screening methods and treatment modalities for cancers of the female reproductive tract.
- Outline the nursing management needed for the most common malignant reproductive tract cancers in women.
- Examine lifestyle changes and health screenings that can reduce the risk of or prevent reproductive tract cancers.
- Assess at least three website resources available for a woman diagnosed with cancer of the reproductive tract.
- Appraise the psychological distress felt by women diagnosed with cancer, and outline information that can help them to cope.

SECTION I: ASSESSING YOUR UNDERSTANDING

Activity A FILL IN THE BLANKS

1. High-grade _____ can progress to invasive cervical cancer; the progression takes up to 2 years.

2. _____ is a microscopic examination of the lower genital tract with use of a magnifying instrument.

3. _____ is the use of liquid nitrogen to freeze abnormal cervical tissue.

4. _____ or uterine cancer is a malignant neoplastic growth of the uterine lining.

5. Pap smear results are classified by the _____ system.

6. _____ refers to the surgical removal of the uterus.

7. _____ is a biologic tumor marker associated with ovarian cancer.

8. The two major types of vulvar intraepithelial neoplasia (VIN) are classic (undifferentiated) and _____ (differentiated).

9. Ovarian cancer usually originates in the ovarian _____.

10. _____ cell carcinomas that begin in the epithelial lining of the vagina tend to spread early by directly invading the bladder and rectal walls.

Activity B MATCHING

Match the stages of endometrial cancer in Column A with the relevant organs affected during that stage in Column B.

Column A

____ **1.** Stage I

____ **2.** Stage II

____ **3.** Stage III

____ **4.** Stage IV

Column B

a. Cervix

b. Muscle wall of the uterus

c. Bladder mucosa, with distant metastases to the lungs, the liver, and bone

d. Bowel or vagina, with metastases to pelvic lymph nodes

Activity C SEQUENCING

Given below, in random order, are some of the steps performed by a nurse while assisting with the collection of a Pap smear. Choose the most likely sequence in which they would have occurred.

1. Provide support to the client as the practitioner obtains a sample.

2. Drape the client with a sheet, leaving the perineal area exposed.

3. Wash hands thoroughly.

4. Transfer the specimen to a container or a slide.

5. Position the client in stirrups or foot pedals so that her knees fall outward.

6. Assemble the equipment.

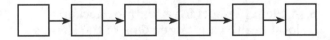

Activity D SHORT ANSWERS

Briefly answer the following.

1. What are the risk factors associated with cervical cancer?

_____

_____

_____

2. What are the treatment options for endometrial cancer?

_____

_____

_____

3. What are the risk factors for ovarian cancer?

_____

_____

_____

4. What is a transvaginal ultrasound used for?

_____

_____

_____

5. What are the nursing interventions when caring for clients with cancers of the female reproductive tract?

_____

_____

_____

6. What are the diagnostic options for endometrial cancer?

_____

_____

_____

SECTION II: APPLYING YOUR KNOWLEDGE

Activity E CASE STUDY

Consider this scenario and answer the questions.

Amy, age 60, has been diagnosed with ovarian cancer. Because this cancer develops slowly, remains silent, and is without symptoms until the cancer is far advanced, it is considered one of the worst gynecologic malignancies.

1. What are the most common symptoms of ovarian cancer?

_____

_____

_____

2. There is still no adequate screening test to identify early cancer of the ovary. What suggestions should a nurse give a client to facilitate early detection of this type of cancer?

_____

_____

_____

3. State the nursing diagnoses related to malignancies of the reproductive tract.

_____

_____

_____

4. Explain the four stages of ovarian cancer.

_____

_____

_____

SECTION III: PRACTICING FOR NCLEX

Activity F NCLEX-STYLE QUESTIONS

Answer the following questions.

1. A nurse is educating a 25-year-old client with a family history of cervical cancer. Which test should the nurse inform the client about to detect cervical cancer at an early stage?

   a. Papanicolaou test

   b. Blood tests for mutations in the BRCA genes

   c. CA-125 blood test

   d. Transvaginal ultrasound

2. A client presents for her annual Pap test. She wants to know about the risk factors that are associated with cervical cancer. Which should the nurse inform the client is a risk factor for cervical cancer?

   a. Early age at first intercourse

   b. Obesity (at least 50 lb [22.7 kg] overweight)

   c. Hypertension

   d. Infertility

3. A client is waiting for the results of an endometrial biopsy for suspected endometrial cancer. She wants to know more about endometrial cancer and asks the nurse about the available treatment options. Which treatment information should the nurse give the client?

   a. Surgery involves removal of the uterus only.

   b. In advanced cancers, radiation and chemotherapy are used instead of surgery.

   c. Surgery involves removal of the uterus, fallopian tubes, and ovaries; adjuvant therapy is used if relevant.

   d. Follow-up care after the relevant treatment should last for at least 6 months after the treatment.

4. A 65-year-old client presents at a local community health care center for a routine checkup. While obtaining her medical history, the nurse learns that the client had her menarche when she was 13 years old. She experienced menopause at 51. She is between 5 and 10 lb (2.3 and 4.5 kg) underweight but is otherwise in good physical condition. The nurse should inform the client of which factor that increases the client's risk of getting ovarian cancer?

   a. The client's age at menarche

   b. The client's present age

   c. The client's age at menopause

   d. The client's weight

5. A client presents at a community health care center for a routine checkup. The client wants to know about any tests that can effectively detect ovarian cancer early. About which test that can aid in the detection of ovarian cancer should the nurse inform the client?

   a. Pap smear

   b. Serum CA-125

   c. Yearly bimanual pelvic examinations

   d. Regular x-rays of the pelvic area

6. A client presents for a routine checkup at a local health care center. One of the client's distant relatives died of ovarian cancer, and the client wants to know about measures that can reduce the risk of ovarian cancer. The nurse informs the client about which measure to reduce the risk of ovarian cancer?

   a. Provide genetic counseling and thorough assessment.

   b. Instruct the client to avoid use of oral contraceptives.

   c. Instruct the client to avoid breastfeeding.

   d. Instruct the client to use perineal talc or hygiene sprays.

7. A nurse is caring for a client who has been diagnosed with genital warts due to human papilloma virus (HPV). The nurse explains to the client that HPV increases the risk of vulvar cancer. Which preventive measure to reduce the risk of vulvar cancer should the nurse explain to the client?

   a. Genital examination should be done only by the primary health care provider.

   b. Genital examination should be done by the client.

   c. The client should avoid tight undergarments.

   d. The client should use over-the-counter (OTC) drugs for self-medication of suspicious lesions.

8. When working in a local community health care center, a nurse is frequently asked about cervical cancer and ways to prevent it. Which information should be provided by the nurse? Select all that apply.

   a. Encourage the use of an intrauterine device (IUD) for contraception.

   b. Encourage cessation of smoking and drinking.

   c. Encourage prevention of sexually transmitted infections (STIs) to reduce risk factors.

   d. Avoid stress and high blood pressure.

   e. Counsel teenagers to avoid early sexual activity.

9. The endometrial biopsy of a client reveals cancerous cells, and the primary health care provider has diagnosed it as endometrial cancer. Which responsibilities of the nurse are part of the treatment of the client? Select all that apply.

   a. Make sure the client understands all the available treatment options.

   b. Inform the client that changes in sexuality are normal and need not be reported.

   c. Inform the client about the possible advantages of a support group.

   d. Offer the family explanations and emotional support throughout the treatment.

   e. Inform the client that follow-up care is not required unless something unusual occurs.

10. A nurse is conducting a session on education about cancers of the reproductive tract and is explaining the importance of visiting a health care professional if certain unusual symptoms appear. Which should the nurse include in her list of symptoms that merit a visit to a health care professional for further evaluation? Select all that apply.

    a. Irregular bowel movements

    b. Irregular vaginal bleeding

    c. Increase in urinary frequency

    d. Persistent low backache not related to standing

    e. Elevated or discolored vulvar lesions

11. A client has been referred for a colposcopy by the physician. The client wants to know more about the examination. Which information regarding a colposcopy should the nurse give to the client?

    a. Client may feel pain in the vaginal area during the examination.

    b. The test is conducted because of abnormal results in Pap smears.

    c. Intercourse should be avoided for at least a week afterward.

    d. Client may experience pain during urination for a week following the test.

12. The results of a Pap smear test have been classified as atypical squamous cells with possible HSIL (ASC-H) as per the 2001 Bethesda system. Which interpretation of the result is correct?

    a. Repeat the Pap smear in 4 to 6 months, or refer for a colposcopy.

    b. Refer for a colposcopy without human papilloma virus (HPV) testing.

    c. Immediate colposcopy; follow-up is based on the results of findings.

    d. No need for any further Pap smear screenings.

13. Which risk factors are associated with vaginal cancer? Select all that apply.

    a. Advancing age

    b. HIV infection

    c. Persistent ovulation over time

    d. Smoking

    e. Hormone replacement therapy for more than 10 years

14. A postmenopausal woman presents to the clinic with painless vaginal bleeding. The health care provider wants to assess for endometrial cancer. The nurse would anticipate the health care provider ordering which procedure **first**?

a. A transvaginal ultrasound

b. An endometrial biopsy

c. A hysterectomy

d. Chemotherapy and radiation

15. A 55-year-old client presents to the clinic with persistent vulvar pruritus, burning, and a lump. She states she has had the symptoms for 5 months and has been trying to treat them with over-the-counter creams. She has a history of multiple sexual partners and HPV and is a smoker. What should the nurse do **next**?

a. Prepare the client for a biopsy of the lesion

b. Determine what creams the client has used

c. Assess how much the client smokes daily

d. Schedule the client for cryosurgery

Violence and Abuse

Learning Objectives

After completion of the chapter, you should be able to:

- Define the key terms.
- Examine the incidence of violence in women.
- Characterize the cycle of violence and appropriate interventions.
- Evaluate the various myths and facts about violence.
- Analyze the dynamics of rape and sexual abuse.
- Select the resources available to women experiencing abuse.
- Outline the role of the nurse who cares for abused women.

SECTION I: ASSESSING YOUR UNDERSTANDING

Activity A FILL IN THE BLANKS

1. A victim of _____ woman syndrome has experienced deliberate and repeated physical or sexual assault at the hands of an intimate partner.

2. _____ is any type of sexual exploitation between blood relatives or surrogate relatives before the victim reaches 18 years of age.

3. _____ rape is sexual activity between an adult and a person below the age of 18 and is considered to have occurred despite the willingness of the underage person.

4. _____, also known as roofies, forget pills, and the drop drug, is a common date rape drug.

5. Female genital mutilation, also known as female _____, refers to procedures involving injury, or partial or total removal of the female genital organs.

6. _____ rape involves someone being forced to have sex by a person he or she knows.

7. Forcing objects into a woman's vagina against her will constitutes _____ abuse.

8. Increased emotional arousal, exaggerated startle response, and irritability are some of the symptoms of _____ during post-traumatic stress disorder (PTSD).

9. To assess for the presence of _____ reactions during PTSD, the nurse should find out if the client feels numb emotionally or tries to avoid thinking of the trauma.

10. During the _____ phase, the abuser is sorry for the abuse inflicted.

Activity B MATCHING

Match the four phases of rape recovery in Column A with the survivor's responses in Column B.

Column A

_____ **1.** Acute phase (disorganization)

_____ **2.** Outward adjustment phase (denial)

_____ **3.** Reorganization

_____ **4.** Integration and recovery

Column B

a. The survivor attempts to make life adjustments by moving or changing jobs and using emotional distancing to cope

b. The survivor appears outwardly composed, refuses to discuss the assault, and denies need for counseling

c. The survivor begins to feel safe, starts to trust others, and may become an advocate for other rape victims

d. The survivor experiences shock, fear, disbelief, anger, shame, guilt, and feelings of being unclean

Activity C SEQUENCING

Given below are the interventions that a nurse performs when caring for a client who has been physically or sexually abused. Choose the order in which the interventions would have occurred.

1. Document and report findings.

2. Screen for abuse during every health care visit.

3. Isolate the client from her partner immediately.

4. Ask direct and indirect questions about abuse.

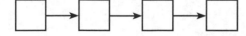

Activity D SHORT ANSWERS

Briefly answer the following.

1. What is the cycle of violence?

_____

_____

_____

2. What is financial abuse?

_____

_____

_____

3. What are the potential nursing diagnoses related to violence against women?

_____

_____

_____

4. What is PTSD? What are its symptoms?

_____

_____

_____

5. What signs should the nurse assess the client for, to find out if she is a victim of abuse?

_____

_____

_____

6. What are the effects of physical abuse on the pregnant woman?

_____

_____

_____

SECTION II: APPLYING YOUR KNOWLEDGE

Activity E CASE STUDY

Consider this scenario and answer the questions.

A visit to a health care agency is an ideal time for women to be assessed for violence. Suzanne, a married 24-year-old, presents to the Women's Center with complaints of pelvic pain, headaches, and sleep disruption. The triage nurse in the center recognizes that Suzanne became uncomfortable when discussing her marital relationship.

1. What are common symptoms of suspected physical abuse?

   _____

   _____

   _____

2. Explain why Suzanne may not seek help when she is in an abusive relationship.

   _____

   _____

   _____

3. What appropriate strategies should the nurse suggest that might help Suzanne to manage the situation?

   _____

   _____

   _____

SECTION III: PRACTICING FOR NCLEX

Activity F NCLEX-STYLE QUESTIONS

Answer the following questions.

1. A nurse is caring for a client who is being hospitalized for physical injuries. She later confides to the nurse that the injuries are a result of a physical assault by her partner when he was drunk. The client feels degraded and ashamed but realizes that her partner was under the influence of alcohol. How should the nurse respond to this client?

   a. "Violent tendencies have gone on for generations; you need to accept it as part of life."

   b. "Try to avoid provoking your partner in any way that might lead to abuse."

   c. "Being drunk is not an excuse for physically assaulting an intimate partner."

   d. "Violence occurs to only a small percentage of women who deserve it."

2. A client is receiving treatment for injuries sustained during a fight with her partner. The nurse observes that the partner visits her daily in the hospital and appears very solicitous and contrite. When questioned, the client tries to convince the nurse that her partner always apologizes and brings gifts after a fight. Which information should the nurse provide this client?

   a. "Sometimes people do things that cause them to be a victim of physical abuse."

   b. "Your partner seems to be genuinely contrite."

   c. "You should try not to upset your partner in the future."

   d. "Although your partner seems sorry, often they will repeat this behavior in the future."

3. A nurse is caring for a client who has been admitted with an ear infection. While discussing her partner with the nurse, the client says that her lover's behavior is "threatening" and "intimidating" at times, even though he has not physically harmed her. She wants to know what emotional abuse is. Which statement **best** describes an example of emotional abuse?

   a. Being overly watchful of the client's every move

   b. Throwing objects at the client

   c. Destroying valued possessions or attacking pets

   d. Forcing the client to have intercourse

4. A nurse is conducting an awareness session on sexual abuse, and she is explaining the psychological profile of an average abuser. Which trait is often displayed by abusers?

   a. They have parents who are divorced.

   b. They exhibit antisocial behaviors.

   c. They belong to the low-income group.

   d. They are usually physically imposing.

5. A nurse is working in a community hospital situated in an area with a history of grievous assaults on women, including rape. The nurse discovers that most rape victims come to the hospital but leave without seeking medical treatment. Which intervention should the nurse perform to ensure that rape victims get legal and medical aid?

   a. Let them wait in waiting rooms to collect their thoughts before approaching them

   b. Treat them as any other client to make them feel more comfortable

   c. Focus on treating them rather than on collecting evidence

   d. Ensure that the appropriate law enforcement agencies are apprised of the incident

6. A client comes to a local community health care facility for a routine checkup. While talking to the nurse, the client happens to mention that every time she has a serious fight with her husband, he forces her to have intercourse with him. The client seems to be very disturbed when revealing this to the nurse. Which is an appropriate response by the nurse?

   a. "Your husband is just trying to reconcile using intimacy."

   b. "It's okay in cases of fights where you're really at fault."

   c. "This behavior is considered sexual abuse."

   d. "Such behavior is considered normal in a married couple."

7. A 13-year-old immigrant from Asia is admitted to the health care facility with vaginal bleeding. A genital examination reveals unhealed circumcision wounds. The client can understand limited English but cannot speak the language fluently. The service of an interpreter is employed. What are the points the nurse should keep in mind when interacting with this client?

   a. She is still a child so convey important information in precise medical terms to ease understanding

   b. Allow the interpreter to question the client directly to assist with data gathering

   c. Use pictures and diagrams to supplement the questions and answers of the client's understanding

   d. Condemn the cultural practice and explain why it is wrong to the client

8. A woman comes to a local community health care facility with her partner. She has a broken arm and bruises on the face that she reports were caused by a fall. The nature of the injuries, however, causes the nurse to be convinced that this is a case of physical abuse. Which intervention should the nurse perform?

   a. Ask the partner directly if he was responsible

   b. Attempt to interview the woman in private

   c. Tell the partner to leave the room immediately

   d. Question the client about the injury in front of the partner

9. A nurse is caring for a client who was raped at gunpoint. The client does not want any photos taken of her injuries. The client also does not want the police to be informed about the incident, even though state laws require reporting life-threatening injuries. Which intervention should the nurse perform to document and report the findings of the case?

   a. Use direct quotes and specific language

   b. Obtain photos to substantiate the client's case in a court of law

   c. Document only descriptions of medical interventions taken

   d. Respect the client's opinion and avoid informing the police

10. A nurse observes telltale signs of injuries from physical abuse on the face and neck of a female client. When questioned, the client tells the nurse that the injuries are the result of a physical attack by her partner and that she has developed palpitations thereafter. Which action should the nurse take to gain the trust of the client and enhance the nurse–client relationship?

    a. Offer referrals so the client can get help that will allow her to heal

    b. Tell the client to forget about the incident to avoid the trauma

    c. Inform the client that there is no connection between the violence and palpitations

    d. Confirm with the partner whether the client's story is true

11. A nurse is caring for a rape victim who was just brought to the local emergency care facility. Which interventions should the nurse perform to minimize risk of pregnancy in this client?

    a. Administer prescribed double dose of emergency contraceptive pills

    b. Wait for first signs of pregnancy before taking action

    c. Apply spermicidal cream or gel near the vaginal area upon arrival

    d. Administer prescribed regular oral contraceptive pills

12. A nurse is caring for a pregnant client and discovers signs of bruises near her neck. On questioning, the nurse learns that the bruises were caused by her husband. The client tells the nurse that her husband had stopped abusing her some time ago, but this was the first time during the pregnancy that she was assaulted. She blames herself because she admits to not paying enough attention to her husband. Which facts about abuse during pregnancy should the nurse tell the client to convince her that the abuse was not her fault? Select all that apply.

    a. Abuse is a result of concern for the unborn child when the mother doesn't fulfill her responsibilities toward the newborn.

    b. Abuse is a result of resentment toward the interference of the growing fetus and change in the woman's shape.

    c. Abuse is a result of the perception of the partner that the baby will be a competitor after he or she is born.

    d. Abuse is a result of insecurity and jealousy of the pregnancy and the responsibilities it brings.

    e. Most men exhibit violent reactions during pregnancy as a way of coping with the stress.

13. A nurse is caring for a 16-year-old female immigrant. The nurse wishes to assess if the client is a victim of human trafficking. Which questions should the nurse ask? Select all that apply.

    a. "Can you leave your job or situation if you wish?"

    b. "Can you come and go as you please?"

    c. "Are you enrolled in school?"

    d. "What do your parents and siblings do?"

    e. "Is there a lock on your door at home so you cannot get out?"

14. A nurse is working in a local community health care facility where she frequently encounters victims of abuse. For which signs should the nurse assess to find out if a client is a victim of abuse? Select all that apply.

    a. Affected by STIs frequently

    b. Mental health problems such as depression, anxiety, or substance abuse

    c. Injuries on the face, head, and neck

    d. Partner of the suspected victim seems relaxed and not overly worried

    e. Reported history of the injury is inconsistent with the presenting problem

15. A nurse is interviewing a rape victim who was assaulted 6 months ago. Which questions should the nurse ask the client to know the extent of physical symptoms of PTSD? Select all that apply.

    a. "Are you having trouble sleeping?"

    b. "Have you felt irritable or experienced outbursts of anger?"

    c. "Do you have heart palpitations or sweating?"

    d. "Do you feel numb emotionally?"

    e. "Do you ever feel as you are reliving the event?"

CHAPTER 10

Fetal Development and Genetics

Learning Objectives

Upon completion of the chapter, you will be able to:

- Characterize the process of fertilization, implantation, and cell differentiation.
- Examine the functions of the placenta, umbilical cord, and amniotic fluid.
- Outline normal fetal development from conception through birth.
- Compare the various inheritance patterns, including nontraditional patterns of inheritance.
- Analyze examples of ethical and legal issues surrounding genetic testing.
- Research the role of the nurse in genetic counseling and genetic-related activities.

SECTION I: ASSESSING YOUR UNDERSTANDING

Activity A   FILL IN THE BLANKS

1. _____ is one of two or more alternative versions of a gene at a given position or locus on a chromosome that imparts the same characteristic of that gene.

2. Any change in gene structure or location leads to a _____, which may alter the type and amount of protein produced.

3. Human beings typically have 22 pairs of nonsex chromosomes or _____ and 1 pair of sex chromosomes.

4. The _____ originates from the ectoderm germ layer during the early stages of embryonic development; it is a thin protective membrane that contains the amniotic fluid.

5. _____ are long, continuous strands of DNA that carry genetic information.

6. The _____ reaches the uterine cavity about 72 hours after fertilization.

7. The pictorial analysis of the number, form, and size of an individual's chromosomes is termed _____.

8. A genetic disorder is a disease caused by an abnormality in an individual's genetic material or _____.

9. The genotype, together with environmental variation that influences the individual, determines the _____, or the observed, outward characteristics of an individual.

Activity B LABELING

Consider the following figure. Identify and describe what the figure depicts.

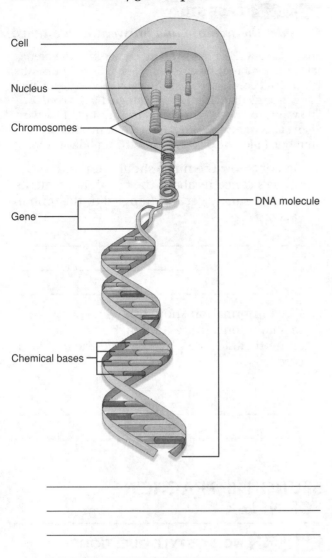

Cell

Nucleus

Chromosomes

Gene

DNA molecule

Chemical bases

_____

_____

_____

_____

_____

Activity C MATCHING

Match the terms related to genetics in Column A with their descriptions in Column B.

Column A

____ **1.** Monosomies

____ **2.** Trisomies

____ **3.** Mosaicism

____ **4.** Homozygous

Column B

a. Both alleles for a trait are the same in the individual

b. Chromosomal abnormalities that do not show up in every cell

c. There is only one copy of a particular chromosome instead of the usual pair

d. There are three copies of a particular chromosome instead of the usual two

Activity D SEQUENCING

Write the correct sequence of events in human development after fertilization in the boxes provided below.

1. Formation of the placenta

2. Development of the fluid-filled blastocyst

3. Development of the morula

4. Formation of the amnion

5. Development of the trophoblast

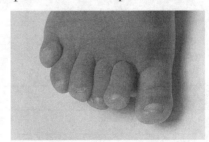

Activity E SHORT ANSWERS

Briefly answer the following.

1. How does conception occur?

   _____

   _____

   _____

2. What are the different stages of fetal development?

   _____

   _____

   _____

3. What determines the sex of a zygote?

   _____

   _____

   _____

4. What happens during differentiation of the zygote?

   _____

   _____

   _____

5. What is amniotic fluid?

   _____

   _____

   _____

6. What are the hormones produced by the placenta?

   _____

   _____

   _____

SECTION II: APPLYING YOUR KNOWLEDGE

Activity F CASE STUDY

Consider the scenario and answer the questions.

Shana is 16 weeks pregnant and comes into the prenatal clinic for a routine check-up. She tells the nurse she is worried because she feels the baby moving a lot and has concerns that "it might get tangled in its cord." She wants to know if this could be true and, if so, why. Shana also wants to know about the functions of amniotic fluid, the placenta, and the umbilical cord.

1. Describe how the nurse should respond to Shana's concerns about the baby's movements and potentially getting "tangled in the umbilical cord."

   _____

   _____

   _____

2. What information should the nurse provide to Shana concerning the function of the amniotic fluid, the placenta, and the umbilical cord?

   _____

   _____

   _____

SECTION III: PRACTICING FOR NCLEX

Activity G NCLEX-STYLE QUESTIONS

Answer the following questions.

1. The nurse is counseling a couple who are concerned because the woman has achondroplasia in her family. The woman is not affected. Which statement by the couple indicates the need for more teaching?

   a. "If the mother has the gene, then there is a 50% chance of passing it on."

   b. "If the father doesn't have the gene, then his son won't have achondroplasia."

   c. "If the father has the gene, then there is a 50% chance of passing it on."

   d. "Since neither one of us has the disorder, we won't pass it on."

2. A client has been informed that the result of her pregnancy test indicates that she is 3 weeks pregnant. Which instructions should the nurse give the client in regard to her condition?

    a. Avoid exercising during pregnancy

    b. Discontinue intercourse until after the baby is born

    c. Stop using drugs, alcohol, and tobacco

    d. Wear comfortable clothes that are not tight or restrictive

3. A nurse is obtaining the genetic history of a pregnant client by eliciting historical information about her family members. Which question is **most** appropriate for the nurse to ask?

    a. "Were there any instances of premature birth in the family?"

    b. "Is there a family history of drinking or drug abuse?"

    c. "What was the cause and age of death for deceased family members?"

    d. "Were there any instances of depression during pregnancy?"

4. A 25-year-old client wants to know if her baby boy is at risk for Down syndrome, because one of her distant relatives was born with it. Which information would the nurse share with the client while counseling her about Down syndrome?

    a. Instances of Down syndrome in the family greatly increases the risk for the baby also having Down syndrome.

    b. Children with Down syndrome have extra genetic material in the 21 chromosomes that occurs during development of the sperm or egg.

    c. Down syndrome occurs only in females, and there is no risk as the baby is male.

    d. Children with Down syndrome are usually born to older mothers.

5. A nurse is interviewing the family members of a pregnant client to obtain a genetic history. While asking questions, which information would be **most** important?

    a. Socioeconomic status of the family members

    b. Avoidance of questions on race or ethnic background

    c. Specific physical characteristics of family members

    d. If couples are related to each other or have blood ties

6. A pregnant client and her husband have had a session with a genetic specialist. What is the role of the nurse after the client has seen a specialist?

    a. Identify the best decision to be taken for the client

    b. Refer the client to another specialist for a second opinion

    c. Review what has been discussed with the specialist

    d. Refer the client for further diagnostic and screening tests

7. A nurse is caring for a 32-year-old Jewish client who is pregnant with a female baby. The parents are not directly related by blood. The mother reports that her husband's cousin had an infant born with Tay–Sachs disease that died 2 years ago and she is concerned about her baby. Which information does the nurse need to give the client to help alleviate her concerns regarding her baby having the same disease?

    a. Tay–Sachs disease affects only male infants so there is no problem with her baby.

    b. The age of the client increases the susceptibility of the baby to Tay–Sachs disease.

    c. There is no risk of Tay–Sachs disease because the parents are not related by blood.

    d. There is a risk to the baby based upon the Jewish background so genetic testing would be recommended.

8. A pregnant client arrives at the community health center for a routine check-up. She informs the nurse that a relative on her mother's side has hemophilia, and she wants to know the chances of her child acquiring hemophilia. Which characteristics of hemophilia should the nurse explain to the client to help her understand the odds of acquiring the disease? Select all that apply.

   a. Affected individuals will have affected parents.

   b. Affected individuals are usually males.

   c. Daughters of an affected male are unaffected and are not carriers.

   d. Female carriers have a 50% chance of transmitting the disorder to their sons.

   e. Females are affected by the condition if it is a dominant X-linked disorder.

9. A nurse is providing genetic counseling to a pregnant client. Which are nursing responsibilities related to counseling the client? Select all that apply.

   a. Explaining basic concepts of probability and disorder susceptibility

   b. Ensuring complete informed consent to facilitate decisions about genetic testing

   c. Instructing the client on the appropriate decision to be taken

   d. Knowing basic genetic terminology and inheritance patterns

   e. Avoiding explanation of ethical or legal issues and concentrating on genetic issues

10. The nurse is caring for a client and her partner who are considering a future pregnancy. The client reports her last two pregnancies ended in stillbirth related to an underlying genetic disorder. What response by the nurse is **most** appropriate?

    a. "You should contact a geneticist after you become pregnant to closely watch your condition."

    b. "Your risk of repeated occurrences likely increases with future pregnancies."

    c. "You are strong to consider such an undertaking."

    d. "Consultation with a genetic counselor before you become pregnant would likely be beneficial."

11. The physician has ordered a karyotype for a newborn. The mother questions what type of information will be provided by the test. What information should be included in the nurse's response?

    a. The karyotype will provide information about the severity of your baby's condition.

    b. A karyotype is useful in determining the potential complications the baby may face as a result of its condition.

    c. The karyotype will assess the baby's chromosomal makeup.

    d. The karyotype will determine the treatment needed for the infant.

12. The nurse is caring for a client at the prenatal clinic. The client reports that she has felt some fluttering sensations in her lower abdomen and she noticed that her waistline is now totally gone. Additionally, she shows the nurse her nipples and the areola are much darker. Based upon this assessment, in which month of pregnancy is this client?

    a. 3rd month

    b. 5th month

    c. 2nd month

    d. 4th month

Maternal Adaptation During Pregnancy

Upon completion of the chapter, you will be able to:

- Define the key terms used in this chapter.
- Differentiate between subjective (presumptive), objective (probable), and diagnostic (positive) signs of pregnancy.
- Appraise maternal physiologic changes that occur during pregnancy.
- Summarize the nutritional needs of the pregnant woman and her fetus.
- Characterize the emotional and psychological changes that occur during pregnancy.

SECTION I: ASSESSING YOUR UNDERSTANDING

Activity A **FILL IN THE BLANKS**

1. During the stress of pregnancy, _____, secreted by the adrenal glands, helps keep up the level of glucose in the plasma by breaking down noncarbohydrate sources.

2. _____, or having conflicting feelings at the same time, is an emotion expressed by most women upon learning they are pregnant.

3. _____, released by the posterior pituitary gland, is responsible for milk ejection during breastfeeding.

4. At birth, as soon as the _____ is expelled, and there is a drop in progesterone, lactogenesis can begin.

5. Palmar erythema, a well-delineated pinkish area on the palmar surface of the hands, is caused by elevated _____ levels.

6. The postural changes of pregnancy coupled with the loosening of the _____ joints may result in lower back pain.

7. Constipation, increased venous pressure, and pressure from the gravid uterus can lead to the formation of _____ during pregnancy.

8. During pregnancy, elevated _____ levels cause smooth-muscle relaxation, which results in delayed gastric emptying and decreased peristalsis.

9. _____ is the creamy, yellowish breast fluid that provides nourishment for the newborn during the first few days of life.

10. Most women experience an increase in a whitish vaginal discharge, called _____, during pregnancy.

Activity B LABELING

Consider the following figure.

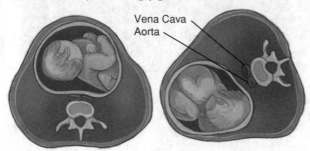

Supine position   Side-lying position

1. What condition is illustrated in the figure above?

   _____

   _____

   _____

2. What causes this condition to occur?

   _____

   _____

   _____

3. What symptoms are associated with this condition?

   _____

   _____

   _____

Activity C MATCHING

Match the parts of the female reproductive tract in Column A with the physiologic changes that occur in them during pregnancy, in Column B.

Column A

____ **1.** Uterus

____ **2.** Cervix

____ **3.** Vagina

____ **4.** Ovaries

____ **5.** Ureters

Column B

a. Between weeks 6 and 8 of gestation, softens due to vasocongestion

b. Elongate, widen, and curve above pelvic rim by 10th gestational week

c. Connective tissue loosens and smooth muscle begins to hypertrophy

d. Active in hormone production to support the pregnancy until about weeks 6 to 7

e. Its size increases from 70 g to about 1,100 to 1,200 g at term

Activity D SEQUENCING

Given in random order are the changes in the uterus as pregnancy progresses. Arrange the items in sequence.

1. Uterus progressively ascends into the abdomen.

2. Fundal height drops as fetus begins to descend and engage into the pelvis.

3. Fundus reaches its highest level at the xiphoid process.

4. Softening and compressibility of the lower uterine segment are noted.

5. Fundus is at the level of the umbilicus and measures 20 cm.

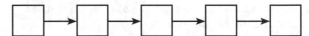

Activity E SHORT ANSWERS

Briefly answer the following.

1. What are stretch marks?

   _____

   _____

   _____

2. Why does hypertrophy of the heart occur in pregnant women?

   _____

   _____

   _____

3. Why do iron requirements increase during pregnancy?

   _____

   _____

   _____

4. What is pica?

_____

_____

_____

5. What is the role of oxytocin?

_____

_____

6. Why do pregnant women develop varicose veins?

_____

_____

_____

SECTION II: APPLYING YOUR KNOWLEDGE

Activity F CASE STUDY

Consider this scenario and answer the questions.

A nurse working in a private doctor's office has been assigned to be the primary nurse for Maggie, age 40, who is in her first trimester of pregnancy. Maggie states that she is very nervous about the pregnancy and is concerned because "she is not very excited." She adds that she is also worried about her baby, avoids travel, stays indoors because she feels nauseous most of the time, and has little interaction with the outside world. She asks the nurse if it is normal to feel this way.

1. Describe how the nurse should respond to the client about her lack of excitement.

_____

_____

_____

2. How should the nurse explain to the client how introversion, or focusing on oneself, may be common in early pregnancy?

_____

_____

_____

3. How should the nurse describe to the client how she may feel in the second trimester?

_____

_____

_____

4. How should the nurse reassure Maggie about her mood swings?

_____

_____

_____

SECTION III: PRACTICING FOR NCLEX

Activity G NCLEX-STYLE QUESTIONS

Answer the following questions.

1. A 28-year-old client states she did not have her menses for the past 3 months and suspects she is pregnant. Which should the nurse do **next**?

a. Determine at what age the client began menses

b. Have the client take a pregnancy test

c. Assess the client for a fetal heart tone

d. Ask the client the date her last menses ended

2. A pregnant client reports an increase in a thick, whitish vaginal discharge. Which response, made by the nurse, would be **most** appropriate?

a. "You should refrain from any sexual activity."

b. "You need to be assessed for a fungal infection."

c. "This discharge is normal during pregnancy."

d. "Use local antifungal agents regularly."

3. A pregnant client states she was unable to breastfeed her last child because her breasts did not produce milk. She desires to breastfeed this child. Which hormones would the nurse monitor during this pregnancy?

a. Estrogen and human placental lactogen (hPL)

b. Relaxin and human chorionic gonadotropin (hCG)

c. Progesterone and relaxin

d. Oxytocin and progesterone

4. A 28-year-old client in her first trimester of pregnancy reports conflicting feelings. She expresses feeling proud and excited about her pregnancy while at the same time feeling fearful and anxious of its implications. Which action should the nurse do **next**?

   a. Schedule the client a consult with a psychiatric health care provider

   b. Determine if the client's significant other is experiencing similar feelings about the pregnancy

   c. Provide the client with information about pregnancy support groups

   d. Inform the client this is a normal response to pregnancy that many women experience

5. A pregnant client arrives at the maternity clinic reporting constipation. Which factors could be the cause of constipation during pregnancy? Select all that apply.

   a. Decreased activity level

   b. Increase in estrogen levels

   c. Use of iron supplements

   d. Reduced stomach acidity

   e. Intestinal displacement

6. A client in her 10th week of gestation arrives at the maternity clinic reporting morning sickness. The nurse needs to inform the client about the body system adaptations during pregnancy. Which factors correspond to the morning sickness period during pregnancy? Select all that apply.

   a. Reduced stomach acidity

   b. Elevated human chorionic gonadotropin (hCG)

   c. Increased red blood cell (RBC) production

   d. Increased estrogen level

   e. Elevated human placental lactogen (hPL)

7. A pregnant client in her first trimester of pregnancy reports spontaneous, irregular, painless contractions. What does this indicate?

   a. Preterm labor

   b. Infection of the gastrointestinal (GI) tract

   c. Braxton Hicks contractions

   d. Acid indigestion

8. A client in her 29th week of gestation reports dizziness and clamminess when assuming a supine position. During the assessment, the nurse observes there is a marked decrease in the client's blood pressure. Which intervention should the nurse implement to help alleviate this client's condition?

   a. Keep the client's legs slightly elevated

   b. Place the client in an orthopneic position

   c. Keep the head of the client's bed slightly elevated

   d. Place the client in the left lateral position

9. A client in her 20th week of gestation expresses concern about her 5-year-old son, who is behaving strangely by not approaching her anymore. He does not seem to be taking the news of a new family member very well. Which of the following strategies can a nurse discuss with the mother to deal with the situation?

   a. Provide constant reinforcement of love and care to the child.

   b. Avoid talking to the child about the new arrival.

   c. Pay less attention to the child to prepare him for the future.

   d. Consult a child psychologist about the situation.

10. When caring for a newborn, the nurse observes that the neonate has developed white patches on the mucus membranes of the mouth. Which condition is the newborn **most** likely experiencing?

    a. Rubella

    b. Thrush

    c. Cytomegalovirus infection

    d. Toxoplasmosis

11. A client in her 39th week of gestation arrives at the maternity clinic stating that earlier in her pregnancy, she experienced shortness of breath. However, for the past few days, she's been able to breathe easily, but she has also begun to experience increased urinary frequency. A nurse is assigned to perform the physical examination of the client. Which observation is **most** likely?

    a. Fundal height has dropped since the last recording.

    b. Fundal height is at its highest level at the xiphoid process.

    c. The fundus is at the level of the umbilicus and measures 20 cm.

    d. The lower uterine segment and cervix have softened.

12. A client in her second trimester of pregnancy is anxious about the blotchy, brown pigmentation appearing on her forehead and cheeks. She also reports increased pigmentation on her breasts and genitalia. Which statement, by the nurse, is **most** appropriate?

    a. "I will let the health care provider know about the pigmentation."

    b. "I understand your concern; I would be concerned too."

    c. "This is called facial melanoma and should fade after your delivery."

    d. "I can tell you are anxious. Are there any other things worrying you?"

13. A client in her 39th week of gestation reports swelling in the legs after standing for long periods of time. The nurse recognizes that this factor increases the client's risk for which condition?

    a. Hemorrhoids

    b. Embolism

    c. Venous thrombosis

    d. Supine hypotension syndrome

14. A nurse is assigned to educate a pregnant client regarding the changes in the structures of the respiratory system taking place during pregnancy. Which conditions are associated with such changes? Select all that apply.

    a. Nasal and sinus stuffiness

    b. Persistent cough

    c. Nosebleed

    d. Kussmaul respirations

    e. Thoracic rather than abdominal breathing

15. During a prenatal visit, a client in her second trimester of pregnancy verbalizes positive feelings about the pregnancy and conceptualizes the fetus. Which is the **most** appropriate nursing intervention when the client expresses such feelings?

    a. Encourage the client to focus on herself, not on the fetus

    b. Inform the primary health care provider about the client's feeling

    c. Inform the client that it is too early to conceptualize the fetus

    d. Offer support and validation about the client's feelings

16. A client in her second trimester of pregnancy reports discomfort during sexual activity. Which instruction should a nurse provide?

    a. Perform frequent douching, and use lubricants

    b. Modify sexual positions to increase comfort

    c. Restrict contact to alternative, noncoital modes of sexual expression

    d. Perform stress-relieving and relaxing exercises

17. A nurse is educating a client about the various psychological feelings experienced by a woman and her partner during pregnancy. Which feeling is experienced by the expectant partner during the second trimester of pregnancy?

    a. Ambivalence along with extremes of emotions

    b. Confusion when dealing with the partner's mood swings

    c. Preparation for the new role as a parent and negotiating his or her role during labor

    d. Sympathetic response to the partner's pregnancy

18. A nurse who has been caring for a pregnant client understands that the client has pica and has been regularly consuming soil. For which condition should the nurse monitor the client?

    a. Iron-deficiency anemia

    b. Constipation

    c. Tooth fracture

    d. Inefficient protein metabolism

19. A client who is in her 6th week of gestation is being seen for a routine prenatal care visit. The client asks the nurse about changes in her eating habits that she should make during her pregnancy. The client informs the nurse that she is a vegetarian. The nurse knows that she has to monitor the client for which risks arising from her vegetarian diet? Select all that apply.

    a. Epistaxis

    b. Iron-deficiency anemia

    c. Decreased mineral absorption

    d. Constipation

    e. Low gestational weight gain

CHAPTER 12

Nursing Management During Pregnancy

Learning Objectives

Upon completion of the chapter, you will be able to:

- Define the key terms used in this chapter.
- Relate the information typically collected at the initial prenatal visit.
- Select the assessments completed at follow-up prenatal visits.
- Evaluate the tests used to assess maternal and fetal well-being, including nursing management for each.
- Outline appropriate nursing management to promote maternal self-care and to minimize the common discomforts of pregnancy.
- Examine the key components of perinatal education.

SECTION I: ASSESSING YOUR UNDERSTANDING

Activity A FILL IN THE BLANKS

1. A _____ is a laywoman trained to provide women and their families with encouragement, emotional and physical support, and information through late pregnancy, labor, and birth.

2. A _____ is a woman who has given birth once after a pregnancy of at least 20 weeks.

3. _____ height is the distance (in cm) measured with a tape measure from the top of the pubic bone to the top of the uterus while the client is lying on her back with her knees slightly flexed.

4. In a pregnant woman, darker pigmentation of the nipple and areola develops, along with enlargement of _____ glands in the breast.

5. Bluish coloration of the cervix and vaginal mucosa is known as _____ sign.

6. _____ is the craving for nonfood substances such as clay, cornstarch, laundry detergent, baking soda, soap, paint chips, dirt, ice, or wax.

7. _____ involves a transabdominal perforation of the amniotic sac to obtain a sample of amniotic fluid for analysis.

8. Alpha-fetoprotein is a substance produced by the fetal _____ between weeks 13 and 20 of gestation.

9. The basis for the _____ test is that the normal fetus produces characteristic fetal heart rate patterns in response to fetal movements.

10. _____ are varicosities of the rectum which occur as a result of progesterone-induced vasodilation and from pressure of the enlarged uterus on the lower intestine and rectum.

Activity B MATCHING

Match the different types of assessment tests conducted to determine fetal well-being in Column A with their uses in Column B.

Column A

___ **1.** Ultrasonography

___ **2.** Doppler flow studies

___ **3.** Nuchal translucency screening (ultrasound)

___ **4.** Percutaneous umbilical blood sampling

___ **5.** Contraction stress test

Column B

a. Conducted between 11 and 14 weeks, this test allows for earlier detection and diagnosis of some fetal chromosomes and structural abnormalities

b. Permits the collection of a blood specimen directly from the fetal circulation for rapid chromosomal analysis

c. Determines the fetal heart rate response under stress, such as during contractions

d. Acts as a guide for the need for invasive intrauterine tests and used to monitor fetal growth and placental location

e. With the help of the ultrasound, this test is used to identify abnormalities in diastolic flow within the umbilical vessels

Activity C SEQUENCING

Pregnant women are at an increased risk for epistaxis (nosebleeds). Given below, in random order, are steps that should be followed when caring for the client who experiences an epistaxis. Rearrange in the correct sequence.

1. Pinch her nostrils with her thumb and forefinger for 10 to 15 minutes.

2. Loosen the clothing around her neck.

3. Apply an ice pack to the bridge of her nose.

4. Sit with her head tilted forward.

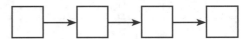

Activity D SHORT ANSWERS

Briefly answer the following.

1. What are the key areas which the nurse should include in preconception care?

_____

_____

_____

2. What is the role of a nurse in preconception care to ensure a positive impact on the pregnancy?

_____

_____

_____

3. Discuss the priority assessment by the nurse during a client's initial prenatal visit.

_____

_____

_____

4. What are the roles of a nurse with regard to providing counseling and education to the client at a prenatal visit?

_____

_____

_____

5. What assessments should a nurse perform when conducting a chest examination for a pregnant client on her first prenatal visit, and what are expectations for each skill performed?

_____

_____

_____

6. What assessments should the nurse perform during follow-up visits?

_____

_____

_____

SECTION II: APPLYING YOUR KNOWLEDGE

Activity E **CASE STUDY**

Consider this scenario and answer the questions.

A pregnant client and her husband are preparing for the birth of their first baby. The couple wants to ensure that they are well prepared for the baby's birth and homecoming and seek guidance from the nurse. The pregnant client also wants to know the importance of breastfeeding and wants to prepare for it.

1. What are the items in the checklist used by the nurse to ensure that the client is well prepared for the newborn's birth and homecoming?

_____

_____

_____

2. What interventions should the nurse perform in preparing the client for breastfeeding?

_____

_____

_____

3. What advantages of breastfeeding should the nurse educate the pregnant client about?

_____

_____

_____

SECTION III: PRACTICING FOR NCLEX

Activity F **NCLEX-STYLE QUESTIONS**

Answer the following questions.

1. Which nursing intervention should the nurse perform when assessing fetal well-being through abdominal ultrasonography in a client?
   a. Inform the client that she may feel hot initially
   b. Instruct the client to refrain from emptying her bladder
   c. Instruct the client to report the occurrence of fever
   d. Obtain and record vital signs of the client

2. A pregnant client wishes to know if sexual intercourse would be safe during her pregnancy. Which should the nurse confirm before educating the client regarding sexual behavior during pregnancy?
   a. Client does not have an incompetent cervix
   b. Client does not have anxieties and worries
   c. Client does not have anemia
   d. Client does not experience facial and hand edema

3. A client in the third trimester of pregnancy has to travel a long distance by car. The client is anxious about the effect the travel may have on her pregnancy. Which instruction should the nurse provide to promote easy and safe travel for the client?
   a. Activate the air bag in the car
   b. Use a lap belt that crosses over the uterus
   c. Apply a padded shoulder strap properly
   d. Always wear a three-point seat belt

4. A client in her third trimester of pregnancy wishes to use the method of feeding formula to her baby. What instruction should the nurse provide?
   a. Mix one scoop of powder with an ounce of water
   b. Feed the infant every 8 hours
   c. Serve the formula at room temperature
   d. Refrigerate any leftover formula

5. A nurse caring for a client in labor has asked her to perform Lamaze breathing techniques to avoid pain. Which should the nurse keep in mind to promote effective Lamaze-method breathing?
   a. Ensure deep abdominopelvic breathing
   b. Ensure abdominal breathing during contractions
   c. Ensure client's concentration on pleasurable sensations
   d. Remain quiet during client's period of imagery

6. A 28-year-old client who has just conceived arrives at a health care facility for her first prenatal visit to undergo a physical examination. Which intervention should the nurse perform to prepare the client for the physical examination?
   a. Ensure that the client is lying down
   b. Ensure that the client's family is present
   c. Instruct the client to empty her bladder
   d. Instruct the client to keep taking deep breaths

7. A client in her third month of pregnancy arrives at the health care facility for a regular follow-up visit. The client reports discomfort due to increased urinary frequency. Which instruction should the nurse offer the client to reduce the client's discomfort?
   a. Avoid consumption of caffeinated drinks
   b. Drink fluids with meals rather than between meals
   c. Avoid an empty stomach at all times
   d. Munch on dry crackers and toast in the early morning

8. A pregnant client has come to a health care provider for her first prenatal visit. The nurse needs to document useful information about the past health history. What are goals of the nurse in the history-taking process? Select all that apply.
   a. To prepare a plan of care that suits the client's lifestyle
   b. To develop a trusting relationship with the client
   c. To prepare a plan of care for the pregnancy
   d. To assess the client's partner's sexual health
   e. To urge the client to achieve an optimal body weight

9. A pregnant client has come to a health care facility for a physical examination. Which assessments should a nurse perform when doing a physical examination of the head and neck? Select all that apply.
   a. Previous injuries and sequelae
   b. Eye movements
   c. Levels of estrogen
   d. Limitations in range of motion
   e. Thyroid gland enlargement

10. A pregnant client in her 12th week of gestation has come to a health care center for a physical examination of her abdomen. Where should the nurse palpate for the fundus in this client?
   a. At the umbilicus
   b. Below the ensiform cartilage
   c. Midway between the symphysis and umbilicus
   d. At the symphysis pubis

11. A pregnant client has come to a clinic for a pelvic examination. What assessments should a nurse perform when examining external genitalia?
   a. Cervix is smooth, long, thick, and closed
   b. Bluish coloration of cervix and vaginal mucosa
   c. Any infection due to hematomas, varicosities, and inflammation
   d. Hemorrhoids, masses, prolapse, and lesions

12. A client in her second trimester arrives at a health care facility for a follow-up visit. During the exam, the client reports constipation. Which instruction should the nurse offer to help alleviate constipation?
   a. Ensure adequate hydration and bulk in the diet
   b. Avoid spicy or greasy foods in meals
   c. Practice Kegel exercises
   d. Avoid lying down for 2 hours after meals

13. A pregnant client's last menstrual period was March 10. Using Naegele's rule, the nurse estimates the date of birth to be:
   a. January 7.
   b. December 17.
   c. February 21.
   d. January 30.

14. A nurse is caring for a pregnant client in her second trimester of pregnancy. The nurse educates the client to look for which danger sign of pregnancy needing immediate attention by the physician?

a. Vaginal bleeding

b. Painful urination

c. Severe, persistent vomiting

d. Lower abdominal and shoulder pain

15. A nurse is caring for a client in her second trimester of pregnancy. During a regular follow-up visit, the client reports varicosities of the legs. Which instruction should the nurse provide to help the client alleviate varicosities of the legs?

a. Avoid sitting in one position for long

b. Refrain from crossing legs when sitting for long periods

c. Apply heating pads on the extremities

d. Refrain from wearing any kind of stockings

CHAPTER 13

Labor and Birth Process

Learning Objectives

Upon completion of the chapter, you will be able to:

- Relate premonitory signs of labor.
- Compare and contrast true versus false labor.
- Categorize the critical factors affecting labor and birth.
- Analyze the cardinal movements of labor.
- Evaluate the maternal and fetal responses to labor and birth.
- Classify the stages of labor and the critical events in each stage.
- Characterize the normal physiologic/psychological changes occurring during all four stages of labor.
- Formulate the concept of pain as it relates to the woman in labor.

SECTION I: ASSESSING YOUR UNDERSTANDING

Activity A FILL IN THE BLANKS

1. Vaginal birth is most favorable with a _____ type of pelvis because the inlet is round and the outlet is roomy.

2. The thinning out process of the cervix during labor is termed _____.

3. The _____ suture is located between the parietal bones and divides the skull into the right and left halves.

4. _____ station is designated when the presenting part is at the level of the maternal ischial spines.

5. _____ occurs when the fetal presenting part begins to descend into the maternal pelvis.

6. An increase in prostaglandins leads to myometrial _____ and to a reduction in cervical resistance.

7. Oxytocin aids in stimulating prostaglandin synthesis through receptors in the _____.

8. The birth _____ is the route through which the fetus must travel to be birthed vaginally.

9. A sudden increase in energy on the part of the expectant woman 24 to 48 hours before the onset of labor is sometimes referred to as _____.

10. The elongated shape of the fetal skull at birth as a result of overlapping of the cranial bones is known as _____.

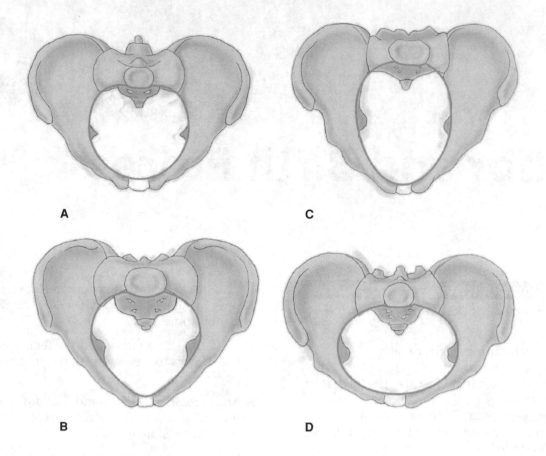

A

C

B

D

Activity B LABELING

Consider the following figures.

1. Identify the four types of pelvic shapes shown in the image. Which one of the four images is most favorable for a vaginal birth?

   _____

   _____

   _____

2. Identify the different types of breech positions shown in the figure. In which clients are such cases observed?

   _____

   _____

   _____

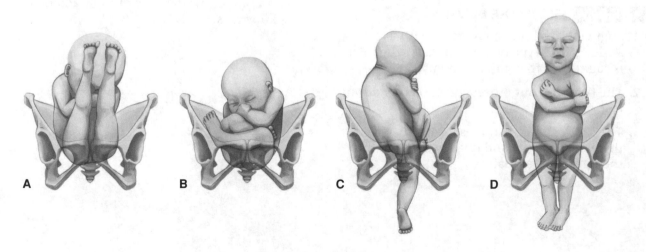

A

B

C

D

Activity C MATCHING

Match the cardinal movements of labor in Column A with the corresponding fetal movements observed in Column B.

Column A

____ **1.** Engagement

____ **2.** Descent

____ **3.** Flexion

____ **4.** Extension

____ **5.** External rotation

Column B

a. Occurs when the greatest transverse diameter of the head in vertex passes through the pelvic inlet

b. Downward movement of the fetal head until it is within the pelvic inlet. A maneuver that occurs throughout the laboring process

c. Allows the shoulders to rotate internally to fit the maternal pelvis

d. The head emerges through extension under the symphysis pubis, along with the shoulders

e. Occurs as the vertex meets resistance from the cervix, walls of the pelvis, or the pelvic floor

Activity D SEQUENCING

Given below, in random order, are the phases of labor. Arrange them in the order of their occurrence. Put the items in correct sequence by writing the letters in the boxes provided below.

1. Pelvic phase

2. Perineal phase

3. Placental expulsion

4. Latent phase

5. Active phase

6. Placental separation

7. Transition phase

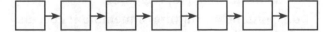

Activity E SHORT ANSWERS

Briefly answer the following.

1. What are the reasons that cause women to adopt back-lying positions during labor?

_____

_____

_____

2. Why should the nurse encourage the pregnant client experiencing contractions to adopt the upright or lateral position?

_____

_____

_____

3. What are the maternal physiologic responses that occur as a woman progresses through childbirth?

_____

_____

_____

4. What are the factors influencing the ability of a woman to cope with labor stress?

_____

_____

_____

5. What are the signs of separation that indicate the placenta is ready to deliver?

_____

_____

_____

6. What are the factors that ensure a positive birth experience for the pregnant client?

_____

_____

_____

SECTION II: APPLYING YOUR KNOWLEDGE

Activity F   CASE STUDY

Consider this scenario and answer the questions.

Becca is a primigravida at 36 weeks' gestation. During her prenatal visit, she asks the nurse the following questions about labor. Describe how the nurse should respond.

1. "How will I know I am in labor?"

   _____

   _____

   _____

2. "When should I come to the hospital?"

   _____

   _____

   _____

3. "My sister just had a baby and she told me that the nurse midwife encouraged her to change positions and to walk to help her labor; will this help me in labor?"

   _____

   _____

   _____

4. "How do we determine that it's time to push?"

   _____

   _____

   _____

SECTION III: PRACTICING FOR NCLEX

Activity G   NCLEX-STYLE QUESTIONS

Answer the following questions.

1. A client in her third trimester of pregnancy arrives at a health care facility with a report of cramping and low back pain; she also notes that she is urinating more frequently and that her breathing has become easier the past few days. Physical examination conducted by the nurse indicates that the client has edema of the lower extremities, along with an increase in vaginal discharge. What should the nurse do **next**?

   a. Notify the health care provider
   b. Continue to monitor the client
   c. Assess the client's blood pressure
   d. Prepare the client for birth

2. The assessment of a pregnant client, who is toward the end of her third trimester, reveals that she has increased prostaglandin levels. For which factors should the nurse assess the client? Select all that apply.

   a. Reduction in cervical resistance
   b. Myometrial contractions
   c. Boggy appearance of the uterus
   d. Softening and thinning of the cervix
   e. Hypotonic character of the bladder

3. A client experiencing contractions presents at a health care facility. Assessment conducted by the nurse reveals that the client has been experiencing Braxton Hicks contractions. The nurse has to educate the client on the usefulness of Braxton Hicks contractions. Which role do Braxton Hicks contractions play in aiding labor?

   a. These contractions help in softening and ripening the cervix.
   b. These contractions increase the release of prostaglandins.
   c. These contractions increase oxytocin sensitivity.
   d. These contractions make maternal breathing easier.

4. A pregnant client wants to know why the labor of a first-time-pregnant woman usually lasts longer than that of a woman who has already delivered once and is pregnant a second time. What explanation should the nurse offer the client?

   a. Braxton Hicks contractions are not strong enough during first pregnancy.
   b. Contractions are stronger during the first pregnancy than the second.
   c. The cervix takes around 12 to 16 hours to dilate during first pregnancy.
   d. Spontaneous rupture of membranes occurs during first pregnancy.

5. A pregnant client is admitted to a maternity clinic for birth. The client wishes to adopt the kneeling position during labor. The nurse knows that which to be an advantage of adopting a kneeling position during labor?

   a. It helps the woman in labor to save energy.

   b. It facilitates vaginal examinations.

   c. It facilitates external belt adjustment.

   d. It helps to rotate fetus in a posterior position.

6. A nurse is caring for a pregnant client who is in labor. Which maternal physiologic responses should the nurse monitor for in the client, as the client progresses through birth? Select all that apply.

   a. Increase in heart rate

   b. Increase in blood pressure

   c. Increase in respiratory rate

   d. Slight decrease in body temperature

   e. Increase in gastric emptying and pH

7. A nurse is caring for a client in labor who is delivering. For which fetal response should the nurse monitor?

   a. Decrease in arterial carbon dioxide pressure

   b. Increase in fetal breathing movements

   c. Increase in fetal oxygen pressure

   d. Decrease in circulation and perfusion to the fetus

8. A client in the third stage of labor has experienced placental separation and expulsion. Why is it necessary for a nurse to massage the woman's uterus briefly until it is firm?

   a. To reduce boggy nature of the uterus

   b. To remove pieces left attached to uterine wall

   c. To constrict the uterine blood vessels

   d. To lessen the chances of conducting an episiotomy

9. A nurse is caring for a pregnant client in labor in a health care facility. The nurse knows that which sign marks the termination of the first stage of labor in the client?

   a. Diffuse abdominal cramping

   b. Rupturing of fetal membranes

   c. Start of regular contractions

   d. Dilation of cervix diameter to 10 cm

10. A nurse is caring for a client who is in the first stage of labor. The client is experiencing extreme pain due to the labor. The nurse understands which to be causes of the extreme pain in the client? Select all that apply.

    a. Lower uterine segment distention

    b. Fetus moving along the birth canal

    c. Stretching and tearing of structures

    d. Spontaneous placental expulsion

    e. Dilation of the cervix

11. A pregnant client in labor has to undergo a sonogram to confirm the fetal position of a shoulder presentation. For which condition associated with shoulder presentation during a vaginal birth should the nurse assess?

    a. Uterine abnormalities

    b. Fetal anomalies

    c. Congenital anomalies

    d. Prematurity

12. A nurse is assigned the task of educating a pregnant client about birth. Which nursing interventions should the nurse perform as a part of prenatal education for the client to ensure a positive birth experience? Select all that apply.

    a. Provide the client clear information on procedures involved

    b. Encourage the client to have a sense of mastery and self-control

    c. Encourage the client to have a positive reaction to pregnancy

    d. Instruct the client to spend some time alone each day

    e. Instruct the client to begin changing the home environment

13. A pregnant client is admitted to a maternity clinic for birth. Which assessment finding indicates that the client's fetus is in the transverse lie position?

    a. Long axis of fetus is at 60 degrees to that of client.

    b. Long axis of fetus is parallel to that of client.

    c. Long axis of fetus is perpendicular to that of client.

    d. Long axis of fetus is at 45 degrees to that of client.

14. A pregnant client is admitted to a maternity clinic after experiencing contractions. The assigned nurse observes that the client experiences pauses between contractions. The nurse knows that which event marks the importance of the pauses between contractions during labor?

a. Effacement and dilation of the cervix

b. Shortening of the upper uterine segment

c. Reduction in length of the cervical canal

d. Restoration of blood flow to uterus and placenta

15. A nurse is caring for a pregnant client during labor. Which methods should the nurse use to provide comfort to the pregnant client? Select all that apply.

a. Hand holding

b. Chewing gum

c. Massaging

d. Acupressure

e. Prescribed pain killers

Nursing Management During Labor and Birth

Upon completion of the chapter, you will be able to:

- Define the key terms related to the labor and birth process.
- Examine the measures used to evaluate maternal status during labor and birth.
- Differentiate the advantages and disadvantages of external and internal fetal monitoring, including the appropriate use for each.
- Choose appropriate nursing interventions to address nonreassuring fetal heart rate patterns.
- Outline the nurse's role in fetal assessment.
- Appraise the various comfort promotion and pain relief strategies used during labor and birth.
- Summarize the assessment data collected on admission to the perinatal unit.
- Relate the ongoing assessments involved in each stage of labor and birth.
- Analyze the nurse's role throughout the labor and birth process.

SECTION I: ASSESSING YOUR UNDERSTANDING

Activity A FILL IN THE BLANKS

1. _____ comfort measures are usually simple, safe, effective, and inexpensive to use.

2. If the woman is a diabetic, it is critical to alert the newborn nursery of potential _____ in the newborn.

3. If the nitrazine test is inconclusive, an additional test, called the _____ test, can be used to confirm rupture of membranes.

4. The nurse reviews the prenatal record to identify risk factors that may contribute to a decrease in _____ circulation during pregnancy and/or labor.

5. The _____ spines serve as landmarks for estimating the descent of the fetal presenting part and have been designated as zero station.

6. The primary power of labor is/are _____ contractions, which are involuntary.

7. The _____ is placed over the uterine fundus in the area of greatest contractility to electronically monitor uterine contractions.

8. _____ describes the irregular variations or absence of fetal heart rate (FHR) due to erroneous causes on the fetal monitor record.

9. Baseline variability represents the interplay between the _____ and sympathetic nervous systems.

10. Fetal _____ are transitory increases in the FHR above the baseline that are associated with sympathetic nervous stimulation.

Activity B MATCHING

Match the extent of the lacerations in Column A with their depths in Column B.

Column A

_____ **1.** First-degree laceration

_____ **2.** Second-degree laceration

_____ **3.** Third-degree laceration

_____ **4.** Fourth-degree laceration

Column B

a. Through the anal sphincter muscle

b. Through the muscles of the perineal body

c. Through the skin

d. Through the anterior rectal wall

Activity C SEQUENCING

Put the items in correct sequence by writing the letters in the boxes provided below.

1. Given below, in random order, are nursing interventions during various stages of labor and birth. Arrange them in the correct order.

a. Check the fundus to ensure that it is firm (size and consistency of a grapefruit), located in the midline and below the umbilicus.

b. Ascertain whether the woman is in true or false labor.

c. Position the woman and cleanse the vulva and perineal areas.

d. Check for lengthening of the umbilical cord protruding from the vagina.

e. Check for crowning, low grunting sounds from the woman, and increase in blood-tinged show.

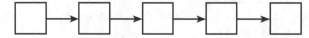

Activity D SHORT ANSWERS

Briefly answer the following.

1. What information should a nurse include when taking the maternal health history?

_____

_____

_____

2. What does the Apgar score assess?

_____

_____

_____

3. What is the purpose of vaginal examination during maternal assessment?

_____

_____

_____

4. What are the advantages and disadvantages of continuous electronic fetal monitoring?

_____

_____

_____

_____

5. What are the typical signs of the second stage of labor?

_____

_____

_____

6. What positions are used for the second stage of labor?

_____

_____

_____

SECTION II: APPLYING YOUR KNOWLEDGE

Activity E CASE STUDY

Consider this scenario and answer the questions.

Susan, a pregnant client, has been admitted to the health care facility because she is in labor. The nurse is prepared to do maternal assessment during labor and delivery. Susan informs the nurse that there is no vaginal bleeding.

1. What nursing intervention should the nurse perform?

_____

_____

_____

2. What is the purpose of vaginal examination during maternal assessment?

_____

_____

_____

3. What is the procedure for conducting vaginal examination?

_____

_____

_____

SECTION III: PRACTICING FOR NCLEX

Activity F NCLEX-STYLE QUESTIONS

Answer the following questions.

1. A 39-week-gestation client presents to the labor and birth unit reporting abdominal pain. What should the nurse do **first**?

   a. Determine if the client is in true or false labor

   b. Ask if this is the client's first pregnancy

   c. Notify the health care provider

   d. Assess to see if the client has any drug allergies

2. A nurse is assigned to conduct an admission assessment on the phone for a pregnant client. Which information should the nurse obtain from the client? Select all that apply.

   a. Estimated due date

   b. History of drug abuse

   c. Characteristics of contractions

   d. Appearance of vaginal blood

   e. History of drug allergy

3. A nurse is caring for a pregnant client who is in the active phase of labor. At what interval should the nurse monitor the client's vital signs?

   a. Every 15 minutes

   b. Every 30 minutes

   c. Every 45 minutes

   d. Every 1 hour

4. A nurse is required to obtain the fetal heart rate (FHR) for a pregnant client. If the presentation is cephalic, which maternal site should the nurse monitor to hear the FHR clearly?

   a. Lower quadrant of the maternal abdomen

   b. At the level of the maternal umbilicus

   c. Above the level of the maternal umbilicus

   d. Just below the maternal umbilicus

5. The nurse is assessing the laboring client to determine fetal oxygenation status. What indirect assessment method will the nurse likely use?

   a. External electronic fetal monitoring

   b. Fetal blood pH

   c. Fetal oxygen saturation

   d. Fetal position

6. A client in labor is administered lorazepam to help her relax enough so that she can participate effectively during her labor process rather than fighting against it. For which adverse effect of the drug should the nurse monitor?

   a. Increased sedation

   b. Newborn respiratory depression

   c. Nervous system depression

   d. Decreased alertness

7. A pregnant client with a history of spinal injury is being prepared for a cesarean birth. Which method of anesthesia is to be administered to the client?

   a. Local infiltration

   b. Epidural block

   c. Regional anesthesia

   d. General anesthesia

8. The nurse is monitoring a pregnant client admitted to a health care center who is in the latent phase of labor. The nurse demonstrates appropriate nursing care by monitoring the fetal heart rate (FHR) with the Doppler at least how often?

   a. Every 15 to 30 minutes

   b. Every 30 minutes

   c. Every hour

   d. Continuously

9. During an admission assessment of a client in labor, the nurse observes that there is no vaginal bleeding yet. What nursing intervention is appropriate in the absence of vaginal bleeding when the client is in the early stage of labor?

   a. Monitor vital signs

   b. Assess amount of cervical dilation

   c. Obtain urine specimen for urinalysis

   d. Monitor hydration status

10. A 29-week-gestation client is admitted with moderate vaginal discharge. The nurse performs a nitrazine test to determine if the membranes have ruptured. The nitrazine tape remains yellow to olive green, with pH between 5 and 6. What should the nurse do **next**?

    a. Prepare the client for birth

    b. Assess the client's cervical status

    c. Notify the health care provider

    d. Perform Leopold's maneuver

11. The nurse is monitoring a client's uterine contractions. Which factors should the nurse assess to monitor uterine contraction? Select all that apply.

    a. Uterine resting tone

    b. Frequency of contractions

    c. Change in temperature

    d. Change in blood pressure

    e. Intensity of contractions

12. The nurse explains Leopold's maneuvers to a pregnant client. For which purposes are these maneuvers performed? Select all that apply.

    a. Determining the presentation of the fetus

    b. Determining the position of the fetus

    c. Determining the lie of the fetus

    d. Determining the weight of the fetus

    e. Determining the size of the fetus

13. A nurse caring for a pregnant client in labor observes that the fetal heart rate (FHR) is below 110 beats per minute. Which interventions should the nurse perform? Select all that apply.

    a. Turn the client on her left side

    b. Reduce intravenous (IV) fluid rate

    c. Administer oxygen by mask

    d. Assess client for underlying causes

    e. Ignore questions from the client

14. The nurse caring for a client in preterm labor observes abnormal fetal heart rate (FHR) patterns. Which nursing intervention should the nurse perform **next**?

    a. Application of vibroacoustic stimulation

    b. Tactile stimulation

    c. Administration of oxygen by mask

    d. Fetal scalp stimulation

15. A nurse is caring for a client who has been administered an epidural block. Which should the nurse assess **next**?

    a. Respiratory rate

    b. Temperature

    c. Pulse

    d. Uterine contractions

16. A client administered combined spinal–epidural analgesia is showing signs of hypotension and associated fetal heart rate (FHR) changes. What intervention should the nurse perform to manage the changes?

    a. Assist client to a supine position

    b. Provide supplemental oxygen

    c. Discontinue intravenous (IV) fluid

    d. Turn client to her right side

17. A pregnant client has opted for hydrotherapy for pain management during labor. Which should the nurse consider when assisting the client during the birthing process?

    a. Initiate the technique only when the client is in active labor

    b. Do not allow the client to stay in the bath for long

    c. Ensure that the water temperature exceeds body temperature

    d. Allow the client into the water only if her membranes have rupture

18. A nurse is teaching a couple about patterned breathing during their birth education. Which technique should the nurse suggest for slow-paced breathing?

    a. Inhale and exhale through the mouth at a rate of 4 breaths every 5 seconds

    b. Inhale slowly through nose and exhale through pursed lips

    c. Punctuated breathing by a forceful exhalation through pursed lips every few breaths

    d. Hold breath for 5 seconds after every 3 breaths

19. A pregnant client requires administration of an epidural block for management of pain during labor. For which conditions should the nurse check the client before administering the epidural block? Select all that apply.

   a. Spinal abnormality

   b. Hypovolemia

   c. Varicose veins

   d. Coagulation defects

   e. Skin rashes or bruises

20. A nurse is caring for a client administered general anesthesia for an emergency cesarean birth. The nurse notes the client's uterus is relaxed upon massage. What would the nurse do **next**?

   a. Continue to monitor the client

   b. Continue to massage the client's fundus

   c. Administer oxygen to the client

   d. Assess the client's vaginal bleeding

Postpartum Adaptations

Learning Objectives

Upon completion of the chapter, you will be able to:

- Define the key terms used in this chapter.
- Examine the systemic physiologic changes occurring in the woman after childbirth.
- Assess the phases of maternal role adjustment and accompanying behaviors.
- Analyze the psychological adaptations occurring in the mother's partner after childbirth.

SECTION I: ASSESSING YOUR UNDERSTANDING

Activity A FILL IN THE BLANKS

1. Within 10 days of birth, the fundus of the uterus usually cannot be palpated because it has descended into the true _____.

2. If retrogressive changes <u>do not occur</u> as a result of retained placental fragments or infection, _____ results.

3. _____ are the painful uterine contractions some women experience during the early postpartum period.

4. Increased prolactin levels and abundant milk supply, combined with inadequate emptying of the breast, may cause breast _____.

5. During pregnancy, stretching of the abdominal wall muscles occurs to accommodate the enlarging _____.

6. _____ elicits the milk letdown reflex so that milk can be ejected from the alveoli to the nipple.

7. For _____ women, menstruation usually resumes 7 to 9 weeks after giving birth.

8. _____ is defined as the secretion of milk by the breasts.

9. _____, which is secreted from the anterior pituitary gland in increasing levels throughout pregnancy, triggers synthesis and secretion of milk after giving birth.

10. The profuse _____ that is common during the early postpartum period is one of the most noticeable adaptations in the integumentary system and is a way of eliminating excess body fluids retained during pregnancy.

Activity B MATCHING

Match the terms in Column A with their descriptions in Column B.

Column A

____ **1.** Engrossment

____ **2.** Involution

____ **3.** Lochia

____ **4.** Puerperium

____ **5.** Atony

Column B

a. The vaginal discharge that occurs after the birth of the placenta

b. Encompasses the time after delivery as the woman's body begins to return to the prepregnant state

c. This state of the uterus allows for excessive bleeding

d. The father's developing a bond with his newborn, which is a time of intense absorption, preoccupation, and interest

e. Involves three retrogressive processes, which include contraction of muscle fibers, catabolism, and regeneration of uterine epithelium

Activity C SEQUENCING

Put the items in correct sequence by writing the letters in the boxes provided below.

1. Lochia refers to the discharge that occurs after birth. Given below, in random order, are the three stages of lochia. Choose the correct sequence in which they appear after birth.

a. Lochia alba

b. Lochia rubra

c. Lochia serosa

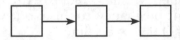

2. Given below, in random order, are the three stages a woman goes through immediately after she gives birth to a child. Choose the correct sequence in which they occur.

a. Letting-go phase

b. Taking-hold phase

c. Taking-in phase

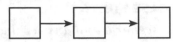

Activity D SHORT ANSWERS

Briefly answer the following.

1. Explain why breastfeeding is not a reliable method of contraception?

_____

_____

2. Why are afterpains more acute in multiparous women?

_____

_____

_____

3. What are the factors that facilitate uterine involution?

_____

_____

_____

4. What are the factors that inhibit uterine involution?

_____

_____

_____

5. Why do women who have had cesarean births tend to have less flow of lochial discharge?

_____

_____

_____

6. Why are afterpains usually stronger during breastfeeding? What can be done to reduce this discomfort?

_____

_____

_____

SECTION II: APPLYING YOUR KNOWLEDGE

Activity E CASE STUDY

Consider this scenario and answer the questions.

A nurse is caring for two clients, one who is breastfeeding and has developed breast engorgement and another who is not breastfeeding and has developed breast engorgement.

1. What relief measures should the nurse suggest to resolve engorgement in the client who is breastfeeding?

   _____

   _____

   _____

2. What relief measures should a nurse suggest for nonbreastfeeding engorgement?

   _____

   _____

   _____

SECTION III: PRACTICING FOR NCLEX

Activity F NCLEX-STYLE QUESTIONS

Answer the following questions.

1. A client who gave birth about 12 hours ago informs the nurse that she has been voiding small amounts of urine frequently. The nurse examines the client and notes the displacement of the uterus from the midline to the right. What intervention would the nurse perform **next**?
   a. Insert a 20-gauge IV
   b. Administer oxytocin IV
   c. Notify the health care provider
   d. Urinary catheterization

2. A client who has given birth a week ago reports discomfort when defecating and ambulating. The birth involved an episiotomy. Which suggestions should the nurse provide to the client to provide local comfort? Select all that apply.
   a. Maintain correct posture
   b. Use of warm sitz baths
   c. Use of anesthetic sprays
   d. Use of witch hazel pads
   e. Use normal body mechanics

3. A nurse is caring for a client who has had a vaginal birth. The nurse understands that pelvic relaxation can occur in any woman experiencing a vaginal birth. Which should the nurse recommend to the client to improve pelvic floor tone?
   a. Kegel exercises
   b. Urinating immediately when the urge is felt
   c. Abdominal crunches
   d. Sitz baths

4. The nurse is caring for a client who had been administered an anesthetic block during labor. For which risks should the nurse watch in the client? Select all that apply.
   a. Incomplete emptying of bladder
   b. Bladder distention
   c. Ambulation difficulty
   d. Urinary retention
   e. Perineal laceration

5. A client who delivered a baby 36 hours ago informs the nurse that she has been passing unusually large volumes of urine very often. How should the nurse explain this to the client?
   a. "Bruising and swelling of the perineum often cause excessive urination."
   b. "Larger than normal amounts of urine frequently occur due to swelling of tissues surrounding the urinary meatus."
   c. "Your body usually retains extra fluids during pregnancy, so this is one way it rids itself of the excess fluid."
   d. "Anesthesia causes decreased bladder tone, which causes you to urinate more frequently."

6. A client reports pain in the lower back, hips, and joints 10 days after the birth of her baby. What instruction should the nurse give the client after birth to prevent low back pain and injury to the joints?

   a. Try to avoid carrying the baby for a few days

   b. Maintain correct posture and positioning

   c. Soak in a warm bath several times a day

   d. Apply ice to the sore joints

7. A concerned client tells the nurse that her husband, who was very excited about the baby before its birth, is apparently happy but seems to be afraid of caring for the baby. What suggestion should the nurse give to the client's husband to resolve the issue?

   a. He begin by holding the baby frequently

   b. He speak to his friends who have children

   c. He read up on parental care

   d. The client speak to the physician on her husband's behalf

8. A client who gave birth 5 days ago reports profuse sweating during the night. What should the nurse recommend to the client in this regard?

   a. "I would suggest that you speak with your physician about this."

   b. "Drink plenty of cold fluids before you go to bed."

   c. "Be sure to change your pajamas to prevent you from chilling."

   d. "I'm not sure why this is occurring since this usually doesn't occur until much later in the postpartum period."

9. A breastfeeding client informs the nurse that she is unable to maintain her milk supply. What instruction should the nurse give to the client to improve milk supply?

   a. Take cold baths

   b. Apply ice to the breasts

   c. Empty the breasts frequently

   d. Perform Kegel exercises

10. A nurse is examining a client who underwent a vaginal birth 24 hours ago. The client asks the nurse why her discharge is such a deep red color. What explanation is **most** accurate for the nurse to give to the client?

    a. "The discharge consists of mucus, tissue debris, and blood; this gives it the deep red color."

    b. "It is normal for the discharge to be deep red since it consists of leukocytes, decidual tissue, RBCs, and serous fluid."

    c. "The discharge at this point in the postpartum period consists of RBCs and leukocytes."

    d. "This discharge is called lochia, and it consists of leukocytes and decidual tissue."

11. A client who had a vaginal delivery 2 days ago asks the nurse when she will be able to breathe normally again. Which response by the nurse is accurate?

    a. "You should notice a change in your respiratory status within the next 24 hours."

    b. "Everyone is different, so it is difficult to say when your respirations will be back to normal."

    c. "It usually takes about 3 months before all of your abdominal organs return to normal, allowing you to breathe normally."

    d. "Within 1 to 3 weeks, your diaphragm should return to normal and your breathing will feel like it did before your pregnancy."

12. The nurse is caring for a client of Asian descent 1 day after she has given birth. Which foods will the client **most** likely refuse to eat when her meal tray is delivered? Select all that apply.

    a. Ice cream

    b. Hot soup

    c. Raw carrots and celery

    d. Orange slices

    e. Mashed potatoes with gravy

13. While caring for a client following a lengthy labor and birth, the nurse notes that the client repeatedly reviews her labor and birth and is very dependent on her family for care. The nurse is correct in identifying the client to be in which phase of maternal role adjustment?

   a. Letting-go

   b. Taking-hold

   c. Taking-in

   d. Acquaintance/attachment

14. A nurse is caring for the client who gave birth a week ago. The client informs the nurse that she experiences painful uterine contractions when breastfeeding the baby. Which should the nurse do **next**?

   a. Tell the client to take an NSAID orally

   b. Have the client stop breastfeeding

   c. Instruct the client to take a warm shower

   d. Ask how often the client is breastfeeding

15. When assessing the uterus of a 2-day postpartum client, which finding would the nurse evaluate as normal?

   a. A scant amount of lochia alba

   b. A moderate amount of lochia alba

   c. A moderate amount of lochia rubra

   d. A scant amount of lochia serosa

16. Which client should the postpartum nurse assess **first** after receiving shift report?

   a. The 3-day postpartum client who has a pulse of 50.

   b. The 12-hour postpartum client who has a temperature of 100.4°F (38°C).

   c. The 2-day postpartum client who has a blood pressure of 138/90.

   d. The 1-day postpartum client who has a respiratory rate of 20.

CHAPTER 16

Nursing Management During the Postpartum Period

Learning Objectives

Upon completion of the chapter, you will be able to:

- Define the key terms.
- Characterize the normal physiologic and psychological adaptations to the postpartum period.
- Determine the parameters that need to be assessed during the postpartum period.
- Compare the bonding and attachment process.
- Select behaviors that enhance or inhibit the attachment process.
- Outline nursing management for the woman and her family during the postpartum period.
- Examine the role of the nurse in promoting successful breastfeeding.
- Plan areas of health education needed for discharge planning, home care, and follow-up.

SECTION I: ASSESSING YOUR UNDERSTANDING

Activity A FILL IN THE BLANKS

1. The _____ is a plastic squeeze bottle filled with warm tap water that is sprayed over the perineal area after each voiding and before applying a new perineal pad.

2. When palpating the breasts, any evidence of any nodules, masses, or areas of warmth, may indicate a plugged duct that may progress to _____ if not treated promptly.

3. Elevations in blood pressure from the woman's baseline might suggest pregnancy-induced _____.

4. _____ is considered the fifth vital sign.

5. _____ hypotension can occur when the woman changes rapidly from a lying or sitting position to a standing one.

6. The top portion of the uterus, also known as the _____, is routinely assessed to determine uterine involution.

7. Women who experience _____ births will have less lochia discharge than those having a vaginal birth.

8. _____ is the process by which the infant's capabilities and behavioral characteristics elicit parental response.

9. _____ refers to the enduring nature of the attachment relationship.

10. Any discharge from the nipple should be described and documented if it is not _____, also called foremilk.

Activity B MATCHING

Match the terms in Column A with their descriptions in Column B.

Column A

___ **1.** Bonding

___ **2.** Proximity

___ **3.** Process of attachment

___ **4.** Postpartum blues

___ **5.** Contact

Column B

a. Physical and psychological experience of the parents being close to their infant

b. Transient emotional disturbances

c. Development of a close emotional attachment to a newborn by the parents during the first 30 to 60 minutes after birth

d. Development of strong affectional ties between an infant and a significant other (e.g., mother, father, sibling, caretaker)

e. Sensory experiences such as touching, holding, and gazing at the newborn

Activity C SHORT ANSWERS

Briefly answer the following.

1. What does the postpartum assessment of the mother include?

_____

_____

_____

2. What nutritional recommendations can a nurse provide to a client during the postpartum period?

_____

_____

_____

3. What are the causes of postpartum stress?

_____

_____

4. What are the postpartum physiologic danger signs?

_____

_____

_____

5. Discuss ways a nurse can model behavior to facilitate parental role adaptation and attachment during the postpartum period.

_____

_____

_____

6. What suggestions can a nurse provide to the parents to minimize sibling rivalry during the postpartum period?

_____

_____

_____

SECTION II: APPLYING YOUR KNOWLEDGE

Activity D CASE STUDY

Consider this scenario and answer the questions.

A nurse is caring for a client who has just delivered a healthy baby girl. The client is aware of the benefits of breastfeeding. She expresses her desire to breastfeed her newborn.

1. What assessments should the nurse perform in this regard?

_____

_____

_____

2. How often should the client breastfeed her infant during the postpartum period?

_____

_____

_____

SECTION III: PRACTICING FOR NCLEX

Activity E **NCLEX-STYLE QUESTIONS**

Answer the following questions.

1. A nurse has been assigned to the care of a client who has just given birth. How frequently should the nurse perform the assessments during the first hour after birth?

   a. Every 30 minutes

   b. Every 15 minutes

   c. After 60 minutes

   d. After 45 minutes

2. During assessment of the mother during the postpartum period, what sign should alert the nurse that the client is likely experiencing uterine atony?

   a. Fundus feels firm

   b. Foul-smelling urine

   c. Purulent vaginal drainage

   d. Boggy or relaxed uterus

3. The nurse observes a 2-in (5-cm) lochia stain on the perineal pad of a 1-day postpartum client. Which of the following should the nurse do **next**?

   a. Reassess the client in 1 hour

   b. Document the lochia as scant

   c. Ask when the peripad was changed

   d. Massage the client's fundus

4. A nurse is caring for a client who has just received an episiotomy. The nurse observes that the laceration extends through the perineal area and continues through the anterior rectal wall. How does the nurse classify the laceration?

   a. First-degree

   b. Second-degree

   c. Third-degree

   d. Fourth-degree

5. A nurse is applying ice packs to the perineal area of a client who has had a vaginal birth. Which intervention should the nurse perform to ensure that the client gets the optimum benefits of the procedure?

   a. Apply ice packs directly to the perineal area

   b. Apply ice packs for 40 minutes continuously

   c. Ensure ice pack is changed frequently

   d. Use ice packs for a week after birth

6. A first-time mother is nervous about breastfeeding. Which intervention would the nurse perform to reduce maternal anxiety about breastfeeding?

   a. Reassure the mother that some newborns "latch on and catch on" right away, and some newborns take more time and patience.

   b. Explain that breastfeeding comes naturally to all mothers.

   c. Tell her that breastfeeding is a mechanical procedure that involves burping once in a while and that she should try finishing it quickly.

   d. Ensure that the mother breastfeeds the newborn using the cradle method.

7. A client who has a breastfeeding newborn reports sore nipples. Which intervention can the nurse suggest to alleviate the client's condition?

   a. Recommend a moisturizing soap to clean the nipples

   b. Encourage use of breast pads with plastic liners

   c. Offer suggestions based on observation to correct positioning or latching

   d. Fasten nursing bra flaps immediately after feeding

8. A client who has given birth is being discharged from the health care facility. She wants to know how safe it would be for her to have intercourse. Which instructions should the nurse provide to the client regarding intercourse after birth?

   a. Avoid use of water-based gel lubricants

   b. Resume intercourse if bright-red bleeding stops

   c. Avoid performing pelvic floor exercises

   d. Use oral contraceptives for contraception

9. A client is Rh negative and has given birth to her newborn. What should the nurse do **next**?

    a. Determine the newborn's blood type and rhesus

    b. Determine if this is the client's first baby

    c. Administer Rh immunoglobulins intramuscularly

    d. Ask if the client received Rh immunoglobulins during the pregnancy

10. A nurse is to care for a client during the postpartum period. The client reports pain and discomfort in her breasts. What signs should a nurse look for to find out if the client has engorged breasts? Select all that apply.

    a. Breasts are hard.

    b. Breasts are tender.

    c. Nipples are fissured.

    d. Nipples are cracked.

    e. Breasts are soft.

11. A nurse is assessing a client during the postpartum period. Which findings indicate normal postpartum adjustment? Select all that apply.

    a. Abdominal pain

    b. Active bowel sounds

    c. Tender abdomen

    d. Passing gas

    e. Nondistended abdomen

12. When teaching the new mother about breastfeeding, the nurse is correct when providing what instructions? Select all that apply.

    a. Give newborns water and other foods to balance nutritional needs.

    b. Help the mother initiate breastfeeding within 30 minutes of birth.

    c. Encourage breastfeeding of the newborn infant on demand.

    d. Provide breastfeeding newborns with pacifiers.

    e. Place baby in uninterrupted skin-to-skin contact with the mother.

13. A postpartum client is having difficulty stopping her urine stream. Which should the nurse do **next**?

    a. Determine if the client is emptying her bladder

    b. Ask the client when she last urinated

    c. Perform an in and out catheter on the client

    d. Educate the client on how to perform Kegel exercises

14. Upon assessment, a nurse notes the client has a pulse of 90 beats per minute, moderate lochia, and a boggy uterus. What should the nurse do **next**?

    a. Notify the health care provider

    b. Assess the client's blood pressure

    c. Change the client's peripad

    d. Massage the client's fundus

15. A client has been discharged from the hospital after a cesarean birth. Which should the nurse include in the discharge teaching?

    a. "Follow-up with your health care provider within 3 weeks of being discharged."

    b. "Notify the health care provider if your temperature is greater than 99°F (37.2°C)."

    c. "You should be seen by your health care provider if you have blurred vision."

    d. "Call your health care provider if you saturate a peripad in less than 4 hours."

CHAPTER 17

Newborn Transitioning

Learning Objectives

Upon completion of the chapter, you will be able to:

- Define the key terms used in this chapter.
- Examine the major physiologic changes that occur as the newborn transitions to extrauterine life.
- Determine the primary challenges faced by the newborn during transition to extrauterine life.
- Differentiate the three behavioral patterns that newborns progress through after birth.
- Assess the five typical behavioral responses triggered by external stimuli of the newborn.

SECTION I: ASSESSING YOUR UNDERSTANDING

Activity A FILL IN THE BLANKS

1. _____ is the newborn's ability to process and respond to visual and auditory stimuli.

2. A _____ is an involuntary muscular response to a sensory stimulus.

3. The immune system's responses may be either natural or _____.

4. _____ is considered the first stool passed by the newborn. It is composed of amniotic fluid, shed mucosal cells, intestinal secretions, and blood.

5. Human breast milk provides a passive mechanism to protect the newborn against the dangers of a deficient _____ defense system.

6. At birth, the pH of the stomach contents is mildly acidic, reflecting the pH of the _____ fluid.

7. _____ refers to the yellowing of the skin, sclera, and mucous membranes as a result of increased bilirubin blood levels.

8. The source of bilirubin in the newborn is the _____ of erythrocytes.

9. Newborn iron stores are determined by total body _____ content and length of gestation.

10. The primary body temperature regulators are located in the _____ and the central nervous system.

Activity B LABELING

Consider the following figures. Identify figures A, B, C, and D by the mechanisms of heat loss for the newborn.

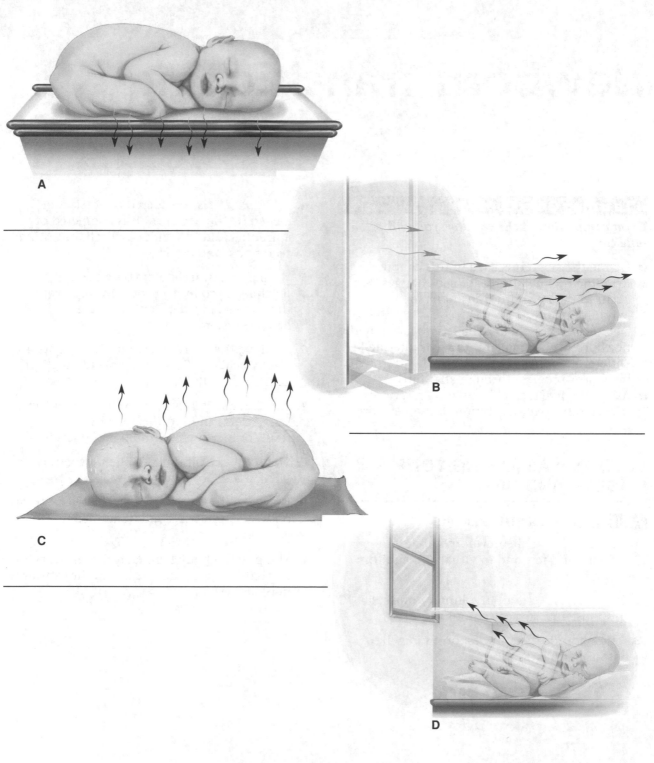

A

_____

B

_____

C

_____

D

_____

Activity C MATCHING

Match the blood-supplying structures in Column A with their corresponding functions in Column B.

Column A

_____ 1. Umbilical vein

_____ 2. Ductus venosus

_____ 3. Foramen ovale

_____ 4. Ductus arteriosus

_____ 5. Placenta

Column B

a. Allows majority of the umbilical vein blood to bypass liver and merge with blood moving through the vena cava, bringing it to the heart sooner

b. Connects pulmonary artery to the aorta, which allows bypassing of the pulmonary circuit

c. Allows more than half the blood entering the right atrium to cross immediately to the left atrium

d. Carries oxygenated blood from placenta to the fetus

e. Provides oxygen and nutrients to the fetus and removes waste products

Activity D SHORT ANSWERS

Briefly answer the following.

1. What is a newborn's response to auditory and visual stimuli?

_____

_____

_____

2. What are the expected neurobehavioral responses of the newborn?

_____

_____

_____

3. What events must occur before a newborn's lungs can maintain respiratory function?

_____

_____

_____

4. How is the amniotic fluid removed from the lungs of a newborn?

_____

_____

_____

5. What are some abnormal signs the nurse should assess while observing a newborn's respiratory effort?

_____

_____

_____

6. What are the nursing interventions that may help minimize regurgitation?

_____

_____

_____

SECTION II: APPLYING YOUR KNOWLEDGE

Activity E CASE STUDY

Consider this scenario and answer the questions.

A newborn is under the observation of a nurse in a health care facility. The child is crying, and its heartbeat has increased. Usually, heartbeats are highest after birth and reach a plateau within a week after birth. During the first few minutes after birth, a newborn's heart rate is approximately 120 to 180 beats per minute. Thereafter, the heart rate begins to decrease to somewhere between 120 and 130 beats per minute.

1. What are the factors that increase the heart rate and blood pressure in a newborn?

_____

_____

_____

2. What are the factors that affect the hematologic values of a newborn?

_____

_____

_____

3. What are the benefits of delayed cord clamping after birth?

_____

_____

_____

SECTION III: PRACTICING FOR NCLEX

Activity F **NCLEX-STYLE QUESTIONS**

Answer the following questions.

1. The nurse cares for a newborn with a congenital cardiac anomaly. What component of nursing care is the **priority** for the newborn?

   a. Maintain oxygen saturation at 95% or above

   b. Accompany the newborn to all radiologic examinations

   c. Prevent pain as much as possible

   d. Teach the parents to take pulse and blood pressure measurements

2. A client delivers a newborn in a local health care facility. What guidance should the nurse give to the client before discharge regarding thermoregulation of the newborn at home?

   a. Ensure cool air is circulating over the newborn to prevent overheating

   b. Keep the newborn wrapped in a blanket, with a cap on its head

   c. Encourage the mother to keep the infant in her bed to ensure that the infant stays warm

   d. Keep the infant's room temperature at least 80 degrees

3. A nurse is explaining the benefits of breast-feeding to a client who has just delivered. Which statement correctly explains the benefits of breast-feeding to this mother?

   a. Immunoglobulin IgA in breast milk boosts a newborn's immune system

   b. Breast-feeding provides more iron and calcium for the infant

   c. Mothers who breast-feed have increased breast size following nursing

   d. Breast-fed infants gain weight faster than formula-fed infants after 6 month of age

4. Which factors could increase the risk of overheating in a newborn? Select all that apply.

   a. Limited ability of diaphoresis

   b. Underdeveloped lungs

   c. Isolette that is too warm

   d. Limited sugar stores

   e. Lack of brown fat

5. A 2-month-old infant is admitted to a local health care facility with an axillary temperature of 96.8°F (36°C). Which observed manifestation would confirm the occurrence of cold stress in this client?

   a. Increased appetite

   b. Increase in the body temperature

   c. Lethargy and hypotonia

   d. Hyperglycemia

6. A primiparous mother delivered a 8-lb 12-oz (4-kg) infant daughter yesterday. She is being bottle fed, is Rh positive, has a cephalohematoma, and received her hepatitis A vaccine last evening. Which factor places the newborn at risk for the development of jaundice?

   a. Formula feeding

   b. Cephalohematoma

   c. Female gender

   d. Hepatitis A vaccine

   e. Rh-positive blood type

7. A 12-hour-old infant is receiving IV fluids for polycythemia. For which complication should a nurse monitor this client?

   a. Tachycardia

   b. Hypotension

   c. Decreased level of consciousness

   d. Fluid overload

8. A client is worried that her newborn's stools are greenish, with an unpleasant odor. The newborn is being formula fed. What instruction should the nurse give this client?

   a. Switch to feeding breast milk

   b. No action is need; this is normal

   c. Increase the newborn's fluid intake

   d. Change to a soy-based formula

9. A breast-feeding mother wants to know how to help her 2-week-old newborn gain the weight lost after birth. Which action should the nurse suggest as the **best** method to accomplish this goal?

   a. The mother pump her breast milk and measure it before feeding

   b. Breast-feed the infant every 2 to 3 hours on demand

   c. Weigh the infant daily to ensure that she is gaining 11/2 to 2 oz per day

   d. Add cereal to the newborn's feedings twice a day

10. A preterm infant is experiencing cold stress after birth. For which symptom should the nurse assess to **best** validate the problem?

    a. Shivering

    b. Hyperglycemia

    c. Apnea

    d. Metabolic alkalosis

11. A client delivers a baby at a local health care facility. The nurse observes that the infant is fussy and begins to move her hands to her mouth and suck on her hand and fingers. How should the nurse interpret these findings?

    a. The infant is entering the habituation state.

    b. The infant is attempting self-consoling maneuvers.

    c. The infant is in a state of hyperactivity.

    d. The infant is displaying a state of alertness.

12. A nurse needs to monitor the blood glucose levels of a newborn under observation at a health care facility. When should the nurse check the newborn's initial glucose level?

    a. After the newborn has received the initial feeding

    b. 24 hours after admission to the nursery

    c. On admission to the nursery

    d. 4 hours after admission to the nursery

13. The nurse wants to maintain a neutral thermal environment for her assigned neonatal clients. Which intervention would **best** ensure that this goal is met?

    a. Promote early breast-feeding for the infants

    b. Avoid skin-to-skin contact with the mother until the infants are 8 hours old

    c. Keep the infant transporter temperature between 80°F and 85°F

    d. Avoid bathing the newborn until they are 24 hours old

14. A nurse is assessing the temperature of a newborn using a skin temperature probe. Which point should the nurse keep in mind while taking the newborn's temperature?

    a. Ensure that the newborn is lying on its abdomen

    b. Tape the temperature probe on the forehead

    c. Place the temperature probe over the liver

    d. Use the skin temperature probe only in open bassinets

15. A nurse is assigned to care for a newborn with an elevated bilirubin level. Which symptom would the nurse expect to find during the infant's physical assessment?

    a. Yellow sclera

    b. Abdominal distension

    c. Heart rate of 130 beats per minute

    d. Respiratory rate of 24

16. The nurse is providing teaching to a new mother who is breast-feeding. The mother demonstrates understanding of teaching when she identifies which characteristics as being true of the stool of breast-fed newborns? Select all that apply.

    a. Formed in consistency

    b. Completely odorless

    c. Firm in shape

    d. Yellowish gold color

    e. Stringy to pasty consistency

17. A nurse is caring for a 5-hour-old newborn. The physician has asked the nurse to maintain the newborn's temperature between 97.7°F and 99.5°F (36.5°C and 37.5°C). Which nursing intervention would be the **best** approach to maintaining the temperature within the recommended range?

    a. Delay weighing the infant, as the scales may be cold

    b. Use the stethoscope over the newborn's garment

    c. Place the newborn's crib close to the outer wall in the room

    d. Place the newborn skin-to-skin with the mother

CHAPTER 18

Nursing Management of the Newborn

Learning Objectives

Upon completion of the chapter, you will be able to:

- Define the key terms.
- Relate the assessments performed during the immediate newborn period.
- Employ appropriate interventions that meet the immediate needs of the term newborn.
- Demonstrate the components of a typical physical examination of a newborn.
- Distinguish common variations that can be noted during a newborn's physical examination.
- Characterize common concerns in the newborn and appropriate interventions.
- Compare the importance of the newborn screening tests.
- Plan for common interventions that are appropriate during the early newborn period.
- Analyze the nurse's role in meeting the newborn's nutritional needs.
- Outline discharge planning content and education needed for the family with a newborn.

SECTION I: ASSESSING YOUR UNDERSTANDING

Activity A FILL IN THE BLANKS

1. The _____ score is used to evaluate newborns at 1 minute and 5 minutes after birth.

2. _____ refers to the soft, downy hair on the newborn's body.

3. _____ babies are babies with placental aging who are born after 42 weeks.

4. Babies weighing more than the 90th percentile on standard growth charts are referred to as _____ for gestational age.

5. Vitamin K, a fat-soluble vitamin, promotes blood clotting by increasing the synthesis of _____ by the liver.

6. Persistent cyanosis of fingers, hands, toes, and feet with mottled blue or red discoloration and coldness is called _____.

7. _____ are unopened sebaceous glands frequently found on a newborn's nose.

8. _____ sign refers to the dilation of blood vessels on only one side of the body, giving the newborn the appearance of paleness on one side of the body and ruddiness on the other.

9. The _____ fontanel of the baby is diamond shaped and closes by age 18 to 24 months.

10. _____ is a localized effusion of blood beneath the periosteum of the skull of the newborn.

Activity B LABELING

Consider the following figure. What is being depicted?

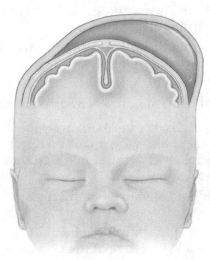

A

_____

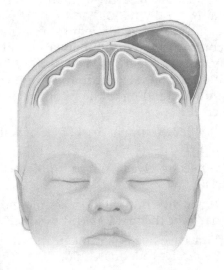

B

1. _____
   _____
   _____

Activity C MATCHING

Match the following anthropometric measurements of a term newborn in Column A with their appropriate value in Column B.

Column A

____ 1. Head circumference

____ 2. Chest circumference

____ 3. Weight

____ 4. Length

Column B

a. 32–38 cm

b. 33–37 cm

c. 2,500–4,000 g

d. 45–55 cm

Activity D SEQUENCING

Arrange the following reflexes in the correct order of their disappearance into adulthood.

1. Stepping
2. Babinski sign
3. Grasp
4. Rooting
5. Gag reflex

☐ → ☐ → ☐ → ☐ → ☐

Activity E SHORT ANSWERS

Briefly answer the following.

1. How can a mother achieve the football-hold position for breast-feeding?

   _____
   _____
   _____

2. What is colostrum?

   _____
   _____
   _____

3. What is the use of fiber optic pads in treatment of physiologic jaundice?

   _____
   _____
   _____

4. How can a nurse test Moro reflex?

_____

_____

_____

5. What is caput succedaneum?

_____

_____

_____

6. What is erythema toxicum?

_____

_____

_____

SECTION II: APPLYING YOUR KNOWLEDGE

Activity F CASE STUDY

Consider this scenario and answer the questions.

Karen, a first-time mother, is worried that her baby does not sleep properly and wakes up every 2 hours. Karen informs the nurse that she often brings the baby to her bed to nurse and falls asleep with the baby in her bed.

1. What information should the nurse offer regarding the sleeping habits of newborns?

_____

_____

_____

2. What safety precautions should the mother take when putting the baby to sleep?

_____

_____

_____

3. What education should the nurse impart to Karen to discourage bed sharing?

_____

_____

_____

SECTION III: PRACTICING FOR NCLEX

Activity G NCLEX-STYLE QUESTIONS

Answer the following questions.

1. The nurse caring for a newborn has to perform assessment at various intervals. When should the nurse complete the second assessment for the newborn?
   a. Within 30 minutes after birth, in the birthing area
   b. Within the first 2 to 4 hours, when the newborn reaches the nursery
   c. Prior to the newborn being discharged
   d. 24 hours after the newborn's birth

2. As a part of the newborn assessment, the nurse examines the infant's skin. Which nursing observation would warrant further investigation?
   a. Bright red, raised bumpy area noted above the right eye
   b. Small pink or red patches on the baby's eyelids, and back of the neck
   c. Fine red rash noted over the chest and back
   d. Blue or purplish splotches on buttocks

3. The nurse is educating a client who is breast-feeding her 2-week-old newborn regarding the nutritional requirements of newborns, according to the recommendations of the American Academy of Pediatrics (AAP). Which response by the mother would validate her understanding of the information she received?
   a. "I will feed him at least 30 cc of water daily."
   b. "I need to give him iron supplements daily."
   c. "I will give him vitamin D supplements daily for the first 2 months of life."
   d. "Since we live in a rural area, I must ensure he receives adequate fluoride supplementation."

4. A first-time mother informs the nurse that she is unable to breast-feed her newborn through the day as she is usually away at work. She adds that she wants to express her breast milk and store it for her newborn to have later. What instruction would be correct to offer the mother to ensure the safety of the stored expressed breast milk?

   a. Use the sealed and chilled milk within 24 hours

   b. Use any frozen milk within 6 months of obtaining it

   c. Use microwave ovens to warm the chilled milk

   d. Refreeze any unused milk for later use if it has not been out more than 2 hours

5. A nurse is educating the mother of a newborn about feeding and burping. Which strategy should the nurse offer to the mother regarding burping?

   a. Hold the newborn upright with the newborn's head on the mother's shoulder

   b. Lay the newborn on its back on its mother's lap

   c. Gently rub the newborn's abdomen while the newborn is in a sitting position

   d. Lay the newborn on its abdomen in the mother's lap and gently pat the buttocks

6. The mother of a formula-fed newborn asks how she will know if her newborn is receiving enough formula during feedings. Which response by the nurse is correct?

   a. "Your newborn should finish a bottle in less than 15 minutes."

   b. "A sign of normal nutrition is when your newborn seems satisfied and is gaining sufficient weight."

   c. "If your newborn is wetting three to four diapers and producing several stools a day, enough formula is likely being consumed."

   d. "Your newborn should be taking about 2 oz of formula for every pound of body weight during each feeding."

7. A nurse, while examining a newborn, observes salmon patches on the nape of the neck and on the eyelids. Which is the **most** likely cause of these skin abnormalities?

   a. Bruising from the birth process

   b. An immature autoregulation of blood flow

   c. An allergic reaction to the soap used for the first bath

   d. Concentration of immature blood vessels

8. A nurse is required to obtain the temperature of a healthy newborn who was placed in an open crib. Which is the **most** appropriate method for measuring a newborn's temperature?

   a. Tape electronic thermistor probe to the abdominal skin

   b. Obtain the temperature orally

   c. Place electronic temperature probe in the midaxillary area

   d. Obtain the temperature rectally

9. A nurse determines that a newborn has a 1-minute Apgar score of 5 points. What conclusion would the nurse make from this finding?

   a. The infant requires immediate and aggressive interventions for survival.

   b. The infant is adjusting well to extrauterine life.

   c. The infant is experiencing moderate difficulty in adjusting to extrauterine life.

   d. The infant probably has either a congenital heart defect or an immature respiratory system.

10. The mother of a newborn observes a diaper rash on her newborn's skin. Which intervention should the nurse instruct the parent to implement to treat the diaper rash?

    a. Expose the newborn's bottom to air several times a day

    b. Use only baby wipes to cleanse the perianal area

    c. Use products such as talcum powder with each diaper change

    d. Place the newborn's buttocks in warm water after each void or stool

11. A nurse is caring for a newborn with transient tachypnea. What nursing interventions should the nurse perform while providing supportive care to the newborn? Select all that apply.

    a. Provide warm water to drink

    b. Provide oxygen supplementation

    c. Massage the newborn's back

    d. Ensure the newborn's warmth

    e. Observe respiratory status frequently

12. A nurse is caring for a newborn with hypoglycemia. For which symptoms of hypoglycemia should the nurse monitor the newborn? Select all that apply.

   a. Lethargy

   b. Low-pitched cry

   c. Cyanosis

   d. Skin rashes

   e. Jitteriness

13. A mother who is 4 days postpartum, and is breast-feeding, expresses to the nurse that her breast seems to be tender and engorged. What education should the nurse give to the mother to relieve breast engorgement? Select all that apply.

   a. Take warm-to-hot showers to encourage milk release

   b. Feed the newborn in the sitting position only

   c. Express some milk manually before breast-feeding

   d. Massage the breasts from the nipple toward the axillary area

   e. Apply warm compresses to the breasts prior to nursing

14. A nurse is performing a detailed newborn assessment of a female newborn. Which observations indicate a normal finding? Select all that apply.

   a. Mongolian spots

   b. Enlarged fontanelles

   c. Swollen genitals

   d. Low-set ears

   e. Short, creased neck

CHAPTER 19

Nursing Management of Pregnancy at Risk: Pregnancy-Related Complications

Learning Objectives

Upon completion of the chapter, you will be able to:

- Evaluate the term "high-risk pregnancy."
- Determine the common factors that might place a pregnancy at high risk.
- Detect the causes of vaginal bleeding during early and late pregnancy.
- Outline nursing assessment and management for the pregnant woman experiencing vaginal bleeding.
- Develop a plan of care for the woman experiencing preeclampsia, eclampsia, and HELLP syndrome.
- Examine the pathophysiology of polyhydramnios and subsequent management.
- Evaluate factors in a woman's prenatal history that place her at risk for premature rupture of membranes (PROM).
- Formulate a teaching plan for maintaining the health of pregnant women experiencing a high-risk pregnancy.

SECTION I: ASSESSING YOUR UNDERSTANDING

Activity A FILL IN THE BLANKS

1. _____ is a decreased amount of amniotic fluid (<500 mL) between 32 and 36 weeks' gestation.

2. _____ is the presence of rhythmic involuntary contractions, most often at the foot or ankle.

3. The time interval from rupture of membranes to the onset of regular contractions is termed the _____ period.

4. Brisk reflexes, or _____, is a common presenting symptom of preeclampsia and is the result of an irritable cortex.

5. Rh _____ is a condition that develops when a woman with Rh-negative blood type is exposed to Rh-positive blood cells and subsequently develops circulating titers of Rh antibodies.

6. _____ twins develop when a single, fertilized ovum splits during the first 2 weeks after conception.

7. A foul odor of amniotic fluid indicates
_____.

8. A _____ abortion refers to the loss of a fetus resulting from natural causes—that is, not elective or therapeutically induced by a procedure.

9. The most common cause for _____ trimester abortions is fetal genetic abnormalities, usually unrelated to the mother.

10. _____ hypertension is characterized by hypertension without proteinuria after 20 weeks' gestation and a return of the blood pressure to normal postpartum.

Activity B MATCHING

Match the following conditions commonly associated with pregnancy-related complications in Column A with their definitions in Column B.

Column A

_____ 1. Spontaneous abortion

_____ 2. Ectopic pregnancy

_____ 3. Gestational trophoblastic disease

_____ 4. Cervical insufficiency

_____ 5. Placenta previa

Column B

a. Spectrum of neoplastic disorders that originate in the human placenta

b. Weak, structurally defective cervix that spontaneously dilates in the absence of contractions in the second trimester, resulting in the loss of the pregnancy

c. Loss of an early pregnancy, usually before the 20th week of gestation

d. Painless bleeding condition that occurs in the last two trimesters of pregnancy

e. Pregnancy in which the fertilized ovum implants outside the uterine cavity

Activity C SEQUENCING

Put the terms in correct sequence by writing the letters in the boxes provided below.

1. Given below, in random order, are the steps for assessing the patellar reflex. Write the correct sequence.

   a. Using a reflex hammer or the side of the hand, strike the area of the patellar tendon firmly and quickly.

   b. Have the woman flex her knee slightly.

   c. Place the woman in the supine position.

   d. Repeat the procedure on the opposite leg.

   e. Note the movement of the leg and foot.

   f. Place a hand under the knee to support the leg and locate the patellar tendon.

   ☐ → ☐ → ☐ → ☐ → ☐ → ☐

Activity D SHORT ANSWERS

Briefly answer the following.

1. What are some possible complications of hyperemesis gravidarum?

2. What are the conditions associated with early bleeding during pregnancy?

3. What are the causes of ectopic pregnancies?

4. What are the risk factors for hyperemesis gravidarum?

5. What should a nurse include in prevention education for ectopic pregnancies?

_____

_____

_____

6. What is the Kleihauer–Betke test?

_____

_____

_____

SECTION II: APPLYING YOUR KNOWLEDGE

Activity E CASE STUDY

Consider this scenario and answer the questions.

The labor and birth triage nurse is admitting Jenna. By completing Jenna's history, the nurse learns that she is a single, 17-year-old African American, G-3 P-0020, who registered for prenatal care at the local clinic at 16 weeks' gestation. Her prenatal course has been unremarkable except for a urinary tract infection at 22 weeks that was treated with antibiotics. She did not return to the clinic for a follow-up urine culture after treatment. She is presenting at the hospital now, at 26 weeks, complaining of lower backache, cramping, and malaise. She reports to the nurse that she feels normal fetal movement and denies vaginal bleeding or discharge. She states that she feels her uterus "balling up" every 5 to 10 minutes. This has been going on all day, even after she came home from school and rested. The external fetal monitor, tocodynamometer, and ultrasound are applied to Jenna. The nurse's initial assessment indicates the client having contractions every 4 to 5 minutes that last 30 to 40 seconds, and the nurse palpates the contractions as mild.

1. Name the symptoms that indicate preterm labor and birth.

_____

_____

_____

2. The nurse caring for Jenna must ensure that she receives basic information about preterm labor, including information about harmful lifestyles, the signs of genitourinary infections, and preterm labor. What information should the nurse provide to the client to help better educate her in prevention strategies?

_____

_____

_____

SECTION III: PRACTICING FOR NCLEX

Activity F NCLEX-STYLE QUESTIONS

Answer the following questions.

1. A pregnant client with hyperemesis gravidarum needs advice on how to minimize nausea and vomiting. Which instruction should the nurse give this client?

a. Lie down or recline for at least 2 hours after eating

b. Avoid dry crackers, toast, and soda

c. Eat small, frequent meals throughout the day

d. Decrease intake of carbonated beverages

2. When caring for a client with premature rupture of membranes (PROM), the nurse observes an increase in the client's pulse. What should the nurse do **next**?

a. Assess the client's temperate

b. Monitor the client for preterm labor

c. Assess for cord compression

d. Monitor the fetus for respiratory distress

3. A nurse is monitoring a client with PROM who is in labor and observes meconium in the amniotic fluid. What does this indicate?

a. Cord compression

b. Fetal distress related to hypoxia

c. Infection

d. Central nervous system "CNS" involvement

4. The nurse is caring for a pregnant client with severe preeclampsia. Which nursing interventions should a nurse perform to institute and maintain seizure precautions in this client?

   a. Provide a well-lit room
   b. Keep head of bed slightly elevated
   c. Place the client in a supine position
   d. Keep the suction equipment readily available

5. A client with preeclampsia is receiving magnesium sulfate to suppress or control seizures. Which nursing intervention should a nurse perform to determine the effectiveness of therapy?

   a. Assess deep tendon reflexes
   b. Monitor intake and output
   c. Assess client's mucous membrane
   d. Assess client's skin turgor

6. A nurse is assessing pregnant clients for the risk of placenta previa. Which of the following clients faces the greatest risk for this condition?

   a. A 23-year-old multigravida client
   b. A client with a history of alcohol abuse
   c. A client with a structurally defective cervix
   d. A client who had a myomectomy to remove fibroids

7. A client is seeking advice for his pregnant wife, who is experiencing mild elevations in blood pressure. In which position should a nurse recommend the pregnant client rest?

   a. Supine position
   b. Lateral recumbent position
   c. Left lateral lying position
   d. Head of the bed slightly elevated

8. A nurse is caring for a client with hyperemesis gravidarum. Which nursing action is the **priority** for this client?

   a. Administer total parenteral nutrition
   b. Administer an antiemetic
   c. Set up for a percutaneous endoscopic gastrostomy
   d. Administer IV NS with vitamins and electrolytes

9. A nurse has been assigned to assess a pregnant client for abruptio placenta. For which classic manifestation of this condition should the nurse assess?

   a. Painless bright red vaginal bleeding
   b. Increased fetal movement
   c. "Knife-like" abdominal pain with vaginal bleeding
   d. Generalized vasospasm

10. A nurse is caring for a client undergoing treatment for ectopic pregnancy. Which symptom is observed in a client if rupture or hemorrhaging occurs before the ectopic pregnancy is successfully treated?

    a. Phrenic nerve irritation
    b. Painless bright red vaginal bleeding
    c. Fetal distress
    d. Tetanic contractions

11. The nurse is required to assess a pregnant client who is reporting vaginal bleeding. Which nursing action is the **priority**?

    a. Monitoring uterine contractility
    b. Assessing signs of shock
    c. Determining the amount of funneling
    d. Assessing the amount and color of the bleeding

12. The nurse is caring for a pregnant client with fallopian tube rupture. Which intervention is the **priority** for this client?

    a. Monitor the client's beta-hCG level
    b. Monitor the mass with transvaginal ultrasound
    c. Monitor the client's vital signs and bleeding
    d. Monitor the fetal heart rate (FHR)

13. The nurse is caring for an Rh-negative nonimmunized client at 14 weeks' gestation. What information would the nurse provide to the client?

    a. Obtain RhoGAM at 28 weeks' gestation
    b. Consume a well-balanced, nutritional diet
    c. Avoid sexual activity until after 28 weeks
    d. Undergo periodic transvaginal ultrasounds

14. A nurse is caring for a pregnant client with eclamptic seizure. Which is a characteristic of eclampsia?

   a. Muscle rigidity is followed by facial twitching.

   b. Respirations are rapid during the seizure.

   c. Coma occurs after seizure.

   d. Respiration fails after the seizure.

15. A nurse is assessing a pregnant client with preeclampsia for suspected dependent edema. Which description of dependent edema is **most** accurate?

   a. Dependent edema leaves a small depression or pit after finger pressure is applied to a swollen area.

   b. Dependent edema occurs only in clients on bed rest.

   c. Dependent edema can be measured when pressure is applied.

   d. Dependent edema may be seen in the sacral area if the client is on bed rest.

16. A pregnant client is brought to the health care facility with signs of premature rupture of the membranes (PROM). Which conditions and complications are associated with PROM? Select all that apply.

   a. Prolapsed cord

   b. Abruptio placenta

   c. Spontaneous abortion

   d. Placenta previa

   e. Preterm labor

17. The nurse is required to assess a client for HELLP syndrome. Which are the signs and symptoms of this condition? Select all that apply.

   a. Blood pressure higher than 160/110

   b. Epigastric pain

   c. Oliguria

   d. Upper right quadrant pain

   e. Hyperbilirubinemia

18. A nurse is monitoring a client with spontaneous abortion who has been prescribed misoprostol. Which symptoms are common adverse effects associated with misoprostol? Select all that apply.

   a. Constipation

   b. Dyspepsia

   c. Headache

   d. Hypotension

   e. Tachycardia

Nursing Management of the Pregnancy at Risk: Selected Health Conditions and Vulnerable Populations

Learning Objectives

Upon completion of the chapter, you will be able to:

- Select at least two conditions present before pregnancy that can have a negative effect on a pregnancy.
- Examine how a condition present before pregnancy can affect the woman physiologically and psychologically when she becomes pregnant.
- Evaluate the nursing assessment and management for a pregnant woman with diabetes from that of a pregnant woman without diabetes.
- Explore how congenital and acquired heart conditions can affect a woman's pregnancy.
- Design the nursing assessment and management of a pregnant woman with cardiovascular disorders and respiratory conditions.
- Differentiate among the types of anemia affecting pregnant women in terms of prevention and management.
- Relate the nursing care needed for the pregnant woman with an autoimmune disorder.

- Compare the most common infections that can jeopardize a pregnancy and propose possible preventive strategies.
- Develop a plan of care for the pregnant woman who is HIV positive.
- Outline the nurse's role in the prevention and management of adolescent pregnancy.
- Determine the impact of pregnancy for a woman over the age of 35.
- Analyze the effects of substance abuse during pregnancy.

SECTION I: ASSESSING YOUR UNDERSTANDING

Activity A FILL IN THE BLANKS

1. Human placental lactogen and growth hormone _____ increase in direct correlation with the growth of placental tissue, causing insulin resistance.

2. _____ diabetes of any severity increases the risk of fetal macrosomia.

3. Asthma is known as reactive _____ disease.

4. The _____ is the major site of involvement in the client with tuberculosis.

5. _____ results in reduced capacity of the blood to carry oxygen to the vital organs of the mother and fetus as a result of reduced quantities of RBCs or hemoglobin.

6. Vaginal and rectal specimens of pregnant women may be cultured for the presence of _____ bacterium.

7. _____ is a widespread parasitic infection caused by a one-celled protozoan that may result from contact with cat feces.

8. _____ spans the time frame from the onset of puberty to the cessation of physical growth, roughly from 11 to 19 years of age.

9. _____ found in cigarettes causes vasoconstriction, transfers across the placenta, and reduces blood flow to the fetus, contributing to fetal hypoxia.

10. Maternal use of _____ early in a pregnancy often results in fetal neural tube defects and microencephaly.

Activity B MATCHING

Match the substances in Column A with their effect on pregnancy in Column B.

Column A

___ 1. Alcohol

___ 2. Caffeine

___ 3. Nicotine

___ 4. Cocaine

___ 5. Narcotics

___ 6. Sedatives

Column B

a. Respiratory problems, feeding difficulties, disturbed sleep

b. Neonatal abstinence syndrome, preterm labor, intrauterine growth restriction (IUGR), and preeclampsia

c. Vasoconstriction, tachycardia, hypertension, abruptio placenta, abortion, prune belly syndrome, IUGR

d. Reduced uteroplacental blood flow, decreased birth weight, abortion, prematurity, abruptio placenta

e. Decreased iron absorption; increased risk of anemia

f. Growth deficiencies, facial abnormalities, CNS impairment, behavioral disorders, and abnormal intellectual development

Activity C SHORT ANSWERS

Briefly answer the following.

1. What are the complications in a pregnant client with hypertension?

   _____

   _____

   _____

2. What elements should be included during the physical examination of pregnant clients with asthma?

   _____

   _____

   _____

3. What are the factors the nurse should include in the teaching plan for a pregnant client with asthma?

   _____

   _____

   _____

4. What is the procedure involved in the assessment of tuberculosis in pregnant clients?

   _____

   _____

   _____

5. What are the developmental tasks associated with adolescent behavior?

_____

_____

_____

6. What are the effects of abuse of sedatives by the mother on her infant?

_____

_____

_____

SECTION II: APPLYING YOUR KNOWLEDGE

Activity D CASE STUDY

Consider this scenario and answer the questions.

A nurse is caring for a pregnant client with asthma. During pregnancy, the respiratory system of the client is affected by hormonal changes, mechanical changes, and prior respiratory conditions.

1. When is a pregnant client likely to suffer an increase in asthma attacks?

_____

_____

_____

2. What does successful management of asthma in pregnancy involve?

_____

_____

_____

3. What are the nursing interventions involved for a client with asthma during labor?

_____

_____

_____

SECTION III: PRACTICING FOR NCLEX

Activity E NCLEX-STYLE QUESTIONS

Answer the following questions.

1. What is the role of the nurse during the preconception counseling of a pregnant client with chronic hypertension?

  a. Stressing the avoidance of dairy products

  b. Stressing the positive benefits of a healthy lifestyle

  c. Stressing the increased use of vitamin D supplements

  d. Stressing regular walks and exercise

2. The nurse is caring for a pregnant client who is in her 30th week of gestation and has congenital heart disease. Which should the nurse recognize as a symptom of cardiac decompensation with this client?

  a. Swelling of the face

  b. Dry, rasping cough

  c. Slow, labored respiration

  d. Elevated temperature

3. A nurse is caring for a pregnant client with heart disease in a labor unit. Which intervention is **most** important in the first 48 hours postpartum?

  a. Limiting sodium intake

  b. Inspecting the extremities for edema

  c. Ensuring that the client consumes a high-fiber diet

  d. Assessing for cardiac decompensation

4. A nurse is caring for a pregnant client with asthma. Which intervention would the nurse perform **first**?

  a. Monitoring temperature frequently

  b. Assessing oxygen saturation

  c. Monitoring frequency of headache

  d. Assessing for feeling nauseated

5. What important instruction should the nurse give a pregnant client with tuberculosis?

  a. Maintain adequate hydration

  b. Avoid direct sunlight

  c. Avoid red meat

  d. Wear light, cotton clothes

6. Which should the nurse identify as a risk associated with anemia during pregnancy?

   a. Newborn with heart problems

   b. Fetal asphyxia

   c. Preterm birth

   d. Newborn with an enlarged liver

7. A nurse is caring for a client with CVD who has just delivered. What nursing interventions should the nurse perform when caring for this client? Select all that apply.

   a. Assess for shortness of breath

   b. Assess for a moist cough

   c. Assess for edema and note any pitting

   d. Auscultate heart sounds for abnormalities

   e. Monitor the client's hemoglobin and hematocrit

8. The nurse is caring for a 2-day-old newborn whose mother was diagnosed with cytomegalovirus during the first trimester. On which health care provider order should the nurse place the **priority**?

   a. Perform a hearing screen test

   b. Obtain a urine specimen

   c. Monitor growth and development

   d. Assess pulse rate

9. A nurse is caring for a pregnant adolescent client, who is in her first trimester, during a visit to the maternal child clinic. Which important area should the nurse address during assessment of the client?

   a. Sexual development of the client

   b. Whether sex was consensual

   c. Options for birth control in the future

   d. Knowledge of child development

10. A nurse is caring for a 45-year-old pregnant client with a cardiac disorder, who has been instructed by her physician to follow class I functional activity recommendations. The nurse correctly instructs the client to follow which limitations?

    a. "You will need to be on bedrest for the remainder of your pregnancy."

    b. "It is important for you to rest after any physical activity in order to prevent any cardiac complications."

    c. "It will be beneficial if you plan rest periods throughout your day."

    d. "You do not need to limit your physical activity unless you experience any problems such as fatigue, chest pain, or shortness of breath."

11. A nurse is caring for a pregnant client who is human immunodeficiency virus (HIV) positive. What is a **priority** issue that the nurse should discuss with the client?

    a. The client's relationship with the spouse

    b. The amount of physical contact that should occur with the infant

    c. The client's plan for future pregnancies

    d. The need for the client to avoid breast-feeding

12. A nurse is caring for a pregnant client. The initial interview reveals that the client is accustomed to drinking coffee at regular intervals. For which increased risk should the nurse make the client aware?

    a. Heart disease

    b. Anemia

    c. Rickets

    d. Scurvy

13. The nurse is caring for a pregnant client who indicates that she is fond of meat, works with children, and has a pet cat. Which instructions should the nurse give this client to prevent toxoplasmosis? Select all that apply.

    a. Eat meat cooked to 160°F (71°C)

    b. Avoid cleaning the cat's litter box

    c. Keep the cat outdoors at all times

    d. Avoid contact with children when they have a cold

    e. Avoid outdoor activities such as gardening

14. A pregnant client has been diagnosed with gestational diabetes. Which are risk factors for developing gestational diabetes? Select all that apply.

    a. Maternal age less than 18 years

    b. Genitourinary tract abnormalities

    c. Obesity

    d. Hypertension

    e. Previous large for gestational age (LGA) infant

15. A nurse is caring for a pregnant client with sickle cell anemia. What should the nursing care for the client include? Select all that apply.

   a. Teach the client meticulous hand-washing

   b. Assess serum electrolyte levels of the client at each visit

   c. Instruct client to consume protein-rich food

   d. Assess hydration status of the client at each visit

   e. Urge the client to drink 8 to 10 glasses of fluid daily

16. A nurse is caring for a newborn with fetal alcohol spectrum disorder. What characteristic of the fetal alcohol spectrum disorder should the nurse assess for in the newborn?

   a. Small head circumference

   b. Decreased blood glucose level

   c. Abnormal breathing pattern

   d. Wide eyes

17. A nurse is documenting a dietary plan for a pregnant client with pregestational diabetes. What instructions should the nurse include in the dietary plan for this client?

   a. Include more dairy products in the diet

   b. Include complex carbohydrates in the diet

   c. Eat only two meals per day

   d. Eat at least one egg per day

18. A nurse caring for a pregnant client suspected substance use during pregnancy. What is the **priority** nursing intervention for this client?

   a. Determine how long the client has been using drugs

   b. Obtain a urine specimen for a drug screening

   c. Determine if the client has emotional support

   d. Provide education material on cessation of substance use

19. A nurse is caring for a pregnant client with gestational diabetes. Which meal should the nurse recommend for this client?

   a. Baked chicken, green beans, and chocolate cake

   b. Pizza, corn, and orange slices

   c. Baked turkey, brown rice, and strawberries

   d. Steak, baked potato with butter, and ice cream

20. During the assessment of a laboring client, the nurse learns that the client has cardiovascular disease (CVD). Which assessment would be **priority** for the newborn?

   a. Respiratory function

   b. Heart rate

   c. Temperature

   d. Urine output

CHAPTER 21

Nursing Management of Labor and Birth at Risk

Learning Objectives

Upon completion of the chapter, you will be able to:

- Propose at least five risk factors associated with dystocia.
- Differentiate the four major abnormalities or problems associated with dysfunctional labor patterns, giving examples of each problem.
- Examine the nursing management for the woman with dysfunctional labor experiencing a problem with the powers, passenger, passageway, and psyche.
- Devise a plan of care for the woman experiencing preterm labor.
- Relate the nursing assessment and management of the woman experiencing a postterm pregnancy.
- Assess four obstetric emergencies that can complicate labor and birth, including appropriate management for each.
- Compare and contrast the nursing management for the woman undergoing labor induction or augmentation, forceps, and vacuum-assisted birth.
- Summarize the plan of care for a woman who is to undergo a cesarean birth.
- Evaluate the key areas to be addressed when caring for a woman who is to undergo vaginal birth after cesarean.

SECTION I: ASSESSING YOUR UNDERSTANDING

Activity A FILL IN THE BLANKS

1. Abnormal or difficult labor is known as _____.

2. _____ presentation is frequently associated with multifetal pregnancies and grand multiparity.

3. _____ maneuver is used to identify deviations in fetal presentation or position.

4. _____ drugs promote uterine relaxation by interfering with uterine contraction.

5. _____ are given to enhance fetal lung maturity between 24 and 34 weeks' gestation.

6. Fetal _____, a glycoprotein produced by the chorion, is found at the junction of the chorion and decidua.

7. _____ score helps to identify women who would be most likely to achieve a successful induction.

8. _____ dilators absorb endocervical and local tissue fluids; as they enlarge, they expand the endocervix and provide controlled mechanical pressure.

9. An _____ involves inserting a cervical hook through the cervical os to artificially rupture the membranes.

10. _____ is produced naturally by the posterior pituitary gland and stimulates contractions of the uterus.

Activity B   LABELING

Consider the following figure. What is being depicted?

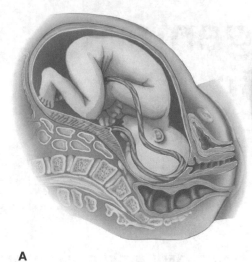 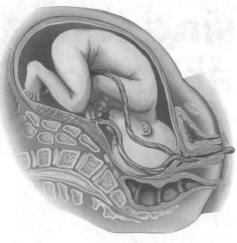

A   B

_____

_____

_____

Activity C   MATCHING

Match the tests in Column A with their purposes in Column B.

Column A

___ **1.** Ultrasound

___ **2.** Pelvimetry

___ **3.** Nonstress test

___ **4.** Phosphatidyl-glycerol level

___ **5.** Nitrazine paper and/or fern test

Column B

a. To rule out fetopelvic disproportion

b. To assess fetal lung maturity

c. To evaluate fetal size, position, and gestational age and to locate the placenta

d. To confirm ruptured membranes

e. To evaluate fetal well being by monitoring the fetal heart tracing

Activity D   SEQUENCING

Given below, in random order, are steps for administering oxytocin. Choose the correct sequence.

1. Use an infusion pump on a secondary line connected to the primary infusion.

2. Prepare the oxytocin infusion by diluting 10 units of oxytocin in 1,000 mL of lactated Ringer solution.

3. Perform or assist with periodic vaginal examinations to determine cervical dilation and fetal descent.

4. Start the oxytocin infusion in mU per minute or mL per hour as ordered.

5. Monitor the characteristics of the FHR, including baseline rate, baseline variability, and decelerations.

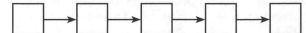

Activity E **SHORT ANSWERS**

Briefly answer the following.

1. What are symptoms of preterm labor?

   _____

   _____

   _____

2. What is cervical ripeness?

   _____

   _____

   _____

3. What is uterine rupture?

   _____

   _____

   _____

4. What are the indications and contraindications of amnioinfusion?

   _____

   _____

   _____

5. What care should the nurse take when assessing the client for risk of cord prolapse?

   _____

   _____

   _____

6. What are maternal and fetal complications in shoulder dystocia?

   _____

   _____

   _____

SECTION II: APPLYING YOUR KNOWLEDGE

Activity F **CASE STUDY**

Consider this scenario and answer the questions.

1. A nurse is caring for an antenatal mother who is advised to undergo amnioinfusion due to oligohydramnios. The nurse prepares the client for the procedure. What nursing

interventions should the nurse follow when caring for the client to prevent maternal and fetal complications?

   _____

   _____

   _____

SECTION III: PRACTICING FOR NCLEX

Activity G **NCLEX-STYLE QUESTIONS**

Answer the following questions.

1. The nurse is caring for a client experiencing a prolonged second stage of labor. The nurse would place **priority** on preparing the client for which intervention?

   a. A forceps- and vacuum-assisted birth

   b. A precipitous birth

   c. Artificial rupture of membranes

   d. A cesarean section

2. A nurse is caring for a client who is experiencing acute onset of dyspnea and hypotension. The physician suspects the client has amniotic fluid embolism. What other signs or symptoms would alert the nurse to the presence of this condition in the client? Select all that apply.

   a. Cyanosis

   b. Arrhythmia

   c. Hyperglycemia

   d. Hematuria

   e. Pulmonary edema

3. A nurse is caring for a client at 38 weeks' gestation who is diagnosed with chorioamnionitis. On which intervention should the nurse place **priority**?

   a. Administer oxytocin

   b. Monitor WBC count

   c. Assess temperature

   d. Assess amniotic fluid

4. A nurse is caring for a client who is scheduled to undergo an amnioinfusion. The nurse would question this order if which is noted upon client assessment?

   a. Uterine hypertonicity

   b. Active genital herpes infection

   c. Blood pressure of 130/88

   d. Decreased urine output

5. A client is experiencing shoulder dystocia during birth. The nurse would place **priority** on performing which assessment postbirth?

   a. Extensive lacerations

   b. Monitor for a cardiac anomaly

   c. Assess for cleft palate

   d. Brachial plexus assessment

6. A full-term pregnant client is being assessed for induction of labor. Her Bishop score is less than 6. Which order would the nurse anticipate?

   a. Insertion of a Foley catheter into the endocervical canal

   b. Prepare the client for a cesarean birth

   c. Administer oxytocin intravenously at 10 mU/min

   d. Artificial rupture of membranes

7. Which postoperative intervention should a nurse perform when caring for a client who has undergone a cesarean birth?

   a. Assess uterine tone to determine fundal firmness

   b. Delay breast-feeding the newborn for a day

   c. Ensure that the client does not cough or breathe deeply

   d. Avoid early ambulation to prevent respiratory problems

8. A client with full-term pregnancy who is not in active labor has been ordered oxytocin intravenously. The nurse would notify the health care provider if which is noted?

   a. Dysfunctional labor pattern

   b. Postterm status

   c. Prolonged ruptured membranes

   d. Overdistended uterus

9. A client who is in labor presents with shoulder dystocia of the fetus. Which is an important nursing intervention?

   a. Assist with positioning the woman in squatting position

   b. Assess for reports of intense back pain in first stage of labor

   c. Anticipate possible use of forceps to rotate to anterior position at birth

   d. Assess for prolonged second stage of labor with arrest of descent

10. A nurse is assessing the following antenatal clients. Which client is at highest risk for having a multiple gestation?

    a. The 41-year-old client who conceived by in vitro fertilization

    b. The 38-year-old client whose spouse is a triplet

    c. The 19-year-old client diagnosed with polycystic ovarian syndrome

    d. The 27-year-old client who delivered twins 2 years ago

11. A client is admitted to the health care facility. The fetus has a gestational age of 42 weeks and is suspected to have cephalopelvic disproportion. Which should the nurse do **next**?

    a. Place the client in lithotomy position for birth

    b. Administer oxytocin intravenously at 4 mU/min

    c. Perform artificial rupture of membranes

    d. Prepare the client for a cesarean birth

12. A nurse is caring for a client who has been diagnosed with precipitous labor. For which potential fetal complication should the nurse monitor?

    a. Facial nerve injury

    b. Cephalhematoma

    c. Intracranial hemorrhage

    d. Facial lacerations

13. The nurse would monitor clients with which conditions for fetal demise? Select all that apply.

    a. Hydramnios

    b. Multifetal gestation

    c. Prolonged pregnancy

    d. Malpresentation

    e. Hypertension

14. A nurse is caring for an antenatal mother diagnosed with umbilical cord prolapse. For which should the nurse monitor the fetus?

    a. Fetal hypoxia
    b. Preeclampsia
    c. Coagulation defects
    d. Placental pathology

15. The nurse is caring for a client after experiencing a placental abruption. Which finding is the **priority** to report to the health care provider?

    a. Hematocrit of 36%
    b. 45 mL urine output in 2 hours
    c. Hemoglobin of 13 g/dL
    d. Platelet count of 150,000 mm^3

CHAPTER 22

Nursing Management of the Postpartum Woman at Risk

- Examine the major conditions that place the postpartum woman at risk.
- Analyze the risk factors, assessment, preventive measures, and nursing management of common postpartum complications.
- Differentiate the causes of postpartum hemorrhage based on the underlying pathophysiologic mechanisms.
- Outline the nurse's role in assessing and managing the care of a woman with a thromboembolic condition.
- Discuss the nursing management of a woman who develops a postpartum infection.
- Identify at least two affective disorders that can occur in women after birth, describing specific therapeutic management for each.

SECTION I: ASSESSING YOUR UNDERSTANDING

Activity A FILL IN THE BLANKS

1. Failure of the uterus to contract and retract immediately after birth is called uterine _____.

2. _____ refers to the incomplete involution of the uterus, or its failure to return to its normal size and condition after birth.

3. In von Willebrand disease, there is a _____ in the von Willebrand factor, which is necessary for platelet adhesion and aggregation.

4. A blood clot within a blood vessel is called a _____.

5. Obstruction of a blood vessel by a blood clot carried by the circulation from the site of origin is called _____.

6. _____ is an infectious condition that involves the endometrium, decidua, and adjacent myometrium of the uterus.

7. A localized inflammation of the breast is called _____.

8. Excessive blood loss that occurs within 24 hours after birth is termed _____ postpartum hemorrhage.

9. Placenta _____ is a condition in which the chorionic villi adhere to the myometrium, causing the placenta to adhere abnormally to the uterus and not separate and deliver spontaneously.

10. A prolapse of the uterine fundus to or through the cervix, so that the uterus is turned inside out after birth, is called uterine _____.

Activity B MATCHING

Match the following causes of postpartum hemorrhage in Column A with their appropriate intervention in Column B.

Column A

___ **1.** Uterine atony

___ **2.** Retained placental tissue

___ **3.** Lacerations or hematoma

___ **4.** Bleeding disorder

___ **5.** von Willebrand disease

Column B

a. Evacuation and oxytocics

b. Massage and oxytocics

c. Provide blood products

d. Surgical repair

e. Administration of desmopressin and plasma concentrates

Activity C SEQUENCING

Arrange the steps for the management of uterine inversion in the proper sequence.

1. Administration of oxytocin

2. Manually push back the uterus into proper position

3. Administration of general anesthetic

4. Administration of antibiotics

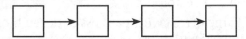

Activity D SHORT ANSWERS

Briefly answer the following.

1. What are the causes of overdistention of the uterus?

_____

_____

_____

2. What is idiopathic thrombocytopenic purpura?

_____

_____

_____

3. Which microorganisms are responsible for postpartum infections?

_____

_____

_____

4. What are baby blues?

_____

_____

_____

5. What are the symptoms of postpartum psychosis?

_____

_____

_____

6. What are the types of venous thrombosis?

_____

_____

_____

SECTION II: APPLYING YOUR KNOWLEDGE

Activity E CASE STUDY

Consider this scenario and answer the questions.

A 37-year-old client complains of calf pain following the vaginal delivery of her third child. On assessment, the nurse finds that the calf area is tender to the touch. The client is diagnosed with superficial venous thrombosis.

1. What are the risk factors for which a nurse should assess for the development of thrombo-embolic complications in a postpartum client?

_____

_____

_____

2. What nursing interventions should the nurse perform to prevent thromboembolic complications in clients?

_____

_____

_____

3. What interventions should the nurse perform to treat the client's condition of superficial venous thrombosis?

_____

_____

_____

SECTION III: PRACTICING FOR NCLEX

Activity F NCLEX-STYLE QUESTIONS

Answer the following questions.

1. A nurse is caring for a postpartum client who has a history of thrombosis during pregnancy and is at high risk of developing a pulmonary embolism. For which sign or symptom should the nurse monitor the client to prevent the occurrence of pulmonary embolism?

   a. Sudden change in mental status

   b. Difficulty in breathing

   c. Calf swelling

   d. Sudden chest pain

2. A nurse is caring for a postpartum client who has been treated for deep vein thrombosis (DVT). Which order would the nurse question?

   a. Wear compression stockings

   b. Plan long rest periods throughout the day

   c. Take aspirin as needed

   d. Take an oral contraceptive daily

3. A nurse is caring for a client with idiopathic thrombocytopenic purpura (ITP). Which intervention should the nurse perform **first**?

   a. Administration of prescribed nonsteroidal anti-inflammatory drugs (NSAIDs)

   b. Administration of platelet transfusions as ordered

   c. Avoiding administration of oxytocics

   d. Continual firm massage of the uterus

4. Two weeks after a vaginal birth, a client presents with low-grade fever. The client also reports a loss of appetite and low energy levels. The health care provider suspects an infection of the episiotomy. What sign or symptom is **most** indicative of an episiotomy infection?

   a. Foul-smelling vaginal discharge

   b. Sudden onset of shortness of breath

   c. Pain in the lower leg

   d. Apprehension and diaphoresis

5. A nurse is caring for a postpartum client diagnosed with von Willebrand disease. What should be the nurse's **priority** for this client?

   a. Check the lochia

   b. Assess the temperature

   c. Monitor the pain level

   d. Assess the fundal height

6. A nurse is caring for a 38-year-old overweight client 24 hours postcesarean birth. The client is reporting calf tenderness. Which should the nurse do **first**?

   a. Assess the client's respiratory rate

   b. Determine the severity of the pain

   c. Administer an anticoagulant

   d. Have the client rest with the extremity elevated

7. A nurse finds that a client is bleeding excessively after a vaginal birth. Which assessment finding would indicate retained placental fragments as a cause of bleeding?

   a. Soft and boggy uterus that deviates from the midline

   b. Firm uterus with trickle of bright-red blood in perineum

   c. Firm uterus with a steady stream of bright-red blood

   d. Large uterus with painless dark-red blood mixed with clots

8. Upon assessment, the nurse notes a postpartum client has increased vaginal bleeding. The client had a forceps birth which resulted in lacerations 4 hours ago. What should the nurse do **next**?

   a. Assess for uterine contractions

   b. Change the client's peripad

   c. Obtain the client's vital signs

   d. Have the client void

9. A nurse is caring for a client who delivered vaginally 2 hours ago. What postpartum complication can the nurse assess within the first few hours following birth?

   a. Postpartal infection

   b. Postpartal blues

   c. Postpartal hemorrhage

   d. Postpartum depression

10. A nurse is a caring for a postpartum client. What instruction should the nurse provide to the client as precautionary measures to prevent thromboembolic complications?

   a. Avoid performing any deep-breathing exercises

   b. Try to relax with pillows under knees

   c. Avoid sitting in one position for long periods of time

   d. Refrain from elevating legs above heart level

11. A postpartum client who was discharged home returns to the primary health care facility after 2 weeks with reports of fever and pain in the breast. The client is diagnosed with mastitis. What education should the nurse give to the client for managing and preventing mastitis?

   a. Discontinue breast-feeding to allow time for healing

   b. Perform hand-washing before and after breast-feeding

   c. Avoid hot or cold compresses on the breast

   d. Discourage manual compression of breast for expressing milk

12. A nurse is caring for a client who has had an intrauterine fetal death with prolonged retention of the fetus. For which signs and symptoms should the nurse watch to assess for an increased risk of disseminated intravascular coagulation? Select all that apply.

   a. Hypertension

   b. Bleeding gums

   c. Tachycardia

   d. Acute renal failure

   e. Lochia less than usual

13. A client in her 7th week of the postpartum period is experiencing bouts of sadness and insomnia. The nurse suspects that the client may have developed postpartum depression. What signs or symptoms are indicative of postpartum depression? Select all that apply.

   a. Inability to concentrate

   b. Loss of confidence

   c. Manifestations of mania

   d. Decreased interest in life

   e. Bizarre behavior

14. A nurse is assessing a client with postpartal hemorrhage; the client is presently on IV oxytocin. Which interventions should the nurse perform to evaluate the efficacy of the drug treatment? Select all that apply.

   a. Assess client's uterine tone

   b. Monitor client's vital signs

   c. Assess client's skin turgor

   d. Get a pad count

   e. Assess deep tendon reflexes

15. A nurse is caring for a client who has just undergone birth. What is the **best** method for the nurse to assess this client for postpartum hemorrhage?

   a. By assessing skin turgor

   b. By assessing blood pressure

   c. By frequently assessing uterine involution

   d. By monitoring hCG titers

CHAPTER 23

Nursing Care of the Newborn with Special Needs

Upon completion of the chapter, you will be able to:

- Evaluate factors that assist in identifying a newborn at risk due to variations in birthweight and gestational age.
- Select contributing factors and common complications associated with dysmature infants and their management.
- Compare and contrast nursing assessment findings and nursing management of a small-for-gestational-age newborn and a large-for-gestational-age newborn; a postterm and preterm newborn.
- Analyze nursing assessment and management of newborn conditions associated with variations in birthweight and gestational ages.
- Outline the nurse's role in helping parents experiencing perinatal grief or loss.
- Integrate knowledge of the risks associated with late preterm births into nursing interventions, discharge planning, and parent education.

SECTION I: ASSESSING YOUR UNDERSTANDING

Activity A FILL IN THE BLANKS

1. _____ is defined as a venous hematocrit of greater than 65%.

2. _____ feedings are used for compromised newborns to minimize energy expenditure from sucking during the feeding process.

3. A newborn who fails to establish adequate, sustained respiration after birth is said to have _____.

4. A _____ infant is born before the completion of 37 weeks.

5. One of the problems that affect the preterm infant's breathing ability and adjustment to extrauterine life includes an unstable chest wall, leading to _____.

6. A _____ newborn is an infant who is born from the first day of week 38 through 42 weeks.

7. _____ of prematurity is a potentially blinding eye disorder that occurs when abnormal blood vessels grow and spread through the retina, eventually leading to retinal detachment.

8. _____ assessment is considered the "fifth vital sign" and should be done as frequently as the other four vital signs.

9. Gestational age at birth is _____ correlated with the risk that the infant will experience physical, neurologic, or developmental sequelae.

10. Fetal growth is dependent on _____, placental, and maternal factors.

Activity B LABELING

Consider the following figure.

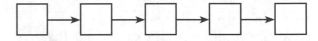

1. What is depicted in the figure?

   _____
   _____
   _____

2. Describe the reasons for using the piece of equipment depicted and how it works.

   _____
   _____
   _____

Activity C MATCHING

Match the heat transfer mechanism in Column A with the ways to prevent heat loss in Column B.

Column A	Column B
____ 1. Convection	a. Warm everything the newborn comes in contact with
____ 2. Conduction	
____ 3. Radiation	b. Provide insulation to prevent heat transfer
____ 4. Evaporation	c. Avoid drafts near the newborn
	d. Delay the first bath until the baby's temperature is stable

Activity D SEQUENCING

Given below, in random order, are a set of actions performed when resuscitating the newborn. Rearrange them in the correct sequence by writing the letters in the boxes provided below.

a. Administer epinephrine and/or volume expansion.
b. Position the head in a "sniffing" position.
c. Clear the airway and stimulate breathing; use suction if necessary.
d. Provide ventilation at a rate of 40 to 60 breaths per minute.
e. Perform chest compressions if heart rate is below 60 beats per minute.

☐ → ☐ → ☐ → ☐ → ☐

Activity E SHORT ANSWERS

Briefly answer the following.

1. What are the physical characteristics of preterm newborns?

   _____
   _____
   _____

2. What are the signs of hypoglycemia in the newborn?

   _____
   _____
   _____

3. What is developmentally supportive care?

_____

_____

_____

4. What are the risk factors to which a preterm infant is susceptible?

5. What are the characteristics of large-for-gestational-age newborns?

_____

_____

_____

6. What are the characteristics of postterm newborns?

_____

_____

_____

SECTION II: APPLYING YOUR KNOWLEDGE

Activity F CASE STUDY

Consider this scenario and answer the questions.

A nurse is caring for a preterm newborn who may not survive. The nurse is in the difficult situation of having to help the newborn's parents.

1. How can a nurse help the parents in the detachment process in the case of a dying newborn?

_____

_____

_____

2. What are the nursing interventions when caring for a family experiencing a perinatal loss?

_____

_____

_____

SECTION III: PRACTICING FOR NCLEX

Activity G NCLEX-STYLE QUESTIONS

Answer the following questions.

1. A nurse is caring for an infant born with polycythemia. Which intervention is **most** appropriate when caring for this infant?

   a. Focus on decreasing blood viscosity by increasing fluid volume

   b. Check blood glucose within 2 hours of birth by reagent test strip

   c. Repeat screening every 2 to 3 hours or before feeds

   d. Focus on monitoring and maintaining blood glucose levels

2. When caring for a preterm infant, what intervention will **best** address the sensorimotor needs of the infant?

   a. Rocking and massaging

   b. Swaddling and positioning

   c. Using minimal amount of tape

   d. Using distraction through objects

3. A nurse is assessing an infant who has experienced asphyxia at birth. Which finding indicates that the resuscitation methods have been successful?

   a. Heart rate of 80 bpm

   b. Jitteriness

   c. Hypotonia

   d. Strong cry

4. A nurse has placed an infant with asphyxia on a radiant warmer. Which sign indicates that the resuscitation methods have been successful?

   a. Heart rate of 80 bpm

   b. Tremors

   c. Bluish tongue

   d. Good cry

5. A nurse is caring for a preterm infant. Which intervention will prepare the newborn's gastrointestinal tract to better tolerate feedings when initiated?

   a. Administer vitamin D supplements

   b. Administer 0.5 mL/kg/hr of breast milk enterally

   c. Administer iron supplements

   d. Administer dextrose intravenously

6. A nurse is caring for an infant. A serum blood sugar of 40 was noted at birth. What care should the nurse provide to this newborn?
   a. Begin early feedings either by the breast or bottle
   b. Give dextrose intravenously before oral feedings
   c. Place infant on radiant warmer immediately
   d. Focus on decreasing blood viscosity by introducing feedings

7. Which maternal factors should the nurse consider contributory to a newborn being large for gestational age? Select all that apply.
   a. Diabetes mellitus
   b. Postdates gestation
   c. Alcohol use
   d. Prepregnancy obesity
   e. Renal infection

8. A nurse is assessing a term newborn and finds the blood glucose level is 23 mg/dL. The newborn has a weak cry, is irritable, and exhibits bradycardia. Which intervention is **most** appropriate?
   a. Administer dextrose intravenously
   b. Monitor the infant's hematocrit levels closely
   c. Administer PO glucose water immediately
   d. Place the infant on a radiant warmer

9. A nurse is caring for an infant born with an elevated bilirubin level. When planning the infant's care, what interventions will assist in reducing the bilirubin level? Select all that apply.
   a. Increase the infant's hydration
   b. Stop breastfeeding until jaundice resolves
   c. Offer early feedings
   d. Administer vitamin supplements
   e. Initiate phototherapy

10. Which symptom would **most** accurately indicate that a newborn has experienced meconium aspiration during the delivery process?
    a. Bluish skin discoloration
    b. Listlessness or lethargy
    c. Stained umbilical cord and skin
    d. Meconium-stained fluids followed by tachypnea

11. The nurse is caring for a client in the early stages of labor. What maternal history factors will alert the nurse to plan for the possibility of a small-for-gestational-age (SGA) newborn? Select all that apply.
    a. Maternal smoking during pregnancy
    b. Hypotension upon admission
    c. Asthma exacerbations during pregnancy
    d. Drug abuse
    e. Pregnancy weight gain of 25 lb

12. Which exemplifies developmental care in the NICU?
    a. Clustering care and activities
    b. Giving a bath
    c. Giving medications
    d. Holding the infant

13. The small-for-gestational-age neonate is at increased risk for which complication during the transitional period?
    a. Anemia probably due to chronic fetal hypoxia
    b. Hyperthermia due to decreased glycogen stores
    c. Hyperglycemia due to decreased glycogen stores
    d. Polycythemia probably due to chronic fetal hypoxia

14. The nurse observes a neonate delivered at 28 weeks' gestation. Which finding would the nurse expect to see?
    a. The skin is pale, and no vessels show through it.
    b. Creases appear on the interior two-thirds of the sole.
    c. The pinna of the ear is soft and flat and stays folded.
    d. The neonate has 7 to 10 mm of breast tissue.

15. An infant born 10 minutes prior was brought into the nursery for its exam. The nurse notices the infant's lip and palate are malformed. The father comes up to door and asks if the baby seems okay. What is the appropriate response by the nurse?
    a. "Oh yeah, the baby seems fine, you can see him soon."
    b. "Come on over and I will explain your infant's exam and findings."
    c. "Wait outside and we will call you later."
    d. "The baby is okay, just wait until your doctor speaks to you."

Nursing Management of the Newborn at Risk: Acquired and Congenital Newborn Conditions

Learning Objectives

Upon completion of the chapter, you will be able to:

- Describe the most common acquired conditions affecting the newborn.
- Characterize the nursing management of a newborn experiencing respiratory distress syndrome.
- Outline the birthing room preparation and procedures necessary to prevent meconium aspiration syndrome in the newborn at birth.
- Differentiate risk factors for the development of necrotizing enterocolitis.
- Analyze the impact of maternal diabetes on the newborn and the care needed.
- Evaluate the assessment and intervention for a newborn experiencing substance withdrawal after birth.
- Develop assessment and nursing management for newborns sustaining trauma and birth injuries.
- Outline the assessment, interventions, prevention, and management of hyperbilirubinemia in newborns.

- Summarize the interventions appropriate for a newborn with neonatal sepsis.
- Research four gastrointestinal system congenital anomalies that can occur in a newborn.
- Formulate a plan of care for a newborn with an acquired or congenital condition.
- Relate the importance of parental participation in care of the newborn with a congenital or acquired condition, including the nurse's role in facilitating parental involvement.

SECTION I: ASSESSING YOUR UNDERSTANDING

Activity A FILL IN THE BLANKS

1. An _____ is a defect of the umbilical ring that allows evisceration of abdominal contents into an external peritoneal sac.

2. _____ is a subperiosteal collection of blood secondary to the rupture of blood vessels between the skull and periosteum.

3. _____ is a condition in which total serum bilirubin level is above 5 mg/dL and exhibited as jaundice.

4. Presence of bacterial, fungal, or viral microorganisms or their toxins in blood or other tissues in newborns is known as neonatal _____.

5. _____ is a synthetic opiate narcotic that is used primarily as maintenance therapy for heroin addiction.

6. Immune hydrops is a severe form of _____ disease of the newborn that occurs when pathologic changes develop in the organs of the fetus secondary to severe anemia.

7. For the newborn with jaundice, regardless of its etiology, _____ is used to convert unconjugated bilirubin to the less toxic water-soluble form that can be excreted.

8. _____ is a herniation of abdominal contents through an abdominal wall defect.

9. Failure to establish adequate, sustained respiration after birth is known as neonatal _____.

10. _____ is a preventable neurologic disorder characterized by encephalopathy, motor abnormalities, hearing and vision loss, and death.

11. In bronchopulmonary dysplasia (BPD), high inspired oxygen concentrations cause an _____ process in the lungs that leads to parenchymal damage.

Activity B MATCHING

Match the commonly abused substances in Column A with their effects on newborns in Column B.

Column A

____ 1. Marijuana

____ 2. Cocaine

____ 3. Methamphet-amines

____ 4. Heroin

____ 5. Tobacco/nicotine

Column B

a. Altered responses to visual stimuli, sleep-pattern abnormalities, photophobia

b. Frantic fist sucking, high-pitched cry, and significant lassitude

c. Stiff and hyper-extended positioning, limb defects, ambiguous genitalia

d. Smaller head circumference, piercing cry, genitourinary tract abnormalities

e. Low birthweight, small for gestational age, SIDS

Activity C SHORT ANSWERS

Briefly answer the following.

1. What are the characteristics of an infant born to a diabetic mother?

_____

_____

_____

2. What are the most common types of malformations in infants of diabetic mothers?

_____

_____

_____

3. What does the treatment of infants born to diabetic mothers focus on?

_____

_____

_____

4. What are the causes of birth trauma?

_____

_____

_____

5. What is meconium aspiration syndrome?

_____

_____

_____

6. What is periventricular/intraventricular hemorrhage (PVH/IVH)?

_____

_____

_____

7. What are the goals of therapy for a newborn with bladder exstrophy?

_____

_____

_____

SECTION II: APPLYING YOUR KNOWLEDGE

Activity D CASE STUDY

Consider this scenario and answer the questions.

A pregnant client visits a health care facility for regular checkups. During the examination, the client reveals that she is addicted to alcohol and tobacco. The client is concerned; she wants to provide a healthy environment for her unborn child and also know how to avoid harmful consequences.

1. What is the role of the nurse in handling substance-abusing mothers?

_____

_____

_____

2. How can the nurse use the "5 As" approach to help this client attempt to quit smoking?

_____

_____

_____

SECTION III: PRACTICING FOR NCLEX

Activity E NCLEX-STYLE QUESTIONS

Answer the following questions.

1. An infant born is suspected of having persistent pulmonary hypertension of the newborn (PPHM). What intervention implemented by the nurse would be **most** beneficial in treating this client?

  a. Encourage the parents to hold the infant for bonding

  b. Place the infant in a cool environment to prevent overheating

  c. Administer anticonvulsants as ordered

  d. Provide oxygen by oxygen hood or ventilator

2. A nurse is assigned to care for a newborn with hyperbilirubinemia. The newborn is relatively large in size and shows signs of listlessness. What **most** likely occurred?

  a. The infant's mother must have had a long labor.

  b. The infant's mother probably had diabetes.

  c. The infant may have experienced birth trauma.

  d. The infant's mother probably used alcohol.

3. A nurse in a local health care facility is caring for a newborn with periventricular hemorrhage-intraventricular hemorrhage (PVH-IVH), who has recently been discharged from a local NICU. For which likely complications should the nurse assess? Select all that apply.

  a. Hydrocephalus

  b. Acid–base imbalances

  c. Pneumonitis

  d. Vision or hearing deficits

  e. Cerebral palsy

4. A nurse is caring for a newborn with asphyxia. What nursing management is involved when treating a newborn with asphyxia?

  a. Ensure adequate tissue perfusion

  b. Ensure effective resuscitation measures

  c. Administer IV fluids

  d. Administer surfactant as ordered

5. A nurse is assigned to care for a newborn with esophageal atresia. What preoperative nursing care is the **priority** for this newborn?

   a. Document the amount and color of esophageal drainage

   b. Administer antibiotics and total parenteral nutrition as ordered

   c. Prevent aspiration by elevating the head of the bed and insert an NG tube to low suction

   d. Provide NG feedings only

6. A newborn is suspected of having gastroschisis at birth. How would the nurse differentiate this problem from other congenital defects?

   a. The abdominal contents are contained within a thin, transparent sac.

   b. The intestines appear reddened and swollen and have no sac around them.

   c. The umbilical cord comes out of middle of the defect.

   d. The skin over the abdomen is wrinkled and looks like a prune.

7. A nurse is caring for a newborn with necrotizing enterocolitis (NEC) who is scheduled to undergo surgery for a bowel resection. The infant's parents wish to know the implications of the surgery. What information should the nurse provide to the parents regarding this surgery?

   a. Surgically treated NEC is a short process.

   b. Surgery will prevent long-term medical problems.

   c. Surgery requires placement of a proximal enterostomy.

   d. Surgery prevents the infant from needing enteral feedings after the repair.

8. The nurse is assessing a newborn suspected of having meconium aspiration syndrome. What sign or symptom would be **most** suggestive of this condition?

   a. High-pitched shrill cry

   b. Bile-stained emesis

   c. Intermittent tachypnea

   d. Expiratory grunting

9. A nurse is caring for an infant born after a prolonged and difficult maternal labor. What nursing intervention should the nurse perform when assessing for trauma and birth injuries in the newborn?

   a. Examine the newborn's skin for cyanosis

   b. Be alert for signs of apathy and listlessness

   c. Assess the baby for any temperature instability

   d. Note any absence of or decrease in deep tendon reflexes

10. A nurse is caring for a newborn whose chest x-ray reveals marked hyperaeration mixed with areas of atelectasis. The infant's arterial blood gas analysis indicates metabolic acidosis. For which dangerous condition should the nurse prepare when providing care to this newborn?

    a. Choanal atresia

    b. Diaphragmatic hernia

    c. Meconium aspiration syndrome

    d. Pneumonia

11. A nurse is caring for a newborn with transient tachypnea. Which is the **priority** nursing intervention?

    a. Administer IV fluids; gavage feedings

    b. Maintain adequate hydration

    c. Monitor for signs of hypotonia

    d. Perform gentle suctioning

12. A nurse is caring for a newborn with jaundice undergoing phototherapy. What intervention is appropriate when caring for the newborn?

    a. Expose the newborn's skin minimally

    b. Shield the newborn's eyes

    c. Discourage feeding the newborn

    d. Discontinue therapy if stools are loose, green, and frequent

13. A nurse is caring for a newborn with meconium aspiration syndrome. Which interventions should the nurse perform when caring for this newborn? Select all that apply.

    a. Perform repeated suctioning and stimulation

    b. Place the newborn under a radiant warmer or in a warmed Isolette

    c. Handle and rub the newborn well with a dry towel

    d. Administer oxygen therapy

    e. Administer broad-spectrum antibiotics

14. When caring for a neonate of a mother with diabetes, which physiologic finding is **most** indicative of a hypoglycemic episode?

   a. Hyperalert state

   b. Jitteriness

   c. Excessive crying

   d. Serum glucose level of 60 mg/dL

15. A client with group AB blood whose husband has group O blood has just given birth. Which complication or test result is a major sign of ABO blood incompatibility that the nurse should look for when assessing this neonate?

   a. Negative Coombs test

   b. Bleeding from the nose or ear

   c. Jaundice after the first 24 hours of life

   d. Jaundice within the first 24 hours of life

CHAPTER 25

Growth and Development of the Newborn and Infant

Upon completion of the chapter, you will be able to:

■ Identify normal developmental changes occurring in the newborn and infant.

■ Identify the gross and fine motor milestones of the newborn and infant.

■ Express an understanding of language development in the first year of life.

■ Describe nutritional requirements of the newborn and infant.

■ Develop a nutritional plan for the first year of life.

■ Identify common issues related to growth and development in infancy.

■ Demonstrate knowledge of appropriate anticipatory guidance for common developmental issues.

SECTION I: ASSESSING YOUR UNDERSTANDING

Activity A FILL IN THE BLANKS

1. Inconsolable crying, known as _____, lasts longer than 3 hours.

2. The education of parents about what to expect in the next phase of development is referred to as _____ guidance.

3. Milk production is stimulated by _____, a hormone secreted by the anterior pituitary.

4. The thin, yellowish fluid called _____ is produced by the breasts for the first 2 to 4 days after birth.

5. Stranger anxiety is an indicator that the infant is recognizing himself as _____ from others.

6. The sequential process by which infants and children gain various skills and function is referred to as _____.

7. The anterior fontanel normally remains open until _____ months of life.

Activity B LABELING

Label the tooth and age of eruption on the figure provided.

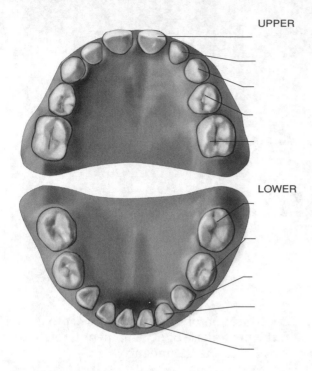

UPPER

LOWER

Activity C MATCHING

1. Match the infant age in Column A with the proper motor skill in Column B.

Column A

___ **1.** 1-month old

___ **2.** 2-month old

___ **3.** 3-month old

___ **4.** 4-month old

___ **5.** 5-month old

___ **6.** 6-month old

Column B

a. Raises head and chest

b. Hold open hand to face

c. Tripod sits

d. Grasps rattle or toy

e. Rolls from prone to supine

f. Lifts head while prone

2. Match the reflex in Column A with the description in Column B.

Column A

___ **1.** Asymmetric tonic neck

___ **2.** Babinski

___ **3.** Moro

___ **4.** Parachute

___ **5.** Root

Column B

a. Fanning and hyperextension

b. Fencing position

c. Prepare to "catch themselves"

d. Hands form "C"

e. Searches with the mouth

Activity D SEQUENCING

List the motor skills of the infant in order of occurrence.

1. Crawls on hands and knees

2. Pokes with index finger

3. Puts objects in container

4. Sits unsupported

5. Transfers object from one hand to the other

Activity E SHORT ANSWER

Briefly answer the following.

1. What are the nursing interventions that will help achieve the Healthy People 2020 objective of increasing the proportion of mothers who breastfeed?

_____

_____

_____

2. In what incidences is breastfeeding contraindicated?

_____

_____

_____

3. When providing education to a new parent about how to tell if her infant is hungry, what behavioral cues should be discussed as early cues of hunger?

_____

_____

_____

4. The nurse is reviewing the adjusted age of an infant. What is the adjusted age and how is it calculated?

_____

_____

_____

5. Identify four primitive reflexes present at birth.

_____

_____

_____

6. What changes normally take place in the cardiovascular system during the first year of life?

_____

_____

_____

SECTION II: APPLYING YOUR KNOWLEDGE

Activity F CASE STUDY

Remember Allison Johnson, the 6-month old from Chapter 4, who was brought to the clinic by her mother and father for her 6-month check-up. As new parents, Allison's mother and father had many questions and concerns.

1. Allison's parents ask "What can we do to encourage Allison's development?"

_____

_____

_____

2. Allison's dad states in college he took a psychology class and remembers there are different development theories. He asks how those relate to Allison right now.

_____

_____

_____

3. During your assessment, Allison's parents ask what findings would concern you. Discuss specific developmental warning signs you are assessing.

_____

_____

_____

_____

SECTION III: PRACTICING FOR NCLEX

Activity G NCLEX-STYLE QUESTIONS

Answer the following questions.

1. The nurse is examining a 6-month-old girl who was born 8 weeks early. Which finding is cause for concern?
   a. The child measures 21 in (53 cm) in length
   b. The child exhibits palmar grasp reflex
   c. Head size has increased 5 in (12 cm) since birth
   d. The child weighs 10 lb 2 oz (4.6 kg)

2. The nurse is caring for the family with a 2-month-old boy with colic. The mother reports feeling very stressed by the baby's constant crying. Which intervention would provide the **most** help in the short term?
   a. Urging the baby's mother to take time for herself away from the child
   b. Educating the parents about when colic stops
   c. Assessing the parents' care and feeding skills
   d. Watching how the parents respond to the child

3. The mother of 1-week-old boy voices concerns about her baby's weight loss since birth. At birth the baby weighed 7 lb (3.2 kg); the baby currently weighs 6 lb 1 oz (2.8 kg). Which response by the nurse is **most** appropriate?
   a. "All babies lose a substantial amount of weight after birth."
   b. "Your baby has lost too much weight and may need to be hospitalized."
   c. "Your baby's weight loss is well within the expected range."
   d. "Your baby has lost a bit more than the normal amount."

4. The nurse is teaching the parents of a 6-month-old boy about proper child dental care. Which action will the nurse indicate as the **most** likely to cause dental caries?
   a. Not cleaning a baby's gums when he is done eating
   b. Putting the baby to bed with a bottle of milk or juice
   c. Using a cloth instead of a brush for cleaning teeth
   d. Failing to clean the teeth with fluoridated toothpaste

5. The nurse is assessing the sleeping practices of the parents of a 4-month-old girl who wakes repeatedly during the night. Which parent comment might reveal a cause for the night waking?
   a. They sing to her before she goes to sleep
   b. They put her to bed when she falls asleep
   c. If she is safe, they lie her down and leave
   d. The child has a regular, scheduled bedtime

6. The nurse is educating the mother of a 6-month-old boy about the symptoms for teething. Which symptom would the nurse identify?
   a. Running a mild fever or vomiting
   b. Choosing soft foods over hard foods
   c. Increased biting and sucking
   d. Frequent loose stools

7. The nurse is teaching healthy eating habits to the parents of a 7-month-old girl. Which recommendation is the **most** valuable advice?
   a. Let the child eat only the foods she prefers
   b. Actively urge the child to eat new foods
   c. Provide small portions that must be eaten
   d. Serve new foods several times

8. The nurse is providing helpful feeding tips to the mother of a 2-week-old boy. Which recommendations will **best** help the child feed effectively?
   a. Maintain a feed-on-demand approach
   b. Apply warm compresses to the breast
   c. Encourage the infant to latch on properly
   d. Maintain adequate diet and fluid intake

9. The nurse is observing a 6-month-old boy for developmental progress. For which typical milestone should the nurse look?
   a. Shifts a toy to his left hand and reaches for another
   b. Picks up an object using his thumb and finger tips
   c. Puts down a little ball to pick up a stuffed toy
   d. Enjoys hitting a plastic bowl with a large spoon

10. The nurse is assessing an infant at his 4-month well-baby check-up. The nurse notes that at birth the baby weighed 8 lb (3.6 kg) and was 20 in (50.8 cm) in length. Which finding is **most** consistent with the normal infant growth and development?
    a. The baby weighs 21 lb (9.5 kg) and is 30 in (76.2 cm) in length
    b. The baby weighs 16 lb (7.3 kg) and is 26 in (66.0 cm) in length
    c. The baby weighs 15 lb (6.8 kg) and is 24 in (61.0 cm) in length
    d. The baby weighs 24 lb (10.9 kg) and is 26 in (66.0 cm) in length

11. The mother of a 1-month-old infant voices concern about her baby's respirations. She states they are rapid and irregular. Which information should the nurse provide?

    a. The normal respiratory rate for an infant at this age is between 20 and 30 breaths per minute.

    b. The respirations of a 1-month-old infant are normally irregular and periodically pause.

    c. An infant at this age should have regular respirations.

    d. The irregularity of the infant's respirations are concerning; I will notify the physician.

12. The nurse is assessing the oral cavity of a 4-month-old infant. Which finding is consistent with a child of this age?

    a. 1 to 3 natal teeth

    b. No teeth

    c. 1 to 2 lower teeth

    d. 1 upper tooth

13. The nurse is educating the mother of a newborn about feeding practices. The nurse correctly advises the mother:

    a. the best feeding schedule offers food every 4 to 6 hours.

    b. most newborns need to eat about four times per day.

    c. the newborn's stomach can hold between one-half to one ounce.

    d. demand scheduled feeding is associated with increased difficulty getting the baby to sleep through the night.

CHAPTER 26

Growth and Development of the Toddler

Learning Objectives

Upon completion of the chapter, you will be able to:

- Explain normal physiologic, psychosocial, and cognitive changes occurring in the toddler.
- Identify the gross and fine motor milestones of the toddler.
- Demonstrate an understanding of language development in the toddler years.
- Discuss sensory development of the toddler.
- Demonstrate an understanding of emotional/social development and moral/spiritual development during toddlerhood.
- Implement a nursing care plan to address common issues related to growth and development in toddlerhood.
- Encourage growth and learning through play.
- Develop a teaching plan for safety promotion in the toddler period.
- Demonstrate an understanding of toddler needs related to sleep and rest, as well as dental health.
- Develop a nutritional plan for the toddler based on average nutritional requirements.
- Provide appropriate anticipatory guidance for common developmental issues that arise in the toddler period.
- Demonstrate an understanding of appropriate methods of discipline for use during the toddler years.

- Identify the role of the parent in the toddler's life and determine ways to support, encourage, and educate the parents about toddler growth, development, and concerns during this period.

SECTION I: ASSESSING YOUR UNDERSTANDING

Activity A FILL IN THE BLANKS

1. When _____ of the spinal cord is achieved around age 2 years, the toddler is capable of exercising voluntary control over the sphincters.

2. The leading cause of unintentional injury and death in children in this country is due to _____.

3. The ability to understand what is being said or asked is called _____ language.

4. The _____ remains short in both the male and female toddler, making them more susceptible to urinary tract infections compared to adults.

5. During the _____ stage of development, according to Piaget, children begin to become more sophisticated with symbolic thought.

Activity B MATCHING

1. Match the word in Column A with the correct description in Column B.

Column A

____ **1.** Echolalia

____ **2.** Regression

____ **3.** Individuation

____ **4.** Ritualism

____ **5.** Egocentrism

____ **6.** Telegraphic speech

Column B

a. Self-interest due to an inability to focus on another's perspective

b. Familiar routine that provides structure and security for the toddler

c. Speech that uses essential words only

d. Repetition of words and phrases without understanding

e. Internalizing a sense of self and one's environment

f. Returning to a prior developmental stage

2. Match the nutrients in Column A with the appropriate food source in Column B.

Column A

____ **1.** Dietary fiber

____ **2.** Folate

____ **3.** Vitamin A

____ **4.** Vitamin C

____ **5.** Calcium

Column B

a. Avocados, broccoli, green peas, dark greens

b. Apricots, cantaloupe, carrots, sweet potatoes

c. Applesauce, carrots, corn, green beans

d. Dairy products, broccoli, tofu, legumes

e. Broccoli, oranges, strawberries, tomatoes

Activity C SEQUENCING

Place the following descriptions of expressive language in the order the toddler will display them.

1. Uses primarily descriptive words (hungry, hot)

2. Talks about something that happened in the past

3. Babbles in what sounds like sentences

4. Uses a finger to point to things

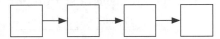

Activity D SHORT ANSWERS

Briefly answer the following.

1. Discuss ways to prevent temper tantrums in toddlers.

_____

_____

_____

2. Describe appropriate discipline for a toddler.

_____

_____

_____

3. Explain the care for the toddler's teeth and gums. How does the care change after the child reaches the age of 2 years?

_____

_____

_____

4. Discuss the changes in the genitourinary system in the toddler that allow for readiness for toilet training.

_____

_____

_____

5. Toddlers generally have a swayback appearance. What is the underlying cause of this manifestation?

_____

_____

_____

SECTION II: APPLYING YOUR KNOWLEDGE

Activity E CASE STUDY

Jose Gonzales is a 2-year-old boy brought to the clinic by his mother and father for his 2-year-old check-up. The following questions refer to him.

1. Jose's parents state "We speak Spanish at home to Jose and are working to make him bilingual." What do you need to consider when assessing language development in Jose?

   _____

   _____

   _____

2. Jose's mother asks what they can do to encourage Jose's language development.

   _____

   _____

   _____

3. Jose's father states that Jose's favorite word is "No." He asks if this is normal at this age. How would you respond? (include a discussion on Erikson stage of development and suggestions for dealing with this)

   _____

   _____

   _____

SECTION III: PRACTICING FOR NCLEX

Activity F NCLEX-STYLE QUESTIONS

Answer the following questions.

1. The parents of an overweight 2-year-old boy admit that their child is a bit "chubby," but argue that he is a picky eater who will eat only junk food. Which response by the nurse is **best** to facilitate a healthier diet?

   a. "You may have to serve a new food 10 or more times."

   b. "Serve only healthy foods. He'll eat when he's hungry."

   c. "Give him more healthy choices with less junk food available."

   d. "Calorie requirements for toddlers are less than infants."

2. The nurse is observing a 36-month-old boy during a well-visit. Which motor skill has he **most** recently acquired?

   a. Undress himself

   b. Push a toy lawnmower

   c. Kick a ball

   d. Pull a toy while walking

3. The nurse is providing anticipatory guidance to the parents of an 18-month-old girl. Which recommendation should be the **most** helpful to the parents?

   a. Giving the child time out for 1 ½ minute

   b. Ignoring bad behavior and praising good behavior

   c. Slapping her hand using one or two fingers

   d. Describing proper behavior when she misbehaves

4. The nurse is teaching a first-time mother with a 14-month-old boy about child safety. Which is the **most** effective overall safety information to provide guidance for the mother?

   a. "Place a gate at the top of each stairway."

   b. "Never let him out of your sight when outdoors."

   c. "Put chemicals in a locked cabinet."

   d. "Don't smoke in the house or car."

5. The parents of a 2-year-old girl are concerned with her behavior. For which behavior would the nurse share their concern?

   a. Refuses to share toys with her sister

   b. Frequently babbles to herself when playing

   c. Likes to change toys frequently

   d. Plays by herself even when other children are present

6. The nurse is discussing sensory development with the mother of a 2-year-old boy. Which parental comment suggests the child may have a sensory problem?

   a. "He wasn't bothered by the paint smell."

   b. "He was licking the dishwashing soap."

   c. "He doesn't respond if I wave to him."

   d. "I dropped a pan behind him and he cried."

7. The nurse is assessing the language development of a 3-year-old girl. Which finding would suggest a problem?

   a. Makes simple conversation

   b. Tells the nurse she saw Na-Na today

   c. Speaks in 2- to 3-word sentences

   d. Tells the nurse her name

8. The nurse is observing a 3-year-old boy in a daycare center. Which behavior might suggest an emotional problem?

   a. Has persistent separation anxiety

   b. Goes from calm to tantrum suddenly

   c. Sucks his thumb periodically

   d. Is unable to share toys with others

9. The nurse is teaching a mother of a 1-year-old girl about weaning her from the bottle and breast. Which recommendation should be part of the nurse's plan?

   a. Wean from breast by 18 months of age at the latest

   b. Give the child an iron-fortified cereal

   c. Switch the child to a no-spill sippy cup

   d. Wean from the bottle at 15 months of age

10. The parents of a 3-year-old boy have asked the nurse for advice about a preschool for their child. Which suggestion is **most** important for the nurse to make?

    a. "Look for a preschool that is clean and has a loving staff."

    b. "Check to make sure your child can attend with the sniffles."

    c. "Make sure that you can easily get an appointment to visit."

    d. "The staff should be trained in early childhood development."

11. The nurse is assessing a 2-year-old boy during a well-child visit. The nurse correctly identifies the child's current stage of Erikson's growth and development as:

    a. trust versus mistrust.

    b. autonomy versus shame and doubt.

    c. initiative versus guilt.

    d. industry versus inferiority.

12. The nurse is assessing a 3-year-old child. The nurse notes the child is able to understand that objects hidden from sight still exist. The nurse correctly documents the child is displaying:

    a. object permanence.

    b. mental combinations.

    c. preoperational thinking.

    d. concrete thinking.

13. The nurse is discussing the activities of a 20-month-old child with his mother. The mother reports the children of her friends seem to have more advanced speech abilities than her child. After assessing the child, which finding is cause for follow up?

a. Inability to point to named body parts

b. Inability to talk with the nurse about something that happened a few days ago

c. Points to pictures in books when asked

d. Understands approximately 200 words

14. The mother of an 18-month-old girl voices concerns about her child's social skills. She reports that the child does not play well with others and seems to ignore other children who are playing at the same time. What response by the nurse is indicated?

a. "It is normal for children to engage in play alongside other children at this age."

b. "Has your child displayed any aggressive tendencies toward other children?"

c. "Perhaps you should consider a preschool to promote more socialization opportunities."

d. "Does your child have opportunities to socialize much with other children?"

Growth and Development of the Preschooler

SECTION I: ASSESSING YOUR UNDERSTANDING

Activity A FILL IN THE BLANKS

1. The over-consumption of cow's milk may result in a deficiency of _____ due to the calcium blocking its absorption.

2. Communication in preschool children is _____ in nature, as they are not yet capable of abstract thought.

3. Preschool-aged children are more susceptible to bladder infections than are adults due to the length of the _____.

4. During a night _____ a child will scream and thrash but not awaken.

5. A nutrient _____ diet along with physical activity is the foundation for obesity prevention in the preschool child.

Activity B MATCHING

Match the theorist and stage in Column A with the proper activities/behaviors in Column B.

Column A

_____ **1.** Erikson – Initiative versus guilt

_____ **2.** Piaget – Preconceptual

_____ **3.** Piaget – Intuitive

_____ **4.** Kohlberg – Punishment–obedience orientation

_____ **5.** Kohlberg – Preconventional morality

_____ **6.** Freud – Phallic stage

Column B

a. Displays animism

b. Able to classify and relate objects

c. Children may learn inappropriate behavior if the parent does not intervene to teach the behavior is wrong

d. Likes to please parents

e. Super-ego is developing and the conscience is emerging

f. Determines good and bad dependent upon associated punishment

Activity C SEQUENCING

Place the following motor skills in the order of acquisition.

1. Swings and climbs well

2. Copies circles and traces squares

3. Throws ball overhand

Activity D SHORT ANSWERS

Briefly answer the following.

1. Describe the cognitive abilities of a child in the intuitive phase.

_____

_____

_____

2. Explain the difference between nightmares and night terrors.

_____

_____

_____

3. Name three ways to promote healthy teeth and gums in preschoolers.

_____

_____

_____

4. What strategies should be used by the parents of a preschool-aged child who has lied?

_____

_____

_____

5. What is the primary social task of the preschool-aged child?

_____

_____

_____

SECTION II: APPLYING YOUR KNOWLEDGE

Activity E CASE STUDY

Remember Nila Patel, the 4-year old from Chapter 5, who was brought to the clinic by her parents for her school checkup.

1. Nila's mother states that "Nila loves to play make-believe. She is constantly playing in a fantasy world. I am not sure if this is healthy behavior." How would you address Mrs. Patel's concerns?

_____

_____

_____

2. Nila's parents express concerns about the transition to Kindergarten. What guidance can you give them regarding this?

_____

_____

_____

3. During your assessment, Nila's mother asks what findings would concern you. Discuss specific developmental warning signs you are assessing for.

_____

_____

_____

SECTION III: PRACTICING FOR NCLEX

Activity F NCLEX-STYLE QUESTIONS

Answer the following questions.

1. The nurse is conducting a well-child assessment of a 4-year old. Which assessment finding warrants further investigation?
   a. Presence of 20 deciduous teeth
   b. Presence of 10 deciduous teeth
   c. Absence of dental caries
   d. Presence of 19 deciduous teeth

2. The nurse is conducting a health screening of a 5-year-old boy as required for kindergarten. The boy is fearful about going to a new school. The mother asks for the nurse's advice. Which response by the nurse is **best**?
   a. "Kindergarten is a big step for a child. Be patient with him."
   b. "Talk to your son's new teacher and schedule a tour with him."
   c. "Be aware that he may have difficulty adjusting being away from home 5 days a week."
   d. "Remind him that kindergarten will be a lot of fun and he'll make new friends."

3. The nurse is conducting a well-child examination of a 4-year old and is assessing the child's height. By how much should the nurse expect the child's height to have increased since last year's examination?
   a. 0.5 to 1 in (1.27 to 2.54 cm)
   b. 1 to 2 in (2.54 to 5.07 cm)
   c. 2.5 to 3 in (6.35 to 7.62 cm)
   d. 3.5 to 4 in (8.89 to 10.16 cm)

4. A nurse is providing a routine wellness examination for a 5-year-old boy. Which response by the parents indicates a need for an additional referral or follow-up?

   a. "He can count to 30 but gets confused after that."

   b. "We often have to translate his speech to others."

   c. "He is always talking and telling detailed stories."

   d. "He knows his name and address."

5. The parents of a 4-year-old girl tell the nurse that their daughter is having frequent nightmares. Which statement indicates that the girl is having night terrors instead of nightmares?

   a. "She screams and thrashes when we try to touch her."

   b. "She is scared after she wakes up."

   c. "She comes and wakes us up after she awakens."

   d. "She has a hard time going back to sleep."

6. The nurse is providing teaching to the mother of a 4-year-old girl about bike safety. Which statement indicates a need for further teaching?

   a. "The balls of her feet should reach both pedals while sitting."

   b. "Pedal back brakes are better for her age group."

   c. "She should always ride on the sidewalk."

   d. "She can ride on the street if I am riding with her."

7. The nurse is conducting a health screening for a 3-year-old boy as required by his new preschool. Which statement by the parents warrants further discussion and intervention?

   a. "The school has a looser environment which is a good match for his temperament."

   b. "The school requires processed foods and high sugar foods be avoided."

   c. "The school is quite structured and advocates corporal punishment."

   d. "There is a very low student teacher ratio and they do a lot of hands on projects."

8. A nurse is caring for a 4-year-old girl. The parents indicate that their daughter often reports that objects in the house are her friends. They are concerned because the girl says that the grandfather clock in the hallway smiles and sings to her. Which response by the nurse is **best**?

   a. "Your daughter is demonstrating animism which is common."

   b. "Attributing life-like qualities to inanimate objects is quite normal at this age."

   c. "Do you think your daughter is hallucinating?

   d. "Is there a family history of mental illness?"

9. The nurse is providing teaching about child safety to the parents of a 4-year-old girl. Which statement by the parents indicates a need for further teaching?

   a. "We need to tell her that her vitamins are candy."

   b. "She still needs a booster seat in the car."

   c. "We need to know the basics of CPR and first aid."

   d. "We need to continually remind her about safety rules."

10. The nurse is providing teaching about proper dental care for the parents of a 5-year-old girl. Which response indicates a need for further teaching?

    a. "Too much fluoride can contribute to fluorosis."

    b. "We should use only a pea-sized amount of toothpaste."

    c. "She needs to floss her teeth before brushing."

    d. "She should see a dentist every 6 months."

11. The father of a preschool boy reports concerns about the short stature of his son. The nurse reviews the child's history and notes the child is 4 years old and is presently 41 in (104 cm) tall and has grown 2.5 in (6.35 cm) in the past year. Which response by the nurse is **most** appropriate?

    a. "Is there a reason you are concerned about your child's height?"

    b. "Your son is slightly below the normal height for his age group but may still grow to be a normal height in the coming year."

c. "Your son is slightly below the normal height for his age but he had demonstrated a normal growth rate this year."

d. "Both your son's height and rate of growth are within normal limits for his age."

12. The mother of a 4-year-old girl reports her daughter has episodes of wetting her pants. The nurse questions the mother about the frequency. The nurse determines these episodes occur about once every 1 to 2 weeks. Which response by the nurse is indicated?

a. "Consider restricting your daughter's fluid intake."

b. "Discipline should be applied after these times."

c. "At this age it is helpful to remind children to go to the bathroom."

d. "The frequency of these wetting episodes may be consistent with a low-grade urinary tract infection."

13. The nurse is caring for a 4-year-old child who is hospitalized and in traction. The child talks about an invisible friend to the nurse. Which action by the nurse is indicated?

a. The nurse should document the reports of hallucinations by the child.

b. The nurse should explain to the child that there are no friends present.

c. The nurse should discourage the child from talking about the imaginary friend.

d. The nurse should recognize this behavior as normal for the child's developmental age and do nothing.

14. The mother of a 4-year-old boy reports her son has voiced curiosity about her breasts. She asks the nurse what she should do. Which information is **best** for the nurse to give the parent?

a. Advise the parent that sexual curiosity is unusual at this age.

b. Encourage the parent to provide a detailed discussion about human sexuality with the child.

c. Encourage the parent to determine what the child's specific questions are and answer them briefly.

d. Advise the parent to explain to the child that he is too young to discuss such things.

15. The mother of a 3-year-old child reports her son is afraid of the dark. She asks the nurse for help. Which advice is **best** for the nurse to offer?

a. Encourage the parent to allow a small night light.

b. Encourage the parent to consider allowing the child to sleep with her.

c. Encourage the mother to check for monsters under the bed in the presence of the child.

d. Encourage the parent to leave on the television in the child's room.

Growth and Development of the School-Age Child

Learning Objectives

Upon completion of the chapter, you will be able to:

- Identify normal physiologic, cognitive, and moral changes occurring in the school-aged child.
- Describe the role of peers and schools in the development and socialization of the school-aged child.
- Identify the developmental milestones of the school-aged child.
- Identify the role of the nurse in promoting safety for the school-aged child.
- Demonstrate knowledge of the nutritional requirements of the school-aged child.
- Identify common developmental concerns in the school-aged child.
- Demonstrate knowledge of the appropriate nursing guidance for common developmental concerns.

SECTION I: ASSESSING YOUR UNDERSTANDING

Activity A FILL IN THE BLANKS

1. An 8-year old who is the size of an 11-year old will think and act like a(n) _____ year old.

2. The Academy of Pediatrics recommends _____ hours or less of television viewing per day.

3. Brain growth is complete by the time the _____ birthday is celebrated.

4. Between the ages of 10 and 12 (the pubescent years for girls), _____ levels remain high, but are more controlled and focused than previously.

5. Motor vehicle accidents are a common cause of _____ in the school-aged child.

6. Most young children are not capable of handling _____ or making decisions on their own before 11 or 12 years of age.

7. Ways to develop self-worth is termed _____.

8. During school children are influenced by _____ and teachers.

9. Compared with the earlier years, caloric needs of the school-aged child are _____.

10. The bladder capacity for a 10-year old would be _____ ounces.

Activity B MATCHING

1. Match the terms in Column A with the descriptions in Column B.

Column A

____ 1. Inferiority

____ 2. Bruxism

____ 3. Malocclusion

____ 4. Caries

____ 5. Secondary sexual characteristics

____ 6. Principle of conservation

Column B

a. Gritting or grinding of teeth

b. Tooth decay

c. Feelings of inability or not measuring up to the abilities of others

d. Matter does not change when forms change

e. Improper teeth alignment

f. Changes in breast development and genitalia during late school age or early adolescence

2. Match the systems in Column A with the capacities in Column B.

Column A

____ 1. Lymph system

____ 2. Heart

____ 3. Bones

Column B

a. Mineralization not complete until maturity

b. Smaller in size, in relation to the rest of the body, than any other developmental stage

c. Continues to grow until the child is 9 years old

3. Match the theorists in Column A with characteristics of their theories for the school-aged child, listed in Column B.

Column A

____ 1. Kohlberg

____ 2. Freud

____ 3. Piaget

____ 4. Erikson

Column B

a. Industry versus inferiority

b. Conventional: "good child, bad child"

c. Latency

d. Concrete operational

Activity C SEQUENCING

Place the following developmental milestones in the proper sequence.

1. Brain growth is complete

2. Fine motor skills develop

3. Frontal sinuses development is complete

4. Gross motor skills develop

5. Lymphatic tissue growth is complete

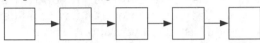

Activity D SHORT ANSWERS

Briefly answer the following.

1. Describe the development of children's gross motor skills as they correspond to age groups.

   _____

   _____

   _____

2. Describe the child who is labeled "slow to warm."

   _____

   _____

   _____

3. Define the nurse's role in school-aged children's growth and development.

   _____

   _____

   _____

4. Detail the sleep requirements for school-aged children.

   _____

   _____

   _____

5. Discuss the importance of body image on the school-aged child.

   _____

   _____

   _____

SECTION II: APPLYING YOUR KNOWLEDGE

Activity E CASE STUDY

Olivia Anderson, 9 years old, is brought to the clinic by her mother for her annual check-up.

1. During your assessment you note the interaction between the mother and the daughter. While asking Olivia about her friends at school, the mother responds "Olivia does not have many friends. I have told her if she would just care more about her appearance, other children will want to spend time with her." How would you respond to the mother?

   _____

   _____

   _____

2. Olivia's mother expresses concerns regarding discipline and how best to approach this. How would you respond?

   _____

   _____

   _____

3. During your assessment, you discover that Olivia spends most of her time watching television and playing video games. What guidance can you give to Olivia and her mother regarding this?

   _____

   _____

   _____

SECTION III: PRACTICING FOR NCLEX

Activity F NCLEX-STYLE QUESTIONS

Answer the following questions.

1. The nurse is about to see a 9-year-old girl for a well-child check-up. Knowing that the child is in Piaget's period of concrete operational thought, which characteristic should the child display?

   a. Consider an action and its consequences

   b. View the world in terms of her own experience

   c. Make generalized assumptions about groups of things

   d. Know lying is bad because she gets sent to her room for it

2. The nurse is educating the parents of a 6-year-old boy how to manage the child's introduction into elementary school. The child has an easy temperament. Which should the nurse suggest?

   a. Comforting the child when he is frustrated

   b. Helping the child deal with minor stresses

   c. Scheduling several visits to the school before classes start

   d. Being firm with episodes of moodiness and irritability

3. The mother of a 7-year-old girl is asking the nurse's advice about getting her daughter a two-wheel bike. Which response by the nurse is **most** important?

   a. "Teach her where she'll land on the grass if she falls."

   b. "Be sure to get the proper size bike."

   c. "She won't need a helmet if she has training wheels."

   d. "Learning to ride the bike will improve her coordination."

4. The school nurse is assessing the nutritional status of an overweight 12-year-old girl. Which question is appropriate for the nurse to ask?

   a. Does your family have rules about foods and how they are prepared?

   b. What does your family do for exercise?

   c. How often does everyone in your family eat together?

   d. Have you gained weight recently?

5. The nurse has taken a health history and performed a physical examination for a 12-year-old boy. Which finding is the **most** likely?

   a. The child's body fat has decreased since last year.

   b. The child has different diet preferences than his parents.

   c. The child has a leaner body mass than a girl at this age.

   d. The child described a somewhat reduced appetite.

6. The nurse is teaching parents of an 11-year-old girl how to deal with the issues relating to peer pressure to use tobacco and alcohol. Which suggestion provides the **best** course of action for the parents?

   a. Avoid smoking in the house or in front of the child.

   b. Hide alcohol out of the child's reach.

   c. Forbid the child to have friends that smoke or drink.

   d. Discuss tobacco and alcohol use with the child.

7. The nurse is assessing the nutritional needs of an 8-year-old girl who weighs 65 lb (29.48 kg). Which of the following amounts would provide the proper daily caloric intake for this child?

   a. 1,895 calories per day

   b. 2,065 calories per day

   c. 2,245 calories per day

   d. 2,385 calories per day

8. The nurse is talking with the parents of an 8-year-old boy who has been cheating at school. Which comment should be the nurse's primary message?

   a. "Punishment should be severe and long lasting."

   b. "Make sure that your behavior around your son is exemplary."

   c. "Resolve this by providing an opportunity for him to cheat and then dealing with it."

   d. "You may be putting too much pressure on him to succeed."

9. A 9-year-old boy has arrived for a health maintenance visit. Which milestone of physical growth should the nurse expect to observe?

   a. Brain growth is complete and the shape of the head is longer.

   b. Lymphatic tissue growth is complete providing greater resistance to infections.

   c. Frontal sinuses are developed while tonsils have decreased in size.

   d. All deciduous teeth are replaced by 32 permanent teeth.

10. The nurse is educating the parents of a 10-year-old girl in ways to help their child avoid tobacco. Which suggestion should be part of the nurse's advice?

    a. "Keep your cigarettes where she can't get to them."

    b. "Always go outside when you have a cigarette."

    c. "Tell her only losers smoke and chew tobacco."

    d. "As parents, you need to be good role models."

11. The parents of a 7-year-old girl report concerns about her seemingly low self-esteem. The parents question how self-esteem is developed in a young girl. Which response by the nurse is **best**?

 a. "The peers of a child at this age are the greatest influence on self-esteem."

 b. "Several interrelated factors are to blame for low self-esteem."

 c. "Your daughter's self-esteem is influenced by feedback from people they view as authorities at this age."

 d. "A child's self-esteem is greatly inborn and environmental influences guide it."

12. The parents of an 8-year-old boy report their son is being bullied and teased by a group of boys in the neighborhood. Which response by the nurse is **best**?

 a. "Perhaps teaching your son self-defense courses will help him to have a greater sense of control and safety."

 b. "Bullying can have lifelong effects on the self-esteem of a child."

 c. "Fortunately the scars of being picked on will fade as your son grows up."

 d. "Your son is at high risk for bullying other children as a result of this situation."

13. During a well-child check at the ambulatory clinic, the mother of a 10-year-old boy reports concerns about her son's frequent discussions about death and dying. Based upon knowledge of this age group the nurse understands that:

 a. at this age, children are not afraid of death.

 b. discussing death and dying may hint at a psychological disorder.

 c. consistent thoughts of death and dying at this age leads to the later development of depression.

 d. preoccupation with death and dying is common in the school-aged child.

14. The parents of a 9-year-old boy report they have been homeschooling their son and now plan to enroll him in the local public school. They voice concerns about the influence of the other children on their son's values. Which information should the nurse provide the parents?

 a. "At your son's age, values are most influenced by peers."

 b. "The values of the family will likely prevail for your son."

 c. "Values are largely inborn and will be impacted only in a limited way by environmental influences."

 d. "The teacher will begin to have the largest influence on a child's values at this age."

15. The nurse is caring for a hospitalized 5-year-old child. The child's mother has reported her child is becoming very "clingy." Which advice should the nurse provide? Select all that apply.

 a. "Regression is normal during hospitalization."

 b. "Be careful not to coddle the child or it will result in regressive behaviors."

 c. "These behaviors are the result of a loss of self-control and are likely temporary."

 d. "Allowing the child to have some input in the care may be helpful in managing these behaviors."

 e. "The child may miss school and interaction with peers."

CHAPTER 29

Growth and Development of the Adolescent

Learning Objectives

Upon completion of the chapter, you will be able to:

- Identify normal physiologic changes, including puberty, occurring in the adolescent.
- Discuss psychosocial, cognitive, and moral changes occurring in the adolescent.
- Identify changes in relationships with peers, family, teachers, and community during adolescence.
- Describe interventions to promote safety during adolescence.
- Demonstrate knowledge of the nutritional requirements of the adolescent.
- Demonstrate knowledge of the development of sexuality and its influence on dating during adolescence.
- Identify common developmental concerns of the adolescent.
- Demonstrate knowledge of the appropriate nursing guidance for common developmental concerns.

SECTION I: ASSESSING YOUR UNDERSTANDING

Activity A FILL IN THE BLANKS

1. Risk-taking behaviors of adolescents are those that could lead to physical or _____ injury.

2. Second only to growth during _____, adolescence provides the most rapid and dramatic changes in size and proportions.

3. Adolescents proceed from thinking in concrete terms to thinking in _____ terms.

4. Families who listen and continue to demonstrate affection for and acceptance of their adolescent have a more _____ outcome.

5. The prevalence of obesity is highest in _____ and African-American teens between the ages of 12 and 19.

6. The family can experience a _____ if an adolescent's striving for independence is met with stricter parental limits.

7. According to Erikson, it is during adolescence that teenagers achieve a sense of _____.

8. The _____ of the skeletal system is completed earlier in girls than in boys.

9. During middle adolescence gross motor skills such as speed, accuracy, and _____ improve.

10. It is important for the nurse to take into consideration the effects culture, ethnicity, and _____ have on adolescents.

Activity B MATCHING

Match the illicit drug in Column A with the proper descriptive phrase in Column B.

Column A

_____ **1.** Amphetamines

_____ **2.** Barbiturates

_____ **3.** Cocaine

_____ **4.** Hallucinogens

_____ **5.** Opiates

_____ **6.** Phencyclidine hydrochloride (PCP)

Column B

a. Pressured speech and anorexia

b. Drowsiness, constricted pupils

c. Depression in children

d. Violence, irrational behavior

e. Hypertension, distorted perceptions

f. Hyperactivity in children

Activity C SEQUENCING

Place the following physiological changes in sequential order beginning with early adolescence to late adolescence according to gender (males then females).

1. Male: Voice changes

2. Male: Adult size genitalia

3. Male: Leggy look

4. Female: Height increases rapidly

5. Female: Menarche begins

6. Female: Breast buds develop

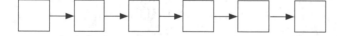

Activity D SHORT ANSWERS

Briefly answer the following.

1. List 10 safety areas that are important to teach to adolescents.

_____

_____

_____

2. Describe the adolescent's achievement of his or her identity, including how previous developmental stages and culture play a role.

_____

_____

_____

3. Explain how the school experience comprises an integral component of the adolescent's preparation for the future.

_____

_____

_____

4. Explain the importance of sexuality discussions between parents and teens.

_____

_____

_____

5. Discuss the physical growth and development of the teenager. What factors influence the growth of teens? How has growth of teens changed over the past few decades?

_____

_____

_____

6. Discuss the cognitive development/ capabilities of the teenaged child.

_____

_____

_____

SECTION II: APPLYING YOUR KNOWLEDGE

Activity E CASE STUDY

Cho Chung, a 15-year old, is brought to the clinic by her mother for her annual school check-up.

1. During your assessment, Cho states she wants to get her belly button pierced but her parents refuse. She states, "They just don't understand that there is really no risk. I have at least 10 friends who have one, and none of them have had any problems." How would you address this?

   _____

   _____

   _____

2. During your assessment, Cho comments that her boyfriend is very protective of her. He often tells her what to wear, he doesn't like many of her friends, and he gets angry when she doesn't respond immediately to his calls or texts. What thoughts do you have on hearing these things from Cho?

   _____

   _____

   _____

3. After the examination, Cho's mother expresses concerns about communicating with her daughter. How would you respond?

   _____

   _____

   _____

SECTION III: PRACTICING FOR NCLEX

Activity F NCLEX-STYLE QUESTIONS

Answer the following questions.

1. The nurse knows that the 13-year-old girl in the examination room is in the process of developing her own set of values. Which activity will this child be experiencing according to Kohlberg's theory?
   a. Wishing her parents were more understanding
   b. Assuming everyone is interested in her favorite pop star
   c. Wondering what is the meaning of life
   d. Comparing morals with those of peers

2. The nurse is promoting safe sex to a 14-year-old boy who is frequently dating. Which of the following points is most likely to be made during the talk?
   a. "Adolescents account for 25% of sexually transmitted infection (STI) cases."
   b. "Contraception is a shared responsibility."
   c. "Be careful or you'll wind up being a teenage dad."
   d. "Girls are more susceptible to STIs than boys."

3. The school nurse is providing nutritional guidance during a ninth grade health class. Which foods should the nurse recommend as good sources for calcium?
   a. Strawberries, watermelon, and raisins
   b. Beans, poultry, and fish
   c. Peanut butter, tomato juice, and whole grain bread
   d. Cheese, yogurt, and white beans

4. The nurse is talking to a 13-year-old boy about choosing friends. Which function do peer groups provide that can have a negative result?
   a. Following role models
   b. Sharing problems
   c. Negotiating differences
   d. Developing loyalties

5. The school nurse is assessing a 16-year-old girl who was removed from class because of disruptive behavior. She arrives in the nurse's office with dilated pupils and is talking rapidly. Which drug might she be using?

a. Opiates

b. Barbiturates

c. Amphetamines

d. Marijuana

6. The nurse is providing anticipatory guidance for violence prevention to a group of parents with adolescents. Which parental action should the nurse include as the most effective in preventing suicide?

a. Watching for aggressive behavior or racist remarks

b. Checking for signs of depression or lack of friends

c. Becoming acquainted with the teen's friends

d. Monitoring video games, TV shows, and music

7. A 16-year-old girl has arrived for her sports physical with a new piercing in her navel. Which response by the nurse is **best**?

a. "Be sure to clean the navel several times a day."

b. "I hope for your sake the needle was clean."

c. "This is a risk for hepatitis, tetanus, and AIDS."

d. "This is a wound and can become infected."

8. The nurse is performing a health surveillance visit with a 12-year-old boy. Which characteristic suggests the boy has entered adolescence?

a. Shows growing interest in attracting girl's attention

b. Feels secure with his body image

c. Experiences frequent mood changes

d. Understands that actions have consequences

9. The nurse is performing a physical assessment on an 11-year-old girl during a health surveillance visit. Which of the following findings would suggest the child has reached adolescence?

a. A significant muscle mass increase

b. Eruption of last four molars

c. Increased shoulder, chest, and hip widths

d. The child has higher blood pressure

10. The nurse is promoting nutrition to a teen who is going through a growth spurt. Which food should the nurse recommended for its high iron content?

a. Fat-free milk

b. Whole grain bread

c. Organic carrots

d. Fresh orange juice

11. The nurse is collecting data from a 15-year-old boy who is being seen at the ambulatory care clinic for immunizations. During the initial assessment, he voices concerns about being shorter than his peers. What response by the nurse is indicated?

a. "Being short is nothing to be ashamed of."

b. "I am sure you are not the shortest guy in your class."

c. "Boys your age will often continue growing a few more years."

d. "Are the other men in your family short?"

12. The nurse is meeting with a 16-year-old girl who reports being physically active on the track and basketball teams at school. The child reports a weight loss of 7 lb (3.2 kg) since she began training for the track season. When reviewing her caloric needs the nurse recognizes the diet should include how many calories?

a. 1,800 calories per day

b. 2,000 calories per day

c. 2,200 calories per day

d. 2,400 calories per day

13. Which behavior by an 18-year old is consistent with successful progression through the stages of Piaget's theory of development?

   a. Has a strong sense of understanding of internal identity

   b. Reflects a strong moral code

   c. Uses critical thought processes to handle a problem

   d. Is able to be part of a large group of peers while maintaining a sense of self

14. The nurse is counseling an overweight, sedentary 15-year-old girl. The nurse is assisting her to make appropriate menu choices. Which statement indicates the adolescent understands how to make appropriate dietary selections?

   a. "I avoid all fat intake."

   b. "Because of my age, my dairy intake is unlimited."

   c. "I need to have four servings of fruit each day."

   d. "To lose weight my protein intake should be limited to two to four servings per day."

15. The nurse is performing an assessment on a 12-year-old boy. Which finding is consistent with the child's age?

   a. No pubic hair

   b. Curling pubic hair

   c. Coarse pubic hair

   d. Sparse pubic hair

16. The nurse is working with a 12-year old who has recently experienced family instability and abuse. When assessing this client in the context of Erikson's developmental theory, the nurse should recognize that the adolescent has a risk of which negative outcome?

   a. Physical and emotional aggression in relationships

   b. Development of an antisocial identity

   c. Confusion about role in the world

   d. Dissociative identity disorder

17. The nurse is providing anticipatory guidance to the parents of a 15-year old who are exasperated with their teenager's sleep habits. They state, "Left to her own devices, I'm sure she'd stay up until 3:00 in the morning on the weekends and sleep until after lunchtime." Which should the nurse explain to the parents?

   a. "I can hear that this is exasperating for you, but know that children do grow out of this in time, with no ill effects."

   b. "That must be hard for you to manage. Perhaps we can explore some strategies with her to establish more predictable sleep patterns."

   c. "This is expected at this stage of development. Are there any ways that you could adjust your family routines to accommodate this?"

   d. "It's very important that you communicate to your daughter that this is unacceptable because it can have a negative effect on her health."

CHAPTER 30

Atraumatic Care of Children and Families

Learning Objectives

Upon completion of the chapter, you will be able to:

- Describe the major principles and concepts of atraumatic care.
- Incorporate atraumatic care to prevent and minimize physical stress for children and families.
- Discuss the major components and concepts of family-centered care.
- Utilize excellent therapeutic communication skills when interacting with children and their families.
- Use culturally competent communication when working with children and their families.
- Describe the process of health teaching as it relates to children and their families.

SECTION I: ASSESSING YOUR UNDERSTANDING

Activity A FILL IN THE BLANKS

1. Therapeutic care that decreases or eliminates the psychological and physical distress experienced by children and their families when receiving health care is referred to as _____ care.

2. Communication that is goal-directed, focused, and purposeful is considered _____ communication.

3. Things such as eye contact and body position are part of _____ communication.

4. A _____ nurse practitioner helps ensure that children and families receive atraumatic care.

5. Clarifying the parent's feelings by paraphrasing parts of a conversation is utilization of _____ communication.

6. Paying attention to what the child and parents are saying by nodding one's head and making eye contact is considered _____ listening.

7. Communicating with a family that speaks a different language than the nurse or with a child that is deaf may require the use of a reliable _____.

Activity B MATCHING

Match the development level in Column A with the communication technique in Column B appropriate for the developmental age.

Column A

____ **1.** Adolescents

____ **2.** Infants

____ **3.** Preschoolers

____ **4.** School-age children

____ **5.** Toddlers

Column B

a. Use a soothing voice

b. Prepare child just before procedure

c. Use diagrams and illustrations

d. Use storytelling and play

e. Define medical words as necessary

Activity C SEQUENCING

Place the following methods of learning in order from lowest percent of information remembered to the highest percent remembered after 2 weeks.

1. Actively discussing

2. Hearing

3. Performing an activity

4. Reading

5. Watching a demonstration

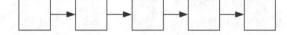

Activity D SHORT ANSWERS

Briefly answer the following.

1. Discuss how therapeutic hugging is beneficial during certain procedures?

_____

_____

_____

2. Describe four ways to evaluate the success of child and family education.

_____

_____

_____

_____

3. What incidents would alert the nurse that a family may be suffering from health literacy difficulties?

_____

_____

_____

4. Name six suggestions to enhance learning if literacy problems exist.

_____

_____

_____

5. How can the nurse help prevent or minimize child and family separation during a child's hospitalization?

_____

_____

_____

SECTION II: APPLYING YOUR KNOWLEDGE

Activity E   CASE STUDY

Emma is a 4-year-old female admitted to your pediatric unit secondary to a suspected head injury from a fall. She was playing at a playground with her babysitter and fell from the top of the slide. Emma also has a laceration to her arm that will require stitches. She is scheduled for a CT scan. Her parents are with her and are very supportive and display no difficulties with health literacy.

1. How would you explain a head CT to Emma?

   _____

   _____

   _____

2. What technique should be used to restrain Emma while she receives her stitches?

   _____

   _____

   _____

SECTION III: PRACTICING FOR NCLEX

Activity F   NCLEX-STYLE QUESTIONS

Answer the following questions.

1. The nurse is assessing the learning needs of the parents of 5-year-old girl who is scheduled for surgery. Which nonverbal cue should the nurse use to show interest in what the family members are saying?
   a. Sit straight with feet flat on the floor
   b. Look at child when the father is talking
   c. Nod head while the mother speaks
   d. Stand several steps away from parents

2. The nurse is caring for a 3-year-old boy who must have a lumbar puncture. Which action provides the greatest contribution toward atraumatic care?
   a. Having a child-life nurse practitioner play with the child

   b. Explaining the lumbar puncture procedure
   c. Letting the child take his teddy bear with him
   d. Keeping the parents calm in front of the child

3. The nurse is caring for a 14-year-old boy, and his parents, who has just been diagnosed with a malignant tumor on his liver. Which intervention is most important to this child and family?
   a. Arranging an additional meeting with the nurse practitioner
   b. Discussing treatment options with the child and parents
   c. Involving the child and family in decision making
   d. Describing postoperative home care for the child

4. The child life nurse practitioner has been assigned to assist the hospitalized child and the child's parents. Which interventions are appropriate for the child life specialist to perform? Select all that apply.
   a. Talking to the family about a scheduled diagnostic test
   b. Giving the child an influenza vaccination
   c. Starting the child's intravenous line
   d. Showing the child where the pediatric play room is located
   e. Speaking to the physician as the child's advocate

5. The child has been admitted to a pediatric unit in a hospital. Which nursing interventions use atraumatic care principles? Select all that apply.
   a. Requesting that parents assist the nurse by "holding the child down"
   b. Applying a numbing cream prior to starting the child's intravenous line
   c. Asking the child if he would like to take a bath before or after he takes his medication
   d. Encouraging the family to bring in the child's favorite stuffed animal from home
   e. Showing the parent how to unfold the chair in the child's room into a bed

6. The nurse is educating a 15-year-old girl with Graves disease and her family about the disease and its treatment. Which method of evaluating learning is least effective?

   a. Having the child and family demonstrate skills

   b. Asking closed-ended questions for specific facts

   c. Requesting the parent to teach the child skills

   d. Setting up a scenario for them to talk through

7. The nurse is caring for a 14-year-old girl with terminal cancer and her family. Which intervention provides the **best** therapeutic communication?

   a. Recognizing the parent's desire to use all options

   b. Supporting the child's desires for treatment

   c. Presenting options for treatment

   d. Informing the child in terms she can understand

8. The nurse is assessing the teaching needs of the parents of an 8-year-old boy with leukemia. Which assessment should the nurse explore as a potential issue with the parent's health literacy?

   a. The parents missed the last scheduled appointment.

   b. The entire family is fluently bilingual.

   c. The parents are taking notes on answers to their questions.

   d. The mother seems to ask most of the questions regarding care.

9. The nurse is teaching a 7-year-old girl about her upcoming tonsillectomy. Which techniques would be appropriate for this child? Select all that apply.

   a. Allowing the child to do as much self care as possible

   b. Explaining the procedure that will happen later in the day

   c. Offering choices of drinks and gelatin after the procedure

   d. Explaining that anesthesia is a lot like falling asleep

   e. Using plays or puppets to help explain the procedure

10. The nurse is educating the family of a 2-year-old boy with bronchiolitis about the disorder and its treatment. The family parents speak only Chinese. Which action, involving an interpreter, can jeopardize the family's trust?

    a. Allowing too little appointment time for the translation

    b. Using a person who is not a professional interpreter

    c. Asking the interpreter questions not meant for the family

    d. Using an older sibling to communicate with the parents

11. The child and her mother are receiving discharge instructions from the nurse. Which statements by the child's mother are "red flags" that the mother may have poor literacy skills? Select all that apply.

    a. "I forgot my glasses today and can't seem to read this form."

    b. "I'm going to take a few notes while you're teaching us."

    c. "The receptionist told me that we missed another appointment."

    d. "I guess I just forgot to give her the medication the way you told me to."

    e. "I'm going to take these instructions home to read them."

12. The nurse is preparing to educate the child about a procedure scheduled for the following morning. Which techniques should the nurse use when communicating with this child? Select all that apply.

   a. Standing at the foot of the child's bed while teaching the child

   b. Using terms that the child will likely understand

   c. Looking for nonverbal cues

   d. Requesting that the parents leave the room during the education

   e. Being patient with the child

13. The nurse is educating a young child about what to expect during an upcoming procedure. Which statements are appropriate for the nurse to use? Select all that apply.

   a. "This little tube will go in your nose and down into your belly."

   b. "I'm going to give you this shot and it will put you to sleep."

   c. "You'll end up in 'ICU' where you'll wake up with some electrodes on your thorax."

   d. "When they come to get you, you'll get on a special rolling bed."

   e. "They're going to give you some special medicine to help the doctor see what's happening inside your belly."

CHAPTER 31

Health Supervision

Learning Objectives

Upon completion of the chapter, you will be able to:

- Describe the principles of health supervision.
- Identify challenges to health supervision for children with chronic illnesses.
- List the three components of a health supervision visit.
- Use instruments appropriately for developmental surveillance and screening of children.
- Demonstrate knowledge of the principles of immunization.
- Identify barriers to immunization.
- Identify the key components of health promotion.
- Describe the role of anticipatory guidance in health promotion.

SECTION I: ASSESSING YOUR UNDERSTANDING

Activity A FILL IN THE BLANKS

1. Because of the impact that hearing loss can have on _____, it is crucial that even slight hearing loss be identified by age 3 months.

2. Screening for iron deficiency at 6 months of age is important because the _____ iron stores of full-term infants are almost depleted.

3. If a client's family has difficulty accessing health care facilities, health promotion activities may be carried out in _____ settings such as schools and churches.

4. Health supervision has three components: screening, _____, and health promotion.

5. When obtaining an immunization history, asking _____ and where the last immunization was received provides more information than asking if immunizations are current.

6. The purpose of hyperlipidemia screening is to reduce the incidence of adult _____ disease.

7. The Weber test screens for hearing by assessing sound conducted via _____.

8. Vaccinations may be postponed if the child has a severe illness with high fever or _____, or has recently received blood products.

9. For children less than 3 years of age, vision screening is based on the child's ability to _____ and follow objects.

10. _____ immunity is acquired when a person's own immune system generates the immune response.

Activity B MATCHING

1. Match the age and developmental warning sign in Column A with the possible developmental concern in Column B.

Column A

___ **1.** Rolls over before 3 months

___ **2.** Persistent head lag after 4 months

___ **3.** Not smiling at 6 months

___ **4.** Not babbling at 6 months

___ **5.** Not walking by 18 months

___ **6.** Hand dominance present before 18 months

Column B

a. Hemiplegia in opposite upper extremity

b. Hypertonia

c. Visual defect or attachment issue

d. Gross motor delay

e. Hypotonia

f. Hearing deficit

2. Match the developmental screening tool in Column A with the descriptive phrase in Column B.

Column A

___ **1.** Ages and Stages Questionnaire (ASQ)

___ **2.** Child Development Inventory (CDI)

___ **3.** Denver II

___ **4.** Goodenough–Harris Drawing test

___ **5.** Parent's Evaluation of Developmental Status (PEDS)

Column B

a. Simple questions about infant, toddler, or preschooler behaviors

b. Uses props provided in kit such as a baby doll, ball, and crayons to assess personal–social, fine motor–adaptive, language and gross motor skills

c. Assesses communication, gross and fine motor, personal–social, and problems-solving skills

d. Screens for developmental, behavioral, and family issues. Tool is available in Spanish.

e. Nonverbal screen for mental ability

3. Match the vision screening tool in Column A with the descriptive phrase in Column B.

Column A

___ **1.** Color Vision Testing Made Easy (CVTME)

___ **2.** Ishihara

___ **3.** LEA symbols or Allen figures

___ **4.** Snellen letters or numbers

___ **5.** Tumbling E

Column B

a. Uses pictures instead of the alphabet

b. Shapes embedded in dots

c. Used to assess the preschooler by asking him to point the direction the letter is pointing

d. Numbers hidden in dots

e. Used in children who know the alphabet

Activity C SEQUENCING

Beginning with an infant who is between birth and 3 months, and progressing in age, place the following developmental warning signs in sequential order.

1. Head lag disappears

2. Uses spoon or crayon

3. Uses imitative play

4. Rolls over

5. Says first word

6. Primitive reflex disappears

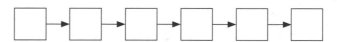

Activity D SHORT ANSWERS

Briefly answer the following.

1. Describe the proper technique for doing the Weber test, including what should be heard and where.

_____

_____

_____

2. What conditions seen in parents or grandparents who are less than 55 years of age would suggest screening for hyperlipidemia in the children?

_____

_____

_____

3. Describe the process of screening for hearing loss in older children, beginning with a history from the primary caregivers.

_____

_____

_____

4. Describe the potential impact of iron deficiency in children. During what periods of time is a child at the greatest risk for the development of the condition?

_____

_____

_____

5. Discuss the recommendations for screening children for hypertension. What factors increase the risk for the development of this condition?

_____

_____

_____

SECTION II: APPLYING YOUR KNOWLEDGE

Activity E CASE STUDY 1

Jasmine Chase, a 15-year-old female, is seen in your clinic for her annual examination. During this health supervision visit, Jasmine expresses concerns about her weight. She states she has been attempting to diet and has reduced her number of meals a day by skipping breakfast. She also decided to give up meat, fish, and poultry, and eats mostly salads for lunch and dinner.

1. During the health interview and examination, what information do you want to elicit?

_____

_____

_____

2. What screening test may be warranted for Jasmine and why?

_____

_____

_____

3. During today's examination, you determine Jasmine's height is 5 feet (1.52 m) and her weight is 150 lb (68.03 kg). What can you do to help promote a healthy weight for Jasmine?

_____

_____

_____

CASE STUDY 2

Claire Rosemount is a 5-year-old female who was recently diagnosed with type 1 diabetes mellitus. Your clinic has been her medical home since birth. Health supervision of a child with a chronic illness can be challenging.

1. What can nurses do to meet these challenges and ensure proper care for Claire and other children with chronic illnesses?

_____

_____

_____

SECTION III: PRACTICING FOR NCLEX

Activity F NCLEX-STYLE QUESTIONS

Answer the following questions.

1. During the health history of a 2-month-old infant, the nurse identified a risk factor for developmental delay and is preparing to screen the child's development. Which risk might the nurse have found?

   a. The child had neonatal conjunctivitis

   b. The parents are both in college

   c. The child was born at 36 weeks

   d. The child has small eyes and chin

2. The nurse is promoting the benefits of achieving a healthy weight to an overweight 12-year-old child and her parents. Which approach is **best**?

   a. Show the family the appropriate weight for the child

   b. Ask what activities she enjoys such as dance or sports

   c. Suggest that the child join a little league softball team

   d. Point out fattening foods and excesses in their diet

3. The nurse is discussing Varicella immunization with a mother of a 13-month old. The mother is reluctant to vaccinate because she feels it is "not necessary." Which comment by the nurse will be most persuasive for immunization?

   a. "Mild reactions occur in 5% to 10% of children."

   b. "Varicella is a highly contagious herpes virus."

   c. "Children not immunized are at risk if exposed to the disease."

   d. "Risk of Varicella is greater than the risk of vaccine."

4. The nurse is doing a health history for a 14-year-old boy during a health supervision visit. The boy says he has outgrown his clothes recently. For which condition should the nurse check, based on this information?

   a. Developmental problems

   b. Hyperlipidemia

   c. Iron deficiency anemia

   d. Systemic hypertension

5. A mother and her 2-week-old infant have arrived for a health supervision visit. Which activity will the nurse perform?

   a. Assess the child for an upper respiratory infection

   b. Take a health history for a minor injury

   c. Administer a Varicella injection

   d. Warn against putting the baby to bed with a bottle

6. During a physical assessment of a 6-year-old child, the nurse observes the child has lost a tooth. The nurse uses the opportunity to promote oral health care with the child and parents. Which comment should the nurse include in this discussion?

   a. "Oral health can affect general health."

   b. "Fluoridated water has significantly reduced cavities."

   c. "Try to keep the child's hands out of the mouth."

   d. "Limit the amount of soft drinks in the child's diet."

7. The mother of a 5-year old with eczema is getting a check-up for her child before school starts. Which action should the nurse take during the visit?

   a. Change the bandage on a cut on the child's hand

   b. Assess how the family is coping with the chronic illness

   c. Discuss systemic corticosteroid therapy

   d. Assess the child's fluid volume

8. The nurse is performing a vision screening for 6-year-old child. Which screening chart is **best** for the nurse use to determine the child's ability to discriminate color?

   a. Snellen

   b. Ishihara

   c. Allen figures

   d. CVTME

9. The nurse is anticipating that health supervision for a 5-year-old child will be challenging. Which indicator supports this concern?

   a. Grandparents play a significant role in the family

   b. The child has a number of chores and responsibilities

   c. The mother dotes on the child

   d. The home is in a high-crime neighborhood

10. During the health history, the parent of a 10-year-old child mentions the child seems to have trouble hearing. Which test is the nurse most likely to use?

    a. Rinne test

    b. Whisper test

    c. Evoked otoacoustic emissions test

    d. Auditory brainstem response test

11. The nurse is collecting data from the mother of a 3-year-old child. Which report warrants further follow-up?

   a. Cannot stack five blocks

   b. Cannot grasp a crayon with the thumb and fingers

   c. Cannot copy a circle

   d. Cannot throw a ball overhand

12. The nurse is preparing to perform the Denver II screening test. Which items should the nurse prepare for use in the assessment? Select all that apply.

   a. Ball

   b. Four plastic rings

   c. Doll

   d. Crayon

   e. Crackers

13. The mother of a 2-year-old child questions when she will need to initially have her child's vision screened. The nurse should inform the mother that vision screening begins at which age?

   a. 1 year of age

   b. 2 years of age

   c. 3 years of age

   d. 4 years of age

14. The nurse is counseling a pregnant adolescent about the health benefits associated with breastfeeding. Which statements by the client indicate understanding?

   a. "Breastfeeding my baby will pass on a type of active immunity."

   b. "Breastfeeding my baby will pass on passive immunity."

   c. "Breastfeeding my baby will provide lifelong immunity against certain diseases."

   d. "Breastfeeding my baby will help to stimulate my baby's immune system to activate."

15. Which child poses the greatest risk for elevated lead levels?

   a. 2-year-old Caucasian child who lives in a city apartment

   b. 18-month-old African-American child who lives in a suburban home

   c. 10-year-old Caucasian child who lives with his grandparents

   d. 2-year-old Asian child who lives with his adopted American parents

Health Assessment of Children

Learning Objectives

Upon completion of the chapter, you will be able to:

- Demonstrate an understanding of the appropriate health history to obtain from the child and the parent or primary caregiver.
- Individualize elements of the health history depending on the age of the child.
- Discuss important concepts related to health assessment in children.
- Perform a health assessment using approaches that relate to the age and developmental stage of the child.
- Describe the appropriate sequence of the physical examination in the context of the child's developmental stage.
- Distinguish normal variations in the physical examination from differences that may indicate serious alterations in health status.
- Determine the sexual maturity of females and males based on evaluation of the secondary sex characteristics.

SECTION I: ASSESSING YOUR UNDERSTANDING

Activity A FILL IN THE BLANKS

1. _____ is an acronym that means pupils are equal, round, reactive to light and accommodation.

2. _____ is the measure of body weight relative to height.

3. The _____ is the area on an infant's head that is not protected by skull bone.

4. Auscultation is listening with a _____.

5. When assessing the thorax and lungs, an inspiratory high-pitched sound is referred to as audible _____.

6. During assessment of the newborn the nurse notes small white papules on the infant's forehead, chin, nose, and cheeks. The nurse is correct in documenting this finding as _____.

7. Following inspection, _____ of the abdomen should be performed next during assessment of the abdomen.

Activity B LABELING

Consider the following figure.

Identify the point of maximal intensity (PMI) or apical impulse, for birth to 4 years, age 4 to 6 years, and 7 years and older.

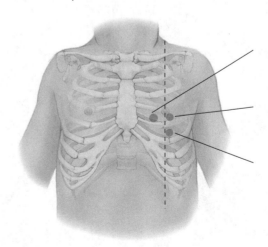

Activity C MATCHING

Match the term in Column A with the proper definition in Column B.

Column A

____ **1.** Acrocyanosis

____ **2.** Cerumen

____ **3.** Lanugo

____ **4.** Stadiometer

____ **5.** Accommodation

Column B

a. Soft downy hair found on the newborn's body

b. Ability of the eyes to focus at different distances

c. Transient blueness in the hands and feet

d. Instrument to measure standing height

e. Waxy substance normally found lubricating and protecting the external ear canal

Activity D SEQUENCING

Place the following questions in the health interview of an adolescent in the proper sequence in the boxes provided below.

1. Are you sexually active?

2. What is your name?

3. What can I help you with today?

4. Do you have any allergies?

Activity E SHORT ANSWERS

Briefly answer the following.

1. Briefly describe the six grades of heart murmurs in children.

_____

_____

_____

2. Differentiate between ecchymosis, petechiae, and purpura.

_____

_____

_____

3. Briefly describe the expected appearance of the healthy ear canal and tympanic membrane.

_____

_____

_____

4. How does the heart rate vary according to a child's age?

_____

_____

_____

5. What are some possible reasons for inaccurate pulse oximetry readings?

_____

_____

_____

6. Identify four risk factors that would indicate the need to assess the blood pressure of a child under the age of 3 years.

_____

_____

_____

SECTION II: APPLYING YOUR KNOWLEDGE

Activity F CASE STUDY

As the nurse on a pediatric unit you are assigned to care for three children. You receive the following information on each child in report. Based on this information, rank in order of priority when to assess each child. Provide rationale for your answers.

1. A 5-year old hospitalized with an acute asthma attack. Vital signs are: heart rate 124, respiratory rate 28 to 30, blood pressure 93/48, and axillary temperature of 98.6°F.

   _____

   _____

   _____

2. A 3-month old hospitalized for rule out sepsis secondary to fever. Vital signs are: heart rate 165, respiratory rate 34, blood pressure 108/64, and rectal temperature of 102.5°F taken immediately before report. No intervention was initiated.

   _____

   _____

   _____

3. A 7-month old hospitalized with pneumonia. Vital signs are heart rate of 165 with brief episodes of dropping into the 60s during the previous shift, respiratory rate of 78, blood pressure 112/72, and axillary temperature of 99.5°F.

   _____

   _____

   _____

SECTION III: PRACTICING FOR NCLEX

Activity G NCLEX-STYLE QUESTIONS

Answer the following questions.

1. The nurse is examining the genitals of a healthy newborn girl. The nurse should observe which normal finding?

   a. Swollen labia minora

   b. Lesions on the external genitalia

   c. Labial adhesions

   d. Swollen labia majora

2. The nurse is caring for a 13-year-old girl. As part of a routine health assessment the nurse needs to address areas relating to sexuality and substance use. Which statement should the nurse say **first** to encourage communication?

   a. "Do you smoke cigarettes or marijuana?"

   b. "I promise not to tell your mother any of your responses."

   c. "Tell me about some of your current activities at school."

   d. " Are you considering sexual activity?"

3. The nurse is caring for a 10-year-old girl and is trying to obtain clues about the child's state of physical, emotional, and moral development. Which question is most likely to elicit the desired information?

   a. "Do you like your school and your teacher?"

   b. "Would you say that you are a good student?"

   c. "Tell me about your favorite activity at school?"

   d. "Do you have a lot of friends at school?"

4. A nurse is caring for a very shy 4-year-old girl. During the course of a well-child assessment, the nurse must take the girl's blood pressure. Which approach is **best**?

   a. "May I take your blood pressure?"

   b. "Your sister did a great job when I took hers"

   c. "Help me take your dolls blood pressure"

   d. "Will you let me put this cuff on your arm?"

5. The nurse is preparing to see a 14-month-old child and needs to establish the chief purpose of the visit. Which approach with the parents would be **best**?

   a. "What is your chief complaint?"

   b. "What can I help you with today?"

   c. "Is your child feeling sick?"

   d. "Has your child been exposed to infectious agents?"

6. A nurse is conducting a physical examination of an uncooperative preschooler. In order to encourage deep breathing during lung auscultation what could the nurse say?

   a. "You must breathe deeply so I can hear your lungs."

   b. "You may not leave until I listen to your breathing."

   c. "Do you think you can blow out my light bulb on this pen?"

   d. "Do you want your mother to listen to your lungs?"

7. The nurse is conducting a physical examination of a healthy 6-year old. Which action should the nurse do **first**?

   a. Observe the skin for its overall color and characteristics

   b. Tap with the knee with a reflex hammer to check for deep tendon reflexes

   c. Palpate the skin for texture and hydration status

   d. Auscultate the heart, lungs, and the abdomen

8. A nurse is assessing an infant's reflexes. The nurse places his or her thumb to the ball of the infant's foot to elicit which reflex?

   a. Parachute

   b. Plantar grasp

   c. Babinski

   d. Palmar grasp

9. The emergency department nurse is caring for a child who is showing signs of anaphylaxis. The nurse evaluates how comprehensive the history of the child should be and determines that which action takes priority?

   a. Taking a problem-focused history

   b. Obtaining a complete and detailed history

   c. Stabilizing the child's physical status

   d. Getting the child's history from other providers

10. The nurse is conducting a physical examination of a 5-year-old girl. The nurse asks the girl to stand still with her eyes closed and arms down by her side. The girl immediately begins to lean. What does this tell the nurse?

    a. The child has poor coordination and poor balance.

    b. The child warrants further testing for cerebellar dysfunction.

    c. The child has a negative Romberg test; no further testing is necessary.

    d. The child warrants further testing for an inner ear infection.

11. The nurse needs to calculate the child's body mass index (BMI). The child's weight is 42 kg. The child is 142 cm in height. Calculate the child's BMI using the metric method. Record your answer using a whole number.

12. The experienced nurse is assessing the child's lungs. Rank the following steps in the proper order of assessment.

  a. The nurse visually inspects the child's thorax

  b. The nurse palpates the child's thorax

  c. The nurse percusses over the child's lungs

  d. The nurse auscultates the child's lungs

Caring for Children in Diverse Settings

Upon completion of the chapter, you will be able to:

■ Identify the major stressors of illness and hospitalization for children.
■ Identify the reactions and responses of children and their families during illness and hospitalization.
■ Explain the factors that influence the reactions and responses of children and their families during illness and hospitalization.
■ Describe the nursing care that minimizes stressors for children who are ill or hospitalized.
■ Discuss the major components of admission for children to the hospital.
■ Discuss appropriate safety measures to use when caring for children of all ages.
■ Review nursing responsibilities related to client discharge from the hospital.
■ Describe the various roles of community and home care nurses.
■ Discuss the variety of settings in which community-based care occurs.
■ Discuss the advantages and disadvantages of home health care.

SECTION I: ASSESSING YOUR UNDERSTANDING

Activity A FILL IN THE BLANKS

1. Therapeutic _____ is the use of a holding position that promotes close physical contact between the child and a parent or caregiver that is used when the child needs to remain still for procedures such as IV insertion.

2. Restraints should be checked every _____ minutes following initial placement, then every hour for proper placement.

3. A good time to assess the skin is during _____ time.

4. Forcing a child to _____ can exacerbate any nausea or vomiting.

5. _____ play allows a child to express his or her feelings and fears, as well as providing a means to promote energy expenditure.

6. Nurses in the school setting develop _____ to plan how the school staff will collaborate with the student and family in meeting the needs of students with complex health care issues.

7. _____ nurses focus on health supervision services and connecting children to needed community resources.

Activity B MATCHING

Match the term in Column A with the proper definition in Column B.

Column A

_____ **1.** Denial

_____ **2.** Regression

_____ **3.** Sensory overload

_____ **4.** Separation anxiety

_____ **5.** Sensory deprivation

Column B

a. Increased stimulation for the child

b. Defense mechanism used by children to avoid unpleasant realities

c. Distress related to being removed from primary caregivers and familiar surroundings

d. Lack of stimulation

e. Defense mechanism used by children to avoid dealing with conflict by returning to a previous stage that may be more comfortable to the child

Activity C SEQUENCING

Place the three stages of separation anxiety in the proper sequence.

1. Despair

2. Denial

3. Protest

Activity D SHORT ANSWERS

Briefly answer the following.

1. How can the nurse address and minimize separation anxiety in the hospitalized child?

_____

_____

_____

2. When does discharge planning begin? Why?

_____

_____

_____

3. What are some common behaviors or methods children use for coping with hospitalization?

_____

_____

_____

4. What are the most common reasons for children to be hospitalized?

_____

_____

_____

5. What are some ways the home care nurse can establish a trusting relationship with the child and caregivers?

_____

_____

_____

SECTION II: APPLYING YOUR KNOWLEDGE

Activity E CASE STUDY

A variety of reactions and responses are seen as a result of the stressors children experience in relation to hospitalization. Nurses often spend more time with children and their families compared to other physicians during hospitalization. Therefore, it is essential that nurses establish strategies to care and intervene in order to help children cope with their experience. Nurses must examine effects of hospitalization within the child's developmental stage and understand the reactions and responses of the child and family to hospitalization.

While working on the pediatric unit, your child care assignment involves children of differing developmental ages. Read the below reactions and identify interventions and rationales for each of the following children in your care.

1. Leslie Lucas, a 6-month-old female with a club foot repair, is hospitalized postsurgery. She has been irritable and difficult to console.

   _____

   _____

   _____

2. Eli Castle, an 18-month-old male admitted with pneumonia, has not slept more than 1 hour without waking.

   _____

   _____

   _____

3. Amelia Lionhart, a 4-year-old female admitted with dehydration, repeatedly wakes up crying after having nightmares.

   _____

   _____

   _____

4. Jamal Anderson, a 10-year-old male, hospitalized secondary to asthma, has eaten very little from his meal trays for the past few days.

   _____

   _____

   _____

5. Cheryl Erikson, a 16-year-old female with lymphoma, expresses a desire to be left alone in her darkened room.

   _____

   _____

   _____

SECTION III: PRACTICING FOR NCLEX

Activity F NCLEX-STYLE QUESTIONS

Answer the following questions.

1. The nurse is caring for an 18-month-old boy hospitalized with a gastrointestinal disorder. The nurse knows that the child is at risk for separation anxiety. The nurse watches for behaviors that indicate the first phase of separation anxiety. For which behavior should the nurse watch?

   a. Crying and acting out

   b. Embracing others who attempt to comfort him

   c. Losing interest in play and food

   d. Exhibiting apathy and withdrawing from others

2. The nurse is caring for a preschooler who is hospitalized with a suspected blood disorder and receives an order to draw a blood sample. Which approach is **best**?

   a. "I need to take some blood."

   b. "We need to put a little hole in your arm."

   c. "I need to remove a little blood."

   d. "Why don't you sit on your mom's lap?"

3. The nurse is caring for a child hospitalized with complications from asthma. Which statement by the parents indicates a need for careful observation of the child's anxiety level?

 a. "My mother passed away here after surgery."

 b. "Our twins were born here 18 months ago."

 c. "My father undergoes kidney dialysis at this hospital."

 d. "We attended a 'living with asthma' class here."

4. A nurse is caring for a 6-year-old boy hospitalized due to an infection requiring intravenous antibiotic therapy. The child's motor activity is restricted and he is acting out, yelling, kicking, and screaming. How should the nurse respond to help promote positive coping?

 a. "Your medicine is the only way you will get better."

 b. "Let me explain why you need to sit still."

 c. "Would you like to read or play video games?"

 d. "Do I need to call your parents?"

5. A nurse is educating the parents on how to help their 10-year-old daughter deal with an extended hospital stay due to surgery, followed by traction. Which response indicates a need for further teaching?

 a. "I should not tell her how long she will be here."

 b. "She will watch our reactions carefully."

 c. "We must prepare her in advance."

 d. "She will be sensitive to our concerns."

6. A nurse is preparing to admit a child for a tonsillectomy. How should the nurse establish rapport?

 a. "Let's take a look at your tonsils."

 b. "Do you understand why you are here?"

 c. "Are you scared about having your tonsils out?"

 d. "Tell me about your cute stuffed dog you have."

7. The nurse is preparing to admit a 4-year old who will be having tympanostomy tubes placed in both ears. Which strategy is most likely to reduce the child's fears of the procedure?

 a. "The doctor is going to insert tympanostomy tubes in your ears."

 b. "Don't worry, you will be asleep the whole time."

 c. "Let me show you how tiny these tubes are."

 d. "Let me show you the operating room."

8. A nurse is developing a preoperative plan of care for a 2-year old. The nurse should pay particular attention to which of the child's age-related fears?

 a. Separation from friends

 b. Separation from parents

 c. Loss of control

 d. Loss of independence

9. The nurse is educating the parents of a 7-year-old boy, scheduled for surgery, to help prepare the child for hospitalization. Which statement by the parents indicates a need for further teaching?

 a. "We should talk about going to the hospital and what it will be like coming home"

 b. "We should visit the hospital and go through the preadmission tour in advance"

 c. "It is best to wait and let him bring up the surgery or any questions he has"

 d. "It is a good idea to read stories about experiences with hospitals or surgery"

10. The nurse is caring for a 7-year-old boy in a body cast. He is shy and seems fearful of the numerous personnel in and out of his room. How can the nurse help reduce his fear?

 a. Remind the boy he will be out of the hospital and going home soon.

 b. Encourage the boy's parents to stay with him at all times to reduce his fears.

 c. Write the name of his nurse on a board and identify all staff on each shift, every day.

 d. Tell him not to worry; explain that everyone is here to care for him.

11. The nurse has applied a restraint to the child's right wrist to prevent the child from pulling out an intravenous line. Which assessment findings ensure that there is proper circulation to the child's right arm? Select all that apply.

    a. Capillary refill is less than 2 seconds in upper extremities bilaterally

    b. Fingers are pink and warm bilaterally

    c. Lungs are clear throughout

    d. Radial pulses are easily palpable bilaterally

    e. Bowel sounds present in all four quadrants

12. The student nurse is assisting the more experienced pediatric nurse. Which statements by the student indicate further education is required? Select all that apply.

    a. "Could you give the nauseated child some medicine before it is time for him to start thinking about ordering lunch?"

    b. "I'm going to redress the child's IV site while she is in the playroom."

    c. "I took our new teenaged child down to show him the playroom."

    d. "It would be easy to perform a straight catheterization while the baby is in his crib."

    e. "I told the child's mom to go ahead and bring in his blanket and stuffed animal."

13. The nurse is documenting the child's intake. The child ate four cups of ice during this shift. How many cups of fluid did the child ingest?

    a. Four cups of fluid

    b. One cup of fluid

    c. Half a cup of fluid

    d. Two cups of fluid

14. The nurse is providing care for a hospitalized child. Rank the following phases in the order of occurrence based on the nurse's statements.

    a. "Hi, my name is Cindy and I'm going to be your nurse for today."

    b. "Let's sit over here and play a game of "Go Fish"."

    c. "Would you like your medicine before or after your mom helps take a bath?"

    d. "You handled that procedure so well! Would you like me to get Mr. Snuggles for you?"

34

Caring for the Special Needs Child

Learning Objectives

Upon completion of the chapter, you will be able to:

- Analyze the impact that being a child with special needs has on the child and family.
- Identify anticipated times when the child and family will require additional support.
- Describe ways that nurses assist children with special needs and their families to obtain optimal functioning.
- Discuss early intervention and public school education for the special needs child.
- Plan for transition of the special needs child from the inpatient facility to the home, and from pediatric to adult medical care.
- Discuss key elements related to pediatric end-of-life care.
- Differentiate developmental responses to death and appropriate interventions.

SECTION I: ASSESSING YOUR UNDERSTANDING

Activity A FILL IN THE BLANKS

1. The Individuals with Disabilities Education Act (IDEA) of 2004 mandates government-funded care coordination and special education for children up to _____ years of age.

2. _____ care provides an opportunity for families to take a break from the daily intensive care giving responsibilities.

3. When working with a dying child, always focus on the _____ as the unit of care.

4. _____ remains the leading cause of death from disease in all children over the age of 1 year.

5. A _____ consent is necessary for organ donation, so the family must be appropriately informed and educated.

6. _____ care provides the best quality of life possible at the end of life while alleviating physical, psychological, emotional, and spiritual suffering.

7. During the last stages of a terminal illness, _____ care allows for family-centered care in the child's home or appropriate facility.

Activity B MATCHING

Match the child's stage in Column A with their needs as they go through the dying process, listed in Column B.

Column A	Column B
____ **1.** Toddler (1 to 3 years)	**a.** Need to know death is not a punishment; need to know that although they will be missed, the family will function without them
____ **2.** 3 to 5 years	
____ **3.** 5 to 10 years	
____ **4.** 10 to 14 years	
____ **5.** 14 to 18 years	**b.** Specific honest details; old enough to help in some decision making
	c. Reinforcement of self-esteem; privacy and time alone, time with peers; participation in decision making
	d. Support through honest, detailed explanations; wants to feel truly involved and listened to
	e. Need familiarity, routine, favorite toys, and physical comfort

Activity C SEQUENCING

Place the Adolescent Health Transition Project (AHTP) recommendations schedule for transitioning child care to adult care for the child with special health care needs in the proper sequence.

1. Explore health care financing for young adults. If needed, notify the local division of vocational rehabilitation by the autumn before the teen is to graduate from high school of the impending transition. Initiate guardianship procedures if appropriate.

2. Ensure that a transition plan is initiated and that the individualized education plan (IEP) reflects post–high school plans.

3. Ensure that the young adult has registered with the Division of Developmental Disabilities for adult services if applicable.

4. Notify the teen that all rights transfer to him or her at the age of majority. Check the teen's eligibility for SSI the month the child turns 18. Determine if the child is eligible for SSI work incentives.

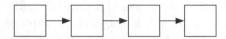

Activity D SHORT ANSWERS

Briefly answer the following.

1. Name four different complementary therapies that might be adopted for treatment of children with chronic illness.

   _____

   _____

   _____

2. Explain dietary requirements and how they are best met for formerly premature infants who need to "catch-up" on weight.

   _____

   _____

   _____

3. How should the nurse explain DNR orders (do not resuscitate) to a family when they are trying to make this decision regarding a terminally ill child?

   _____

   _____

   _____

4. List the principles that the Last Acts Palliative Care Task Force has established regarding the care of children with a terminal illness.

   _____

   _____

   _____

5. Since the body requires less nutrition during the dying process, what are some important care measures to keep in mind for the dying child?

   _____

   _____

   _____

SECTION II: APPLYING YOUR KNOWLEDGE

Activity E CASE STUDY

1. Preet Singh is a 2-year-old boy born at 27 weeks' gestation and has a history of hydrocephalus and developmental delay. What role can the nurse play in assisting the family to obtain optimal functioning?

   _____

   _____

   _____

2. Georgia Lansing, a 7-year-old girl, has been diagnosed with lymphoma. She recently had a relapse and has not responded to treatment. The family has decided on palliative care. Discuss ways the nurse can support the dying child and family.

   Include the type of support and education that the dying child needs according to the developmental stage.

   _____

   _____

   _____

SECTION III: PRACTICING FOR NCLEX

Activity F NCLEX-STYLE QUESTIONS

Answer the following questions.

1. The nurse is caring for the family of a medically fragile 2-year-old girl. Which activity is **most** effective in building a therapeutic relationship?

   a. Helping access an early intervention program

   b. Teaching physiotherapy techniques

   c. Listening to parents' triumphs and failures

   d. Getting free samples of the child's medications

2. A 14-year-old boy is aware that he is dying. Which action **best** meets the child's need for self-esteem and sense of worth?

   a. Providing full participation in decision making

   b. Initiating conversations about his feelings

   c. Giving direct, honest answers to his questions

   d. Listening to his fears and concerns about dying

3. A 10-year-old girl with bone cancer is near death. Which action should **best** minimize her 8-year-old sister's anxiety?

   a. Correcting her when she says her sister won't die

   b. Telling her that her sister won't need food any more

   c. Discouraging the child's questions about death

   d. Explaining how the morphine drip works

4. A 15-year-old boy with special needs is attending high school. Which nursing intervention will be **most** beneficial to his education?

   a. Collaborating with the school nurse about his care

   b. Serving on his individualized education plan (IEP) committee

   c. Advocating for financial aid for a motorized wheelchair

   d. Assessing how attending school will affect his health

5. A 6-month-old girl is significantly underweight. Which assessment finding points to an inorganic cause of failure to thrive?

   a. Infant refuses the nipple

   b. Child avoids eye contact

   c. Premature birth

   d. Risk factors in the health history

6. The nurse is caring for the family of a 9-year-old boy with cerebral palsy. Which intervention will best improve communication between the nurse and the family?

   a. Giving direct, understandable answers

   b. Sharing cell phone numbers with the parents

   c. Using reflective listening techniques

   d. Saying the same thing in different ways

7. It is difficult for the father of a technologically dependent 7-year-old girl to leave his work. Which nursing intervention would **best** involve him in family-centered care?

   a. Leave a voice mail for the father at work.

   b. Email a status report to the father's office.

   c. Urge the father to come to the hospital at lunch.

   d. Schedule education sessions in the evening.

8. The nurse is caring for the family of a medically fragile child in the hospital. Which intervention is **most** important to the parents?

   a. Educating the parents about the course of treatment

   b. Evaluating the emotional strength of the parents

   c. Preparing a list of supplies the family will need

   d. Assessing the adequacy of the home environment

9. The nurse at a hospice care facility is caring for a 12-year-old girl. Which intervention **best** meets the needs of this child?

   a. Assuring her the illness is not her fault

   b. Urging her to invite her friends to visit

   c. Acting as the child's personal confidant

   d. Explaining her condition to her in detail

10. The nurse is caring for a 15-year-old boy with cystic fibrosis. Which intervention will help avert risky behavior?

    a. Assessing for signs of depression

    b. Encouraging participation in activities

    c. Monitoring compliance with treatment

    d. Urging that he join a support group

11. The infant was born preterm. Which assessment findings may indicate that the child is suffering from a medical condition associated with being born preterm?

    a. The child's parents stated that the child began losing baby teeth earlier than their other children.

    b. The child's hearing is not within normal limits and the child requires a hearing aid.

    c. The child eyes deviate inward.

    d. The child is noted to be above the 95th percentile for height and at the 85th percentile for weight.

    e. The child started speaking multiword sentences at 18 months old.

12. The child has been diagnosed with vulnerable child syndrome. Which statements by the child's parent are associated with the presence of this syndrome? Select all that apply.

    a. "I discipline all three of my kids very fairly."

    b. "He was always a sweet and happy baby."

    c. "For the first few weeks of his life, he was so yellow I was afraid he would glow."

    d. "When she was a toddler she developed meningitis and the doctors told me they didn't think she'd make it."

    e. "She was born with a cleft lip and palate I was so afraid she wasn't getting enough formula."

13. The nurse is planning the care of a 5-year-old child with developmental disabilities whose weight is on the 12th percentile for age. The care team and the child's parents have agreed that interventions are necessary. Which intervention should be added to the plan of care?

   a. Encourage the parents to maintain a detailed log of the child's food and fluid intake.

   b. Facilitate the insertion of a peripherally inserted central catheter for parenteral nutrition.

   c. Allow the child to choose which foods to eat and which food to reject.

   d. Encourage the family to provide a low-fat, high-carbohydrate diet.

14. The child has been hospitalized for failure to thrive. The child weighs 23.2 kg. The child is to receive 120 kcal/kg of weight per day. How many kilocalories should the child eat each day? Record your answer using a whole number.

15. The infant was born at 32 weeks' gestation and is now 9 months old. What is the infant's corrected age? Record your answer using a whole number.

Key Pediatric Nursing Interventions

Learning Objectives

Upon completion of the chapter, you will be able to:

- Describe the "rights" of pediatric medication administration.
- Explain the physiologic differences in children affecting a medication's pharmacodynamic and pharmacokinetic properties.
- Accurately determine recommended pediatric medication doses.
- Demonstrate the proper technique for administering medication to children via the oral, rectal, ophthalmic, otic, intravenous, intramuscular, and subcutaneous routes.
- Integrate the concepts of atraumatic care in medication administration for children.
- Identify the preferred sites for peripheral and central intravenous medication administration.
- Describe nursing management related to maintenance of intravenous infusions in children, as well as prevention of complications.
- Explain nursing care related to enteral tube feedings.
- Describe nursing management of the child receiving total parenteral nutrition.

SECTION I: ASSESSING YOUR UNDERSTANDING

Activity A FILL IN THE BLANKS

1. A port-a-cath is a type of _____ central venous access device.

2. _____ is the behavior of a medication at the cellular level.

3. Encouraging the child to count aloud or asking a child to blow bubbles during a medical procedure is a method to create a _____.

4. When inserting a rectal suppository for any child under the age of 3, the nurse should use the _____ finger.

5. _____ typically occurs with too rapid cessation of TPN (total parenteral nutrition).

6. _____ tubes are inserted through the nose and terminate in the stomach and are used for short-term enteral feeding.

7. Administration of medication into the eyes is referred to as the _____ route.

Activity B LABELING

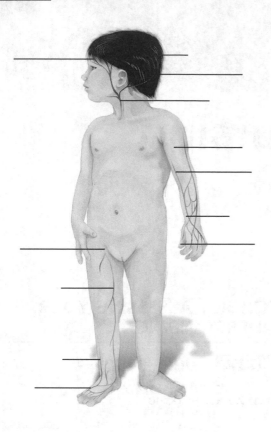

Provide labels for the preferred peripheral sites for IV insertion.

a. Dorsal arch

b. Great saphenous

c. Basilic

d. Superficial temporal

e. Femoral

f. Cephalic

g. Frontal

h. Dorsal arch

i. External jugular

j. Occipital

k. Digital

l. Small saphenous

Activity C MATCHING

Match the term in Column A with the proper definition in Column B.

Column A

1. Gavage feedings

2. Enteral nutrition

3. Bolus feeding

4. Parenteral nutrition

5. Residual

Column B

a. Nutrition delivered directly into the intestinal tract

b. Administration of a specified feeding solution at specific intervals, usually over a short period of time

c. Intravenous delivery of nutritional substances

d. The amounts of contents remaining in the stomach indicating gastric emptying time

e. Feeding administered via a tube into the stomach or intestines

Activity D SEQUENCING

Place the steps of administering a gavage enteral feeding in the proper sequence.

1. Measure the amount of gastric residual.

2. Flush the tube with water and administer the feeding.

3. Check tube for placement.

4. Flush the tube with water.

Activity E SHORT ANSWERS

Briefly answer the following.

1. What is the rationale for performing all invasive procedures outside of the child's hospital room?

   _____

   _____

   _____

2. There are eight rights of pediatric medication administration. How can the nurse ensure that the medication is being administered to the right child?

   _____

   _____

   _____

3. What are the key measures to reduce the risk of complications related to the use of central venous access devices and total parenteral nutrition?

   _____

   _____

   _____

4. What are the eight rights of medication administration for children?

   _____

   _____

   _____

5. Briefly explain the methods for verifying proper feeding tube placement.

   _____

   _____

   _____

SECTION II: APPLYING YOUR KNOWLEDGE

Activity F CASE STUDY

Jennifer Michels, a 7-month old, has a rectal temperature of 102.5°F. As the nurse caring for her, you are preparing to administer oral acetaminophen per the physicians order. Jennifer's weight is 15 lb (6.80 kg).

1. Discuss the steps you will take for administering a PRN dose of oral acetaminophen for Jennifer. Include rationale for your actions.

   _____

   _____

   _____

2. The physician ordered 70 mg PO every 4 hours for fever or discomfort. Calculate the correct dose for Jennifer's weight based on recommended dosing for acetaminophen of 10 to 15 mg/kg every 4 to 6 hours. Is the physician's order a safe and therapeutic dose?

   _____

   _____

   _____

3. Obtain the amount to be drawn up using a concentration of acetaminophen infant drops 80 mg/0.8 ml.

   _____

   _____

   _____

SECTION III: PRACTICING FOR NCLEX

Activity G   NCLEX-STYLE QUESTIONS

Answer the following questions.

1. The nurse is preparing to administer a medication via a syringe pump as ordered for a 2-month-old girl. Which is the **priority** nursing action?
   a. Gather the medication
   b. Verify the medication order
   c. Gather the necessary equipment and supplies
   d. Wash hands and put on gloves

2. A nurse is educating the parents how to administer daily oral medication to their 5-year-old boy. Which response indicates a need for further teaching?
   a. "I should never refer to the medicine as candy."
   b. "We should never bribe our child to take the medicine."
   c. "He needs to take his medicine or he will lose a privilege."
   d. "We checked that the medicine can be mixed with yogurt or applesauce."

3. A nurse is preparing to administer an ordered IM injection to an infant. The nurse knows that the **most** appropriate injection site for this child is which muscle?
   a. Deltoid
   b. Ventrogluteal
   c. Dorsogluteal
   d. Vastus lateralis

4. The nurse is educating the parents of a 5-month old how to administer an oral antibiotic. Which response indicates a need for further teaching?
   a. "We can mix the antibiotics into his formula or food."
   b. "We can follow his medicine with some applesauce or yogurt."
   c. "We can place the medicine along the inside of his cheek."
   d. "We should not forcibly squirt the medication in the back of his throat."

5. The nurse is assessing the aspirate of a gavage feeding tube to confirm placement. Which assessment finding indicates intestinal placement?
   a. Clear aspirate
   b. Yellow aspirate
   c. Tan aspirate
   d. Green aspirate

6. The nurse is preparing to administer medication to a 10-year old who weighs 70 lb (32 kg). The prescribed single dose is 3 to 4 mg/kg/day. Which dose range is appropriate for this child?
   a. 96 to 128 mg
   b. 105 to 140 mg
   c. 210 to 280 mg
   d. 420 to 560 mg

7. Age affects how the medication is distributed throughout the body. Which factors affect how medication distribution is altered in infants and young children? Select all that apply.
   a. Infants and young children have an increased percentage of water in their bodies.
   b. Infants and young children have an increased percentage of body fat.
   c. Infants and young children have an increased number of plasma proteins available for binding to drugs.
   d. The blood–brain barrier in infants and young children does not easily allow permeation by many medications.
   e. The livers of infants and young children are immature.

8. The nurse is caring for a 4-year old who requires a venipuncture. To prepare the child for the procedure, which explanation is **most** appropriate?
   a. "The doctor will look at your blood to see why you are sick."
   b. "The doctor wants to see if you have strep throat."
   c. "The doctor needs to take your blood to see why you are sick."
   d. "The doctor needs to culture your blood to see if you have strep."

9. The nurse is caring for a child with an intravenous device in his hand. Which sign would alert the nurse that infiltration is occurring?

   a. Warmth, redness

   b. Cool, puffy skin

   c. Induration

   d. Tender skin

10. The nurse is preparing to remove an IV device from the arm of a 6-year-old girl. Which approach is **best** for minimizing fear and anxiety?

    a. "This won't be painful; you'll just feel a tug and a pinch."

    b. "The first step is for you to help me remove this dressing from your IV."

    c. "Be sure to keep your hands clear of the scissors so I don't cut you."

    d. "Please be a big girl and don't cry when I remove this."

11. A nurse is caring for a child who requires intravenous maintenance fluid. The child weighs 30 kg. Which is the child's daily maintenance fluid requirement?

    a. 1,500 mL

    b. 1,600 mL

    c. 1,700 mL

    d. 1,800 mL

12. The child weighs 47 lb (21.31 kg). How many kilograms does the child weigh? Record your answer using one decimal place.

13. The child weighs 27 kg. Using the following formula, calculate how many milliliters of intravenous fluids should be administered to the child in a 24 hour period. Record your answer using a whole number

Formula:

   100 mL/kg of body weight for the first 10 kg
   50 mL/kg of body weight for the next 10 kg
   20 mL/kg of body weight for the remainder
     of body weight in kilograms

14. The adolescent weighs 113 lb (51.36 kg). The nurse closely monitors the child's urine output. How many milliliters of urine is the least amount that the adolescent should make during an 8-hour shift? Record your answer using a whole number.

15. The nurse is calculating the urinary output for the infant. The infant's diaper weighed 40 g prior to placing the diaper on the infant. After removal of the wet diaper, the diaper weighed 75 g. How many milliliters of urine can the nurse document as urinary output? Record your answer using a whole number.

Pain Management in Children

SECTION I: ASSESSING YOUR UNDERSTANDING

Activity A FILL IN THE BLANKS

1. Two of the most commonly used agents for conscious sedation are _____ and fentanyl.

2. EMLA should be applied _____ minutes before a superficial procedure such as a heel stick or venipuncture.

3. Conscious sedation is a medically controlled state of _____ consciousness.

4. _____ is considered the "gold standard" for all opioid agonists and is the drug to which all other opioids are compared.

5. Patient-controlled analgesia is usually reserved for use by children _____ years of age and older.

6. The point at which an individual feels the lowest intensity of the painful stimulus is referred to as the _____.

7. _____ is the pain rating scale that is used for children that uses photographs of facial expressions.

Activity B MATCHING

1. Match the term in Column A with the proper definition in Column B.

Column A	Column B
___ 1. Somatic pain	a. Process of nociceptor activation
___ 2. Transduction	b. Pain due to the activation of the A delta fibers and C fibers by noxious stimulant
___ 3. Nociceptive pain	
___ 4. Neuromodulators	c. Situated within the spinal canal, on or outside the dura mater
___ 5. Epidural	d. Pain that develops in the tissues
	e. Substances that modify the perception of pain

2. Match the medication in Column A with its action in Column B.

Column A

____ **1.** Morphine

____ **2.** Pentazocine

____ **3.** Ibuprofen

____ **4.** Acetamino-
phen

Column B

a. Inhibition of prostaglandin synthesis

b. Opioid agonist acting primarily at μ-receptor sites

c. Direct action of hypothalamic heat regulating center

d. Antagonist at μ-receptor sites agonist at κ-receptor sites

Activity C SEQUENCING

Place the physiologic events that lead to the sensation of pain in the proper sequence.

1. Modulation

2. Transmission

3. Transduction

4. Perception

Activity D SHORT ANSWERS

Briefly answer the following.

1. What is the difference between superficial somatic pain and deep somatic pain?

_____

_____

_____

2. What are the three general principles that guide pain management in children?

_____

_____

_____

3. Which of the factors that influence a child's perception of pain can be changed?

_____

_____

_____

4. What is conscious sedation? What are the advantages of conscious sedation? What agents may be used to achieve conscious sedation?

_____

_____

_____

5. Discuss the administration of epidural anesthesia.

_____

_____

_____

SECTION II: APPLYING YOUR KNOWLEDGE

Activity E CASE STUDY

Owen Nelson, 6 months old, is admitted to your unit post club foot repair. His parents are at the bedside and concerned about Owen's comfort. They state "We have heard that infants do not feel pain like adults do but we want to make sure Owen is not in pain. How do we do this?"

1. How would you address Owen's parents' concerns?

_____

_____

_____

2. During your assessment you find that Owen is lying in his crib with his legs elevated, his face is relaxed, he appears restless but moves easily, cries occasionally but is consoled by his mother's or father's touch and voice. Using the appropriate pain assessment tool for Owen's age and development, assess Owen's pain level based on the above information. What further assessment information may be helpful in determining if Owen is in pain?

_____

_____

_____

_____

3. Based on your above assessment, you intervene by providing pain medication to Owen per the physician's order to. What nonpharmacologic interventions can you discuss with the parents to help decrease Owen's discomfort?

_____

_____

_____

SECTION III: PRACTICING FOR NCLEX

Activity F **NCLEX-STYLE QUESTIONS**

Answer the following questions.

1. The nurse is providing postsurgical care for a 5-year old. The nurse knows to avoid which question when assessing the child's pain level?

   a. Would you say that the pain you are feeling is sharp or dull?

   b. Would you point to the cartoon face that best describes your pain?

   c. Would you point to the spot where your pain is?

   d. Would you please show me which photograph and number **best** describes your hurt?

2. The nurse is assisting with the administration of the child's initial dose of parenteral opioids. Which action should the nurse take **first**?

   a. Ensure naloxone is readily available

   b. Assess for any adverse reaction

   c. Assess the status of bowel sounds

   d. Premedicate with acetaminophen

3. The nurse is caring for a child who has received postoperative epidural analgesia. Which nursing assessment is **priority**?

   a. Urinary retention

   b. Pruritus

   c. Nausea and vomiting

   d. Respiratory depression

4. A nurse is applying EMLA as ordered. The nurse understands that EMLA is contraindicated in which situation?

   a. Infants less than 6 weeks of age

   b. Children with darker skin

   c. Infants less than 12 months of age receiving methemoglobin-inducing agents

   d. Children undergoing venous cannulation or intramuscular injections

5. A nurse is caring for a 4-year-old child who is exhibiting extreme anxiety and behavior upset prior to receiving stitches for a deep chin laceration. Which nursing intervention is **priority**?

   a. Ensuring that emergency equipment is readily available.

   b. Serving as an advocate for the family to ensure appropriate pharmacologic agents are chosen.

   c. Conducting an initial assessment of pain to serve as a baseline from which options for relief can be chosen.

   d. Ensuring the lighting is adequate for the procedure but not so bright to cause discomfort.

6. A nurse is interviewing the mother of a sleeping 10-year-old girl to assess the level of the child's postoperative pain. Which comment should trigger additional questions and necessitate further teaching?

   a. "She is asleep, so she must not be in pain."

   b. "She has never had surgery before."

   c. "She is very articulate and will tell you how she feels."

   d. "She has a very easygoing temperament."

7. The nurse is caring for a 9-year-old boy with episodes of chronic pain. The nurse is educating the parents how to help the child manage pain nonpharmacologically. Which statement indicates a need for further teaching?

   a. "We should perform the techniques along with him."

   b. "We should start the method after he feels pain."

   c. "We need to identify the ways in which he shows pain."

   d. "We should select a method that he likes the best."

8. A nurse is assessing the pain level of an infant. Which finding is not a typical physiologic indicator of pain?

    a. Decreased oxygen saturation

    b. Decreased heart rate

    c. Palmar sweating

    d. Plantar sweating

9. The nurse is preparing to assess the postsurgical pain level of a 6-year-old boy. The child has appeared unwilling or unable to accurately report his pain level. Which assessment tool is most appropriate for this child?

    a. FACES Pain Rating Scale

    b. FLACC Behavioral Scale

    c. Oucher Pain Rating Scale

    d. Visual Analog and Numerical scales

10. The nurse is preparing to assess the pain of a developmentally and cognitively delayed 8-year old. Which pain rating scales should the nurse choose?

    a. FACES Pain Rating Scale

    b. Word-Graphic Rating Scale

    c. Adolescent Pediatric Pain Tool

    d. Visual Analog and Numerical Scales

11. A pregnant teen voices concerns related to potential paralysis during a discussion about an epidural anesthetic to be administered. What information can be provided to the teen?

    a. "Paralysis is not a serious concern for the procedure."

    b. "The spinal cord will not be damaged by the insertion of the epidural catheter."

    c. "The spinal cord ends above the area where the epidural is inserted."

    d. "The risk of paralysis is limited because your physician is skilled in the administration of epidurals."

12. The nurse is assigned to care for a 14-year-old child who is hospitalized in traction for serious leg fractures after an automobile accident. The parents ask the nurse to avoid administering analgesics to their child to help prevent him from becoming addicted. Which response by the nurse is indicated?

    a. "We can talk with the physician to see about reducing the amount of medications given to reduce the potential for addiction."

    b. "If there is no history of drug abuse in the family there should be no increased risk for the development of addiction."

    c. "Administering medications to manage reports of pain is not going to cause addiction."

    d. "Your child is too young to experience drug addiction."

13. The nurse is caring for a 5-year-old child who underwent a painful surgical procedure earlier in the day. The nurse notes the child has not reported pain to any of the nursing staff. Which action by the nurse is indicated?

    a. Contact the physician to report the child's condition

    b. Administer prophylactic analgesics

    c. Observe for behavioral cues consistent with pain

    d. Encourage the child to report pain

14. The nurse is preparing to administer a dose of ketorolac to a 15-year-old adolescent. How should the nurse administer the medication to reduce the potential for gastrointestinal upset?

    a. Before meals

    b. With milk

    c. With meals

    d. With a citrus beverage

Nursing Care of the Child With an Infectious or Communicable Disorder

Learning Objectives

Upon completion of the chapter, you will be able to:

- Discuss anatomic and physiologic differences in children versus adults in relation to the infectious process.
- Identify nursing interventions related to common laboratory and diagnostic tests used in the diagnosis and management of infectious conditions.
- Identify appropriate nursing assessments and interventions related to medications and treatments for childhood infectious and communicable disorders.
- Distinguish various infectious illnesses occurring in childhood.
- Devise an individualized nursing care plan for the child with an infectious or communicable disorder.
- Develop child/family teaching plans for the child with an infectious or communicable disorder.

SECTION I: ASSESSING YOUR UNDERSTANDING

Activity A FILL IN THE BLANKS

1. The trigger of prostaglandins to increase the body's temperature set point is caused by _____.

2. Monocytes use _____ as a means to eliminate pathogens.

3. B cells use _____ to attack specific foreign substances.

4. Fever can increase the production of _____ and slow the growth of bacteria and viruses.

5. Acetaminophen and _____, administered at the appropriate dose and interval, are safe and effective for reducing fever in children.

Activity B MATCHING

1. Match the infection chain link in Column A with the proper word or phrase in Column B.

Column A

____ **1.** Infectious agent

____ **2.** Mode of transmission

____ **3.** Portal of entry

____ **4.** Portal of exit

____ **5.** Reservoir

____ **6.** Susceptible host

Column B

a. Child

b. Rickettsiae

c. Gastrointestinal tract

d. Animal

e. Fomite

f. Respiratory tract

2. Match the vector-borne illness in Column A with the means of infection in Column B.

Column A

____ **1.** Endemic typhus

____ **2.** Pediculosis pubis

____ **3.** Rickettsialpox

____ **4.** Roundworm

____ **5.** Scabies

Column B

a. Mouse mite bite

b. Rat flea feces

c. Sexual contact

d. Close, prolonged contact

e. Ingested fecal matter

Activity C SEQUENCING

Place the following stages of an infectious disease in the proper order.

1. Convalescence

2. Illness

3. Incubation

4. Prodromal

☐ → ☐ → ☐ → ☐

Activity D SHORT ANSWERS

Briefly answer the following.

1. Name five risk factors for sepsis that are related to pregnancy and labor.

_____

_____

_____

2. Describe the nursing management of mumps.

_____

_____

_____

3. Explain postexposure prophylaxis after an animal bite.

_____

_____

_____

4. Explain the role of fever in the child with an infection.

_____

_____

_____

5. Explain sepsis. What is septic shock?

_____

_____

_____

SECTION II: APPLYING YOUR KNOWLEDGE

Activity E CASE STUDY

Jennifer Mikelson, a 16-year-old female, is seen in your clinic. She presents with complaints of abnormal vaginal discharge and pain with urination. Jennifer is visibly upset and not very willing to answer questions at this time. She states "can't you just give me some medicine to take."

1. How would you proceed with your assessment?

_____

_____

_____

2. Jennifer is diagnosed with Chlamydia. What home care instructions and education should you provide?

_____

_____

_____

3. By the end of the assessment Jennifer is opening up. She states she recently began having sexual relations with her boyfriend. He does not like condoms so the majority of the sexual interactions have been unprotected. How would you respond?

_____

_____

_____

SECTION III: PRACTICING FOR NCLEX

Activity F **NCLEX-STYLE QUESTIONS**

Answer the following questions.

1. A 10-year-old girl with long hair is brought to the emergency room because she began acting irritable, reported a headache, and was very sleepy. Which question is **most** appropriate for the nurse to ask the parents?
   a. "Has she done this before?"
   b. "How long has she been acting like this?"
   c. "What were you doing prior to her beginning to feel sick?"
   d. "What medications is she currently taking?"

2. A 6-year-old boy is suspected of having late-stage Lyme disease. Which assessment should the nurse use to produce findings supporting this concern?
   a. Inspecting for erythema migraines
   b. Asking the child if his knees hurt
   c. Observing for facial palsy
   d. Examining for conjunctivitis

3. The nurse is preparing to administer acetaminophen to a 4-year-old girl to provide comfort to the child. Which precaution is specific to antipyretics?
   a. Check for medicine allergies
   b. Take entire course of medication
   c. Ensure proper dose and interval
   d. Warn of possible drowsiness

4. A 10-year-old boy has an unknown infection and will need to provide a urine specimen for culture and sensitivity. To assure that the sensitivity results are accurate, which step is most important?
   a. Ensure that the specimen is obtained from proper area
   b. Collect three specimens on three different days
   c. Use aseptic technique when getting the specimen
   d. Obtain specimen before antibiotics are given

5. The nurse at an outpatient facility is obtaining a blood specimen from a 9-year-old girl. Which technique would **most** likely be used?
   a. Puncturing a vein on the dorsal side of the hand
   b. Administering sucrose prior to beginning
   c. Accessing an indwelling venous access device
   d. Using an automatic lancet device on the heel

6. Which child needs to be seen immediately in the physician's office?
   a. 10-month old with a fever and petechiae who is grunting
   b. 2-month old with a slight fever and irritability after getting immunizations the previous day
   c. 4-month old with a cough, elevated temperature, and wetting eight diapers every 24 hours
   d. 8-month old who is restless, irritable, and afebrile

7. The nurse is administering a chicken pox vaccination to a 12-month-old girl. Which concern is unique to varicella?

   a. This disease can reactivate years later and cause shingles.

   b. Vitamin A is indicated for children younger than 2 years.

   c. Dehydration is caused by mouth lesions.

   d. Children with this disease need to avoid pregnant women.

8. The pediatric nurse knows that there are a number of anatomic and physiologic differences between children and adults. Which statement about the immune systems of infants and young children is true?

   a. Children have an immature immune response.

   b. Cellular immunity is not functional in children.

   c. Children have an increased inflammatory response.

   d. Passive immunity overlaps immunizations.

9. The nurse is taking a health history for an 8-year-old boy who is hospitalized. Which is a risk factor for sepsis in a hospitalized child?

   a. Maternal infection or fever

   b. Use of immunosuppression drugs

   c. Lack of juvenile immunizations

   d. Resuscitation or invasive procedures

10. The nurse is caring for a 5-year-old girl with scarlet fever. Which intervention will **most** likely be part of her care?

    a. Exercising both standard and droplet precautions

    b. Palpating for and noting enlarged lymph nodes

    c. Monitoring for changes in respiratory status

    d. Teaching proper administration of penicillin V

11. The nurse is caring for a 10-year-old child with a skin rash. The nurse should include which intervention to manage the associated pruritis?

    a. Encourage warm baths

    b. Apply hot compresses

    c. Press the pruritic area

    d. Rub powder on the pruritic area

12. The student nurse is discussing the plan of care for a child admitted to the hospital for treatment of an infection. Which action should be taken **first**?

    a. Obtain blood cultures

    b. Initiate antibiotic therapy

    c. Obtain urine specimen for analysis

    d. Initiate intravenous therapy

13. The nurse is reviewing the assessment data from a 4-year old admitted to the hospital for management of early onset sepsis. Which finding supports the diagnosis?

    a. The child is unhappy about having to stay in bed

    b. The child's tympanic temperature is 98.8°F (37.11°C)

    c. The child is hypotensive

    d. The child is irritable

14. The nurse is providing education to the parents of a 5-year old with a fever. Which statements indicate the need for further instruction? Select all that apply.

    a. "Fever has many therapeutic properties."

    b. "I can administer two baby aspirin tablets to my child every 4 to 6 hours for the fever."

    c. "Sponging my child with cold water can be a soothing way to manage the fever."

    d. "I should use a cooling fan in my child's room to keep the fever down."

    e. "Ibuprofen has been shown to be more beneficial than acetaminophen when managing a fever."

Nursing Care of the Child With an Alteration in Intracranial Regulation/ Neurologic Disorder

Learning Objectives

Upon completion of the chapter, you will be able to:

- Compare how the anatomy and physiology of the neurologic system in children differs from adults.
- Identify various factors associated with neurologic disease in infants and children.
- Discuss common laboratory and other diagnostic tests useful in the diagnosis of neurologic conditions.
- Discuss common medications and other treatments used for treatment and palliation of neurologic conditions.
- Recognize risk factors associated with various neurologic disorders.
- Distinguish among different neurologic illnesses based on the signs and symptoms associated with them.
- Discuss nursing interventions commonly used for neurologic illnesses.
- Devise an individualized nursing care plan for the child with a neurologic disorder.
- Develop child and family teaching plans for the child with a neurologic disorder.
- Describe the psychosocial impact of chronic neurologic disorders on children.

SECTION I: ASSESSING YOUR UNDERSTANDING

Activity A FILL IN THE BLANKS

1. The _____ sign is an indication of meningitis.

2. Lack of response to _____ stimuli can indicate a life-threatening condition.

3. Variation in head _____ percentiles over time may indicate abnormal brain or skull growth.

4. Changes in _____, muscle tone, or strength may indicate certain neurologic problems.

5. The _____ maneuver can be helpful in assessing cranial nerves III, IV, and VI in an infant, uncooperative child, or comatose child.

6. When assessing sensory function in an infant, limit the examination to _____ or pain.

7. _____ pressure is inversely related to level of consciousness.

8. During auscultation, a loud or localized _____ indicates the need for immediate further investigation.

Activity B LABELING

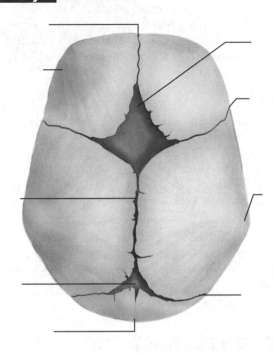

Label the skull structures in the infant.

a. Parietal bone

b. Occipital bone

c. Sagittal suture

d. Lambdoid suture

e. Frontal bone

f. Anterior fontanel

g. Coronal suture

h. Frontal suture

i. Posterior fontanel

Activity C MATCHING

Match the condition in Column A with the proper approach to management in Column B.

Column A

____ 1. Febrile seizures

____ 2. Reye syndrome

____ 3. Craniosynostosis

____ 4. Aseptic meningitis

____ 5. Positional plagiocephaly

Column B

a. Treat aggressively with intravenous antibiotics initially

b. Position the infant so that the flatten area is up

c. Surgical correction to allow brain growth

d. Rectal diazepam

e. Maintain cerebral perfusion, manage ICP, manage hydration, and safety measures

Activity D SEQUENCING

Place the following levels of consciousness in the proper order from lowest to highest using the boxes provided below:

1. Coma

2. Confusion

3. Full consciousness

4. Obtunded

5. Stupor

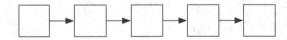

Activity E SHORT ANSWERS

Briefly answer the following.

1. Describe how to test for Kernig sign, what indicates a positive sign, and what disorder is indicated.

_____

_____

_____

2. Describe the opisthotonic position, what age a child would assume this position, and what neurologic disorder is implicated.

_____

_____

_____

3. What are the proper positions for a lumbar puncture for an infant and child?

_____

_____

_____

4. What is the purpose of a ventriculoperitoneal (VP) shunt, what causes it to malfunction, and what are the symptoms the malfunction produces?

_____

_____

_____

5. In regard to the Glasgow Coma Scale, what are the three major areas of assessment, and what does a low score indicate?

_____

_____

_____

SECTION II: APPLYING YOUR KNOWLEDGE

Activity F CASE STUDY

Consider this scenario and answer the questions.

Jessica Clark, 5 years old, is admitted to the neurologic unit at a pediatric hospital after having a seizure at school. Her mother reports that Jessica has a history of seizures and is taking phenobarbital to control them. The mother states, "Ever since Jessica started school this year, it has been more difficult to get her to take her medicine."

1. What diagnostic and laboratory tests can you anticipate?

_____

_____

_____

2. Minutes after leaving the room, the mother calls you back because Jessica is having another seizure. Identify nursing interventions related to the care of this child during and immediately following a seizure. List in order of priority.

_____

_____

_____

3. What teaching will the nurse do with this child's family? Include a discussion on ways to increase compliance with the seizure medication.

_____

_____

_____

_____

SECTION III: PRACTICING FOR NCLEX

Activity G NCLEX-STYLE QUESTIONS

Answer the following questions.

1. The nurse is providing education to the parents of a 3-year-old girl with hydrocephalus who has just had an external ventricular drainage system placed. Which question is **best** to begin the teaching session?
   a. "What questions or concerns do you have about this device?"
   b. "Do you understand why you clamp the drain before she sits up?"
   c. "What do you know about her autoregulation mechanism failing?"
   d. "Why do you always keep her head raised 30 degrees?"

2. During physical assessment of a 2-month-old infant, the nurse suspects the child may have a lesion on the brain stem. Which symptom was observed?
   a. Only one eye is dilated and reactive
   b. Sudden increase in head circumference
   c. Horizontal nystagmus
   d. Closed posterior fontanel

3. After a difficult birth, the nurse observes that a newborn has swelling on part of his head. Which sign suggests cephalohematoma?

   a. Swelling does not cross the suture lines.

   b. Swelling crosses the midline of the infant's scalp.

   c. Infant had a low birthweight when born at 37 weeks.

   d. Infant has facial abnormalities.

4. The nurse is caring for an 8-year-old girl who was in a car accident. Which symptom suggests the child has a cerebral contusion?

   a. Trouble focusing when reading

   b. Difficulty concentrating

   c. Vomiting

   d. Bleeding from the ear

5. The nurse caring for an infant with craniosynostosis, specifically positional plagiocephaly, should prioritize which activity?

   a. Moving the infant's head every 2 hours

   b. Measuring the intake and output every shift

   c. Massaging the scalp gently every 4 hours

   d. Giving the infant small feedings whenever he is fussy

6. The nurse is caring for a near-term pregnant woman who has not taken prenatal vitamins or folic acid supplements. Which congenital defect is **most** likely to occur based on the mother's prenatal history?

   a. Neonatal conjunctivitis

   b. Facial deformities

   c. A neural tube defect

   d. Incomplete myelinization

7. The nurse is caring for a 3-year-old boy who is experiencing seizure activity. Which diagnostic test will determine the seizure area in the brain?

   a. Cerebral angiography

   b. Lumbar puncture

   c. Video electroencephalogram

   d. Computed tomography

8. A pregnant client asks if there is any danger to the development of her fetus in the first few weeks of her pregnancy. How should the nurse respond?

   a. "As long as you were taking good care of your health before becoming pregnant, your fetus should be fine during the first few weeks of pregnancy."

   b. "Bones begin to harden in the first 5 to 6 weeks of pregnancy so vitamin D consumption is particularly important."

   c. "During the first 3 to 4 weeks of pregnancy brain and spinal cord development occur and are affected by nutrition, drugs, infection, or trauma."

   d. "The respiratory system matures during this time so good prenatal care during the first weeks of pregnancy is very important."

9. The nurse has developed a nursing plan for the care of a 6-year-old girl with congenital hydrocephalus whose shunt has become infected. The **most** important discharge teaching point for this family is:

   a. maintaining effective cerebral perfusion.

   b. ensuring the parents know how to properly give antibiotics.

   c. establishing seizure precautions for the child.

   d. encouraging development of motor skills.

10. The young child has been diagnosed with bacterial meningitis. Which nursing interventions are appropriate? Select all that apply.

   a. Initiate droplet isolation

   b. Identify close contacts of the child who will require postexposure prophylactic medication

   c. Administer antibiotics as ordered

   d. Monitor the child for signs and symptoms associated with decreased intracranial pressure

   e. Initiate seizure precautions

11. The meningococcal vaccine should be offered to high-risk populations. If never vaccinated, who has an increased risk of becoming infected with meningococcal meningitis? Select all that apply.

   a. 18-year-old student who is preparing for college in the fall and has signed up to live in a dormitory with two other suite mates

   b. 12-year-old child with asthma

   c. 5-year-old child who routinely travels in the summer with her parents on mission trips to Haiti

   d. 9-year-old child who was diagnosed with diabetes mellitus when he was 7 years old

   e. 8-year-old child who is in good health

12. An 11-year-old child was recently diagnosed with chickenpox. His parents gave him aspirin for a fever and the child is now hospitalized. Which nursing interventions are appropriate for this child? Select all that apply.

   a. Request order for an antiemetic

   b. Assess intake and output every shift

   c. Assess child's skin for the development of distinctive rash every 4 hours

   d. Request order for anticonvulsant

   e. Monitor the child's laboratory values related to pancreatic function

13. The young boy was involved in a motor vehicle accident and was admitted to the pediatric intensive care unit with changes in level of consciousness and a high-pitched cry. Which are late signs of increased intracranial pressure? Select all that apply.

   a. The child states that he feels a little "dizzy."

   b. The child's toes are pointed downward, his head and neck are arched backward, and his arms and legs are extended.

   c. The sclera of the eyes is visible above the iris.

   d. The child's heart rate is 56 beats per minute.

   e. The child's pupils are fixed and dilated.

Nursing Care of the Child With an Alteration in Sensory Perception/ Disorder of the Eyes or Ears

Learning Objectives

Upon completion of the chapter, you will be able to:

- Differentiate between the anatomic and physiologic differences of the eyes and ears in children as compared with adults.
- Identify various factors associated with disorders of the eyes and ears in infants and children.
- Discuss common laboratory and other diagnostic tests useful in the diagnosis of disorders of the eyes and ears.
- Discuss common medications and other treatments used for treatment and palliation of conditions affecting the eyes and ears.
- Recognize risk factors associated with various disorders of the eyes and ears.
- Distinguish between different disorders of the eyes and ears based on the signs and symptoms associated with them.
- Discuss nursing interventions commonly used in regard to disorders of the eyes and ears.
- Devise an individualized nursing care plan for the child with a sensory impairment or other disorder of the eyes or ears.
- Develop patient/family teaching plans for the child with a disorder of the eyes or ears.
- Describe the psychosocial impact of sensory impairments on children.

SECTION I: ASSESSING YOUR UNDERSTANDING

Activity A FILL IN THE BLANKS

1. According to *Healthy People 2020* recommendations, visual acuity testing should begin at _____ years of age.

2. Short length and _____ position of eustachian tubes leads to greater susceptibility of acute otitis media in children less than 2 years of age.

3. Systemic _____ are used to treat periorbital cellulitis.

4. Permanent visual _____ can be averted with early identification and treatment of amblyopia.

5. Vision or hearing impairment impedes _____ progress.

6. The spherical shape of the newborn's lens does not allow for _____ accommodation.

Activity B MATCHING

Match the condition in Column A with the description in Column B.

Column A

_____ 1. Contusion

_____ 2. Corneal abrasion

_____ 3. Eyelid injury

_____ 4. Foreign body

_____ 5. Scleral hemorrhage

Column B

a. Vision is usually unaffected

b. Discoloration and edema of eyelid

c. Erythema that resolves gradually without intervention

d. May require ointment to sooth injury or antibiotic ointment

e. Requires careful removal only by a health care professional

Activity C SEQUENCING

Place the following vision and hearing milestones in the proper order:

1. Binocular vision

2. Eye color

3. Functional hearing

4. Visual acuity of 20/20

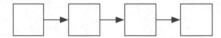

Activity D SHORT ANSWERS

Briefly answer the following.

1. List at least five signs and symptoms of children with hearing loss at (a) infant, (b) young child, and (c) older child stages.

_____

_____

_____

2. Describe how to interact with a visually impaired child, especially the use of one's voice and ways to act as the child's eyes.

_____

_____

_____

3. List at least three signs and symptoms that would lead the nurse to suspect a child is visually impaired at (a) infant, (b) young child, or (c) older child stages.

_____

_____

_____

4. List at least five factors that increase the risk of a child developing acute otitis media.

_____

_____

_____

5. Discuss the characteristics that increase the risk of a child having difficulty with the development of speech or language, or having learning difficulties.

_____

_____

_____

SECTION II: APPLYING YOUR KNOWLEDGE

Activity E CASE STUDY

Brandon, age 6 months, has been brought to the pediatrician's office for a well-baby checkup. Brandon's mother tells the nurse that she is concerned about Brandon's left eye. She tells the nurse that Brandon's eyes do not seem to be looking in the same place. Upon assessment the nurse finds asymmetry of the corneal light reflex. Brandon is referred for further assessment to an ophthalmologist.

1. Brandon is diagnosed with amblyopia. What information would the nurse know to include in a teaching plan for Brandon's family at this first visit?

   _____

   _____

   _____

2. Why is it important to treat amblyopia as soon as it is found and what treatments might be used in the treatment of Brandon's condition?

   _____

   _____

   _____

SECTION III: PRACTICING FOR NCLEX

Activity F NCLEX-STYLE QUESTIONS

Answer the following questions.

1. The nurse is caring for a 2-year-old girl with persistent otitis media with effusion. Which intervention is most important to the developmental health of the child?
   a. Informing the parents to avoid nonprescription drugs
   b. Telling parents not to smoke in the house
   c. Educating the parents about proper antibiotic use
   d. Reassessing for language acquisition

2. The nurse is caring for an 8-year-old boy with otitis media with effusion. Which situation may have caused this disorder?
   a. He frequently goes swimming
   b. He has good attendance at school
   c. He is experiencing recurrent nasal congestion
   d. He had recent bacterial conjunctivitis

3. A 10-year-old boy has just been treated for otitis externa and now the nurse is teaching the boy and his parents about prevention. Which recommendation should the nurse include?
   a. Using alcohol and vinegar for soreness
   b. Using cotton swabs to keep the inner ear dry
   c. Using a hair dryer on cool to dry the ears
   d. Washing the hair only when necessary

4. The nurse works in a pediatrician office. Which children, who have been diagnosed with acute otitis media, does the nurse expect the physician to treat with antibiotics? Select all that apply.
   a. 12-year-old child who reports he has some mild ear pain with a temperature of 101.4°F (38.6°C)
   b. 8-year-old child who is crying due to ear pain and has a temperature of 103°F (39.4°C)
   c. 2-month-old child who is having difficulty sleeping and has a fever of 102.6°F (39.2°C)
   d. 5-month-old child who is fussy and pulling at her ears
   e. 22-month-old child who is irritable with the presence of purulent drainage from her right ear

5. The nurse is explaining information to the parents of a 3-year-old boy who may have strabismus. The nurse should explain that which examinations will be performed **first** to find out if he has strabismus?
   a. Refractive examination
   b. Visual acuity test
   c. Corneal light reflex test
   d. Ophthalmologic examination

6. The nurse is caring for a 10-year-old girl with acute periorbital cellulitis. Which nursing intervention (therapy) is primary for this disorder?

   a. Applying heated aqua pad to site

   b. Administering antibiotics IV as ordered

   c. Administering morphine sulfate as ordered

   d. Monitoring for increased intracranial pressure

7. The nurse is caring for a 24-month-old boy with regressed retinopathy of prematurity. Which intervention is **priority** for this child?

   a. Assessing the child for asymmetric corneal light reflex

   b. Observing for rubbing, shutting the eyes, or squinting

   c. Referring the child to the local district of early intervention

   d. Teaching the parents to check how the child's glasses fit

8. The nurse is caring for a 7-year-old girl in an outpatient clinic diagnosed with amblyopia that is unrelated to any other disorder. Which intervention should be most helpful at this time?

   a. Discouraging the child from roughhousing

   b. Explaining postsurgical treatment of the eye

   c. Ensuring follow-up visits with the ophthalmologist

   d. Educating parents on how to use prescribed atropine drops

9. The nurse is educating the parents of a 4-year-old boy with strabismus. Teaching for the parents would include the:

   a. need for ultraviolet-protective glasses postoperatively.

   b. importance of completing the full course of oral antibiotics.

   c. possibility that multiple operations may be necessary.

   d. importance of patching as prescribed.

10. The nurse is educating the parents of a 5-year-old girl with infectious conjunctivitis about the disorder. Which information is most important to provide to prevent the spread of the disorder?

    a. Properly applying the prescribed antibiotic

    b. Staying home from school

    c. Washing hands frequently

    d. Keeping hands away from eyes

11. The nurse is teaching parents of a 9-year-old girl about the importance of wearing the prescribed glasses. Which subject is least important to promoting compliance?

    a. Getting scheduled eye examinations on time

    b. Checking condition and fit of glasses monthly

    c. Watching for signs that prescription needs changing

    d. Encouraging the use of eye protection for sports

12. The pediatric office nurse notes that several of the young children that are waiting to see the physician may have conjunctivitis. Which findings are consistent with bacterial conjunctivitis? Select all that apply.

    a. Only the right eye is involved

    b. The drainage is yellow and thick

    c. The drainage is white

    d. There is clear, watery drainage from both eyes

    e. The child suffers from seasonal allergies

13. A child has been diagnosed with bacterial conjunctivitis. Which statements by the child's parent indicate the need for further education? Select all that apply.

    a. "I'll continue to use eye drops to help with the redness."

    b. "All of us at home need to wash our hands really well."

    c. "We should not use a towel that he has used."

    d. "He can go back to school in 4 hours after that thick yellow drainage is gone."

    e. "This is really contagious."

14. The young child has been diagnosed with a corneal abrasion. Which findings are most consistent with this diagnosis? Select all that apply.

    a. The child's pupils are equal, round, reactive to light and accommodation.

    b. The child denies any eye pain.

    c. The child reports that it hurts to look toward bright light.

    d. The child has a large purple bruise over the eye and edema on the eyelid.

    e. The child's eye is draining clear fluid and the child says it feels like it is full of tears.

Nursing Care of the Child With an Alteration in Gas Exchange/Respiratory Disorder

Learning Objectives

Upon completion of the chapter, you will be able to:

- Distinguish differences between the anatomy and physiology of the respiratory system in children versus adults.
- Identify various factors associated with respiratory illness in infants and children.
- Discuss common laboratory and other diagnostic tests useful in the diagnosis of respiratory conditions.
- Describe nursing care related to common medications and other treatments used for management and palliation of respiratory conditions.
- Recognize risk factors associated with various respiratory disorders.
- Distinguish different respiratory disorders based on their signs and symptoms.
- Discuss nursing interventions commonly used for respiratory illnesses.
- Devise an individualized nursing care plan for the child with a respiratory disorder.

- Develop child/family teaching plans for the child with a respiratory disorder.
- Describe the psychosocial impact of chronic respiratory disorders on children.

SECTION I: ASSESSING YOUR UNDERSTANDING

Activity A FILL IN THE BLANKS

1. A _____ is a surgical construction of a respiratory opening in the trachea.

2. Allergic rhinitis is associated with _____ dermatitis and asthma.

3. Cough and _____ are symptoms of influenza for both children and adults.

4. Pulse oximetry is an _____ measurement of oxygen saturation in arterial blood.

5. Auscultation of the lungs might reveal _____ or rales in the younger child with pneumonia.

6. Tuberculin skin testing is also known as a _____ test.

7. Pseudoephedrine is an example of a _____ used for the treatment of runny or stuffy nose associated with the common cold.

Activity B   LABELING

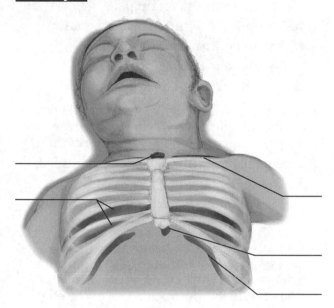

Label the image using the following terms:

a. Intercostal

b. Substernal

c. Supraclavicular

d. Subcostal

e. Suprasternal

Activity C   MATCHING

Match the piece of equipment in Column A with the appropriate description in Column B.

Column A

_____ **1.** Nasal cannula

_____ **2.** Non-rebreather mask

_____ **3.** Partial rebreather mask

_____ **4.** Simple face mask

_____ **5.** Venturi mask

Column B

a. Minimum flow rate of 6 L/min

b. Oxygen reservoir bag

c. Mixes room air and oxygen

d. Must have patent nasal passages

e. One-way valve

Activity D   SEQUENCING

Place the following steps for using a bulb syringe in the proper order:

1. Clean the bulb syringe

2. Compress the bulb

3. Empty the bulb

4. Instill saline nose drops

5. Place the bulb in the nose

6. Release pressure on bulb

7. Remove the bulb from nose

8. Tilt the infant's head back

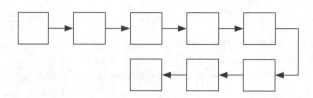

Activity E   SHORT ANSWERS

Briefly answer the following.

1. Discuss common signs and symptoms that are seen with sinusitis.

_____

_____

_____

2. Discuss common laboratory and diagnostic tests that the nurse anticipates to be ordered for a child suspected of having cystic fibrosis and identify findings that indicate cystic fibrosis.

_____

_____

_____

3. Compare the similarities and differences of croup and epiglottitis.

_____

_____

_____

4. Discuss the therapeutic management of the common cold.

_____

_____

_____

5. What is the most common cause of bronchiolitis and discuss the peak incidence of the disorder.

_____

_____

_____

SECTION II: APPLYING YOUR KNOWLEDGE

Activity F CASE STUDY

Consider this scenario and answer the questions.

James Jackson, an 8-year-old boy, is admitted to the pediatric hospital because of dyspnea, coughing, and wheezing. James states "my chest feels really tight." Physical findings include pallor, tachypnea, tachycardia, and bilateral wheezing on auscultation. This is the first time James has experienced these symptoms.

1. What health history information is important for the nurse to collect?

_____

_____

_____

2. List four nursing diagnoses that would pertain to James. Prioritize and provide rationale.

James has been diagnosed with asthma and is prescribed a bronchodilator and a metered dose inhaler while in the health care facility and for home. His breathing becomes easier and he states the tightness has gone away.

_____

_____

_____

3. Since this is James' first episode of asthma, what will be important discharge teaching for him and his family?

_____

_____

_____

SECTION III: PRACTICING FOR NCLEX

Activity G NCLEX-STYLE QUESTIONS

Answer the following questions.

1. The nurse is assessing several children. Which child is **most** at risk for dysphagia?

a. 7-month-old with erythematous rash

b. 8-year-old with fever and fatigue

c. 5-year-old with epiglottitis

d. 2-month-old with toxic appearance

2. The nurse is caring for a 14-month-old boy with cystic fibrosis. Which sign of ineffective family coping requires urgent intervention?

a. Compliance with therapy is diminished.

b. The family becomes overvigilant.

c. The child feels fearful and isolated.

d. Siblings are jealous and worried.

3. The nurse is taking a health history for a 3-year-old girl suspected of having pneumonia who presents with a fever, chest pain, and cough. Which information places the child at risk for pneumonia?

a. The child is a triplet.

b. The child was a postmaturity date infant.

c. The child has diabetes.

d. The child attends day care.

4. The nurse is auscultating the lungs of a lethargic, irritable 6-year-old boy and hears wheezing. The nurse will **most** likely include which teaching point if the child is suspected of having asthma?

a. "I'm going to have the respiratory therapist get some of the mucus from your lungs."

b. "I'm going to have this hospital worker take a picture of your lungs."

c. "We're going to go take a look at your lungs to see if there are any sores on them."

d. "I'm going to hold your hand while the phlebotomist gets blood from your arm."

5. The nurse is caring for a 3-year-old girl who is cyanotic and breathing rapidly. Which intervention is **best** to relieve these symptoms?

   a. Suction

   b. Oxygen administration

   c. Saline lavage

   d. Saline gargles

6. The nurse knows that respiratory disorders in children are sometimes attributed to anatomical and physiological differences from adults. Which statement is accurate?

   a. Adults have twice as many alveoli as newborns.

   b. The tongue is proportionately smaller in infants than in adults.

   c. Infants consume twice as much oxygen as adults.

   d. Hypoxemia occurs later in children than adults.

7. The nurse is developing a teaching plan for the parents of a 10-year-old boy with cystic fibrosis. The plan should include teaching about the use of a:

   a. flutter valve device.

   b. metered dose inhaler.

   c. nebulizer.

   d. peak flow meter.

8. The nurse is caring for a 10-year-old girl with allergic rhinitis. Which intervention helps prevent secondary bacterial infection?

   a. Using normal saline nasal washes

   b. Teaching parents how to avoid allergens

   c. Discussing anti-inflammatory nasal sprays

   d. Educating parents about oral antihistamines

9. The nurse is discussing the differences between children's and adult's respiratory systems. Which statements by the nurse are accurate? Select all that apply.

   a. "Children are less likely to develop problems associated with swelling of the airways."

   b. "Children's tongues are proportionally smaller."

   c. "The only time that newborns can breathe through their mouths is when they cry."

   d. "A newborn's respiratory tract is drier because the newborn doesn't make very much mucus."

   e. "Children under the age of 6 years are more prone to developing sinus infections."

10. The child has been admitted to the hospital with a possible diagnosis of pneumonia. Which findings are consistent with this diagnosis? Select all that apply.

    a. The child's temperature is 98.4°F (36.9°C).

    b. The child's chest x-ray indicates the presence of perihilar infiltrates.

    c. The child's white blood cell count is elevated.

    d. The child's respiratory rate is rapid.

    e. The child is producing yellow purulent sputum.

11. The young child is wearing a nasal cannula. The oxygen is set at 3 L/min. Calculate the percentage of oxygen the child is receiving? Record your answer using a whole number.

12. The young child has been diagnosed with group A streptococcal pharyngitis. The physician orders amoxicillin 45 mg/kg in three equally divided doses. The child weighs 23 lb (10.45 kg). Calculate how many milligrams the child will receive with each dose of amoxicillin. Record your answer using a whole number.

13. The child has been diagnosed with asthma and the child's physician is using a stepwise approach. Rank the following in the order the nurse should administer these medications as the child's condition worsens.

    a. Albuterol as needed.

    b. Low-dose inhaled corticosteroid

    c. Medium-dose inhaled corticosteroid

    d. Medium-dose inhaled corticosteroid and salmeterol

Nursing Care of the Child With an Alteration in Perfusion/ Cardiovascular Disorder

SECTION I: ASSESSING YOUR UNDERSTANDING

Activity A FILL IN THE BLANKS

1. Cardiac _____ is the radiographic study of the heart and coronary vessels after injection of contrast medium.

2. Cardiac catheterization may be categorized as diagnostic, interventional, or _____.

3. Coarctation of the aorta is defined as _____ of the aorta.

4. Examples of defects with increased _____ blood flow are patent ductus arteriosus (PDA), atrial septal defect (ASD), and ventricular septal defect (VSD).

5. Most cases of heart failure in children with congenital heart defects occur by the age of _____.

6. Cardiac disorders that are not congenital are considered _____ disorders.

7. _____ is a delayed disorder resulting from group A streptococcal pharyngeal infection.

Activity B MATCHING

Match the medication in Column A with its use in Column B.

Column A

____ **1.** Alprostadil

____ **2.** Furosemide

____ **3.** Heparin

____ **4.** Ace inhibitors

____ **5.** Niacin

Column B

a. Management of edema associated with heart failure

b. Temporary maintenance of ductus arteriosus patency in infants with ductal-dependent congenital heart defects

c. Management of hypertension

d. Prophylaxis and treatment of thromboembolic disorders especially after cardiac surgery

e. Medication to lower blood cholesterol levels

Activity C SEQUENCING

Place the following changes that occur in the cardiopulmonary system immediately following birth in proper order:

1. Drop in pulmonary artery pressure

2. Reduction of pulmonary vascular resistance to blood flow

3. Decreased pressure in the right atrium

4. Lungs inflate

5. Closure of the ductus arteriosus

6. Closure of the foramen ovale

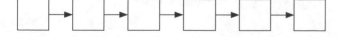

Activity D SHORT ANSWERS

Briefly answer the following.

1. Describe the action and indications for digoxin (Lanoxin). What are the key considerations when administering digoxin?

_____

_____

_____

2. Heart murmurs must be evaluated on the basis of what characteristics?

_____

_____

_____

3. What are the three types of atrial septal defects?

_____

_____

_____

4. Discuss the incidence of ventricular septal defect (VSD) and common assessment findings.

_____

_____

_____

5. What are the risk factors for the development of infective endocarditis?

_____

_____

_____

SECTION II: APPLYING YOUR KNOWLEDGE

Activity E CASE STUDY

The nurse is caring for a 2-year-old girl who was admitted to the hospital to undergo a cardiac catheterization for a suspected cardiac defect.

1. Discuss preprocedure nursing care for the child and family.

   _____

   _____

   _____

2. Discuss postprocedure nursing care following a cardiac catheterization.

   _____

   _____

   _____

SECTION III: PRACTICING FOR NCLEX

Activity F NCLEX-STYLE QUESTIONS

Answer the following questions.

1. The nurse is caring for an 8-month-old infant with a suspected congenital heart defect. The nurse examines the child and documents which expected finding?
   a. Steady weight gain since birth
   b. Softening of the nail beds
   c. Appropriate mastery of developmental milestones
   d. Intact rooting reflex

2. The nurse is assessing the heart rate of a healthy 6-month old. In which range should the nurse expect the infant's heart rate?
   a. 60 to 68 bpm
   b. 70 to 80 bpm
   c. 80 to 105 bpm
   d. 90 to 160 bpm

3. The nurse is conducting a physical examination of a 7-year-old girl prior to a cardiac catheterization. The nurse knows to pay particular attention to assessing the child's pedal pulses. How can the nurse best facilitate their assessment after the procedure?
   a. Mark the location of the child's peripheral pulses with an indelible marker.
   b. Mark the child's pedal pulses with an indelible marker, then document.
   c. Document the location and quality of the child's pedal pulses.
   d. Assess the location and quality of the child's peripheral pulses.

4. The nurse is assessing the past medical history of an infant with a suspected cardiovascular disorder. Which response by the mother warrants further investigation?
   a. "His Apgar score was an 8."
   b. "I was really nauseous throughout my whole pregnancy."
   c. "I am on a low dose of steroids."
   d. "I had the flu during my last trimester."

5. A nurse is assessing the skin of a 12-year old with suspected right ventricular heart failure. Where should the nurse expect to note edema in this child?
   a. Lower extremities
   b. Face
   c. Presacral region
   d. Hands

6. A nurse is palpating the pulse of a child with suspected aortic regurgitation. Which assessment finding should the nurse expect to note?
   a. Appropriate mastery of developmental milestones
   b. Bounding pulse
   c. Preference to resting on the right side
   d. Pitting periorbital edema

7. The nurse is conducting a physical examination of an infant with a suspected cardiovascular disorder. Which assessment finding is suggestive of sudden ventricular distention?

   a. Decreased blood pressure

   b. Heart murmur

   c. Cool, clammy, pale extremities

   d. Accentuated third heart sound

8. The nurse performs a cardiac assessment and notes a loud heart murmur with a precordial thrill. This murmur would be classified as a:

   a. Grade I.

   b. Grade II.

   c. Grade III.

   d. Grade IV.

9. The nurse is assessing the blood pressure of an adolescent. In which range should the nurse expect the blood pressure measurement for a healthy 13-year-old boy?

   a. 80 to 90/40 to 64 mm Hg

   b. 80 to 100/64 to 80 mm Hg

   c. 94 to 112/56 to 60 mm Hg

   d. 100 to 120/70 to 80 mm Hg

10. The nurse is auscultating heart sounds of a child with a mitral valve prolapse. The nurse should expect which assessment finding?

    a. Mild to late ejection click at the apex

    b. Abnormal splitting of S2 sounds

    c. Clicks on the upper left sternal border

    d. Intensifying of S2 sounds

11. The young child had a chest tube placed during cardiac surgery. Which findings may indicate the development of cardiac tamponade? Select all that apply.

    a. The chest tube drainage had been averaging 15 to 25 mL out per hour and now there is no drainage from the chest tube.

    b. The child's heart rate has increased from 88 bpm to 126 bpm.

    c. The child's right atrial filling pressure has decreased.

    d. The child is resting quietly.

    e. The child's apical heart rate is strong and easily auscultated.

12. The pediatric nurse has digoxin ordered for each of five children. The nurse should withhold digoxin for which children? Select all that apply.

    a. 4-month-old child with an apical heart rate of 102 bpm

    b. 12-year-old child whose digoxin level was 0.9 ng/ mL on a blood draw this morning

    c. 16-year-old child with a heart rate of 54 bpm

    d. 2-year-old child whose digoxin level was 2.4 ng/mL from a blood draw this morning

    e. 5-year-old child who developed vomiting and diarrhea, and is difficult to arouse

13. Which findings are major criteria used to help the physician diagnose acute rheumatic fever in a child? Select all that apply.

    a. Elevated erythrocyte sedimentation rate

    b. Temperature of 101.2°F (38.4°C)

    c. Painless nodules located on the wrists

    d. Pericarditis with the presence of a new heart murmur

    e. Heart block with a prolonged PR interval

14. The child has returned to the nurse's unit following a cardiac catheterization. The insertion site is located at the right groin. Peripheral pulses were easily palpated in bilateral lower extremities prior to the procedure. Which finding should be reported to the child's physician?

    a. The right groin is soft without edema.

    b. The child's right foot is cool with a pulse assessed only with the use of a Doppler.

    c. The child has a temperature of 102.4°F (39.1°C).

    d. The child is reporting nausea.

    e. The child has a runny nose.

15. The infant has been hospitalized and develops hypercyanosis. The physician has ordered the nurse to administer 0.1 mg of morphine sulfate per every kilogram of the infant's body weight. The infant weighs 15.2 lb (6.81 kg). Calculate the infant's morphine sulfate dose. Record your answer using one decimal place.

42

Nursing Care of the Child With an Alteration in Bowel Elimination/ Gastrointestinal Disorder

Learning Objectives

Upon completion of the chapter, you will be able to:

■ Compare the differences in the anatomy and physiology of the gastrointestinal system between children and adults.

■ Discuss common medical treatments for infants and children with alterations in bowel elimination (gastrointestinal disorders).

■ Discuss common laboratory and diagnostic tests used to identify disorders of the gastrointestinal tract.

■ Discuss medication therapy used in infants and children with alterations in bowel elimination (gastrointestinal disorders).

■ Recognize risk factors associated with various gastrointestinal illnesses.

■ Differentiate between acute and chronic gastrointestinal disorders.

■ Distinguish common gastrointestinal illnesses of childhood.

■ Discuss nursing interventions commonly used for gastrointestinal illnesses.

■ Devise an individualized nursing care plan for infants/children with an alteration in bowel elimination/gastrointestinal disorder.

■ Develop teaching plans for family/patient education for children with gastrointestinal illnesses.

■ Describe the psychosocial impact that chronic gastrointestinal illnesses have on children.

SECTION I: ASSESSING YOUR UNDERSTANDING

Activity A FILL IN THE BLANKS

1. Vomiting is a reflex with three different phases. The first phase is the prodromal period, the second phase is _____, and the third phase is vomiting.

2. Biliary _____ is an absence of some or all of the major biliary ducts, resulting in obstruction of bile flow.

3. Chronic diarrhea is diarrhea that lasts for more than _____ weeks.

4. Oral candidiasis is a _____ infection of the oral mucosa.

5. Cholelithiasis is the presence of _____ in the gallbladder.

6. _____ supplementation while a child is taking antibiotics for other disorders may reduce the incidence of antibiotic-related diarrhea.

7. The proximal segment of the bowel telescoping into a more distal segment of the bowel is known as _____.

Activity B LABELING

Identify which is the colostomy and which is the ileostomy.

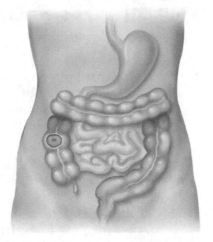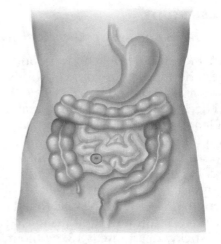

Activity C MATCHING

Match the procedure or condition in Column A with the proper definition in Column B.

Column A

_____ **1.** Bowel prep

_____ **2.** Cleansing enema

_____ **3.** Icteric

_____ **4.** Total parenteral nutrition (TPN)

_____ **5.** Ostomy

Column B

a. Long-term NPO status, swallowing or absorption difficulties

b. Colonoscopy or bowel surgery

c. Severe constipation or impaction

d. Jaundiced or yellow in color

e. Imperforate anus, gastroschisis, Hirschsprung disease

Activity D SEQUENCING

Place the steps of abdominal assessment in the proper sequence.

1. Palpation

2. Inspection

3. Percussion

4. Auscultation

Activity E SHORT ANSWERS

Briefly answer the following.

1. What does the acronym S.T.O.M.A. stand for?

_____

_____

_____

2. Infants and children repeatedly put objects to their mouth for exploration. Why is this considered a risk factor for gastrointestinal illnesses?

_____

_____

_____

3. How is acute hepatitis typically treated?

_____

_____

_____

4. What complications are of most concern during infancy for the child with a cleft palate?

_____

_____

_____

5. Discuss the signs and symptoms that would indicate that an infant had pyloric stenosis.

_____

_____

_____

SECTION II: APPLYING YOUR KNOWLEDGE

Activity F CASE STUDY

Consider this scenario and answer the questions.

Nico Taylor, a 1-month-old boy who was born at 33 weeks' gestation is seen in your clinic. His birth weight was 4 lb 12 oz and length was 18 in. At his 2-week checkup he weighed 5 lb 4 oz and was 18.5 in in length. His mother reports that he has always spit up quite a bit, but eats well. A few days ago she noted increased irritability with a hoarse cry and arching of his back with feedings. On physical examination, he weighs 4 lb 14 oz with a length of 19 in. His head is round with a sunken anterior fontanel, and his mucous membranes are sticky. Heart rate is 152 without a murmur, and breath sounds are clear with a respiratory rate of 42. His abdomen is soft and nondistended with positive bowel sounds in all four quadrants. Nico's skin turgor is poor.

1. Which part of your physical assessment findings is concerning to you?

   _____
   _____
   _____

2. What interventions are anticipated for Nico?

   _____
   _____
   _____

3. How would you evaluate Nico's progress?

   _____
   _____
   _____

4. Nico is diagnosed with gastroesophageal reflux. What education will you provide for the family regarding Nico's care?

   _____
   _____
   _____

SECTION III: PRACTICING FOR NCLEX

Activity G NCLEX-STYLE QUESTIONS

Answer the following questions.

1. A 4-month-old has had a fever, vomiting, and loose watery stools every few hours for 2 days. The mother calls the physician's office and asks the nurse what she should do. Which response by the nurse is **most** appropriate?

   a. "Do not give the child anything to drink for 4 hours. If the fever goes down and the loose stools stop, you can resume breastfeeding."

   b. "Continue breastfeeding as you have been doing. The fluid from the breast milk is important to maintain fluid balance."

   c. "Give a clear pediatric electrolyte replacement for the next few hours, then call back to report on how your child is doing."

   d. "Bring the child to the office today so we can evaluate her fluid balance and determine the best treatment."

2. The nurse is caring for a 13-year-old girl with suspected autoimmune hepatitis. The girl inquires about the testing required to evaluate the condition. How should the nurse respond?

   a. "You will most likely have a blood test to check for certain antibodies."

   b. "You will most likely have an ultrasound evaluation."

   c. "You will most likely have viral studies."

   d. "You will most likely be tested for ammonia levels."

3. The nurse is obtaining the history of an infant with a suspected intestinal obstruction. Which response regarding newborn stool patterns would indicate a need for further evaluation for Hirschsprung disease?

   a. Passed a meconium stool in the first 24 to 48 hours of life

   b. Has had diarrhea for 3 days

   c. Constipated and passing gas for 2 days

   d. Passed a meconium plug

4. A nurse is caring for a 6-year-old girl recently diagnosed with celiac disease and is discussing dietary restrictions with the girl's mother. Which response indicates a need for further teaching?

   a. "My daughter is eating more vegetables."

   b. "There is gluten hidden in unexpected foods."

   c. "There are many types of flour besides wheat."

   d. "My daughter can eat any kind of fruit."

5. The nurse is providing instructions to the parents of a 10-year-old boy who has undergone a barium swallow/upper and lower GI for suspected inflammatory bowel disease. Which of the following instructions is **most** important?

   a. "Please be aware of any signs of infection."

   b. "It is very important to drink lots of water and fluids after the test is finished."

   c. "Your child could have diarrhea for several days afterward."

   d. "Your child might have lighter stools for the next few days."

6. The nurse is assessing a 10-day-old infant for dehydration. Which finding indicates severe dehydration?

   a. Pale and slightly dry mucosa

   b. Blood pressure of 80/42 mm Hg

   c. Tenting of skin

   d. Soft and flat fontanels

7. A nurse is caring for a 6-year-old boy with a history of encopresis. What is the **best** way to approach the parents to assess for proper laxative use?

   a. "Tell me about his daily stool patterns."

   b. "Are you giving him the laxatives properly?"

   c. "Are the laxatives working?"

   d. "Describe his bowel movements for the past week."

8. Which client **most** likely has ulcerative colitis rather than Crohn disease?

   a. 16-year-old female with continuous distribution of disease in the colon, distal to proximal

   b. 14-year-old female with full-thickness chronic inflammation of the intestinal mucosa

   c. 18-year-old male with abdominal pain

   d. 12-year-old with oral temperature of 101.6°F (38.7°C)

9. The nurse is conducting a physical examination of an infant with suspected pyloric stenosis. Which finding indicates pyloric stenosis?

   a. Sausage-shaped mass in the upper mid abdomen

   b. Perianal fissures and skin tags

   c. Abdominal pain and irritability

   d. Hard, movable "olive-like mass" in the upper right quadrant

10. The young child has been diagnosed with hepatitis B. Which of the following statements by the child's mother indicates that further education is required?

    a. "We went swimming in a local lake 2 months ago and I just knew she drank some of the lake water."

    b. "Could I have this virus in my body, too?"

    c. "The virus is the reason her skin looks a little yellowish."

    d. "The only way you can get this virus is from intravenous drug use."

    e. "Her fever and rash are probably related to this virus."

11. The adolescent has been diagnosed with gastroesophageal reflux disease (GERD). Which statements by the teen indicate that adequate learning has occurred? Select all that apply.

    a. "This famotidine may make me tired."

    b. "The omeprazole could give me a headache."

    c. "It sounds like the physician is reluctant to give me a prokinetic because of the side effects."

    d. "I will probably need a laxative because of the omeprazole."

    e. "I should try to lie down right after I eat."

12. A 3-year-old child has been brought to the clinic for assessment because of frequent episodes of constipation. After ruling out an organic cause, the child's plan of care should **prioritize:**

    a. teaching the child's caregivers the need to toilet the child hourly during the day.

    b. administering over the counter stool softeners on a temporary basis.

    c. teaching the child habits that promote normal bowel function.

    d. teaching the child's caregivers how to safely administer an enema.

13. The emergency department nurse is assessing a child who has presented with a 2-day history of nausea and vomiting with pain that is isolated to the right upper quadrant of the abdomen. Which action is **most** appropriate?

    a. Prepare the child for admission to the hospital

    b. Assess the child's usual urinary voiding pattern

    c. Encourage fluid intake

    d. Administer antacids as ordered

14. The infant is listless with sunken fontanels and has been diagnosed with dehydration. The infant is still producing at least 1 mL/kg each hour of urine. The infant weighs 13.2 lb (6 kg). At the minimum, how many milliliters of urine will the infant produce during the next 8-hour shift? Record your answer using a whole number.

15. The child has been diagnosed with severe dehydration. The physician has ordered the nurse to administer a bolus of 20 mL/kg of normal saline over a 2-hour period. The child weighs 63.5 lb (28.8 kg). At which mL/hr should the nurse set the child's intravenous administration pump? Record your answer using a whole number.

Nursing Care of the Child With an Alteration in Urinary Elimination/ Genitourinary Disorder

Upon completion of the chapter, you will be able to:

- Compare anatomic and physiologic differences of the genitourinary system in infants and children versus adults.
- Describe nursing care related to common laboratory and diagnostic testing used in the medical diagnosis of pediatric genitourinary conditions.
- Distinguish alterations in urinary elimination and genitourinary disorders common in infants, children, and adolescents.
- Identify appropriate nursing assessments and interventions related to medications and treatments for alterations in urinary elimination and pediatric genitourinary disorders.
- Develop an individualized nursing care plan for the child with an alteration in urinary elimination or genitourinary disorder.
- Describe the psychosocial impact of chronic genitourinary disorders on children.
- Devise a nutrition plan for the child with renal insufficiency.
- Develop child/family teaching plans for the child with an alteration in urinary elimination or genitourinary disorder.

SECTION I: ASSESSING YOUR UNDERSTANDING

Activity A FILL IN THE BLANKS

1. Cytotoxic drugs cause bone marrow _____.

2. Human chorionic gonadotropin is used to precipitate _____ descent.

3. A creatinine (serum) clearance test is used to diagnose impaired _____ function.

4. Urodynamic studies measures the urine _____ during micturition.

5. Desmopressin is a medication commonly used to treat nocturnal _____.

6. Bladder capacity of the newborn is _____.

Activity B LABELING

Indicate which image represents:

1. Hypospadias

2. Epispadias

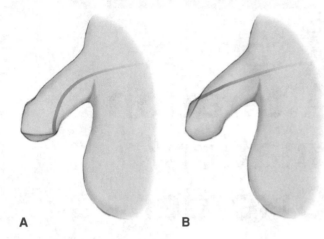

A   B

Activity C MATCHING

1. Match the condition in Column A with its description in Column B.

Column A

____ **1.** Anuria

____ **2.** Anasarca

____ **3.** Menorrhagia

____ **4.** Oliguria

____ **5.** Hyperlipidemia

Column B

a. Profuse menstrual bleeding

b. Significant decrease in urinary output

c. Elevated lipid levels in the blood stream

d. Severe generalized edema

e. Absence of urine formation

2. Match the treatment in Column A with the appropriate indication in Column B.

Column A

____ **1.** Peritoneal dialysis

____ **2.** Foley catheter

____ **3.** Nephrostomy tube

____ **4.** Bladder augmentation

Column B

a. Decreased bladder capacity

b. Used to drain an obstructed kidney

c. Acute or chronic renal failure

d. Unable to void postoperatively

Activity D SEQUENCING

Review the steps of care needed for the child scheduled to undergo a voiding cystourethrogram (VCUG). Place them in the correct order.

1. Bladder filled with contrast material

2. Insertion of urinary catheter

3. Bladder emptied

4. Child scanned using fluoroscope

5. Fluoroscopy completed

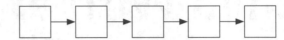

Activity E SHORT ANSWERS

Briefly answer the following.

1. How will the urine appear after a bladder augmentation is done?

_____

_____

_____

2. What are the key nursing implications following cystoscopy?

_____

_____

_____

3. What medications/supplements are commonly used to treat the complications of end-stage renal disease?

_____

_____

_____

4. Discuss testicular torsion.

_____

_____

_____

5. The nurse has completed the newborn assessment for a baby boy. The assessment reveals the right testicle is undescended. How will this condition be managed?

_____

_____

_____

SECTION II: APPLYING YOUR KNOWLEDGE

Activity F CASE STUDY

Corey Bond is a 5-year-old female. She was brought to the clinic by her mother. She presented with fever and lethargy for the past 24 hours. A urinalysis and culture confirmed that Corey has a urinary tract infection. This is Corey's first urinary tract infection and her mother is concerned and states "I do not understand how a 5-year old can get a urinary tract infection?"

1. How will you address the mother's concerns?

   _____

   _____

   _____

2. Corey is started on oral antibiotics at home. What education can you provide the family regarding treatment and providing comfort?

   _____

   _____

   _____

3. What can Corey and her family do to try to prevent the recurrence of a urinary tract infection?

   _____

   _____

   _____

SECTION III: PRACTICING FOR NCLEX

Activity G NCLEX-STYLE QUESTIONS

Answer the following questions.

1. The nurse is conducting a follow-up visit for a 13-year-old girl who has been treated for pelvic inflammatory disease. Which remark indicates a need for further teaching?
   a. "I should be tested for other sexually transmitted diseases."
   b. "Douching is not necessary and can cause bacteria to flourish."
   c. "I cannot have sex again until my partner is treated."
   d. "My partner needs to be treated with antibiotics."

2. The nurse is caring for the parents of a newborn who has an undescended testicle. Which comment by the parents indicates understanding of the condition?
   a. "Our son may need surgery on his testes before we are discharged to go home."
   b. "Our son may have to go through life without two testes."
   c. "Our son's condition may resolve on its own."
   d. "Our son will likely have a high risk of cancer in his teen years as a result of this condition."

3. The nurse is caring for a child with epididymitis. When planning care which intervention may be included?
   a. Scrotal elevation
   b. Warm compresses
   c. Corticosteroid therapy
   d. Catheterization

4. The nurse is planning the discharge instructions for the parents of a 1-month-old infant who has had a circumcision completed. Which information should be included in the education provided?
   a. Use petroleum jelly on the head of the penis for the first 2 weeks after the procedure
   b. Report any bleeding to the physician
   c. Reduce the child's fluid intake to reduce voiding during the first 24 hours
   d. Report redness or swelling on the penile shaft

5. The nurse is caring for a 10-year-old girl presenting with fever, dysuria, flank pain, urgency, and hematuria. The nurse would expect to help obtain which test **first**?
   a. Total protein, globulin, and albumin
   b. Creatinine clearance
   c. Urinalysis
   d. Urine culture and sensitivity

6. The nurse is caring for a 12-year-old boy diagnosed with acute glomerulonephritis. When reviewing the boy's health history which finding will likely be noted?

   a. History of recurrent urinary tract infections

   b. Family history of renal disorders

   c. Recent history of an upper respiratory infection

   d. History of hypotension

7. The nurse is caring for a child who is undergoing peritoneal dialysis. Immediately after draining the dialysate, which action should the nurse should take immediately?

   a. Empty the old dialysate

   b. Weigh the old dialysate

   c. Weigh the new dialysate

   d. Start the process over with a fresh bag

8. A nurse is caring for a 12-year-old girl recently diagnosed with end-stage renal disease. The nurse is discussing dietary restrictions with the girl's mother. Which response indicates a need for further teaching?

   a. "My daughter can eat what she wants when she is hooked to the machine."

   b. "My daughter must avoid high sodium foods."

   c. "She needs to restrict her potassium intake."

   d. "She can eat whatever she wants on dialysis days."

9. The nurse is administering cyclophosphamide as ordered for a 12-year-old boy with nephrotic syndrome. Which instruction is most accurate regarding administration?

   a. Administer in the evening on an empty stomach.

   b. Provide adequate hydration and encourage voiding.

   c. Administer in the morning, encourage fluids and voiding during and after administration.

   d. Encourage fluids, adequate food intake, and voiding before and after administration.

10. A nurse is caring for a 10-year-old boy with nocturnal enuresis with no physiologic cause. He says he is embarrassed and wishes he could stop immediately. How should the nurse respond?

    a. "You will grow out of this eventually; you just need to be patient."

    b. "There are several things we can do to help you achieve this goal."

    c. "There are almost 5 million people that have enuresis."

    d. "The pull-ups look just like underwear; no one has to know."

11. The nurse is assessing an infant with suspected hemolytic uremic syndrome. Which characteristics of this condition should the nurse expect to assess or glean from chart review?

    a. Hemolytic anemia, acute renal failure, and hypotension

    b. Dirty green colored urine, elevated erythrocyte sedimentation, and depressed serum complement level

    c. Hemolytic anemia, thrombocytopenia, and acute renal failure

    d. Thrombocytopenia, hemolytic anemia, and nocturia several times each night

12. A nurse is caring for a 13-year-old boy with end-stage renal disease who is preparing to have his hemodialysis treatment in the dialysis unit. Which nursing action is appropriate?

    a. Administer his routine medications as scheduled

    b. Take his blood pressure measurement in extremity with AV fistula

    c. Withhold his routine medication until after dialysis is completed

    d. Assess the Tenckhoff catheter site

13. The nurse is caring for a child who receives dialysis via an AV fistula. Which finding indicates an immediate need to notify the physician?

    a. Presence of a bruit

    b. Presence of a thrill

    c. Dialysate without fibrin or cloudiness

    d. Absence of a thrill

14. The nurse is caring for a child diagnosed with hydronephrosis. Which manifestation is consistent with complications of the disorder?

   a. Hypertension

   b. Hypotension

   c. Hypothermia

   d. Tachycardia

15. The nurse is caring for a child who has been admitted to the acute care facility with manifestations consistent with hydronephrosis. Which tests will confirm the diagnosis? Select all that apply.

   a. Intravenous pyelogram (IVP)

   b. Urinalysis

   c. Voiding cystourethrogram (VCUG)

   d. Complete blood cell count (CBC)

   e. Renal ultrasound

Nursing Care of the Child With an Alteration in Mobility/Neuromuscular or Musculoskeletal Disorder

Learning Objectives

Upon completion of the chapter, you will be able to:

- Compare differences between the anatomy and physiology of the neuromuscular and musculo-skeletal systems in children versus adults.
- Identify nursing interventions related to common laboratory and diagnostic tests used in the diagnosis and management of neuromuscular and musculoskeletal conditions.
- Identify appropriate nursing assessments and interventions related to medications and treatments used for childhood neuromuscular and musculoskeletal conditions.
- Distinguish various neuromuscular and musculoskeletal disorders occurring in childhood.
- Devise an individualized nursing care plan for the child with a neuromuscular and musculoskeletal disorder.
- Develop child/family teaching plans for the child with a neuromuscular and musculoskeletal disorder.
- Describe the psychosocial impact of chronic neuromuscular and musculoskeletal disorders on the growth and development of children.

SECTION I: ASSESSING YOUR UNDERSTANDING

Activity A FILL IN THE BLANKS

1. The _____ is where ossification of new bone occurs.

2. Kyphosis refers to excessive _____ curvature of the spine resulting in a hump-back appearance.

3. Atrophy is a _____ or wasting in size of a muscle.

4. Spasticity is _____ muscle contractions that are not coordinated with other muscles.

5. Decreased muscle tone is called _____.

6. The structural disorders of spina bifida occulta, meningocele, and myelomeningocele are all considered _____.

7. Transient _____ of the hip is the most common cause of hip pain in children.

Activity B **LABELING**

Provide the appropriate labels for the following images.

1. Normal spine

2. Spine showing spina bifida occulta

3. Spine showing meningocele

4. Spine showing myelomeningocele

A

B

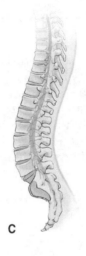

C

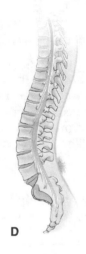

D

Activity C **MATCHING**

Match the medication in Column A with the appropriate action in Column B.

Column A

___ 1. Baclofen

___ 2. Corticosteroids

___ 3. Botulin toxin

___ 4. Benzodiaze-
        pines

___ 5. Oxybutynin

Column B

a. Central acting skeletal muscle relaxant

b. Anticonvulsant

c. Anti-inflammatory

d. Neurotoxin

e. Antispasmodic

Activity D **SHORT ANSWERS**

Briefly answer the following.

1. What are the four classifications of cerebral palsy? Which is the most common form? Which is the rarest form?

_____

_____

_____

2. According to the text, what is the appropriate nursing management focus for a child with myelomeningocele?

_____

_____

_____

3. List and explain the four types of fractures seen in children.

_____

_____

_____

4. What factors increase the risk of a fetus developing a neural tube defect?

_____

_____

_____

5. Discuss the commonalities of the various forms of muscular dystrophy. What is the most common childhood type of muscular dystrophy?

_____

_____

_____

SECTION II: APPLYING YOUR KNOWLEDGE

Activity E CASE STUDY 1

Elijah Jefferson, a 2-year-old boy, was recently diagnosed with cerebral palsy (CP). He was born at 28 weeks' gestation after a complicated and prolonged delivery. Elijah's parents have many questions and concerns about their son's diagnosis. They ask "Can Elijah outgrow this disorder with proper physical and occupational therapy?"

1. How can you help Elijah's parents to have an accurate perception of CP?

_____

_____

_____

2. What are some assessment findings on examination that are characteristic of CP?

_____

_____

_____

3. Discuss the focus of nursing management when caring for a child with CP.

_____

_____

_____

CASE STUDY 2

You are caring for a 2-year-old boy who was brought to the clinic by his mother. He presented with right arm bruising, swelling, and wrist point tenderness. An x-ray confirmed he had a right wrist fracture. The doctor decided he needed a cast.

1. What assessments and interventions should you perform after application of the cast?

_____

_____

_____

2. What education will the family need for home care of their son?

_____

_____

_____

SECTION III: PRACTICING FOR NCLEX

Activity F NCLEX-STYLE QUESTIONS

Answer the following questions.

1. A nurse is assisting the parents of a child who requires a Pavlik harness. The parents are apprehensive about how to care for their baby. The nurse should stress which teaching point?

   a. "The baby needs the harness only for 2 to 3 weeks."

   b. "It is important that the harness be worn continuously."

   c. "The harness does not hurt the baby."

   d. "Let me teach you how to make appropriate adjustments to the harness."

2. The nurse is conducting a routine physical examination of a newborn to screen for DDH. The nurse correctly assesses the infant by placing the infant:

   a. in a prone position, noting asymmetry of the thigh or gluteal folds.

   b. with both legs extended and observes the hip and knee joint relationship.

   c. with both legs extended and observes the feet.

   d. in a supine position with both legs extended and observes the tibia/fibula.

3. A 5-year-old child is in traction and at risk for impaired skin integrity due to pressure. Which intervention is most effective?

   a. Inspect the child's skin for rashes, redness, irritation, or pressure sores

   b. Apply lotion to dry skin

   c. Gently massage the child's back to stimulate circulation

   d. Keep the child's skin clean and dry

4. A nurse is conducting a physical examination of an infant with suspected metatarsus adductus. Type II metatarsus adductus is indicates when the forefoot is:

   a. inverted and turned slightly upward.

   b. flexible past neutral actively and passively.

   c. flexible passively past neutral, but only to midline actively.

   d. rigid, does not correct to midline even with passive stretching.

5. A nurse is providing instructions for home cast care. Which response by the parent indicates a need for further teaching?

   a. "We must avoid causing depressions in the cast."

   b. "Pale, cool, or blue skin coloration is to be expected."

   c. "The casted arm must be kept still."

   d. "We need be aware of odor or drainage from the cast."

6. A nurse is caring for a 6-year-old boy with a fractured ulna. He is fearful about the casting process and is resisting treatment. How should the nurse respond?

   a. "The application of the cast will not hurt."

   b. "Would you like to pick out your favorite color?"

   c. "Look over there at the neon fish in our aquarium."

   d. "Will you please take this medicine for pain?"

7. The nurse is providing postoperative care for a boy who has undergone surgical correction for pectus excavatum. The nurse should emphasize which instruction to the child's parents?

   a. "Please watch for signs of infection."

   b. "Be sure to monitor his vital capacity."

   c. "Do not allow him to lie on either side."

   d. "Do not allow him to lie on his stomach."

8. A nurse is caring for an 11-year old with an Ilizarov fixator and is providing teaching regarding pin care. The nurse should provide which instruction?

   a. "Cleansing by showering should be sufficient."

   b. "You must clean the pin sites with saline."

   c. "The pin site should be cleaned with antibacterial solution."

   d. "Please make sure that the pin site is cleansed with betadine swabs after showering."

9. The nurse is caring for an infant girl in an outpatient setting. The infant has just been diagnosed with developmental dysplasia of the hip (DDH). The mother is very upset about the diagnosis and blames herself for her daughter's condition. Which response best addresses the mother's concerns?

   a. "There are simple noninvasive treatment options."

   b. "Your daughter will likely wear a Pavlik harness."

   c. "Don't worry; this is a relatively common diagnosis."

   d. "This is not your fault and we will help you with her care and treatment."

10. The nurse is conducting a physical examination of a newborn with suspected osteogenesis imperfecta. Which finding is common?

    a. Foot is drawn up and inward

    b. Sole of foot faces backward

    c. Dimpled skin, hair in lumbar region

    d. Blue sclera

11. The young child is experiencing muscle spasms and has been given lorazepam. Which statements by the child indicate that the child may be experiencing some common side effects? Select all that apply.

    a. "I feel sort of dizzy."

    b. "I need to take a nap."

    c. "My muscle cramps are getting worse."

    d. "I think I'm going to throw up."

    e. "My belly hurts."

12. The young boy has fractured his left leg and has had a cast applied. The nurse educates the boy and his parents prior to discharge

from the hospital. The parents should call the physician when which indents occur? Select all that apply.

a. The boy experiences mild pain when wiggling his toes.

b. The boy has had a fever of greater than 102°F (38.9°C) for the last 36 hours.

c. New drainage is seeping out from under the cast.

d. The outside of the boy's cast got wet and had to be dried using a hair dryer.

e. The boy's toes are light blue and very swollen.

13. The child has been diagnosed with slipped capital femoral epiphysis. Which characteristics about the client are risk factors associated with the development of this condition? Select all that apply.

a. The child is noted to be underweight by the nurse.

b. The child is 13 years old.

c. The child is African American.

d. The child's parents state that the child has recently experienced a "growth spurt."

e. The child is male.

14. The nurse is taking the history of a 4-year-old boy. His mother mentions that he seems weaker and unable to keep up with his 6-year-old sister on the playground. Which question should the nurse ask to elicit the most helpful information?

a. "Has he achieved his developmental milestones on time?"

b. "Would you please describe the weakness you are seeing in your son?"

c. "Do you think he is simply fatigued?"

d. "Has his pace of achieving milestones diminished?"

15. The nurse is conducting a physical examination of a 9-month-old infant with a suspected neuromuscular disorder. Which finding would warrant further evaluation?

a. Presence of symmetrical spontaneous movement

b. Absence of Moro reflex

c. Absence of tonic neck reflex

d. Presence of Moro reflex

16. The nurse is conducting a wellness examination of a 6-month-old child. The mother points out some dimpling and skin discoloration in the child's lumbosacral area. How should the nurse respond?

a. "This could be an indicator of spina bifida; we need to evaluate this further."

b. "This can be considered a normal variant with no indication of a problem; however, the doctor will want to take a closer look."

c. "Dimpling, skin discoloration, and abnormal patches of hair are often indicators of spina bifida occulta."

d. "This is often an indicator of spina bifida occulta as opposed to spina bifida cystica."

17. A nurse is caring for an infant with a meningocele. Which finding alerts the nurse that the lesion is increasing in size?

a. Leaking cerebrospinal fluid

b. Increasing ICP

c. Constipation and bladder dysfunction

d. Increasing head circumference

18. A nurse is teaching the parents of a boy with a neurogenic bladder about clean intermittent catheterization. Which response indicates a need for further teaching?

a. "We must be careful to use latex-free catheters."

b. "The very first step is to apply water-based lubricant to the catheter."

c. "My son may someday learn how to do this for himself."

d. "We need to soak the catheter in a vinegar and water solution daily."

19. A nurse is caring for a 13-year-old boy with Duchenne muscular dystrophy. He says he feels isolated and that there is no one who understands the challenges of his disease. How should the nurse respond?

a. "You need to remain as active as possible and have a positive attitude."

b. "There are many things that you can do like crafts, computers, or art."

c. "There are a lot of kids with the same type of muscular dystrophy you have at the MDA support group."

d. "You have to go to a support group; it will be very helpful."

20. The nurse is conducting a physical examination of a 10-year-old boy with a suspected neuromuscular disorder. Which finding is a sign of Duchenne muscular dystrophy?

    a. Gowers sign

    b. Appearance of smaller than normal calf muscles

    c. Indications of hydrocephalus

    d. Lordosis

21. A nurse is caring for a 2-year-old girl with cerebral palsy. The child is having difficulty with proper nutrition and is not gaining adequate weight. How can the nurse elicit additional information to establish a diagnosis?

    a. "Let's see if she is dehydrated and we'll assess her respiratory system."

    b. "Does she have difficulty swallowing or chewing?"

    c. "Does she like to feed herself or do you feed her?"

    d. "Let's offer her a snack now and you can tell me about her diet on a typical day."

22. The nurse is caring for a 5-year-old child with Guillain–Barré syndrome. Which would be the best way to assess the level of paralysis?

    a. Gentle tickling

    b. Observe for symmetrical flaccid weakness

    c. Monitor for ataxia

    d. Inquire about sensory disturbances

23. The nurse is providing presurgical care for a newborn with myelomeningocele. Which action is the central nursing **priority**?

    a. Maintain infant's body temperature

    b. Prevent rupture or leaking of cerebrospinal fluid

    c. Maintain infant in prone position

    d. Keep lesion free from fecal matter or urine

24. The child has a meningocele and a neurogenic bladder. Which topics should the nurse include in the teaching plan when educating the child and the child's caregivers? Select all that apply.

    a. How and when to administer oxybutynin chloride

    b. The importance of antibiotic use to prevent urinary tract infections from occurring

    c. How and when to perform clean intermittent urinary catheterization

    d. Signs and symptoms of a urinary tract infection

    e. Different types of surgeries used to treat this condition

25. The nurse is assessing a young boy who has been brought to the physician for mobility and balance issues by his parents. Which findings are positively associated with the presence of Duchenne muscular dystrophy? Select all that apply.

    a. Serum creatine kinase levels are elevated.

    b. An electromyogram demonstrates the problem is within the nerves, not the muscles.

    c. A muscle biopsy shows an absence of dystrophin.

    d. The child is unable to rise easily into a standing position when placed on the floor.

    e. Genetic testing indicates the presence of a gene associated with spinal muscular atrophy.

26. The nurse learns that the child has been admitted with clinical manifestations associated with cholinergic crisis. Which findings are associated with this condition? Select all that apply.

    a. The child exhibits diaphoresis

    b. The child's apical heart rate is 52 beats per minute

    c. The child's blood pressure is 172/94

    d. The child is complaining that his muscles are very weak

    e. The child is drooling excessively

27. The young girl has been prescribed corticosteroids for dermatomyositis. Which statements by her mother indicate the need for further education? Select all that apply.

    a. "I give it to her first thing in the morning before breakfast."

    b. "We are taking her to Disney in the summer."

    c. "The physician said when it's time for her to stop taking this medication; he will gradually start reducing her dose."

    d. "She's got to take this medication to help with the calcium deposits that can form."

    e. "She might recover completely from this condition."

28. The child has been diagnosed with rickets. The child's mother is educated about the importance of providing the child with 10 µg (400 International Units) of an oral vitamin D supplement each day. The child's mother purchases over-the-counter vitamin D drops. The supplement is noted to contain 5 µg of vitamin D in each 0.5 mL. How much of the supplement should the mother administer to the child each day? Record your answer using one decimal place.

29. The young child has been diagnosed with Guillain–Barré syndrome and it is progressing in a classic manner. Rank the following sequence of events in the order that they typically occur.

a. The child reports numbness and tingling in his toes.

b. The child states that it is difficult to move his legs.

c. The child states that it is difficult to move his arms.

d. The child is having difficulty producing facial expressions.

Nursing Care of the Child With an Alteration in Tissue Integrity/ Integumentary Disorder

Learning Objectives

Upon completion of the chapter, you will be able to:

- Compare anatomic and physiologic differences of the integumentary system in infants and children versus adults.
- Describe nursing care related to common laboratory and diagnostic tests used in the medical diagnosis of integumentary disorders/ alterations in tissue integrity in infants, children, and adolescents.
- Distinguish alterations in tissue integrity/ integumentary disorders common in infants, children, and adolescents.
- Identify appropriate nursing assessments and interventions related to pediatric integumentary disorders/alterations in tissue integrity.
- Develop an individualized nursing care plan for the child with an alteration in tissue integrity integumentary disorder.
- Describe the psychosocial impact of a chronic integumentary disorder on children or adolescents.
- Develop child/family teaching plans for the child with an integumentary disorder/tissue integrity alteration.

SECTION I: ASSESSING YOUR UNDERSTANDING

Activity A FILL IN THE BLANKS

1. Diaper wearing _____ the skin's pH, activating fecal enzymes that further contribute to skin maceration.

2. Serum _____ may be elevated in the child with atopic dermatitis.

3. Urticaria is a type I _____ reaction.

4. Seborrhea in infants is commonly referred to as _____.

5. Acne neonatorum occurs as a response to the presence of maternal _____.

Activity B **MATCHING**

1. Match the term related to findings in skin conditions, in Column A, with the correct definition in Column B.

Column A

____ **1.** Annular

____ **2.** Papule

____ **3.** Vesicle

____ **4.** Macule

____ **5.** Scaling

Column B

a. A flat discolored area on the skin

b. In a circle or ring shape

c. Small raised bump on the skin

d. A fluid-filled bump on the skin

e. Flaking of the skin

2. Match the treatment in Column A with the condition in Column B.

Column A

____ **1.** Silver sulfadiazine 1%

____ **2.** Isotretinoin

____ **3.** Coal tar preparations

____ **4.** Benzoyl peroxide

Column B

a. Psoriasis, atopic dermatitis

b. Mild acne vulgaris

c. Cystic acne

d. Burns

Activity C **SEQUENCING**

List in order the stages in the progression of an impetigo lesion.

1. Formation of a crust on an ulcer-like base

2. Papules

3. Painless pustules with an erythematous border

4. Honey-colored exudate

5. Vesicles

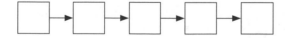

Activity D **SHORT ANSWERS**

Briefly answer the following.

1. Review the different cutaneous reactions commonly found in dark-skinned children compared to children with lighter skin.

_____

_____

2. According to the text, what are the four criteria used to describe lesions?

_____

_____

_____

3. What are the differences between bullous impetigo and nonbullous impetigo?

_____

_____

4. List the risk factors that are associated with the development of pressure ulcers. What sites are more prone for pressure ulcer development?

_____

_____

_____

5. Explain the relationship between puberty and acne vulgaris.

_____

_____

_____

SECTION II: APPLYING YOUR KNOWLEDGE

Activity E CASE STUDY

Eva Lopez is a 1-year-old child. She has presented at the ambulatory care clinic with reports of itching and scratching that is worse at night. The assessment reveals dry patches of skin. She has evidence of bleeding at the wrists from scratching. A diagnosis of atopic dermatitis (eczema) is made.

1. The mother states, "I do not understand why the rash comes and goes and only seems to appear after Eva has been scratching." Address the mother's concerns.

   _____

   _____

   _____

2. What education will the family need to help manage atopic dermatitis?

   _____

   _____

   _____

SECTION III: PRACTICING FOR NCLEX

Activity F NCLEX-STYLE QUESTIONS

Answer the following questions.

1. The nurse is conducting a primary survey of a child with burns. Which assessment finding points to airway injury from burn or smoke inhalation?
   a. Burns on hands
   b. Cervical spine injury
   c. Stridor
   d. Internal injuries

2. The nurse is conducting a physical examination of a child with severe burns. Which internal physiologic manifestation should the nurse expect to occur **first**?
   a. Insulin resistance
   b. Hypermetabolic response with increased cardiac output
   c. Decrease in cardiac output
   d. Increased protein catabolism

3. The nurse is caring for a 10-month old with a rash. The child's mother reports that the onset was abrupt. The nurse assesses diffuse erythema and skin tenderness with ruptured bullae in the axillary area with red weeping surface. The nurse suspects which bacterial infection?
   a. Folliculitis
   b. Impetigo
   c. Nonbullous impetigo
   d. Scalded skin syndrome

4. A nurse providing teaching on ways to promote skin hydration for the parents of an infant with atopic dermatitis. Which response indicates a need for further teaching?
   a. "We need to avoid any skin product containing perfumes, dyes, or fragrances."
   b. "We should use a mild soap for sensitive skin."
   c. "We should bathe our child in hot water, twice a day."
   d. "We should use soap to clean only dirty areas."

5. A nurse is caring for a child with tinea pedis. Which assessment finding should the nurse expect?
   a. Red scaling rash on soles and between the toes
   b. Patches of scaling in the scalp with central hair loss
   c. Inflamed boggy mass filled with pustules
   d. Erythema, scaling, maceration in the inguinal creases and inner thighs

6. A nurse assessing a 6-month-old girl with an integumentary disorder. The nurse notes three virtually identically sized, round red circles with scaling that are symmetrically spaced on both of the girl's inner thighs. Which should the nurse ask the mother?
   a. "Has she been exposed to poison ivy?"
   b. "Does she wear sleepers with metal snaps?"
   c. "Do you change her diapers regularly?"
   d. "Tell me about your family history of allergies."

7. The nurse is conducting a physical examination of a boy with erythema multiforme. Which assessment finding should the nurse expect?

   a. Lesions over the hands and feet, and extensor surfaces of the extremities with spread to the trunk

   b. Thick or flaky/greasy yellow scales

   c. Silvery or yellow-white scale plaques and sharply demarcated borders

   d. Superficial tan or hypopigmented oval-shaped scaly lesions especially on upper back and chest and proximal arms

8. A nurse is caring for a child with a wasp sting. Which nursing intervention is **priority**?

   a. Remove jewelry or restrictive clothing

   b. Apply ice intermittently

   c. Administer diphenhydramine per protocol

   d. Cleanse wound with mild soap and water

9. The nurse is examining a child for indications of frostbite and notes blistering with erythema and edema. The nurse notes which degree of frostbite?

   a. First degree frostbite

   b. Second degree frostbite

   c. Third degree frostbite

   d. Fourth degree frostbite

10. The nurse is providing teaching on ways to maintain skin integrity and prevent infection for the parents of a boy with atopic dermatitis. Which response indicates a need for further teaching?

    a. "We should avoid using petroleum jelly."

    b. "We should keep his fingernails short and clean."

    c. "We should avoid tight clothing and heat."

    d. "We need to develop ways to prevent him from scratching."

11. The nurse is providing education to a teenaged boy diagnosed with impetigo. Which statement by the boy indicates the need for further education?

    a. "I will need to cover my son's skin lesions with bandages until it has healed."

    b. "It is important to remove the crusts before applying any topical medications."

    c. "This condition is contagious."

    d. "I can continue to attend school while taking the prescribed antibiotics."

12. A 16-year-old male who diagnosed with tinea pedis questions the nurse about how he may have contracted the condition. How should the nurse respond?

    a. "It is unlikely you will be able to determine the cause of the infection."

    b. "This condition is common in individuals with lowered immunity."

    c. "You may have gotten the condition from a community shower or gym area."

    d. "You likely had an infection in another area of your body and it has spread."

13. The nurse is discussing the use of over-the-counter ointments to manage a mild case of diaper rash. What ingredients should the nurse instruct the parents to look for in a compound? Select all that apply.

    a. Vitamin A

    b. Zinc

    c. Vitamin D

    d. Vitamin B6

    e. Vitamin B12

14. The nurse is discussing dietary intake with the parents of a 4-year-old child who has been diagnosed with atopic dermatitis. Later, the nurse notes the menu selection made by the parents for the child. Which selection indicates the need for further instruction?

    a. Peanut butter and jelly sandwich

    b. Chicken nuggets

    c. Tomato soup

    d. Carrot and celery sticks

15. The nurse is developing the plan of care for a 3-year-old child diagnosed with atopic dermatitis. Which client outcomes are common focuses for a child with this diagnosis? Select all that apply.

    a. Pain management

    b. Promotion of skin hydration

    c. Maintenance of skin integrity

    d. Reduction in anxiety

    e. Prevention of infection

Nursing Care of the Child With an Alteration in Cellular Regulation/ Hematologic or Neoplastic Disorder

Learning Objectives

Upon completion of the chapter, you will be able to:

- Identify major hematologic disorders that affect children.
- Compare childhood and adult cancers.
- Identify types of cancer common in infants, children, and adolescents.
- Determine priority assessment information for children with alterations in cellular regulation/ hematologic and neoplastic disorders.
- Analyze laboratory data and describe nursing care related to common laboratory and diagnostic testing used in alterations in cellular regulation/ hematologic and neoplastic disorders.
- Develop an individualized nursing care plan for the child with cancer or a hematologic disorder.
- Identify priority interventions for children with alterations in cellular regulation.
- Develop a teaching plan for the family of children with hematologic disorders or cancer.
- Devise a nutrition plan for the child with cancer.
- Describe the psychosocial impact of cancer on children and their families.
- Identify resources for children and families with hematologic disorders, nutrition deficits, or cancer.

SECTION I: ASSESSING YOUR UNDERSTANDING

Activity A FILL IN THE BLANKS

1. The complete blood count is also called the CBC or _____.

2. Anemia is the reduction of red blood cells or hemoglobin in the total blood _____.

3. Untreated, neutropenia can lead to _____ and should be treated with IV antibiotics immediately.

4. Mean corpuscular volume (MCV) is a measure of the average _____ of the RBC.

5. Bone cancer may be treated with a combination of _____ procedure, radiation, and chemotherapy.

6. _____ is the measurement of the size of the platelets.

7. If the levels of RBCs and Hgb are lower than normal _____ is present.

8. _____ is the most frequently occurring type of childhood cancer.

Activity B   LABELING

Place the following labels in the appropriate location on the diagram.

Multipotent stem cell

Neutrophil

Lymphocyte

Monocyte

Megakaryocyte/erythroid progenitor

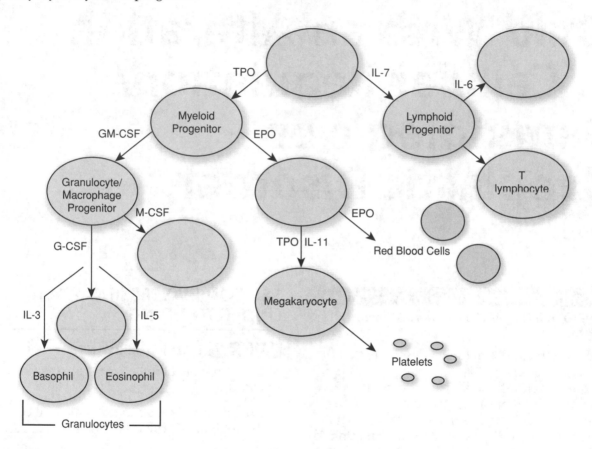

Activity C   MATCHING

1. Match the medication in Column A with the appropriate indication in Column B.

Column A

____ **1.** Factor VII

____ **2.** Deferoxamine

____ **3.** Intravenous immune globulin (IVIG)

____ **4.** Penicillin

____ **5.** Chelating agents

Column B

a. Blood lead levels greater than 45 μg/dL

b. Prophylaxis of infection in asplenia

c. Iron toxicity

d. Idiopathic thrombocytopenic purpura

e. Hemophilia

2. Match the medical treatment in Column A with the proper word or phrase in Column B.

Column A

____ **1.** Biopsy

____ **2.** Central venous catheter

____ **3.** Implanted port

____ **4.** Leukapheresis

____ **5.** Radiation therapy

Column B

a. High-energy x-ray

b. Long-term IV medication

c. May be done with needle

d. Vena cava or subclavian vein

e. White blood cell extraction

Activity D SHORT ANSWERS

Briefly answer the following.

1. Discuss three ways how childhood cancer differs from adult cancer.

   _____

   _____

   _____

2. According to the American Academy of Pediatrics, what is the recommended action for a blood lead level of 20 to 44 μg/dL?

   _____

   _____

   _____

3. Signs of changes in the hematologic system are often subtle and overlooked. What are some of the first signs of a problem developing?

   _____

   _____

   _____

4. Discuss the incidence of sickle cell anemia.

   _____

   _____

   _____

5. Discuss how iron deficiency anemia occurs and which age groups it is most prevalent in.

   _____

   _____

   _____

SECTION II: APPLYING YOUR KNOWLEDGE

Activity E CASE STUDY 1

Jayda Johnson, 15-months old, is brought to the clinic for a routine examination. Her parents state she has been irritable lately. Assessment findings reveal pallor of the mucous membranes and conjunctivae, heart rate of 120 and a heart murmur heard upon auscultation.

1. What other assessment information about the home environment is important for the nurse to gather.

   _____

   _____

   _____

2. Laboratory results revealed hemoglobin of 10 g/dL and hematocrit of 29%. The physician decides to start Jayda on a daily dose of ferrous sulfate. What instructions should be given to the child's parents?

   _____

   _____

   _____

3. What sociocultural influences may be related to the child's condition?

   _____

   _____

   _____

CASE STUDY 2

A 4-year-old boy is brought to the clinic by his parents due to fever. After further assessment the diagnosis of acute lymphoblastic leukemia (ALL) was confirmed. The child was admitted to your unit and started on treatment immediately. Upon assessment and review of his laboratory work today you find his temperature to be 101.2°F, HR 100, RR 24. His absolute neutrophil count (ANC) is <500.

1. What will be your priority nursing interventions?

   _____

   _____

   _____

2. One week later, John is ready to be discharged home and will receive his treatment in the outpatient setting. What education will you review with the family regarding preventing infection?

_____

_____

_____

3. The mother asks, "How can we help John's development not fall behind other children his age?"

_____

_____

_____

SECTION III: PRACTICING FOR NCLEX

Activity F **NCLEX-STYLE QUESTIONS**

Answer the following questions.

1. The nurse is teaching the parents of a 15-year-old boy who is being treated for acute myelogenous leukemia about the side effects of chemotherapy. For which symptoms should the parents seek medical care immediately?
   a. Earache, stiff neck, or sore throat
   b. Blisters, ulcers, or a rash appear
   c. Temperature of 101°F (38.3°C) or greater
   d. Difficulty or pain when swallowing

2. The nurse is assessing a 2-year-old girl whose parents noticed that one of her pupils appeared to be white. Which assessments should the nurse expect to find if the girl has retinoblastoma? Select all that apply.
   a. Observation of eyes reveals yellow discharge.
   b. Parents report that the child has headaches.
   c. Observation confirms cat's eye reflex in pupil.
   d. Assessment discloses hyphema in one eye.
   e. History reveals strabismus.

3. The nurse is providing preoperative care for a 7-year-old boy with a brain tumor and his parents. Which intervention is **priority**?
   a. Assessing the child's level of consciousness
   b. Providing a tour of the intensive care unit
   c. Educating the child and parents about shunts
   d. Having the child talk to another child who has had this surgery

4. The nurse is assessing a 14-year-old girl with a tumor. Which finding indicates Ewing sarcoma?
   a. Child reports dull bone pain just below her knee.
   b. Palpation reveals swelling and redness on the right ribs.
   c. Child reports persistent pain from minor ankle injury.
   d. Palpation discloses asymptomatic mass on the upper back.

5. The nurse is teaching a group of 13-year-old boys and girls about screening and prevention of reproductive cancers. Which subjects would not be included in the nurse's teaching plan? Select all that apply.
   a. Self-examination is an effective screening method for testicular cancer.
   b. Testicular cancer is one of the most difficult cancers to cure.
   c. A papanicolaou (PAP) smear does not require parent consent in most states.
   d. Sexually transmitted disease is a risk factor for cervical cancer.
   e. Provide information regarding the benefits of receiving the HPV vaccine.

6. The nurse is caring for a 4-year-old boy following surgical removal of a stage I neuroblastoma. Which intervention is most appropriate for this child?
   a. Applying aloe vera lotion to irradiated areas of skin
   b. Administering antiemetics as prescribed for nausea
   c. Giving medications as ordered via least invasive route
   d. Maintaining isolation as prescribed to avoid infection

7. The nurse is caring for a 6-year-old girl with leukemia who is having an oncologic emergency. Which signs and symptoms would indicate hyperleukocytosis?

    a. Bradycardia and distinct S1 and S2 sounds

    b. Wheezing and diminished breath sounds

    c. Respiratory distress and poor perfusion

    d. Tachycardia and respiratory distress

8. The nurse is assessing a 3-year-old boy whose mother reports that he is listless and has been having trouble swallowing. Which finding suggests the child may have a brain tumor?

    a. Observation reveals nystagmus and head tilt

    b. Vital signs show blood pressure measures 120/80 mm Hg

    c. Examination shows temperature of 101.4°F (38.6°C) and headache

    d. Observation reveals a cough and labored breathing

9. The nurse is assessing a 4-year-old girl whose mother reports that she is not eating well, is losing weight, and has started vomiting after eating. Which risk factor from the health history suggests the child may have a Wilms tumor?

    a. The child has Down syndrome.

    b. The child has Beckwith–Wiedemann syndrome.

    c. The child has Shwachman syndrome.

    d. There is a family history of neurofibromatosis.

10. The nurse is educating the parents of a 16-year-old boy who has just been diagnosed with Hodgkin disease. Which discussion is most appropriate at this time?

    a. Describing the two ways of staging the disease

    b. Telling about the drugs and side effects of chemotherapy

    c. Informing the parents about postoperative care

    d. Explaining how to care for skin after radiation therapy

11. The child has been diagnosed with cancer and is being treated with chemotherapy. Which findings are common side effects of this type of treatment? Select all that apply.

    a. The child's mother states, "It seems like he catches every bug that comes along."

    b. The child's teeth are enlarged.

    c. The child has no hair on his head.

    d. The child's mother states that she often has to repeat herself because he can't hear very well.

    e. The child reports feeling nauseated.

12. The child has been admitted to the hospital. Her absolute neutrophil count is 450 and the child has been placed in neutropenic precautions. Which nursing interventions indicate that the nurse requires further education? Select all that apply.

    a. The child has been placed in a semiprivate room

    b. The child is being transported to radiology for an x-ray and the nurse places gloves on the child's hands

    c. The nurse monitors the child's vital signs every 2 to 4 hours

    d. The nurse assesses the child for clinical manifestations of an infection every 4 to 8 hours

    e. The nurse carefully washes his hands before and after providing care for the child

13. The nurse is caring for a child with disseminated intravascular coagulation. The nurse notices signs of neurologic deficit. Which nursing action is appropriate?

    a. Continue to monitor neurologic signs

    b. Notify the physician

    c. Evaluate respiratory status

    d. Inspect for signs of bleeding

14. The nurse is examining the hands of a child with suspected iron deficiency anemia. Which finding should the nurse expect?

    a. Capillary refill in less than 2 seconds

    b. Pink palms and nail beds

    c. Absence of bruising

    d. Spooning of nails

15. The nurse is evaluating the complete blood count of a 7-year-old child with a suspected hematologic disorder. Which finding is associated with an elevated mean corpuscular volume (MCV)?

    a. Macrocytic red blood cells (RBCs)

    b. Decreased white blood cells (WBCs)

    c. Platelet count of 250,000

    d. Hemoglobin (Hgb) of 11.2 g/dL

16. A nurse is caring for a newborn whose screening test result indicates the possibility of sickle cell anemia (SCA) or sickle cell trait. The nurse would expect the test result to be confirmed by which laboratory tests?

a. Reticulocyte count

b. Peripheral blood smear

c. Erythrocyte sedimentation rate

d. Hemoglobin electrophoresis

17. A nurse is providing dietary interventions for a 5-year old with an iron deficiency. Which response indicates a need for further teaching?

a. "Red meat is a good option; he loves the hamburgers from the drive-thru."

b. "He will enjoy tuna casserole and eggs."

c. "There are many iron fortified cereals that he likes."

d. "I must encourage a variety of iron-rich foods that he likes."

18. A nurse is caring for a 7-year-old boy with hemophilia who requires an infusion of factor VIII. He is fearful about the process and is resisting treatment. How should the nurse respond?

a. "Would you like to administer the infusion?"

b. "Would you help me dilute this and mix it up?"

c. "Will you help me apply this band-aid?"

d. "Please be brave; we need to stop the bleeding"

19. The nurse is providing teaching about iron supplement administration to the parents of a 10-month-old child. It is critical that the nurse emphasize which teaching point to the parents?

a. "You must precisely measure the amount of iron."

b. "Your child may become constipated from the iron."

c. "Please give him plenty of fluids and encourage fiber."

d. "Place the liquid behind the teeth; the pigment can cause staining."

20. A nurse in the emergency department is examining a 6-month old with symmetrical swelling of the hands and feet. The nurse immediately suspects:

a. Cooley anemia.

b. idiopathic thrombocytopenic purpura (ITP).

c. sickle cell disease.

d. hemophilia.

21. The nurse is caring for a child with aplastic anemia. The nurse is reviewing the child's blood work and notes the granulocyte count is about 500, platelet count is over 20,000, and the reticulocyte count is over 1%. The parents ask if these values have any significance. Which response by the nurse is appropriate?

a. "The doctor will discuss these findings with you when he comes to the hospital."

b. "These values will help us monitor the disease."

c. "These labs are just common labs for children with this disease."

d. "I'm really not allowed to discuss these findings with you."

22. The nurse is caring for an 18-month old with suspected iron deficiency anemia. Which laboratory results confirm the diagnosis?

a. Increased hemoglobin and hematocrit, increased reticulocyte count, microcytosis, and hypochromia

b. Increased serum iron and ferritin levels, decreased FEP level, microcytosis and hypochromia

c. Decreased hemoglobin and hematocrit, decreased reticulocyte count, microcytosis, and hypochromia, decreased serum iron and ferritin levels and increase FEP level

d. Increased hemoglobin and hematocrit, increased reticulocyte, microcytosis and hypochromia, increased serum iron and ferritin levels and decreased FEP level

23. The young girl has been diagnosed with a hematologic disorder. Her erythrocyte count is below normal. The mean corpuscular volume is below normal. The girl's mean corpuscular hemoglobin (Hgb) concentration is below normal. Which statements by the nurse are true regarding this girl? Select all that apply.

    a. "She's anemic."

    b. "Her red blood cells are macrocytic."

    c. "Her red blood cells are hypochromic."

    d. "The amount of hemoglobin in her red blood cells is very dilute."

    e. "Her red blood cells are smaller than normal."

24. The young boy has had his spleen surgically removed. Which statements by the boy's parents prior to discharge indicate that an adequate amount of learning has occurred?

    a. "If he gets a fever, I'm going to call our physician right away."

    b. "If he does get sick, then we'll need to put on his medic alert bracelet."

    c. "Before he goes to the dentist, we'll make sure he gets antibiotics."

    d. "He's going to need several vaccines."

    e. "He's going to get really good at washing his hands."

25. The boy has anemia and iron supplements will be administered by his parents at home. Which statements by the child's parents indicate that further education is required? Select all that apply.

    a. "It's better if I give the iron with orange juice."

    b. "I can give the iron mixed with chocolate milk."

    c. "If the iron is mixed in a drink, then he should drink it with a straw."

    d. "He may develop diarrhea."

    e. "His urine may look dark."

26. The child has been diagnosed with severe iron deficiency anemia. The child requires 5 mg/kg of elemental iron per day in three equally divided doses. The child weighs 47.3 lb (21.5 kg). How many milligrams of elemental iron should the child receive with each dose? Record your answer using a whole number.

27. The physician requests the nurse to calculate the child's absolute neutrophil count (ANC). The complete blood count indicates that the child's "segs" are 14%, bands are 9%, and white blood cells (WBC) are 15,000. Calculate the child's absolute neutrophil count. Record your answer using a whole number.

28. The child has been prescribed chemotherapy. In order to properly calculate the child's dose, the nurse must first figure the child's body surface area (BSA). The child is 130 cm tall and weighs 27 kg. Calculate the child's BSA. Record your answer using two decimal places.

29. The blood cell becomes an erythrocyte. Rank the following steps in the proper order of occurrence.

    a. The bone marrow releases a stem cell.

    b. Thrombopoietin acts on the cell.

    c. The myeloid cell becomes a megakaryocyte.

    d. Erythropoietin helps the cell turn into a red blood cell.

30. The child has been diagnosed with leukemia. Rank the following medications used to treat leukemia in order based on the stage of treatment.

    a. Oral steroids and vincristine through an intravenous line

    b. High-dose methotrexate and 6-mercaptopurine

    c. Low doses of 6-mercaptopurine and methotrexate

    d. Chemotherapy through an intrathecal catheter

Nursing Care of the Child With an Alteration in Immunity or Immunologic Disorder

Learning Objectives

Upon completion of the chapter, you will be able to:

- Explain anatomic and physiologic differences of the immune system in infants and children versus adults.
- Describe nursing care related to common laboratory and diagnostic testing used in the medical diagnosis of pediatric immune and autoimmune disorders.
- Distinguish immune, autoimmune, and allergic disorders common in infants, children, and adolescents.
- Identify appropriate nursing assessments and interventions related to medications and treatments for pediatric immune, autoimmune, and allergic disorders.
- Develop an individualized nursing care plan for the child with an immune or autoimmune disorder.
- Describe the psychosocial impact of chronic immune disorders on children.
- Devise a nutrition plan for the child with immunodeficiency.
- Develop child/family teaching plans for the child with an immune or autoimmune disorder.

SECTION I: ASSESSING YOUR UNDERSTANDING

Activity A FILL IN THE BLANKS

1. In systemic lupus erythematosus (SLE), autoantibodies react with the child's _____ to form immune complexes.

2. _____ is the movement of white blood cells to an inflamed or infected area of the body in response to chemicals released by neutrophils, monocytes, and the suffering tissue.

3. Primary immune deficiencies such as SCID and Wiskott–Aldrich syndrome are cured only by _____ or stem cell transplantation.

4. The malar rash of SLE resembles the shape of a _____.

5. For most children only allergies to fish, shellfish, tree nuts, and _____ persist into adulthood.

6. A _____ rash is often an early sign of a graft-versus-host disease that is developing in response to a bone marrow or stem cell transplant.

7. HIV infects the CD4 cells, also known as the _____ cells.

Activity B MATCHING

Match the medication in Column A with the appropriate indication in Column B.

Column A

_____ **1.** Cyclophospha-mide

_____ **2.** Protease inhibitors

_____ **3.** Cyclosporine A

_____ **4.** Methotrexate

_____ **5.** NSAIDs

Column B

a. Severe polyarticular juvenile idiopathic arthritis (JIA)

b. Prevention of rejection of renal transplants

c. JIA

d. Treatment of HIV as part of three-drug regimen

e. Severe SLE

Activity C SEQUENCING

Place the following anaphylaxis treatment priorities in the proper sequence.

1. Administration of corticosteroids

2. Injection of intramuscular epinephrine

3. Administration of intravenous diphenhydramine

4. Assessment of airway and support of the airway, breathing, and circulation

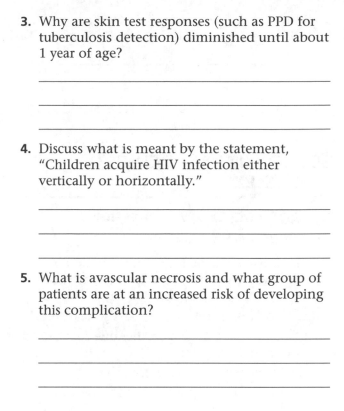

Activity D SHORT ANSWERS

Briefly answer the following.

1. What is the complement in relation to the immune system?

_____

_____

_____

2. Which laboratory test for HIV requires serial testing? Why?

_____

_____

_____

3. Why are skin test responses (such as PPD for tuberculosis detection) diminished until about 1 year of age?

_____

_____

_____

4. Discuss what is meant by the statement, "Children acquire HIV infection either vertically or horizontally."

_____

_____

_____

5. What is avascular necrosis and what group of patients are at an increased risk of developing this complication?

_____

_____

_____

SECTION II: APPLYING YOUR KNOWLEDGE

Activity E CASE STUDY

A 15-year-old female presents with complaints of pain and swelling in her joints, weight gain, and fatigue. After further assessment the physician suspects SLE.

1. What laboratory and diagnostic tests may you expect the physician to order?

_____

_____

_____

2. The mother asks, "Will these tests confirm whether or not my daughter has lupus?" How would you respond?

_____

_____

_____

3. If the diagnosis is confirmed, what education will be necessary for the girl and her mother?

_____

_____

_____

SECTION III: PRACTICING FOR NCLEX

Activity F NCLEX-STYLE QUESTIONS

Answer the following questions.

1. The nurse is caring for a 6-month-old boy with Wiskott–Aldrich syndrome. The nurse teaches the parents which of the following:

   a. "Don't use a tub bath for daily cleansing."

   b. "Don't encourage a pacifier due to possible oral malformation."

   c. "Do not insert anything in the rectum."

   d. "Do not use a sponge bath for light cleaning."

2. The nurse is preparing to administer intravenous immunoglobulin (IVIG) for a child who has not had an IVIG infusion in over 10 weeks. The nurse knows to first:

   a. begin infusion slowly increasing to prescribed rate.

   b. assess for adverse reaction.

   c. obtain baseline physical assessment.

   d. premedicate with acetaminophen or diphenhydramine.

3. The nurse is providing instructions to the parents of a child with a severe peanut allergy. Which statement by the parents indicates a need for further teaching about the use of an epinephrine auto-injector?

   a. "We must massage the area for 10 seconds after administration."

   b. "We must make sure that the black tip is pointed downward."

   c. "The epinephrine autoinjector should be jabbed into the upper arm."

   d. "The epinephrine autoinjector must be held firmly for 10 seconds."

4. A nurse is caring for an infant whose mother is human immunodeficiency (HIV) positive. The nurse knows that which diagnostic test result will be positive even if the child is not infected with the virus?

   a. Erythrocyte sedimentation rate

   b. Immunoglobulin electrophoresis

   c. Polymerase chain reaction test

   d. Enzyme-linked immunosorbent assay (ELISA)

5. A nurse is providing dietary interventions for a 12-year old with a shellfish allergy. Which response indicates a need for further teaching?

   a. "He will likely outgrow this."

   b. "He must avoid lobster and shrimp."

   c. "We must order carefully when dining out."

   d. "Wheezing is a sign of a severe reaction."

6. A nurse is conducting a physical examination of a 12-year-old girl with suspected systemic lupus erythematosus (SLE). How would the nurse best interview the girl?

   a. "Do you notice any wheezing when you breathe or a runny nose?"

   b. "Do you have any shoulder pain or abdominal tenderness?"

   c. "Have you noticed any new bruising or different color patterns on your skin?"

   d. "Have you noticed any hair loss or redness on your face?"

7. The nurse is providing teaching about food substitutions when cooking for the child with an allergy to eggs. Which response indicates a need for further teaching?

   a. "I must not feed my child eggs in any form."

   b. "I can use the egg white when baking, but not the yolk."

   c. "1 tsp yeast and ¼ cups warm water is a substitute in baked goods."

   d. "1 teaspoon baking powder equals one egg in a recipe."

8. A nurse in the emergency department is examining an 18-month old with lip edema, urticaria, stridor, and tachycardia. The nurse immediately suspects:

   a. severe polyarticular juvenile idiopathic arthritis.

   b. anaphylaxis.

   c. systemic lupus erythematosus.

   d. severe combined immunodeficiency.

9. The nurse is providing teaching for the parents of a child with a latex allergy. The nurse tells the client to avoid which food?

   a. Blueberries

   b. Pumpkins

   c. Bananas

   d. Pomegranates

10. The nurse is caring for a child with juvenile idiopathic arthritis (JIA). There is involvement of five or more small joints and it is affecting the body symmetrically. This tells the nurse which information about the child?

    a. Has polyarticular JIA

    b. Has systemic JIA

    c. Has pauciarticular JIA

    d. Is at risk for anaphylaxis

11. The child has a peanut allergy and accidentally ate food that contained peanuts. Which clinical manifestations of anaphylaxis should the nurse expect to find? Select all that apply.

    a. The child's pulse is 52 beats per minute.

    b. The child states that his tongue feels "too big" for his mouth.

    c. The child has developed hives on his face and trunk.

    d. The child states he feels like he might "throw up".

    e. The child states that he feels like he might faint.

12. The nurse is preparing to administer the child's dose of intravenous immune globulin (IVIG). Which actions should the nurse take? Select all that apply.

    a. Prepare to administer the medication ventrogluteal site as an intramuscular injection.

    b. Take baseline vital signs and monitor the vital signs during the infusion.

    c. Prepare to give acetaminophen to the child.

    d. Prepare to give diphenhydramine to the child.

    e. Mix the medication with the child's intravenous antibiotic.

13. The nurse is assessing children in a physician's office. Who may have a primary immunodeficiency? Select all that apply.

    a. Child diagnosed with six episodes of acute otitis media during the previous year.

    b. Child with oral thrush that is unresolved with treatment.

    c. Child admitted to the hospital three times within the last year with pneumonia.

    d. Child diagnosed with a severe case of acute sinusitis during the last year.

    e. Child who has taken antibiotics for the last 3 months without evidence of clearing of the infection.

14. The young girl has been diagnosed with juvenile idiopathic arthritis (JIA) and has been prescribed methotrexate. Which statements by the child's parent indicate that adequate learning has occurred? Select all that apply.

    a. "We'll need to bring her back in for some laboratory tests after she starts methotrexate."

    b. "She can take methotrexate with yogurt or chocolate milk."

    c. "She may start feeling better by next week."

    d. "Swimming sounds like a good exercise for her."

    e. "A warm bath before bed might help her sleep better."

15. The nurse is assessing a child with a complex medical history that includes fatigue, Raynaud phenomenon, anemia, and photosensitivity. The nurse should anticipate that this child may require which treatment?

    a. Antiretroviral therapy

    b. Administration of intravenous immunoglobulin (IVIG)

    c. Phototherapy

    d. Corticosteroid therapy

Nursing Care of the Child With an Alteration in Metabolism/ Endocrine Disorder

Learning Objectives

Upon completion of the chapter, you will be able to:

■ Describe the major components and functions of a child's endocrine system.

■ Differentiate between the anatomic and physiologic differences of the endocrine system in children versus adults.

■ Identify the essential assessment elements, common diagnostic procedures, and laboratory tests associated with the diagnosis of endocrine disorders in children.

■ Identify the common medications and treatment modalities used for palliation of endocrine disorders in children.

■ Distinguish specific disorders of the endocrine system affecting children.

■ Link the clinical manifestations of specific disorders in the endocrine system of a child with the appropriate nursing diagnoses.

■ Establish the nursing outcomes, evaluative criteria, and interventions for a child with specific disorders in the endocrine system.

■ Develop child/family teaching plans for the child with an endocrine disorder.

SECTION I: ASSESSING YOUR UNDERSTANDING

Activity A FILL IN THE BLANKS

1. Insulin is developed and secreted by beta cells, located in the islets of _____ in the pancreas.

2. Ophthalmic changes, due to hyperthyroidism, include _____, which is less pronounced in children.

3. The most common initial symptoms of diabetes mellitus reported are _____ and polydipsia.

4. Twitching of the extremities, referred to as _____, is related to hypocalcemia in children with hypoparathyroidism.

5. Slow, deep _____ respirations are characteristic of air hunger during metabolic acidosis.

6. Dwarfism is due to a growth hormone _____.

7. The presence of a goiter is typically associated with _____.

Activity B LABELING

Circle the areas on the body corresponding with insulin injection sites.

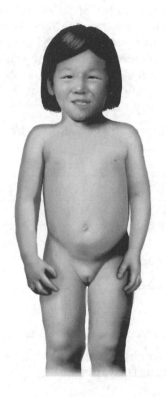
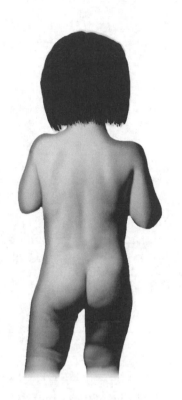

Activity C MATCHING

Match the gland in Column A with the proper word or phrase in Column B.

Column A

____ **1.** Adrenal gland

____ **2.** Pancreas

____ **3.** Parathyroid

____ **4.** Thymus

____ **5.** Thyroid

Column B

a. Humoral factors

b. Calcium and phosphorus concentration

c. Glucagon and somatostatin

d. Regulation of metabolism, growth, and bone development

e. Mineralocorticoids

Activity D SEQUENCING

Place the following insulin types in the proper order of their onset times:

1. Lispro

2. NPH

3. Regular

4. Glargine

Activity E **SHORT ANSWERS**

Briefly answer the following.

1. What are the teaching topics needed to educate parents of children with diabetes mellitus?

   _____

   _____

   _____

2. List signs and symptoms of hypothyroidism and hyperthyroidism.

   _____

   _____

   _____

3. What are the nursing implications when teaching, discussing, and caring for children with diabetes mellitus in the following age groups: (a) infants and toddlers, (b) preschoolers, (c) school age, (d) and adolescent?

   _____

   _____

   _____

4. Discuss how *Healthy People 2020* suggests addressing the goal of reducing the annual number of new cases of diagnosed diabetes in the population.

   _____

   _____

   _____

5. What teaching points should the nurse discuss with the parents of a child receiving growth hormone in regards to possible adverse reactions?

   _____

   _____

   _____

SECTION II: APPLYING YOUR KNOWLEDGE

Activity F **CASE STUDY**

A 12-year-old boy is admitted to the pediatric unit with weakness, fatigue, blurred vision, headaches, and mood and behavior changes. After further assessment he was diagnosed with diabetes mellitus type 2 (DM type 2). His mother states, "I know a little about diabetes and I thought type 2 diabetes was seen only in adults?"

1. How would you address the mother's question?

   _____

   _____

   _____

2. What will be the focus of your nursing management for Carlos and his family?

   _____

   _____

   _____

3. What challenges may you anticipate with educating Carlos?

   _____

   _____

   _____

SECTION III: PRACTICING FOR NCLEX

Activity G **NCLEX-STYLE QUESTIONS**

Answer the following questions.

1. The nurse is providing acute care for an 11-year-old boy with hypoparathyroidism. Which intervention is **priority**?

   a. Providing administration of calcium and vitamin D

   b. Ensuring patency of the IV site to prevent tissue damage

   c. Monitoring fluid intake and urinary calcium output

   d. Administering intravenous calcium gluconate as ordered

2. The nurse is assessing a 4-year-old girl with ambiguous genitalia. Which finding suggests congenital adrenal hyperplasia?

   a. Irregular heartbeat on auscultation

   b. Pubic hair and hirsutism

   c. Pain from constipation on palpation

   d. Hyperpigmentation of the skin

3. The nurse is assessing a 7-year-old girl with a headache, irritability, and vomiting. Her health history reveals she has had meningitis. Which intervention is **priority**?

   a. Notifying the physician of the neurologic findings

   b. Setting up safety precautions to prevent injury

   c. Monitoring urine volume and specific gravity

   d. Restoring fluid balance with IV sodium

4. The nurse is caring for a 4-year-old boy during a growth hormone stimulation test. Which task is **priority** in the care of this child?

   a. Providing a wet washcloth to suck

   b. Educating family about side effects

   c. Monitoring blood glucose levels

   d. Monitoring intake and output

5. The nurse is assessing a 1-month-old girl who, according to the mother, doesn't eat well. Which assessment suggests the child has congenital hypothyroidism?

   a. Frequent diarrhea

   b. Enlarged tongue

   c. Tachycardia

   d. Warm, moist skin

6. The nurse is caring for an obese 15-year-old girl who missed two periods and is afraid she is pregnant. Which finding indicates polycystic ovary syndrome?

   a. Acanthosis nigricans

   b. Blurred vision and headaches

   c. Increased respiratory rate

   d. Hypertrophy and weakness

7. The nurse is assessing a 16-year-old boy who has had long-term corticosteroid therapy. Which finding, along with the use of the corticosteroids, indicates Cushing disease?

   a. History of rapid weight gain

   b. Round, child-like face

   c. High weight-to-height ratio

   d. Delayed dentition

8. The nurse is caring for a 10-year-old girl with hyperparathyroidism. Which would be a primary nursing diagnosis for this child?

   a. Disturbed body image related to hormone dysfunction

   b. Imbalanced nutrition: more than body requirements

   c. Deficient fluid volume related to electrolyte imbalance

   d. Deficient knowledge related to treatment of the disease

9. The nurse is caring for a 12-year-old girl with hypothyroidism. Which information should be part of the nurse's teaching plan for the child and family?

   a. How to recognize vitamin D toxicity

   b. How to maintain fluid intake regimens

   c. Administering methimazole with meals

   d. Reporting irritability or anxiety

10. Which adolescents may have delayed puberty? Select all that apply.

    a. 14-year-old female who has not developed breasts

    b. 13-year-old female who has no pubic hair

    c. 15-year-old male who has had no changes to the size of testicles

    d. 14-year-old male who has no pubic hair

    e. 13-year-old male who has no changes in the appearance of his scrotum

11. The child may have developed thyroid storm. Which clinical manifestations of thyroid storm should the nurse expect to find? Select all that apply.

    a. Temperature of 103.2°F (39.6°C)

    b. Wet bed linen and report of feeling "sweaty"

    c. Apical heart rate of 172 beats per minute

    d. Report of feeling very tired and wanting to nap

    e. Mild-mannered and compliant demeanor

12. The nurse is teaching an 11-year-old boy and his family how to manage his diabetes. Which instruction does not focus on glucose management?

    a. Teaching that 50% of daily calories should be carbohydrates

    b. Instructing the child to rotate injection sites

    c. Encouraging the child to maintain the proper injection schedule

    d. Promoting higher levels of exercise than previously maintained

13. The child has developed hypothyroidism and has been prescribed sodium L-thyroxine. The starting dose is 12 mg/kg of body weight each day. The child weighs 72 lb (32.73 kg). Calculate the child's dose in micrograms. Record your answer using a whole number.

14. The young child has been diagnosed with a secondary growth hormone deficiency. The child weighs 58 lb (26.36 kg). The physician orders the child to receive 0.2 mg of growth hormone for each kilogram of body weight per week, divided into daily doses. How many milligrams of growth hormone would the child receive with each dose? Record your answer using three decimal places.

15. Rank the different types of insulin based on their duration of action beginning with the shortest to the longest duration.

    a. Lispro

    b. Humulin R

    c. Humulin N

    d. Lantus

Nursing Care of the Child With an Alteration in Genetics

Learning Objectives

Upon completion of the chapter, you will be able to:

- Discuss various inheritance patterns, including nontraditional patterns of inheritance.
- Discuss ethical and legal issues associated with genetic testing.
- Discuss genetic counseling and the role of the nurse.
- Discuss the nurse's role and responsibilities when caring for a child diagnosed with a genetic disorder and his or her family.
- Identify nursing interventions related to common laboratory and diagnostic tests used in the diagnosis and management of genetic conditions.
- Distinguish various genetic disorders occurring in childhood.
- Devise an individualized nursing care plan for the child with a genetic disorder.
- Develop child/family teaching plans for the child with a genetic disorder.

SECTION I: ASSESSING YOUR UNDERSTANDING

Activity A FILL IN THE BLANKS

1. Many time genes for the same trait have two or more _____ or versions that may be expressed.

2. Close blood relationship, referred to as _____, is a risk factor for genetic disorders.

3. The physical appearance, or _____, is the expression of a dominant gene or two recessive genes.

4. When a child receives different genes from the mother and father for the same trait, the child's genes are _____, and usually the dominant gene will be expressed.

5. Trisomy 21 is a disorder caused by _____ or an error in cell division during meiosis.

6. The _____ of an organism is its entire hereditary information encoded in the DNA.

7. A _____ is a long, continuous strand of DNA that carries genetic information.

Activity B MATCHING

Match the disorder in Column A with the description in Column B.

Column A

_____ **1.** Achondroplasia

_____ **2.** Apert syndrome

_____ **3.** CHARGE syndrome

_____ **4.** Marfan syndrome

_____ **5.** VATER association

Column B

a. No single feature present in all individuals

b. Not a diagnosis

c. Disorder of connective tissue

d. Disordered growth

e. Older paternal age

Activity C SHORT ANSWERS

Briefly answer the following.

1. Describe at least five major complications a child with Down syndrome can experience.

_____

_____

_____

2. Summarize the guiding principles for nurses providing support and education to families of children with genetic abnormalities.

_____

_____

_____

3. Briefly describe how the four errors of metabolism disorders are associated with specific odors of a child's excretions.

_____

_____

_____

4. Discuss the incidence of Trisomy 21.

_____

_____

_____

5. What are the common clinical manifestations that would alert the nurse to the likelihood that an infant has Trisomy 13?

_____

_____

_____

SECTION II: APPLYING YOUR KNOWLEDGE

Activity D CASE STUDY

A 1-week-old baby girl named Chloe is seen in your clinic secondary to abnormal newborn screening results. Her mother states, "Chloe has been doing great. She eats well, every 2 to 3 hours. I do not understand why we are here today. The nurse called and mentioned something about an inborn error of metabolism. I do not understand what that is and how Chloe could have that? She is not even sick."

1. How would you address the mother's concerns?

_____

_____

_____

2. The newborn screen came back positive for a fatty acid oxidation disorder, medium-chain acyl-CoA dehydrogenase deficiency. After further testing the diagnosis was confirmed. What education and nursing management will you provide?

_____

_____

_____

SECTION III: PRACTICING FOR NCLEX

Activity E NCLEX-STYLE QUESTIONS

Answer the following questions.

1. The nurse is assessing a newborn boy. Which findings indicate the possibility of neurofibromatosis? Select all that apply.

   a. History shows a grandparent had neurofibromatosis.

   b. Measurement shows a slightly larger head size.

   c. Inspection discloses several café au lait spots on the trunk.

   d. Observation reveals freckles on the lower extremities.

   e. Assessment reveals abnormal curvature of the spine.

2. The nurse is caring for a 9-year-old girl with Marfan syndrome. Which interventions should be part of the nursing plan of care for this child? Select all that apply.

   a. Arranging for respiratory therapy at home

   b. Promoting annual ophthalmology examinations

   c. Monitoring for bone and joint problems

   d. Encouraging use of antibiotics before dentistry

   e. Arranging for in home physical therapy

3. The nurse is examining an 8-year-old boy with chromosomal abnormalities. Which sign or symptom suggests the boy has Angelman syndrome?

   a. Palpation discloses reduced muscular tonicity.

   b. Observation reveals moonlike round face.

   c. History shows surgery for cleft palate repair.

   d. Observation shows jerky ataxic movement.

4. The nurse is caring for an 8-year-old girl who has just been diagnosed with fragile X syndrome. Which interventions is **priority**?

   a. Explain care required due to the disorder

   b. Assess family's ability to learn about the disorder

   c. Educate the family about available resources

   d. Screen to determine current level of functioning

5. The nurse is assessing a 2-week-old boy who was born at home and has not had metabolic screening. Which sign or symptom indicates phenylketonuria?

   a. Increased reflex action on palpation

   b. Signs of jaundice

   c. Musty or mousy odor to the urine

   d. Report of seizures

6. The nurse is examining a 2-year-old girl with VATER association. Which sign or symptom should be noted?

   a. Use of hearing aid

   b. Underdeveloped labia

   c. Cleft in the iris

   d. History of corrective surgery for anal atresia

7. The nurse is assessing infants in the newborn nursery. Who is most likely to have a major anomaly?

   a. 12-hour-old Caucasian male with café-au-lait spots on his trunk

   b. 16-hour-old African-American male with polydactyly

   c. Set of 6-hour-old Indian-American identical twin females with syndactyly

   d. 4-hour-old Asian-American female with protruding ears

8. The nurse is caring for a newborn girl with galactosemia. Which intervention will be necessary for her health?

   a. Adhering to a low-phenylalanine diet

   b. Eliminating dairy products from the diet

   c. Eating frequent meals and never fasting

   d. Supplementing with thiamine throughout the lifespan

9. The nurse is assessing a 3-year-old boy with Sturge–Weber syndrome. Which finding is most indicative of the disorder?

   a. Record shows the boy has seizures

   b. Observation shows behavior problems

   c. Inspection reveals a port-wine stain

   d. Observation indicates mild retardation

10. The 14-year-old boy may have Klinefelter syndrome. Which findings should the nurse expect? Select all that apply.

    a. Long trunk and short legs

    b. Shorter than average for his age

    c. Diagnosis of dyslexia

    d. Smaller than normal scrotum

    e. Significant amount of breast tissue

11. The nurse is inspecting a newborn with trisomy 18. Which findings should the nurse expect? Select all that apply.

    a. Very small head

    b. Extra fingers or toes

    c. Major heart problem

    d. Webbed fingers and toes

    e. Low-placed ears

12. The nurse is counseling a couple who are concerned that the woman has achondroplasia in her family. The woman is not affected. Which statement by the couple indicates the need for more teaching?

    a. "If the mother has the gene, then there is a 50% chance of passing it on."

    b. "If the father doesn't have the gene, then his son won't have achondroplasia."

   c. "If the father has the gene, then there is a 50% chance of passing it on."

   d. "Since neither one of us has the disorder, we won't pass it on."

13. The nurse is interviewing parents after their newborn was diagnosed with a genetic disorder. Which statements by the mother are associated with risk factors of genetic disorders? Select all that apply.

    a. "Our obstetrician told us that I wasn't making enough amniotic fluid during this pregnancy."

    b. "My husband is 55 years old."

    c. "Our alpha-fetoprotein came back negative when I was 18 weeks' pregnant."

    d. "My sister's baby was born with trisomy 18."

    e. "He is our first child."

14. The nurse is reviewing patterns of inheritance regarding genetic disorders. Which disorders are considered monogenic? Select all that apply.

    a. Autosomal dominant

    b. Autosomal recessive

    c. X-linked dominant

    d. Mitochondrial inheritance

    e. Genomic imprinting

15. The nurse is working for an obstetrician. Which couples may benefit from genetic counseling? Select all that apply.

    a. The mother-to-be is 29 years old.

    b. The father-to-be is 58 years old.

    c. The parents-to-be are cousins.

    d. The parents-to-be are African American.

    e. The parents-to-be have a child who was born blind and deaf.

Nursing Care of the Child With an Alteration in Behavior, Cognition, or Development

Upon completion of the chapter, you will be able to:

- Discuss the impact of alterations in mental health on the growth and development of infants, children, and adolescents.
- Describe techniques used to evaluate the status of mental health in children.
- Identify appropriate nursing assessments and interventions related to therapy and medications for the treatment of childhood and adolescent mental health disorders.
- Distinguish mental health disorders common in infants, children, and adolescents.
- Develop an individualized nursing care plan for the child with a mental health disorder.
- Develop child/family teaching plans for the child with a mental health disorder.

SECTION I: ASSESSING YOUR UNDERSTANDING

Activity A FILL IN THE BLANKS

1. Purging is self-induced vomiting or evacuation of the _____.

2. For a diagnosis of attention deficit/hyperactivity disorder (ADHD), the symptoms of impulsivity and hyperactivity begin before 7 years of age and must persist longer than _____ months.

3. Children with _____ experience difficulty with reading, writing, and spelling.

4. Burns that appear in a _____ or glove pattern are highly suspicious of inflicted burns.

5. _____ is defined as failure to provide a child with appropriate food, clothing, shelter, medical care, and schooling.

6. A disorder in which an adult meets her own psychological needs by having an ill child is known as _____.

7. Pervasive developmental disorder is another name for _____.

Activity B LABELING

Mark an X on all of the areas that indicate injury sites that are suspicious for abuse.

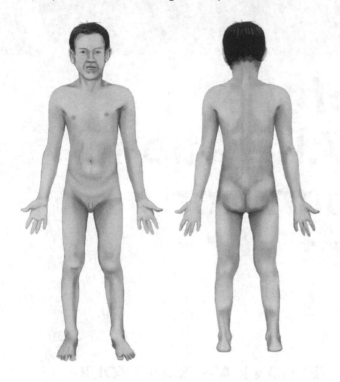

Activity C MATCHING

Match the term in Column A with the proper definition in Column B.

Column A

____ **1.** Affect

____ **2.** Anxiety

____ **3.** Binging

____ **4.** Dysgraphia

____ **5.** Dyscalculia

Column B

a. Feelings of dread, worry, discomfort

b. Emotional reaction associated with an experience

c. Problems with math and computation

d. Rapid excessive consumption of food or drink

e. Difficulty producing the written word

Activity D SHORT ANSWERS

Briefly answer the following.

1. What are some common behavior management techniques that can be utilized in the hospital, clinic, classroom, or home setting?

_____

_____

_____

2. According to the text, what common laboratory and diagnostic studies are ordered for the assessment of abuse?

_____

_____

_____

3. What is generalized anxiety disorder?

_____

_____

_____

4. Discuss the data that should be collected if the nurse suspects an adolescent patient is suffering from depression.

_____

_____

_____

5. What are the common classifications of medications used to treat ADHD and what is the intended goal of medication treatment?

_____

_____

_____

SECTION II: APPLYING YOUR KNOWLEDGE

Activity E CASE STUDY

Elisa, a 6-month-old female is seen in your clinic for her wellness check-up. Her mother states "I have seen so much about autism in the news lately. What is autism and how would I know if Elisa has this disorder?"

1. How would you explain autism to Elisa's mother?

   _____

   _____

   _____

2. What signs and symptoms would be exhibited by an infant or toddler who has autism?

   _____

   _____

   _____

SECTION III: PRACTICING FOR NCLEX

Activity F NCLEX-STYLE QUESTIONS

Answer the following questions.

1. A nurse is caring for a child with intellectual challenge. The medical chart indicates an IQ of 37. The nurse understands that the degree of disability is classified as:
   a. mild.
   b. moderate.
   c. severe.
   d. profound.

2. A nurse is caring for a 10-year old intellectually challenged girl hospitalized for a scheduled cholecystectomy. The girl expresses fear related to her hospitalization and unfamiliar surroundings. How should the nurse respond?
   a. "Don't worry, you will be going home soon."
   b. "Tell me about a typical day at home."
   c. "Have you talked to your parents about this?"
   d. "Do you want some art supplies?"

3. The nurse is examining a child with fetal alcohol syndrome (FAS). Which assessment finding should the nurse expect?
   a. Macrocephaly
   b. Low nasal bridge with short upturned nose
   c. Clubbing of fingers
   d. Short philtrum with thick upper lip

4. The school-aged child has been diagnosed with dysgraphia and dyslexia. Which tasks should this child find difficult? Select all that apply.
   a. Hopping on one foot
   b. Adding and subtracting numbers
   c. Jumping rope
   d. Writing words
   e. Spelling his name

5. The nurse is conducting a well-child assessment of a 3-year old. Which statement by the parents would warrant further investigation?
   a. "He spends a lot of time playing with his little cars."
   b. "He spends hours repeatedly lining up his cars."
   c. "He is very active and keeps very busy."
   d. "He would rather run around than sit on my lap and read a book."

6. The mother of a 10-year-old boy with attention deficit/hyperactivity disorder (ADHD) contacts the school nurse. She is upset because her son has been made to feel different by his peers because he has to visit the nurse's office for a lunch time dose of medication. The boy is threatening to stop taking his medication. How should the nurse respond?

   a. "He will need to learn to ignore the children, he needs this medication."

   b. "I can have the teacher speak with the other children."

   c. "You may want to talk to your physician about an extended release medication."

   d. "Remind him that his schoolwork may deteriorate."

7. The nurse is conducting an examination of a boy with Tourette syndrome. Which finding should the nurse expect to observe?

   a. Toe walking

   b. Sudden, rapid stereotypical sounds

   c. Spinning and hand flapping

   d. Lack of eye contact

8. A nurse is providing a routine wellness examination and follow-up for a 3-year old recently diagnosed with autism spectrum disorder (ASD). Which response indicates a need for additional referral or follow-up?

   a. "We have recently completed his individualized education plan."

   b. "We really like the treatment plan that has been created by his school."

   c. "We try to be flexible and change his routine from day to day."

   d. "We have a couple of baby sitters who know how to handle his needs."

9. The nurse is caring for a girl with anorexia who has been hospitalized with unstable vital signs and food refusal. The girl requires enteral nutrition. The nurse is alert for which complications that signal refeeding syndrome?

   a. Cardiac arrhythmias, confusion, seizures

   b. Orthostatic hypotension and hypothermia

   c. Hypothermia and irregular pulse

   d. Bradycardia with ectopy and seizures

10. A nurse is conducting a physical examination of an adolescent girl with suspected bulimia. Which assessment finding should the nurse expect?

    a. Eroded dental enamel

    b. Dry sallow skin

    c. Soft sparse body hair

    d. Thinning scalp hair

11. The nurse is providing teaching about medication management of attention deficit/hyperactivity disorder (ADHD). Which response indicates a need for further teaching?

    a. "We should give it to him after he eats breakfast."

    b. "This may cause him to have difficulty sleeping."

    c. "If he takes this medicine he will no longer have ADHD."

    d. "We should see an improvement in his schoolwork."

12. The 18-month-old toddler has been brought into the pediatrician's office by his parents. The nurse interviews the parents regarding the child's abilities. Which findings are warning signs that the toddler may have autism spectrum disorder? Select all that apply.

    a. Has never "babbled"

    b. Does not exhibit attempts to communicate by pointing to objects

    c. Does not use any words

    d. Does not speak in short sentences

    e. Cannot stand on tiptoe

13. The child has been diagnosed with attention deficit/hyperactivity disorder (ADHD) and has begun taking methylphenidate. Which findings are most likely adverse effects related to this medication? Select all that apply.

    a. Weight gain

    b. Occasional headache

    c. Increased amount of sleep

    d. Increased irritability

    e. Abdominal pain

14. The child has been diagnosed with a mental health disorder and the child's parents are beginning to incorporate behavior management techniques. Which statements by the child's parent indicate the need for further education? Select all that apply.

   a. "I use a higher pitched voice when I communicate with her."

   b. "I am quick to point out the things that she does that make me crazy."

   c. "We have set some boundaries that are nonnegotiable."

   d. "We tell her when she is doing something well."

   e. "We're trying to make her accountable and responsible for her own behavior."

15. The parents of an adolescent are concerned about his mental health and have brought the adolescent into the physician's office for an evaluation. Which statements by the parents indicate that the child may have a mental health disorder? Select all that apply.

   a. "He has started sleeping for only 3 hours each night."

   b. "He has lost 10 pounds over the last 4 months."

   c. "He hangs out with the same kids he always has."

   d. "He used to be a straight-A student and now he's bringing home Cs and Ds."

   e. "He still enjoys playing a lot of baseball."

CHAPTER 51

Nursing Care During a Pediatric Emergency

Learning Objectives

Upon completion of the chapter, you will be able to:

■ Identify various factors contributing to emergency situations among infants and children.
■ Discuss common treatments and medications used during pediatric emergencies.
■ Conduct a health history of a child in an emergency situation, specific to the emergency.
■ Perform a rapid cardiopulmonary assessment.
■ Discuss common laboratory and other diagnostic tests used during pediatric emergencies.
■ Integrate the principles of the American Heart Association and Pediatric Advanced Life Support in the comprehensive management of pediatric emergencies, such as respiratory arrest, shock, cardiac arrest, near drowning, poisoning, and trauma.

SECTION I: ASSESSING YOUR UNDERSTANDING

Activity A   FILL IN THE BLANKS

1. Children as old as 18 years of age should be managed using the _____ advanced life support guidelines.

2. Use the mnemonic _____ to remember which drugs may be given via the tracheal route.

3. The assessment and management of the _____ of a prearresting or arresting child is always the first intervention in a pediatric emergency situation.

4. A nonreactive _____ indicates the need for immediate relief of increased intracranial pressure.

5. Circumoral pallor or _____ is a late and often ominous sign of respiratory distress.

6. To open the airway of a victim suspected of having a neck injury the rescuer should utilize the _____ technique.

7. The best place to check the pulse in a child is either at the _____ or carotid site.

Activity B **LABELING**

Identify the arrhythmia by placing the proper arrhythmia type under the appropriate illustration.

1. Supraventricular tachycardia
2. Ventricular tachycardia
3. Sinus tachycardia
4. Coarse ventricular fibrillation

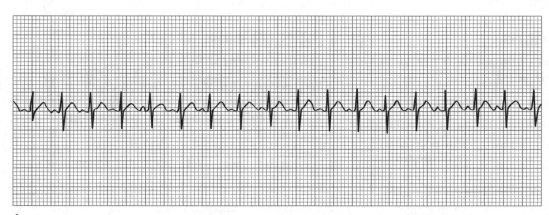

A

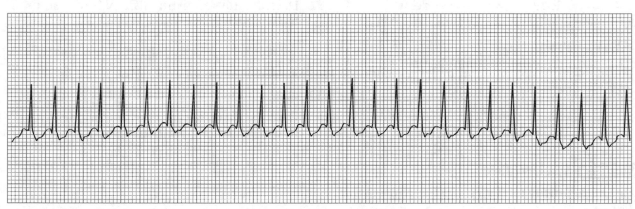

B

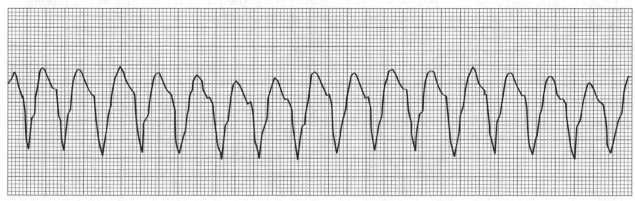

C

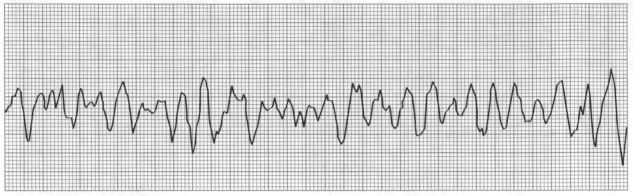

D

Activity C MATCHING

Match the test in Column A with the correct statement in Column B.

Column A

_____ **1.** Arterial blood gas

_____ **2.** Chest X-ray

_____ **3.** Computerized tomography

_____ **4.** Toxicology panel

_____ **5.** Urinalysis

Column B

a. Usually available in emergency department

b. Accompany the child to observe and manage

c. Never delay resuscitation efforts pending results

d. Notify laboratory of drugs the child is taking

e. Standards vary with agency used

Activity D SEQUENCING

Place the following CPR steps in the proper order:

1. Administer 100% oxygen

2. Evaluate heart rate and pulses

3. Look, listen, feel for respirations

4. Position to open airway

5. Suction

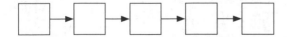

Activity E SHORT ANSWERS

Briefly answer the following.

1. Describe rates of compression to breaths and the hand positions used with CPR for infants and children for both one-person and two-person CPR.

_____

_____

_____

2. Describe how to distinguish SVT from sinus tachycardia.

_____

_____

_____

3. Describe the proper procedure for one person to ventilate a child with a bag valve mask.

_____

_____

_____

4. What is the purpose of using cricoid pressure during resuscitation?

_____

_____

_____

5. Discuss the mnemonic "DOPE" in regards to a child who is intubated.

_____

_____

_____

SECTION II: APPLYING YOUR KNOWLEDGE

Activity F CASE STUDY

A nurse is providing training for pediatric emergencies to a day care staff, including CPR, use of a defibrillator, poisonings, and near-drowning interventions. One of the day care providers states that she didn't think automatic external defibrillators (AEDs) were used for children. Another day care provider questions how the chain of survival is different for children compared to adults since she was certified in adult CPR several months ago.

1. How would you respond to the question regarding the use of AEDs with children?

    _____

    _____

    _____

2. How does the chain of survival for children differ from the chain of survival for adults?

    _____

    _____

    _____

SECTION III: PRACTICING FOR NCLEX

Activity G NCLEX-STYLE QUESTIONS

Answer the following questions.

1. A 6-year-old girl who is being treated for shock is pulseless with an irregular heart rate of 32 bpm. Which intervention is **priority**?
    a. Give three doses of epinephrine
    b. Administer two consecutive defibrillator shocks
    c. Initiate cardiac compressions
    d. Defibrillate once followed by three cycles of cardiopulmonary resuscitation (CPR)

2. The parents of a 7-month-old boy with a broken arm agree on how the accident happened. Which account would lead the nurse to suspect child abuse?
    a. "He was climbing out of his crib and fell."
    b. "He fell out of a shopping cart in the store."
    c. "Mom turned and he fell from changing table."
    d. "The gate was open and he fell down three steps."

3. A 3-year-old girl had a near-drowning incident when she fell into a wading pool. Which intervention is the highest **priority**?
    a. Suctioning the upper airway to ensure airway patency
    b. Inserting a nasogastric tube to decompress stomach
    c. Covering the child with warming blankets
    d. Assuring the child stays still during an x-ray

4. A 2-year-old boy is in respiratory distress. Which nursing assessment finding would suggest the child aspirated a foreign body?
    a. Hearing dullness when percussing the lungs
    b. Noting absent breath sounds in one lung
    c. Auscultating a low-pitched, grating breath sound
    d. Hearing a hyperresonant sound on percussion

5. The nurse is ventilating a 9-year-old girl with a bag valve mask. Which action would most likely reduce the effectiveness of ventilation?
    a. Checking the tail for free flow of oxygen
    b. Setting the oxygen flow rate at 15 L/minute
    c. Pressing down on the mask below the mouth
    d. Referring to Broselow tape for bag size

6. The nurse is examining a 10-year-old boy with tachypnea and increased work of breathing. Which finding is a late sign that the child is in shock?
    a. Blood pressure slightly less than normal
    b. Equally strong central and distal pulses
    c. Significantly decreased skin elasticity
    d. Delayed capillary refill with cool extremities

7. The nurse is examining a 10-month-old girl who has fallen from the back porch. Which assessment will directly follow evaluation of the "ABCs?"
   a. Observing skin color and perfusion
   b. Palpating the abdomen for soreness
   c. Auscultating for bowel sounds
   d. Palpating the anterior fontanel

8. The nurse is caring for a 10-month-old infant with signs of respiratory distress. Which is the best way to maintain this child's airway?
   a. Placing the hand under the neck
   b. Inserting a small towel under shoulders
   c. Using the head tilt chin lift technique
   d. Employing the jaw-thrust maneuver

9. The nurse is caring for a 4-year-old boy who is receiving mechanical ventilation. Which intervention is the **priority** when moving this child?
   a. Auscultating the lungs for equal air entry
   b. Checking the CO_2 monitor for a yellow display
   c. Watching for disconnections in the breathing circuit
   d. Monitoring the pulse oximeter for oxygen saturation

10. Cardiopulmonary resuscitation (CPR) is in progress on an 8-year-old boy who is in shock. Which nursing intervention is **priority**?
    a. Using a large bore catheter for peripheral venous access
    b. Inserting an indwelling urinary catheter to measure urine output
    c. Attaining central venous access via the femoral route
    d. Drawing a blood sample for arterial blood gas analysis

11. The child needs a tracheal tube placed. The child is 8 years old. Calculate the size, in millimeters, of the tracheal tube that should be used for this child. Record your answer using a whole number.

12. The nurse must calculate the adolescent's cardiac output. The child's heart rate is 76 bpm and the stroke volume is 75 mL. Calculate the child's cardiac output. Record your answer using a whole number.

13. The child's physician requests that the nurse should notify her if the child's urine output is less than 1 mL/kg of body weight each hour. The child weighs 56 lb (25.46 kg). Calculate the minimum amount of urine output the child should produce each hour. Record your answer using a whole number.

14. The child's ability to perfuse is poor due to inadequate circulation. The physician writes an order for the child to receive 20 mL of normal saline for each kilogram of body weight. The child will receive the normal saline as a bolus through a central intravenous line. The child weighs 78 lb (35.46 kg). Calculate the amount of normal saline the nurse should administer as a bolus. Record your answer using a whole number.

15. The nurse has been monitoring the child's vital signs. The child is 7 years old. Calculate the child's minimum acceptable systolic blood pressure. Record your answer using a whole number.

Answers

CHAPTER 1

SECTION I: ASSESSING YOUR UNDERSTANDING

Activity A FILL IN THE BLANKS

1. doula
2. family
3. emancipated
4. competence
5. morbidity
6. unintentional
7. guardians
8. protective
9. spirituality
10. easy

Activity B MATCHING

1. d **2.** e **3.** c **4.** a **5.** b

Activity C SEQUENCING

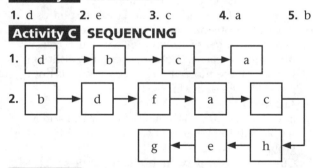

Activity D SHORT ANSWERS

1. Nurses need to look beyond the obvious "crushing chest pain" textbook symptom that heralds a heart attack in men. Risk factors of heart disease differ between men and women in several other ways—for example, menopause (associated with a signifi-cant rise in coronary events); diabetes, high cholesterol levels, and left ventricular hypertrophy; and repeated episodes of weight loss and gain (increased coronary morbidity and mortality).
2. A positive family history of breast cancer, aging, and irregularities in the menstrual cycle at an early age are major risk factors. Other risk factors include excess weight, not having children, oral contracep-tive use, excessive alcohol consumption, a high-fat diet, and long-term use of hormone replacement therapy.

3. The maternal mortality rate is the annual number of deaths from any cause related to or aggravated by pregnancy or its management (excluding accidental or incidental causes) during pregnancy and childbirth or within 42 days of termination of pregnancy, irre-spective of the duration and site of the pregnancy, per 100,000 live births, for a specified year.
4. Congenital anomalies remain the leading cause of infant mortality in the United States. In addition, low birth weight and prematurity are major indicators of infant health and significant predictors of infant mortality.
5. The Women, Infants, Children program provides nutritional supplementation and education to low-income families, women who are pregnant, postpartum or lactating, and infants and children up to age 5.
6. For positive reinforcement to be effective, feedback must be immediate, consistent, and frequent.

SECTION II: APPLYING YOUR KNOWLEDGE

Activity E CASE STUDY

1. Barriers may include: Financial barriers such as lack of insurance, not enough insurance, or inability to pay for services; sociocultural and ethnic factors such as lack of transportation and the need for both parents to work; knowledge barriers (e.g., lack of understanding of the importance of preventive health care), language barriers (e.g., speaking a different language than the health care providers), or spiritual barriers (e.g., religious beliefs discourag-ing some forms of treatment); health care delivery system barriers, such as the cost containment move-ment and possible limited access to specialty care—which greatly affects clients with chronic or long-term illnesses, facility hours of operation and inability to meet the needs of the clients and the possible negative attitudes of health care workers.
2. As the family is Hispanic, you need to remember that the father is viewed as the source of strength, wisdom, and self-confidence and the mother is the caretaker and decision-maker for health. Children are viewed as people to continue the family and culture. This family would also view health as God's will and may use folk medicine practices and payers, herbal teas and poultices for illness treatment.

SECTION III: PRACTICING FOR NCLEX

Activity F NCLEX-STYLE QUESTIONS

1. **Answer: B**
   RATIONALE: Breastfeeding reduces the rates of infection in infants and helps to improve long-term maternal health. Placing the infant on his or her back to sleep prevents SIDS but does not prevent infections in the infant. Feeding solids early is not recommended and has no effect on prevention of infections. Vitamins will not prevent infections by themselves and only help meet daily nutritional requirements and may not be necessary.

2. **Answer: D**
   RATIONALE: According to the ANA's code of ethics, the nurse could make arrangements for alternate care providers for a client undergoing an abortion, if the nurse ethically opposes the procedure. Nurses need to make their values and beliefs known to their managers before the situation occurs so that alternate staffing arrangement can be made. Under the ANA's code of ethics for nurses, the nurse need not provide emotional support to the client nor should he or she involve the client's family in convincing the client against an abortion.

3. **Answer: D**
   RATIONALE: The nurse should instruct the client to place the infant on his or her back to sleep to prevent SIDS. Wrapping the infant in warm clothes, providing very soft bedding, or feeding only breast milk will not prevent SIDS in the infant and may increase the risk.

4. **Answer: C**
   RATIONALE: The best way to have a positive impact on perinatal outcomes and reduce prematurity is to improve women's access to prenatal care. Tracking the incidence of violent crime does not give information on how to improve outcomes, nor does examining health disparities between ethnic groups or identifying specific national goals related to maternal and infant care without acting on the information. None of these address the true problem.

5. **Answer: C**
   RATIONALE: In the Arab American culture, women often are subordinate to men. The nurse would deal directly and exclusively with the husband. Arab women are not comfortable in mixed gender birthing classes either. If they were to attend a birthing class, they would be accompanied by a female relative. Inquiring about folk remedies used may be appropriate with African American families but not Arab cultures. Use of birth control to limit the number of children in an Arab family is looked down upon because children are valued.

6. **Answer: B**
   RATIONALE: Clients have the right to refuse medical treatment, based on the American Hospital Association's Patient Care Partnership (Bill of Rights). The nurse needs to heed the client's wishes and not give the medication.

7. **Answer: D**
   RATIONALE: The nurse should tell the client that the law specifically states that it is the client's decision who can have access to her health records and who cannot.

8. **Answer: C**
   RATIONALE: In cases of abuse and violence, nurses can serve their clients best by not trying to rescue them but by helping them build on their strengths, providing support, and empowering them to help themselves. Counseling the client's partner against abuse, helping the client know the legal impact of her situation, and introducing the client to a women's rights group to garner support are not the best ways of serving the client.

9. **Answer: B**
   RATIONALE: Congenital anomalies and chromosomal abnormalities are the leading causes of infant mortality in the United States. Abuse and neglect can be contributory to infant deaths but are not major predictors of infant mortality. SIDS is a cause of infant mortality but is not the greatest cause. Infant mortality statistics go from age 1 month to 1 year of age, not starting at birth.

10. **Answer: C**
    RATIONALE: Cardiovascular disease is the leading cause of death of women in the United States. Interventions that address reduction of this risk would be a priority. Elevations in death rates are in part attributed to the difficulty recognizing cardiovascular concerns in women. The second leading cause of death in women is cancer, specifically lung and cervical. Lower respiratory tract infections have increased over recent years as a cause of death in women but is not the number one cause. Alzheimer disease, although impacting the mortality rates of women, is not the greatest cause of death.

11. **Answer: A, C, E**
    RATIONALE: Culture is a view of the world and a set of traditions that are used by a specific social group and are transmitted to the next generation. Culture is a complex phenomenon involving many components, such as beliefs, values, language, time, personal space, and view of the world, all of which shape a person's actions and behavior. Race refers to ethnicity of an individual. The level of education provides information on an individual's socioeconomic status.

12. **Answer: D**
    RATIONALE: Extended families consist of parents, children, aunts, uncles, and/or grandparents. Blended families consist of parents who have children from previous marriages and potentially children from the new marriage. Groups of individuals who are not necessarily related by blood ties but who are living together to raise their families are referred to as communal families. In the binuclear family, children are members of two families as a result of custody or "joint parenting" arrangements.

13. **Answer: B**

RATIONALE: The behaviors most associated with traditional Hispanic culture include a desire to have their mother and female relative present during labor. There is a desire for privacy, making wish to be unclothed during labor unlikely. Hispanic women normally are very expressive during labor instead of being stoic.

14. **Answer: C**

RATIONALE: Assessing the child's daily oxygen supplement needs addresses the child's physical health but not the contemporary issue of quality of life. Helping the child modify trendy clothing to his needs, consulting with the school nurse, and adapting technologies for use outside of the home will improve the child's quality of life by building independence and self-esteem.

15. **Answer: B**

RATIONALE: It is important to log off whenever leaving the computer. The person that shares the nurse's log-on session may get called away from the computer leaving the nurse responsible for any breech in security. Keeping IDs and passwords confidential is basic computer security. E-mail is not a safe way to transmit confidential information for transmittal. Printing is safer. Closing patient files before stepping away from the computer helps ensure privacy.

16. **Answer: B**

RATIONALE: One of the factors associated with childhood injuries is parental drug or alcohol abuse. This is the leading cause for child mortality. Low–birth-weight babies are at higher risk for infant mortality. Foreign-born adoption is a factor for childhood morbidity. The child's hostility toward other children may be an environmental or psychosocial factor for childhood morbidity.

17. **Answer: D**

RATIONALE: Making phone calls to the parents of the children who were determined to need counseling is least important to the nursing plan of care. It is, no doubt, mandatory for the nurse to inform and support the parents. However, this intervention is the least important based on the nursing diagnosis of the children's need for counseling, the intervention to arrange for a counselor, and the adaptation of the intervention by providing counseling for the friends of the injured child.

18. **Answer: D**

RATIONALE: The consent of a parent or guardian is required for completion of a surgical procedure such as a circumcision. The parent in this case is under age. She may, however, consent for health care treatment of her child.

19. **Answer: D**

RATIONALE: Requests of the parents and child must be documented. The surgeon does not have the automatic authority to override the parents'

wishes. The child is under age and does not have decision-making authority.

20. **Answer: B**

RATIONALE: Questions of risks versus benefits often require the care team to examine options in the light of nonmaleficence; that is, the responsibility to avoid undue harm. Encouraging an adolescent to take ownership of her health will likely involve the principle of autonomy. Mediating in a family dispute or providing empathic care is less likely to involve the principle of nonmaleficence.

CHAPTER 2

SECTION I: ASSESSING YOUR UNDERSTANDING

Activity A FILL IN THE BLANKS

1. case management
2. Nonverbal
3. Community
4. Primary
5. encounters
6. Health

Activity B MATCHING

1. d   **2.** c   **3.** b   **4.** a

Activity C SEQUENCING

| 5 | → | 2 | → | 1 | → | 3 | → | 4 |

Activity D SHORT ANSWERS

1. Maternal and pediatric nurses provide care at the primary, secondary, and tertiary levels of prevention. The concept of primary prevention involves preventing the disease or condition before it occurs through health promotion activities, environmental protection, and specific protection against disease or injury. Its focus is on health promotion to reduce the person's vulnerability to any illness by strengthening the person's capacity to withstand physical, emotional, and environmental stressors. Secondary prevention is the early detection and treatment of adverse health conditions. This level of prevention is aimed at halting the disease, thus shortening its duration and severity to get the person back to a normal state of functioning. Tertiary prevention is designed to reduce or limit the progression of a permanent, irreversible disease or disability. The purpose of tertiary prevention is to restore individuals to their maximum potential.

2. Case management involves advocacy, communication, and resource management; client-focused comprehensive care across a continuum; and coordinated care with an interdisciplinary approach.

3. Some of the techniques that the nurse can use to enhance learning include:
   - Slowing down and repeating information often
   - Speaking in conversational style using plain, nonmedical language
   - "Chunking" information and teaching it in small bites using logical steps
   - Prioritizing information and teaching "survival skills" first
   - Using visuals, such as pictures, videos, and models
   - Teaching using an interactive, "hands-on" approach

4. The four main purposes of nursing documentation are as follows: the client's medical record serves as a communication tool that the entire interdisciplinary team can use to keep track of what the client and family has learned already and what learning still needs to occur. Next, it serves to testify to the education the family has received if and when legal matters arise. Third, it verifies standards set by the Joint Commission on Accreditation of Healthcare Organizations, Centers for Medicare and Medicaid Services (CMS), and other accrediting bodies that hold health care providers accountable for client and family education activities. And finally, it informs third-party payers of goods and services provided for reimbursement purposes.

5. Both contribute to improved transition from the hospital to the community for women, children, their families, and the health care team.

6. Community health nursing focuses on prevention and improvement of the health of populations and communities, addressing current and potential health needs of the population or community, promoting and preserving the health of a population regardless of a particular age group or diagnosis.

7. A birthing center provides a cross between a home birth and a hospital birth. Birthing centers offer a homelike setting with close proximity to a hospital in case of complications. Midwives are often the sole care providers in freestanding birthing centers, with obstetricians as backups in case of emergencies. Birthing centers usually have fewer restrictions and guidelines for families to follow and allow for more freedom in making laboring decisions. Birthing centers aim to provide a relaxing home environment and promote a culture of normalcy.

SECTION II: APPLYING YOUR KNOWLEDGE
Activity E CASE STUDY

1. Our hospital defines "family-centered care" as the delivery of safe, satisfying, high-quality health care that focuses on and adapts to the physical and psychosocial needs of the family. It is a cooperative effort of families and other caregivers that recognizes the strength and integrity of the family. What that really means is that when you come in to have your baby, we will not only take care of you and your newborn, but also include your husband as part of your family unit. We will listen to what you and your husband want and include it in your plan of care as best we can.

2. "Evidence-based nursing practice" involves the use of research or evidence in establishing a plan of care and implementing that care. It is a clinical decision making approach involving the integration of the best scientific evidence, client values and preferences, clinical circumstances, and clinical expertise to promote best outcomes.

SECTION III: PRACTICING FOR NCLEX
Activity F NCLEX-STYLE QUESTIONS

1. **Answer: D**
   RATIONALE: Case management focuses on coordinating health care services while balancing quality and cost outcomes. The nurse would be most likely involved with scheduling speech and respiratory services, ensuring these services are integrated into the client's plan of care in a coordinated manner. Helping a person learn a procedure or assessing the sanitary conditions of the home and establishing eligibility are not activities associated with case management.

2. **Answer: A**
   RATIONALE: Key elements in the provision of family-centered care include demonstrating interpersonal sensitivity, providing general health information and being a valuable resource, communicating specific health information, and treating people respectfully. Giving as much control as possible to the client and their family is essential in family-centered care. Give all the health information, both good and bad, that the client or their family request. Be culturally sensitive to your client and their family.

3. **Answer: B**
   RATIONALE: Promoting the health and safety of a group of clients is a common goal of nurses in all community settings. Removing health barriers to learning is the community nurse's goal. Determining the type of care a client needs is the goal of a triage nurse. Ensuring the health and well-being of women and their families is a goal of family-centered home care.

4. **Answer: B**
   RATIONALE: The nurse should instruct the client to take folic acid supplements, as consumption of folic acid supplements reduces the risk of developing NTDs in the growing fetus. Taking vitamin E supplements and consuming legumes and citrus fruits regularly during pregnancy do not reduce the risk of developing NTDs.

5. **Answer: D**
   RATIONALE: The nurse should inform the women that comprehensive community-centered care should be given to women during their reproductive years. This is because as their reproductive goals change, as does their health care needs.

A women's immune system does not weaken immediately after birth. Similarly, women do not have more health problems specifically during their reproductive years, nor are they more susceptible to stress during their reproductive years.

6. **Answer: B**

   RATIONALE: The nurse should include the monitoring of the physical and emotional well-being of the client's family members as part of her postpartum care in the home environment. The nurse should provide hands-on experience in infant care instead of providing self-help books to the client. The nurse should include parental needs along with the infant needs and focus on each of its areas while preparing her discharge plan, as the nurse should identify potential or developing complications not only in the infant but also in the client.

7. **Answer: A**

   RATIONALE: A nurse who thinks stereotypically may assign a client to a staff member who is of the same culture as the client because the nurse assumes that all people of that culture are alike. The nurse also may believe that clients with the same skin color may react in the same manner in similar social situations. Because stereotypes are preconceived ideas unsupported by facts, they may not be real or accurate. In fact, they can be dangerous because they are dehumanizing and interfere with accepting others as unique individuals.

8. **Answer: B**

   RATIONALE: Feng shui is the Chinese art of place-ment in which objects in the environment are position to induce harmony with chi. Reflexology is the use of deep massage on identified points of the foot and hand to scan and rebalance body parts that correspond to each point. Therapeutic touch involves the balancing of energy by center-ing. Aromatherapy involves the use of essential oils to stimulate the sense of smell for balancing mind, body, and spirit.

9. **Answer: C**

   RATIONALE: Asking questions or having private con-versations with the interpreter may make the family uncomfortable and destroy the nurse/client relation-ship. Translation takes longer than a same-language explanation and the family may need additional to clarify terms, and this must be considered so that the family is not rushed. Use of a nonprofessional may result in some inaccuracy in translating medical terminology but should not impact the trust of the family. Using a relative can upset the family relation-ships or cause legal problems but also does not affect trust with the healthcare providers.

10. **Answer: A**

    RATIONALE: Recognizing family strengths and indi-viduality is a key element of family-centered home care. Ensuring a safe, nurturing environment is

part of the assessment process prior to preparing the nursing plan of care. Equipment maintenance is important but not a part of family-centered care. The nurse should respect the family's different methods of coping rather than correcting them.

11. **Answer: D**

    RATIONALE: Atraumatic care refers to the delivery of care that minimizes or eliminates the psychological and physical distress experienced by children and their families in the health care system. The key principles of atraumatic care include preventing or minimizing physical stressors, preventing or minimizing separation of the child from the family, and promoting a sense of control. Allowing the parents to stay, allowing the child to touch the stethoscope, and explaining that the stethoscope may feel cold are appropriate. Wrapping the child so that he cannot move would be stressful and traumatic.

12. **Answer: D**

    RATIONALE: Trust, respect, and empathy are three factors needed to create and foster effective therapeutic communication between people. Literacy would be important for education.

13. **Answers: B, C, E**

    RATIONALE: To enhance learning, the nurse should speak in a conversational style using plain, non-medical language, chunk information with breaks every 10 to 15 minutes, prioritize and teach the "survival skills" or need-to-know information first, and use visuals such as pictures, videos, and models to facilitate learning.

14. **Answer: A, B, C**

    RATIONALE: Primary prevention activities would include drug education programs for schools, smoking cessation programs, and poison preven-tion educational programs. Cholesterol monitor-ing and fecal occult blood testing are examples of secondary prevention activities.

15. **Answer: C**

    RATIONALE: When working with an interpreter, it is important to allow additional time because, in some languages it takes longer to say the words than it does when speaking in English. The nurse should place herself so that she is facing the fam-ily and the family is facing her. The interpreter is the communication bridge, not the content expert. The nurse should talk directly to the family, not to the interpreter.

16. **Answer: A**

    RATIONALE: The first step to cultural competence is cultural awareness in which the person becomes aware of, appreciates, and becomes sensitive to the values, beliefs, customs, and behaviors that have shaped one's culture. Next, the nurse would obtain knowledge about various worldviews and then assess each client's unique cultural beliefs, values, and practices, ultimately engaging in cross-cultural interactions with people from culturally diverse backgrounds.

CHAPTER 3

SECTION I: ASSESSING YOUR UNDERSTANDING

Activity A FILL IN THE BLANKS

1. rugae
2. Prolactin
3. epididymis
4. urethra
5. endometrium
6. Skene
7. episiotomy
8. prostate
9. uterus
10. scrotum

Activity B MATCHING

1. e   2. c   3. b   4. d   5. a

Activity C SEQUENCING

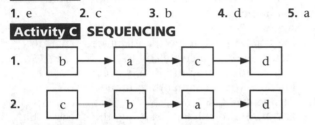

1. b → a → c → d

2. c → b → a → d

Activity D SHORT ANSWERS

1. The external female reproductive organs collectively are called the vulva. The vulva serves to protect the urethral and vaginal openings. The structures that make up the vulva include the mons pubis, the labia majora and minora, the clitoris, the structures within the vestibule, and the perineum.
2. Colostrum is a dark yellow fluid that contains more minerals and protein, but less sugar and fat, than mature breast milk. It is initially produced during pregnancy. After birth, colostrum is secreted for approximately a week, with a gradual conversion to mature breast milk. Colostrum is rich in maternal antibodies, especially immunoglobulin A, which offers protection for the newborn against enteric pathogens.
3. During the perimenopausal years, women may experience physical changes associated with decreasing estrogen levels, which may include vasomotor symptoms of hot flashes, irregular menstrual cycles, sleep disruptions, forgetfulness, irritability, mood disturbances, decreased vaginal lubrication, fatigue, vaginal atrophy, and depression.
4. Nurses can play a major role in assisting menopausal women by educating and counseling them about the multitude of options available for disease prevention, treatment for menopausal symptoms, and health promotion during this time of change in their lives.
5. The testes produce sperm and synthesize testosterone, which is the primary male sex hormone. Sperm is produced in the seminiferous tubules of the testes.
6. The bulbourethral (Cowper) glands are two small structures about the size of peas, located inferior to the prostate gland. They are composed of several tubes whose epithelial linings secrete a mucus-like fluid. It is released in response to sexual stimulation and lubricates the head of the penis in preparation for sexual intercourse. They gradually diminish in size with advancing age.

SECTION II: APPLYING YOUR KNOWLEDGE

Activity E CASE STUDY

1. The nurse should inform Susan about the following: the main function of the reproductive cycle is to stimulate growth of a follicle to release an egg and prepare a site for implantation if fertilization occurs; menstruation, the monthly shedding of the uterine lining, marks the beginning of a new cycle; the menstrual cycle involves a complex interaction of hormones; the ovarian cycle is the series of events associated with a developing oocyte (ovum or egg) within the ovaries; at ovulation, a mature follicle ruptures in response to a surge of LH, releasing a mature oocyte (ovum); the endometrial cycle is divided into three phases: the follicular or proliferative phase, the luteal or secretory phase, and the menstrual phase; the endometrium, ovaries, pituitary gland, and hypothalamus are all involved in the cyclic changes that help prepare the body for fertilization; the menstrual cycle results from a functional hypothalamic–pituitary–ovarian axis and a precise sequencing of hormones that lead to ovulation; if conception doesn't occur, menses ensues; and the one thing to remember is that whether a women's cycle is 28 or 120 days, ovulation takes place 14 days before menstruation.
2. The nurse should inform Susan that cycles vary in frequency from 21 to 36 days; bleeding lasts 3 to 8 days; blood loss averages 20 to 80 mL; the average cycle is 28 days long, but this varies; and irregular menses can be associated with irregular ovulation, stress, disease, and hormonal imbalances.
3. The range for the onset of menstruation is between 8 and 18 years. The average age is 12.8 years. There are several factors that influence the age of menstruation onset. Genetics is the most important factor in determining the age at which menarche starts, but geographic location, nutrition, weight, general health, nutrition, and cultural and social practices are also potential variables.

SECTION III: PRACTICING FOR NCLEX

Activity F NCLEX-STYLE QUESTIONS

1. **Answer: B**
   RATIONALE: To increase the chances of conceiving, the best time for intercourse is 1 or 2 days before ovulation. This ensures that the sperm meets the ovum at the right time. The average life of a sperm cell is 2 to 3 days, and the sperm cells will not be able to survive until ovulation if intercourse occurs a week before ovulation. The chances of conception are minimal for intercourse after ovulation.

2. **Answer: B**
   RATIONALE: The nurse should inform the client that the yellow fluid is called colostrum, and it contains more minerals and protein, but less sugar and fat, than mature breast milk and is also rich in maternal antibodies. The nurse should inform the client that, gradually, the production of colostrum stops and the production of regular breast milk begins, but there is no need to avoid breastfeeding when colostrum is being produced, if the client's culture allows for it. There is no need to modify diet or to feed formula to the infant.

3. **Answer: C**
   RATIONALE: During ovulation, some women can feel a pain around the time the egg is released on one side of the abdomen. Discomfort is referred to as mittelschmerz. The pain is not a sign of pregnancy, as the client experiences this pain regularly during ovulation. The pain is also not related to an irregular menstruation cycle or the client's exercise regimen.

4. **Answer: B**
   RATIONALE: There should be a significant increase in temperature, usually 0.5° to 1° F, within a day or two after ovulation has occurred. The temperature remains elevated for 12 to 16 days, until menstruation begins. The cause of this rise in temperature is the hormone progesterone. If there is no change in the woman's monthly temperature, the progesterone level should be assessed.

5. **Answer: B**
   RATIONALE: After menopause, the uterus shrinks and gradually atrophies. A full bladder, not menopause, causes the uterus to tilt backward. Cervical muscle content does not increase during menopause. Menopause has no significant effect on the outer layer of the cervix.

6. **Answer: D**
   RATIONALE: Progesterone is called the hormone of pregnancy because it reduces uterine contractions, thus producing a calming effect on the uterus, allowing pregnancy to be maintained. FSH is primarily responsible for the maturation of the ovarian follicle. LH is required for both the final maturation of preovulatory follicles and the luteinization of the ruptured follicle. Estrogen is crucial for the development and maturation of the follicle.

7. **Answer: C**
   RATIONALE: During cold conditions, the scrotum is pulled closer to the body for warmth or protection. The cremaster muscles in the scrotal wall contract to allow the testes to be pulled closer to the body. Frequency of urination has no significant impact in maintaining the scrotal temperature. Increase in blood flow to the genital area occurs primarily during erection and is not due to climatic conditions.

8. **Answer: C**
   RATIONALE: The nurse should inform the client that the duration of the flow is about 3 to 7 days. An average cycle length is about 21 to 36 days, not 15 to 20 days. In the ovary, 2 million oocytes are present at birth, and about 400,000 follicles are still present at puberty. Blood loss averages 20 to 80 mL, not 120 to 150 mL.

9. **Answer: C**
   RATIONALE: At ovulation, a mature follicle ruptures, releasing a mature oocyte (ovum). Ovulation always takes place 14 days, not 10 days, before menstruation. The lifespan of the ovum is only about 24 hours, not 48 hours; unless it meets a sperm on its journey within that time, it will die. When ovulation occurs, there is a drop, not a rise, in estrogen levels.

10. **Answer: B**
    RATIONALE: GnRH is secreted from the hypothalamus in a pulsatile manner throughout the reproductive cycle. It induces the release of FSH and LH to assist with ovulation, both of which are secreted by the anterior pituitary gland. Estrogen is secreted by the ovaries and is crucial for the development and maturation of the follicle.

11. **Answer: B**
    RATIONALE: The mature ovum is released from the ovary, resulting in the corpus luteum. Progesterone is produced by the corpus luteum. Estrogen is secreted by the ovaries. Glycogen is secreted by the endometrial glands during the luteal phase. Luteinizing hormone is not a product of the corpus luteum.

12. **Answer: A**
    RATIONALE: Cervical mucus should be alkaline to protect sperm from the acidic environment of the vagina. Colostrum, the dark yellow substance secreted from the breasts following birth, is a normal finding in a 1-day postdelivery client. The vaginal should have an acidic environment to aid in preventing ascending infections. The shape of the cervical os should be a transverse slit following birth.

13. **Answer: D**
    RATIONALE: During ovulation, the cervix produces thin, clear, stretchy, slippery mucus that is designed to capture the man's sperm, nourish it, and help the sperm travel up through the cervix to meet the ovum for fertilization.

14. **Answer: B**
    RATIONALE: The testes should have two nut-like structures present in males. The third mass could indicate a tumor or other anomaly. All the remaining clients have normal, expected findings.

15. **Answer: 3, 5, 1, 4, 2**
    RATIONALE: Bartholin glands, when stimulated, secrete mucus that supplies lubrication for intercourse. Endocrine glands secrete hormones for various bodily functions. The pituitary gland releases follicle-stimulating hormone to stimulate the ovary to produce follicles. Skene glands secrete a small amount of mucus to keep the opening to the urethra moist and lubricated for the passage of urine.

CHAPTER 4

SECTION I: ASSESSING YOUR UNDERSTANDING

Activity A FILL IN THE BLANKS

1. Adenomyosis
2. prostaglandin
3. Laparoscopy
4. perimenopause
5. vasectomy
6. medical
7. Osteoporosis
8. spinnbarkeit
9. basal
10. minipills

Activity B MATCHING

1. c **2.** d **3.** a **4.** e **5.** b

Activity C SEQUENCING

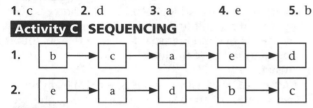

Activity D SHORT ANSWERS

1. Common laboratory tests ordered to determine the cause of amenorrhea are karyotype, ultrasound to detect ovarian cysts, pregnancy test, thyroid function studies, prolactin level, FSH level, LH level, 17-ketosteroids tests, laparoscopy, and CT scan of head.
2. Menopause refers to the cessation of regular menstrual cycles. It is the end of menstruation and childbearing capacity. Natural menopause is defined as 1 year without a menstrual period. The average age at which it occurs is 51 years.
3. The risk factors associated with endometriosis are increasing age, family history of endometriosis, short menstrual cycle, long menstrual flow, young age at menarche, and few or no pregnancies.
4. Infertility refers to the inability to conceive a child after a year of regular sexual intercourse unprotected by contraception, or the inability to carry a pregnancy to term. Secondary infertility results when an individual is unable to conceive after having done so in the past.
5. In the Two-Day Method, women observe the presence or absence of cervical secretions by examining toilet paper or underwear or by monitoring their physical sensations. Every day, the woman asks two simple questions: "Did I note any secretions yesterday?" and "Did I note any secretions today?" If the answer to either question is yes, she considers herself fertile and avoids unprotected intercourse. If the answers are no, she is unlikely to become pregnant from unprotected intercourse on that day.
6. Intrauterine systems (IUSs) are small, plastic, T-shaped objects that are placed inside the uterus to provide contraception. They prevent pregnancy by making the endometrium of the uterus hostile to implantation of a fertilized ovum, by causing a nonspecific inflammatory reaction.

SECTION II: APPLYING YOUR KNOWLEDGE

Activity E CASE STUDY

1. Amenorrhea is a normal feature in prepubertal, pregnant, and postmenopausal women. The two categories of amenorrhea are primary and secondary amenorrhea. Primary amenorrhea is defined as either absence of menses by age 14, with absence of growth and development of secondary sexual characteristics, or absence of menses by age 16, with normal development of secondary sexual characteristics. Ninety-eight percent of American girls menstruate by age 16.
2. Causes of primary amenorrhea related to Alexa may include extreme weight gain or loss, stress from a major life event, excessive exercise, or eating disorders such as anorexia nervosa or bulimia. Primary amenorrhea is also caused by congenital abnormalities of the reproductive system, Cushing disease, polycystic ovarian syndrome, hypothyroidism, and Turner syndrome; other causes are imperforate hymen, chronic illness, pregnancy, cystic fibrosis, congenital heart disease, and ovarian or adrenal tumors.
3. The treatment of primary amenorrhea involves correcting any underlying disorders as well as providing estrogen replacement therapy to stimulate the development of secondary sexual characteristics. If a pituitary tumor is the cause, it might be treated with drug therapy, surgical resection, or radiation therapy. Surgery might be needed to correct any structural abnormalities of the genital tract.
4. The nurse should address the diverse causes of amenorrhea, the relationship to sexual identity, and the possibility of infertility and more serious problems. In addition, the nurse should inform Alexa about the purpose of each diagnostic test, how it is performed, and when the results will be available. Sensitive listening, interviewing, and presenting treatment options are of paramount importance to gaining the client's cooperation and understanding. Nutritional counseling is also vital in managing this disorder, especially when the client has findings suggestive of an eating disorder. Although not all causes can be addressed by making lifestyle changes, the nurse can still emphasize maintaining a healthy lifestyle.

SECTION III: PRACTICING FOR NCLEX

Activity F NCLEX-STYLE QUESTIONS

1. **Answer: D**
   RATIONALE: The nurse should instruct the client to deliver the semen sample to the laboratory for analysis within 1 to 2 hours after ejaculation. The client should also be instructed to collect the sample in a specimen container, not a condom or

plastic bag. The client needs to abstain from sexual activity for at least 24 hours before giving the sample, but he need not avoid strenuous activity.

2. **Answer: D**
   RATIONALE: When assessing a client for amenorrhea, the nurse should document facial hair and acne as possible evidence of androgen excess secondary to a tumor. The nurse may observe and should document hypothermia, bradycardia, hypotension, and reduced subcutaneous fat in women with anorexia nervosa; however, these are not symptoms of excess androgen.

3. **Answer: B**
   RATIONALE: The nurse should explain to the client that the fertility awareness method relies on the assumption that the "unsafe period" is approximately 6 days; 3 days before and 3 days after ovulation. The method also assumes that sperm can live up to 5 days, not just 24 hours after intercourse. An ovum lives up to 24 hours after being released from the ovary. The exact time of ovulation cannot be determined, so 2 to 3 days are added to the beginning and end to avoid pregnancy.

4. **Answer: B, D, E**
   RATIONALE: When instructing a client with dysmenorrhea on how to manage her symptoms, the nurse should ask her to increase water consumption, use heating pads or take warm baths, and increase exercise and physical activity. Water consumption serves as a natural diuretic, heating pads or warm baths help increase comfort, and exercise increases endorphins and suppresses prostaglandin release. The nurse should also tell the client to limit salty foods to prevent fluid retention during menstruation and to keep legs elevated while lying down, because this helps increase comfort.

5. **Answer: D**
   RATIONALE: The nurse should prepare the client for a laparoscopy to obtain a definitive diagnosis; laparoscopy allows for direct visualization of the internal organs and helps confirm the diagnosis. A hysterosalpingogram assesses tubal patency, and a clomiphene citrate challenge test determines ovarian function; these tests are not used to determine the extent of endometriosis.

6. **Answer: C**
   RATIONALE: The nurse should explain that during ovulation, the cervix is high or deep in the vagina. The os is slightly open during ovulation. Under the influence of estrogen during ovulation, the cervical mucus is copious and slippery and can be stretched between two fingers without breaking. It becomes thick and dry after ovulation, under the influence of progesterone.

7. **Answer: C**
   RATIONALE: Recent studies have shown that the extended use of active OC pills carries the same safety profile as the conventional 28-day regimen. This option helps reduce the number of periods

and is as effective as the conventional regimen. There is no evidence to suggest that discontinuation of active OCs will not ensure restoration of fertility. Depo-Provera, not active OC pills, prevents pregnancy for 3 months at a time.

8. **Answer: D**
   RATIONALE: The client should be instructed to take her temperature before rising and record it on a chart. If using this method by itself, the client should avoid unprotected intercourse until the BBT has been elevated for 3 days. The client should be informed that other fertility awareness methods should be used along with BBT for better results. The oral method is better suited than the axillary method for taking the temperature in this case.

9. **Answer: D**
   RATIONALE: The best option for a client who is not well educated would be the Standard Days Method with CycleBeads, as the 32 color-coded CycleBeads are easy to use and understand. An injection of medroxyprogesterone would also suit this client, as it works by suppressing ovulation and the production of follicle-stimulating hormone and luteinizing hormone by the pituitary gland and prevents pregnancy for 3 months at a time. BBT requires the client to take and chart her body temperature; this may be difficult for the client to follow. Coitus interruptus is a method in which the man controls his ejaculation and ejaculates outside the vagina; this suggests that the client rely solely on the cooperation and judgment of her spouse. The lactational amenorrhea method works as a temporary method of contraception only for breastfeeding mothers.

10. **Answer: A, C, E**
    RATIONALE: The nurse should tell the client to inspect the cervical cap before insertion for cracks, holes, or tears and to wait approximately 30 minutes after insertion before engaging in sexual intercourse to be sure that a seal has formed between the rim and the cervix. In addition, the cap should not be used during menses because of the potential for toxic shock syndrome; an alternative method such as condoms should be used during this time. The client should be told not to apply spermicide to the rim because it may interfere with the seal. It should be left in place for a minimum of 6 hours after sexual intercourse.

11. **Answer: B**
    RATIONALE: Considering the client's smoking habit, combination oral contraceptives may be contraindicated. Oral contraceptives are highly effective when taken properly, but can aggravate many medical conditions, especially in women who smoke. The medroxyprogesterone injection or copper intrauterine devices are not contraindicated in this client and can be used with certain precautions. Implantable contraceptives are subdermal time release implants that deliver synthetic

progestin; these are highly effective and are not contraindicated in this client.

12. **Answer: B**
    RATIONALE: The client is seeking a medical abortion. The nurse should inform the client that such medications are effectively used to terminate a pregnancy only during the first trimester, not the second. The medications are available as a vaginal suppository or in oral form and do not present a high risk of respiratory failure. Sterilization, not abortion, is considered a permanent end to fertility.

13. **Answer: B**
    RATIONALE: Because the client has multiple sex partners, condoms will help offer protection against sexually transmitted infections (STIs) and are best suited for her needs. The client cannot use an IUD because of her history of various pelvic infections. Although OCs will help the client as a means of contraception, this method is not the best choice for her because it does not offer protection against STIs. Tubal ligation is a sterilization procedure and does not suit the client's purpose.

14. **Answer: B, C, E**
    RATIONALE: The nurse needs to clear up misconceptions by explaining to clients that taking birth control pills does not protect against STIs and that irregular menstruation or douching after sex does not prevent pregnancy. The nurse also needs to confirm that breastfeeding does not protect against pregnancy and that pregnancy can occur during menses.

15. **Answer: A**
    RATIONALE: The nurse should inform the client that IUDs cause monthly periods to become lighter, shorter, and less painful. Monthly periods reduce in number with use of oral contraceptives, but not with use of IUDs.

16. **Answer: B, C, D**
    RATIONALE: The nurse should instruct the client to wet the sponge before inserting it, to insert it 24 hours before intercourse, and to leave it in place for at least 6 hours following intercourse, to be effective. The sponge should not be replaced every 2 hours because this will reduce its efficacy. A contraceptive sponge covers the cervix and releases spermicide. It does not protect against STIs. Therefore, keeping the sponge for more than 30 hours will not prevent STIs, but will increase risk of toxic shock syndrome.

17. **Answer: A**
    RATIONALE: Because the client has a history of cardiac problems, long-term hormone replacement therapy is contraindicated. This is because there is an increased risk of heart attacks and strokes. The client should instead be asked to consider options with minimized risk, such as lipid-lowering agents, or nonhormonal therapies, such as bisphosphonates and selective estrogen receptor modulators.

18. **Answer: C**
    RATIONALE: The client is likely to be experiencing vaginal atrophy, which occurs during menopause because of declining estrogen levels. The condition can be managed with the use of over-the-counter moisturizers and lubricants. A positive outlook on sexuality and a supportive partner may make the sexual experience enjoyable and fulfilling, whereas a support group may reduce the client's anxiety. However, these will not alleviate the client's discomfort. Menopause can be a physically and emotionally challenging time for women because of the stigma of an "aging" body; the nurse should be sensitive to the client's feelings when discussing these changes.

CHAPTER 5

SECTION I: ASSESSING YOUR UNDERSTANDING

Activity A FILL IN THE BLANKS

1. Trichomoniasis
2. tertiary
3. Ectoparasites
4. Scabies
5. thrush
6. Syphilis
7. liver
8. chlamydia
9. CD4
10. chlamydia

Activity B LABELING

1. a. The disease in the photograph is genital herpes simplex.
   b. The clinical manifestations of genital herpes include blister-like lesions. Additional symptoms may include dysuria, headache, fever, and muscle aches.
   c. The disease is not curable. Pharmacologic management may include antiviral therapies such as acyclovir (Zovirax), famciclovir (Famvir), or valacyclovir (Valtrex).

2. a. The disease in the photograph is an STI known as genital warts.
   b. Risk factors associated with genital warts include multiple sex partners, age (15 to 25), sex with a male who has had multiple sexual partners, and first intercourse at 16 or younger.
   c. Treatments used in for genital warts include:
      • Topical trichloroacetic acid 80% to 90%
      • Liquid nitrogen cryotherapy
      • Topical imiquimod 5% cream (Aldara)
      • Topical podophyllin 10% to 25%
      • Laser carbon dioxide vaporization
      • Client-applied Podofilox 0.5% solution or gel
      • Simple surgical excision
      • Loop electrosurgical excisional procedure
      • Intralesional interferon therapy

Activity C MATCHING

1. c **2.** a **3.** b **4.** f **5.** d **6.** e

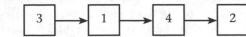

Activity D SEQUENCING

3 → 1 → 4 → 2

Activity E SHORT ANSWERS

1. Predisposing factors that may increase the chances of vulvovaginal candidiasis include pregnancy; use of oral contraceptives with a high estrogen content; use of broad-spectrum antibiotics; diabetes mellitus; use of steroids and immunosuppressive drugs; HIV infection; wearing tight, restrictive clothes and nylon underpants; and trauma to vaginal mucosa from chemical irritants or douching.

2. Hepatitis A produces flulike symptoms with malaise, fatigue, anorexia, nausea, pruritus, fever, and upper right quadrant pain.

3. HIV is transmitted by intimate sexual contact; by sharing needles for intravenous drug use; from mother to fetus during pregnancy; or by transfusion of blood or blood products.

4. AIDS is a breakdown in the immune function caused by HIV, a retrovirus. The infected person develops opportunistic infections or malignancies that become fatal. Progression from HIV infection to AIDS occurs at a median of 11 years after infection.

5. There can be hundreds of causes of vaginitis, but more often than not the cause is infection by one of three organisms: Candida, a fungus; Trichomonas, a protozoan; or Gardnerella, a bacterium.

6. The clinical manifestations of chlamydia are muco-purulent vaginal discharge, urethritis, bartholinitis, endometritis, salpingitis, and dysfunctional uterine bleeding.

SECTION II: APPLYING YOUR KNOWLEDGE

Activity F CASE STUDY

1. In pregnant women, gonorrhea is associated with chorioamnionitis, premature labor, premature rupture of membranes, and postpartum endometritis. It can also be transmitted to the newborn in the form of ophthalmia neonatorum during birth by direct contact with gonococcal organisms in the cervix. Ophthalmia neonatorum is highly contagious and, if untreated, leads to blindness of the newborn.

2. The nurse should be aware of the following factors:
   • Sensitivity and confidentiality: There is a social stigma attached to STIs, so women need to be reassured about confidentiality.
   • Education and counseling skills: The nurse should possess the necessary education and counseling skills to help the client deal with the infection.
   • Level of knowledge: The nurse's level of knowledge about chlamydia and gonorrhea should include treatment strategies, referral sources, and preventive measures.
   • Assessment: Assessment involves taking a health history that includes a comprehensive sexual history. Questions about the number of sex partners and the use of safer sex practices are appropriate. Previous and current symptoms should be reviewed. Seeking treatment and informing sex partners should be emphasized.

3. High-risk groups who may develop gonorrhea include individuals who
   • have low socioeconomic status.
   • live in an urban area.
   • are single.
   • practice inconsistent use of barrier contraceptives.
   • have multiple sex partners.

SECTION III: PRACTICING FOR NCLEX

Activity G NCLEX-STYLE QUESTIONS

1. **Answer: A**
   RATIONALE: As a preventive measure for the client with frequent vulvovaginal candidiasis, the nurse should instruct the client to wear white, 100% cotton underpants. The nurse should instruct the client to use pads instead of superabsorbent tampons, to avoid douching the affected area (as it washes away protective vaginal mucus), and to reduce her dietary intake of simple sugars and soda.

2. **Answer: B**
   RATIONALE: The nurse should instruct the client to use high-protein supplements such as Boost to provide quick and easy protein and calories. The nurse should also instruct the client to eat dry crackers upon arising, not after every meal, and to eat six small meals a day, not three. Drinking fluids constantly while eating is not recommended. The nurse should instruct the client to separate the intake of food and fluids.

3. **Answer: B**
   RATIONALE: The nurse should inform the client that even after warts are removed, HPV still remains and viral shedding will continue. The nurse should instruct the client to avoid applying steroid creams, sprays, or gels to vaginal area. All women above the age of 30 should undergo an HPV test, and women between 9 and 26 years of age should consider HPV vaccination with Gardasil. The use of latex condoms has been associated with a decreased risk, not an increased risk, of cervical cancer.

4. **Answer: D**
   RATIONALE: The nurse should counsel the client taking metronidazole to avoid alcohol during the treatment because mixing the two causes severe nausea and vomiting. Avoiding extremes of temperature to the genital area is a requirement for clients with genital ulcers, not trichomoniasis. The nurse should instruct the client to avoid sex, regardless of using condoms, until she and her sex partners are cured, that is, when therapy has been completed and both partners are symptom-free. It is not required to increase fluid intake during treatment.

5. **Answer: A**
RATIONALE: Symptoms of bacterial vaginosis include a characteristic "stale fish" odor and thin, white homogeneous vaginal discharge, not heavy yellow discharge. Dysfunctional uterine bleeding is a sign of Chlamydia, not bacterial vaginosis. Erythema in the vulvovaginal area is a symptom of vulvovaginal candidiasis, not bacterial vaginosis.

6. **Answer: D**
RATIONALE: Genital herpes simplex is characterized by lesions, frequently located on the vulva, vagina, and perineal areas. Rashes on the face are not symptoms of HSV. Alopecia is one of the symptoms of syphilis, not of primary HSV. Vaginal discharge during the primary stage of herpes is mucopurulent, not yellow-green.

7. **Answer: C**
RATIONALE: As a nursing strategy to prevent the spread of STIs, the nurse should discuss reducing the number of sex partners to diminish the risk of acquiring STIs. Oral contraceptives are not effective in preventing STIs, and barrier methods (condoms, diaphragms) should be promoted. The nurse should counsel and encourage sex partners of persons with STIs to seek treatment. Maintaining good body hygiene or not sharing personal items with others does not reduce the risk of spreading STIs.

8. **Answer: B**
RATIONALE: The nurse should instruct all community members to get vaccinated for prevention of hepatitis B. Ensuring that drinking water is disease free and educating people about the risks involved with injecting drugs may help prevent hepatitis A, not hepatitis B. Delaying the start of sexual activity by teenagers may not protect them from hepatitis B in the long run.

9. **Answer: A**
RATIONALE: Although the reasons for bacterial vaginosis are not yet fully understood, sex with multiple partners increases the risk, and therefore it should be avoided. Using oral contraceptives and smoking have not been associated with bacterial vaginosis. A colposcopy test is recommended for clients with high-risk HPV, not for diagnosing bacterial vaginosis.

10. **Answer: C**
RATIONALE: The nurse should inform the client that there is no evidence to suggest that antiviral therapy is completely safe during pregnancy. HSV cannot be cured completely, even with timely antiviral drug therapy, and there may be recurrences. The viral shedding process continues for 2 weeks during the primary episode, and kissing during this period may transmit the disease. Recurrent HSV-infection episodes are shorter and milder.

11. **Answer: B, C, E**
RATIONALE: The nurse should instruct the client with pelvic inflammatory disease to avoid douching, limit the number of sex partners, and complete the antibiotic therapy. Use of an intrauterine device is one of the risk factors associated with PID and should be avoided. Increasing fluid intake does not help alleviate the client's condition.

12. **Answer: A, C, D**
RATIONALE: The nurse should instruct the client to wear nonconstricting clothes and to wash her hands with soap and water after touching lesions to avoid autoinoculation. If urination is painful because of the ulcers, instruct the client to urinate in water but to avoid extremes of temperature such as ice packs or hot pads to the genital area. The client should abstain from intercourse during the prodromal period and when lesions are present. The ulcer disappears during the latency period.

13. **Answer: A, B, C**
RATIONALE: The nurse should give opportunities to practice negotiation techniques and encourage women to develop refusal skills so that they can respond positively in situations where they might be at risk for HIV infection. To reduce risk of HIV infection, the nurse should encourage the use of female condoms. Supporting youth-development activities to reduce sexual risk-taking and identifying or encouraging women to lead a healthy lifestyle may not be effective enough in empowering women to develop control over their lives.

14. **Answer: C, D, E**
RATIONALE: The nurse should ensure that the client understands the dosing regimen and schedule. The client should be informed that unpleasant side effects such as nausea and diarrhea are common. The nurse should provide written material describing diet, exercise, and medications to promote compliance and ensure a healthy lifestyle. There is no evidence to suggest that exposure of the fetus to antiretroviral agents during pregnancy is completely safe in the long run. HIV is a lifelong condition, and antiretroviral therapy may delay the onset of AIDS but not prevent it.

15. **Answer: B, D, E**
RATIONALE: When educating the client about cervical cancer, the nurse should inform the client that recurrence of genital warts increases the risk of cervical cancer and that she should obtain regular Pap smears to detect cervical cancer. Use of latex condoms reduces the risk of cervical cancer. Abnormal vaginal discharge does not necessarily indicate cervical cancer. There is no significant link between use of broad-spectrum antibiotics and increased risk of cervical cancer.

16. **Answer: B**
RATIONALE: The hepatitis B vaccine consists of a series of three injections given within 6 months. The vaccine is safe and well tolerated by most babies, including those who are underweight or premature. Vaccines are given after birth in most hospitals, not 6 months later. All babies are

vaccinated, not just those whose mothers are identified as at high risk for hepatitis.

17. Answer: B
RATIONALE: To prevent gonococcal ophthalmia neonatorum in the baby, the nurse should instill a prophylactic agent in the eyes of the newborn. Cephalosporins are administered to the mother during pregnancy to treat gonorrhea but not to prevent infection in the newborn. Performing a cesarean operation will not prevent gonococcal ophthalmia neonatorum in the newborn. An antiretroviral syrup is administered to the newborn only if the mother is HIV-positive and will not help prevent gonococcal ophthalmia neonatorum in the baby.

18. Answer: D
RATIONALE: Antiretroviral syrup is administered to the infant within 12 hours after birth to reduce the risk of transmission of HIV to the baby. Delivering the baby via cesarean does not significantly lower the risk of transmitting AIDS to the baby. A triple-combination HAART is used to treat HIV in adults, not babies. The nurse should counsel the client to avoid breastfeeding and use formula instead, because HIV can be spread to the infant through breastfeeding.

CHAPTER 6

SECTION I: ASSESSING YOUR UNDERSTANDING

Activity A FILL IN THE BLANKS

1. Ultrasound
2. Brachytherapy
3. estrogen
4. Lumpectomy
5. Mammography
6. Chemotherapy
7. mastectomy
8. Hemoccult
9. Immunotherapy
10. Fibroadenomas

Activity B MATCHING

1. e **2.** d **3.** c **4.** b **5.** a

Activity C SEQUENCING

1.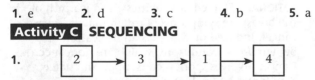

Activity D SHORT ANSWERS

1. A benign breast disorder is any noncancerous breast abnormality. Though not life threatening, benign disorders can cause pain and discomfort and account for a large number of visits to primary care providers. The most commonly encountered benign breast disorders in women include fibrocystic breasts, fibroadenomas, intraductal papilloma, mammary duct ectasia, and mastitis.

2. The three aspects on which breast cancers are classified are tumor size, extent of lymph node involvement, and evidence of metastasis.

3. Breast-conserving surgery, the least invasive procedure, is the wide local excision (or lumpectomy) of the tumor along with a 1-cm margin of normal tissue. A lumpectomy is often used for early-stage localized tumors. The goal of breast-conserving surgery is to remove the suspicious mass along with tissue free of malignant cells to prevent recurrence. The results are less drastic and emotionally less scarring to the woman. Women undergoing breast-conserving therapy receive radiation after lumpectomy with the goal of eradicating residual microscopic cancer cells to limit locoregional recurrence. In women who do not require adjuvant chemotherapy, radiation therapy typically begins 2 to 4 weeks after surgery to allow healing of the lumpectomy incision site. Radiation is administered to the entire breast at daily doses over a period of several weeks.

4. Adjunct therapy is supportive or additional therapy that is recommended after surgery. Adjunct therapies include local therapy such as radiation therapy and systemic therapies such as chemotherapy, hormonal therapy, and immunotherapy.

5. The typical side effects of chemotherapy include nausea and vomiting, diarrhea, or constipation.

6. The status of the axillary lymph nodes is an important prognostic indicator in early-stage breast cancer. The presence or absence of malignant cells in lymph nodes is highly significant. The more lymph nodes involved and the more aggressive the cancer, the more powerful chemotherapy will have to be, in terms of both the toxicity of drugs and the duration of treatment.

SECTION II: APPLYING YOUR KNOWLEDGE

Activity E CASE STUDY

1. The nurse should ask the following questions:
   • When did she first notice this lump?
   • Where is the lump located, and is it freely moveable or fixed?
   • Does the client have any nipple discharge? If yes, describe its color and consistency.
   • Does the client have a feeling of fullness in the breast?
   • Is the pain dull, burning, or itchy? Can she describe the pain?
   • Is there any skin dimpling or nipple retraction?

2. Mrs. Taylor needs the following education regarding breast health:
   • Monthly breast self-examination
   • Yearly clinical breast examination
   • Yearly mammography

3. The treatment modalities available to Mrs. Taylor in case of a malignancy are:
   • Local treatments such as surgery, and radiation
   • Systemic treatments such as chemotherapy, hormonal therapy, and immunotherapy

4. Mrs. Taylor will need the following community referrals:
   - Telephone counseling by the nurse
   - American Cancer Society's (ACS) Reach for Recovery
   - Organizations or charities that support cancer research
   - Participation in breast cancer walks to raise awareness
   - Emotional support groups

SECTION III: PRACTICING FOR NCLEX

Activity F NCLEX-STYLE QUESTIONS

1. **Answer: C**
   RATIONALE: To determine if the client is experiencing fibrocystic breast changes, the nurse must first examine the client's breasts. It is not important to know if the client has a mammography at this time. Cryoablation is done to remove a tumor.

2. **Answer: B**
   RATIONALE: As the physician suspects fibroadenomas, it is important for the nurse to know whether the client is pregnant or lactating since the incidence of fibroadenomas is more frequent among pregnant and lactating women. Taking oral contraceptives assists a client with fibrocystic breast changes, but is not necessary for a client with fibroadenomas. Fibroadenomas usually occur in women between 20 and 30 years of age. Smoking and a high-fat diet will make the client more susceptible to cancer, not fibroadenomas.

3. **Answer: A**
   RATIONALE: The nurse should instruct the client with mastitis to increase her fluid intake. A client with mastitis is instructed to continue breastfeeding as tolerated and to frequently change positions while nursing. The nurse should also instruct the client to apply warm, not cold, compresses to the affected breast area or to take a warm shower before breastfeeding.

4. **Answer: B**
   RATIONALE: When preparing a client for mammography, the nurse should ensure the client has not applied deodorant or powder on the day of testing because these products can appear on the x-ray film as calcium spots. It is not necessary for the client to avoid fluid intake 1 hour prior to testing. Mammography has to be scheduled just after the client's menses to reduce chances of breast tenderness, not when the client is going to start her menses. The client can take aspirin or acetaminophen after the completion of the procedure to ease any discomfort, but these medications are not taken before mammography.

5. **Answer: D**
   RATIONALE: The side effects of chemotherapy are constipation, hair loss, weight loss, vomiting, diarrhea, immunosuppression, and, in extreme cases, bone marrow suppression. The nurse should monitor for these side effects when caring for the client undergoing chemotherapy. Vaginal discharge, headache, and chills are not side effects of chemotherapy. Vaginal discharge is one of the side effects of SERMs as a part of hormonal therapy, which is used to prevent cancer from spreading further into the body. Headache is a side effect of aromatase inhibitors under hormonal therapy to counter cancer. Chills are a side effect of immunotherapy.

6. **Answer: D**
   RATIONALE: The nurse should inform the client that intraductal papillomas and fibrocystic breasts, although considered benign, carry a cancer risk with prolific masses and hyperplastic changes within the breasts. Other benign breast disorders such as mastitis, mammary duct ectasia, and fibroadenomas carry little risk.

7. **Answer: A**
   RATIONALE: The nurse should inform the client that removing only the sentinel lymph node prevents side effects such as lymphedema, which is otherwise associated with a traditional axillary lymph node dissection. It does not help reveal the hormonal status of the cancer. Hormone-receptor status can be revealed through normal breast epithelium, which has hormone receptors and responds specifically to the stimulatory effects of estrogen and progesterone. A sentinel lymph node biopsy will determine how powerful a chemotherapy regimen the client will have to undergo, but undergoing a sentinel lymph node biopsy will not lessen the aggressiveness of the chemotherapy. Degree of HER-2/neu oncoprotein will be revealed through the HER-2/neu genetic marker, not through a sentinel lymph node biopsy.

8. **Answer: B**
   RATIONALE: When providing care to the client, the nurse should instruct the client to elevate the affected arm on a pillow. As part of the respiratory care, the nurse should instruct the client to turn, cough, and breathe deeply every 2 hours; rapid breathing is not encouraged. Active range-of-motion and arm exercises are necessary. To counter any pain experienced by the client, analgesics are administered as needed; intake of medication is not restricted.

9. **Answer: C**
   RATIONALE: Skin edema, redness, and warmth of the breast are symptoms of inflammatory breast cancer. Induced discharge is an indication of benign breast conditions, which are noncancerous. Cancer involves spontaneous nipple discharge. Papillomas and palpable mobile cysts are characteristics of fibroadenomas, intraductal papilloma, and mammary duct ectasia, which are benign breast conditions and are noncancerous.

10. **Answer: D**
    RATIONALE: The symptom of mammary duct ectasia include the presence of green, brown, straw-colored, reddish, gray, or cream-colored nipple discharge with a consistency of toothpaste. Treatment includes antibiotic therapy with penicillinase-resistant

penicillin or cephalosporin, pain medication, and warm compresses to the inflamed area.

11. **Answer: C**
RATIONALE: When caring for a client who is being administered selective estrogen receptor modulator, the nurse should monitor for side effects such as hot flashes, vaginal discharge, bleeding, and cataract formation. Hot flashes are an expected side effect of SERM; therefore the nurse should document the finding in the chart.

12. **Answer: A, C, D**
RATIONALE: The modifiable risk factors for breast cancer are postmenopausal use of estrogen and progestins, not having children until after the age of 30, and failing to breastfeed for up to a year after pregnancy. Early menarche or late menopause and previous abnormal breast biopsy are the nonmodifiable risk factors for breast cancer.

13. **Answer: D**
RATIONALE: When performing the breast self-examination, the nurse should instruct the client to apply hard pressure down to the ribs. Light, not medium, pressure should be applied when moving the skin without moving the tissue underneath. Medium, not light, pressure should be applied midway into the tissue. Client need not specifically palpate the areolar area during breast self-examination.

14. **Answer: A**
RATIONALE: Adverse effects of trastuzumab include cardiac toxicity, vascular thrombosis, hepatic failure, fever, chills, nausea, vomiting, and pain with first infusion. The nurse should monitor for these adverse effects with the first infusion of trastuzumab. The nurse would notify the health care provider since the client is showing signs of hepatic failure.

15. **Answer: A**
RATIONALE: A nurse would monitor for signs of anorexia as it is a likely side effect of radiation therapy, along with swelling and heaviness of the breast, local edema, inflammation, and sunburn-like skin changes. The nurse would continue to monitor the client since this is a common, expected side effect of radiation.

16. **Answer: B**
RATIONALE: When caring for a client who has just undergone surgery for intraductal papilloma, the nurse should instruct the client to continue monthly breast self-examinations along with yearly clinical breast examinations. Applying warm compresses to the affected breast and wearing a supportive bra 24 hours a day are instructions given in cases of mastitis but not for intraductal papilloma. The nurse should instruct clients to refrain from consuming salt in the diet in cases of fibrocystic breast changes but not in cases of intraductal papilloma.

17. **Answer: B, D, E**
RATIONALE: Lumpectomy is contraindicated for women who have previously undergone radiation to the affected breast, those whose connective tissue is reported to be sensitive to radiation, and those whose surgery will not result in a clean margin of tissue. Clients who have had an early menarche or late onset of menopause and clients who have failed to breastfeed for up to 1 year after pregnancy are at risk for developing breast cancer. Lumpectomy is a treatment option for clients with breast cancer.

18. **Answer: A, B, D**
RATIONALE: The client is more susceptible to lymphedema if the affected arm is used for drawing blood or measuring blood pressure, if she engages in activities like gardening without using gloves, or if she's not wearing a well-fitted compression sleeve to promote drainage return. Consuming foods rich in phytochemicals is essential to prevent the incidence of cancer, not lymphedema. Not consuming a diet high in fiber and protein will not make the client susceptible to lymphedema.

19. **Answer: B, D, E**
RATIONALE: The nurse should instruct the client with fibrocystic breast changes to avoid caffeine. Caffeine acts as a stimulant that can lead to discomfort. It is important to maintain a low-fat diet rich in fruits, vegetables, and grains to maintain a healthy body weight. Taking diuretics is important to counteract fluid retention and swelling of the breasts. Practicing good hand-washing techniques and increasing fluid intake are important for clients with mastitis but may not help clients with fibrocystic breast changes.

20. **Answer: A, B, C**
RATIONALE: The nurse should instruct the client to restrict intake of salted foods, limit intake of processed foods, and consume seven or more daily portions.

CHAPTER 7

SECTION I: ASSESSING YOUR UNDERSTANDING

Activity A FILL IN THE BLANKS

1. Cystocele
2. prolapse
3. pessary
4. Polyps
5. leiomyomas
6. Kegel
7. rectum
8. urethra
9. Metrorrhagia
10. Transvaginal

Activity B MATCHING

1. a　　**2.** e　　**3.** b　　**4.** c　　**5.** d

Activity C SHORT ANSWERS

1. Pelvic organ prolapse could be caused by the following:
   • Constant downward gravity because of erect human posture

- Atrophy of supporting tissues with aging and decline of estrogen levels
- Weakening of pelvic support related to childbirth trauma
- Reproductive surgery
  - Instrumental childbirth
  - Multiparity
  - Uncontrolled rapid birth
  - Young age at first birth
  - Obesity
  - Respiratory problems or chronic coughing
- Family history of pelvic organ prolapse
- Young age at first birth
- Connective tissue disorders
- Infant birth weight of greater than 4,500 g
- Pelvic radiation
- Increased abdominal pressure secondary to lifting of children or heavy objects, straining due to chronic constipation, respiratory problems or chronic coughing, or obesity

2. Kegel exercises strengthen the pelvic floor muscles to support the inner organs and prevent further prolapse. They help increase the muscle volume, which will result in a stronger muscular contraction. These exercises might limit the progression of mild prolapse and alleviate mild prolapse symptoms, including low back pain and pelvic pressure. Clients with severe uterine prolapse may not benefit from Kegel exercises.

3. Several factors contribute to urinary incontinence:
   - Intake of fluids, especially alcohol, carbonated drinks, and caffeinated beverages
   - Constipation, which alters the position of pelvic organs and puts pressure on the bladder
   - Habitual preventive emptying, which may result in training the bladder to hold small amounts of urine
   - Anatomic changes due to advanced age, which decrease pelvic support
   - Pregnancy and childbirth, which cause damage to the pelvis structure during birthing process
   - Obesity, which increases abdominal pressure

4. The Colpexin sphere is a polycarbonate sphere with a locator string that is fitted above the hymenal ring to support the pelvis floor muscle. The sphere is used in conjunction with pelvic floor muscle exercises, which should be performed daily. The sphere supports the pelvic floor muscle and facilitates rehabilitation of the pelvic floor muscles.

5. Uterine fibroids may be medically managed by UAE. UAE is an option in which polyvinyl alcohol pellets are injected into selected blood vessels via a catheter to block circulation to the fibroid, causing shrinkage of the fibroid and resolution of the symptoms. After treatment, most fibroids are reduced by 50% within 3 months, but they might recur. The failure rate is approximately 10% to 15%, and this therapy should not be performed on women desiring to retain their fertility.

6. Bartholin glands are two mucus-secreting glandular structures with duct openings bilaterally at the base of the labia minora, near the opening of the vagina, that provide lubrication during sexual arousal. A Bartholin cyst is a fluid-filled, swollen, saclike structure that results from a blockage of one of the ducts of the Bartholin gland. The cyst may become infected and an abscess may develop in the gland. Bartholin cysts are the most common cystic growths in the vulva, affecting approximately 2% of women at some time in their lives.

SECTION II: APPLYING YOUR KNOWLEDGE
Activity D CASE STUDY

1. Pelvic support disorders increase with age and are a result of weakness of the connective tissue and muscular support of the pelvic organs. Vaginal childbirth, obesity, lifting, chronic cough, straining at defecation secondary to constipation, and estrogen deficiency all contribute to pelvic support disorders.

2. Symptoms of uterine prolapse include low back pain, pelvic pressure, urinary frequency, retention, and/or incontinence. These symptoms are likely to affect Mrs. Scott's daily activities.

3. Nonsurgical interventions include regular Kegel exercises, estrogen replacement therapy, dietary and lifestyle modifications, and pessaries. Kegel exercises might limit the progression of mild prolapse and alleviate mild prolapse symptoms, including low back pain and pelvic pressure. Estrogen replacement therapy may help to improve the tone and vascularity of the supporting tissue in perimenopausal and menopausal women by increasing blood perfusion and elasticity to the vaginal wall. Dietary and lifestyle modifications may help prevent pelvic relaxation and chronic problems later in life. Pessaries may be indicated for uterine prolapse or cystocele, especially among elderly clients for whom surgery is contraindicated. Surgical interventions include anterior and posterior colporrhaphy and vaginal hysterectomy. Anterior and posterior colporrhaphy may be effective for a first-degree prolapse. A vaginal hysterectomy is the treatment of choice for uterine prolapse because it removes the prolapsed organ that is bringing down the bladder and rectum with it.

SECTION III: PRACTICING FOR NCLEX
Activity E NCLEX-STYLE QUESTIONS

1. **Answer: C**
   RATIONALE: Weakening of the pelvic floor muscles causes a feeling of dragging and a "lump" in the vagina; these are symptoms of pelvic organ prolapse. These symptoms do not indicate urinary incontinence, endocervical polyps, or uterine fibroids. Urinary incontinence is the involuntary loss of urine. The symptoms of endocervical

polyps are abnormal vaginal bleeding or discharge. In cases of uterine fibroids, the uterus is enlarged and irregularly shaped.

2. **Answer: B**
   RATIONALE: Before starting estrogen replacement therapy, each woman must be evaluated on the basis of a thorough medical history to validate her risk for complications such as endometrial cancer, myocardial infarction, stroke, breast cancer, pulmonary emboli, or deep vein thrombosis. The effective dose of estrogen required, the dietary modifications, and the cost of estrogen replacement therapy can be discussed at a later stage when the client understands the risks associated with estrogen replacement therapy and decides to use hormone therapy.

3. **Answer: A**
   RATIONALE: The nurse should instruct the client to increase dietary fiber and fluids to prevent constipation. A high-fiber diet with an increase in fluid intake alleviates constipation by increasing stool bulk and stimulating peristalsis. Straining to pass a hard stool increases intra-abdominal pressure, which, over time, causes the pelvic organs to prolapse. Avoiding caffeine products would not help in the management of this condition. In addition to recommending increasing the amount of fiber in her diet, the nurse should also encourage the woman to drink eight 8-oz glasses of fluid daily. The nurse should instruct the client to avoid high-impact aerobics to minimize the risk of increasing intra-abdominal pressure.

4. **Answer: D**
   RATIONALE: The disadvantage of myomectomy is that the fibroids may grow back in the future. Fertility is not jeopardized because this procedure leaves the uterine wall intact. Weakening of the uterine walls, scarring, and adhesions are caused by laser treatment, not myomectomy.

5. **Answer: B**
   RATIONALE: Kegel exercises might limit the progression of mild prolapse and alleviate mild prolapse symptoms, including low back pain and pelvic pressure. Intake of food is not required before performing Kegel exercises. Surgical interventions do not interfere with Kegel exercises. Kegel exercises do not cause an increase in blood pressure.

6. **Answer: A, B, D**
   RATIONALE: The predisposing factors for uterine fibroids are age (late reproductive years), nulliparity, obesity, genetic predisposition, and African American ethnicity. Smoking and hyperinsulinemia are not predisposing factors for uterine fibroids.

7. **Answer: B**
   RATIONALE: Vaginal dryness is one of the side effects of GnRH medications. The other side effects of GnRH medications are hot flashes, headaches, mood changes, musculoskeletal malaise, bone loss, and depression. Increased vaginal discharge,

urinary tract infections, and vaginitis are side effects of a pessary, not GnRH medications.

8. **Answer: C**
   RATIONALE: The nurse should instruct the client using a pessary to report any discomfort or difficulty with urination or defecation. Avoiding high-impact aerobics, jogging, jumping, and lifting heavy objects, as well as wearing a girdle or abdominal support, are recommended for a client with prolapse as part of lifestyle modifications and may not be necessary for a client using a pessary.

9. **Answer: B**
   RATIONALE: The most common recommendation for pessary care is removing the pessary twice weekly and cleaning it with soap and water. In addition, douching with diluted vinegar or hydrogen peroxide helps to reduce urinary tract infections and odor, which are side effects of using a pessary. Estrogen cream is applied to make the vaginal mucosa more resistant to erosion and strengthen the vaginal walls. Removing the pessary before sleeping or intercourse is not part of the instructions for pessary care.

10. **Answer: D**
    RATIONALE: The nurse should monitor the client with ultrasound scans every 3 to 6 months. Monitoring gonadotropin level and blood sugar level and scheduling periodic Pap smears are not important assessments for the client with small ovarian cysts.

11. **Answer: A**
    RATIONALE: The nurse should teach the client turning, deep breathing, and coughing prior to the surgery to prevent atelectasis and respiratory complications such as pneumonia. Reducing activity level and the need for pelvic rest are instructions related to discharge planning after the client has undergone a hysterectomy. A high-fat diet need not be avoided before undergoing hysterectomy; avoiding a high-fat diet is required for clients with pelvic organ prolapse to reduce constipation.

12. **Answer: B, C, E**
    RATIONALE: If the client is at high risk of recurrent prolapse after a surgical repair, is morbidly obese, or has chronic obstructive pulmonary disease, then the client is not a good candidate for surgical repair. Low back pain and pelvic pressure are common to almost all pelvic organ prolapses and do not help to decide whether the client should opt for surgical repair. A client with severe pelvic organ prolapse may be a candidate for surgical repair.

13. **Answer: A, B, D**
    RATIONALE: The teaching guidelines include continuing pelvic floor (Kegel) exercises, increasing fiber in the diet to reduce constipation, and controlling blood glucose levels to prevent polyuria. The nurse should instruct the client to reduce the intake of fluids and foods that are bladder irritants, such as orange juice, soda, and caffeine, and the client should wipe from front to back to prevent urinary tract infections.

14. **Answer: A, D, E**
    RATIONALE: The postoperative care plan for a client who has undergone a hysterectomy includes administering analgesics promptly and using a PCA pump, frequent ambulation, and administering antiemetics to control nausea and vomiting. The nurse should change the position of the client frequently and use pillows for support to promote comfort and pain management. Ambulation is key in the prevention of postoperative complications. An excess of carbonated beverages in the diet does not affect the postoperative healing process.

15. **Answer: A**
    RATIONALE: The nurse should stress follow-up care to the client with polycystic ovarian syndrome so that the client does not overlook this benign disorder. Increasing intake of fiber-rich foods, increasing fluid intake, and performing Kegel exercises help to control pelvic organ prolapse, not polycystic ovarian syndrome.

CHAPTER 8

SECTION I: ASSESSING YOUR UNDERSTANDING

Activity A FILL IN THE BLANKS

1. dysplasia
2. Colposcopy
3. Cryotherapy
4. Endometrial
5. Bethesda
6. Hysterectomy
7. CA-125
8. simplex
9. epithelium
10. Squamous

Activity B MATCHING

1. b   **2.** a   **3.** d   **4.** c

Activity C SEQUENCING

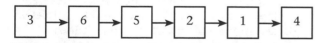

3 → 6 → 5 → 2 → 1 → 4

Activity D SHORT ANSWERS

1. Risk factors for developing cervical cancer are as follows:
   - Early age of first intercourse (within 1 year of menarche)
   - Lower socioeconomic status
   - Promiscuous male partners
   - Unprotected sexual intercourse
   - Family history of cervical cancer (mother or sisters)
   - Sexual intercourse with uncircumcised men
   - Female offspring of mothers who took diethylstilbestrol (DES)
   - Infections with genital herpes or chronic chlamydia
   - History of multiple sex partners
   - Cigarette smoking
   - Immunocompromised state
   - HIV infection
   - Oral contraceptive use
   - Moderate dysplasia on Pap smear within past 5 years
   - HPV infection

2. Treatment options for endometrial cancer are as follows:
   - Treatment of endometrial cancer depends on the stage of the disease and usually involves surgery, with adjunct therapy based on pathologic findings.
   - Surgery most often involves removal of the uterus (hysterectomy) and the fallopian tubes and ovaries (salpingo-oophorectomy).
   - In more advanced cancers, radiation and chemotherapy are used as adjunct therapies to surgery.
   - Routine surveillance intervals for follow-up care are typically every 3 to 4 months for the first 2 years, since 85% of recurrences occur in the first 2 years after diagnosis.

3. The following are possible risk factors for ovarian cancer:
   - Nulliparity
   - Early menarche (<12 years old)
   - Late menopause (>55 years old)
   - Increasing age (>50 years of age)
   - High-fat diet
   - Obesity
   - Persistent ovulation over time
   - First-degree relative with ovarian cancer
   - Use of perineal talcum powder or hygiene sprays
   - Older than 30 years at first pregnancy
   - Positive BRCA-1 and BRCA-2 mutations
   - Personal history of breast, bladder, or colon cancer
   - Hormone replacement therapy for more than 10 years
   - Infertility

4. Transvaginal ultrasound can be used to evaluate the endometrial cavity and measure the thickness of the endometrial lining. It can be used to detect endometrial hyperplasia.

5. The following are the nursing interventions in caring for clients with cancers of the female reproductive tract:
   - Validate the client's feelings and provide realistic hope.
   - Use basic communication skills in a sincere way during all interactions.
   - Provide useful, nonjudgmental information to all women.
   - Individualize care to address the client's cultural traditions.
   - Carry out postoperative care and instructions as prescribed.
   - Discuss postoperative issues, including incision care, pain, and activity level.
   - Instruct the client on health-maintenance activities after treatment.

- Inform the client and family about available support resources.

6. The following are the diagnostic options for endometrial cancer:
   - Endometrial biopsy: An endometrial biopsy is the procedure of choice to make the diagnosis. It can be done in the health care provider's office without anesthesia. A slender suction catheter is used to obtain a small sample of tissue for pathology. It can detect up to 90% of cases of endometrial cancer in the woman with postmenopausal bleeding, depending on the technique and experience of the health care provider. The woman may experience mild cramping and bleeding after the procedure for about 24 hours, but typically mild pain medication will reduce this discomfort.
   - Transvaginal ultrasound: A transvaginal ultrasound can be used to evaluate the endometrial cavity and measure the thickness of the endometrial lining. It can be used to detect endometrial hyperplasia. If the endometrium measures less than 4 mm, then the client is at low risk for malignancy.

SECTION II: APPLYING YOUR KNOWLEDGE

Activity E CASE STUDY

1. • Back pain
   - Abdominal bloating
   - Fatigue
   - Urinary frequency
   - Constipation
   - Abdominal pressure
2. The most common early symptoms include abdominal bloating, early satiety, fatigue, vague abdominal pain, urinary frequency, diarrhea or constipation, and unexplained weight loss or gain. The later symptoms include anorexia, dyspepsia, ascites, palpable abdominal mass, pelvic pain, and back pain. Early detection of ovarian cancer is possible if the clients are informed about yearly bimanual pelvic examination and transvaginal ultrasound to identify ovarian masses.
3. Disturbed body image related to:
   - Loss of body part
   - Loss of good health
   - Altered sexuality patterns
   Anxiety related to:
   - Threat of malignancy
   - Potential diagnosis
   - Anticipated pain/discomfort
   - Effect of condition treatment on future
   Deficient knowledge related to:
   - Disease process and prognosis
   - Specific treatment options
   - Diagnostic procedures needed
4. In Stage I, the ovarian cancer is limited to the ovaries. In Stage II, the growth involves one or both ovaries, with pelvic extension. In Stage III, the cancer spreads to the lymph nodes and other organs or structures inside the abdominal cavity. In Stage IV, the cancer has metastasized to distant sites. Treatment options for ovarian cancer vary, depending on the stage and severity of the disease. Usually a laparoscopy (abdominal exploration with an endoscope) is performed for diagnosis and staging, as well as evaluation for further therapy.

SECTION III: PRACTICING FOR NCLEX

Activity F NCLEX-STYLE QUESTIONS

1. **Answer: A**
   RATIONALE: The client should have Papanicolaou tests regularly to detect cervical cancer during the early stages. Blood tests for mutations in the BRCA genes indicate the lifetime risk of the client of developing breast or ovarian cancer. CA-125 is a biologic tumor marker associated with ovarian cancer, but it is not currently sensitive enough to serve as a screening tool. The transvaginal ultrasound can be used to detect endometrial abnormalities.

2. **Answer: A**
   RATIONALE: Early onset of sexual activity, within the first year of menarche, increases the risk of acquiring cervical cancer later on. Obesity, infertility, and hypertension are risk factors that are associated with endometrial cancer.

3. **Answer: C**
   RATIONALE: The nurse should inform the client that surgery most often involves removal of the uterus (hysterectomy) and the fallopian tubes and ovaries (salpingo-oophorectomy). Removal of the tubes and ovaries, not just the uterus, is recommended because tumor cells spread early to the ovaries, and any dormant cancer cells could be stimulated to grow by ovarian estrogen. In advanced cancers, radiation and chemotherapy are used as adjuvant therapies to surgery. Routine surveillance intervals for follow-up care are typically every 3 to 4 months for the first 2 years.

4. **Answer: B**
   RATIONALE: The client's present age increases her risk of developing ovarian cancer, as women who are older than 50 are at a greater risk. The client's age at menarche (older than 12) and menopause (younger than 55) are both normal. The client is underweight and not obese, so her weight is not a risk factor for ovarian cancer.

5. **Answer: C**
   RATIONALE: To identify ovarian masses in their early stages, the client needs to have yearly bimanual pelvic examinations. Pap smears are not effective enough to detect ovarian masses. The U.S. Preventive Services Task Force recommends against routine screening for ovarian cancer with serum CA-125 because the potential harm could outweigh the potential benefits. X-rays of the pelvic area do not detect ovarian masses.

6. Answer: A
RATIONALE: Only 5% of ovarian cancers are genetic in origin. However, the nurse needs to tell the client to seek genetic counseling and thorough assessment to reduce her risk of ovarian cancer. Oral contraceptives reduce the risk of ovarian cancer and should be encouraged. Breastfeeding should be encouraged as a risk-reducing strategy. The nurse should instruct the client to avoid using perineal talc or hygiene sprays.

7. Answer: B
RATIONALE: The nurse should teach the client genital self-examination to assess for any unusual growths in the vulvar area. The nurse should instruct the client to seek care for any suspicious lesions and to avoid self-medication. Wearing restrictive undergarments is not associated with vulvar cancer.

8. Answer: B, C, E
RATIONALE: To reduce the risk of cervical cancer, the nurse should encourage clients to avoid smoking and drinking. In addition, because STIs such as HPV increase the risk of cervical cancers, care should be taken to prevent STIs. Teenagers also should be counseled to avoid early sexual activity because it increases the risk of cervical cancer. The use of barrier methods of contraception, not IUDs, should be encouraged. Avoiding stress and high blood pressure will not have a significant impact on the risk of cervical cancer.

9. Answer: A, C, D
RATIONALE: The responsibilities of a nurse while caring for a client with endometrial cancer include ensuring that the client understands all the treatment options available, suggesting the advantages of a support group and providing referrals, and offering the family explanations and emotional support throughout the treatment. The nurse should also discuss changes in sexuality with the client as well as stress the importance of regular follow-up care after the treatment and not just in cases where something unusual occurs.

10. Answer: B, D, E
RATIONALE: Irregular vaginal bleeding, persistent low backache not related to standing, and elevated or discolored vulvar lesions are some of the symptoms that should be immediately brought to the notice of the primary health care provider. Increase in urinary frequency and irregular bowel movements are not symptoms related to cancers of the reproductive tract.

11. Answer: B
RATIONALE: The nurse should explain to the client that the colposcopy is done because the physician has observed abnormalities in Pap smears. The nurse should also explain to the client that the procedure is painless and there are no adverse effects, such as pain during urination. There is no need to avoid intercourse for a week after the colposcopy.

12. Answer: B
RATIONALE: According to the 2001 Bethesda system for classifying Pap smear results, a result of ASC-H means that the client is to be referred for colposcopy without HPV testing. Atypical squamous cells of undetermined significance (ASC-US) mean that the test has to be repeated in 4 to 6 months or the client has to be referred for colposcopy. Atypical glandular cells (AGC) or adenocarcinoma in situ (AIS) results indicate immediate colposcopy, with the follow-up based on the results of findings.

13. Answer: A, B, D
RATIONALE: Although direct risk factors for the initial development of vaginal cancer have not been identified, associated risk factors include advancing age (greater than 60 years old), human immunodeficiency virus (HIV) infection, smoking, previous pelvic radiation, exposure to diethylstilbestrol (DES) in utero, vaginal trauma, history of genital warts (human papilloma virus [HPV] infection), cervical cancer, chronic vaginal discharge, and low socioeconomic level. Persistent ovulation over time and hormone replacement therapy for more than 10 years are risk factors associated with ovarian cancer.

14. Answer: A
RATIONALE: Abnormal and painless vaginal bleeding is a major initial symptom of endometrial cancer. A transvaginal ultrasound can be used to evaluate the endometrial cavity and measure the thickness of the endometrial lining. If the endometrium measures less than 4 mm, then the client is at low risk for malignancy. A biopsy is not indicted when endometrial thickness is >4 mm in a postmenopausal client with bleeding, thereby avoiding invasive measures.

15. Answer: A
RATIONALE: The client has classic symptoms of vulvar cancer. All clients with vulvar lumps should be biopsied even if they are asymptomatic. Cryosurgery may be scheduled if the biopsy confirms the diagnosis of vulvar cancer. It is not important to know what creams the client has used and how much she smokes at this time.

CHAPTER 9

SECTION I: ASSESSING YOUR UNDERSTANDING

Activity A FILL IN THE BLANKS

1. battered
2. Incest
3. Statutory
4. Rohypnol
5. circumcision
6. Acquaintance
7. sexual
8. hyperarousal
9. avoidance
10. honeymoon

Activity B MATCHING

1. d   2. b   3. a   4. c

Activity C SEQUENCING

$$2 \rightarrow 3 \rightarrow 4 \rightarrow 1$$

Activity D SHORT ANSWERS

1. The cycle of violence occurs in an abusive relationship. It includes three distinct phases: the tension-building phase, the acute battering phase, and the honeymoon phase. The cyclic behavior begins with a time of tension-building arguments, progresses to violence, and settles into a making-up or calm period. With time, this cycle of violence increases in frequency and severity as it is repeated over and over again. The cycle can cover a long or short period of time. The honeymoon phase gradually shortens and eventually disappears altogether.

2. An abuser may financially abuse the partner in the following ways:
   - Preventing the woman from getting a job
   - Sabotaging the current job
   - Controlling how all money is spent
   - Refusing to contribute financially

3. The potential nursing diagnoses related to violence against women include the following:
   - Deficient knowledge related to understanding of the cycle of violence and availability of resources
   - Fear related to possibility of severe injury to self or children during cycle of violence
   - Low self-esteem related to feelings of worthlessness
   - Hopelessness related to prolonged exposure to violence
   - Compromised individual and family coping related to persistence of victim–abuser relationship

4. PTSD develops when an event outside the range of normal human experience occurs that produces marked distress in the person. Symptoms of PTSD are divided into three groups:
   - Intrusion (re-experiencing the trauma, including nightmares, flashbacks, recurrent thoughts)
   - Avoidance (avoiding trauma-related stimuli, social withdrawal, emotional numbing)
   - Hyperarousal (increased emotional arousal, exaggerated startle response, irritability)

5. The nurse should screen the client for the following signs to determine whether she is a victim of abuse:
   - Injuries: bruises, scars from blunt trauma, or weapon wounds on the face, head, and neck
   - Injury sequelae: headaches, hearing loss, joint pain, sinus infections, teeth marks, clumps of hair missing, dental trauma, pelvic pain, breast or genital injuries
   - The reported history of the injury doesn't seem to add up to the actual presenting problem
   - Mental health problems: depression, anxiety, substance abuse, eating disorders, suicidal ideation, or suicide attempts
   - Frequent health care visits for chronic, stress-related disorders such as chest pain, headaches, back or pelvic pain, insomnia, and gastrointestinal disturbances
   - Partner's behavior at the health care visit: appears overly solicitous or overprotective, unwilling to leave client alone with the health care provider, answers questions for her, and attempts to control the situation in the health care setting

6. Abuse during pregnancy threatens the well-being of the mother and fetus. Physical violence to the pregnant woman brings injuries to the head, face, neck, thorax, breasts, and abdomen. Mental health consequences are also significant. Women assaulted during pregnancy are at a risk for depression, chronic anxiety, insomnia, poor nutrition, excessive weight gain or loss, late entry into prenatal care, preterm labor, miscarriage, stillbirth, premature and low-birth-weight infants, placental abruption, uterine rupture, chorioamnionitis, vaginitis, STIs, urinary tract infections, or smoking and substance abuse.

SECTION II: APPLYING YOUR KNOWLEDGE

Activity E CASE STUDY

1. Some of the common symptoms of physical abuse include depression, sexual dysfunction, backaches, STIs, fear or guilt, or phobias.

2. Suzanne may not seek help in the abusive relationship for the following reasons:
   - She may feel responsible for the abuse.
   - She may feel she deserved the abuse.
   - She may have been abused as a child and has low self-esteem.

3. The following strategies may help Suzanne to manage the situation:
   - Teaching coping strategies to manage stress
   - Encouraging the establishment of realistic goals
   - Teaching problem-solving skills
   - Encouraging social activities to connect with other people
   - Explaining that abuse is never okay

SECTION III: PRACTICING FOR NCLEX

Activity F NCLEX-STYLE QUESTIONS

1. **Answer: C**
   RATIONALE: The nurse should inform the client that alcohol, drugs, money problems, depression, or jealousy do not cause violence and are excuses given by the abuser for losing control. Even though violence against women was common in the past, the police, justice system, and society are beginning to make domestic violence socially unacceptable. The nurse also needs to emphasize that physical abuse is not the result of provocation from the female but an expression of inadequacy of the perpetrator. Violence against women is widespread, and whatever the cause of the assault, there is no justification for physical or sexual assault.

2. **Answer: D**

RATIONALE: The nurse should clearly explain to the client that whatever the cause of the incident, no one deserves to be a victim of physical abuse and abusive behaviors are often repeated. Even though the partner appears to be genuinely contrite, most people who attack their spouses are serial abusers and there is no certainty that they will not repeat their actions. The client should realize that even if she tries her best not to upset her partner, her partner may abuse her again. The client should never accept battering as a normal part of any relationship.

3. **Answer: C**

RATIONALE: Attacking pets and destroying valued possessions are examples of emotional abuse. Observing the client's movements closely may be a sign of suspicion. Throwing objects at the client is physical abuse. Forcing the client to have intercourse against her will is an act of sexual abuse.

4. **Answer: B**

RATIONALE: Abusers are most likely to exhibit antisocial behavior or childlike aggression. They use aggression to control their victims. Abusers come from all walks of life; they are not just restricted to low-income groups, nor are they necessarily products of divorced parents. The physical characteristics of the abusers vary, and they are not necessarily physically imposing.

5. **Answer: D**

RATIONALE: For every rape victim who turns up, the nurse should ensure that the appropriate law enforcement agencies are apprised of the incident. Victims should not be made to wait long hours in the waiting room, as they may leave if no one attends to them. Victims of rape should be treated with more sensitivity than other clients. Although the primary job of a nurse is to medically care for the rape victim, a nurse should also pay due attention to collecting evidence to substantiate the victim's claim in a court of law.

6. **Answer: C**

RATIONALE: The nurse should tell the client that she is a victim of sexual abuse because her partner forces her to have intercourse against her will. The nurse should also explain to the client that she is in no way responsible for such incidents and that she has a right to refuse sexual intimacy. There is no justification for sexual abuse, and the client should not regard it as "normal" behavior.

7. **Answer: C**

RATIONALE: The nurse should use pictures and diagrams to ensure that the client understands what is being asked and explained. Instead of using medical terms, the nurse should use simple, accurate terms as much as possible. Condemning the practice will only alienate the girl and serve no useful purpose.

8. **Answer: B**

RATIONALE: If the nurse suspects physical abuse, the nurse should attempt to interview the woman in private. Many abusers will not leave their partners for fear of being reported. The nurse should use subtle ways of doing this, such as telling the woman a urine specimen is required and showing her the way to the restroom, providing the nurse and client some private time. Asking the partner directly if he was responsible will not help because the partner may not admit his culpability. Telling the partner to leave the room immediately may rouse the suspicions of the partner. Questioning the client about the injury in front of the partner may trigger another abusive episode and should be avoided. Precaution should be taken to prevent the abuser from punishing the woman when she returns home.

9. **Answer: A**

RATIONALE: The nurse should use direct quotes and specific language as much as possible when documenting. The nurse should not obtain photos of the client without informed consent. The nurse should, however, document the refusal of the client to be photographed. Documentation must include details as to the frequency and severity of abuse and the location, extent, and outcome of injuries, not just a description of the interventions taken. The nurse is required by law to inform the police of any injuries that involve knives, firearms, or other deadly weapons or that present life-threatening injuries.

10. **Answer: A**

RATIONALE: The nurse should offer referrals to the client, such as support groups or specialists, so that the client gets professional help in recovering from the incident. The nurse should help the client cope with the incident rather than telling the client to forget about it. The nurse should also educate the client about the connection between the violence and some of the symptoms that she has developed recently, like palpitations. Confirming with the partner whether the client's story is true will create further problems for the client, and the nurse may lose the client's trust.

11. **Answer: A**

RATIONALE: To minimize risk of pregnancy, the nurse should ensure that the client takes a double dose of emergency contraceptive pills: the first dose within 72 hours of the rape and the second dose 12 hours after the first dose, if not sooner. It is better to use contraceptive measures immediately than to wait for signs of pregnancy. Using spermicidal creams or gels or regular oral contraceptive pills will not prove effective in preventing unwanted pregnancies.

12. **Answer: B, C, D**

RATIONALE: Some of the factors that may lead to abuse during pregnancy are resentment toward the interference of the growing fetus and change in the woman's shape, perception of the baby as a competitor once he or she is born, and insecurity and jealousy of the pregnancy and the responsibilities it brings. Concern for the child will never result in physical abuse, as the unborn child is also at risk through assault during pregnancy. Serial abusers may exhibit violent tendencies during pregnancy, and such behavior is unacceptable.

13. **Answer: A, B, E**
    RATIONALE: Victims of human trafficking have restrictions on their daily movements, so the nurse should ask questions to learn whether the client can move around freely. The nurse should also find out if the client could leave her present job or situation if she wants to. Asking clients what their parents do or what their educational background is does not help determine whether they are victims of human trafficking.

14. **Answer: B, C, E**
    RATIONALE: To screen for abuse, the nurse should assess for mental health problems or injuries. The nurse should also be alert for inconsistencies regarding the reporting of the injury and the actual problem. Having STIs frequently is not a sign of physical or sexual abuse. Usually, partners of suspected victims seem overprotective and they do not leave the client alone.

15. **Answer: A, B, C, E**
    RATIONALE: To learn whether the client is having physical symptoms of PTSD, the nurse should ask the client if she is having trouble sleeping and whether she is emotionally stable or given to bursts of irritability. The nurse should also find out if the client experiences heart palpitations or sweating. Reliving the event is called flashback and is a physical response to the event. Asking the client if she is feeling numb emotionally assesses the presence of avoidance reactions, not physical manifestation of PTSD. The nurse should ask the client whether she has upsetting thoughts and nightmares to assess for the presence of intrusive thoughts.

CHAPTER 10

SECTION I: ASSESSING YOUR UNDERSTANDING

Activity A FILL IN THE BLANKS

1. Allele
2. mutation
3. autosomes
4. amnion
5. Chromosomes
6. morula
7. karyotype
8. genome
9. phenotype

Activity B LABELING

The figure depicts fetal circulation. Arrows indicate the path of blood. The umbilical vein carries oxygen-rich blood from the placenta to the liver and through the ductus venosus. From there it is carried to the inferior vena cava to the right atrium of the heart. Some of the blood is shunted through the foramen ovale to the left side of the heart, where it is routed to the brain and upper extremities. The rest of the blood travels down to the right ventricle and through the pulmonary artery. A small portion of the blood travels to the nonfunctioning lungs, while the remaining blood is shunted through the ductus arteriosus into the aorta to supply the rest of the body.

Activity C MATCHING

1. c **2.** d **3.** b **4.** a

Activity D SEQUENCING

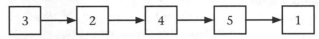

3 → 2 → 4 → 5 → 1

Activity E SHORT ANSWERS

1. For conception or fertilization to occur, a healthy ovum from the woman has to be released from the ovary. It passes into an open fallopian tube and starts its journey downward. Sperm from the male must be deposited into the vagina and be able to swim approximately 7 in to meet the ovum where one spermatozoa penetrates the ovum's thick outer membrane. Fertilization takes place in the outer third of the ampulla of the fallopian tube.

2. The three different stages of fetal development during pregnancy are:
   - Pre-embryonic stage: begins with fertilization through the 2nd week
   - Embryonic stage: begins 15 days after conception and continues through week 8
   - Fetal stage: begins from the end of the 8th week and lasts until birth

3. The sex of the zygote is determined at fertilization. It depends on whether the ovum is fertilized by a Y-bearing sperm or an X-bearing sperm. An XX zygote will become a female, and an XY zygote will become a male.

4. Concurrent with the development of the trophoblast and implantation, further differentiation of the inner cell mass of the zygote occurs. Some of the cells become the embryo itself, and others give rise to the membranes that surround and protect it. The three embryonic layers of cells formed are:
   - Ectoderm—forms the central nervous system, special senses, skin, and glands
   - Mesoderm—forms the skeletal, urinary, circulatory, and reproductive organs
   - Endoderm—forms the respiratory system, liver, pancreas, and digestive system

5. Amniotic fluid is derived from fluid transported from the maternal blood across the amnion and fetal urine. Its volume changes constantly as the fetus swallows and voids. Amniotic fluid is composed of 98% water and 2% organic matter. It is slightly alkaline and contains albumin, urea, uric acid, creatinine, bilirubin, lecithin, sphingomyelin, epithelial cells, vernix, and fine hair called lanugo.

6. The placenta produces hormones that control the basic physiology of the mother in such a way that the fetus is supplied with the necessary nutrients and oxygen needed for successful growth. The placenta produces the following hormones necessary for normal pregnancy:
- Human chorionic gonadotropin
- Human placental lactogen
- Estrogen (estriol)
- Progesterone (progestin)
- Relaxin

SECTION II: APPLYING YOUR KNOWLEDGE

Activity F CASE STUDY

1. Shana should be reassured that she will continue to feel fetal movement throughout her pregnancy and that it is not common for a fetus to get "tangled in its umbilical cord."

2. The nurse should explain the following functions of the amniotic fluid:
- Helps maintain a constant body temperature for the fetus
- Permits symmetric growth and development of the fetus
- Cushions the fetus from trauma
- Allows the umbilical cord to be free of compression
- Promotes fetal movement to enhance musculoskeletal development
- Amniotic fluid volume can be important in determining fetal well-being

The nurse should explain the following functions of the placenta:
- Makes hormones to ensure implantation of the embryo and to control the mother's physiology to provide adequate nutrients and water to the growing fetus
- Transports oxygen and nutrients from the mother's bloodstream to the developing fetus
- Protects the fetus from immune attack by the mother
- Removes fetal waste products
- Near term, produces hormones to mature fetal organs in preparation for extrauterine life

The nurse should also explain the following about the umbilical cord:
- The lifeline from the mother to the fetus
- Formed from the amnion and contains one large vein and two small arteries
- Wharton jelly surrounds the vessels to prevent compression
- At term, the average length is 22 in and the average width is 1 in

SECTION III: PRACTICING FOR NCLEX

Activity G NCLEX-STYLE QUESTIONS

1. Answer: B
RATIONALE: This disorder is not X-linked. Either the father or the mother can pass the gene along regardless of whether their mate has the gene or not. The only way that an autosomal-dominant gene is not expressed is if it does not exist. If only one of the parents has the gene, then there is a 50% chance it will be passed on to the child.

2. Answer: C
RATIONALE: The nurse should instruct the client to stop using drugs, alcohol, and tobacco, as these harmful substances may be passed on to the fetus from the mother. There is no need to avoid exercise during pregnancy as long as the client follows the prescribed regimen. Wearing comfortable clothes is not as important as the client's health. The client does not need to avoid intercourse during pregnancy unless complications arise.

3. Answer: C
RATIONALE: The nurse should find out the age and cause of death for deceased family members, as it will help establish a genetic pattern. Although inquiry of a history of premature birth or depression during pregnancy are important and should be included in the data collection, they do not relate to genetically inherited disorders. A family history of drinking or drug abuse does not increase the risk of genetic disorders.

4. Answer: B
RATIONALE: Down syndrome occurs because of the presence of an extra chromosome in the body that is in either the sperm or the egg. Down syndrome is not genetically inherited, except in incidences of translocation which are very rare. Both males and females are equally at risk for Down syndrome. Most children with Down syndrome are born to younger mothers.

5. Answer: D
RATIONALE: While obtaining the genetic history of the client, the nurse should find out if the members of the couple are related to each other or have blood ties, as this increases the risk of many genetic disorders. The socioeconomic status or the physical characteristics of family members do not have any significant bearing on the risk of genetic disorders. The nurse should ask questions about race or ethnic background because some races are more susceptible to certain disorders than others.

6. Answer: C
RATIONALE: After the client has seen the specialist, the nurse should review what the specialist has discussed with the family and clarify any doubts the couple may have. The nurse should never make the decision for the client but rather should present all the relevant information and aid the couple in making an informed decision. There is no need for the nurse to refer the client to another specialist or for further diagnostic and screening tests unless instructed to do so by the specialist.

7. Answer: D
RATIONALE: Tay–Sachs disease affects both male and female babies. The age of the client does not significantly increase the risk of Tay–Sachs disease. Even though the client and her husband are not

related by blood, because of their background their baby is at a greater risk. There is a chance that the offspring may have Tay–Sachs disease even if both parents don't have it because they could be carriers, so genetic testing would be advisable.

8. **Answer: B, D, E**
   RATIONALE: The nurse should explain to the client that individuals with hemophilia are usually males. Female carriers have a 50% chance of transmitting the disorder to their sons, and females are affected by the condition if it is a dominant X-linked disorder. Offspring of nonhemophilic parents may be hemophilic. Daughters of an affected male are usually carriers.

9. **Answer: A, B, D**
   RATIONALE: The responsibilities of the nurse while counseling the client include knowing basic genetic terminology and inheritance patterns and explaining basic concepts of probability and disorder susceptibility. The nurse should ensure complete informed consent to facilitate decisions about genetic testing. The nurse should explain ethical and legal issues related to genetics as well. The nurse should never instruct the client on which decision to make and should let the client make the decision.

10. **Answer: D**
    RATIONALE: Prepregnancy screening with a genetic counselor would be helpful to the client who has a history of fetal loss as a result of a genetic disorder. The screening would allow the family to closely be evaluated for risk factors and have access to potential screening options.

11. **Answer: C**
    RATIONALE: The pictorial analysis of the number, form, and size of an individual's chromosomes is referred to as a karyotype. This analysis commonly uses white blood cells and fetal cells in amniotic fluid. The chromosomes are numbered from the largest to the smallest, 1 to 22, and the sex chromosomes are designated by the letter X or the letter Y. The severity and related complications of a disorder are not determined by the karyotype. Condition management is not determined by the karyotype.

12. **Answer: D**
    RATIONALE: Based upon the presenting findings, the mother is in her 4th month of pregnancy. This is when quickening occurs—the beginning of feeling fetal movement. Also, the mother now has lost her waistline and the breast areola has begun to darken.

CHAPTER 11

SECTION I: ASSESSING YOUR UNDERSTANDING

Activity A FILL IN THE BLANKS

1. cortisol
2. Ambivalence
3. Oxytocin
4. placenta
5. estrogen
6. sacroiliac
7. hemorrhoids
8. progesterone
9. Colostrum
10. leukorrhea

Activity B LABELING

1. The condition illustrated is supine hypotensive syndrome.
2. When the inferior vena cava is in the supine position, vena cava compression results from pressure of the gravid uterus. This causes a reduction in venous return and decreases cardiac output and blood pressure, with increasing orthostatic stress.
3. Symptoms associated with supine hypotensive include weakness, lightheadedness, nausea, dizziness, or syncope.

Activity C MATCHING

1. e   **2.** a   **3.** c   **4.** d   **5.** b

Activity D SEQUENCING

4 → 1 → 5 → 3 → 2

Activity E SHORT ANSWERS

1. Striae gravidarum, or stretch marks, are irregular reddish streaks that may appear on the abdomen, breasts, and buttocks in about half of pregnant women. Striae are most prominent by 6 to 7 months and occur in up to 90% of pregnant women. They are caused by reduced connective tissue strength resulting from elevated adrenal steroid levels and stretching of the structures secondary to growth. They are more common in younger women, women with larger infants, and women with higher body mass indices. Nonwhites and women with a history of breast or thigh striae or a family history of striae gravidarum are also at higher risk.

2. There is slight hypertrophy, or enlargement of the heart, during pregnancy to accommodate the increase in blood volume and cardiac output. The heart works harder and pumps more blood to supply the oxygen needs of the fetus as well as those of the mother. Both heart rate and venous return are increased in pregnancy, contributing to the increase in cardiac output seen throughout gestation.

3. Iron requirements during pregnancy increase because of the oxygen and nutrient demands of the growing fetus and the resulting increase in maternal blood volume. The fetal tissues take predominance over the mother's tissues with respect to use of iron stores. With the accelerated production of RBCs, iron is necessary for hemoglobin formation, the oxygen-carrying component of RBCs.

4. Pica is the compulsive ingestion of nonfood substances. The three main substances consumed by women with pica are soil or clay (geophagia),

ice (pagophagia), and laundry starch (amylophagia). Nutritional implications of pica include iron-deficiency anemia, parasitic infection, and constipation.

5. Oxytocin is responsible for stimulating uterine contractions. After delivery, oxytocin secretion causes the myometrium to contract and helps constrict the uterine blood vessels, decreasing the amount of vaginal bleeding after delivery. Oxytocin is also responsible for milk ejection during breast-feeding. Stimulation of the breasts through sucking or touching stimulates the secretion of oxytocin from the posterior pituitary gland.

6. Varicose veins during pregnancy are the result of venous distention and instability, from poor circulation secondary to prolonged standing or sitting. Venous compression from the heavy gravid uterus places pressure on the pelvic veins, also preventing efficient venous return.

SECTION II: APPLYING YOUR KNOWLEDGE
Activity F CASE STUDY

1. The realization of a pregnancy can lead to fluctuating responses, possibly at opposite ends of the spectrum. For example, regardless of whether the pregnancy was planned, it is normal to be fearful and anxious of the implications. The woman's reaction may be influenced by several factors, including the way she was raised by her family, her current family situation, the quality of the relationship with the expectant father, and her hopes for the future. It is common for some women to express concern over the timing of the pregnancy, wishing that goals and life objectives had been met before becoming pregnant. Other women may question how a newborn or infant will affect their careers or their relationships with friends and family. These feelings can cause conflict and confusion about the impending pregnancy.

  Ambivalence, or having conflicting feelings at the same time, is a universal feeling and is considered normal when preparing for a lifestyle change and new role. Pregnant women commonly experience ambivalence during the first trimester. Usually ambivalence evolves into acceptance by the second trimester, when fetal movement is felt.

2. A pregnant woman may withdraw and become increasingly preoccupied with herself and her fetus. As a result, participation with the outside world may be less, and she may appear passive to her family and friends. This introspective behavior is a normal psychological adaptation to motherhood for most women. Introversion seems to heighten during the first and third trimesters, when the woman's focus is on behaviors that will ensure a safe and healthy pregnancy outcome. Women may also feel disinterested in certain activities because of nausea and fatigue experienced in the first trimester. Couples need to be aware of this behavior

and be informed about measures to maintain and support the focus on the family.

3. During the second trimester, as the pregnancy progresses, the physical changes of the growing fetus, along with an enlarging abdomen and fetal movement, bring reality and validity to the pregnancy. The pregnant woman feels fetal movement and may hear the heartbeat. She may see the fetal image on an ultrasound screen and feel distinct parts, which allow her to identify the fetus as a separate individual. Many women will verbalize positive feelings of the pregnancy and will conceptualize the fetus. In addition, a reduction in physical discomfort will bring about an improvement in mood and physical well-being in the second trimester.

4. Frequently, pregnant women will start to cry without any apparent cause. Some feel as though they are riding an "emotional roller coaster." These extremes in emotion can make it difficult for partners and family members to communicate with the pregnant woman without placing blame on themselves for the woman's mood changes. Emotional liability is characteristic throughout most pregnancies. One moment a woman can feel great joy, and within a short time span feel shock and disbelief.

SECTION III: PRACTICING FOR NCLEX
Activity G NCLEX-STYLE QUESTIONS

1. **Answer: B**
   RATIONALE: Absence of menstruation, along with consistent nausea, fatigue, breast tenderness, and urinary frequency, are the presumptive signs of pregnancy. To determine if the client may be pregnant, a pregnancy test is indicated.

2. **Answer: C**
   RATIONALE: During pregnancy, the vaginal secretions become more acidic, white, and thick. Most women experience an increase in a whitish vaginal discharge, called leukorrhea, during pregnancy. The nurse should inform the client that the vaginal discharge is normal except when it is accompanied by itching and irritation, possibly suggesting Candida albicans infection, a monilial vaginitis, which is a very common occurrence in this glycogen-rich environment. Monilial vaginitis is a benign fungal condition and is treated with local antifungal agents. The client need not refrain from sexual activity when there is an increase in a thick, whitish vaginal discharge.

3. **Answer: A**
   RATIONALE: Estrogen aids in developing the ductal system of the breasts in preparation for lactation during pregnancy. hPL prepares the mammary glands for lactation. Progesterone supports the endometrium of the uterus to provide an environment conducive to fetal survival. Oxytocin is responsible for uterine contractions, both before and after birth. Oxytocin is also responsible for milk ejection during breastfeeding.

4. **Answer: D**
   RATIONALE: The maternal emotional response experienced by the client is ambivalence. Ambivalence, or having conflicting feelings at the same time, is universal and is considered normal when preparing for a lifestyle change and new role. Pregnant women commonly experience ambivalence during the first trimester.

5. **Answer: A, C, E**
   RATIONALE: Constipation during pregnancy is due to changes in the gastrointestinal system. Constipation can result from decreased activity level, use of iron supplements, intestinal displacement secondary to a growing uterus, slow transition time of food throughout the GI tract, a low-fiber diet, and reduced fluid intake. Increase in progesterone, not estrogen levels, causes constipation during pregnancy. Reduced stomach acidity does not cause constipation. Morning sickness has been linked to stomach acidity.

6. **Answer: A, B, D**
   RATIONALE: hCG levels in a normal pregnancy usually double every 48 to 72 hours, until they reach a peak at approximately 60 to 70 days after fertilization. This elevation of hCG corresponds to the morning sickness period of approximately 6 to 12 weeks during early pregnancy. Reduced stomach acidity and high levels of circulating estrogens are also believed to cause morning sickness. Elevation of hPL and RBC production do not cause morning sickness. hPL increases during the second half of pregnancy, and it helps in the preparation of mammary glands for lactation and is involved in the process of making glucose available for fetal growth by altering maternal carbohydrate, fat, and protein metabolism. The increase in RBCs is necessary to transport the additional oxygen required during pregnancy.

7. **Answer: C**
   RATIONALE: Spontaneous, irregular, painless contractions, called Braxton Hicks contractions, begin during the first trimester. These contractions are not the signs of preterm labor, infection of the GI tract, or acid indigestion. Acid indigestion causes heartburn. Acid indigestion or heartburn (pyrosis) is caused by regurgitation of the stomach contents into the upper esophagus and may be associated with the generalized relaxation of the entire digestive system.

8. **Answer: D**
   RATIONALE: The symptoms experienced by the client indicate supine hypotension syndrome. When the pregnant woman assumes a supine position, the expanding uterus exerts pressure on the inferior vena cava. The nurse should place the client in the left lateral position to correct this syndrome and optimize cardiac output and uterine perfusion. Elevating the client's legs, placing the client in an orthopneic position, or keeping the head of the bed elevated will not help alleviate the client's condition.

9. **Answer: A**
   RATIONALE: The nurse should instruct the parents to provide constant reinforcement of love and care to reduce the sibling's fear of change and possible replacement by the new family member. The parents should neither avoid talking to the child about the new arrival nor pay less attention to the child. The nurse should urge parents to include siblings in this event and make them feel a part of the preparations for the new infant. The nurse should instruct the parents to continue to focus on the older sibling after the birth to reduce regressive or aggressive behavior that might manifest toward the newborn. The child is exhibiting sibling rivalry, which results from the child's fear of change in the security of his relationships with his parents. This behavior is common and does not require the intervention of a child psychologist.

10. **Answer: B**
    RATIONALE: Monilial vaginitis is a benign fungal condition that is uncomfortable for women; it can be transmitted from an infected mother to her newborn at birth. Neonates develop an oral infection known as thrush, which presents as white patches on the mucus membranes of the mouth. Although rubella, toxoplasmosis, and cytomegalovirus are infections transmitted to the newborn by the mother, this newborn is not experiencing any of these infections. Rubella causes fetal defects, known as congenital rubella syndrome; common defects of rubella are cataracts, deafness, congenital heart defects, cardiac disease, and intellectual disability. Possible fetal effects due to toxoplasmosis include stillbirth, premature birth, microcephaly, hydrocephaly, seizures, and intellectual disability, whereas possible effects of cytomegalovirus infection include small for gestational age (SGA), microcephaly, hydrocephaly, and intellectual disability.

11. **Answer: A**
    RATIONALE: Between 38 and 40 weeks of gestation, the fundal height drops as the fetus begins to descend and engage into the pelvis. Because it pushes against the diaphragm, many women experience shortness of breath. By 40 weeks, the fetal head begins to descend and engage into the pelvis. Although breathing becomes easier because of this descent, the pressure on the urinary bladder now increases, and women experience urinary frequency. The fundus reaches its highest level at the xiphoid process at approximately 36, not 39, weeks. By 20 weeks' gestation, the fundus is at the level of the umbilicus and measures 20 cm. At between 6 and 8 weeks of gestation, the cervix begins to soften (Goodell sign) and the lower uterine segment softens (Hegar sign).

12. **Answer: C**
    RATIONALE: The skin and complexion of pregnant women undergo hyperpigmentation, primarily as a result of estrogen, progesterone, and melanocyte stimulating hormone levels. The increased

pigmentation that occurs on the breasts and geni-talia also develops on the face to form the "mask of pregnancy," or facial melasma (cholasma). This is a blotchy, brownish pigment that covers the forehead and cheeks in dark-haired women. The nurse would inform the client that this is a normal occurrence in pregnancy and should fade once she delivers the child.

13. **Answer: C**

    RATIONALE: During pregnancy, there is an increase in the client's blood components. These changes, coupled with venous stasis secondary to venous pooling, which occurs during late pregnancy after standing long periods of time (with the pressure exerted by the uterus on the large pelvic veins), contribute to slowed venous return, pooling, and dependent edema. These factors also increase the woman's risk for venous thrombosis. The symptoms experienced by the client do not indicate that she is at risk for hemorrhoids, embolism, or supine hypotension syndrome. Supine hypotension syndrome occurs when the uterus expands and exerts pressure on the inferior vena cava, which causes a reduction in blood flow to the heart. A client with supine hypotension syndrome experiences dizziness, clamminess, and a marked decrease in blood pressure.

14. **Answer: A, C, E**

    RATIONALE: Changes in the structures of the respiratory system take place to prepare the body for the enlarging uterus and increased lung volume. Increased vascularity of the respiratory tract is influenced by increased estrogen levels, leading to congestion. This congestion gives rise to nasal and sinus broadening with a conversion from abdominal breathing to thoracic breathing. Persistent cough, Kussmaul respirations, and dyspnea are not associated with the changes in the respiratory tract during pregnancy.

15. **Answer: D**

    RATIONALE: During the second trimester, many women will verbalize positive feelings about the pregnancy and will conceptualize the fetus. The woman may accept her new body image and talk about the new life within her. Generating a discussion about the woman's feelings and offering support and validation at prenatal visits are important nursing interventions. The nurse should encourage the client in her first trimester to focus on herself, not on the fetus; this is not required when the client is in her second trimester. The client's feelings are normal for the second trimester of pregnancy; hence, it is not necessary either to inform the primary health care provider about the client's feelings or to tell the client that it is too early to conceptualize the fetus.

16. **Answer: B**

    RATIONALE: The nurse should instruct the client to change sexual positions to increase comfort as the pregnancy progresses. Although the nurse should also encourage her to engage in alternative, noncoital modes of sexual expression, such as cuddling, caressing, and holding, the client need not restrict herself to such alternatives. It is not advisable to perform frequent douching, because this is believed to irritate the vaginal mucosa and predispose the client to infection. Using lubricants or performing stress-relieving and relaxation exercises will not alleviate discomfort during sexual activity.

17. **Answer: B**

    RATIONALE: During the second trimester of pregnancy, partners go through acceptance of their role of breadwinner, caretaker, and support person. They come to accept the reality of the fetus when movement is felt, and they experience confusion when dealing with the woman's mood swings and introspection. During the first trimester, the expectant partner may experience couvade syndrome—a sympathetic response to the partner's pregnancy—and may also experience ambivalence with extremes of emotions. During the third trimester, the expectant partner prepares for the reality of the new role and negotiates what his or her role will be during the labor and birthing process.

18. **Answer: A**

    RATIONALE: Pica is characterized by a craving for substances that have no nutritional value. Consumption of these substances can be dangerous to the client and her developing fetus. The nurse should monitor the client for iron-deficiency anemia as a manifestation of the client's compulsion to consume soil. Consumption of ice due to pica is likely to lead to tooth fractures. The nurse should monitor for inefficient protein metabolism if the client has been consuming laundry starch as a result of pica. The nurse should monitor for constipation in the client if she has been consuming clay.

19. **Answer: B, C, E**

    RATIONALE: When caring for a pregnant client who follows a vegetarian diet, the nurse should monitor her for iron-deficiency anemia, decreased mineral absorption, and low gestational weight gain. Risk of epistaxis and increased risk of constipation are not reported to be associated with a vegetarian diet.

CHAPTER 12

SECTION I: ASSESSING YOUR UNDERSTANDING

Activity A FILL IN THE BLANKS

1. doula
2. primipara
3. Fundal
4. Montgomery
5. Chadwick
6. Pica

7. Amniocentesis
8. liver
9. nonstress
10. Hemorrhoids

Activity B MATCHING

1. d **2.** e **3.** a **4.** b **5.** c

Activity C SEQUENCING

2 → 4 → 1 → 3

Activity D SHORT ANSWERS

1. The nurse should include the following key areas when providing preconception care:
   - Immunization status
   - Underlying medical conditions, such as cardiovascular or respiratory problems or genetic disorders
   - Reproductive health data such as pelvic examinations, use of contraceptives, and STIs
   - Sexuality and sexual practices, such as safe sex practices and body image issues
   - Nutrition
   - Lifestyle practices, including occupation and recreational activities
   - Psychosocial issues such as levels of stress and exposure to abuse and violence
   - Medication and drug use, including use of tobacco, alcohol, over-the-counter and prescription medications, and illicit drugs
   - Support system, including family, friends, and community

2. Nurses can enter into a collaborative partnership with a woman and her partner, enabling them to examine their own health and its influence on the health of their future baby. The nurse performs the following interventions as part of preconception care to ensure a positive impact on the pregnancy:
   - Stress the importance of taking folic acid to prevent neural tube defects.
   - Urge the woman to achieve optimal weight before pregnancy.
   - Ensure that the woman's immunizations are up to date.
   - Address substance use issues, including smoking and taking drugs.
   - Identify victims of violence and assist them in getting help.
   - Manage chronic conditions such as diabetes and asthma.
   - Educate the woman about environmental hazards, including metals and herbs.
   - Offer genetic counseling to identify carriers.
   - Suggest the availability of support systems, if needed.

3. The assessments to be made by a nurse on a client's initial prenatal visit are as follows:
   - Screen for factors that place the client and her fetus at risk.
   - Educate the client about changes that will affect her life.

4. Counseling and educating the pregnant client and her partner are important to healthy outcomes for the mother and her infant. The role of a nurse in providing counseling and education to the client during a prenatal visit is as follows:
   - Provide anticipatory guidance.
   - Make appropriate community referrals.
   - Answer questions that the client and her partner may have regarding the pregnancy. It is important for the nurse to clarify all the misinformation or misconceptions in the minds of the client and her partner.

5. The nurse should perform the following assessments when conducting a chest examination of the client:
   - Auscultate heart sounds, noting any abnormalities.
   - A soft systolic murmur caused by the increase in blood volume may be noted.
   - Anticipate an increase in heart rate by 10 to 15 beats per minute secondary to increases in cardiac output and blood volume.
   - Note adaptation of the body with peripheral dilatation.
   - Auscultate the chest for breath sounds, which should be clear.
   - Note symmetry of chest movement and thoracic breathing patterns.
   - Expect a slight increase in respiratory rate to accommodate the increase in tidal volume and oxygen consumption.
   - Inspect and palpate the breasts: increases in estrogen and progesterone and blood supply make the breasts feel full and more nodular, with increased sensitivity to touch.
   - Blood vessels become more visible, and there is an increase in breast size.
   - Striae gravidarum may be visible in women with large breasts.
   - Darker pigmentation of the nipple and areola is present, along with enlargement of Montgomery glands.
   - Teach and reinforce breast self-examination.

6. The nurse should perform the following assessments during a follow-up visit:
   - Weight and blood pressure, which are compared to baseline values
   - Urine testing for protein, glucose, ketones, and nitrites
   - Fundal height measurement to assess fetal growth
   - Assessment for quickening/fetal movement to determine well-being
   - Assessment of fetal heart rate (should be 120 to 160 beats per minute)
   - Answer questions
   - Provide anticipatory guidance and education
   - Review nutritional guidelines
   - Evaluate the client for compliance with prenatal vitamin therapy
   - Encourage the woman's partner to participate if possible

SECTION II: APPLYING YOUR KNOWLEDGE
Activity E CASE STUDY

1. The items in the checklist used by the nurse to ensure that the client is well prepared for the newborn's birth and homecoming are as follows:
   - Attend childbirth preparation classes and practice breathing techniques.
   - Purchase an infant safety seat.
   - Select a feeding method.
   - Decide whether a boy will be circumcised.
   - Select and arrange for a birth setting.
   - Tour the birthing facility.
   - Choose a family planning method to be used after the birth.
   - Communicate needs and desires concerning pain management.
   - Understand signs and symptoms of labor.
   - Provide for care of other siblings during labor (when applicable).
   - Discuss the possibility of a cesarean birth.
   - Prepare for the birthing facility when labor starts.
   - Discuss possible names for the newborn.
   - Know how to reach a health care professional when labor starts.
   - Decide on a pediatrician.
2. The nurse should perform the following interventions in preparing a client for breastfeeding:
   - Encourage the client to attend a La Leche League or breastfeeding class.
   - Provide the client with sources of information about infant feeding.
   - Suggest that the client reads a good reference book about lactation.
3. The nurse should educate the pregnant client about the following advantages of breastfeeding:
   - Human milk is digestible, economical, and requires no preparation
   - Promotes bonding between mother and child
   - Costs less than purchasing formula
   - Suppresses ovulation
   - Reduces the risk of ovarian cancer and premenopausal breast cancer
   - Uses extra calories, which promote weight loss gradually without dieting
   - Releases oxytocin, which promotes rapid uterine involution with less bleeding
   - Suckling helps in developing the muscles in the infant's jaw
   - Improves absorption of lactose and minerals in the newborn
   - Helps prevent infections in the baby
   - Composition of breast milk adapts to meet the infant's changing needs
   - Prevents constipation in the baby, with adequate intake
   - Helps lessen chance that the baby will develop food allergies
   - Reduces the incidence of otitis media and upper respiratory infections in the infant and the risk of adult obesity
   - Makes the baby less prone to vomiting

SECTION III: PRACTICING FOR NCLEX
Activity F NCLEX-STYLE QUESTIONS

1. **Answer: B**
   RATIONALE: When assessing fetal well-being through abdominal ultrasonography, the nurse should instruct the client to refrain from emptying her bladder. The nurse must ensure that abdominal ultrasonography is conducted on a full bladder and should inform the client that she is likely to feel cold, not hot, initially in the test. The nurse should obtain the client's vital records and instruct the client to report the occurrence of fever when the client has to undergo amniocentesis, not ultrasonography.
2. **Answer: A**
   RATIONALE: The nurse should inform the client that sexual activity is permissible during pregnancy unless there is a history of incompetent cervix, vaginal bleeding, placenta previa, risk of preterm labor, multiple gestation, premature rupture of membranes, or presence of any infection. Anemia and facial and hand edema would be contraindications to exercising but not intercourse. Freedom from anxieties and worries contributes to adequate sleep promotion.
3. **Answer: D**
   RATIONALE: To promote easy and safe travel for the client, the nurse should instruct the client to always wear a three-point seat belt to prevent ejection or serious injury from collision. The nurse should instruct the client to deactivate the air bag if possible. The nurse should instruct the client to apply a nonpadded shoulder strap properly, ensuring that it crosses between the breasts and over the upper abdomen, above the uterus. The nurse should instruct the client to use a lap belt that crosses over the pelvis below—not over—the uterus.
4. **Answer: C**
   RATIONALE: The nurse should instruct the client to serve the formula to her infant at room temperature. The nurse should instruct the client to follow the directions on the package when mixing the powder because different formulas may have different instructions. The infant should be fed every 3 to 4 hours, not every 8 hours. The nurse should specifically instruct the client to avoid refrigerating the formula for subsequent feedings. Any leftover formula should be discarded.
5. **Answer: D**
   RATIONALE: According to the Lamaze method of preparing for labor and birth, the nurse must remain quiet during the client's period of imagery and focal point visualization to avoid breaking her concentration. The nurse should ensure deep abdominopelvic breathing by the client according

to the Bradley method, along with ensuring the client's concentration on pleasurable sensations. The Bradley method emphasizes the pleasurable sensations of birth and involves teaching women to concentrate on these sensations when "turning on" to their own bodies. The nurse should ensure abdominal breathing during contractions when using the Dick-Read method.

6. **Answer: C**

   RATIONALE: When preparing the client for a physical examination, the nurse should instruct the client to empty her bladder; the nurse should then collect the urine sample so that it can be sent for laboratory tests to detect possibilities of a urinary tract infection. The client need not lie down, take deep breaths, or have the family present; however, it is important for the nurse to ensure that the client feels comfortable.

7. **Answer: A**

   RATIONALE: To reduce the client's urinary frequency, the nurse should instruct the client to avoid consuming caffeinated drinks, since caffeine stimulates voiding patterns. The nurse instructs the client to drink fluids between meals rather than with meals if the client reports nausea and vomiting. The nurse instructs the client to avoid an empty stomach at all times, to prevent fatigue. The nurse also instructs the client to munch on dry crackers or toast early in the morning before arising if the client experiences nausea and vomiting; this would not help the client experiencing urinary frequency.

8. **Answer: A, B, C**

   RATIONALE: When documenting a comprehensive health history while caring for a client, it is important for the nurse to prepare a care plan that suits the client's lifestyle, to develop a trusting relationship with the client, and to prepare a plan of care for the pregnancy. The nurse does not need to assess the client's partner's sexual health during the history-taking process or urge the client to achieve an optimal body weight. Achieving optimal body weight before conception helps the client to achieve a positive impact on the pregnancy.

9. **Answer: A, D, E**

   RATIONALE: While conducting a physical examination of the head and neck, the nurse assesses for any previous injuries and sequelae, evaluates for limitations in range of motion, and palpates the thyroid gland for enlargement. The nurse should also assess for any edema of the nasal mucosa or hypertrophy of gingival tissue, as well as palpate for enlarged lymph nodes or swelling. The nurse need not check the client's eye movements; pregnancy does not affect the eye muscles. The nurse should check for levels of estrogen when examining the extremities of the client.

10. **Answer: D**

    RATIONALE: In the 12th week of gestation, the nurse should palpate the fundus at the symphysis pubis. The nurse should palpate for the fundus below the ensiform cartilage when the client is in the 36th week of gestation; midway between symphysis and umbilicus in the 16th week of gestation; and at the umbilicus in the 20th week of gestation.

11. **Answer: C**

    RATIONALE: While examining external genitalia, the nurse should assess for any infection due to hematomas, varicosities, inflammation, lesions, and discharge. The nurse assesses for a long, smooth, thick, and closed cervix when examining the internal genitalia. Other assessments when examining the internal genitalia include assessing for bluish coloration of cervix and vaginal mucosa and conducting a rectal examination to assess for lesions, masses, prolapse, or hemorrhoids.

12. **Answer: A**

    RATIONALE: To help alleviate constipation, the nurse should instruct the client to ensure adequate hydration and bulk in the diet. The nurse should instruct the client to avoid spicy or greasy foods when a client reports heartburn or indigestion. The nurse also should instruct the client to avoid lying down for 2 hours after meals if the client experiences heartburn or indigestion. The nurse should instruct the client to practice Kegel exercises when the client experiences urinary frequency.

13. **Answer: B**

    RATIONALE: Naegele's rule can be used to establish the estimated date of birth (EDB). Using this rule, the nurse should subtract 3 months and then add 7 days to the first day of the last normal menstrual period. On the basis of Naegele's rule, the EDB will be December 17, because the client started her last menstrual period on March 10. January 7, February 21, and January 30 are not the EDB according to Naegele's rule.

14. **Answer: A**

    RATIONALE: In a client's second trimester of pregnancy, the nurse should educate the client to look for vaginal bleeding as a danger sign of pregnancy needing immediate attention from the physician. Generally, painful urination, severe/persistent vomiting, and lower abdominal and shoulder pain are the danger signs that the client has to monitor for during the first trimester of pregnancy.

15. **Answer: B**

    RATIONALE: To help the client alleviate varicosities of the legs, the nurse should instruct the client to refrain from crossing her legs when sitting for long periods. The nurse should instruct the client to avoid standing, not sitting, in one position for long periods of time. The nurse should instruct the client to wear support stockings to promote better circulation, though the client should stay away from constrictive stockings and socks. Applying heating pads on the extremities is not reported to alleviate varicosities of the legs.

CHAPTER 13

SECTION I: ASSESSING YOUR UNDERSTANDING

Activity A FILL IN THE BLANKS

1. gynecoid
2. effacement
3. sagittal
4. Zero
5. Lightening
6. sensitization
7. decidua
8. passageway
9. nesting
10. molding

Activity B LABELING

1. The pelvic shapes in images A to D are as follows. The gynecoid shape (Figure A) is the most favorable shape for a vaginal delivery.
   A. **Gynecoid:** This is considered the true female pelvis, occurring in about 50% of all women. Vaginal birth is most favorable with this type of pelvis because the inlet is round and the outlet is roomy.
   B. **Android:** This type of pelvic is characterized by its funnel shape. Descent of the fetal head into the pelvis is slow, and failure of the fetus to rotate is common. Prognosis for labor is poor, subsequently leading to cesarean birth.
   C. **Anthropoid:** Vaginal birth is more favorable with this pelvic shape (deep pelvis, wider front-to-back than side-to-side) compared to the android or platypelloid shape.
   D. **Platypelloid** (or flat pelvis): This is the least common type of pelvic structure. The pelvic cavity is shallow but widens at the pelvic outlet, making it difficult for the fetus to descend through the midpelvis. It is not favorable for a vaginal birth unless the fetal head can pass through the inlet. Women with this type of pelvis usually require cesarean birth.
2. The figure shows four breech presentations which are identified below. Breech presentations are associated with prematurity, placenta previa, multiparity, uterine abnormalities (fibroids), and some congenital anomalies such as hydrocephaly.
   A. Frank breech
   B. Complete breech
   C. Single footling breech
   D. Double footling breech

Activity C MATCHING

1. a   **2.** b   **3.** e   **4.** d   **5.** c

Activity D SEQUENCING

$$4 \rightarrow 5 \rightarrow 7 \rightarrow 1 \rightarrow 2 \rightarrow 6 \rightarrow 3$$

Activity E SHORT ANSWERS

1. Well-controlled research validates that nonmoving, back-lying positions during labor are not healthy. Despite this, most women lie flat on their backs. This position is preferred during labor mostly for the following reasons:
   - Laboring women need to conserve their energy and not tire themselves.
   - Nurses can keep track of clients more easily if they are not ambulating.
   - The supine position facilitates vaginal examinations and external belt adjustment.
   - A bed is simply where one is usually supposed to be in a hospital setting.
   - It is believed that this practice is convenient for the delivering health professional.
   - Laboring women are "connected to things" that impede movement.
2. The nurse should encourage the pregnant client to adopt the upright or lateral position because such a position
   - Reduces the duration of the second stage of labor
   - Reduces the number of assisted deliveries (vacuum and forceps)
   - Reduces episiotomies and perineal tears
   - Contributes to fewer abnormal fetal heart rate patterns
   - Increases comfort and reduces requests for pain medication
   - Enhances a sense of control reported by mothers
   - Alters the shape and size of the pelvis, which assists descent
   - Assists gravity to move the fetus downward
   - Reduces the length of labor
3. Maternal physiologic responses that occur as a woman progresses through childbirth include:
   - Increase in heart rate, by 10 to 20 beats per minute
   - Increase in cardiac output, by 12% to 31% during the first stage of labor and by 50% during the second stage of labor
   - Increase in blood pressure, up to 35 mm Hg during uterine contractions in all labor stages
   - Increase in white blood cell count, to 25,000 to 30,000 cells per mm^3, perhaps as a result of tissue trauma
   - Increase in respiratory rate, along with greater oxygen consumption, related to the increase in metabolism
   - Decrease in gastric motility and food absorption, which may increase the risk of nausea and vomiting during the transition stage of labor
   - Decrease in gastric emptying and gastric pH, which increase the risk of vomiting with aspiration
   - Slight elevation in temperature, possibly as a result of an increase in muscle activity
   - Muscular aches/cramps, as a result of a stressed musculoskeletal system involved in the labor process

- Increase in basal metabolic rate (BMR) and decrease in blood glucose levels because of the stress of labor
4. The factors that influence the ability of a woman to cope with labor stress include:
   - Previous birth experiences and their outcomes
   - Current pregnancy experience
   - Cultural considerations
   - Involvement of support system
   - Childbirth preparation
   - Expectations of the birthing experience
   - Anxiety level and fear of labor experience
   - Feelings of loss of control
   - Fatigue and weariness
   - Anxiety levels
5. The signs of separation that indicate the placenta is ready to deliver are the following:
   - Uterus rises upward.
   - Umbilical cord lengthens.
   - Blood trickles suddenly from the vaginal opening.
   - Uterus changes its shape to globular.
6. The following factors ensure a positive birth experience for the pregnant client:
   - Clear information on procedures
   - Positive support; not being alone
   - Sense of mastery, self-confidence
   - Trust in staff caring for her
   - Positive reaction to the pregnancy
   - Personal control over breathing
   - Preparation for the childbirth experience

SECTION II: APPLYING YOUR KNOWLEDGE
Activity F CASE STUDY

1. Many women fear being sent home from the hospital with "false labor." All women feel anxious when they feel contractions, but they should be informed that labor can be a long process, especially if it is their first pregnancy. With first pregnancies, the cervix can take up to 20 hours to dilate completely. False labor is a condition occurring during the latter weeks of some pregnancies, in which irregular uterine contractions are felt but the cervix is not affected. In contrast, true labor is characterized by contractions occurring at regular intervals that increase in frequency, duration, and intensity with the contraction starting in the back and radiating around toward the front of the abdomen. True labor contractions bring about progressive cervical dilation and effacement.

2. The client should follow the instructions of her health care provider, but generally the client is instructed to stay home until contractions are 5 minutes apart, lasting 45 to 60 seconds and strong enough so that a conversation during one is not possible. Variables, such as rural versus urban setting, time to the hospital/distance from hospital, traffic at certain times of day, are taken into consideration when giving instructions on when to leave to travel to the hospital. She should be

instructed to drink fluids and walk to assess if there is any change in her contractions. In true labor, contractions are regular, become closer together, and become stronger with time. The contraction starts in the back and radiates around toward the front of the abdomen.

3. Changing positions and moving around during labor and birth do offer several benefits. Maternal position can influence pelvic size and contours. Changing position and walking affect the pelvis joints, which facilitate fetal descent and rotation. Squatting enlarges the pelvic diameter, whereas a kneeling position removes pressure on the maternal vena cava and assists to rotate the fetus in the posterior position.

   The client should be encouraged to ask the nurse caring for her during labor if she can walk and have the nurse suggest positions to try.

4. Pushing occurs during the second stage of labor, which begins with complete cervical dilation (10 cm) and effacement and ends with the birth of the newborn. Although the previous stage of labor primarily involved the thinning and opening of the cervix, this stage involves moving the fetus through the birth canal and out of the body. The cardinal movements of labor occur during the early phase of passive descent in the second stage of labor.

   Additional second-stage characteristics that help indicate that pushing can occur include contractions that occur every 2 to 3 minutes, last 60 to 90 seconds, and are described as strong by palpation. During this expulsive stage, the client may feel more in control and less irritable and agitated and be focused on the work of pushing. During the second stage of labor, pushing can either follow a spontaneous urge or be directed by the nurse and/or health provider.

SECTION III: PRACTICING FOR NCLEX
Activity G NCLEX-STYLE QUESTIONS

1. **Answer: B**
   RATIONALE: The nurse knows that the client is experiencing lightening. Lightening occurs when the fetal presenting part begins to descend into the maternal pelvis, and may occur 2 weeks or more before labor. The uterus lowers and moves into a more anterior position. The client may report increased respiratory capacity, decreased dyspnea, increased pelvic pressure, cramping, and low back pain. She may also note edema of the lower extremities as a result of the increased stasis of blood pooling, an increase in vaginal discharge, and more frequent urination. The nurse would continue to monitor the client as this is a normal progression of pregnancy.

2. **Answer: A, B, D**
   RATIONALE: Upon seeing the increased prostaglandin levels, the nurse should assess for myometrial contractions, leading to a reduction in cervical

resistance and subsequent softening and thinning of the cervix. The uterus of the client will appear boggy during the fourth stage of birth, after the completion of pregnancy and birth. Hypotonic character of the bladder is also marked during the fourth stage of pregnancy, not when the prostaglandin levels rise, marking the onset of labor.

3. **Answer: A**
RATIONALE: Braxton Hicks contractions assist in labor by ripening and softening the cervix and moving the cervix from a posterior position to an anterior position. Prostaglandin levels increase late in pregnancy secondary to elevated estrogen levels; this is not due to the occurrence of Braxton Hicks contractions. Braxton Hicks contractions do not help in bringing about oxytocin sensitivity. Occurrence of lightening, not Braxton Hicks contractions, makes maternal breathing easier.

4. **Answer: C**
RATIONALE: The labor of a first-time-pregnant woman lasts longer because during the first pregnancy the cervix takes between 12 and 16 hours to dilate completely. The intensity of the Braxton Hicks contractions stays the same during the first and second pregnancies. Spontaneous rupture of membranes may occur before the onset of labor during each birth, not only during the first birth.

5. **Answer: D**
RATIONALE: The advantage of adopting a kneeling position during labor is that it helps to rotate the fetus in a posterior position. Facilitating vaginal examinations, facilitating external belt adjustment, and helping the woman in labor to save energy are advantages of the back-lying maternal position.

6. **Answer: A, B, C**
RATIONALE: When caring for a client in labor, the nurse should monitor for an increase in the heart rate by 10 to 20 beats per minute, an increase in blood pressure by as much as 35 mm Hg, and an increase in respiratory rate. During labor, the nurse should monitor for a slight elevation in body temperature as a result of an increase in muscle activity. The nurse should also monitor for decreased gastric emptying and gastric pH, which increase the risk of vomiting with aspiration.

7. **Answer: D**
RATIONALE: When monitoring fetal responses in a client experiencing labor, the nurse should monitor for a decrease in circulation and perfusion to the fetus secondary to uterine contractions. The nurse should monitor for an increase, not a decrease, in arterial carbon dioxide pressure. The nurse should also monitor for a decrease, not an increase, in fetal breathing movements throughout labor. The nurse should monitor for a decrease in fetal oxygen pressure with a decrease in the partial pressure of oxygen.

8. **Answer: C**
RATIONALE: The nurse must massage the client's uterus briefly after placental expulsion to constrict the uterine blood vessels and minimize the possibility of hemorrhage. Massaging the client's uterus will not lessen the chances of conducting an episiotomy. In addition, an episiotomy, if required, is conducted in the second stage of labor, not the third. The client's uterus may appear boggy only in the fourth stage of labor, not in the third stage. Ensuring that all sections of the placenta are present and that no piece is left attached to the uterine wall is confirmed through a placental examination after expulsion.

9. **Answer: D**
RATIONALE: The first stage of labor terminates with the dilation of the cervix diameter to 10 cm. Diffused abdominal cramping and rupturing of the fetal membrane occur during the first stage of labor. Regular contractions occur at the beginning of the latent phase of the first stage; they do not mark the end of the first stage of labor.

10. **Answer: A, C, E**
RATIONALE: The nurse knows that lower uterine segment distention, stretching and tearing of the structures, and dilation of the cervix cause pain in the first stage. The fetus moves along the birth canal during the second stage of labor, when the client is more in control and less agitated. Spontaneous expulsion of the placenta occurs in the third stage of labor, not the first.

11. **Answer: B**
RATIONALE: The nurse, along with the physician, has to assess for fetal anomalies, which are usually associated with a shoulder presentation during a vaginal birth. The other conditions include placenta previa and multiple gestations. Uterine abnormalities, congenital anomalies, and prematurity are conditions associated with a breech presentation of the fetus during a vaginal birth.

12. **Answer: A, B, C**
RATIONALE: To ensure a positive birth experience for the client, the nurse should provide the client clear information on procedures involved, encourage the client to have a sense of mastery and self-control, and encourage the client to have a positive reaction to pregnancy. Instructing the client to spend some time alone is not an appropriate intervention; instead, the nurse should instruct the client to obtain positive support and avoid being alone. The client does not need to change the home environment; this does not ensure a positive birth experience.

13. **Answer: C**
RATIONALE: If the long axis of the fetus is perpendicular to that of the mother, then the client's fetus is in the transverse lie position. If the long axis of the fetus is parallel to that of the mother, the client's fetus is in the longitudinal lie position. The long axis of the fetus being at 45 or 60 degrees to that of the client does not indicate any specific position of the fetus.

14. **Answer: D**
RATIONALE: The pauses between contractions during labor are important because they allow the restoration of blood flow to the uterus and the placenta. Shortening of the upper uterine segment, reduction in length of the cervical canal, and effacement and dilation of the cervix are other processes that occur during uterine contractions.

15. **Answer: A, C, D**
RATIONALE: To provide comfort to the pregnant client, the nurse should make use of massage, hand holding, and acupressure to bring comfort to the pregnant client during labor. It is not advisable to provide chewing gum to a client in labor; it may cause accidental asphyxiation. Pain killers are not prescribed for a client experiencing labor.

CHAPTER 14

SECTION I: ASSESSING YOUR UNDERSTANDING

Activity A FILL IN THE BLANKS

1. Nonpharmacologic
2. hypoglycemia
3. fern
4. uteroplacental
5. ischial
6. uterine
7. tocotransducer
8. Artifact
9. parasympathetic
10. accelerations

Activity B MATCHING

1. c   **2.** b   **3.** a   **4.** d

Activity C SEQUENCING

1. b → a → c → e → d

Activity D SHORT ANSWERS

1. The nurse should include biographical data such as the woman's name and age, and the name of the delivering health care provider, prenatal record data, past health and family history, prenatal education, medications, risk factors, reason for admission, history of previous preterm births, allergies, the last time the client ate, method for infant feeding, name of birth attendant and pediatrician, and pain management plan.
2. The Apgar score assesses five parameters—heart rate (absent, slow, or fast), respiratory effort (absent, weak cry, or good strong yell), muscle tone (limp, or lively and active), response to irritation stimulus, and color—that evaluate a newborn's cardiorespiratory adaptation after birth.
3. The purpose of vaginal examination is to assess the amount of cervical dilation, the percentage of cervical effacement, and the fetal membrane status, and to gather information about presentation, position, and station. If the presentation is cephalic, the degree of fetal head flexion and presence of fetal skull swelling or molding can be determined during the vaginal examination.
4. Advantage: Electronic fetal monitoring produces a continuous record of the FHR, unlike intermittent auscultation, when gaps are likely.
Disadvantage: Continuous monitoring can limit maternal movement and encourages her to lie in the supine position, which reduces placental perfusion.
5. The typical signs of the second stage of labor are as follows:
   • Increase in apprehension or irritability
   • Spontaneous rupture of membranes
   • Sudden appearance of sweat on upper lip
   • Increase in blood-tinged show
   • Low grunting sounds from the woman
   • Complaints of rectal and perineal pressure
   • Beginning of involuntary bearing-down efforts
6. Positions used for the second stage of labor are as follows:
   • Lithotomy with feet up in stirrups: most convenient position for caregivers
   • Semisitting with pillows underneath knees, arms, and back
   • Lateral/side-lying with curved back and upper leg supported by partner
   • Sitting on birthing stool: opens pelvis, enhances the pull of gravity, and helps with pushing
   • Squatting/supported squatting: gives the woman a sense of control
   • Kneeling with hands on bed and knees comfortably apart

SECTION II: APPLYING YOUR KNOWLEDGE
Activity E CASE STUDY

1. If there was no vaginal bleeding on admission, the nurse should perform a vaginal examination to assess cervical dilation, after which it is monitored periodically as necessary to identify progress.
2. The purpose of vaginal examination is to assess the amount of cervical dilation, the percentage of cervical effacement, and the fetal membrane status and to gather information about presentation, position, and station. If the presentation is cephalic, the degree of fetal head flexion and presence of fetal skull swelling or molding can be assessed. The vaginal examination will also reveal the presence of a breech presentation.
3. Procedure for conducting vaginal examination:
   • Instruct the client on the purpose of the vaginal examination.
   • Place the client in a lithotomy position.
   • Put on sterile gloves.

- Use water as lubricant to check membrane status, if needed.
- Use antiseptic solution to prevent infection if the membrane has ruptured.
- Insert index and middle fingers into the vaginal introitus.
- Palpate cervix to assess dilation, effacement, and position.

SECTION III: PRACTICING FOR NCLEX

Activity F NCLEX-STYLE QUESTIONS

1. **Answer: A**
   RATIONALE: When a nurse first comes in contact with a pregnant client, it is important to first ascertain whether the woman is in true or false labor. Information regarding the number of pregnancies or history of drug allergy is not important criteria for admitting the client. The health care provider should be notified once the nurse knows the client's current status.

2. **Answer: A, C, D**
   RATIONALE: When conducting an admission assessment on the phone for a pregnant client, the nurse needs to obtain information regarding the estimated due date, characteristics of contractions, and appearance of vaginal blood to evaluate the need to admit her. History of drug abuse or a drug allergy is usually recorded as part of the client's medical history.

3. **Answer: B**
   RATIONALE: When a pregnant client is in the active phase of labor, the nurse should monitor the vital signs every 30 minutes. The nurse should monitor the vital signs every 30 to 60 minutes if the client is in the latent phase of labor and every 15 to 30 minutes during the transition phase of labor. Temperature is usually monitored every 4 hours in the active phase of labor.

4. **Answer: A**
   RATIONALE: In a cephalic presentation, the FHR is best heard in the lower quadrant of the maternal abdomen. In a breech presentation, it is heard at or above the level of the maternal umbilicus.

5. **Answer: A**
   RATIONALE: Analysis of the FHR using external electronic fetal monitoring is one of the primary evaluation tools used to determine fetal oxygen status indirectly. Fetal pulse oximetry measures fetal oxygen saturation directly and in real time. It is used with electronic fetal monitoring as an adjunct method of assessment when the FHR pattern is abnormal or inconclusive. Fetal scalp blood is obtained to measure the pH. The fetal position can be determined through ultrasonography or abdominal palpation but is not indicative of fetal oxygenation.

6. **Answer: A**
   RATIONALE: Increased sedation is an adverse effect of lorazepam. Diazepam and midazolam cause

central nervous system depression for both the woman and the newborn. Opioids are associated with newborn respiratory depression and decreased alertness.

7. **Answer: D**
   RATIONALE: General anesthesia is administered in emergency cesarean births. Local anesthetic is injected into the superficial perineal nerves to numb the perineal area generally before an episiotomy. Although an epidural block is used in cesarean births, it is contraindicated in clients with spinal injury. Regional anesthesia is contraindicated in cesarean births.

8. **Answer: C**
   RATIONALE: During the latent phase of labor, the nurse should monitor the FHR every 30 to 60 minutes. FHR should be monitored every 30 minutes in the active phase and every 15 to 30 minutes in the transition phase of labor. Continuous monitoring is done when an electronic fetal monitor is used.

9. **Answer: B**
   RATIONALE: If vaginal bleeding is absent during admission assessment, the nurse should perform vaginal examination to assess the amount of cervical dilation. Hydration status is monitored as part of the physical examination. A urine specimen is obtained for urinalysis to obtain a baseline. Vital signs are monitored frequently throughout the maternal assessment.

10. **Answer: C**
    RATIONALE: The nitrazine tape shows a pH between 5 and 6, which indicates an acidic environment with the presence of vaginal fluid and less blood. If the membranes had ruptured, amniotic fluid was present, or there was excess blood, the nitrazine test tape would have indicated an alkaline environment. The nurse would notify the health care provider for further assessment of the client.

11. **Answer: A, B, E**
    RATIONALE: The nurse should assess the frequency of contractions, intensity of contractions, and uterine resting tone to monitor uterine contractions. Monitoring changes in temperature and blood pressure is part of the general physical examination and does not help to monitor uterine contraction.

12. **Answer: A, B, C**
    RATIONALE: Leopold maneuvers help the nurse to determine the presentation, position, and lie of the fetus. The approximate weight and size of the fetus can be determined with ultrasound sonography or abdominal palpation.

13. **Answer: A, C, D**
    RATIONALE: The nurse should turn the client on her left side to increase placental perfusion, administer oxygen by mask to increase fetal oxygenation, and assess the client for any underlying contributing causes. The client's questions should not be ignored; instead, the client should be reassured that interventions are to

effect FHR pattern change. A reduced IV rate would decrease intravascular volume, affecting the FHR further.

14. **Answer: C**
RATIONALE: The client should be administered oxygen by mask because the abnormal FHR pattern could be due to inadequate oxygen reserves in the fetus. Because the client is in preterm labor, it is not advisable to apply vibroacoustic stimulation, tactile stimulation, or fetal scalp stimulation.

15. **Answer: A**
RATIONALE: The nurse must monitor for respiratory depression. Monitoring the client's respiratory rate will be the best indicator of respiratory depression.

16. **Answer: B**
RATIONALE: The nurse should provide supplemental oxygen if a client who has been administered combined spinal–epidural analgesia exhibits signs of hypotension and associated FHR changes. The client should be assisted to a semi-Fowler position; the client should not be kept in a supine position or be turned on her left side. Discontinuing IV fluid will cause dehydration.

17. **Answer: A**
RATIONALE: The recommendation for initiating hydrotherapy is that women be in active labor (>5 cm dilated) to prevent the slowing of labor contractions secondary to muscular relaxation. Women are encouraged to stay in the bath or shower as long as they feel they are comfortable. The water temperature should not exceed body temperature. The woman's membranes can be intact or ruptured.

18. **Answer: B**
RATIONALE: For slow-paced breathing, the nurse should instruct the woman to inhale slowly through her nose and exhale through pursed lips. In shallow or modified-paced breathing, the woman should inhale and exhale through her mouth at a rate of 4 breaths every 5 seconds. In pattern-paced breathing, the breathing is punctuated every few breaths by a forceful exhalation through pursed lips. Holding the breath for 5 seconds after every 3 breaths is not recommended in any of the three levels of patterned breathing.

19. **Answer: A, B, D**
RATIONALE: The nurse should check for any abnormality of the spine, hypovolemia, or coagulation defects in the client. An epidural is contraindicated in women with these conditions. Varicose veins and skin rashes or bruises are not contraindications for an epidural block. They are contraindications for massage used for pain relief during labor.

20. **Answer: B**
RATIONALE: The nurse should monitor the client for uterine relaxation. If this is noted, the nurse would continually massage the client's fundus until it no longer felt boggy.

CHAPTER 15

SECTION I: ASSESSING YOUR UNDERSTANDING

Activity A FILL IN THE BLANKS

1. pelvis
2. subinvolution
3. Afterpains
4. engorgement
5. uterus
6. Oxytocin
7. nonlactating
8. Lactation
9. Prolactin
10. diaphoresis

Activity B MATCHING

1. d   **2.** e   **3.** a   **4.** b   **5.** c

Activity C SEQUENCING

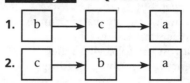

1. b → c → a
2. c → b → a

Activity D SHORT ANSWERS

1. The timing of the first menses and ovulation after birth differs considerably in lactating and nonlactating women. In nonlactating women, menstruation resumes 7 to 9 weeks after giving birth; the first cycle is anovulatory. In lactating women, the return of menses depends on the frequency and duration of breastfeeding. It usually resumes anytime from 2 to 18 months after childbirth, and the first postpartum menses is usually heavier and frequently anovulatory. However, ovulation may occur before menstruation, so breastfeeding is not a reliable method of contraception.

2. Afterpains are more acute in multiparous women secondary to repeated stretching of the uterine muscles, which reduces muscle tone, allowing for alternate uterine contraction and relaxation.

3. Factors that facilitate uterine involution are
   • Complete expulsion of amniotic membranes and placenta at birth
   • Complication-free labor and birth process
   • Breastfeeding
   • Ambulation

4. Factors that inhibit involution include
   • Prolonged labor and difficult birth
   • Incomplete expulsion of amniotic membranes and placenta
   • Uterine infection
   • Overdistention of the uterine muscles due to:
     a. Multiple gestation, hydramnios, or large singleton fetus
     b. Full bladder, which displaces uterus and interferes with contractions

    c. Anesthesia, which relaxes uterine muscles

    d. Close childbirth spacing, leading to frequent and repeated distention and thus decreasing uterine tone and causing muscular relaxation

5. Women who have had cesarean births tend to have less flow because the uterine debris is removed manually with delivery of the placenta.

6. Afterpains are usually stronger during breastfeeding because oxytocin released by the sucking reflex strengthens uterine contractions. Mild analgesics can be used to reduce this discomfort.

SECTION II: APPLYING YOUR KNOWLEDGE

Activity E CASE STUDY

1. The nurse should suggest the following measures to resolve engorgement in the client who is breastfeeding:

    Empty the breasts frequently to minimize discomfort and resolve engorgement.

    Stand in a warm shower or apply warm compresses to the breasts to provide some relief.

2. The nurse should suggest the following relief measures for the client with nonbreastfeeding engorgement:

- Wear a tight, supportive bra 24 hours daily.
- Apply ice to the breasts for approximately 15 to 20 minutes every other hour.
- Do not stimulate the breasts by squeezing or manually expressing milk from the nipples.
- Avoid exposing the breasts to warmth.

SECTION III: PRACTICING FOR NCLEX

Activity F NCLEX-STYLE QUESTIONS

1. Answer: D
RATIONALE: Displacement of the uterus from the midline to the right and frequent voiding of small amounts suggest urinary retention with overflow. Catheterization may be necessary to empty the bladder to restore tone. An IV and oxytocin are indicated if the client experiences hemorrhage due to uterine atony from being displaced. The health care provider would be notified if no other interventions help the client.

2. Answer: B, C, D
RATIONALE: The nurse should tell the client to use warm sitz baths, witch hazel pads, and anesthetic sprays to provide local comfort. Using normal body mechanics and maintaining a correct position are important to prevent lower back pain and injury to the joints.

3. Answer: A
RATIONALE: The nurse should recommend that the client practice Kegel exercises to improve pelvic floor tone, strengthen the perineal muscles, and promote healing. Sitz baths are useful in promoting local comfort in a client who had an episiotomy during the birth. Abdominal crunches would not

be advised during the initial postpartum period and would not help tone the pelvic floor as much as Kegel exercises.

4. Answer: A, B, D
RATIONALE: Many women have difficulty with feeling the sensation to void after giving birth if they have received an anesthetic block during labor, which inhibits neural functioning of the bladder. This client will be at risk for incomplete emptying, bladder distention, difficulty voiding, and urinary retention. Ambulation difficulty and perineal lacerations are due to episiotomy.

5. Answer: C
RATIONALE: Postpartum diuresis is due to the buildup and retention of extra fluids during pregnancy. Bruising and swelling of the perineum, swelling of tissues surrounding the urinary meatus, and decreased bladder tone due to anesthesia cause urinary retention.

6. Answer: B
RATIONALE: The nurse should recommend that clients maintain correct position and normal body mechanics to prevent pain in the lower back, hips, and joints. Avoiding carrying her baby and soaking several times per day are unrealistic. Application of ice is suggested to help relieve breast engorgement in nonbreastfeeding clients.

7. Answer: A
RATIONALE: The nurse should suggest that the father care for the newborn by holding and talking to the child. Reading up on parental care and speaking to his friends or the physician will not help the father resolve his fears about caring for the child.

8. Answer: C
RATIONALE: The nurse should encourage the client to change her pajamas to prevent chilling and reassure the client that it is normal to have postpartal diaphoresis. Drinking cold fluids at night will not prevent postpartum diaphoresis.

9. Answer: C
RATIONALE: The nurse should tell the client to frequently empty the breasts to improve milk supply. Encouraging cold baths and applying ice on the breasts are recommended to relieve engorgement in nonbreastfeeding clients. Kegel exercises are encouraged to promote pelvic floor tone.

10. Answer: A
RATIONALE: The nurse should explain to the client that lochia rubra is a deep red mixture of mucus, tissue debris, and blood. Discharge consisting of leukocytes, decidual tissue, RBCs, and serous fluid is called lochia serosa. Discharge consisting of only RBCs and leukocytes is blood. Discharge consisting of leukocytes and decidual tissue is called lochia alba.

11. Answer: D
RATIONALE: The abdominal organs, including the diaphragm, typically return to prepregnancy state

within 1 to 3 weeks after birth. Discomforts such as shortness of breath and rib aches lessen, and tidal volume and vital capacity return to normal values.

12. **Answer: A, C, D**
    RATIONALE: Many people of Latin American, African, and Asian descent believe that normal health involves a balance of heat and cold. The blood loss during birth is considered loss of warmth, leaving the woman in a cold state. Therefore, cold foods are avoided during this time. Hot soup and mashed potatoes with gravy would provide the warm foods that are desired.

13. **Answer: C**
    RATIONALE: The taking-in phase occurs during the first 24 to 48 hours following the birth of the newborn and is characterized by the mother taking on a very passive role in caring for herself, as well as recounting her labor experience. The second maternal adjustment phase is the taking-hold phase and usually lasts several weeks after the birth. This phase is characterized by both dependent and independent behavior, with increasing autonomy. During the letting-go phase the mother reestablishes relationships with others and accepts her new role as a parent. Acquaintance/attachment phase is a newer term that refers to the first 2 to 6 weeks following birth when the mother is learning to care for her baby and is physically recuperating from the pregnancy and birth.

14. **Answer: A**
    RATIONALE: The nurse should explain to the client that the afterpains are due to oxytocin released by the sucking reflex, which strengthens uterine contractions. An NSAID such as ibuprofen will decrease the discomfort from the afterpains. The client should not discontinue breastfeeding as this could decrease her milk supply. A warm shower may help relax the client; however, the NSAID would be more appropriate at this time.

15. **Answer: C**
    RATIONALE: The client should have lochia rubra for 3 to 4 days postpartum. The client would then progress to lochia serosa being expelled from day 3 to 10. Last the client would have lochia alba from day 10 to 14 until 3 to 6 weeks.

16. **Answer: C**
    RATIONALE: Involution involves three retrogressive processes. The first of these is contraction of muscle fibers, which serves to reduce those previously stretched during pregnancy. Next, catabolism reduces enlarged, individual myometrial cells. Finally, there is regeneration of uterine epithelium from the lower layer of the decidua after the upper layers have been sloughed off and shed during lochia. The breasts do not return to their prepregnancy size as the uterus does. Urinary retention inhibits uterine involution.

CHAPTER 16

SECTION I: ASSESSING YOUR UNDERSTANDING

Activity A FILL IN THE BLANKS

1. peribottle
2. mastitis
3. hypertension
4. Pain
5. Orthostatic
6. fundus
7. cesarean
8. Reciprocity
9. Commitment
10. colostrum

Activity B MATCHING

1. c   **2.** a   **3.** d   **4.** b   **5.** e

Activity C SHORT ANSWERS

1. Postpartum assessment of the mother typically includes vital signs, pain level, and a systematic head-to-toe review of the body systems: breasts, uterus, bladder, bowels, lochia, episiotomy/perineum, extremities, and emotional status.

2. The new mother might ignore her own needs for health and nutrition. She should be encouraged to take good care of herself and eat a healthy diet so that the nutrients lost during pregnancy can be replaced and she can return to a healthy weight. The nurse should provide nutritional recommendations, such as:
   • Eating a wide variety of foods with high nutrient density
   • Using foods and recipes that require little or no preparation
   • Avoiding high-fat, fast foods and fad weight-reduction diets
   • Drinking plenty of fluids
   • Avoiding harmful substances such as alcohol, tobacco, and drugs
   • Avoiding excessive intake of fat, salt, sugar, and caffeine
   • Eating the recommended daily servings from each food group

3. The physical stress of pregnancy and birth, the required caregiving tasks associated with a newborn, meeting the needs of other family members, and fatigue can cause the postpartum period to be quite stressful for the mother.

4. Postpartum danger signs include:
   • Fever more than 38°C (100.4°F) after the first 24 hours following birth
   • Foul-smelling lochia or an unexpected change in color or amount
   • Visual changes, such as blurred vision or spots, or headaches

- Calf pain experienced with dorsiflexion of the foot
- Swelling, redness, or discharge at the episiotomy site
- Dysuria, burning, or incomplete emptying of the bladder
- Shortness of breath or difficulty breathing
- Depression or extreme mood swings

5. The nurse should model behavior to family members as follows:
   - Holding the newborn close and speaking positively
   - Referring to the newborn by name in front of the parents
   - Speaking directly to the newborn in a calm voice
   - Encouraging both parents to pick up and hold the newborn
   - Monitoring newborn's response to parental stimulation
   - Pointing out positive physical features of the newborn

6. The nurse should suggest the following to the family to avoid sibling rivalry:
   - Expect and tolerate some regression
   - Discuss the new infant during relaxed family times
   - Teach safe handling of the newborn with a doll
   - Encourage older children to verbalize emotions about the newborn
   - Move the sibling from the crib to a youth bed months in advance of the birth of the newborn

---

SECTION II: APPLYING YOUR KNOWLEDGE

Activity D CASE STUDY

1. The nurse should perform the following assessments in a client intending to breastfeed her baby:
   - Inspect the breasts for size, contour, asymmetry, engorgement, or areas of erythema.
   - Check the nipples for cracks, redness, fissures, or bleeding.
   - Palpate the breasts to ascertain if they are soft, filling, or engorged, and document findings.
   - Palpate the breasts for any nodules, masses, or areas of warmth, which may indicate a plugged duct that may progress to mastitis if not treated promptly.
   - Describe and document any discharge from the nipple that is not creamy yellow or bluish white.

2. The client is encouraged to offer frequent feedings, at least every 2 to 3 hours, using manual expression just before feeding to soften the breast so the newborn can latch on more effectively. The client should be told to allow the newborn to feed on the first breast until it softens before switching to the other side.

SECTION III: PRACTICING FOR NCLEX

Activity E NCLEX-STYLE QUESTIONS

1. **Answer: B**
   RATIONALE: Postpartum assessment is typically performed every 15 minutes for the first hour. After the second hour, assessment is performed every 30 minutes. The client has to be monitored closely during the first hour after birth; assessment frequencies of 45 or 60 minutes are too long.

2. **Answer: D**
   RATIONALE: A boggy or relaxed uterus is a sign of uterine atony. This can be the result of bladder distention, which displaces the uterus upward and to the right, or retained placental fragments. Foul-smelling urine and purulent drainage are signs of infections but are not related to uterine atony. The firm fundus is normal and is not a sign of uterine atony.

3. **Answer: B**
   RATIONALE: "Scant" would describe a 1- to 2-in (2.5- to 5-cm) lochia stain on the perineal pad, or an approximate 10-mL loss. This is a normal finding in the postpartum client. The nurse would document this and continue to assess the client as ordered.

4. **Answer: D**
   RATIONALE: The nurse should classify the laceration as fourth degree because it continues through the anterior rectal wall. First-degree laceration involves only skin and superficial structures above muscle; second-degree laceration extends through perineal muscles; and third-degree laceration extends through the anal sphincter muscle but not through the anterior rectal wall.

5. **Answer: C**
   RATIONALE: The nurse should ensure that the ice pack is changed frequently to promote normal hygiene and to allow for periodic assessments. Ice packs are wrapped in a disposable covering or clean washcloth and then applied to the perineal area, not directly. The nurse should apply the ice pack for 20 minutes, not 40 minutes. Ice packs should be used for the first 24 hours, not for a week after birth.

6. **Answer: A**
   RATIONALE: The nurse should reassure the mother that some newborns "latch on and catch on" right away, and some newborns take more time and patience; this information will help to reduce the feelings of frustration and uncertainty about their ability to breastfeed. The nurse should also explain that breastfeeding is a learned skill for both parties. It would not be correct to say that breastfeeding is a mechanical procedure. In fact, the nurse should encourage the mother to cuddle and caress the newborn while feeding. The nurse should allow sufficient time to the mother and child to enjoy each other in an unhurried atmosphere. The nurse

should teach the mother to burp the newborn frequently. Different positions, such as cradle and football holds and side-lying positions, should be shown to the mother.

7. Answer: C
RATIONALE: The nurse should observe positioning and latching-on technique while breastfeeding so that she may offer suggestions based on observation to correct positioning/latching. This will help minimize trauma to the breast. The client should use only water, not soap, to clean the nipples to prevent dryness. Breast pads with plastic liners should be avoided. Leaving the nursing bra flaps down after feeding allows nipples to air dry.

8. Answer: B
RATIONALE: The nurse should inform the client that intercourse can be resumed if bright-red bleeding stops. Use of water-based gel lubricants can be helpful and should not be avoided. Pelvic floor exercises may enhance sensation and should not be avoided. Barrier methods such as a condom with spermicidal gel or foam should be used instead of oral contraceptives.

9. Answer: A
RATIONALE: The nurse first needs to determine the rhesus of the newborn to know if the client needs Rh immunoglobulins. Mothers who are Rh negative and have given birth to an infant who is Rh positive should receive an injection of Rh immunoglobulin within 72 hours after birth; this prevents a sensitization reaction to Rh-positive blood cells received during the birthing process. Women should receive the injection regardless of how many children they have had in the past.

10. Answer: A, B
RATIONALE: Engorged breasts are hard and tender, and the nurse should assess for these signs. Improper positioning of the infant on the breast, not engorged breasts, results in cracked, blistered, fissured, bruised, or bleeding nipples in the breastfeeding woman.

11. Answer: B, D, E
RATIONALE: Finding active bowel sounds, verification of passing gas, and a nondistended abdomen are normal assessment results. The abdomen should be nontender and soft. Abdominal pain is not a normal assessment finding and should be immediately looked into.

12. Answer: B, C, E
RATIONALE: The nurse should show mothers how to initiate breastfeeding within 30 minutes of birth. To ensure bonding, place the baby in uninterrupted skin-to-skin contact with the mother. Breastfeeding on demand should be encouraged. Pacifiers do not help fulfill nutritional requirements and are not a part of breastfeeding instruction. The nurse should also ensure that no food or drink other than breast milk is given to newborns.

13. Answer: D
RATIONALE: Client should begin Kegel exercises on the first postpartum day to increase the strength of the perineal floor muscles. Priority for this client would be to educate her how to perform Kegel exercises as strengthening these muscles will allow her to stop her urine stream.

14. Answer: D
RATIONALE: Tachycardia and a boggy fundus in the postpartum woman indicate excessive blood loss. The nurse would massage the fundus to promote uterine involution. It is not priority to notify the health care provider, assess blood pressure, or change the peripad at this time.

15. Answer: C
RATIONALE: The client needs to notify the health care provider for blurred vision as this can indicate preeclampsia in the postpartum period. The client should also notify their health care provider for a temperature greater than 100.4°F (38°C) or if a peripad is saturated in less than 1 hour. The nurse should ensure that the follow-up appointment is fixed for within 2 weeks after hospital discharge.

CHAPTER 17

SECTION I: ASSESSING YOUR UNDERSTANDING

Activity A FILL IN THE BLANKS

1. Habituation
2. reflex
3. acquired
4. Meconium
5. intestinal
6. amniotic
7. Jaundice
8. hemolysis
9. hemoglobin
10. hypothalamus

Activity B LABELING

A. Conduction
B. Convection
C. Evaporation
D. Radiation

Activity C MATCHING

1. d   **2.** a   **3.** c   **4.** b   **5.** e

Activity D SHORT ANSWERS

1. The newborn's response to auditory and visual stimuli is demonstrated by the following:
   - Moving the head and eyes to focus on stimulus
   - Staring at the object intently
   - Using sensory capacity to become familiar with people and objects
2. The expected neurobehavioral responses of the newborn include:
   - Orientation
   - Habituation

- Motor maturity
- Self-quieting ability
- Social behaviors

3. The following events must occur before the newborn's lungs can maintain respiratory function:
   - Initiation of respiratory movement
   - Expansion of the lungs
   - Establishment of functional residual capacity (ability to retain some air in the lungs on expiration)
   - Increased pulmonary blood flow
   - Redistribution of cardiac output

4. The amniotic fluid is removed from the lungs of a newborn by the following actions:
   - The passage through the birth canal squeezes the thorax, which helps eliminate the fluids in the lungs
   - The action of the pulmonary capillaries and lymphatics removes the remaining fluid

5. The nurse should look for the following signs of abnormality in the newborn's respiration:
   - Labored respiratory effort
   - Respiratory rate less than 30 breaths per minute or greater than 60 breaths per minute
   - Asymmetric chest movements
   - Periodic breathing
   - Apneic periods lasting more than 15 seconds with cyanosis and heart rate changes

6. The nursing interventions that may help minimize regurgitation are
   - Avoiding overfeeding
   - Stimulating frequent burping

SECTION II: APPLYING YOUR KNOWLEDGE

Activity E CASE STUDY

1. Normal factors that increase the heart rate and blood pressure in a newborn are
   - Wakefulness
   - Movement
   - Crying

2. Normal factors affecting the hematologic values of a newborn are
   - Site of the blood sampling
   - Placental transfusion
   - Gestational age

3. The benefits of delayed cord clamping after birth are
   - Improved cardiopulmonary adaptation and oxygen transport
   - Prevention of anemia
   - Increased blood pressures and RBC flow

SECTION III: PRACTICING FOR NCLEX

Activity F NCLEX-STYLE QUESTIONS

1. **Answer: C**
   RATIONALE: Providing comfort measures to the newborn who will be subjected to a variety of painful procedures is the highest priority. Be vigilant in ensuring the newborn's comfort, since it cannot report or describe pain. Experiencing pain will cause stress in the infant and increase the workload on the heart. Assist in preventing pain as much as possible; interpret the newborn's cues suggesting pain and manage it appropriately. Maintaining a set saturation may not be a possibility dependent upon the heart defect the infant has.

2. **Answer: B**
   RATIONALE: The nurse should instruct the mother to wrap the infant in a blanket, with a cap on its head. This ensures that the newborn is kept warm and helps prevent cold stress. Allowing cool air to circulate over the newborn's body leads to heat loss and is not desirable. Co-sleeping with a newborn is not advised due to the risk of suffocation. The nurse should not instruct the client keep the nursery temperature too warm. The infant does not need that much heat.

3. **Answer: A**
   RATIONALE: Breast milk is a major source of IgA, so breast-feeding is believed to have significant immunologic advantages over formula feeding. Breast-feeding does not provide more iron or calcium to the infant, maternal breast size does not increase and most breast-fed infants gain weight faster the first 2 months and then weight gain slows down.

4. **Answer: A, C**
   RATIONALE: Limited sweating ability, a crib that is too warm or one that is placed too close to a sunny window, and limited insulation are factors that predispose a newborn to overheating. The immaturity of the newborn's central nervous system makes it difficult to create and maintain balance between heat production, heat gain, and heat loss. Underdeveloped lungs do not increase the risk of overheating. Lack of brown fat will make the infant feel cold, because the infant will not have enough fat stores to burn in response to cold; it does not, however, increase the risk of overheating.

5. **Answer: C**
   RATIONALE: The nurse should look for signs of lethargy and hypotonia in the newborn in order to confirm the occurrence of cold stress. Cold stress leads to a decrease, not increase, in the newborn's body temperature, blood glucose, and appetite.

6. **Answer: B**
   RATIONALE: Risk factors for the development of jaundice include bruising as seen in a cephalohematoma, male gender, and being breastfed. Blood type incompatibility is only an issue if the infant's blood type differs from the mother and the maternal blood type is not stated. Administering hepatitis A vaccine does not increase the risk of jaundice.

7. **Answer: D**
   RATIONALE: The possibility of fluid overload is increased and must be considered by a nurse when

administering IV therapy to a newborn. IV therapy does not significantly increase heart rate or change blood pressure, as well as the level of consciousness, unless fluid overload occurs.

8. **Answer: B**
   RATIONALE: The nurse should tell the client not to worry because it is perfectly normal for the stools of a formula-fed newborn to be greenish, loose, pasty, or formed in consistency, with an unpleasant odor. There is no need to change the formula, increase the newborn's fluid intake, or switch from formula to breast milk.

9. **Answer: B**
   RATIONALE: Breast-feeding the newborn every 2 to 3 hours on demand is the best way to help the infant gain weight the fastest. Normal weight gain for this age infant is 2/3 to 1 oz per day, not 11/2 to 2 oz. Cereal is never given to infants this young. The mother does not need to pump her breast milk to measure it. As long as the newborn is feeding well and has 6+ wet diapers and 3+ stools, the infant is receiving adequate nutrition.

10. **Answer: C**
    RATIONALE: Preterm newborns are at a greater risk for cold stress than term or postterm newborns. Cold stress can cause hypoglycemia, increased respiratory distress and apnea, and metabolic acidosis. Preterm infants lack the ability to shiver in response to cold stress.

11. **Answer: A**
    RATIONALE: The hand-to-mouth movement of the baby indicates the self-quieting and consoling ability of a newborn. The other options are states of behavior of a newborn but are not applicable to this situation.

12. **Answer: C**
    RATIONALE: Typically, a newborn's blood glucose levels are assessed with use of a heel-stick sample of blood on admission to the nursery, not 4 or 24 hours after admission to the nursery. It is also not necessary or even reasonable to check the glucose level only after the newborn has been fed.

13. **Answer: A**
    RATIONALE: The nurse should promote early breast-feeding to provide fuels for nonshivering thermogenesis. The nurse can bathe the newborn if he or she is medically stable. The nurse can also use a radiant heat source while bathing the newborn to maintain the temperature. Skin-to-skin contact with the mother should be encouraged, not discouraged, if the newborn is stable. The infant transporter should be kept fully charged and heated at all times.

14. **Answer: C**
    RATIONALE: The nurse should place the temperature probe over the newborn's liver. Skin temperature probes should not be placed over a bony area like the forehead or used in an open bassinet with no heat source. The newborn should be in a supine or side-lying position.

15. **Answer: A**
    RATIONALE: The nurse should monitor for yellow skin or sclera in a newborn at risk for developing jaundice due to a high bilirubin. A heart rate of 130 beats per minute is normal for a newborn, as is a respiratory rate of 24. Abdominal distension is not a consequence of an elevated bilirubin.

16. **Answer: D, E**
    RATIONALE: The stools of a breast-fed newborn are yellowish gold in color. They are not firm in shape or solid. The smell is usually sour. A formula-fed infant's stools are formed in consistency, whereas a breast-fed infant's stools are stringy to pasty in consistency.

17. **Answer: D**
    RATIONALE: The nurse should place the newborn skin-to-skin with mother. This is the best way to help maintain the newborn's temperature as well as promoting breast-feeding and bonding between the mother and newborn. The nurse can weigh the infant as long as a warmed cover is placed on the scale. The stethoscope should be warmed before it makes contact with the infant's skin, rather than using the stethoscope over the garment because it may obscure the reading. The newborn's crib should not be placed close to the outer walls in the room to prevent heat loss through radiation.

CHAPTER 18

SECTION I: ASSESSING YOUR UNDERSTANDING

Activity A FILL IN THE BLANKS

1. Apgar
2. Lanugo
3. Postmature
4. large
5. prothrombin
6. acrocyanosis
7. Milia
8. Harlequin
9. anterior
10. Cephalhematoma

Activity B LABELING

The figure depicts (A) caput succedaneum and (B) cephalhematoma, which are one of several variations in head sizes and appearance for the newborn after delivery. Caput succedaneum describes localized edema on the scalp that occurs from the pressure of the birth process. It is commonly observed after prolonged labor. Cephalhematoma is localized effusion of blood beneath the periosteum of the skull. This condition is due to disruption of the vessels during birth. It occurs after prolonged labor and use of obstetric interventions such as low forceps or vacuum extraction.

Activity C MATCHING

1. b　　**2.** a　　**3.** c　　**4.** d

Activity D SEQUENCING

1 → 3 → 4 → 2 → 5

Activity E SHORT ANSWERS

1. The football hold is achieved by holding the infant's back and shoulders in the palm of the mother's hand and tucking the infant's body under the mother's arm. The infant's ear, shoulder, and hip should be in a straight line. The mother's hand should support the breast in a C-position and bring it to the infant's lips to latch on until the infant begins to nurse. This position allows the mother to see the infant's mouth as she guides her infant to the nipple. This is a great position for mothers who have had a cesarean birth, as they can avoid pressure on the incision lines by adopting the football-hold position for breast-feeding.

2. Colostrum is a thick, yellowish substance secreted during the first few days after birth. It is high in protein, minerals, and fat-soluble vitamins. It is rich in immunoglobulins (e.g., IgΛ), which help protect the newborn's GI tract against infections. It is a natural laxative to help rid the intestinal tract of meconium quickly.

3. Fiber optic pads (Biliblanket or Bilivest) are used for treatment of physiologic jaundice and can be wrapped around newborns or newborns can lie upon them. These pads consist of a light that is delivered from a tungsten–halogen bulb through a fiber optic cable and is emitted from the sides and ends of the fibers inside a plastic pad. They work on the premise that phototherapy can be improved by delivering higher-intensity therapeutic light to decrease bilirubin levels. The pads do not produce appreciable heat like banks of lights or spotlights do, so insensible water loss is not increased. Eye patches are also not needed; thus, parents can feed and hold their newborns continuously to promote bonding.

4. The Moro reflex, or the embrace reflex, occurs when the neonate is startled. To elicit this reflex, the newborn is placed on his back. The upper body weight of the supine newborn is supported by the arms with use of a lifting motion, without lifting the newborn off the surface. When the arms are released suddenly, the newborn will throw the arms outward and flex the knees; arms then return to the chest. The fingers also spread to form a C. The newborn initially appears startled and then relaxes to a normal resting position.

5. Caput succedaneum is a localized edema on the scalp that occurs from the pressure of the birth process. It is commonly observed after prolonged labor. Clinically, it appears as a poorly demarcated soft tissue swelling that crosses suture lines. Pitting edema and overlying petechiae and ecchymosis are noted. The swelling will gradually dissipate in about 3 days without any treatment. Newborns who were delivered via vacuum extraction usually have a caput in the area where the cup was used.

6. Erythema toxicum is a benign, idiopathic, very common, generalized, transient rash occurring in as many as 70% of all newborns during the first week of life. It consists of small papules or pustules on the skin resembling flea bites. The rash is common on the face, chest, and back. One of the chief characteristics of this rash is its lack of pattern. It is caused by the newborn's eosinophils reacting to the environment as the immune system matures. It does not require any treatment, and it disappears in a few days.

SECTION II: APPLYING YOUR KNOWLEDGE

Activity F CASE STUDY

1. The nurse should inform the mother that newborns usually sleep for up to 20 hours daily, for periods of 2 to 4 hours at a time, but not through the night. This is because their stomach capacity is too small to go long periods of time without nourishment. All newborns develop their own sleep patterns and cycles.

2. The nurse should ask the mother to place the newborn on her back to sleep; remove all fluffy bedding, quilts, sheepskins, stuffed animals, and pillows from the crib to prevent potential suffocation. Parents should avoid unsafe conditions such as placing the newborn in the prone position, using a crib that does not meet federal safety guidelines, allowing window cords to hang loose and in close proximity to the crib, or having the room temperature too high, causing overheating.

3. The nurse should educate Karen about potential risks of bed sharing. Bringing a newborn into bed to nurse or quiet her down and then falling asleep with the newborn is not a safe practice. Infants who sleep in adult beds are up to 40 times more likely to suffocate than those who sleep in cribs. Suffocation also can occur when the infant gets entangled in bedding or caught under pillows, or slips between the bed and the wall or the headboard and mattress. It can also happen when someone accidentally rolls against or on top of them. Therefore, the safest sleeping location for all newborns is in their crib, without any movable objects close.

SECTION III: PRACTICING FOR NCLEX

Activity G NCLEX-STYLE QUESTIONS

1. Answer: B
   RATIONALE: The nurse should complete the second assessment for the newborn within the first 2 to 4 hours, when the newborn is in the nursery. The nurse should complete the initial newborn assessment in the birthing area and the third assessment before the newborn is discharged, whenever that may be.

2. **Answer: A**
RATIONALE: A red bumpy area noted above the right eye is a hemangioma and needs further investigation to determine whether the hemangioma could interfere with the infant's vision. They may grow larger during the first year then fade and usually disappear by age 9. Stork bites or salmon patches, as described in B, and blue or purple splotches on buttocks (Mongolian spots) are common skin variations and are not concerning. Erythema toxicum, seen as a fine red rash over the chest and back, is also a normal skin variant that will disappear within a few days.

3. **Answer: C**
RATIONALE: As per the recommendations of AAP, all newborns should receive a daily supplement of vitamin D during the first 2 months of life to prevent rickets and vitamin D deficiency. There is no need to feed the newborn water, as breast milk contains enough water to meet the newborn's needs. Iron supplements need not be given, as the newborn is being breastfed. Infants over 6 months of age are given fluoride supplementation if they are not receiving fluoridated water.

4. **Answer: A**
RATIONALE: The nurse should instruct the woman to use the sealed and chilled milk within 24 hours. The nurse should not instruct the woman to use frozen milk within 6 months of obtaining it, to use microwave ovens to warm chilled milk, or to refreeze the used milk and reuse it. Instead, the nurse should instruct the woman to use frozen milk within 3 months of obtaining it, to avoid using microwave ovens to warm chilled milk, and to discard any used milk and never refreeze it.

5. **Answer: A**
RATIONALE: The nurse should instruct the mother to hold the newborn upright with the newborn's head on her mother's shoulder. Alternatively, the nurse can also suggest the mother sit with the newborn on her lap with the newborn lying face down. Gently rubbing the newborn's abdomen, giving frequent sips of warm water to the infant, and patting the buttocks will not significantly induce burping; burping is induced by the newborn's position. Placing the newborn on her back while trying to elicit burping after feeding may cause choking or aspiration.

6. **Answer: B**
RATIONALE: A sign of adequate formula intake is when the newborn seems satisfied and is gaining weight regularly. The formula-fed newborn should take 30 minutes or less to finish a bottle, not less than 15 minutes. The newborn does normally produce several stools per day, but should wet 6 to 10 diapers rather than 3 to 4 per day. The newborn should consume approximately 2 oz of formula per pound of body weight per day, not per feeding.

7. **Answer: D**
RATIONALE: A concentration of immature blood vessels causes salmon patches. Bruising does not look like salmon patches but would be more bluish purple in appearance. Harlequin sign is a result of immature autoregulation of blood flow and is commonly seen in low–birth-weight newborns. An allergic reaction would be more generalized and would not be salmon colored.

8. **Answer: C**
RATIONALE: The nurse should obtain a newborn's temperature by placing an electronic temperature probe in the midaxillary area. The nurse should not tape an electronic thermistor probe to the abdominal skin, as this method is applied only when the newborn is placed under a radiant heat source. Rectal temperatures are no longer taken because of the risk of perforation. Oral temperature readings are not taken for newborns.

9. **Answer: C**
RATIONALE: The nurse should conclude that the newborn is facing moderate difficulty in adjusting to extrauterine life. The nurse should not conclude that the infant is in severe distress requiring immediate interventions for survival or has a congenital heart or respiratory disorder. If the Apgar score is 8 points or higher, it indicates that the condition of the newborn is better. An Apgar score of 0 to 3 points represents severe distress in adjusting to extrauterine life.

10. **Answer: A**
RATIONALE: The nurse should instruct the parent to expose the newborn's bottom to air several times per day to treat and prevent diaper rashes. Use of baby wipes and products such as powder should be avoided. The parent should be instructed to place the newborn's buttocks in warm water after having had a diaper on all night but not with every diaper change.

11. **Answer: B, D, E**
RATIONALE: The nurse should give the newborn oxygen, ensure the newborn's warmth, and observe the newborn's respiratory status frequently. The nurse need not give the newborn warm water to drink or massage the newborn's back.

12. **Answer: A, C, E**
RATIONALE: The nurse should monitor the newborn for lethargy, cyanosis, and jitteriness. Low-pitched crying or rashes on the infant's skin are not signs generally associated with hypoglycemia.

13. **Answer: A, C, E**
RATIONALE: To relieve breast engorgement in the client, the nurse should educate the client to take warm-to-hot showers to encourage milk release, express some milk manually before breast-feeding, and apply warm compresses to the breasts before nursing. The mother should be asked to feed the newborn in a variety of positions—sitting up and then lying down. The breasts should be massaged from under the axillary area, down toward the nipple.

14. **Answer: A, C, E**
    RATIONALE: Mongolian spots, swollen genitals in the female newborn, and a short, creased neck are normal findings in a newborn. Mongolian spots are blue or purple splotches that appear on the lower back and buttocks of newborns. Female babies may have swollen genitals as a result of maternal estrogen. The newborn's neck will appear almost nonexistent because it is so short. Creases are usually noted. Enlarged fontanelles are associated with hydrocephaly; congenital hypothyroidism; trisomies 13, 18, and 21; and various bone disorders such as osteogenesis imperfecta. Low-set ears are characteristic of many syndromes and genetic abnormalities such as trisomies 13 and 18, and internal organ abnormalities involving the renal system.

CHAPTER 19

SECTION I: ASSESSING YOUR UNDERSTANDING

Activity A FILL IN THE BLANKS

1. Oligohydramnios
2. Clonus
3. latent
4. hyperreflexia
5. incompatibility
6. Monozygotic
7. infection
8. spontaneous
9. first
10. Gestational

Activity B MATCHING

1. c   2. e   3. a   4. b   5. d

Activity C SEQUENCING

1. c → b → f → a → e → d

Activity D SHORT ANSWERS

1. Possible complications of hyperemesis gravidarum include persistent, uncontrollable nausea, dehydration, acid–base imbalances, electrolyte imbalances, and weight loss. If the condition is allowed to continue, it jeopardizes fetal well being.
2. Conditions commonly associated with early bleeding (first half of pregnancy) include spontaneous abortion, ectopic pregnancy, and gestational trophoblastic disease.
3. Ectopic pregnancies usually result from conditions that obstruct or slow the passage of the fertilized ovum through the fallopian tube to the uterus. This may be a physical blockage in the tube or failure of the tubal epithelium to move the zygote (the cell formed after the egg is fertilized) down the tube into the uterus. In the general population, most cases are the result of tubal scarring secondary

to PID. Organisms such as *Neisseria gonorrhoeae* and *Chlamydia trachomatis* preferentially attack the fallopian tubes, producing silent infections.
4. Risk factors for hyperemesis gravidarum include young age, nausea and vomiting with previous pregnancy, history of intolerance of oral contraceptives, nulliparity, trophoblastic disease, multiple gestation, emotional or psychological stress, gastroesophageal reflux disease, primigravida status, obesity, hyperthyroidism, and *Helicobacter pylori* seropositivity.
5. A nurse should include the following in prevention education for ectopic pregnancies:
   - Reducing risk factors such as sexual intercourse with multiple partners or intercourse without a condom
   - Avoiding contracting STIs that lead to PID
   - Obtaining early diagnosis and adequate treatment of STIs
   - Avoiding the use of an intrauterine contraception (IUC) as a contraceptive method to reduce the risk of repeat ascending infections responsible for tubal scarring
   - Using condoms to decrease the risk of infections that cause tubal scarring
   - Seeking prenatal care early if pregnant, to confirm location of pregnancy
6. The Kleihauer–Betke test detects fetal RBCs in the maternal circulation, determines the degree of fetal–maternal hemorrhage, and helps calculate the appropriate dosage of RhoGAM to give for Rh-negative clients.

SECTION II: APPLYING YOUR KNOWLEDGE

Activity E CASE STUDY

1. Recognizing preterm labor at an early stage requires that the expectant mother and her health care team identify the subtle symptoms of preterm labor. These may include:
   - Change or increase in vaginal discharge
   - Pelvic pressure (pushing down sensation)
   - Low, dull backache
   - Menstrual-like cramps
   - Uterine contractions, with or without pain
   - Intestinal cramping, with or without diarrhea
2. The nurse must teach Jenna how to palpate and time uterine contractions. Provide written materials to support this education at a level and in a language appropriate for her. Also, educate Jenna about the importance of prenatal care, risk reduction, and recognizing the signs and symptoms of preterm labor. The nurse may also include:
   - Stressing good hydration and consumption of a nutritious diet
   - Advising against any activity, such as sexual activity or nipple stimulation, that might stimulate oxytocin release and initiate uterine contractions
   - Assessing stress levels of client and family and making appropriate referrals

- Providing emotional support and client empowerment throughout
- Emphasizing the possible need for more frequent office visits and for notifying the health care provider if she has questions or concerns.

SECTION III: PRACTICING FOR NCLEX

Activity F NCLEX-STYLE QUESTIONS

1. Answer: C

RATIONALE: The nurse should instruct the client with hyperemesis gravidarum to eat small, frequent meals throughout the day to minimize nausea and vomiting. The nurse should also instruct the client to avoid lying down or reclining for at least 2 hours after eating and to increase the intake of carbonated beverages. The nurse should instruct the client to try foods that settle the stomach such as dry crackers, toast, or soda.

2. Answer: A

RATIONALE: A temperature elevation or an increase in the pulse of a client with PROM would indicate infection. Increase in the pulse does not indicate preterm labor or cord compression. The nurse should monitor FHR patterns continuously, reporting any variable decelerations suggesting cord compression. Respiratory distress syndrome is one of the perinatal risks associated with PROM.

3. Answer: B

RATIONALE: When meconium is present in the amniotic fluid, it typically indicates fetal distress related to hypoxia. Meconium stains the fluid yellow to greenish brown, depending on the amount present. A decreased amount of amniotic fluid reduces the cushioning effect, thereby making cord compression a possibility. A foul odor of amniotic fluid indicates infection. Meconium in the amniotic fluid does not indicate CNS involvement.

4. Answer: D

RATIONALE: The nurse should institute and maintain seizure precautions such as padding the side rails and having oxygen, suction equipment, and call light readily available to protect the client from injury. The nurse should provide a quiet, darkened room to stabilize the client. The nurse should maintain the client on complete bed rest in the left lateral lying position and not in a supine position. Keeping the head of the bed slightly elevated will not help maintain seizure precautions.

5. Answer: A

RATIONALE: If the client is receiving magnesium sulfate to suppress or control seizures, assess deep tendon reflexes to determine the effectiveness of therapy. Common sites utilized to assess deep tendon reflexes are the biceps reflex, triceps reflex, patellar reflex, Achilles reflex, and plantar reflex. Assessing the mucous membranes for dryness and skin turgor for dehydration are the required

interventions when caring for a client with hyperemesis gravidarum. Monitoring intake and output will not help to determine the effectiveness of therapy.

6. Answer: D

RATIONALE: A previous myomectomy to remove fibroids can be associated with the cause of placenta previa. Risk factors also include advanced maternal age (greater than 30 years old). A structurally defective cervix cannot be associated with the cause of placenta previa. However, it can be associated with the cause of cervical insufficiency. Alcohol ingestion is not a risk factor for developing placenta previa but is associated with abruptio placenta.

7. Answer: B

RATIONALE: The nurse should encourage a client with mild elevations in blood pressure to rest as much as possible in the lateral recumbent position to improve uteroplacental blood flow, reduce blood pressure, and promote diuresis. The nurse should maintain the client with severe preeclampsia on complete bed rest in the left lateral lying position. Keeping the head of the bed slightly elevated will not help to improve the condition of the client with mild elevations in blood pressure.

8. Answer: D

RATIONALE: The first choice for fluid replacement is generally NS with vitamins and electrolytes added. If the client does not improve after several days of bed rest, "gut rest," IV fluids, and antiemetics, then total parenteral nutrition or percutaneous endoscopic gastrostomy tube feeding is instituted to prevent malnutrition.

9. Answer: C

RATIONALE: The classic manifestations of abruptio placenta are painful dark red vaginal bleeding, "knife-like" abdominal pain, uterine tenderness, contractions, and decreased fetal movement. Painless bright red vaginal bleeding is the clinical manifestation of placenta previa. Generalized vasospasm is the clinical manifestation of preeclampsia and not of abruptio placenta.

10. Answer: A

RATIONALE: The symptoms if rupture or hemorrhaging occurs before successfully treating the pregnancy are lower abdomen pain, feelings of faintness, phrenic nerve irritation, hypotension, marked abdominal tenderness with distension, and hypovolemic shock. Painless bright red vaginal bleeding occurring during the second or third trimester is the clinical manifestation of placenta previa. Fetal distress and tetanic contractions are not the symptoms observed in a client if rupture or hemorrhaging occurs before successfully treating an ectopic pregnancy.

11. Answer: D

RATIONALE: When the woman arrives and is admitted, assessing her vital signs, the amount and color of the bleeding, and current pain rating on a scale of 1 to 10 are the priorities. Assessing the signs of shock, monitoring uterine contractility, and determining the amount of funneling are not priority assessments when a pregnant woman complaining of vaginal bleeding is admitted to the hospital.

12. **Answer: C**
RATIONALE: A nurse should closely monitor the client's vital signs, bleeding (peritoneal or vaginal) to identify hypovolemic shock that may occur with tubal rupture. Beta-hCG level is monitored to diagnose an ectopic pregnancy or impending abortion. Monitoring the mass with transvaginal ultrasound and determining the size of the mass are done for diagnosing an ectopic pregnancy. Monitoring the FHR does not help to identify hypovolemic shock.

13. **Answer: A**
RATIONALE: The current recommendation is that every Rh-negative nonimmunized woman receives RhoGAM at 28 weeks' gestation and again within 72 hours after giving birth. Consuming a well-balanced nutritional diet and avoiding sexual activity until after 28 weeks will not help to prevent complications of blood incompatibility. Transvaginal ultrasound helps to validate the position of the placenta and will not help to prevent complications of blood incompatibility.

14. **Answer: C**
RATIONALE: The nurse should know that coma usually follows an eclamptic seizure. Muscle rigidity occurs after facial twitching. Respirations do not become rapid during the seizure; they cease. Coma usually follows the seizure activity, with respiration resuming.

15. **Answer: D**
RATIONALE: The nurse should know that dependent edema may be seen in the sacral area if the client is on bed rest. Pitting edema leaves a small depression or pit after finger pressure is applied to a swollen area and can be measured. Dependent edema may occur in clients who are both ambulatory and on bed rest.

16. **Answer: A, B, E**
RATIONALE: The associated conditions and complications of premature rupture of the membranes are infection, prolapsed cord, abruptio placenta, and preterm labor. Spontaneous abortion and placenta previa are not associated conditions or complications of premature rupture of the membranes.

17. **Answer: B, D, E**
RATIONALE: The signs and symptoms of HELLP syndrome are nausea, malaise, epigastric pain, upper right quadrant pain, demonstrable edema, and hyperbilirubinemia. Blood pressure higher than 160/110 and oliguria are the symptoms of severe preeclampsia rather than HELLP syndrome.

18. **Answer: B, D, E**
RATIONALE: Adverse effects commonly associated with misoprostol include dyspepsia, hypotension, tachycardia, diarrhea, abdominal pain, and vomiting. Constipation and headache are not adverse effects commonly associated with misoprostol.

CHAPTER 20

SECTION I: ASSESSING YOUR UNDERSTANDING

Activity A FILL IN THE BLANKS

1. somatotropin
2. Gestational
3. airway
4. lung
5. Anemia
6. Group B streptococcus
7. Toxoplasmosis
8. Adolescence
9. Nicotine
10. cocaine

Activity B MATCHING

1. f   2. e   3. d   4. c   5. b   6. a

Activity C SHORT ANSWERS

1. The most common complications in a pregnant client with hypertension are:
   - Increased risk for developing preeclampsia
   - Decreased uteroplacental perfusion
2. The nurse should include the following elements during the physical examination of pregnant clients with asthma:
   - Rate, rhythm, and depth of respirations
   - Auscultation of lung sounds
   - Skin color
   - Blood pressure
   - Pulse rate
   - Evaluation for signs of fatigue
3. The nurse should include the following factors in the teaching plan for a client with asthma:
   - Signs and symptoms of asthma progression and exacerbation
   - Importance and safety of medication to fetus and to herself
   - Warning signs; potential harm to fetus and self by undertreatment or delay in seeking help
   - Prevention and avoidance of known triggers
   - Home use of metered-dose inhalers
   - Adverse effects of medications
4. Assessment of tuberculosis in pregnant clients includes the following:
   - At antepartum visits, the nurse should be alert for clinical manifestations of tuberculosis such as fatigue, fever or night sweats, nonproductive cough, slow weight loss, anemia, hemoptysis, and anorexia.
   - If tuberculosis is suspected or the woman is at risk for developing tuberculosis, the nurse should

anticipate screening with purified protein derivative administered by intradermal injection; if the client has been exposed to tuberculosis, a reddened induration will appear within 72 hours.
- A follow-up chest x-ray with a lead shield over the abdomen and sputum cultures will confirm the diagnosis.

5. The developmental tasks associated with adolescent behavior are:
- Seeking economic and social stability
- Developing a personal value system
- Building meaningful relationships with others
- Becoming comfortable with their changing bodies
- Working to become independent from their parents
- Learning to verbalize conceptually

6. The effects of sedatives by the mother on her infant are as follows:
- Sedatives easily cross the placenta and cause birth defects and behavioral problems
- Infants born to mothers who abuse sedatives may be physically dependent on the drugs and prone to respiratory problems, feeding difficulties, disturbed sleep, sweating, irritability, and fever

SECTION II: APPLYING YOUR KNOWLEDGE
Activity D CASE STUDY

1. The greatest increase in asthma attacks in the pregnant client usually occurs between 24 and 36 weeks' gestation; flare-ups are rare during the last 4 weeks of pregnancy and during labor.
2. Successful management of asthma in pregnancy involves:
- Drug therapy
- Client education
- Elimination of environmental triggers
3. The following are the nursing interventions involved when caring for the pregnant client with asthma during labor:
- Monitor client's oxygen saturation by pulse oximetry.
- Provide pain management through epidural analgesia.
- Continuously monitor the fetus for distress during labor and assess FHR patterns for indications of hypoxia.
- Assess the newborn for signs and symptoms of hypoxia.

SECTION III: PRACTICING FOR NCLEX
Activity E NCLEX-STYLE QUESTIONS

1. **Answer: B**
   RATIONALE: The nurse should stress the positive benefits of a healthy lifestyle during the preconception counseling of a client with chronic hypertension. The client need not avoid dairy products or increase intake of vitamin D supplements. It may not be advisable for a client with chronic hypertension to exercise without consultation.

2. **Answer: A**
   RATIONALE: Swelling of the face is a symptom of cardiac decompensation, along with moist, frequent cough and rapid respirations. Dry, rasping cough; slow, labored respiration; and an elevated temperature are not symptoms of cardiac decompensation.

3. **Answer: D**
   RATIONALE: The nurse should assess the client with heart disease for cardiac decompensation, which is most common from 28 to 32 weeks' gestation and in the first 48 hours postpartum. Limiting sodium intake, inspecting the extremities for edema, and ensuring that the client consumes a high-fiber diet are interventions during pregnancy, not in the first 48 hours postpartum.

4. **Answer: B**
   RATIONALE: The nurse should evaluate for signs of a respiratory complication with asthma clients. The nurse need not monitor the client's temperature, frequency of headache, or feelings of nausea because these conditions are not related to asthma.

5. **Answer: A**
   RATIONALE: The nurse should instruct the pregnant client with tuberculosis to maintain adequate hydration as a health-promoting activity. The client need not avoid direct sunlight or red meat, or wear light clothes; these have no impact on the client's condition.

6. **Answer: C**
   RATIONALE: The nurse should identify preterm birth as a risk associated with anemia during pregnancy. Anemia during pregnancy does not increase the risk of a newborn with heart problems, an enlarged liver, or fetal asphyxia.

7. **Answer: A, C, D**
   RATIONALE: The nurse should assess for possible fluid overload in a client with cardiovascular disease who has just delivered. Signs of fluid overload in the client who has just labored include cough, progressive dyspnea, edema, palpitations, and crackles in the lung bases. Hemoglobin and hematocrit levels are not affected by laboring of the client with cardiovascular disease.

8. **Answer: A**
   RATIONALE: Symptoms of CMV in the fetus and newborn, known as CMV inclusion disease, include hepatomegaly, thrombocytopenia, IUGR, jaundice, microcephaly, hearing loss, chorioretinitis, and intellectual disability. A hearing screen would be priority over monitoring growth and development because that will have to be done over an extended period of time. Urine and pulse are not important with this diagnosis.

9. **Answer: D**
   RATIONALE: The nurse should address the client's knowledge of child development during assessment of the pregnant adolescent client. The nurse need not address the sexual development of the client

or whether sex was consensual. This would not be an opportune time to discuss birth control methods to be used after the pregnancy.

10. **Answer: D**
    RATIONALE: Class I recommendations (no physical activity limitations) are suggested for clients who are asymptomatic and exhibit no objective evidence of cardiac disease. The functional classification system consists of class I to IV, based on past and present disability and physical signs resulting from cardiac disease.

11. **Answer: D**
    RATIONALE: The nurse should stress the avoidance of breast-feeding when counseling a pregnant client who is HIV positive. The client's relationship with the spouse, contact with the infant, and the plan for future pregnancies are not the highest priority at this time.

12. **Answer: B**
    RATIONALE: The nurse should make the client aware of increased risk of anemia as a possible effect of maternal coffee consumption during pregnancy, as it decreases iron absorption. Maternal coffee consumption during pregnancy does not increase the risk of heart disease, rickets, or scurvy.

13. **Answer: A, B, E**
    RATIONALE: To minimize risk of toxoplasmosis, the nurse should instruct the client to eat meat that has been cooked to an internal temperature of 160°F (71°C) throughout and to avoid cleaning the cat's litter box or performing activities such as gardening. Avoiding children with colds is unreasonable when working with children, and contact with children with colds is not a cause of toxoplasmosis. The cat should be kept indoors to prevent it from hunting and eating birds or rodents.

14. **Answer: C, D, E**
    RATIONALE: Obesity, hypertension, and a previous infant weighing more than 9 lb are risk factors for developing gestational diabetes. Maternal age less than 18 years and genitourinary tract abnormalities do not increase the risk of developing gestational diabetes.

15. **Answer: A, D, E**
    RATIONALE: The nurse caring for a pregnant client with sickle cell anemia should teach the client meticulous hand-washing to prevent the risk of infection, assess the hydration status of the client at each visit, and urge the client to drink 8 to 10 glasses of fluid daily. The nurse need not assess serum electrolyte levels of the client at each visit or instruct the client to consume protein-rich food.

16. **Answer: A**
    RATIONALE: The nurse should assess for small head circumference in a newborn being assessed for fetal alcohol spectrum disorder. Fetal alcohol spectrum disorder does not cause decreased blood glucose level, an abnormal breathing pattern, or wide eyes.

17. **Answer: B**
    RATIONALE: The nurse should stress the inclusion of complex carbohydrates in the diet in the dietary plan for a pregnant woman with pregestational diabetes. The pregnant client with pregestational diabetes need not include more dairy products in the diet, eat only two meals per day, or eat at least one egg per day; these have no impact on the client's condition.

18. **Answer: B**
    RATIONALE: Substance use during pregnancy is associated with preterm labor, abortion, low birth weight, central nervous system and fetal anomalies, and long-term childhood developmental consequences. It is most important to know what the client is taking in order to provide the best care for the client and newborn.

19. **Answer: C**
    RATIONALE: The nurse should recommend foods high in whole grains, lean meats, high fiber, and naturally low in fat and sodium.

20. **Answer: A**
    RATIONALE: The nurse should identify respiratory distress syndrome as a major risk that can be faced by the offspring of a client with cardiovascular disease. While the other assessments are important, they are not a priority.

CHAPTER 21

SECTION I: ASSESSING YOUR UNDERSTANDING

Activity A FILL IN THE BLANKS

1. dystocia
2. Breech
3. Leopold
4. Tocolytic
5. Steroids
6. fibronectin
7. Bishop
8. Hygroscopic
9. amniotomy
10. Oxytocin

Activity B LABELING

The figures depict prolapsed cord. **A.** Prolapse within the uterus. **B.** Prolapse with the cord visible at the vulva.

Activity C MATCHING

1. c **2.** a **3.** e **4.** b **5.** d

Activity D SEQUENCING

2 → 1 → 4 → 5 → 3

Activity E SHORT ANSWERS

1. The symptoms of preterm labor are:
   • Change or increase in vaginal discharge
   • Pelvic pressure (pushing down sensation)
   • Low, dull backache
   • Menstrual-like cramps
   • Heaviness or aching in the thighs

- Uterine contractions, with or without pain
- Intestinal cramping, with or without diarrhea

2. Cervical ripeness is an assessment of the readiness of the cervix to efface and dilate in response to uterine contractions. It is an important variable when labor induction is being considered. A ripe cervix is shortened, centered (anterior), softened, and partially dilated. An unripe cervix is long, closed, posterior, and firm. Cervical ripening usually begins before the onset of labor contractions and is necessary for cervical dilatation and the passage of the fetus.

3. Uterine rupture is a catastrophic tearing of the uterus at the site of a previous scar into the abdominal cavity. The onset is often marked only by sudden fetal bradycardia, and the obliteration of intrauterine pressure/cessation of contractions. Treatment requires rapid surgical attention. In uterine rupture, fetal morbidity occurs secondary to catastrophic hemorrhage, fetal anoxia, or both.

4. Indications of amnioinfusion are severe variable decelerations due to cord compression, oligohydramnios due to placental insufficiency, postmaturity or rupture of membranes, preterm labor with premature rupture of membranes, and thick meconium fluid. Vaginal bleeding of unknown origin, umbilical cord prolapse, amnionitis, uterine hypertonicity, and severe fetal distress are contraindications to amnioinfusion.

5. The nurse assesses each client to help predict her risk status. The nurse should be aware that cord prolapse is more common in pregnancies involving malpresentation, growth restriction, prematurity, ruptured membranes with a fetus at a high station, hydramnios, grand multiparity, and multifetal gestation. The client and fetus should be thoroughly assessed to detect changes and evaluate the effectiveness of any interventions performed.

6. Shoulder dystocia can cause postpartum hemorrhage, secondary to uterine atony or vaginal lacerations in the mother. In the fetus, shoulder dystocia can result in transient and/or permanent Erb or Duchenne brachial plexus palsies and clavicular or humeral fractures, as well as hypoxic encephalopathy.

SECTION II: APPLYING YOUR KNOWLEDGE

Activity F CASE STUDY

1. The nurse should perform the following interventions during amnioinfusion to prevent maternal and fetal complications:
   - Explain the need for the procedure, what it involves, and how it may solve the problem.
   - Inform the mother that she will need to remain on bed rest during the procedure.
   - Assess the mother's vital signs and associated discomfort level.
   - Maintain adequate intake and output records.

- Assess the duration and intensity of uterine contractions frequently to identify overdistention or increased uterine tone.
- Monitor FHR pattern to determine whether the amnioinfusion is improving the fetal status.
- Prepare the mother for a possible cesarean birth if the FHR does not improve after the amnioinfusion.

SECTION III: PRACTICING FOR NCLEX

Activity G NCLEX-STYLE QUESTIONS

1. **Answer: A**
   RATIONALE: A forceps- and-vacuum-assisted birth is required for the client having a prolonged second stage of labor. The client may require a cesarean section if the fetus cannot be delivered with assistance. A precipitous birth occurs when the entire labor and birth process occur very quickly. Artificial rupture of membranes is done during the first stage of labor.

2. **Answer: A, E**
   RATIONALE: The nurse should monitor cyanosis and pulmonary edema when caring for a client with amniotic fluid embolism. Other signs and symptoms of this condition include hypotension, cyanosis, seizures, tachycardia, coagulation failure, disseminated intravascular coagulation, uterine atony with subsequent hemorrhage, adult respiratory distress syndrome, and cardiac arrest. Arrhythmia, hematuria, and hyperglycemia are not known to occur in cases of amniotic fluid embolism. Hematuria is seen in clients having uterine rupture.

3. **Answer: A**
   RATIONALE: Chorioamnionitis is an indication for labor induction. The WBC, temperature, and amniotic fluid are not priority to assess because the nurse already knows the client has chorioamnionitis.

4. **Answer: A**
   RATIONALE: The nurse should ensure that the client does not have uterine hypertonicity to confirm that amnioinfusion is not contraindicated. Other factors that enforce contraindication of amnioinfusion include vaginal bleeding of unknown origin, umbilical cord prolapse, amnionitis, and severe fetal distress. Active genital herpes infection is a condition that enforces contraindication of labor induction rather than amnioinfusion. Urine output and blood pressure do not determine a client's ability to receive amnioinfusion.

5. **Answer: D**
   RATIONALE: The nurse should identify nerve damage as a risk to the fetus in cases of shoulder dystocia. Other fetal risks include asphyxia, clavicle fracture, central nervous system injury or dysfunction, and death. Extensive lacerations are abnormal maternal outcomes due to the occurrence of shoulder dystocia. Cleft palate and cardiac anomalies are not related to shoulder dystocia.

6. **Answer: A**
   RATIONALE: A Bishop score of less than 6 indicates that a cervical ripening method should be used before inducing labor. A low Bishop score is not an indication for cesarean birth; there are several other factors that need to be considered for a cesarean birth. A Bishop score of less than 6 indicates that vaginal birth will be unsuccessful and prolonged because the duration of labor is inversely correlated with the Bishop score.

7. **Answer: A**
   RATIONALE: When caring for a client who has undergone a cesarean birth, the nurse should assess the client's uterine tone to determine fundal firmness. The nurse should assist with breast-feeding initiation and offer continued support. The nurse can also suggest alternate positioning techniques to reduce incisional discomfort while breast-feeding. Delaying breast-feeding may not be required. The nurse should encourage the client to cough, perform deep-breathing exercises, and use the incentive spirometer every 2 hours. The nurse should assist the client with early ambulation to prevent respiratory and cardiovascular problems.

8. **Answer: D**
   RATIONALE: Overdistended uterus is a contraindication for oxytocin administration. Postterm status, dysfunctional labor pattern, and prolonged ruptured membranes are indications for administration of oxytocin.

9. **Answer: A**
   RATIONALE: The nurse caring for the client in labor with shoulder dystocia of the fetus should assist with positioning the client in squatting position. The client can also be helped into the hands and knees position or lateral recumbent position for birth, to free the shoulders. Assessing for complaints of intense back pain in first stage of labor, anticipating possible use of forceps to rotate to anterior position at birth, and assessing for prolonged second stage of labor with arrest of descent are important interventions when caring for a client with persistent occiput posterior position of fetus.

10. **Answer: A**
    RATIONALE: The nurse should assess infertility treatment as a contributor to increased probability of multiple gestations. Multiple gestations do not occur with an adolescent birth; instead, chances of multiple gestations are known to increase due to the increasing number of women giving birth at older ages.

11. **Answer: D**
    RATIONALE: Cephalopelvic disproportion is associated with postterm pregnancy. This client will not be able to vaginally deliver and should be prepared for a cesarean birth. Lithotomy position, artificial rupture of membranes, and oxytocin are interventions for a vaginal birth.

12. **Answer: C**
    RATIONALE: The nurse should assess for fetal complications such as head trauma associated with intracranial hemorrhage, nerve damage, and hypoxia in cases of precipitous labor. Facial and scalp lacerations, facial nerve injury, and cephalhematoma are all newborn traumas associated with the use of the forceps of vacuum extractors during birth. These conditions are not neonatal complications associated with precipitous labor.

13. **Answer: C, E**
    RATIONALE: Prolonged pregnancy and hypertension are causes of intrauterine fetal demise in late pregnancy that the nurse should be aware of. Other factors resulting in intrauterine fetal demise include infection, advanced maternal age, Rh disease, uterine rupture, diabetes, congenital anomalies, cord accident, abruption, premature rupture of membranes, or hemorrhage. Hydramnios, multifetal gestation, and malpresentation are not the causes of intrauterine fetal demise in late pregnancy; they are causes of umbilical cord prolapse.

14. **Answer: A**
    RATIONALE: The nurse should monitor for fetal hypoxia in cases of umbilical cord prolapse. Because this is the fetus's only lifeline, fetal perfusion deteriorates rapidly. Complete occlusion renders the fetus helpless and oxygen deprived. Preeclampsia, coagulation defects, and placental pathology are not risks associated with umbilical cord prolapse.

15. **Answer: B**
    RATIONALE: The nurse knows a placental abruption places the client at high risk of hemorrhage. A decreased urine output indicates decreased perfusion from blood loss. The hematocrit, hemoglobin, and platelet counts are all within expected levels.

CHAPTER 22

SECTION I: ASSESSING YOUR UNDERSTANDING

Activity A FILL IN THE BLANKS

1. atony
2. Subinvolution
3. decrease
4. thrombus
5. thromboembolism
6. Metritis
7. mastitis
8. early
9. accreta
10. inversion

Activity B MATCHING

1. b   2. a   3. d   4. c   5. e

Activity C SEQUENCING

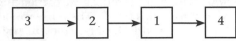

Activity D SHORT ANSWERS

1. Overdistention of the uterus can be caused by multifetal gestation, fetal macrosomia, polyhydramnios, fetal abnormality, or placental fragments. Overdistention of the uterus is a major risk factor for uterine atony, the most common cause of early postpartum hemorrhage, which can lead to hypovolemic shock.

2. Idiopathic thrombocytopenic purpura (ITP) is characterized by increased platelet destruction caused by the development of autoantibodies to platelet membrane antigens. The incidence of ITP in adults is approximately 66 cases per 1 million per year. The characteristic features of the disorder are thrombocytopenia, capillary fragility, and increased bleeding time. Clients with ITP present with easy bruising, bleeding from mucous membranes, menorrhagia, epistaxis, bleeding gums, hematomas, and severe hemorrhage after a cesarean birth or lacerations.

3. Postpartum infections are usually polymicrobial and involve *Staphylococcus aureus, Escherichia coli, Klebsiella* species, *Gardnerella vaginalis,* gonococci, coliform bacteria, group A or B hemolytic streptococci, *Chlamydia trachomatis,* and the anaerobes that are common to bacterial vaginosis.

4. Most postpartum women experience baby blues. The woman exhibits mild depressive symptoms of anxiety, irritability, mood swings, tearfulness, and increased sensitivity, feelings of being overwhelmed, and fatigue after the birth of the baby. The condition typically peaks on postpartum days 4 and 5 and usually resolves by postpartum day 10. Baby blues are usually self-limiting and require no formal treatment other than reassurance and validation of the woman's experience, as well as assistance in caring for herself and the newborn.

5. Symptoms of postpartum psychosis surface within 3 weeks of giving birth. The main symptoms include sleep disturbances, fatigue, depression, and hypomania. The mother will be tearful, confused, and preoccupied with feelings of guilt and worthlessness. The symptoms may escalate to delirium, hallucinations, anger toward herself and her infant, bizarre behavior, manifestations of mania, and thoughts of hurting herself and the infant. The mother frequently loses touch with reality and experiences a severe regressive breakdown, associated with a high risk of suicide or infanticide.

6. A thrombosis refers to the development of a blood clot in the blood vessel. It can cause an inflammation of the blood vessel lining, which in turn can lead to a possible thromboembolism. Thrombi can involve the superficial or deep veins in the legs or pelvis:

- Superficial venous thrombosis usually involves the saphenous venous system and is confined to the lower leg. The lithotomy position during birth can cause superficial thrombophlebitis in some women.
- Deep venous thrombosis (DVT) can involve deep veins from the foot to the calf, to the thighs, or to the pelvis.

In both locations, thrombi can dislodge and migrate to the lungs, causing a pulmonary embolism.

SECTION II: APPLYING YOUR KNOWLEDGE

Activity E CASE STUDY

1. The major causes of thrombus formation are venous stasis, injury to the innermost layer of the blood vessel, and hypercoagulation. Venous stasis and hypercoagulation are common in the postpartum period. The risk factors for thrombosis are as follows:
- Prolonged bed rest
- Diabetes
- Obesity
- Cesarean birth
- Smoking
- Severe anemia
- History of previous thrombosis
- Varicose veins
- Advanced maternal age (greater than 35 years)
- Multiparity
- Use of oral contraceptives before pregnancy

2. The nurse should perform the following nursing interventions to prevent thromboembolic complications in a client:
- Educate the client on the need for early and frequent ambulation.
- Encourage activities that cause leg muscles to contract (leg exercises and walking) to promote venous return in order to prevent venous stasis.
- Use intermittent sequential compression devices, which cause passive leg contractions until the client is ambulatory.
- Elevate the client's legs above heart level to promote venous return.
- Ensure antiembolism stockings are applied and removed every day for inspections of the legs.
- Encourage the client to perform passive exercises on the bed.
- Ensure that the client is involved in postoperative deep-breathing exercises; this improves venous return.
- In order to prevent venous pooling, avoid placing pillows under the knees or keeping the legs in stirrups for a long time or using the knee gatch on the bed.
- Ensure the use of bed cradles; this helps in keeping linens and blankets off the extremity.

3. For clients with superficial venous thrombosis, the nurse should perform the following interventions:
- Administer NSAIDs for analgesic effect as prescribed.
- Provide rest and elevation of the affected leg.

- Apply warm compresses over the affected area to promote healing.
- Use antiembolism stockings, which promote circulation to the extremities.

SECTION III: PRACTICING FOR NCLEX

Activity F NCLEX-STYLE QUESTIONS

1. **Answer: C**
   RATIONALE: The nurse should monitor the client for swelling in the calf. Swelling in the calf, erythema, and pedal edema are early manifestations of deep vein thrombosis, which may lead to pulmonary embolism if not prevented at an early stage. Sudden change in the mental status, difficulty in breathing, and sudden chest pain are manifestations of pulmonary embolism, beyond the stage of prevention.

2. **Answer: D**
   RATIONALE: When caring for a client with DVT, the nurse should instruct the client to avoid using oral contraceptives. Cigarette smoking, use of oral contraceptives, sedentary lifestyle, and obesity increase the risk for developing DVT. The nurse should encourage the client with DVT to wear compression stockings. The nurse should instruct the client to avoid using products containing aspirin when caring for clients with bleeding, but not for clients with DVT. Prolonged rest periods should be avoided. Prolonged rest involves staying motionless; this could lead to venous stasis, which needs to be avoided in cases of DVT.

3. **Answer: B**
   RATIONALE: When caring for a client with ITP, the nurse should administer platelet transfusions as ordered to control bleeding. Glucocorticoids, intravenous immunoglobulins, and intravenous anti-Rho D are also administered to the client. The nurse should not administer NSAIDs when caring for this client since nonsteroidal anti-inflammatory drugs cause platelet dysfunction.

4. **Answer: A**
   RATIONALE: The nurse should monitor for foul-smelling vaginal discharge to verify the presence of an episiotomy infection. Sudden onset of shortness of breath, and apprehension and diaphoresis are signs of pulmonary embolism and do not indicate episiotomy infection. Pain in the lower leg is indicative of a thrombosis.

5. **Answer: A**
   RATIONALE: The nurse should assess the client for prolonged bleeding time. von Willebrand disease is a congenital bleeding disorder, inherited as an autosomal dominant trait, that is characterized by a prolonged bleeding time, a deficiency of von Willebrand factor, and impairment of platelet adhesion. A fever of 100.4°F (30.0°C) after the first 24 hours following birth and pain indicate infection. A client with a postpartum fundal height that is higher than expected may have subinvolution of the uterus.

6. **Answer: D**
   RATIONALE: The client is probably experiencing a deep vein thrombosis (DVT). The nurse would maintain bed rest with the effected extremity elevated until the diagnosis could be confirmed. Once the diagnosis is confirmed, and anticoagulant may be ordered. It is not priority to determine the severity of the pain or a respiratory rate.

7. **Answer: D**
   RATIONALE: The presence of a large uterus with painless dark-red blood mixed with clots indicates retained placental fragments in the uterus. This cause of hemorrhage can be prevented by carefully inspecting the placenta for intactness. A firm uterus with a trickle or steady stream of bright-red blood in the perineum indicates bleeding from trauma. A soft and boggy uterus that deviates from the midline indicates a full bladder, interfering with uterine involution.

8. **Answer: A**
   RATIONALE: The nurse needs to identify whether the bleeding is from lacerations or uterine atony. This can be done by looking for a well-contracted uterus with bright-red vaginal bleeding. Lacerations commonly occur during forceps birth. In subinvolution of the uterus, there is inadequate contraction, resulting in bleeding. A boggy uterus with vaginal bleeding is seen in uterine atony. Once the nurse knows the cause of the bleeding, the condition can be treated.

9. **Answer: C**
   RATIONALE: Early postpartal hemorrhage can be assessed within the first few hours following birth. Postpartal infection may be noticed as a rise in temperature after the first 24 hours following birth. Postpartal blues and postpartum depression are emotional disorders noticed much later, in the days to weeks following birth.

10. **Answer: C**
    RATIONALE: To help prevent the occurrence of postpartum thromboembolic complications, the nurse should instruct the client to avoid sitting or standing in one position for long periods of time. This prevents venous pooling. The nurse should instruct the client to perform postoperative deep-breathing exercises to improve venous return by relieving the negative thoracic pressure on leg veins. The nurse should instruct the client to prevent venous pooling by avoiding the use of pillows under the knees. Elevating the legs above heart level promotes venous return, and therefore the nurse should encourage it.

11. **Answer: B**
    RATIONALE: The nurse should educate the client to perform hand-washing before and after breast-feeding to prevent mastitis. Discontinuing breast-feeding to allow time for healing, avoiding hot or cold compresses on the breast, and discouraging manual compression of breast for expressing milk

are inappropriate interventions. The nurse should educate the client to continue breast-feeding, because it reverses milk stasis, and to manually compress the breast to express excess milk. Hot and cold compresses can be applied for comfort.

12. **Answer: B, C, D**
   RATIONALE: The nurse should monitor for bleeding gums, tachycardia, and acute renal failure to assess for an increased risk of disseminated intravascular coagulation in the client. The other clinical manifestations of this condition include petechiae, ecchymosis, and uncontrolled bleeding during birth. Hypotension and amount of lochia greater than usual are findings that might suggest a coagulopathy or hypovolemic shock.

13. **Answer: A, B, D**
   RATIONALE: The nurse should monitor the client for symptoms such as inability to concentrate, loss of confidence, and decreased interest in life to verify the presence of postpartum depression. Manifestations of mania and bizarre behavior are noted in clients with postpartum psychosis.

14. **Answer: A, B, D**
   RATIONALE: A nurse should evaluate the efficacy of IV oxytocin therapy by assessing the uterine tone, monitoring vital signs, and getting a pad count. Assessing the skin turgor and assessing deep tendon reflexes are not interventions applicable to administration of oxytocin.

15. **Answer: C**
   RATIONALE: The nurse should closely assess the woman for hemorrhage after giving birth by frequently assessing uterine involution. Assessing skin turgor and blood pressure and monitoring hCG titers will not help to determine hemorrhage.

CHAPTER 23

SECTION I: ASSESSING YOUR UNDERSTANDING

Activity A FILL IN THE BLANKS

1. Polycythemia
2. Gavage
3. asphyxia
4. preterm
5. atelectasis
6. term
7. Retinopathy
8. Pain
9. inversely
10. genetic

Activity B LABELING

1. The figure displays a low–birth-weight newborn (or a newborn) in an Isolette.
2. An Isolette keeps the newborn warm to conserve energy and prevent cold stress. The Isolette may be warmed or may have an overhead radiant warmer.

Activity C MATCHING

1. c   **2.** a   **3.** b   **4.** d

Activity D SEQUENCING

b → c → d → e → a

Activity E SHORT ANSWERS

1. The common physical characteristics of preterm newborns include:
   • Birth weight of less than 5.5 lb
   • Scrawny appearance
   • Head disproportionately larger than chest circumference
   • Poor muscle tone
   • Minimal subcutaneous fat
   • Undescended testes
   • Plentiful lanugo (a soft downy hair), especially over the face and back
   • Poorly formed ear pinna with soft, pliable cartilage
   • Fused eyelids
   • Soft and spongy skull bones, especially along suture lines
   • Matted scalp hair, wooly in appearance
   • Absent or only a few creases in the soles and palms
   • Minimal scrotal rugae in male infants; prominent labia and clitoris in female infants
   • Thin, transparent skin with visible veins
   • Breast and nipples not clearly delineated
   • Abundant vernix caseosa

2. The clinical signs of hypoglycemia in the newborn are often subtle and include lethargy, apathy, drowsiness, irritability, tachypnea, weak cry, temperature instability, jitteriness, seizures, apnea, bradycardia, cyanosis or pallor, feeble suck and poor feeding, hypotonia, and coma. Blood glucose level below 40 mg/dL in term newborns and below 20 mg/dL in preterm newborns is indicative of hypoglycemia in the newborn.

3. Developmentally supportive care is defined as care of a newborn or an infant to support growth and development. Developmental care focuses on what newborns or infants can do at that stage of development; it uses therapeutic interventions only to the point that they are beneficial; and it provides for the development of the newborn–family unit.

4. Preterm infants are at a high risk for neurodevelopmental disorders such as cerebral palsy or intellectual disability, intraventricular hemorrhage, congenital anomalies, neurosensory impairment, behavioral disadaptation, and chronic lung disease.

5. The characteristics of large-for-gestational-age newborns are as follows:
   • Large body; appears plump and full faced
   • Increase in body size is proportional
   • Head circumference and body length in upper limits of intrauterine growth
   • Poor motor skills
   • Difficulty in regulating behavioral states
   • More difficult to arouse to a quiet alert state

6. Postterm newborns typically exhibit the following characteristics:
   - Dry, cracked, wrinkled skin
   - Long, thin extremities
   - Creases that cover the entire soles of the feet
   - Wide-eyed, alert expression
   - Abundant hair on scalp
   - Thin umbilical cord
   - Limited vernix and lanugo
   - Meconium-stained skin
   - Long nails

SECTION II: APPLYING YOUR KNOWLEDGE
Activity F CASE STUDY

1. A nurse can help the parents in the detachment process in the following ways:
   - To see their newborn through the maze of equipment
   - Explain the various procedures and equipment
   - Encourage them to express their feelings about the fragile newborn's status
   - Provide the parents time to spend with their dying newborn

2. The nursing interventions when caring for a family experiencing a perinatal loss are as follows:
   - Help the family to accept the reality of death by using the word "died."
   - Acknowledge their grief and the fact that their newborn has died.
   - Help the family to work through their grief by validating and listening.
   - Provide the family with realistic information about the causes of death.
   - Offer condolences to the family in a sincere manner.
   - Initiate spiritual comfort by calling the hospital clergy if needed.
   - Acknowledge variations in spiritual needs and readiness.
   - Encourage the parents to have a funeral or memorial service to bring closure.
   - Encourage the parents to take photographs, make memory boxes, and record their thoughts in a journal.
   - Suggest that the parents plant a tree or flowers to remember the infant.
   - Explore with family members how they dealt with previous losses.
   - Discuss meditation and relaxation techniques to reduce stress.
   - Provide opportunities for the family to hold the newborn if they choose to do so.
   - Assess the family's support network.
   - Address attachment issues concerning subsequent pregnancies.
   - Reassure the family that their feelings and grieving responses are normal.
   - Provide information about local support groups.
   - Provide anticipatory guidance regarding the grieving process.
   - Recommend that family members maintain a healthy diet and get adequate rest and exercise to preserve their health.

SECTION III: PRACTICING FOR NCLEX
Activity G NCLEX-STYLE QUESTIONS

1. **Answer: A**
   RATIONALE: The nurse should focus on decreasing blood viscosity by increasing fluid volume in the newborn with polycythemia. Checking blood glucose within 2 hours of birth by a reagent test strip and screening every 2 to 3 hours or before feeds are not interventions that will alleviate the condition of an infant with polycythemia. The nurse should monitor and maintain blood glucose levels when caring for a newborn with hypoglycemia, not polycythemia.

2. **Answer: A**
   RATIONALE: When preterm infants receive sensorimotor interventions such as rocking, massaging, holding, or sleeping on waterbeds, they gain weight faster, progress in feeding abilities more quickly, and show improved interactive behavior. Interventions such as swaddling and positioning, use of minimal amount of tape, and use of distraction through objects are related to pain management.

3. **Answer: D**
   RATIONALE: A good cry or good breathing efforts are signs that the resuscitation has been successful. A pulse above 100 bpm, not 80 bpm, is an indication of a successful resuscitation. Hypotonia indicates a poor oxygen supply to the brain. Jitteriness is associated with the signs of hypothermia or hypoglycemia; this is not a sign of successful resuscitation.

4. **Answer: D**
   RATIONALE: A good cry or good breathing effort is a sign that the resuscitation has been successful. A pulse above 100 bpm, not 80 bpm, is an indication of a successful resuscitation. Pink tongue, not blue tongue, indicates a good oxygen supply to the brain. Tremors are associated with the signs of hypothermia; this is not a sign of successful resuscitation.

5. **Answer: B**
   RATIONALE: The nurse should administer 0.5 to 1 mL/kg/hr of breast milk enterally to induce surges in gut hormones that enhance maturation of the intestine. Administering vitamin D supplements, iron supplements, or intravenous dextrose will not significantly help the preterm newborn's gut overcome feeding difficulties.

6. **Answer: A**
   RATIONALE: The nurse should provide some nutrition to any infant born with hypoglycemia. Dextrose should be given intravenously only if

the infant refuses oral feedings, not before offering the infant oral feedings. Placing the infant on a radiant warmer will not help maintain blood glucose levels. The nurse should focus on decreasing blood viscosity in an infant who is at risk for polycythemia, not hypoglycemia.

7. **Answer: A, B, D**
RATIONALE: Diabetes mellitus, postdates gestation, and prepregnancy obesity are the maternal factors the nurse should consider that could lead to a newborn being large for gestational age. Renal condition and maternal alcohol use are not factors associated with a newborn's being large for gestational age.

8. **Answer: A**
RATIONALE: The infant is demonstrating signs and symptoms of significant hypoglycemia. IV dextrose should be administered to the term newborn intravenously when the blood glucose level is less than 40 mg/dL, and the newborn is symptomatic for hypoglycemia. Administration of IV glucose assists in stabilizing blood glucose levels. Providing oral glucose feedings or placing the infant on a radiant warmer will not help maintain the glucose level. Monitoring the infant's hematocrit level is not a priority and not related to the problem at hand.

9. **Answer: A, C, E**
RATIONALE: Hydration, early feedings, and phototherapy are measures that the nurse should take to reduce bilirubin levels in the newborn. Stopping breastfeeding or administering vitamin supplements will not help reduce bilirubin levels in the infant.

10. **Answer: D**
RATIONALE: Meconium-stained cord and skin indicates a potential of meconium aspiration, and the nurse should inform the primary care provider but if the infant actually experiences respiratory distress following a delivery with meconium-stained fluids, the likelihood of meconium aspiration is greatly increased. Listlessness or lethargy by themselves does not indicate meconium aspiration. Bluish skin discoloration is normal in infants shortly after birth until the infant' respiratory system clears out all the amniotic fluid.

11. **Answer: A, C, D**
RATIONALE: The nurse should be alert to the possibility of an SGA newborn if the history of the mother reveals smoking, chronic medical conditions (such as asthma), and drug abuse. Additional maternal factors that increase the risk for an SGA newborn include hypertension, genetic disorders, and multiple gestations.

12. **Answer: A**
RATIONALE: Clustering care and activities in the NICU decreases stress and helps developmentally support premature and sick infants. Developmental care can decrease assistance needed and length of hospital stay. The other choices are part of basic infant care.

13. **Answer: D**
RATIONALE: The small-for-gestational-age neonate is at risk for developing polycythemia during the transitional period in an attempt to decrease hypoxia. This neonate is also at increased risk for developing hypoglycemia and hypothermia due to decreased glycogen stores.

14. **Answer: C**
RATIONALE: The ear has a soft pinna that is flat and stays folded. Pale skin with no vessels showing through and 7 to 10 mm of breast tissue are characteristic of a neonate at 40 weeks' gestation. Creases on the anterior two-thirds of the sole are characteristic of a neonate at 36 weeks' gestation.

15. **Answer: C**
RATIONALE: The nurse should include the parents and notify them of any visible anomalies right away. An in-depth discussion can take place later when the diagnosis is more definitive. Although the family may be in shock or denial, the nurse should give a realistic appraisal of the condition of their baby. Keeping communication lines open will lessen the family's feelings of helplessness and support their parental role.

CHAPTER 24

SECTION I: ASSESSING YOUR UNDERSTANDING
Activity A FILL IN THE BLANKS
1. omphalocele
2. Cephalohematoma
3. Hyperbilirubinemia
4. sepsis
5. Methadone
6. hemolytic
7. phototherapy
8. Gastroschisis
9. asphyxia
10. Kernicterus
11. inflammatory

Activity B MATCHING
1. a   2. d   3. b   4. c   5. e

Activity C SHORT ANSWERS
1. The characteristics of an infant born to a diabetic mother are as follows:
   - Full rosy cheeks with a ruddy skin color
   - Short neck with a buffalo hump over the nape of the neck
   - Massive shoulders showing full intrascapular area
   - Distended upper abdomen resulting from organ overgrowth
   - Excessive subcutaneous fat tissue, producing fat extremities

2. The most common types of malformations in infants of diabetic mothers involve anomalies in the following systems:
   - Cardiovascular
   - Skeletal
   - Central nervous system
   - Gastrointestinal
   - Genitourinary
3. The treatment of infants born to diabetic mothers focuses on correcting hypoglycemia, hypocalcemia, hypomagnesemia, dehydration, and jaundice. Oxygenation and ventilation for the newborn are supported as necessary.
4. Birth trauma may result from the pressure of birth, especially in a prolonged or abrupt labor, abnormal or difficult presentation, cephalopelvic disproportion, or mechanical forces such as a forceps or vacuum used during delivery.
5. Meconium aspiration syndrome occurs when the newborn inhales particulate meconium mixed with amniotic fluid into the lungs while still in utero or on taking the first breath after birth. It is a common cause of newborn respiratory distress and can lead to severe illness.
6. PVH/IVH is defined as bleeding that usually originates in the subependymal germinal matrix region of the brain, with extension into the ventricular system. It is a common problem of preterm infants, especially those born before 32 weeks.
7. The goals of therapy include restoring urinary continence, preserving renal function, and reconstructing functional and cosmetically acceptable genitalia.

SECTION II: APPLYING YOUR KNOWLEDGE

Activity D CASE STUDY

1. The role of the nurse in handling substance-abusing mothers includes:
   - Being knowledgeable about issues of substance abuse
   - Being alert for opportunities to identify, prevent, manage, and educate clients and families about this key public health issue
2. The nurse can use the "5 As" approach in the following way:
   - Ask: Ask the client if she smokes and if she would like to quit.
   - Advise: Encourage the use of clinically proved treatment plans.
   - Assess: Provide motivation by discussing the 5 Rs:
     - Relevance of quitting to the client
     - Risk of continued smoking to the fetus
     - Rewards of quitting for both
     - Roadblocks to quitting
     - Repeat at every visit
   - Assist: Help the client to protect her fetus and newborn from the negative effects of smoking.
   - Arrange: Schedule follow-up visits to reinforce the client's commitment to quit.

SECTION III: PRACTICING FOR NCLEX

Activity E NCLEX-STYLE QUESTIONS

1. **Answer: D**
   RATIONALE: The nurse should administer oxygen to the infant in whatever manner needed to help maintain the infant's oxygen levels. Anticonvulsants are not necessary in treating this disorder, the infant's physical environment should be warm, not cool and stimulation should be limited for these patients.
2. **Answer: B**
   RATIONALE: The nurse should know that the infant's mother more than likely was a diabetic. The large size of the infant born to a diabetic mother is secondary to exposure to high levels of maternal glucose crossing the placenta into the fetal circulation. Common problems among infants of diabetic mothers include macrosomia, respiratory distress syndrome, birth trauma, hypoglycemia, hypocalcemia and hypomagnesemia, polycythemia, hyperbilirubinemia, and congenital anomalies. Listlessness is also a common symptom noted in these infants. Infants born to clients who have abused alcohol, infants who have experienced birth traumas, or infants whose mothers have had long labors are not known to exhibit these particular characteristics, although these conditions do not produce very positive pregnancy outcomes. Infants with fetal alcohol syndrome or alcohol exposure during pregnancy do not usually have hypoglycemia problems.
3. **Answer: A, D, E**
   RATIONALE: A nurse should associate obstructive hydrocephalus, vision or hearing defects, and cerebral palsy with newborns who had a PVH/IVH. Acid–base imbalances are complications occurring during exchange transfusion for lowering serum bilirubin levels. Pneumonitis is a complication associated with esophageal atresia.
4. **Answer: B**
   RATIONALE: Ensuring effective resuscitation measures is the nursing intervention involved when treating a newborn for asphyxia. Ensuring adequate tissue perfusion and administering surfactant are nursing interventions involved in the care of newborns with meconium aspiration syndrome. Similarly, administering IV fluids is a nursing intervention involved in the care of newborns with transient tachypnea.
5. **Answer: C**
   RATIONALE: The preoperative nursing care focuses on preventing aspiration by elevating the head of the bed and insertion of an NG tube to low suction to prevent aspiration. Documenting the amount and color of drainage is not needed with the NG tube in place. An infant with esophageal atresia is NPO and fed nothing until after repairing the defect. Administering antibiotics and total parenteral nutrition is a postoperative nursing

intervention when caring for a newborn with esophageal atresia.

6. **Answer: B**

RATIONALE: The nurse should know that gastroschisis is a herniation of abdominal contents in which there is no peritoneal sac protecting herniated organs. A peritoneal sac is present in omphalocele. In gastroschisis, the herniated organs are not normal; they are unprotected and become thickened, edematous, and inflamed because of exposure to amniotic fluid. Gastroschisis is not a defect of the abdomen related to the musculature, that is, Prune belly syndrome, whereby the abdominal musculature is poorly developed. This herniation of abdominal contents occurs to the right of the umbilical cord, not into the base of it. That is an omphalocele.

7. **Answer: C**

RATIONALE: The nurse should inform the parents that surgery for NEC requires the placement of a proximal enterostomy and ostomy care. Surgically treated NEC is a lengthy process, and the amount of bowel that has necrosed, as determined during the bowel resection, significantly increases the likelihood that infants requiring surgery for NEC may have long-term medical problems. If surgery for NEC is required, enteral feedings may be required for a protracted period of time.

8. **Answer: D**

RATIONALE: Expiratory grunting, a barrel-shaped chest with an increased anterior–posterior chest diameter, prolonged tachypnea, progression from mild-to-severe respiratory distress, intercostal retractions, cyanosis, surfactant dysfunction, airway obstruction, hypoxia, and chemical pneumonitis with inflammation of pulmonary tissues are seen in a newborn with meconium aspiration syndrome. A high-pitched cry may be noted in periventricular hemorrhage/intraventricular hemorrhage. Bile-stained emesis occurs in necrotizing enterocolitis. Intermittent tachypnea can be indicative of transient tachypnea of the newborn or any mild respiratory distress problem.

9. **Answer: D**

RATIONALE: Noting any absence of or decrease in deep tendon reflexes is a nursing intervention when assessing a newborn with a risk of trauma. The nurse should examine the skin for cyanosis, should be alert for signs of apathy and listlessness, and should assess for any temperature instability when caring for a newborn born to a diabetic mother. These interventions are not required to assess for trauma or birth injuries in a newborn.

10. **Answer: C**

RATIONALE: The nurse should assess for meconium aspiration syndrome in the newborn. Meconium aspiration involves patchy, fluffy infiltrates unevenly distributed throughout the lungs and marked hyperaeration mixed with areas of atelectasis that can be seen through chest x-rays. Direct visualization of the vocal cords for meconium staining using a laryngoscope can confirm aspiration. Lung auscultation typically reveals coarse crackles and rhonchi. Arterial blood gas analysis will indicate metabolic acidosis with a low blood pH, decreased PaO_2, and increased $PaCO_2$. Newborns with choanal atresia, diaphragmatic hernia, and pneumonia do not exhibit these manifestations.

11. **Answer: A**

RATIONALE: The nurse should administer IV fluids and gavage feedings until the respiratory rate decreases enough to allow oral feedings when caring for a newborn with transient tachypnea. Maintaining adequate hydration and performing gentle suctioning are relevant nursing interventions when caring for a newborn with respiratory distress syndrome. The nurse need not monitor the newborn for signs and symptoms of hypotonia because hypotonia is not known to occur as a result of transient tachypnea. Hypotonia is observed in newborns with inborn errors of metabolism or in cases of periventricular hemorrhage/intraventricular hemorrhage.

12. **Answer: B**

RATIONALE: The nurse should shield the newborn's eyes and cover the genitals to protect these areas from becoming irritated or burned when using direct lights and to ensure exposure of the greatest surface area. The nurse should place the newborn under the lights or on the fiberoptic blanket, exposing as much skin as possible. Breast or bottle feedings should be encouraged every 2 to 3 hours. Loose, green, and frequent stools indicate the presence of unconjugated bilirubin in the feces. This is normal; therefore, there is no need for therapy to be discontinued. Lack of frequent green stools is a cause for concern.

13. **Answer: B, D, E**

RATIONALE: When caring for a newborn with meconium aspiration syndrome, the nurse should place the newborn under a radiant warmer or in a warmed Isolette, administer oxygen therapy as ordered via a nasal cannula or with positive pressure ventilation, and administer broad-spectrum antibiotics to treat bacterial pneumonia. Repeated suctioning and stimulation should be limited to prevent overstimulation and further depression in the newborn. The nurse should also ensure minimal handling to reduce energy expenditure and oxygen consumption that could lead to further hypoxemia and acidosis. Handling and rubbing the newborn with a dry towel is needed to stimulate the onset of breathing in a newborn with asphyxia.

14. **Answer: B**

RATIONALE: Hypoglycemia in a neonate is expressed as jitteriness, lethargy, diaphoresis, and a serum glucose level below 40 mg/dL. A hyperalert state in a neonate is more suggestive of neuralgic irritability and has no correlation to blood glucose levels. Excessive crying is not found in hypoglycemia. A serum glucose level of 60 mg/dL is a normal level.

15. Answer: D

RATIONALE: The neonate with an ABO blood incompatibility with its mother will have jaundice within the first 24 hours of life. The neonate would have a positive Coombs test result. Jaundice after the first 24 hours of life is physiologic jaundice. Bleeding from the nose and ear should be investigated for possible causes but probably is not related to ABO incompatibility.

CHAPTER 25

SECTION I: ASSESSING YOUR UNDERSTANDING

Activity A FILL IN THE BLANKS

1. Colic
2. Anticipatory
3. Prolactin
4. Colostrum
5. Separate
6. Development
7. 12 to 18

Activity B LABELING

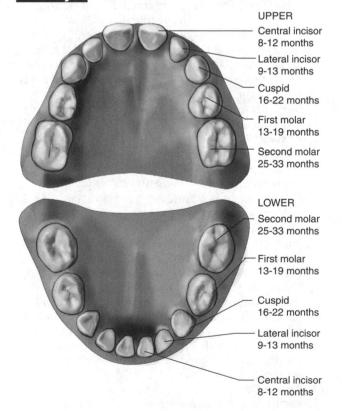

UPPER
Central incisor
8-12 months

Lateral incisor
9-13 months

Cuspid
16-22 months

First molar
13-19 months

Second molar
25-33 months

LOWER
Second molar
25-33 months

First molar
13-19 months

Cuspid
16-22 months

Lateral incisor
9-13 months

Central incisor
8-12 months

Activity C MATCHING

Exercise 1
1. f   2. a   3. b   4. e   5. d   6. c

Exercise 2
1. b   2. a   3. d   4. c   5. e

Activity D SEQUENCING

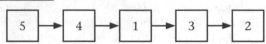

5 → 4 → 1 → 3 → 2

Activity E SHORT ANSWER

1. Encourage breastfeeding in all mothers beginning with the prenatal visit if applicable. Provide accurate education related to breastfeeding.

   Be available for questions or problems related to initiation and continuation of breastfeeding. Consult lactation consultant as needed or available.

   Encourage pumping of breast milk when mother returns to work in order to continue breastfeeding.

   Refer to local breastfeeding support groups such as La Leche League.

2. Breastfeeding or feeding of expressed human milk is recommended for all infants, including sick or premature newborns (with rare exceptions). The exceptions include infants with galactosemia, maternal use of illicit drugs and a few prescription medications, maternal untreated active tuberculosis, and maternal human immunodeficiency virus (HIV) infection in developed countries.

3. Early cues of hunger in a baby include making sucking motions, sucking on hands, or putting the fist to the chin.

4. When assessing the growth and development of a premature infant, use the infant's adjusted age to determine expected outcomes. To determine adjusted age, subtract the number of weeks that the infant was premature from the infant's chronological age.

5. Primitive reflexes are subcortical and involve a whole-body response. Selected primitive reflexes present at birth include moro, root, suck, asymmetric tonic neck, plantar and palmar grasp, step, and Babinski. Except for the Babinski, which disappears around 1 year of age, these primitive reflexes diminish over the first few months of life, giving way to protective reflexes.

6. The heart doubles in size over the first year of life. As the cardiovascular system matures, the average pulse rate decreases from 120 to 140 in the newborn to about 100 in the 1-year old. Blood pressure steadily increases over the first 12 months of life, from an average of 60/40 in the newborn to 100/50 in the 12-month-old. The peripheral capillaries are closer to the surface of the skin, thus making the newborn and young infant more susceptible to heat

loss. Over the first year of life, thermoregulation (the body's ability to stabilize body temperature) becomes more effective: the peripheral capillaries constrict in response to a cold environment and dilate in response to heat.

SECTION II: APPLYING YOUR KNOWLEDGE

Activity F CASE STUDY

1. The discussion should include the following points:

    Play is the work of children and is the natural way they learn. It is critical to their development. It allows them to explore their environment, practice new skills, and problem solve. They practice gross, fine motor and language skills through play. Young infants love to watch people's faces and will often appear to mimic the expressions they see. Parents can talk to and sing to their child while participating in the daily activities that infants need such as feeding, bathing, and changing. As infants become older, toys may be geared toward the motor skills or language skills that are developing currently. Appropriate toys for this age group include fabric or board books, different types of music, easy to hold toys that do things or make noise (fancy rattles), floating, squirting bath toys, and soft dolls or animals. Books are also very important toys for infants. Reading aloud and sharing books during early infancy are critical to the development of neural networks that are important in the later tasks of reading and word recognition. Reading books increases listening comprehension. Infants demonstrate their excitement about picture books by kicking and waving their arms and babbling when looking at them. Reading to all ages of infants is appropriate and the older infant develops fine motor skills as he learns to turn book pages. Reading picture books and simple stories to infants starts a good habit that should be continued throughout childhood.

2. The discussion should include the following points:

    Erikson's stage of psychosocial development is trust versus mistrust. Development of a sense of trust is crucial in the first year, as it serves as the foundation for later psychosocial tasks. The parent or primary caregiver is in a position to significantly impact the infant's development of a sense of trust. When the infant's needs are consistently met, the infant develops this sense of trust. Caregivers respond to these basic needs by feeding, changing diapers, and cleaning, touching, holding, and talking to infants. If the parent or caregiver is inconsistent in meeting the infant's needs in a timely manner, then over time the infant develops a sense of mistrust. As the infant gets older, the nervous system matures. The infant begins to realize a separation between self and caregivers. The infant learns to tolerate small amounts of frustration, and learns to trust the caregivers even if

gratification is delayed, because the infant understands that needs will eventually be provided.

    The first stage of Jean Piaget's theory of cognitive development is referred to as the sensorimotor stage (birth to 2 years). Infants learn about themselves and the world around them through developing sensory and motor capacities. Infants between 4 and 8 months repeat actions to achieve wanted results, such as shaking a rattle to hear the noise it makes. At this age their actions are purposeful, though do not always have an end goal in mind.

3. The discussion should include the following points:

    Inability to sit with assistance, does not turn to locate sound, crosses eyes most of the time, does not laugh or squeal, does not smile or seem to enjoy people.

SECTION III: PRACTICING FOR NCLEX

Activity G NCLEX-STYLE QUESTIONS

1. **Answer: C**
   RATIONALE: The child's head size is large for his adjusted age of 4 months, which would be cause for concern. Normal growth would be 3.6 in (9 cm). At 10 lb, 2 oz (12 cm), the child is the right weight for a 4-month-old adjusted age. Palmar grasp reflex disappears between 4 and 6 months adjusted age, so this would not be a concern yet. The child is of average weight for a 4-month-old adjusted age.

2. **Answer: A**
   RATIONALE: Urging the parents to get time away from the child would be most helpful in the short term, particularly if the parents are stressed. Educating the parents about when colic stops would help them see an end to the stress. Observing how the parents respond to the child helps to determine if the parent–child relationship was altered. Assessing the parents' care and feeding skills may identify other causes for the crying.

3. **Answer: D**
   RATIONALE: The normal newborn may lose up to 10% of their birth weight. The baby in question has lost just below this amount. This will likely not require hospitalization. Expressing to the mother that her baby will likely be hospitalized is rash and will most likely not occur.

4. **Answer: B**
   RATIONALE: The nurse will warn against putting the baby to bed with a bottle of milk or juice because this allows the sugar content of these fluids to pool around the baby's teeth at night. Not cleaning a baby's gums when he is done eating will have minimal impact on the development of dental caries, as will using a cloth instead of a brush for cleaning teeth when they erupt. Failure to clean the teeth with fluoridated toothpaste is not a problem if the water supply is fluoridated.

5. **Answer: B**
   RATIONALE: If the parents are keeping the child up until she falls asleep, they are not creating a

bedtime routine for her. Infants need a transition to sleep at this age. If the parents are singing to her before she goes to bed, if she has a regular, scheduled bedtime, and if they check on her safety when she wakes at night, then lie her down and leave, they are using good sleep practices.

6. **Answer: C**
   RATIONALE: The nurse would advise the mother to watch for increased biting and sucking. Mild fever, vomiting, and diarrhea are signs of infection. The child would more likely seek out hard foods or objects to bite on.

7. **Answer: D**
   RATIONALE: When introducing a new food to an infant, it may take multiple attempts before the child will accept it. Parents must demonstrate patience. Letting the child eat only the foods she prefers, forcing her to eat foods she does not want, or actively urging the child to eat new foods can negatively affect eating patterns.

8. **Answer: A**
   RATIONALE: The best way to ensure effective feeding is by maintaining a feed-on-demand approach rather than a set schedule. Applying warm compresses to the breast helps engorgement. Encouraging the infant to latch on properly helps prevent sore nipples. Maintaining proper diet and fluid intake for the mother helps ensure an adequate milk supply.

9. **Answer: C**
   RATIONALE: At 6 months of age, the child is able to put down one toy to pick up another. He will be able to shift a toy to his left hand to reach for another with his right hand by 7 months. He will pick up an object with his thumb and finger tips at 8 months, and he will enjoy hitting a plastic bowl with a large spoon at 9 months.

10. **Answer: B**
    RATIONALE: The average infant's weight doubles at 4 months and will triple at 1 year of life. The infant's length will increase by 50% by the first year.

11. **Answer: B**
    RATIONALE: The normal respiratory rate for a 1-month-old infant is 30 to 60 breaths per minute. By 1 year of age the rate will be 20 to 30 breaths per minute. The respiratory patterns of the 1-month-old infant are irregular. There may normally be periodic pauses in the rhythm.

12. **Answer: B**
    RATIONALE: Normally infants are not born with teeth. Occasionally there are one or more teeth at birth. These are termed natal teeth and are often associated with anomalies. The first primary teeth typically erupt between the ages of 6 and 8 months.

13. **Answer: C**
    RATIONALE: The capacity of the normal newborn's stomach is between 1½ and 1 oz. The recommended feeding plan is to use a demand schedule. Newborns may eat as often as 1½ to 3 hours. Demand scheduled feedings are not associated with problems sleeping at night.

CHAPTER 26

SECTION I: ASSESSING YOUR UNDERSTANDING

Activity A FILL IN THE BLANKS
1. Myelinization
2. Drowning
3. Receptive
4. Urethra
5. Preoperational

Activity B MATCHING
Exercise 1
1. d   2. f   3. e   4. b   5. a   6. c
Exercise 2
1. c   2. a   3. b   4. e   5. d

Activity C SEQUENCING

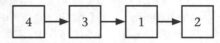

4 → 3 → 1 → 2

Activity D SHORT ANSWERS
1. Prevention is best concerning temper tantrums. Fatigue or hunger may limit the toddler's coping abilities, so adhering to reasonable food and sleep schedules help prevent tantrums. When parents note the beginnings of frustrations during activities, friendly warnings, distractions, refocusing, or removal from the situation may prevent the tantrum.
2. Toddler discipline should focus on clear limit setting, consistency, negotiation, and techniques to assist the toddler to learn problem solving. Positive reinforcement should be used as much as possible while avoiding spanking and other forms of corporal punishment.
3. At the age of 1, every child should have an initial dental visit. To prevent the development of dental caries children should be weaned by 15 months of age. In addition, the use of sippy cups should be limited. Cleaning of the toddler's teeth should progress from brushing simply with water to using a very small pea-sized amount of fluoridated toothpaste with brushing beginning at age 2.
4. Changes in the anatomy of the toddler's genitourinary system make toilet training possible. The kidney functions reach adult levels between 16 and 24 months of age. The bladder is able to hold urine for increased periods of time.
5. The abdominal musculature is weak in the young toddler. This causes a pot-bellied appearance. In addition the child appears sway-backed. As the muscles mature, this resolves.

SECTION II: APPLYING YOUR KNOWLEDGE

Activity E CASE STUDY

Jose Gonzales is a 2-year-old boy brought to the clinic by his mother and father for his 2-year-old check-up. The following questions refer to him:

1. The potentially bilingual child may blend two languages, that is, parts of the word in both languages are blended into one word or may language mix within a sentence; he will combine languages or grammar within a sentence. The assessment of adequate language development is more complicated in bilingual children.

2. Talking and singing to the toddler during routine activities such as feeding and dressing provides an environment that encourages conversation. Frequent, repetitive naming helps the toddler learn appropriate words for objects. Be attentive to what the toddler is saying as well as to his moods. Listen to and answer the toddler's questions. Encouragement and elaboration convey confidence and interest to the toddler. Give the toddler time to complete his or her thoughts without interrupting or rushing. Remember that the toddler is just starting to be able to make the connections necessary to transfer thoughts and feelings into language.

   Do not overreact to the child's use of the word "no." Give the toddler opportunities to appropriately use the word "no" with silly questions such as "Can a cat drive a car?" Teach the toddler appropriate words for body parts and objects. Help the toddler choose appropriate words to label feelings and emotions. Toddlers' receptive language and interpretation of body language and subtle signs far surpasses their expressive language especially at a younger age.

   Encourage the use of both English and Spanish in the home.

   Reading to the toddler every day is one of the best ways to promote language and cognitive development. Toddlers particularly enjoy books about feelings, family, friends, everyday life, animals and nature, and fun and fantasy. Board books have thick pages that are easier for young toddlers to turn. The toddler may also enjoy "reading" the story to the parent.

3. Erikson defines the toddler period as a time of autonomy versus shame and doubt. It is a time of exerting independence. Exertion of independence often results in the toddler's favorite response, "No." The toddler will often answer "no" even when he or she really means "yes." Always saying "no," referred to as negativism, is a normal part of healthy development.

   If there is no option of avoiding an action, do not ask toddlers if they want to do something. Avoid closed ended yes/no questions, as the toddler's usual response is "No," whether he means it or not. Offer the child simple choices such as "Do you want to use the red cup or the blue cup?" This helps give the toddler a sense of control. When getting ready to leave, do not ask the child if he wants to put his shoes on. Simply state in a matter of fact tone that shoes must be worn outside and give the toddler a choice on type of shoe or color of socks. If the child continues with negative answers, then the parent should remain calm and make the decision for the child.

SECTION III: PRACTICING FOR NCLEX

Activity F NCLEX-STYLE QUESTIONS

1. **Answer: C**
   RATIONALE: Suggesting that the parents transition the child to a healthier diet by serving him more healthy choices along with smaller portions of junk food will reassure them that they are not starving their child. The parents would have less success with an abrupt change to healthy foods. Explaining calorie requirements and the time line for acceptance of a new food do not offer a practical reason for making a change in diet.

2. **Answer: A**
   RATIONALE: This child has most recently acquired the ability to undress himself. Pushing a toy lawnmower and kicking a ball are things he learned at about 24 months. He was able to pull a toy while walking at about 18 months.

3. **Answer: D**
   RATIONALE: Stopping the child when she is misbehaving and describing proper behavior sets limits and models good behavior and will be the most helpful advice to the parents. The child is too young to use time out or extinction as discipline. Slapping her hand, even done carefully with two fingers, is corporal punishment, which has been found to have negative effects on child development.

4. **Answer: B**
   RATIONALE: Because they are curious and mobile, toddlers require direct observation and cannot be trusted to be left alone, especially when outdoors. The priority guidance is to never let the child be out of sight. Gating stairways, locking up chemicals, and not smoking around the child are excellent, but specific, safety interventions.

5. **Answer: B**
   RATIONALE: The nurse would be concerned if the child is babbling to herself rather than using real words. By this age, she should be using simple sentences with a vocabulary of 50 words. Being unwilling to share toys, playing parallel with other children, and moving to different toys frequently are typical toddler behaviors.

6. **Answer: C**
   RATIONALE: The fact that the child does not respond when the mother waves to him suggests he may have a vision problem. The toddler's sense of smell is still developing, so he may not be affected by odors. Their sense of taste is not well developed either, and this allows him to eat or

drink poisons without concern. The child's crying at a sudden noise assures the nurse that his hearing is adequate.

7. **Answer: C**
RATIONALE: If the child is still speaking telegraphically in only two- to three-word sentences, it suggests there is a language development problem. If the child makes simple conversation, tells about something that happened in the past, or tells the nurse her name she is meeting developmental milestones for language.

8. **Answer: A**
RATIONALE: Separation anxiety should have disappeared or be subsiding by 3 years of age. The fact that it is persistent suggests there might be an emotional problem. Emotional lability, self soothing by thumb sucking, or the inability to share are common for this age.

9. **Answer: B**
RATIONALE: The nurse would be sure to tell the mother to feed her child iron-fortified cereal and other iron-rich foods when she weans her child off the breast or formula. Weaning from the breast is dependent upon the mother's need and desires with no set time. Weaning from the bottle is recommended at 1 year of age in order to prevent dental caries. Use of a no-spill sippy cup is not recommended because it too is associated with dental caries.

10. **Answer: D**
RATIONALE: The nurse would recommend a preschool where the staff is trained in early childhood development and cardiopulmonary resuscitation. Cleanliness and a loving staff are not enough without competence. Good hygiene procedures require that a sick child not be allowed to attend. It is also important that parents are allowed to visit any time without an appointment.

11. **Answer: B**
RATIONALE: The Erickson stage of development for the toddler is autonomy versus shame and doubt. During this period of time the child works to establish independence. Trust versus mistrust is the stage of infancy. Initiative versus guilt is the stage for the preschooler. Industry versus inferiority is the stage for school-aged children.

12. **Answer: A**
RATIONALE: Object permanence means that the child knows that objects that are out of sight still exist.

13. **Answer: D**
RATIONALE: The 20-month-old toddler should have a vocabulary greater than 40 to 50 words and should comprehend approximately 200 words. The ability to point to named body points, discuss past events, and point to pictures in a book when asked are communication skills associated with an older child.

14. **Answer: A**
RATIONALE: The social skills of the toddler at this age include parallel play. During parallel play children will play alongside each other, rather than cooperatively. There is no indication that the aggression level of the child needs to be investigated. There is no indication the child needs increased socialization with other children.

CHAPTER 27

SECTION I: ASSESSING YOUR UNDERSTANDING

Activity A FILL IN THE BLANKS

1. Iron
2. Concrete
3. Urethra
4. Terror
5. Dense

Activity B MATCHING

1. d   2. a   3. b   4. f   5. c   6. e

Activity C SEQUENCING

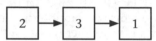

Activity D SHORT ANSWERS

1. The child in the intuitive phase can count 10 or more objects, correctly name at least 4 colors, can understand the concept of time, and knows about things that are used in everyday life such as appliances, money, and food.

2. A nightmare is a scary or bad dream. After a nightmare, the child is aroused and interactive. Night terrors are different. A short time after falling asleep, the child seems to awaken and is screaming. The child usually does not respond much to the parent's soothing, eventually stops screaming, and goes back to sleep. Night terrors are often frightening for parents, because the child does not seem to be responding to them.

3. The preschooler should have his or her teeth brushed and flossed daily with a pea-sized amount of toothpaste. Cariogenic foods should continue to be avoided. If sugary foods are consumed, the mouth should be rinsed with water if it is not possible to brush the teeth directly after their consumption. The preschool-aged child should visit the dentist every 6 months.

4. The parent should ascertain the reason for the lie before punishing the child. If the child has broken a rule and fears punishment, then the parent must determine the truth. The child needs to learn that lying is usually far worse than the misbehavior itself. The punishment for the misbehavior should be lessened if the child admits the truth. The parent should remain calm and serve as a role model of an even temper.

5. The primary psychosocial task of the preschool period is developing a sense of initiative.

SECTION II: APPLYING YOUR KNOWLEDGE
Activity E CASE STUDY

1. Magical thinking and playing make believe are a normal part of preschool development. The preschool-age child believes her thoughts to be all-powerful. The fantasy experienced through magical thinking and make believe allows the preschooler to make room in his world for the actual or the real and to satisfy her curiosity about differences in the world around her. Encouraging pretend play and providing props for dress-up stimulate and develop curiosity and creativity. Fantasy play is usually cooperative in nature and encourages the preschooler to develop social skills like turn-taking, communication, paying attention, and responding to one another's words and actions. Fantasy play also allows preschoolers to explore complex social ideas such as power, compassion, and cruelty.

2. Kindergarten may be a significant change for some children. The hours are usually longer than preschool and it is usually held 5 days per week. The setting and personnel are new and rules and expectations are often very different. When talking about starting kindergarten with Nila, do so using an enthusiastic approach. Keep the conversation light and positive. Meet with Nila's teacher prior to the start of school and discuss any specific needs or concerns the nurse may have. A tour of the school and attending the school's open house can help ease the transition also. Incorporate and practice the new daily routine prior to school starting. This can help the child adjust to the changes that are occurring.

3. The discussion should include the following points:
   - Cannot jump in place or ride a tricycle
   - Cannot stack four blocks
   - Cannot throw ball overhand
   - Does not grasp crayon with thumb and fingers
   - Difficulty with scribbling
   - Cannot copy a circle
   - Does not use sentences with three or more words
   - Cannot use the words "me" and "you" appropriately
   - Ignores other children or does not show interest in interactive games
   - Will not respond to people outside the family, still clings or cries if parents leave

SECTION III: PRACTICING FOR NCLEX
Activity F NCLEX-STYLE QUESTIONS

1. **Answer: B**
   RATIONALE: The presence of only 10 deciduous teeth would warrant further investigation. The preschooler should have 20 deciduous teeth present. The absence of dental caries or presence of 19 teeth does not warrant further investigation.

2. **Answer: B**
   RATIONALE: The nurse should encourage the mother to schedule a meeting with the teacher prior to school's start date and set up a time to tour the classroom and school so the boy knows what to expect. The other statements are not helpful and do not address the mother's or boy's concerns.

3. **Answer: C**
   RATIONALE: The average preschool child will grow 2.5 to 3 inch (6.35 to 7.62 cm) per year. Thus, the nurse would expect that the child's height would have increased 2.5 to 3 inch (6.35 to 7.62 cm) since last year's well-child examination.

4. **Answer: B**
   RATIONALE: By the age of 5, persons outside of the family should be able to understand most of the child's speech without the parents "translation." The other statements would not warrant additional referral or follow-up. A child of 5 years should be able to count to at least 10, know his or her address, and participate in long detailed conversations.

5. **Answer: A**
   RATIONALE: During a night terror, a child is typically unaware of the parent's presence and may scream and thrash more if restrained. During a nightmare, a child is responsive to the parent's soothing and reassurances. The other statements are indicative of a nightmare.

6. **Answer: D**
   RATIONALE: The preschooler is not mature enough to ride a bicycle in the street even if riding with adults, so the nurse should emphasize that the girl should always ride on the sidewalk even if the mother is riding with her daughter. The other statements are correct.

7. **Answer: C**
   RATIONALE: The nurse needs to emphasize that there are number of reasons that a parent should not choose a preschool that utilizes corporal punishment. It may negatively affect a child's self-esteem as well as ability to achieve in school. It may also lead to disruptive and violent behavior in the classroom and should be discouraged. The other statements would not warrant further discussion or intervention.

8. **Answer: B**
   RATIONALE: The nurse should explain to the parents that attributing life-like qualities to inanimate objects is quite normal. Telling the parents that their daughter is demonstrating animism is correct, but it would be better to explain what animism is and then remind them that it is developmentally appropriate. Asking whether they think their daughter is hallucinating or whether there is a family history of mental history is inappropriate and does not teach.

9. **Answer: A**
   RATIONALE: The nurse needs to remind the parents not to coax a child to take a vitamin supplement, tablet, or pill by calling it candy. The other statements are correct.

10. **Answer: C**
    RATIONALE: It is important to remind the parents that they should perform flossing in the preschool period because the child is unable to perform this task. The other statements are correct.

11. **Answer: D**
    RATIONALE: The average 4-year-old child is 40.5 inch (103 cm). The average rate of growth per year is between 2.5 and 3 inch (6.35 and 7.62 cm). The child in the scenario demonstrates normal stature and growth patterns.

12. **Answer: C**
    RATIONALE: Preschool-aged children may become occupied with activities around them and not remember to void. Reminding them to void is helpful. Discipline should not be applied to infrequent episodes of incontinence. There is no indication the child has an infection.

13. **Answer: D**
    RATIONALE: Preschool-aged children often interact with imaginary friends. The nurse should recognize this as normal for the age group. No special actions are needed.

14. **Answer: C**
    RATIONALE: Sexual curiosity is normal in the preschool-aged child. The parents should be encouraged to provide brief, honest answers to the child. The parents must also determine the type of curiosity the child has. Explanations should be within the level of understanding of the child.

15. **Answer: A**
    RATIONALE: Fears are normal in the preschool-aged child. Some children are afraid of the dark. The parents should be advised to show patience with their child as he works through this fear. Refusing a night light will further increase the stress of the child. Parents should not give credibility to the fear by checking under the bed for monsters. Parents should not use the television to soothe the child, rather develop a routine that relaxing such as one-on-time with the child. Parents should disrupt the usual bedtime routine by allowing the child to sleep with them.

CHAPTER 28

SECTION I: ASSESSING YOUR UNDERSTANDING

Activity A FILL IN THE BLANKS

1. 8
2. 2
3. 10th
4. Energy
5. Injury
6. Stress
7. Industry
8. Peers
9. Lower
10. 12

Activity B MATCHING

Exercise 1
1. c **2.** a **3.** e **4.** b **5.** f **6.** d

Exercise 2
1. c **2.** b **3.** a

Exercise 3
1. b **2.** c **3.** d **4.** a

Activity C SEQUENCING

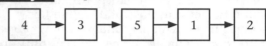

| 4 | → | 3 | → | 5 | → | 1 | → | 2 |

Activity D SHORT ANSWERS

1. Children aged 6 to 8 enjoy bicycling, skating, and swimming. Children between 8 and 10 years of age have greater rhythm and gracefulness of muscular movements; they enjoy activities such as sports. Those aged 10 to 12 years, especially girls, are more controlled and focused, similar to adults.

2. The child typically feels discomfort in new situations, requires additional time to adjust, and exhibits frustration with tears or somatic complaints. Also described as irritable and moody, the child could benefit from patience, firmness, and understanding when faced with new situations.

3. The nurse's role includes promotion of healthy growth and development through anticipatory guidance, goal attainment, playing, learning, education, and reading. The nurse's role also includes addressing common developmental concerns, assessing the individual child, and recommending intervention or referral where needed.

4. Children between ages 6 and 8 years require approximately 12 hours of sleep per night; those between 8 and 10 years of age require 10 to 12 hours of sleep per night. Children between 10 and 12 years of age require 9 to 10 hours of sleep per night. Some children, regardless of their age group, may need an occasional nap.

5. Body image refers to the perception of one's body. This age group models themselves after parents, peers and persons in movies and television. It is important for them to feel accepted by peers; if they feel different and are teased, there may be lifelong effects.

SECTION II: APPLYING YOUR KNOWLEDGE

Activity E CASE STUDY

1. The discussion should include the following points:
   The role of the family in promoting healthy growth and development is critical. Respectful interchange of communication between the parent and child will foster self-esteem and self-confidence. This respect will give the child confidence in achieving personal, educational, and social goals appropriate for his or her age. During your exam, model appropriate behaviors by listening to the child and making appropriate responses. Serve as a

resource for parents and as an advocate for the child in promoting healthy growth and development. Negative comments to the child concerning her appearance may be counterproductive and harm her self-esteem.

2. The discussion should include the following points:

The school-aged child is able to see how her actions affect others and to realize that her behaviors can have consequences. Therefore, discipline techniques with consequences often work well. For example, the child refuses to put away his or her toys, so the parent forbids him or her to play with those toys. Parents need to teach children the rules established by the family, values, and social rules of conduct. This will help give the child guidelines to what behaviors are acceptable and unacceptable. Parents need to be role models and demonstrate appropriate expressions of feelings and emotions and allow the child to express emotions and feelings. They should never belittle the child, and they need to preserve the child's self-esteem and dignity. Parents should be encouraged to discipline with praise. This positive acknowledgment can encourage appropriate behavior.

When misbehaviors occur, the type and amount of discipline should be based upon the developmental level of the child and the parents, severity of misbehavior, established roles of the family, temperament of the child, and response of the child to rewards. The child should participate in developing a plan of action for his or her misbehavior. Consistency in discipline, along with providing it in a nurturing, is essential.

3. The discussion should include the following points:

Although some television shows and video games can have positive influences on children, guidelines on the use of television and video games are important. Research has shown that the amount of time watching television or playing video games can lead to aggressive behavior, less physical activity, and altered body image.

Parents should set limits on how much television the child is allowed to watch. The Academy of Pediatrics recommends 2 hours or less of television viewing per day. The parent should establish guidelines on when the child can watch television, and television watching should not be used as a reward. The parents should monitor what the child is watching, and they should watch the programs together and use that opportunity to discuss the subject matter with the child.

Parents should also prohibit television or video games with violence. There should be no television during dinner and no television in the child's room. The parents need to set examples for the child and encourage sports, interactive play, and reading. They should encourage their child to read instead of watching television or to do a physical activity together as a family. If the television causes fights or arguments, it should be turned off for a period of time.

SECTION III: PRACTICING FOR NCLEX
Activity F NCLEX-STYLE QUESTIONS

1. **Answer: A**
   RATIONALE: The child will be able to consider an action and its consequences in Piaget's period of concrete operational thought. However, she is now able to empathize with others. She is more adept at classifying and dividing things into sets. Defining lying as bad because she gets punished for it is a Kohlberg characteristic.

2. **Answer: B**
   RATIONALE: The child with an easy temperament will adapt to school with only minor stresses. The slow-to-warm child will experience frustration. The difficult child will be moody and irritable and may benefit from a preschool visit.

3. **Answer: B**
   RATIONALE: It is very important to get a bike of the proper size for the child. Getting a bike that the child can "grow into" is dangerous. Training wheels and grass to fall on are not acceptable substitutes for the proper protective gear. The child should already demonstrate good coordination in other playing skills before attempting to ride a bike.

4. **Answer: C**
   RATIONALE: Asking how often the family eats together is an appropriate question for the girl. All the others should be directed to the parents.

5. **Answer: C**
   RATIONALE: The nurse would have found that the child still has a leaner body mass than girls at this age. Both boys and girls increase body fat at this age. Food preferences will be highly influenced by those of her parents. Although caloric intake may diminish, appetite will increase.

6. **Answer: D**
   RATIONALE: Parents are major influences on school-aged children and should discuss the dangers of tobacco and alcohol use with the child. Not smoking in the house and hiding alcohol send mixed messages to the child. Open and honest discussion is the best approach rather than forbidding the child to make friends with kids that use tobacco or alcohol.

7. **Answer: B**
   RATIONALE: The girl would need approximately 2,065 calories per day (29.5 kg × 70 calories per day per kg = 2,065 calories per day).

8. **Answer: B**
   RATIONALE: Because they are role models for their children, parents must first realize the importance of their own behaviors. It is possible that the parents are pressuring the child, but that is not the primary message. Punishment should be appropriate, consistent, and not too severe.

9. **Answer: B**
   RATIONALE: Lymphatic tissue growth is complete by age 9 better helping to localize infections and produce antibody–antigen responses. Brain growth

will be complete by age 10. Frontal sinuses are developed at age 7. Third molars do not erupt until the teen years.

10. **Answer: D**
RATIONALE: The nurse would recommend that the parents be good role models and quit smoking. Locking up or hiding your cigarettes and going outside to smoke is not as effective as having a tobacco-free environment in the home.

11. **Answer: C**
RATIONALE: Self-esteem is developed early in childhood. The feedback a child receives from those perceived in authority such as parents and educators impact the child's sense of self-worth. As the child ages, the influences of peers and their treatment of the child begin to have an increasing influence on self-esteem.

12. **Answer: B**
RATIONALE: The child can be permanently scarred by negative experiences such a bullying. Activities such as self-defense and sports can promote a sense of accomplishment but do relate directly to the problem of bullying. There is no indication the child in the scenario will become a bully.

13. **Answer: D**
RATIONALE: School-aged children are often preoccupied with thoughts of death and dying. There is no indication these thoughts will lead to mental health issues or the development of depression. School-aged children fear death but are fascinated by death and dying.

14. **Answer: B**
RATIONALE: The values of a child are determined largely by the influences of their parents. As the child ages the impact of peers does begin to enter the picture. Children may also begin to test the values with their actions. In most cases the values of the family will prevail.

15. **Answer: A, D, E**
RATIONALE: During hospitalization the school-aged child may exhibit increased clinging behaviors. The child may also demonstrate regression. It will be helpful to promote the child be able to make some decisions or have some age-appropriate sense of control. The school-aged child may miss school and the interactions with his or her peers. Ignoring the behaviors may be counterproductive.

CHAPTER 29

SECTION I: ASSESSING YOUR UNDERSTANDING

Activity A FILL IN THE BLANKS

1. Psychosocial
2. Infancy
3. Abstract
4. Positive

5. Hispanic
6. Crisis
7. Identity
8. Ossification
9. Coordination
10. Socioeconomics

Activity B MATCHING

1. c   **2.** f   **3.** a   **4.** e   **5.** b   **6.** d

Activity C SEQUENCING

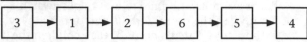

Activity D SHORT ANSWERS

Briefly answer the following.

1. Motor vehicle, bike safety, skateboards, water, firearms, fire safety, sports, machinery, sun, and toxins.

2. The adolescent tries out various roles when interacting with peers, family, community, and society; this strengthens his or her sense of self. Past stages revisited tend to be those of trust (who/what to believe in), autonomy (expression of individuality), initiative (vision for what he or she might become), and industry (choices in school, community, church, and at work).

3. Completing school prepares the adolescent for college and/or employment. Schools that support peer bonds, promote health and fitness, encourage parental involvement, and strengthen community relationships lead to better student outcomes. Teachers, coaches, and counselors provide guidance and support to the adolescent.

4. The nurse should encourage parents and teens to have sexuality discussions. Sexuality discussions increase the teen's knowledge and strengthen his or her ability to make responsible decisions about sexual behavior.

5. Diet, exercise, and hereditary factors influence the height, weight, and body build of the adolescent. Over the past three decades, adolescents have become taller and heavier than their ancestors and the beginning of puberty is earlier. During the early adolescent period, there is an increase in the percentage of body fat and the head, neck, and hands reach adult proportions.

6. According to Piaget, the adolescent progresses from a concrete framework of thinking to an abstract one. It is the formal operational period. During this period, the adolescent develops the ability to think outside of the present; that is, he or she can incorporate into thinking concepts that do exist as well as concepts that might exist. Her thinking becomes logical, organized, and consistent. She is able to think about a problem from all points of view, ranking the possible solutions while solving the problem. Not all adolescents achieve formal operational reasoning at the same time.

SECTION II: APPLYING YOUR KNOWLEDGE

Activity E CASE STUDY

1. The discussion should include the following points:
   Today, piercing of the tongue, lip, eyebrow, naval, and nipple are common. Generally, body piercing is harmless, but Cho should be cautioned about receiving these procedures under nonsterile conditions and about the risk of complications. Qualified personnel using sterile needles should perform the procedure, and proper cleansing of the area at least twice a day is important. Although body piercing is common and considered relatively harmless, complications can occur. The complications of body piercing vary by site. Infections from body piercing usually result from unclean tools of the trade. Some of the infections that may occur as a result of unclean tools include hepatitis, tetanus, tuberculosis, and HIV. These complications may not become evident for some time after the piercing has been performed. Also, keloid formation and allergies to metal may occur. The naval is an area prone for infection since it is a moist area that endures friction from clothing. Once a naval infection occurs, it may take up to a year to heal.

2. The discussion should include the following points:
   Violent behavior that takes place in a context of dating or courtship is not a rare event and can have serious short-term and lifelong effects. Dating violence in the teen years is a risk factor for continued violence exposure in adulthood. Nurses need to assess for and provide interventions to those teens experiencing dating violence or those at risk for being a victim. Education on development of healthy relationships is important.

3. The discussion should include the following points:
   Families and parents of adolescents experience changes and conflicts that require adjustments and understanding of the development of the adolescent. The adolescent is striving for self-identity and increased independence. Maintaining open lines of communication is essential but often difficult during this time. Parents sense that they have less influence on the adolescent as they spend more time with peers, questions family values, and become more mobile.
   To help improve communication, encourage Cho's mother to set aside an appropriate amount of time to discuss matters without interruptions. Encourage her to talk face-to-face with Cho and to be aware of both her and Cho's body language. Suggest that she ask questions about what Cho is feeling and offer Cho suggestions and advice. Cho's mother should choose her words carefully and be aware of her tone of voice and body language. Cho's mother should listen to what Cho has to say and should speak to her as an equal. It is important that her mother does not pretend to know all the answers and admits her mistakes. The mother should be reminded to give praise and approval to Cho often and to ensure rules and limits are set fairly and discussed.

SECTION III: PRACTICING FOR NCLEX

Activity F NCLEX-STYLE QUESTIONS

1. **Answer: C**
   RATIONALE: Asking broad, unanswerable questions, such as what the meaning of life is, is a Kohlberg activity for early adolescence. An example of Piaget activities for middle adolescence is wondering why things can't change (like wishing her parents were more understanding) and assuming everyone shares her interests. Comparing morals with those of peers is a Kohlberg activity for middle adolescence.

2. **Answer: B**
   RATIONALE: Since most contraception methods are designed for females, it is important to teach the boy that contraception is a shared responsibility. Statistics about adolescent cases of STIs and warnings about getting the girl pregnant can easily be ignored by the child's sense of invulnerability. The fact that girls are more susceptible to STIs may give the boy a false sense of security.

3. **Answer: D**
   RATIONALE: Cheese, yogurt, white beans, milk, and broccoli are good sources of calcium. Strawberries, watermelon, raisins, peanut butter, tomato juice, and whole grain bread are all foods high in iron.

4. **Answer: A**
   RATIONALE: Peers serve as role models for social behaviors, so their impact on an adolescent can be negative if the group is using drugs, or the group leader is in trouble. Sharing problems with peers helps the adolescent work through conflicts with parents. The desire to be part of the group teaches the child to negotiate differences and develop loyalties.

5. **Answer: C**
   RATIONALE: Amphetamine use manifests as euphoria with rapid talking and dilated pupils. Signs of opiate use are drowsiness and constricted pupils. Barbiturates typically cause a sense of euphoria followed by depression. Marijuana users are typically relaxed and uninhibited.

6. **Answer: B**
   RATIONALE: Checking for signs of depression or lack of friends would be most effective for preventing suicide. All other choices are more effective for preventing violence to others.

7. **Answer: A**
   RATIONALE: The best response is to describe the proper care using frequent cleansing with antibacterial soap. It is too late for warnings about the dangers of piercing such as skin- or blood-borne infections, or disease from unclean needles.

8. **Answer: C**
   RATIONALE: If the boy has just entered adolescence, he is likely to exhibit frequent mood changes. A

growing interest in attracting girls' attention and understanding that actions have consequences are typical of the middle stage of adolescence. Feeling secure with his body image does not occur until late adolescence.

9. **Answer: D**
   RATIONALE: Increased blood pressure to adult levels indicates the child is in the early stage of adolescence. Increased shoulder, chest, and hip widths and muscle mass increase occurs in mid-adolescence. Eruption of the last four molars occurs in late adolescence.

10. **Answer: B**
    RATIONALE: Whole grain bread contains high amounts of iron and is a type of food the child would not have an aversion to. Milk is a good source of vitamin D. Carrots are high in vitamin A. Orange juice is a good source for vitamin C.

11. **Answer: C**
    RATIONALE: Teen age boys can experience growth in height until age 17.5. The nurse should reassure the teen that this may happen for him. Telling the client not to be ashamed, or assuring him it is not as short as his peers fails to provide information or support. Determining the height of the other men in the family may be indicated at a later time but is not the most appropriate initial comment.

12. **Answer: C**
    RATIONALE: The dietary intake for active teen females should include be approximately 2,200 calories daily.

13. **Answer: C**
    RATIONALE: Piaget developmental theories focus on the cognitive maturation of the child. The ability to critically think is a sign of successful cognitive maturation. A sense of internal identity is consistent with Erikson theories of development. Kohlberg theories development focuses on morals and values.

14. **Answer: C**
    RATIONALE: The sedentary teen needs to consume approximately 1,600 calories each day. The recommended numbers of servings of fruit needed daily are four. A balanced diet includes a small amount of fat. To avoid all fat could place the child's health at risk. Protein intake is important for the development of tissue. The teen will need about 5 oz of protein daily.

15. **Answer: B**
    RATIONALE: The teenaged male has pubic hair that is beginning to curl. This takes place between ages 11 and 14. Absent or sparse pubic hair is consistent with a younger child. Coarse pubic hair is seen in older teens and adult men.

16. **Answer: C**
    RATIONALE: Erikson identifies the primary developmental task of early adolescence as identity versus role confusion. That is, unsuccessful development results in confusion about role and identity. This does not necessarily result in aggression or antisocial behavior. Dissociative identity disorder is a specific psychiatric disorder.

17. **Answer: B**
    RATIONALE: It is common for adolescents to adopt habits of going to bed late and awakening late, especially on weekends. Despite the fact that this is common, it is not ideal; the nurse should explore strategies for changing the adolescent's behavior in a collaborative and inclusive manner. Simply communicating that it is unacceptable is unlikely to bring about change.

CHAPTER 30

SECTION I: ASSESSING YOUR UNDERSTANDING

Activity A FILL IN THE BLANKS
1. Atraumatic
2. Therapeutic
3. Nonverbal
4. Child life
5. Verbal
6. Active
7. Interpreter

Activity B MATCHING
Match the development level in Column A with the communication technique in Column B appropriate for the developmental age.

1. e   **2.** a   **3.** d   **4.** e   **5.** b

Activity C SEQUENCING

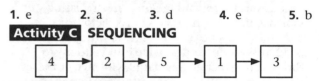

Activity D SHORT ANSWERS
1. Therapeutic hugging is a method of safely preventing a child from harm during a painful or uncomfortable procedure that decreases fear and anxiety. The parent or caregiver holds the child in a position that promotes close physical contact in a way that restrains the child as necessary for the procedure to be performed successfully. This technique provides atraumatic care during procedures such as injections, venipunctures, and other invasive procedures.
2. The child or family will be able to demonstrate a skill, repeat information in their own words, answer open-ended questions, and act out the proper care procedure.
3. Signs exhibited by families or children that should alert the nurse of problems with health literacy include difficulty completing registration forms or health care forms that are incomplete, frequently missed appointments, noncompliance with prescribed treatment, history of medication errors, claiming to have forgotten glasses or asking to take forms home to complete in regards to reading material or filling out forms, inability to answer questions about health care or avoiding asking questions regarding health care.

4. Draw pictures or use medical illustrations, use videos, color-code medications or steps of a procedure, record an audio tape, repeat verbal information often and "chunk" it into small bites, and teach a "back-up" family member.

5. The nurse should be an advocate of family-centered care in order to prevent separation, resulting in anxiety of both the family and child during hospitalization. The nurse can provide comfortable accommodations for the family and allow the family to choose if they want to be present for procedures that are uncomfortable for their child.

SECTION II: APPLYING YOUR KNOWLEDGE

Activity E CASE STUDY

1. The discussion should include the following:

The nurse should avoid using terms that Emma may not understand or interpret differently from the intended meaning. The nurse could tell Emma that she will be taken to another room on a "special bed with wheels" rather than on a "stretcher." When describing the CT equipment the nurse could use an explanation such as, "there will be a big machine in the room that works like a camera. It will take pictures of your head since you hurt it when you fell. Your mommy and daddy will be able to go to this room with you and they will stand right outside the room when the camera takes the pictures."

2. The discussion should include the following:

Therapeutic hugging should be utilized since this will allow Emma's parents to provide a comforting way of safely holding her so that the stitches can be placed with decreased trauma. The nurse should be sure that the parents understand how to hold Emma properly so that the procedure can be performed successfully while maintaining safety and security.

SECTION III: PRACTICING FOR NCLEX

Activity F NCLEX-STYLE QUESTIONS

1. Answer: C

RATIONALE: Nodding the head while the other person speaks indicates interest in what they are saying. When children and parents feel they are being heard, it builds trust. Sitting straight with feet flat on the floor, looking away from the speaker, and keeping distance from the family may send a message of disinterest.

2. Answer: A

RATIONALE: Having a child life specialist play with the child would provide the greatest support for the child and make the greatest contribution to atraumatic care. It is important to explain the procedure to the child and parents, let the child have a favorite toy and keep the parents calm, but these interventions are not as effective for atraumatic care.

3. Answer: C

RATIONALE: Since the child has just been diagnosed, concerns about postoperative home care would be least important. Arranging an additional meeting with the specialist and discussing treatment options may be necessary at some point, but involving the child and family in decision making is always a goal and is a part of family-centered care.

4. Answer: A, D, E

RATIONALE: The child life specialist commonly assists with nonmedical preparation for diagnostic testing, provides tours, assists in play therapy, and is the child's advocate. The child's nurse gives medication, vaccines, and starts intravenous lines.

5. Answer: B, C, D, E

RATIONALE: When following the principles of atraumatic care, it is appropriate to apply numbing cream prior to starting the child's intravenous line. It is appropriate to empower the child with choices about care, if possible. It is appropriate for the child to have a security item present in the hospital. It is helpful for the family if the parent is able to stay with the child because it helps make the environment less stressful. The nurse should avoid using the phrase "holding the child down" and replace this with "therapeutic hugging."

6. Answer: B

RATIONALE: Asking questions is a valid way to evaluate learning. However, it is far more effective to ask open-ended questions because they will better expose missing or incorrect information. As with teaching, evaluation of learning that involves active participation is more effective. This includes the child and family demonstrating skills, teaching skills to each other, and acting out scenarios.

7. Answer: D

RATIONALE: Informing the child in terms that she can understand is the best example of therapeutic communication, which is goal, focused, purposeful communication. Recognizing the parents' and child's desire regarding treatment options is part of family-entered care. Presenting options for treatment is vague.

8. Answer: A

RATIONALE: Missing appointments is one of the red flags to health literacy problems as the parents may not have understood the importance of the appointment or may not have been able to read or understand appointment reminders. Being bilingual does not indicate health literacy issues. Taking notes or one parent being the primary leader of the child's health care are not unusual practices.

9. Answer: A, C, D

RATIONALE: School-age children better understand about and participate in their own care than preschoolers and toddlers. They need time to prepare themselves mentally for the procedure and should be given 3 to 7 days. Plays and puppets are more appropriate for preschoolers. Active involvement in self-care will help them adjust and learn. Giving them choices to make allows them control and involvement in the process.

10. **Answer: C**
RATIONALE: Asking questions or having private conversations with the interpreter may make the family uncomfortable and destroy the child–nurse relationship. Translation takes longer than a same-language appointment, and must be considered so that the family is not rushed. Using a nonprofessional runs the risk that they won't be able to adequately translate medical terminology. Using an older sibling can upset the family relationships or cause legal problems.

11. **Answer: A, C, D, E**
RATIONALE: Taking notes is an indicator that the mother is literate. All of the other options are "red flags" that indicate the mother may not be literate.

12. **Answer: B, C, E**
RATIONALE: The nurse should position himself or herself at the child's level. The nurse should ensure that the child's parents are present during education. It is appropriate to use words that the child will understand. It is appropriate to show patience during the interaction and to look for nonverbal cues that indicate understanding or confusion.

13. **Answer: A, D, E**
RATIONALE: It is appropriate to use the word "tube" and not a "catheter." It is appropriate to call a "gurney" a "rolling bed." It is better to call "dye" special medicine. Terms used in the other options may be misunderstood by the child.

CHAPTER 31

SECTION I: ASSESSING YOUR UNDERSTANDING

Activity A FILL IN THE BLANKS

1. Development
2. In-utero
3. Community
4. Prevention
5. When
6. Coronary
7. Bone
8. Immunosuppression
9. Fixate
10. Active

Activity B MATCHING

Exercise 1

1. b   2. e   3. c   4. f   5. d   6. a

Exercise 2

1. c   2. a   3. b   4. e   5. d

Exercise 3

1. b   2. d   3. a   4. e   5. c

Activity C SEQUENCING

4 → 1 → 6 → 2 → 5 → 3

Activity D SHORT ANSWERS

Briefly answer the following.

1. Place a vibrating tuning fork in the middle of the top of the head. Ask if the sound is in one ear or both ears. The sound should be heard in both ears.
2. Conditions in parents or grandparents what would suggest screening for hyperlipidemia in children includes coronary atherosclerosis, myocardial infarction, angina pectoris, peripheral vascular disease, cerebrovascular disease, and sudden cardiac death.
3. If problems are noted in the provided history, objective audiometry should be performed. When the child is capable of following simple commands, the nurse can perform basic procedures to screen for hearing loss. The "whisper," Weber, and Rinne tests can be used to screen for sensorineural or conductive hearing loss.
4. Iron deficiency is the leading nutritional deficiency in the United States. Iron deficiency can cause cognitive and motor deficits resulting in developmental delays and behavioral disturbances. The increased incidence of iron deficiency anemia is directly associated with periods of diminished iron stores, rapid growth, and high metabolic demands. At 6 months of age, the in utero iron stores of a full-term infant are almost depleted. The adolescent growth spurt warrants constant iron replacement. Pregnant adolescents are at even higher risk for iron deficiency due to the demands of the mother's growth spurt and the needs of the developing fetus.
5. Universal hypertension screening for children beginning at 3 years of age is recommended. If the child has risk factors for systemic hypertension, such as preterm birth, very low birth weight, renal disease, organ transplant, congenital heart disease or other illnesses associated with hypertension, then screening begins when the risk factor becomes apparent.

SECTION II: APPLYING YOUR KNOWLEDGE

Activity E CASE STUDY 1

1. The discussion should include the following points:
Nutritional history should be collected directly from Jasmine. There must be a discussion of her activity levels. Her height and weight should be plotted on a growth chart to observe trends.
2. The discussion should include the following points:
Screening for iron deficiency is warranted for Jasmine. Iron deficiency is the leading nutritional deficiency in the United States. The increased incidence of iron deficiency anemia is directly associated with periods of rapid growth and high

metabolic demands. The adolescent growth spurt warrants constant iron replacement. The Centers for Disease Control and Prevention recommends universal screening of high-risk children at various age intervals. Jasmine demonstrates risk factors for iron deficiency anemia, including the rapid growth spurt of adolescence, meal skipping and dieting, and low intake of fish, meat, and poultry. The American Academy of Pediatrics (AAP) recommends universal screening of all adolescent females during all routine physical examinations, therefore placing Jasmine in this category.

3. The discussion should include the following points:
Your focus of healthy weight promotions should be health-centered, not weight-centered. Emphasize the benefits of health through an active lifestyle and nutritious eating pattern. Gear the education to focus on Jasmine's growing autonomy in making self-care decisions. Encourage healthy eating habits and healthy activity. Limit sedentary activities such as television viewing, computer usage, and video games.

CASE STUDY 2

1. The discussion should include the following points:
Children with chronic illnesses require repeated assessments to determine their health maintenance needs. How their illnesses impact their functional health patterns determines if standard health supervision visits need to be augmented to meet the individual child's situation.

Nurses need to ensure comprehensive health supervision with frequent repeated assessments that include psychosocial assessments. The assessments should cover issues such as health insurance coverage, availability of transportation, financial stressors, family coping, and school personnel response to the child's chronic illness. The nurse needs to help develop an effective partnership between the child's medical home, family, and community.

Coordination of care and access to resources is vital and enhances the quality of life for children with chronic illnesses. Nurses need to assist families in finding support groups and community-based resources, as well as financial and medical assistance programs. The nurse can also educate school personnel about the child's illness and assist them in maximizing the child's potential for academic success.

SECTION III: PRACTICING FOR NCLEX

Activity F NCLEX-STYLE QUESTIONS

1. **Answer: D**
   RATIONALE: Congenital facial malformations are developmental warning signs. Neonatal conjunctivitis, when properly treated, has no long-term effects on development. Parents who are college students are not risk factors as would be high school dropouts. A 36-week birth is not a warning sign, but 33 weeks or less is.

2. **Answer: B**
   RATIONALE: Asking what activities to promote exercise for the child is best for several reasons. It provides assessment of the child's activity preferences and whether the child is health-centered (positive) or weight-centered (negative). It also offers variety. If one sport doesn't work, others might. Emphasizing appropriate weight or dietary shortcomings can lead to eating disorders or body hatred. Suggesting only softball limits the success of the healthy weight promotion.

3. **Answer: C**
   RATIONALE: The most compelling argument for vaccinating for Varicella is that children not immunized are at risk if exposed to the disease. The mother needs to know about the chance of her child contracting the illness if not immunized. The contagious nature of the disease, low risk of the vaccine, or the low incidence of reactions is not appropriate explanation for why the child should have the vaccine.

4. **Answer: C**
   RATIONALE: Iron deficiency anemia could be present because the iron stores in the boy's body may have diminished by the adolescent's growth spurt. This would be checked for by blood work. Developmental problems are not caused by the adolescent's growth spurt. Hyperlipidemia could be possible if the child's diet included an excessive amount of fat. Hypertension might be a problem if a family member had the condition in early adulthood or if many family members had this condition.

5. **Answer: D**
   RATIONALE: The nurse will provide information to prevent injury or disease such as discussing the hazards of putting the baby to sleep with a bottle. Assessing for an infection and taking a health history for an injury are not part of a health supervision visit. Administering a vaccination for Varicella would not occur until 12 months of age.

6. **Answer: A**
   RATIONALE: The nurse will advise the parents that poor oral health can have significant negative effects on systemic health. Discussing fluoridation and community health may have little interest to the mother. Placing the hands in the mouth exposes the child to pathogens and is appropriate for personal hygiene promotion. Soft drink consumption is better covered during healthy diet promotion.

7. **Answer: B**
   RATIONALE: Maintaining proper therapy for eczema can be exhausting both physically and mentally. Therefore it is essential that the nurse assesses parents' ability to cope with this stress. Changing a bandage is not part of a health supervision visit. Skin hydration is important for a child with eczema; however, fluid volume is not a concern. Systemic corticosteroid therapy is very rarely used and the success of the current therapy needs to be assessed first.

8. **Answer: B**
   RATIONALE: The Ishihara chart is best for the 6-year old because the child will know numbers. CVTME charts are designed to assess color vision discrimination for preschoolers. The Allen figures chart and the Snellen charts are for assessing visual acuity.

9. **Answer: D**
   RATIONALE: Neighborhoods with high crime, high poverty, and lack of resources may contribute to poor health care and illness. If the aged grandparents have healthy lifestyles, they would be positive partners. Developmentally appropriate chores and responsibilities could be positive signs of parental guidance. The doting mother could make a strong health supervision partner.

10. **Answer: A**
    RATIONALE: The Rinne test compares air conduction of sound with bone conduction of sound and can be performed in the office. The whisper test requires a quiet room with no distractions. Auditory Brainstem Response (ABR) and the Evoked Otoacoustic Emissions (EOAE) are indicated for newborns and are usually done by an audiologist.

11. **Answer: C**
    RATIONALE: A 3-year-old child should have the ability to copy a circle. Stacking five blocks, grasping a crayon, and throwing a ball overhand are not reasonable accomplishments for a 3-year-old child.

12. **Answer: A, C, D**
    RATIONALE: The Denver II screening test employs props. These include dolls, crayons, and balls.

13. **Answer: C**
    RATIONALE: In the absence of risk factors vision screening should begin in children once they reach the age of 3.

14. **Answer: B**
    RATIONALE: Passive immunity results when immunoglobulins are passed from one person to another. This immunity is temporary. This is the type of immunity that takes place when a mother breastfeeds her child. Active immunity results when an individual's own immunity generates an immune response.

15. **Answer: D**
    RATIONALE: Populations at an increased risk for elevated blood lead levels include immigrants, refugees, or international adoptees.

CHAPTER 32

SECTION I: ASSESSING YOUR UNDERSTANDING

Activity A FILL IN THE BLANKS

1. PERRLA
2. BMI
3. Fontanel
4. Stethoscope
5. Stridor

6. Milia
7. Auscultation

Activity B LABELING

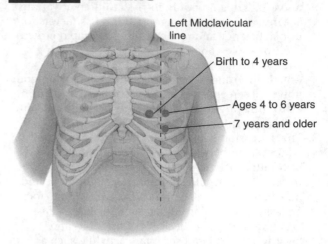

Left Midclavicular line

Birth to 4 years

Ages 4 to 6 years

7 years and older

Activity C MATCHING

1. c   **2.** e   **3.** a   **4.** d   **5.** b

Activity D SEQUENCING

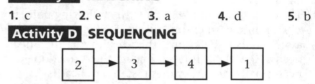

2 → 3 → 4 → 1

Activity E SHORT ANSWERS

1. Grade one is barely audible, sometimes heard, sometimes not. Grade two is quiet, yet heard each time the chest is auscultated. Grade three and four are audible with grade three having an intermediate intensity and grade four having a palpable thrill. Grade five is loud and is audible with the edge of stethoscope lifted off the chest. Grade six is very loud and audible with the stethoscope placed near but not touching the chest.

2. Ecchymosis is a purplish discoloration (bruise) that changes from blue, to brown to black. It is common on the lower extremities in young children.
   Petechiae are pinpoint reddish purple macules that do not blanch when pressed. They are broken tiny blood vessels that occur with coughing, bleeding disorders, and meningococcemia. Purpura is purple larger macules caused by bleeding under the skin and occurs with bleeding disorders and meningococcemia.

3. The canal should be pink, have tiny hairs, and be free from scratches, drainage, foreign bodies, and edema. The tympanic membrane should appear pearly pink or gray and be translucent allowing visualization of the bony landmarks.

4. The heart rate of the child gradually decreases from infancy to adolescence. The infant's normal heart rate ranges from 80 to 150 beats per minute, with the toddlers heart rate decreasing slightly to 70 to 120 beats per minute. The preschooler and school-aged child have similar normal heart rates at 65 to

110 and 60 to 100, respectively. The adolescent's normal heart rate drops to 55 to 95 beats per minute.

5. Inaccurate pulse oximetry readings may result from the child having a low hemoglobin value, hypotension, hypothermia, hypovolemia, skin breakdown, carbon monoxide poisoning, interference with the ambient light, and movement of the extremity.

6. Possible risk factors that indicate the need for BP measurement of children under the age of 3 years include history of prematurity, very low birth weight, or other neonatal complications; congenital heart disease; recurrent urinary tract infections or any other renal complication; any malignancy or transplant; any treatment that causes the BP to increase; systemic illnesses that affect the BP; and increased intracranial pressure.

SECTION II: APPLYING YOUR KNOWLEDGE
Activity F CASE STUDY

FIRST PRIORITY: A 7-month-old hospitalized with pneumonia. Vital signs are heart rate of 165 with brief episodes of dropping into the 60 second during the previous shift, respiratory rate of 78, blood pressure 112/72, and axillary temperature of 99.5°F.
RATIONALE: This child is the most unstable. The tachypnea, tachycardia with bradycardic episodes can be indicative of a potentially unstable airway. The increased blood pressure may also indicate acute distress.

SECOND PRIORITY: A 3-month-old hospitalized for rule out sepsis secondary to fever. Vital signs are heart rate of 165, respiratory rate of 34, blood pressure 108/64, rectal temperature of 102.5°F taken immediately before report. No intervention was initiated.
RATIONALE: This child is potentially unstable. The tachycardia and increased blood pressure are most likely due to fever and stress. The increased temperature (without intervention) is a concern but overall this child's vital signs are less life-threatening than the tachypnea and bradycardia present in the first priority child.

THIRD PRIORITY: A 5-year old hospitalized with an acute asthma attack. Vital signs are heart rate 124, respiratory rate 28 to 30, blood pressure 93/48, and axillary temperature of 98.6°F.
RATIONALE: This child has an acute illness and may be potentially unstable due to slightly increased respiratory rate and mild tachycardia. This child warrants close monitoring but at this time is more stable than either of the other two children.

SECTION III: PRACTICING FOR NCLEX
Activity G NCLEX-STYLE QUESTIONS

1. **Answer: A**
   RATIONALE: The newborn's labia minora is typically swollen from the effects of maternal estrogen. The minora will decrease in size and be hidden by the labia majora within the first weeks. Lesions on the external genitalia are indicative of sexually transmitted infection. Labial adhesions are not a normal finding for a healthy newborn. Swollen labia majora is not a normal finding.

2. **Answer: C**
   RATIONALE: The nurse should first begin with open-ended questions regarding work, hobbies, activities, and friendship in order to make the teen feel comfortable. Once a trusting rapport has been established, the nurse should move on to the more emotionally charged questions. While it is important to assure confidentiality, the nurse should first establish rapport.

3. **Answer: C**
   RATIONALE: A good health history includes open-ended questions that allow the child to narrate their experience. The other questions would most likely elicit a yes or no response.

4. **Answer: C**
   RATIONALE: It is best to approach a shy 4-year old by introducing the equipment slowly and demonstrating the process on the girl's doll first. Toddlers are egocentric; referring to how another child performed probably will not be helpful in gaining the child's cooperation. The other questions would most likely elicit a "no" response.

5. **Answer: B**
   RATIONALE: Asking "What can I help you with?" is very welcoming and allows for a variety of responses that may include functional problems, developmental concerns, or disease. Asking about the chief complaint may not be clear to all parents. Asking if the child feels sick will most likely elicit a yes or no answer and no other helpful details. Asking whether the child has been exposed to infectious agents is unclear and would not open a dialogue.

6. **Answer: C**
   RATIONALE: Preschoolers like to play games. To encourage deep breathing, the nurse should elicit the child's cooperation by engaging the child in a game to blow out the light bulb on the penlight. Telling the child that he or she may not leave or must breathe deeply would not engage the child. Asking whether the child would allow his or her caregiver to listen would most likely elicit a no.

7. **Answer: A**
   RATIONALE: The physical examination of children, just as for adults always begins with a systematic inspection, followed by palpation or percussion, then by auscultation.

8. **Answer: B**
   RATIONALE: Touching the thumb to the ball of the infant's foot would elicit the plantar grasp reflex. The other reflexes are not elicited by this method.

9. **Answer: C**
   RATIONALE: The nurse knows that some of the history must be delayed until after the child is stabilized. After the child is stabilized the nurse

can take a detailed history. The child who has received routine health care and presents with a mild illness would need only a problem-focused history. The nurse should be sensitive to repetitive interviews in hospital situations but should not assume that the child's history can be obtained from other providers. A complete and detailed history would be in order if physicians rarely see the child or if the child is critically ill.

10. **Answer: B**
    RATIONALE: This indicates a positive Romberg test which warrants further testing for possible cerebellar dysfunction.

11. **Answer: 21**
    RATIONALE: Using the metric method, the formula is:
    weight in kilograms divided by height in meters squared
    weight (kg)/height (m^2)
    $42/1.42^2$
    $42/2.0164 = 20.8292$
    Rounded to 21

12. **Correct Order: A, B, C, D**
    RATIONALE: The proper order of the assessment of the thorax is to inspect, palpate, percuss, and auscultate.

CHAPTER 33

SECTION I: ASSESSING YOUR UNDERSTANDING

Activity A FILL IN THE BLANKS

1. Hugging
2. 15
3. Bath
4. Eat
5. Therapeutic
6. Individualized Health Plans (IHPs)
7. Health department

Activity B MATCHING

Match the term in Column A with the proper definition in Column B.

1. b   **2.** e   **3.** a   **4.** c   **5.** d

Activity C SEQUENCING

Place the three stages of separation anxiety in the proper sequence.

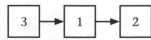

Activity D SHORT ANSWERS

Briefly answer the following.

1. The nurse can address and minimize separation anxiety by: Understanding the stages of separation anxiety and be able to recognize them in children; realizing that behaviors demonstrated during the first stage do not indicate that the child is "bad"; encouraging the family to stay with the child when appropriate; helping the family deal with various reactions and intervene before the behaviors of detachment occur; using guided imagery based on the use of the child's imagination and enjoyment of play in order to help the child relax.

2. Discharge planning actually begins upon admission. The nurse should assess the family's resources and knowledge level upon admission to determine the need for education and possible referrals.

3. Some common coping behaviors/methods include stoicism, ignoring or negating problem, acting out, anger, withdrawal, rejection, and intellectualizing.

4. Under the age of 5 years, children are most commonly admitted to the hospital for respiratory issues. Older children are typically hospitalized for issues such as diseases of the respiratory system, mental health problems, injuries, and gastrointestinal disorders. In regards to adolescents, problems related to pregnancy, birth, mental health, and injury account for the majority of hospitalizations.

5. The home care nurse should be sure to include the child in the conversation; address the caregivers formally unless asked to address them otherwise; be friendly and respectful, and use a soft, calm voice; use good listening skills; and be sure to schedule the first visit when the primary caregiver is present.

SECTION II: APPLYING YOUR KNOWLEDGE

Activity E CASE STUDY

1. **INTERVENTIONS:** Assess if irritability is related to surgical intervention, including pain.
   RATIONALE: The irritability could be related to the surgery, especially pain, resulting from the procedure. Once this is ruled out address the infant's basic needs (trust versus mistrust).
   INTERVENTIONS: Encourage and facilitate family presence at the bedside and rooming-in. Provide consistent nursing staff. Arrange to have a volunteer hold and rock the baby when family is not present at bedside. Place the baby in a room near the nurse's station.
   RATIONALE: Infants gain a sense of trust in the world through reciprocal patterns of contact. Crying without comfort and lack of stimulation can lead to distress in the infant. By 5 to 6 months infants are acutely aware of the absence of their primary caregiver and may be fearful of unfamiliar persons. Providing caregivers who will address the comfort and care needs of the infant consistently is important for the developing infant. Response time to crying may be reduced by placing the infant near the nurse's station.

2. **INTERVENTIONS:** Address discomfort or pain that may be associated with disease process. Promote home routine related to bedtime and naptime. Provide a quiet, darkened room. Allow the parent to lie in bed or crib next to toddler if possible. Group care activities and allow undisturbed periods of rest during designated nap/sleep times.
   • Pain and discomfort could be contributing to lack of rest. Once ruled out, address the toddler's

developmental needs. The change in routine caused by the hospitalization could be contributing to the lack of rest. Maintaining home rituals can help to normalize naptime and bedtime. Toddlers have a need of familiarity and the closeness of a primary caregiver. Providing parental comfort can help to minimize the toddler's distress. Allowing undisturbed times for naps can also help promote adequate rest.

3. **INTERVENTIONS:** Address pain management needs. Explain procedures honestly, using concrete terms. Encourage expression of feelings using therapeutic play. Consult child life physician if available. Encourage family member to room in. Leave a small light on at night.

   • Fantasy and magical thinking may be heightened when pain and discomfort are experienced. Once ruled out address the preschoolers developmental needs. Preschoolers fear mutilation and are afraid of intrusive procedures. They interpret words literally and have an active imagination. Explaining procedures in terms the child can understand can help allay fears. Therapeutic play can help the child express and work through fears. Child life physician are excellent resources to encourage medical play and assist with preparation of the child. Presence of family provides comfort and security. Simply having a small amount of light in the room can help prevent fantasies and fears related to darkness leading to nightmares.

4. **INTERVENTIONS:** Talk to the child about the reasons for his lack of eating. Provide the child's favorite foods and allow the child to choose his meals (allow foods from home, if possible allow child to go to cafeteria to pick out food).

   • The refusal to eat may be related to a lack of appetite due to disease process. Once ruled out, focus on the school-aged child's developmental needs. Lack of eating may be a reaction to the hospitalization or a dislike of the foods provided. Offering favorite foods and asking the child the reasons he is not eating may help determine the cause of the lack of appetite. School-aged children are accustomed to controlling self-care and they like being involved. They are used to making decisions about their meals and activities. By allowing them to pick their food the nurse give them the opportunity to maintain independence, retain self-control, enhance self-esteem, and continue to work toward achieving a sense of industry.

5. **INTERVENTIONS:** Establish rapport with the adolescent. Encourage her to discuss her feelings. Provide a phone at her bedside. Encourage her to call her friends and family. Encourage her friends to visit. Encourage use of a journal. Collaborate with a psychologist if appropriate.

   • Adolescents typically do not experience separation anxiety from being away from their parents; instead, their anxiety comes from separation from their friends. They typically do not like to be different than their peers and appearance is an important factor for them. Adolescents with a chronic illness may become depressed due to prolonged separation from peers, altered body image, lack of self-esteem, and feeling different. Loss of control may lead to behaviors of anger, withdrawing, and general uncooperativeness. Developing rapport with the adolescent and encouraging discussion and expression of her feelings can help the adolescent cope. Also connecting the adolescent with her peers can be an important factor in improving coping. Collaboration with a psychologist may be appropriate if depression seems severe.

SECTION III: PRACTICING FOR NCLEX

Activity F NCLEX-STYLE QUESTIONS

1. **Answer: A**
   RATIONALE: Children in the first phase, protest, react aggressively to this separation, and reject others who attempt to comfort the child. The other behaviors are indicators of the second phase, despair.

2. **Answer: D**
   RATIONALE: It is best to include the families whenever possible so they can assist the child in coping with their fears. Preschoolers fear mutilation and are afraid of intrusive procedures. Their magical thinking limits their ability to understand everything, requiring communication and intervention to be on their level. Telling the child that we need to put a little hole in their arm might scare the child.

3. **Answer: A**
   RATIONALE: Previous experience with hospitalization can either add to the positive aspects of preparation or distract if the experiences were perceived as negative. If the child associates the hospital with the death of a relative, the experience is likely viewed as negative. The other statements would most likely indicate that the child's previous experiences were viewed as positive.

4. **Answer: C**
   RATIONALE: Distraction with books or games would be the best remedy to provide an outlet to distract the child from his restricted activity. The other responses would be unlikely to affect a change in the behavior of a 6-year old.

5. **Answer: A**
   RATIONALE: Parents who do not tell their child the truth or do not answer the child's questions confuse, frighten, and may weaken the child's trust in them. The other statements are effective forms of communication.

6. **Answer: D**
   RATIONALE: The nurse should start the initial contact with children and their families as a foundation for developing a trusting relationship. Asking about a favorite toy would be a good starting point. The nurse should allow the child to participate in the conversation without the

pressure of having to comply with a request or undergo any procedures.

7. **Answer: C**
   RATIONALE: The nurse needs to describe the procedure and equipment in terms the child can understand. For a 4-year old, a simple explanation along with the chance to touch and feel the tiny tubes would be best. Using the term tympanostomy tubes is not age appropriate and does not teach. Telling the child that he or she will be asleep the whole time might increase fear. Showing the child the operating room might increase fear with all of the strange and imposing equipment.

8. **Answer: B**
   RATIONALE: A toddler is most likely to develop anxiety and fears due to separation from the parents. Separation from friends, loss of control, and loss of independence are fears typically experienced by an adolescent.

9. **Answer: C**
   RATIONALE: It is important to be honest and encourage the child to ask questions rather than wait for the child to speak up. The other statements are correct.

10. **Answer: C**
    RATIONALE: The best approach would be to write the name of his nurse on a small board and then identify all staff members working with the child (each shift and each day). Reminding the boy he will be going home soon or telling him not to worry does not address his concerns or provide solutions. Encouraging the boy's parents to stay with him at all times may be unrealistic and may place undue stress on the family.

11. **Answer: A, B, D**
    RATIONALE: It is important to assess the child's peripheral vascular circulation especially when the child has a restraint placed on an extremity. Capillary refill, color, temperature, and pulses are appropriate to assess to ensure that the child's peripheral vascular circulation has not been compromised.

12. **Answer: B, C, D**
    RATIONALE: Even minor nursing interventions should not be performed in the playroom. The playroom should be referred to as the "activity room" or "social room" instead of "playroom" when speaking with adolescent children. It is inappropriate to perform procedures in the child's crib. It is better to perform procedures in the treatment room. It is important to give antiemetics prior to mealtimes. Parents can be encouraged to bring in security items to help reduce the child's level of stress.

13. **Answer: D**
    RATIONALE: Ice is approximately equivalent to half the same amount of water which in this instance would be 2 cups of fluid.

14. **Correct Order: A, B, C, D**
    RATIONALE: Nursing care for a hospitalized child typically occurs in four phases: introduction, building a trusting relationship, decision-making phase, and providing comfort and reassurance.

CHAPTER 34

SECTION I: ASSESSING YOUR UNDERSTANDING

Activity A FILL IN THE BLANKS

1. 3
2. Respite
3. Family
4. Cancer
5. Written
6. Palliative
7. Hospice

Activity B MATCHING

Match the child's stage in Column A with their needs as they go through the dying process, listed in Column B.

1. e   2. a   3. b   4. c   5. d

Activity C SEQUENCING

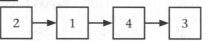

Activity D SHORT ANSWERS

1. Answers may include homeopathic and herbal medicine, pet therapy, hippotherapy, massage or music. Discharge planning actually begins upon admission. The nurse should assess the family's resources and knowledge level upon admission to determine the need for education and possible referrals.

2. Formerly premature infants need extra calories for growth. They also need extra calcium and phosphorus for adequate bone mineralization. Their diet consists of breast milk fortified with additional nutrients or a commercially prepared formula specific for premature infants.

3. The nurse should explain that DNR (do not resuscitate) refers to withholding cardiopulmonary resuscitation should the child's heart stop beating. It is important to ensure that this does not mean they are giving up on their child. Nurses must educate families that resuscitation may be inappropriate and lead to more suffering than if death were allowed to occur naturally. Families may wish to specify a certain extent of resuscitation that they feel more comfortable with (e.g., allowing supplemental oxygen but not providing chest compressions). Some institutions are now replacing the DNR terminology with "allow natural death" (AND), which may be more acceptable to families facing the decision to withhold resuscitation.

4. Respect for the child's goals, preferences, and choices; acknowledgement and addressing of caregiver concerns; provision of a comprehensive, interdisciplinary continuum of care in the community, and competent and ethical care (Association of Pediatric Oncology Nurses, 2003).

5. Do not excessively try to get the child to eat or drink; offer small frequent meals or snacks, such as soups or shakes; provide the child with foods they request; administer antiemetics as needed; provide good mouth care; ensure environment is free of odors and is conducive to eating.

SECTION II: APPLYING YOUR KNOWLEDGE
Activity E CASE STUDY

1. Children with special health care needs require comprehensive and coordinated care from multiple health care professionals. The nurse can facilitate communication and help to ensure collaboration to address the child's health, educational, psychological, and social service needs. The nurse needs to promote family-centered care and work with the parents as a team. Include both parents and other caregivers in learning skills needed to care for this child. The nurse can assist the family to incorporate the child's medical needs into daily life and to minimize the child's self-perception of being different. Developing a trusting and permanent relationship with the family will allow the nurse to identify the family's changing needs and will allow better two-way communication. The nurse should support and empower the family and assist parents and families to find support systems and resources.

2. The nurse needs to be attuned to the entire family's needs and emotions and be fully present with the child and family. Listen to the child and family and foster respect for the whole child. Respect the parents and help them to honor the commitments they have made to their child. Work collaboratively with the family and health care team. Acknowledge that the parents have diverse needs for information and encourage participation in decision making. The school-aged child has a concrete understanding of death. Give Georgia specific honest details when they are requested. Encourage participation in decision making and help the child to establish a sense of control.

SECTION III: PRACTICING FOR NCLEX
Activity F NCLEX-STYLE QUESTIONS

1. **Answer: C**
   RATIONALE: A good therapeutic relationship is built on trust and communication. It is strengthened by listening to the parents, acknowledging their triumphs, and supporting them when they fail. Continuing to educate them, helping them access resources, and helping them to save money on medications are good interventions, but not as effective at building a trusting relationship.

2. **Answer: A**
   RATIONALE: Providing full participation in decision making gives the adolescent a sense of worth and builds his self-esteem. The adolescent may have difficulty initiating conversation, but wants and needs to voice his fears and concerns. He also requires direct, honest answers to his questions. However, these needs are not as effective in meeting his need for sense of self-worth or self-esteem.

3. **Answer: D**
   RATIONALE: School-aged children need specific details about procedures related to dying. Explaining how a morphine drip keeps her sister comfortable would best minimize the child's anxiety. Saying her sister won't need food any more when she dies is more appropriate for a younger child. School-aged children are curious about death and may deny that it is impending. These behaviors should be handled with understanding and patience.

4. **Answer: B**
   RATIONALE: Serving on his individualized education plan committee will be most beneficial to his education because this plan is designed to meet his individual educational needs. Collaborating with the school nurse and assessing the health effects of attending school, and getting a motorized wheel chair do not address his educational needs.

5. **Answer: B**
   RATIONALE: Watching the interaction between mother and child to see if the child maintains eye contact may indicate that the child is being neglected which is an inorganic cause for failure to thrive. Refusing the nipple is a sign of organic cause for failure to thrive. Prematurity is a risk factor for failure to thrive. Checking the health history may disclose other organic causes for failure to thrive.

6. **Answer: C**
   RATIONALE: Communication can best be improved if the nurse uses reflective listening techniques to show the parents that their input is heard and valued. Giving direct, understandable answers and saying the same thing in different ways helps ensure effective communication with the parents but does nothing to build communication between the nurse and family. Sharing cell phone numbers only allows the nurse and family to talk to each other.

7. **Answer: D**
   RATIONALE: A good way to involve the father and gain his input regarding in the child's care is to schedule education sessions in the evening when he can get away from the office. Leaving voice mails and sending email reports leave him isolated from care group. Lunchtime visits are not long enough for him to focus on the situation.

8. **Answer: A**
   RATIONALE: Nurses can help parents build on their strengths and empower them to care for their child by educating them about the course of treatment and the child's expected outcome. Evaluating emotional strength, assessing the home, and preparing a list of supplies do not empower the parents for the task ahead of them.

9. **Answer: B**
   RATIONALE: Young adolescents require time with their peers. Encouraging her to have visitors would best meet this need. Assuring her illness is not her fault and acting as her personal confidant are interventions suited to school-aged children. Explaining her condition in detail meets the needs of an older adolescent.

10. **Answer: C**
    RATIONALE: The child may be struggling to fit in with his peers by avoiding his treatment regimen in an effort to hide his illness. Monitoring his compliance would disclose this risky behavior. Assessing for depression, encouraging participation in activities, and joining a support group would not address risky behavior.

11. **Answer: B, C**
    RATIONALE: Hearing deficits and strabismus are associated with being preterm.

12. **Answer: C, D, E**
    RATIONALE: Risk factors for the development of vulnerable child syndrome include newborn jaundice, an illness that the child was not expected to recover from, and congenital anomalies.

13. **Answer: A**
    RATIONALE: A food log provides a detailed and objective record of a child's food intake. Parenteral nutrition would not normally be a first-line intervention and having the child choose his own diet would not likely maximize nutritional foods. There is no need for a low-fat diet.

14. **Answer: 2,784**
    RATIONALE: 23.2 kg × 120 kcal/1 kg = 2,784 kcal

15. **Answer: 7**
    RATIONALE: When assessing growth and development of the infant or child who was born prematurely, determine the child's adjusted or corrected age so that the nurse can perform an accurate assessment. 40 weeks minus 32 weeks is 8 weeks or 2 months. The child was born 2 months early.

CHAPTER 35

SECTION I: ASSESSING YOUR UNDERSTANDING

Activity A FILL IN THE BLANKS

1. Implanted
2. Pharmacodynamics
3. Distraction
4. Fifth
5. Hypoglycemia
6. Nasogastric
7. Ophthalmic

Activity B LABELING

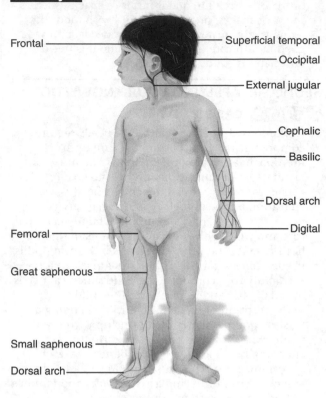

Frontal — Superficial temporal — Occipital — External jugular — Cephalic — Basilic — Dorsal arch — Digital — Femoral — Great saphenous — Small saphenous — Dorsal arch

Activity C MATCHING

1. e   **2.** a   **3.** b   **4.** c   **5.** d

Activity D SEQUENCING

3 → 1 → 2 → 4

Activity E SHORT ANSWERS

1. The child's room should remain a safe and secure area. In the hospital, all invasive procedures should be performed in the treatment room.

2. Check identification since children may deny their identity in attempt to avoid unpleasant situations, play in another child's bed, or remove ID bracelet; confirm identity each time medication is given; verify the child's name with the caregiver to provide additional assurance of identification.

3. Monitor the child's vital signs closely for changes; adhere to strict aseptic technique when caring for the catheter and administering TPN; ensure that the system remains a closed system at all times, including securing all connections, using occlusive dressings, and clamping catheter or having child perform the Valsalva maneuver during tubing and cap changes; follow agency policy for flushing of catheter and maintaining catheter patency; assess intake and output frequently; monitor blood glucose levels and obtain laboratory tests as ordered to evaluate for changes in fluid and electrolytes.

4. The eight rights of medication administration for children are the right: medication, client, time, route of administration, dose, documentation, to be educated, and to refuse.

5. A feeding tube can be checked for placement by checking the pH (results vary between gastric and intestinal tubes); observing the appearance of the fluid removed from the tube upon aspiration; instilling air and performing gastric auscultation; checking external markings on tube and external tube length; assessing for signs indicative of feeding tube misplacement; and reviewing any chest or abdominal x-rays for placement. Always follow agencies policy and procedures.

SECTION II: APPLYING YOUR KNOWLEDGE
Activity F CASE STUDY

1. a. Identify the need for the PRN medication based on the order. Rationale: Identification of the child's condition that warrants the medication is the first step in administering a PRN medication. Jennifer's rectal temperature of 102.5°F demonstrates a need for acetaminophen for fever (per the order).
b. Verify medication order. Rationale: To ensure appropriate medication will be administered.
c. Calculate the correct dose. Rationale: To ensure that the amount of medication is appropriate for the child based on weight.
d. Calculate amount to be drawn up from the bottle of acetaminophen. Rationale: To ensure the appropriate amount of medication is given based on the available medication concentration.
e. Wash hands. Rationale: To prevent infection
f. Verify correct medication and expiration date of medication. Verify time of last dose given and ensure at least 4 hours ago. Verify oral route is the ordered route of administration. Draw up acetaminophen from the bottle using an oral syringe. Rationale: Right medication, right time, and right route of administration are 3 of the 8 right parts of medication administration. A syringe is the best way to accurately measure the liquid medication. It is also the best way to administer medicine to an infant.
g. Prepare a bottle of juice, formula, or breastmilk. Rationale: It is recommended to have a "chaser" for the infant to drink immediately after the medication is given.
h. Educate Jennifer's parents at the bedside regarding why the medicine is needed, what the child will experience and the desired effect of the medication, what is expected of the child and how the parents can participate and support their child. Rationale: Parent teaching is an important part of medication administration. Involvement of parents in medication administration can reduce stress for the infant.

i. Invite the parents to assist and/or give suggestions for techniques. Rationale: The parents may have helpful suggestions for how their child best takes medications. Involvement of parents in medication administration can reduce stress for the infant, validates their roles as caregivers, and may increase the likelihood of successful medication administration.
j. Check identification of the child. Rationale: To ensure medicine is given to correct child.
k. Administer the medication into the back of the infant's mouth between the teeth and gums. Give small amounts and allow the child to swallow before more medicine is placed in the mouth. Have the child upright or at least 45-degree angle. Rationale: Allows infant to swallow the medication and decreases the likelihood of spitting, coughing up, or aspirating the medication.
l. Offer the infant a sip from the prepared bottle. Rationale: The juice can help rinse the medication taste from the mouth and sucking on the bottle often will help soothe and calm the infant.
m. Document the medication administration and within 30 to 60 minutes document the child's response (recheck temperature). Rationale: Documentation should be done after the medication is administered. Since this is a PRN medication the infant's response should be noted.

2. Dosing for acetaminophen is 10 to 15 mg/kg every 4 to 6 hours. Convert 15 lb to kg (1 kg = 2.2 lb). Therefore 15 lb equals 6.8 kg multiplied by 10 = 68 mg; 6.8 multiplied by 15 = 102 mg. The range of acetaminophen Jennifer can receive is 68 mg to 102 mg every 4 to 6 hours; therefore 70 mg every 4 hours po is a safe and therapeutic dose.

3. Ratio method:
Proportion method:

$$\frac{70\ mg}{x} \times \frac{80\ mg}{0.8\ mL}\ \text{(cross multiply)} = 56 = 80x\ \text{solve for x, x} = 0.7\ mL$$

70 mg:x = 80 mg:0.8 mL, multiply means and extremes and get 56 = 80x, solve for x, x = 0.7 mL

SECTION III: PRACTICING FOR NCLEX
Activity G NCLEX-STYLE QUESTIONS

1. Answer: B
RATIONALE: The priority nursing action is to verify the medication ordered. The first step in the eight rights of pediatric medication administration is to ensure that the child is receiving the right medication. After verifying the order, the nurse would then gather the medication, the necessary equipment and supplies, wash hands, and put on gloves.
2. Answer: C
RATIONALE: The nurse should emphasize that the parents should never threaten the child in order to make him take his medication. It is more

appropriate to develop a cooperative approach that will elicit the child's cooperation since he needs ongoing, daily medication. The other statements are correct.

3. **Answer: D**
RATIONALE: The preferred injection site for infants is the vastus lateralis muscle. An alternative site is the rectus femoris muscle. The dorsogluteal is not a recommended site for the infant. The deltoid muscle, which is a small muscle mass, is used as an IM injection site in children after the age of 4 to 5 years of age due to the small muscle mass.

4. **Answer: A**
RATIONALE: Never mix a medication with formula or food. The child may associate the bitter taste with the food and later refuse to eat it.

5. **Answer: B**
RATIONALE: Yellow or bile-stained aspirate indicates intestinal placement. Clean, tan, or green aspirate indicates gastric placement.

6. **Answer: A**
RATIONALE: The nurse should use the child's weight in kilograms. The nurse would then multiply the child's weight in kilograms by 3 mg (32 kg × 3 mg = 96 mg) for the low end and then by 4 mg for the high end (32 lb × 4 mg = 128 mg).

7. **Answer: A, E**
RATIONALE: It is true that infants and young children have an increased percentage of water in their bodies. Infants and young children have immature livers.

8. **Answer: A**
RATIONALE: The nurse should provide a description of and reason for the procedure in age-appropriate language. The nurse should avoid the use of terms such as culture or strep throat as it is not age appropriate for a 4-year old. The nurse should also avoid confusing terms like "take your blood" that might be interpreted literally.

9. **Answer: B**
RATIONALE: Signs of infiltration included cool, puffy, or blanched skin. Warmth, redness, induration, and tender skin are signs of inflammation.

10. **Answer: B**
RATIONALE: The nurse should explain what is to occur and enlist the child's help in the removal of the tape or dressing. This provides the child with a sense of control over the situation and also encourages his or her cooperation. The nurse should avoid using scissors to remove the tape or dressing and the comment regarding cutting may be perceived as threatening and/or frightening. Telling the child to be a big girl is inappropriate and does not teach. Telling the child the procedure will not hurt and using the terms tug and pinch could increase the child's fear and lead to misunderstanding.

11. **Answer: C**
RATIONALE: The child's daily intravenous fluid maintenance is 1,700 mL. The child requires 100 mL/kg for the first 10 kg, plus 50 mL/kg for the next 10 kg, plus 20 mL/kg for each kg more than 20 kg. This equals the number of kg required for 24 hours. (10 × 100) + (10 × 50) + (10 × 20) = 1,700.

12. **Answer: 21.4**
RATIONALE: There are 2.2 lb per kg. 47 lb × 1 kg/2.2 lb = 21.363636 kg. When rounded to the tenth place, the answer is 21.4 kg.

13. **Answer: 1640**
RATIONALE: (First 10 kg) 10 kg × 100 mL/kg = 1,000 mL
(Second 10 kg) 10 kg × 50 mL/kg = 500 mL
(remaining kilograms of body weight) 7 kg × 20 mL/kg = 140 mL
1,000 + 500 + 140 = 1,640 mL

14. **Answer: 411**
RATIONALE: The child weighs 113 lb (51.36 kg).
51.36 kg × 1 mL/1 kg = 51.36 mL/hour;
51.36 × 8 hours = 410.90;
Rounded to the nearest whole number = 411 mL

15. **Answer: 35**
RATIONALE: The diaper must be weighed before being placed on the infant and after removal to determine urinary output. For each 1 g of increased weight, this is the equivalent of 1 mL of fluid.
75 g − 40 g = 35 g = 35 mL

CHAPTER 36

SECTION I: ASSESSING YOUR UNDERSTANDING

Activity A FILL IN THE BLANKS

1. Midazolam
2. 60
3. Depressed
4. Morphine
5. Seven
6. Pain threshold
7. Oucher

Activity B MATCHING

Exercise 1
1. d   2. a   3. b   4. e   5. c

Exercise 2
1. b   2. d   3. a   4. c

Activity C SEQUENCING

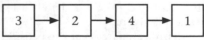

$$3 \rightarrow 2 \rightarrow 4 \rightarrow 1$$

Activity D SHORT ANSWERS

1. Somatic pain refers to pain that develops in the tissues. Superficial somatic pain is also called cutaneous pain. It involves stimulation of nociceptors in the skin, subcutaneous tissue, or mucous membranes. It is typically well localized and described as sharp, pricking, or burning sensation. Tenderness is common. Deep somatic pain typically involves the muscles tendons, joints, fascia, and

bones. It can be localized or diffused and is usually described as dull, aching, or cramping.

2. The three principles that guide pain management in children are:
   - Individualize interventions based on the amount of pain experiences during procedure and the child's personality
   - Use nonpharmacologic approaches to ease or eliminate the pain
   - Use aggressive pharmacologic treatment with the first procedure

3. The situation factors can be changed. They include behavioral, cognitive, and emotional aspects.

4. Conscious sedation utilizes medications to place the child in a depressed state. This is used to allow the physician to perform procedures. Conscious sedation enables the child to retain protective reflexes. The child is then able to maintain a patent airway and respond to verbal and physical stimuli. Medications used to achieve conscious sedation may include morphine, fentanyl, midazolam, chloral hydrate, or diazepam.

5. Epidural anesthesia is administered after the placement of a catheter in the epidural space. The locations used are L 1–2, L 3–4, or L 4–5. Medications used include fentanyl or morphine. The medications enter the cerebrospinal fluid and cross the dura mater to the spinal cord.

SECTION II: APPLYING YOUR KNOWLEDGE
Activity E CASE STUDY

1. The discussion should include the following:

   Recent research supports that infants do feel pain and short- and long-term consequences of inadequately treating their pain do occur. Infants cannot tell us in words that they feel pain like older children or adults but they do give cues with their behaviors, expressions, and vital signs. Infants will act differently when they are in pain than when they are comfortable. Typically, infants respond to pain with irritability, crying, withdrawal, pushing away, restless sleeping, and poor feeding. They may indicate pain by their facial expressions. A facial expression with brows lowered and drawn together, eyes tightly closed, and mouth opened can be a sign of pain. They are preverbal so this facial expression, diffuse body movements and other signs, as indicated above, provide feedback that the infant is in pain. As parents you play an important role in helping us assess Owen's pain and informing us of changes in his behavior that may indicate pain.

2. The discussion should include the following:

   The FLACC scale is an appropriate pain assessment tool for an infant. Based on the scale (refer to Table 14.6 in Essentials of Pediatric Nursing textbook) Owen's pain level is a three at this time.

   Owen's vital signs including oxygen saturation as well as how well Owen is feeding may be helpful. (Children in acute pain will often have an increased heart rate, respiratory rate, or elevated blood pressure. Decreased oxygen saturation may be seen secondary to pain. Also, infants in pain will often demonstrate poor feeding.)

3. The discussion should include the following:

   Parents are important components in both pain assessment and intervention. Many of the nonpharmacologic techniques can be done by parents and are often received better from the parents. Holding the child with as much skin to skin contact as possible, repositioning, rocking, and massaging the child can help decrease pain. Nonnutritive sucking, breastfeeding, or sucrose or other sweet tasting solutions such as glucose water can decrease discomfort. Distracting the infant with a soothing voice, music, stories, and songs can also be helpful.

SECTION III: PRACTICING FOR NCLEX
Activity F NCLEX-STYLE QUESTIONS

1. **Answer: A**
   RATIONALE: A preschooler may have difficulty distinguishing between the types of pain such as if the pain is sharp or dull. It also limits the information being obtained by the nurse. They can, however, tell someone where it hurts and can use various tools such as the FACES scale (cartoon faces) or the OUCHER scale (photograph and corresponding numbers) to rate their pain.

2. **Answer: A**
   RATIONALE: When administering parenteral or epidural opioids, the nurse should always have naloxone readily available in order to reverse the opioids effects, should respiratory distress occur. Premedication with acetaminophen is not required with opioids. After administration, the nurse should continually assess for adverse reaction. The nurse should assess bowel sounds for decreased peristalsis after administration.

3. **Answer: D**
   RATIONALE: Respiratory depression, although rare when epidural analgesia is used, is always a possibility. However, when it does occur it usually occurs gradually over a period of several hours after the medication is initiated. This allows adequate time for early detection and prompt intervention. The nurse should also monitor for pruritus, urinary retention, and nausea and vomiting but the priority is to monitor for respiratory depression.

4. **Answer: C**
   RATIONALE: EMLA is contraindicated in children less than 12 months who are receiving methemoglobin-inducing agents such as sulfonamides, phenytoin, phenobarbital, and acetaminophen. Children with darker skin may require longer application times to ensure effectiveness. EMLA is not contraindicated for children less than 6 weeks of age or those undergoing venous cannulation or intramuscular injections.

5. **Answer: B**
RATIONALE: When a child is manifesting extreme anxiety and behavioral upset, the priority nursing intervention is to serve as an advocate for the family and ensure that the appropriate pharmacologic agents are chosen to alleviate the child's distress. Ensuring emergency equipment is readily available and lighting is adequate for the procedure is also part of nursing function, but secondary interventions. Conducting an initial assessment of pain is important but would likely be difficult if the child was crying inconsolably or extremely anxious.

6. **Answer: A**
RATIONALE: Just because the girl is sleeping does not mean she is not in pain. Sleep may be a coping strategy or reflect excessive exhaustion due to coping with pain. An easygoing temperament and the ability to articulate how she feels will be helpful for the nurse to establish a baseline assessment. If the girl had never had surgery before, she is less likely to have previous memories or episodes of prolonged or severe pain.

7. **Answer: B**
RATIONALE: The parents must understand that they should begin the technique or method chosen before the child experiences pain or when he first indicates he is anxious about or beginning to experience pain. The other statements are accurate.

8. **Answer: B**
RATIONALE: Decreased heart rate is not a physiologic response to pain. Instead, infants demonstrate an increased heart rate, usually averaging approximately 10 beats per minute with possible bradycardia in preterm newborns. Decreased oxygen saturation and palmar and plantar sweating are common physiologic responses to pain in the infant.

9. **Answer: B**
RATIONALE: The FLACC behavioral scale is a behavioral assessment tool that is useful in assessing a child's pain when the child is unable to report accurately his or her level of pain or discomfort and is reliable for children from age 2 months to 7 years. The preferred base age for the visual analog and numerical scales is 7 years. The FACES pain rating scale and OUCHER pain rating scale are appropriate for children as young as 3; however, in this situation the FLACC is required due to the child's inability to report his level of pain.

10. **Answer: A**
RATIONALE: The nurse should select the pain assessment tool that is appropriate for the child's cognitive abilities. The FACES pain rating scale is designed for use with children ages 3 and up. A child with limited reading skills or vocabulary may have difficulty with some of the words listed to describe pain on the word graphic scale. Some of the concepts might be too difficult on the visual analog and numerical scales for a developmentally disabled child. The base age for the adolescent pediatric pain tool is 8 years, but its use would

likely be inappropriate for an 8-year old with cognitive delays.

11. **Answer: D**
RATIONALE: The epidural is placed at the level of L 1–2, L 3–4, or L 4–5. This is below the area of the spinal cord. Advising the child and family that paralysis is not a serious concern trivializes the concerns and does little to promote therapeutic communication. Nurses have the responsibility to provide education to the child and caregivers. Simply telling them that the cord ends above the area of the epidural does not provide the needed information to promote reassurance. Assuring the child and family that their physician has skills does not meet the needed education.

12. **Answer: C**
RESPONSIBLE nursing care requires the nurse administer pain medication as needed. The nurse has the authority to discuss the child's pain control needs with the parents. There is no need to discuss the reduction of medications with the physician. Family history of drug abuse is not a factor in the care of this child. Young children can become addicted to analgesics. There is, however, no indication that addiction is a valid concern with this child.

13. **Answer: C**
RATIONALE: Children may underreport feelings of pain. They may assume that adults know how they are feeling or they may feel worried about appearing to lose control. The nurse should assess for the presence of behavioral cues that might be consistent with pain. The nurse should not simply administer analgesics without cause.

14. **Answer: C**
RATIONALE: Ketorolac is a nonsteroidal anti-inflammatory drug (NSAID). It is associated with gastrointestinal upset. To reduce this side effect the nurse may administer the medication with food.

CHAPTER 37

SECTION I: ASSESSING YOUR UNDERSTANDING

Activity A FILL IN THE BLANKS

1. Pyrogens
2. Phagocytosis
3. Antibodies
4. Neutrophils
5. Ibuprofen

Activity B MATCHING

Exercise 1

| 1. b | 2. e | 3. f | 4. c | 5. d | 6. a |

Exercise 2

| 1. b | 2. c | 3. a | 4. e | 5. d |

Activity C   SEQUENCING

$$3 \rightarrow 4 \rightarrow 2 \rightarrow 1$$

Activity D   SHORT ANSWERS

1. Risk factors for sepsis associated with pregnancy include:
   - premature or prolonged rupture of membranes
   - difficult birth
   - maternal infection or fever, including sexually transmitted infections
   - resuscitation and other invasive procedures
   - positive maternal group beta streptococcal vaginosis

2. The nurse primarily manages the client's symptoms. Acetaminophen may be given for fever management. Narcotic analgesics may be required for pain management. Oral fluids prevent dehydration. If orchitis is present, ice packs and gentle support for the testicles may be necessitated. Hospitalized children should be confined to respiratory isolation. Children are considered to no longer be contagious after 9 days following the onset of parotid swelling.

3. Concurrent use of passive and active immunoprophylaxis is recommended. It consists of a regimen of one dose of immune globulin and five doses of human rabies vaccine over a 28-day period. Rabies immune globulin and the first dose of rabies vaccine should be given as soon as possible after exposure, ideally within 24 hours. Additional doses of rabies vaccine should be given on days 3, 7, 14, and 28 after the first vaccination. Rabies immune globulin is infiltrated into and around the wound with any remaining volume administered intramuscularly at a site distant from the vaccine inoculation. Human rabies vaccine is administered intramuscularly into the anterolateral thigh or deltoid depending on the age and size of the child.

4. Fever is a protective mechanism the body uses to fight infection. Evidence exists that an elevated body temperature actually enhances various components of the immune response. Fever can slow the growth of bacteria and viruses and increase neutrophil production and T-cell proliferation (Crocetti & Serwint, 2005). Studies have shown that the use of antipyretics may prolong illness. Another concern is that reducing fever may hide signs of serious bacterial illness.

5. Sepsis is a systemic over response to infection resulting from bacteria (most common), fungi, viruses, or parasites. It can lead to septic shock, which results in hypotension, low blood flow, and multisystem organ failure. Septic shock is a medical emergency and children are usually admitted to an intensive care unit. The cause of sepsis may not be known, but common causative organisms in children include *Neisseria meningitidis, Streptococcus pneumoniae,* and *Haemophilus influenzae.* Sepsis can affect any age group but is more common in neonates and young infants. Neonates and young infants have a higher susceptibility due to their immature immune system, inability to localize infections, and lack of IgM immunoglobulin, which is necessary to protect against bacterial infections.

SECTION II: APPLYING YOUR KNOWLEDGE

Activity E   CASE STUDY

1. The discussion should include the following points:
   Continue attempting to open dialogue with Jennifer. Make sure your style, content, and message are appropriate to her developmental level. Do not talk down to her and approach her in a direct and nonjudgmental manner. Work on identifying risk factors and risk behaviors.

2. The discussion should include the following points:
   Encourage completion of antibiotic prescription. Encourage sexual partners to get an evaluation, testing, and treatment.

   Once risk factors and risk behaviors have been identified, guide Jennifer to develop specific individualized actions of prevention. The nurse can encourage abstinence at this point along with encouraging Jennifer to minimize her lifetime number of sexual partners, to use barrier methods consistently and correctly, and to be aware of the connection between drug and alcohol use and the incorrect use of barrier methods.

3. The discussion should include the following points:
   Reinforce the risk she is putting herself at and continue to guide her to develop individualized actions of prevention. For possible discussion about other STIs common in adolescents (refer to Table 15.9). Discuss barriers to condom use and ways to overcome them (refer Table 15.10).

   To address specific concerns – condoms are uncomfortable and sex with condoms is not as exciting or as good.

   Encourage Jennifer and her boyfriend to try condoms and provide suggestions such as trying smaller or larger condom sizes, placing a drop of water based lubricant or salvia inside the tip of the condom or on the glans of the penis prior to putting on the condom. Try a thinner latex condom or a different brand for more lubrication. Encourage the incorporation of condom use during foreplay. Remind Jennifer that peace of mind may enhance pleasure for herself and her partner.

   Instruct Jennifer on proper condom use (refer to Teaching Guideline 15.3).

   The discussion should include the following points:
   - Use latex condoms.
   - Use a new condom with each sexual act of intercourse and never reuse a condom.
   - Handle condoms with care to prevent damage from sharp objects such as nails and teeth.
   - Ensure condom has been stored in a cool, dry place away from direct sunlight. Do not store

condoms in wallet or automobile or any place where they are exposed to extreme temperatures.
- Do not use a condom if it appears brittle, sticky, or discolored. These are signs of aging.
- Place condom on before any genital contact.
- Place condom on when penis is erect and ensure it is placed so it will readily unroll.
- Hold the tip of the condom while unrolling. Ensure there is a space at the tip for semen to collect but make sure no air is trapped in the tip.
- Ensure adequate lubrication during intercourse. If external lubricants are used only use water-based lubricants such as KY jelly with latex condoms. Oil-based or petroleum-based lubricants, such as body lotion, massage oil, or cooking oil, can weaken latex condoms.
- Withdraw while penis is still erect and hold condom firmly against base of pen.

SECTION III: PRACTICING FOR NCLEX
Activity F NCLEX-STYLE QUESTIONS

1. **Answer: C**
   RATIONALE: If the family had been camping or in a wooded area, the girl could have been bitten by a tick which would not be easy to discover because of her long hair. Ticks like dark, hair-covered areas and the signs and symptoms presented are neurological, with a rapid onset, which can be characteristic of a tick bite. The other questions are important but are not focusing on the causative agent.

2. **Answer: B**
   RATIONALE: Recurrent arthritis in large joints, such as the knees, is an indication of late-stage Lyme disease. The appearance of erythema migraines would suggest early-localized stage of the disease. Facial palsy or conjunctivitis would suggest the child is in the early disseminated stage of the disease.

3. **Answer: C**
   RATIONALE: It is very important to ensure that the proper dose is given at the proper interval because an overdose can be toxic to the child. Concerns with allergies and taking the entire, prescribed dose are precaution when administering antibiotics and all medications. Drowsiness is not a side effect of antipyretics.

4. **Answer: D**
   RATIONALE: In order to ensure a successful culture, the nurse must determine if the child is taking antibiotics. Throat cultures require specimens taken from the pharyngeal or tonsillar area. Stool cultures may require three specimens, each on a different day. The nurse would use aseptic technique when getting a blood specimen as well as the urine, but antibiotics cannot be received by the child prior to the test being done.

5. **Answer: A**
   RATIONALE: The usual sites for obtaining blood specimens are veins on the dorsal side of the hand or the antecubital fossa. Administration of sucrose prior to beginning helps control pain for young infants. Accessing an indwelling venous access device may be appropriate if the child is in an acute care setting. An automatic lancet device is used for capillary puncture of an infant's heel.

6. **Answer: A**
   RATIONALE: The presence of petechiae can indicate serious infection in an infant. Grunting is abnormal, indicating respiratory difficulty. The behavior of the 2-month-old is normal after immunizations. The 4-month-old needs to be watched but is adequately hydrated and the 8-month-old also needs to be watched. What the 8-month-old is experiencing is common in infants who are teething and is not indicative of illness.

7. **Answer: A**
   RATIONALE: Varicella zoster results in a life-long latent infection. It can reactivate later in life resulting in shingles. The American Academy of Pediatrics recommends consideration of Vitamin A supplementation in children 6 months to 2 years hospitalized for measles. Dehydration caused by mouth lesions is a concern with foot and mouth disease. Avoiding exposure to pregnant women is a concern with rubella, rubeola, and erythema infectiosum.

8. **Answer: A**
   RATIONALE: Infants and young children are more susceptible to infection due to the immature responses of their immune systems. Cellular immunity is generally functional at birth; humoral immunity develops after the child is born. Newborns have a decreased inflammatory response. Young infants lose the passive immunity from their mothers, but disease protection from immunizations is not complete.

9. **Answer: B**
   RATIONALE: The use of immunosuppression drugs is a risk factor for the hospitalized child. Maternal infection or fever and resuscitation or invasive procedures are sepsis risk factors related to pregnancy and labor. Lack of juvenile immunizations is a risk factor affecting the overall health of the child but does not impact the chance of sepsis.

10. **Answer: D**
    RATIONALE: Penicillin V or erythromycin is the preferred antibiotic for treatment of scarlet fever. Scarlet fever transmission is airborne, not via droplet. Lymphadenopathy occurs with cat scratch disease and diphtheria. Close monitoring of airway status is critical with diphtheria because the upper airway becomes swollen.

11. **Answer: C**
    RATIONALE: Pruritus may be managed by pressing on the area instead of scratching. Increases in temperature will result in vasodilation and increase the pruritus. Warm baths and hot compresses should be avoided. Rubbing may result in increased itching.

12. **Answer: A**
    RATIONALE: When treating a child suspected of having an infection, the blood cultures must be obtained first. The administration of antibiotics may impact the culture's results. A urine specimen may be obtained but is not the priority action. Intravenous fluids will likely be included in the plan of care but are not the priority action.

13. **Answer: D**
    RATIONALE: Sepsis may be associated with lethargy, irritability, or changes in level of consciousness. The septic child will likely not be anxious to have a high activity level and would prefer to remain in bed. The temperature elevation of 98.8°F (37.11°C) is not significant and does not confirm the presence of sepsis.

14. **Answer: B, C, D**
    RATIONALE: Aspirin should be avoided in children with fever. It may be associated with Reyes syndrome. Activities that result in overcooling or chilling such as using fans and cold baths should be avoided.

CHAPTER 38

SECTION I: ASSESSING YOUR UNDERSTANDING

Activity A   FILL IN THE BLANKS

1. Kernig
2. painful
3. circumference
4. gait
5. doll's eye
6. touch
7. Intracranial
8. bruit

Activity B   LABELING

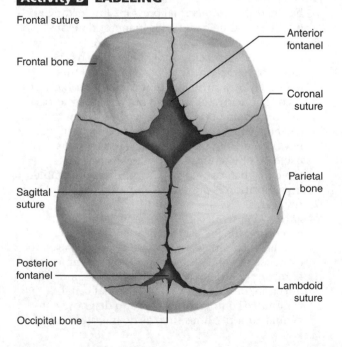

Activity C   MATCHING

1. d   **2.** e   **3.** c   **4.** a   **5.** b

Activity D   SEQUENCING

$$\boxed{1} \rightarrow \boxed{5} \rightarrow \boxed{4} \rightarrow \boxed{2} \rightarrow \boxed{3}$$

Activity E   SHORT ANSWERS

1. Kernig sign is tested by flexing the legs at the hip and knee, then extending the knee. A positive report of pain along the vertebral column is a positive sign and indicates irritation of the meninges, or the presence of meningitis.
2. An infant will hyperextend its head and neck assuming an opisthotonic position in order to relieve discomfort due to bacterial meningitis.
3. Proper positioning for newborns is upright with the head flexed forward. An older infant or child is positioned on its side with head flexed forward and knees flexed toward the abdomen.
4. A ventriculoperitoneal (VP) shunt is designed to relieve the buildup of CSF in hydrocephalus children and maintain proper intracranial pressure. Malfunctions may be due to kinking, clogging, or separation of the tubing. The most common malfunction, however, is due to blockage. Signs and symptoms include vomiting, lethargy, headache in the older child, and altered, diminished, or change in the level of consciousness.
5. The Glasgow Coma scale is a tool used to standardize the degree of consciousness in the child. It consists of three parts: eye opening, verbal response, and motor response. A low score indicates a decreased level of consciousness or responsiveness.

SECTION II: APPLYING YOUR KNOWLEDGE

Activity F   CASE STUDY

1. The nurse should anticipate the following diagnostic and laboratory tests: complete blood count (CBC); electrolytes; culture (if febrile); phenobarbital level; toxicology if ingestion of medicine or chemicals is suspected; lumbar puncture (LP) if signs of central nervous system infection are present; and imaging studies, such as CT or MRI, if head injury is suspected.
2. Interventions should include:
   • If child is standing or sitting ease child to the ground if possible, cradle head, place on soft area. Do not attempt to restrain. Place child on one side and open airway if possible.
   • Place blow-by oxygen by child and have suction ready if needed.
   • Remove any sharp or potentially dangerous objects. Tight clothing and jewelry around the neck should be loosened if possible.
   • Observe length of seizure and activity such as movements noted, as well as cyanosis or loss of

bladder or bowel control, and any other characteristics about the child's condition during the seizure.
- If child's condition deteriorates or seizures persist, call for help.
- Report seizures to physician promptly.
- Administer anticonvulsants as ordered.
- Remain with child until fully conscious.
- Allow postictal behavior without interfering while providing environmental protection.
- When possible, reorient child.
- Accurately document information in chart, including preseizure activity.
- Provide emotional support and education to family.
- Obtain anticonvulsant levels as ordered.

3. Teaching should include:
- Discuss seizure warning signs.
- Teach the family to recognize warning signs and how to care for the child during and after a seizure (refer to Teaching Guidelines 38.1).
- Discuss the disease process and prognosis of condition and life-long need for treatment if indicated.
- Teach parents the need for routine medical care and that it is important for the child to wear a medical bracelet.
- Review medication regimen and the importance of maintaining a therapeutic medication level and administering all prescribed doses.
- Encourage parents to discuss with the child why she does not want to take the medicine.
- Explain to the child in simple terms why the medicine is needed and how it will help her. Encourage participation from physician and parents.
- Discuss alternative ways to administer phenobarbital, such as crushed tablets or elixir, with the physician and family.
- Explain to the family to use an understanding and gentle yet firm approach with medication administration.
- Encourage the family to give medicine at same time and place, which helps create a routine.
- Help the family to identify creative strategies to gain the child's cooperation, such as using a sticker chart and allowing child to do more, such as administering the medication.
- Offer choices when possible, such as "Do you want your medicine before or after your bath, and would you like to have apple or grape juice after your medicine?"
- Praise the child's improvements.

SECTION III: PRACTICING FOR NCLEX
Activity G NCLEX-STYLE QUESTIONS

1. **Answer: A**
   RATIONALE: Always start by assessing the family's knowledge. Ask them what they need to know. Knowing when to clamp the drain is important, but they might not be listening if they have another question on their minds. Autoregulation is too technical. Teaching should be based on the parents' level of understanding. Keeping her head elevated is not part of the information which would be taught regarding the drainage system.

2. **Answer: C**
   RATIONALE: Horizontal nystagmus is a symptom of lesions on the brain stem. A sudden increase in head circumference is a symptom of hydrocephalus suggesting that there is a buildup of fluid in the brain. An intracranial mass would cause only one eye to be dilated and reactive. A closed posterior fontanel is not unusual at 2 months of age.

3. **Answer: A**
   RATIONALE: The fact that swelling did not cross the midline or suture lines suggests cephalohematoma. Swelling that crosses the midline of the infant's scalp indicates caput succedaneum which is common. Low birthweight is not an accompanying factor for cephalohematoma. Facial abnormalities may accompany encephalocele, not cephalohematoma.

4. **Answer: A**
   RATIONALE: Signs and symptoms for cerebral contusions include disturbances to vision, strength, and sensation. A child suffering a concussion will be distracted and unable to concentrate. Vomiting is a sign of a subdural hematoma. Bleeding from the ear is a sign of a basilar skull fracture.

5. **Answer: A**
   RATIONALE: Positional plagiocephaly can occur because the infant's head is allowed to stay in one position for too long. Because the bones of the skull are soft and moldable, they can become flattened if the head is allowed to remain in the same position for a long period of time. Massaging the scalp will not affect the skull. Measuring the intake and output is important but has no effect on the skull bones. Small feedings are indicated whenever an infant has increased intracranial pressure, but feeding an infant each time he fusses is inappropriate care.

6. **Answer: C**
   RATIONALE: Folic acid supplementation has been found to reduce the incidence of neural tube defects by 50%. The fact that the mother has not used folic acid supplements puts her baby at risk for spina bifida occulta, one type of neural tube defect. Neonatal conjunctivitis can occur in any newborn during birth and is caused by virus, bacteria, or chemicals. Facial deformities are typical of babies of alcoholic mothers. Incomplete myelinization is present in all newborns.

7. **Answer: C**
   RATIONALE: A video electroencephalogram can determine the precise localization of the seizure area in the brain. Cerebral angiography is used to diagnose vessel defects or space-occupying lesions. Lumbar puncture is used to diagnose hemorrhage, infection, or obstruction in the spinal canal. Computed tomography is used to diagnose congenital abnormalities such as neural tube defects.

8. Answer: C

RATIONALE: Brain and spinal cord development occur during the first 3 to 4 weeks of gestation. Infection, trauma, teratogens (any environmental substance that can cause physical defects in the developing embryo and fetus), and malnutrition during this period can result in malformations in brain and spinal cord development and may affect normal central nervous system (CNS) development. Good health before becoming pregnant is important but must continue into the pregnancy. Hardening of bones occurs during 13 to 16 weeks' gestation, and the respiratory system begins maturing around 23 weeks' gestation.

9. Answer: B

RATIONALE: Educating parents how to properly give the antibiotics would be the priority intervention because the child's shunt has become infected. Maintaining cerebral perfusion is important for a child with hydrocephalus, but the priority intervention for the parents at this time is in regard to the infection. Establishing seizure precautions is an intervention for a child with a seizure disorder. Encouraging development of motor skills would be appropriate for a microcephalic child.

10. Answer: A, B, C, E

RATIONALE: The child with bacterial meningitis should be placed in droplet isolation until 24 hours following the administration of antibiotics. Close contacts of the child should receive antibiotics to prevent them from developing the infection. The nurse should administer antibiotics and initiate seizure precautions. Children with bacterial meningitis have an increased risk of developing problems associated with an increased intracranial pressure.

11. Answer: A, B, C, D

RATIONALE: The following people have an increased risk of becoming infected with meningococcal meningitis: college freshman living in dormitories, children 11 years old or older, children who travel to high-risk areas, and children with chronic health conditions.

12. Answer: A, B, D

RATIONALE: This child likely has Reye syndrome and may require an antiemetic for severe vomiting. The nurse should monitor the child's intake and output every shift for the development of fluid imbalance. The child may require an anticonvulsant due to an increased intracranial pressure that may induce seizures. A distinctive rash is associated with the development of meningococcal meningitis. The nurse should monitor the Reye syndrome child's laboratory values for indications that the liver is not functioning well.

13. Answer: B, D, E

RATIONALE: Late signs of increased intracranial pressure are decerebrate posturing, bradycardia, and pupils that are fixed and dilated. The other options are early signs of increased intracranial pressure.

CHAPTER 39

SECTION I: ASSESSING YOUR UNDERSTANDING

Activity A FILL IN THE BLANKS

1. 3
2. Horizontal
3. Antibiotics
4. Deterioration
5. Developmental
6. Distance

Activity B MATCHING

1. b **2.** d **3.** a **4.** e **5.** c

Activity C SEQUENCING

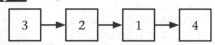

Activity D SHORT ANSWERS

1. Signs and symptoms of children with a hearing loss include:
   a. Infant:
   - Wakes only to touch, not environmental noises
   - Does not startle to loud noises
   - Does not turn to sound by 4 months of age
   - Does not babble at 6 months of age
   - Does not progress with speech development
   b. Young child:
   - Does not speak by 2 years of age
   - Communicates needs through gestures
   - Does not speak distinctly, as appropriate for his or her age
   - Displays developmental (cognitive) delays
   - Prefers solitary play
   - Displays immature emotional behavior
   - Does not respond to ringing of the telephone or doorbell
   - Focuses on facial expressions when communicating
   c. Older child
   - Often asks for statements to be repeated
   - Is inattentive or daydreams
   - Performs poorly at school
   - Displays monotone or other abnormal speech
   - Gives inappropriate answers to questions except when able to view face of speaker
2. According to the Delta Gamma Center for Children with Visual Impairments, there are several ways to successfully interact with the visually impaired child, including:
   - Use the child's name to gain attention.
   - Identify yourself and let the child know you are there before you touch the child.
   - Encourage the child to be independent while maintaining safety.
   - Name and describe people/objects to make the child more aware of what is happening.
   - Discuss upcoming activities with the child.

- Explain what other children or individuals are doing.
- Make directions simple and specific.
- Allow the child additional time to think about the response to a question or statement.
- Use touch and tone of voice appropriate to the situation.
- Use parts of the child's body as reference points for the location of items.
- Encourage exploration of objects through touch.
- Describe unfamiliar environments and provide reference points.
- Use the sighted-guide technique when walking with a visually impaired child.

3. Signs and symptoms that would lead the nurse to suspect that a child was visually impaired include:
   a. Infants:
      - Does not fix and follow
      - Does not make eye contact
      - Unaffected by bright light
      - Does not imitate facial expression
   b. Toddlers and older children:
      - Rubs, shuts, covers eyes
      - Squinting
      - Frequent blinking
      - Holds objects close or sits close to television
      - Bumping into objects
      - Head tilt, or forward thrust

4. Possible risk factors for acute otitis media (AOM) in children include any of the following:
   - Eustachian tube dysfunction
   - Recurrent upper respiratory infection
   - First episode of AOM before 3 months of age
   - Day care attendance (increases exposure to viruses causing upper respiratory infections)
   - Previous episodes of AOM
   - Family history
   - Passive smoking
   - Crowding in the home or large family size
   - Native American, Inuit, or Australian aborigine ethnicity
   - Absence of infant breastfeeding
   - Immunocompromise
   - Poor nutrition
   - Craniofacial anomalies
   - Presence of allergies

5. Children with permanent hearing loss, suspected or diagnosed speech and/or language delay, craniofacial disorders, and pervasive developmental disorders are at risk for difficulty with the development of speech or language, or having learning difficulties. Other children at risk include those with genetic disorders or syndromes, cleft palate, and blindness or significant visual impairment.

SECTION II: APPLYING YOUR KNOWLEDGE
Activity E CASE STUDY

1. The nurse should anticipate the following diagnostic and laboratory tests: Complete blood count (CBC); electrolytes; blood culture (if febrile); pheno-

barbital level; toxicology if ingestion of medicine or chemicals is suspected; lumbar puncture (LP) if signs of central nervous system infection are present; and imaging studies, such as CT or MRI, if head injury is suspected.

2. Interventions should include:
   - If the child is standing or sitting ease the child to the ground if possible, cradle head, place on soft area. Do not attempt to restrain. Place the child on one side and open airway if possible.
   - Place blow-by oxygen by the child and have suction ready if needed.
   - Remove any sharp or potentially dangerous objects. Tight clothing and jewelry around the neck should be loosened if possible.
   - Observe length of seizure and activity such as movements noted, as well as cyanosis or loss of bladder or bowel control, and any other characteristics about the child's condition during the seizure.
   - If the child's condition deteriorates or seizures persist, call for help.
   - Report seizures to physician promptly.
   - Administer anticonvulsants as ordered.
   - Remain with the child until fully conscious.
   - Allow postictal behavior without interfering while providing environmental protection.
   - When possible, reorient child.
   - Accurately document information in chart, including preseizure activity.
   - Provide emotional support and education to family.
   - Obtain anticonvulsant levels as ordered.

SECTION III: PRACTICING FOR NCLEX
Activity F NCLEX-STYLE QUESTIONS

1. **Answer: D**
   RATIONALE: Reassessing for language acquisition would be most important to the health of the child. There is a risk of otitis media with effusion causing hearing loss, as well as speech, language, and learning problems. Parents should not use over-the-counter drugs to alleviate the child's symptoms, nor should they smoke around her. In addition, proper antibiotic use is important; however, language acquisition is directly related to developmental health.

2. **Answer: C**
   RATIONALE: Recurrent nasal congestion contributes to the presence of otitis media with effusion. Frequent swimming would put the child at risk for otitis externa. Attendance at school is a risk factor for infective conjunctivitis. Although otitis media is a risk factor for infective conjunctivitis, infective conjunctivitis is not a risk factor for otitis media with effusion.

3. **Answer: C**
   RATIONALE: A mixture of ½ rubbing alcohol and ½ vinegar squirted into the canal and then allowed to run out is a good preventative measure, but not when inflammation is present. Cotton swabs

should not be placed in the ears to dry them. He can wash his hair as needed. Using a hair dryer on a cool setting to dry the ears works well as long as the vent is clean and free from dust and hair that may have accumulated.

4. **Answer: B, C, D, E**
   RATIONALE: Children who are 2 years old or younger and have a severe form of acute otitis media with a temperature of 102.2°F (39°C) or higher will most likely receive antibiotics to treat the infection. Children who are older than 2 years of age with severe otalgia and a fever higher than 102.2°F (39°C) typically receive antibiotics. Children who are older than 2 years of age and have mild otalgia and a fever lower than 102.2°F (39°C) have a nonsevere illness. In these cases, the physician may just observe the children to see if their symptoms persist over time or get worse.

5. **Answer: C**
   RATIONALE: The corneal light reflex is extremely helpful in assessment of strabismus. It consists of shining a flashlight into the eyes to see if the light reflects at the same angle in both eyes. Strabismus is present if the reflections are not symmetrical. The visual acuity test measures how well the child sees at various distances. Refractive and ophthalmologic examinations are comprehensive and are performed by optometrists and ophthalmologists.

6. **Answer: B**
   RATIONALE: Intravenous antibiotics will be the primary therapy for this child, followed by oral antibiotics. Warm compresses will be applied for 20 minutes every 2 to 4 hours. However, narcotic analgesics are not necessary to handle the pain associated with this disorder.

7. **Answer: A**
   RATIONALE: Assessing for asymmetric corneal light reflex is the priority intervention as strabismus may develop in the child with regressed retinopathy of prematurity. Observing for signs of visual impairment is not be critical for this child, nor is teaching the parents to check how the glasses fit the child. Referral to early intervention would be appropriate if the child was visually impaired.

8. **Answer: D**
   RATIONALE: Therapeutic management of amblyopia may be achieved by using atropine drops in the better eye. Educating parents on how to use atropine drops is the most helpful intervention. Explaining postsurgical treatment and discouraging the child from roughhousing would be appropriate only if the amblyopia required surgery. While follow-up visits to the ophthalmologist are important, compliance with treatment is priority.

9. **Answer: D**
   RATIONALE: Teaching the parents the importance of patching the child's eye as prescribed is most important for the treatment of strabismus. The need for ultraviolet-protective glasses postoperatively is a subject for the treatment of cataracts.

The possibility of multiple operations is a teaching subject for infantile glaucoma. Teaching the importance of completing the full course of oral antibiotics is appropriate to periorbital cellulitis.

10. **Answer: C**
    RATIONALE: Proper handwashing is the single most important factor to reduce the spread of acute infectious conjunctivitis. Proper application of the antibiotic is important for the treatment of the infection, not prevention of transmission; keeping the child home from school until she is no longer infectious and encouraging the child to keep her hands away from her eyes are sound preventative measures, but not as important as frequent hand-washing.

11. **Answer: D**
    RATIONALE: Encouraging the use of eye protection for sports would be more appropriate if the child was wearing contact lenses that may fall out during athletics. A sport strap would be more appropriate for this child. The child is less likely to wear her glasses if improper fit or incorrect prescription is causing a problem or if the glasses are unattractive. It is important to get scheduled eye examinations on time; watch for signs that the prescription needs changing; and check the condition and fit of glasses monthly.

12. **Answer: A, B**
    RATIONALE: Bacterial infections are usually present unilaterally. Drainage from eyes that have been diagnosed with bacterial conjunctivitis is often thick and purulent.

13. **Answer: A, D**
    RATIONALE: Eye drops are not appropriate to use because rebound vasoconstriction may occur and it is not actually treating the infection. The child can go back to school 24 to 48 hours after the mucopurulent drainage is no longer present.

14. **Answer: A, C, E**
    RATIONALE: The child with a corneal abrasion may have a normal assessment of the pupils bilaterally. The child may experience photophobia and tearing noted in the eye. The child with a corneal abrasion will typically experience eye pain. The child with a simple contusion of the eye will have bruising and edema around the eye.

CHAPTER 40

SECTION I: ASSESSING YOUR UNDERSTANDING

Activity A FILL IN THE BLANKS

1. tracheostomy
2. atopic
3. coryza
4. indirect
5. wheezes
6. Mantoux
7. decongestant

Activity B LABELING

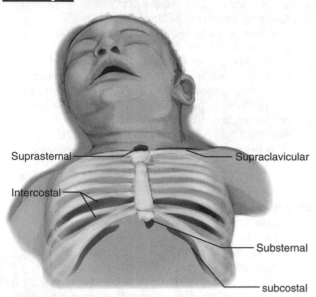

Suprasternal — Supraclavicular

Intercostal —

Substernal

subcostal

Activity C MATCHING

1. d **2.** e **3.** b **4.** a **5.** c

Activity D SEQUENCING

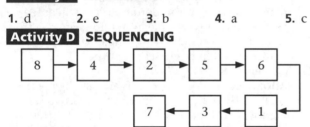

Activity E SHORT ANSWERS

1. Signs and symptoms of sinusitis are similar to those found with a cold, with the difference being that sinusitis signs and symptoms are more persistent than with a cold, with nasal discharge lasting more than 7 to 10 days. Common signs and symptoms include cough, fever, halitosis in preschoolers and older children, eyelid edema, irritability, and poor appetite. Facial pain may or may not be present.

2. Laboratory and diagnostic tests typically ordered for the child suspected of having cystic fibrosis and possible findings indicative of cystic fibrosis include the sweat chloride test (above 50 mEq/L is considered suspicious levels and above 60 mEq is indicative); pulse oximetry (oxygen saturation is usually decreased); chest x-ray (hyperinflation, bronchial wall thickening); and pulmonary function tests (decreased forced vital capacity and forced expiratory volume with increases in residual volume).

3. There is typically no illness that precedes croup or epiglottitis other than possibly mild coryza with croup or a mild upper respiratory infection with epiglottitis. Both have a rapid or sudden onset, with croup frequently occurring at night. Several differences exist between the two illnesses including age groups usually affected (3 months to 3 years with croup and 1 to 8 years for epiglottitis); fever (variable with croup and high with epiglottitis); barking cough and hoarseness with croup; dysphagia and toxic appearance with epiglottitis; lastly, the cause of croup is generally viral whereas the cause of epiglottitis is generally *Haemophilus influenzae* type B.

4. Relief of symptoms is the goal of treatment of the common cold. This may be achieved through a number of methods including relief of nasal congestion by providing a humidified environment or using saline nasal sprays or washes. Saline washes are followed by suctioning with a bulb syringe. Over-the-counter cold remedies may reduce the symptoms of the cold, but not the duration and should not be used in children less than 6 years of age due to possible side effects. Additionally, antihistamines should be avoided as they cause excess drying of secretions.

5. Respiratory syncytial virus (RSV) is the most common cause of bronchiolitis, which is an acute inflammation of the bronchioles. The peak incidence of this disorder occurs in the winter and spring seasons. RSV infection is common in all children, with bronchiolitis RSV occurring most often in infants and toddlers. The severity of the infection typically decreases with age.

SECTION II: APPLYING YOUR KNOWLEDGE

Activity F CASE STUDY

1. The discussion should include the following points:
   - Is there a family history of atopy?
   - Does James have a history of allergic rhinitis or atopic dermatitis?
   - When did James first develop symptoms?
   - Which symptoms developed first?
   - Are there any factors that could have precipitated the attack?
   - Describe James' home environment (include pets, smokers, type of heating use)
   - Does James have any allergies to food or medication?
   - Does James have a seasonal response to environmental pollen or dust allergies?
   - Is James taking any medication?

2. The discussion should include the following points:
   - Ineffective airway clearance related to inflammation and increased secretions as evidenced by dyspnea, coughing and wheezing, pallor, tachypnea, tachycardia and bilateral wheezing on auscultation, and c/o chest tightness.
   - Inflammation and increased mucous secretions can contribute to the narrowing of air passages and interfere with airflow during an acute asthma attack. This is the highest priority nursing diagnosis. Ineffective breathing pattern related to inflammatory or infectious process as evidenced by dyspnea, coughing and wheezing, pallor, tachypnea, tachycardia and bilateral wheezing on auscultation, and c/o chest tightness.
   - Tachypnea and increased work of breathing can lead to inadequate ventilation. Risk for impaired gas exchange related to dyspnea, coughing and

wheezing, pallor, tachypnea, tachycardia and bilateral wheezing on auscultation, and c/o chest tightness.
- Unresolved ineffective airway clearance or ineffective breathing pattern may lead to deficits in oxygenation and carbon dioxide retention and hypoxia. Risk for anxiety related to respiratory distress.
- Respiratory distress and related hypoxia may lead to agitation and anxiety as the child struggles to breathe.

3. The discussion should include the following points:
Education should include a discussion about the pathophysiology, asthma triggers, and prevention and treatment strategies. The nurse should explain that asthma is a chronic, inflammatory airway disorder that decreases the size of the airways leading to respiratory distress. Teaching should include information regarding how attacks of asthma can be prevented by avoiding environmental and emotional triggers (refer to Teaching Guidelines 18.4). Discussion of appropriate use of medication delivery devices, including the nebulizer and metered-dose inhaler are important. Teaching should include the purposes, functions, and side effects of the prescribed medications. It is essential to require return demonstration of equipment use to ensure that children and families are able to utilize equipment properly (refer to Teaching Guidelines 18.5).

SECTION III: PRACTICING FOR NCLEX

Activity G NCLEX-STYLE QUESTIONS

1. **Answer: C**
RATIONALE: The 5-year-old with epiglottitis has a sore, swollen throat placing the child at risk for dysphagia (difficulty swallowing). Erythematous rash and mild toxic appearance are typical of influenza. Fever and fatigue are symptoms of a common cold. Influenza and the common cold may cause sore throats but would not be the highest risk for dysphagia.

2. **Answer: A**
RATIONALE: Until the family adjusts to the demands of the disease, they can become overwhelmed and exhausted, leading to noncompliance, resulting in worsening of symptoms. Typical challenges to the family are becoming overvigilant, the child feeling fearful and isolated, and the siblings being jealous or worried.

3. **Answer: D**
RATIONALE: Attending day care is a known risk factor for pneumonia. Being a triplet is a factor for bronchiolitis. Prematurity rather than postmaturity is a risk factor for pneumonia. Diabetes is a risk factor for influenza.

4. **Answer: B**
RATIONALE: The nurse should teach the child using terms a 6-year-old will understand. A chest x-ray is usually ordered for the assessment of asthma to check for hyperventilation. A sputum culture is

indicated for pneumonia, cystic fibrosis, and tuberculosis; fluoroscopy is used to identify masses or abscesses as with pneumonia; and the sweat chloride test is indicated for cystic fibrosis.

5. **Answer: B**
RATIONALE: Oxygen administration is indicated for the treatment of hypoxemia. Suctioning removes excess secretions from the airway caused by cold or flu. Saline lavage loosens mucus that may be blocking the airway so that it may be suctioned out. Saline gargles are indicated for relieving throat pain as with pharyngitis or tonsillitis.

6. **Answer: C**
RATIONALE: Infants consume twice as much oxygen (6 to 8 L) as adults (3 to 4 L). This is due to higher metabolic and resting respiratory rates. Term infants are born with about 50 million alveoli, which is only 17% of the adult number of around 300 million. The tongue of the infant, relative to the oropharynx is larger than adults. Infants and children will develop hypoxemia more rapidly than adults when in respiratory distress.

7. **Answer: A**
RATIONALE: A flutter valve device is used to assist with mobilization of secretions for older children and adolescents with cystic fibrosis. Teaching regarding the use of metered dose inhalers, nebulizers, and the peak flow meter is typically for asthma therapy.

8. **Answer: A**
RATIONALE: Using nasal washes to improve air flow will help prevent secondary bacterial infection by preventing the mucus from becoming thick and immobile. Teaching parents how to avoid allergens such as tobacco smoke, dust mites, and molds helps prevent recurrence of allergic rhinitis. Discussing anti-inflammatory nasal sprays and teaching parents about using oral antihistamines would help in prevention and treatment of the disorder.

9. **Answer: C, D**
RATIONALE: Until 4 weeks of age, newborns are obligatory nose breathers and breathe only through their mouths when they are crying. A newborn's respiratory tract makes very little mucus. Children have an increased risk of developing problems associated with airway edema. Children's tongues are proportionally larger than adults. Children under the age of 6 years have a reduced risk of developing sinus infections.

10. **Answer: B, C, D, E**
RATIONALE: Children with pneumonia may exhibit the following: a chest x-ray with perihilar infiltrates, an elevated leukocyte level, an increased respiratory rate, and a productive cough. The child with pneumonia typically has a fever.

11. **Answer: 33**
RATIONALE: Room air is 21%. Each 1 L of oxygen flow is equal to an additional 4% of oxygen. The child is receiving 3 L of oxygen. 21% (room air) + 3(4%) = 33% of oxygen.

12. **Answer: 157**
    RATIONALE: Dose should be calculated using weight kilograms.
    $10.45 \text{ kg} \times 45 \text{ g/kg} = 470.45 \text{ mg}$
    $470.45 \text{ mg}/3 = 156.82 \text{ mg}$
    Rounded to 157 mg per dose
13. **Correct Order: 1, 2, 3, 4**
    RATIONALE: The first step is to administer a short acting beta 2-agonist as needed. The second step is to administer a low-dose inhaled corticosteroid. The third step is to administer a medium-dose inhaled corticosteroid. The fourth step is to administer a medium-dose inhaled corticosteroid and a long-acting beta 2-agonist.

CHAPTER 41

SECTION I: ASSESSING YOUR UNDERSTANDING

Activity A FILL IN THE BLANKS

1. Angiography
2. Electrophysiologic
3. Narrowing
4. Pulmonary
5. 6 months
6. Acquired
7. Rheumatic fever

Activity B MATCHING

1. b   **2.** a   **3.** d   **4.** c   **5.** e

Activity C SEQUENCING

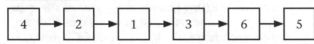

$$4 \rightarrow 2 \rightarrow 1 \rightarrow 3 \rightarrow 6 \rightarrow 5$$

Activity D SHORT ANSWERS

1. Digoxin is prescribed to increase contractility of the heart muscle by decreasing conduction and increasing force. It is commonly indicated for HF, atrial fibrillation, atrial flutters, and supraventricular tachycardia. Digoxin should be given at regular intervals, every 12 hours, such as 8 A.M. and 8 P.M., 1 hour before or 2 hours after feeding. If a digoxin dose is missed and more than 4 hours have elapsed, give the missed dose. If the child vomits digoxin, a second dose should not be given. Potassium levels should be carefully monitored as a decrease enhances the effects of digitalis causing toxicity. Digoxin should not be held if the child's heart rate is below or above normal ranges.

2. Heart murmurs must be evaluated on the basis of the following characteristics:
    Location
    Relation to the heart cycle and duration
    Intensity Grades I to VI
    Quality-harsh, musical, or rough in high, medium, or low pitch
    Variation with position (sitting, lying, standing)

3. The three types of ASDs are identified based on the location of the opening:
    Ostium primum (ASD1): the opening is located at the lower portion of the septum.
    Ostium secundum (ASD2): the opening is located near the center of the septum.
    Sinus venosus defect: the opening is located near the junction of the superior vena cava and the right atrium.

4. Ventricular septal defect (VSD) accounts for 30% of all congenital heart defects. By the age of 2 years approximately 50% of small VSDs spontaneously close, and VSDs that require surgical intervention have a high rate of success. Upon assessment, newborns may not exhibit any signs or symptoms. Signs and symptoms of heart failure typically occur at 4 to 6 weeks of age and may include easily tiring and/or color changes and diaphoresis during feeding; lack of thriving; pulmonary infections, tachypnea, or shortness of breath; edema; murmurs; thrill in the chest upon palpation.

5. Risk factors for infective endocarditis include children with:
    Congenital heart defects;
    Prosthetic heart valves;
    Central venous catheters;
    Intravenous drug use.

SECTION II: APPLYING YOUR KNOWLEDGE

Activity E CASE STUDY

1. The discussion should include:
    Prepare the parents and child for the procedure by discussing what the procedure involves, how long it will take, special instructions from the physician, and what to expect after the procedure is complete. Inform the parents of the possible complications that might occur, such as bleeding, low-grade fever, loss of pulse in the extremity used for the catheterization, and arrhythmias. Explain that the child will have a dressing over the catheter site and the leg may need to remain straight for several hours after the procedure. Discuss that frequent monitoring will be required after the procedure. Use a variety of teaching methods such as videotapes, books, and pamphlets. Discussion with the child should be age appropriate.
    Preprocedure care includes a thorough history and physical examination, including vital signs, to establish a baseline. The nurse should obtain height and weight to assist in determining medication dosages. The child should be assessed for allergies, especially iodine or shellfish, because some contrast material contain iodine as a base. The medication history as well as laboratory testing results should be reviewed. The nurse should keep in mind that some medications, such as anticoagulants, are typically held prior to the procedure to reduce the risk of bleeding. Peripheral pulses, including pedal pulses, should be assessed. The location of the child's pedal pulses should be marked in order to facilitate their

assessment after the procedure. Ensure informed consent has been obtained and a signed form is in the chart. Premedications ordered should be administered, and the parents should be allowed to accompany the child to the catheterization area if permitted.

2. Discussion should include:

Following the procedure, the child should be monitored for complications of bleeding, arrhythmia, hematoma, and thrombus formation and infection. Assessment includes vital signs, neurovascular status of the lower extremities (pulses, color, temperature, and capillary refill), and the pressure dressing over the catheterization site every 15 minutes for the first hour and then every 30 minutes for 1 hour (depending on hospital policy). Monitoring of cardiac rhythm and oxygen saturation levels for the first few hours after the procedure should occur. Maintain bedrest in the immediate post procedure period. The leg might need to be kept straight for approximately 4 to 8 hours, depending on the approach used and facility policy. Reinforcement of the pressure dressing as necessary should be performed, and any evidence of drainage on the dressing should be noted. The infant's intake and output should be monitored closely. The parents should be provided with post-care and follow-up care education prior to discharge.

SECTION III: PRACTICING FOR NCLEX

Activity F NCLEX-STYLE QUESTIONS

1. **Answer: B**
   RATIONALE: Softening of nail beds is the first sign of clubbing due to chronic hypoxia. Rounding of the fingernails is followed by shininess and thickness of nail ends.

2. **Answer: D**
   RATIONALE: The normal infant heart rate averages 90 to 160 beats per minute (bpm); the toddler's or preschooler's is 80 to 115, the school-aged child's is 60 to 100 bpm, and the adolescent's heart rate average 60 to 68 bpm.

3. **Answer: B**
   RATIONALE: The nurse should pay particular attention to assessing the child's peripheral pulses, including pedal pulses. Using an indelible pen, the nurse should mark the location of the child's pedal pulses as well as document the location and quality in the child's medical records.

4. **Answer: C**
   RATIONALE: Some medications, like corticosteroids, taken by pregnant women may be linked with the development of congenital heart defects. Reports of nausea during pregnancy and an Apgar score of 8 would not trigger further questions. Febrile illness during the first trimester, not the third, may be linked to an increased risk of congenital heart defects.

5. **Answer: A**
   RATIONALE: Edema of the lower extremities is characteristic of right ventricular heart failure in older children. In infants, peripheral edema occurs first in the face, then the presacral region, and the extremities.

6. **Answer: B**
   RATIONALE: A bounding pulse is characteristic of patent ductus arteriosis or aortic regurgitation. Narrow or thready pulses may occur in children with heart failure or severe aortic stenosis. A normal pulse would not be expected with aortic regurgitation.

7. **Answer: D**
   RATIONALE: An accentuated third heart sound is suggestive of sudden ventricular distention. Decreased blood pressure, cool, clammy, and pale extremities, and a heart murmur are all associated with cardiovascular disorders; however, these findings do not specifically indicate sudden ventricular distention.

8. **Answer: D**
   RATIONALE: A heart murmur characterized as loud with a precordial thrill is classified as Grade IV. Grade II is soft and easily heard. Grade I is soft and hard to hear. Grade III is loud without thrill.

9. **Answer: D**
   RATIONALE: The normal adolescent's blood pressure averages 100 to 120/70 to 80 mm Hg. The average infant's blood pressure is about 80/55 mm Hg. The toddler or preschooler's blood pressure averages 90 to 110/55 to 75 mm Hg. The normal school-ager's blood pressure averages 100 to 120/60 to 75 mm Hg.

10. **Answer: A**
    RATIONALE: A mild to late ejection click at the apex is typical of a mitral valve prolapse. Abnormal splitting or intensifying of S2 sounds occurs in children with heart problems, not mitral valve prolapse. Clicks on the upper left sternal border are related to the pulmonary area.

11. **Answer: A, B**
    RATIONALE: Abrupt cessation of chest tube output and an increased heart rate are indicators that the child may have developed cardiac tamponade. The child's right atrial filling pressure will increase. The child may be anxious and their apical heart rate may be faint and difficult to auscultate.

12. **Answer: C, D, E**
    RATIONALE: The nurse should not administer digoxin to children with the following issues: The adolescent with an apical pulse under 60 beats per minute, the child with a digoxin level above 2 ng/mL, and the child who exhibiting signs of digoxin toxicity.

13. **Answer: C, D**
    RATIONALE: Subcutaneous nodules and carditis are considered major criteria used in the diagnosing of acute rheumatic fever. The other options are minor criteria.

14. **Answer: B, C, D**
    RATIONALE: The following information should be reported to the physician following a cardiac

catheterization because they are indicative of possible complications: Negative changes to the child's peripheral vascular circulatory status (cool foot with poor pulse), a fever over 100.4°F (37.8°C), and nausea or vomiting.

15. Answer: 0.7

RATIONALE: The dose should be calculated weight in kilograms.

The infant weighs 6.81 kg. For each kilogram of body weight, the infant should receive 0.1 mg of morphine sulfate.

6.81 kg × 0.1 mg/1 kg = 0.681 mg

Rounded to the tenth place = 0.7 mg

The infant will receive 0.7 mg of morphine sulfate.

CHAPTER 42

SECTION I: ASSESSING YOUR UNDERSTANDING

Activity A FILL IN THE BLANKS

1. retching
2. atresia
3. 2
4. fungal
5. stones
6. Probiotic
7. intussusception

Activity B LABELING

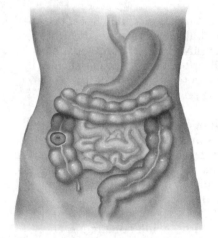 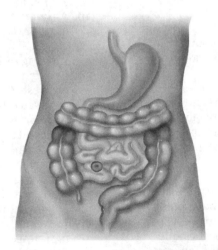

Activity C MATCHING

1. b   **2.** a   **3.** d   **4.** c   **5.** e

Activity D SEQUENCING

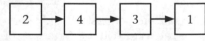

Activity E SHORT ANSWERS

1. (S) set up equipment, (T) take off the pouch, (O) observe the stoma and surrounding skin, (M) measure the stoma and mark the new pouch backing, (A) apply the new pouch.

2. The mouth is highly vascular making it a common entry point for infectious invaders. This increases the infant's and young child's risk for contraction of infectious agents via the mouth.
3. Acute hepatitis is mainly treated with rest, hydration, and nutrition.
4. Complications of a cleft palate that are of most concern during infancy pertain to feeding. The deformity often prevents the infant from being able to form an adequate seal around a nipple, preventing the ability to suction nutrients and cause excessive air intake. Feeding times are greatly extended, which causes insufficient intake and fatigue—both being precursors to problems with normal growth. Cleft palate during infancy also leads to gagging, choking, and nasal regurgitation of milk during feedings.
5. Data collected during the health history that would indicate pyloric stenosis include forceful, nonbilious vomiting that is not related to the feeding position of the infant, with subsequent weight loss, dehydration, and lethargy. These symptoms most commonly occur 2 to 4 weeks after birth. A positive family history of the disorder also increases the risk for pyloric stenosis. Physical assessment findings reveal a hard, movable "olive-like" area palpated in the right upper quadrant of the abdomen.

SECTION II: APPLYING YOUR KNOWLEDGE

Activity F CASE STUDY

1. The discussion should include weight loss of 6 oz in 2 weeks, sunken anterior fontanel, sticky mucous membranes, and poor skin turgor.
2. The discussion should include the following: The nurse should anticipate interventions that are going to rehydrate and restore Nico's fluid volume. Oral rehydration with pedialyte may be sufficient (refer to Teaching Guidelines 42.2). If dehydration appears to be severe, intravenous fluids may be

necessary with a bolus of 20 mL/kg of normal saline or lactated ringers. Blood for electrolytes may need to be drawn to assess the extent of dehydration.

3. To evaluate Nico's hydration status the nurse should assess his fontanels, mucous membranes, skin turgor, urine output, pulses, capillary refill, temperature of extremities, and eyes.

4. Medical management of gastroesophageal reflux disease (GERD) usually begins with appropriate positioning such as elevating the head of the crib 30 degrees and keeping the infant or child upright for 30 to 45 minutes after feeding. Smaller more frequent feedings with a nipple that controls flow well may be helpful. Explain to the family to frequently burp the infant during feeds. Thickening of formula or pumped breast milk with products such as rice cereal can help in keeping the feedings and gastric contents down. Positioning of an infant for sleep with GERD is controversial; infants can be positioned safely on their sides or upright in a car seat to minimize the risk of aspiration while on their backs. However, always check with the physician to discuss his or her recommendations regarding sleeping positions for infants with GERD. If reflux does not improve with these measures, medications are prescribed to decrease acid production and stabilize the pH of the gastric contents. Also, prokinetic agents may be used to help empty the stomach more quickly, minimizing the amount of gastric contents in the stomach that the child can reflux. If prescribed, thoroughly explain medications and their side effects and or adverse reactions. If the GERD cannot be medically managed effectively or requires long-term medication therapy, surgical intervention may be necessary. Explain to Nico's parents that reflux is usually limited to the first year of life; though, in some cases, it may persist. Teach Nico's parents and caregivers the signs and symptoms of potential complications. GERD symptoms can often involve the airway. In rare instances, GERD can cause apnea or acute life-threatening events (ALTEs). Teach parents how to deal with these episodes, as anxiety is very high. Provide CPR instruction to all parents whose children have had ALTE previously, and use of an apnea or bradycardia monitor may be warranted. The monitor requires a physician's order and can be ordered through a home health company.

SECTION III: PRACTICING FOR NCLEX

Activity G NCLEX-STYLE QUESTIONS

1. **Answer: D**
   RATIONALE: Infants are comprised of a high percentage of fluid that can be lost very quickly when vomiting, fever, and diarrhea are all present. This infant needs to be seen by the physician based on her age and symptoms; hospitalization may be necessary for intravenous rehydration depending upon her status when assessed.

2. **Answer: A**
   RATIONALE: Antinuclear antibodies are one of the diagnostic tests performed to diagnose autoimmune hepatitis. Ultrasound is to assess for liver or spleen abnormalities. Viral studies are performed to screen for viral causes of hepatitis. Ammonia levels may be ordered if hepatic encephalopathy is suspected.

3. **Answer: D**
   RATIONALE: If the parent reports that the child passed a meconium plug, the infant should be evaluated for Hirschsprung disease. Constipation, not diarrhea, is associated with this condition; however, constipation alone would not necessarily warrant further evaluation for Hirschsprung disease. Passing a meconium stool in the first 24 to 48 hours of life is normal.

4. **Answer: D**
   RATIONALE: While most fruits and fruit juices are allowed, the nurse needs to make sure the mother knows that some fruit pie fillings and dried fruit may contain gluten.

5. **Answer: B**
   RATIONALE: It is very important to encourage large amounts of water/fluids after this test to avoid barium-induced constipation. It is also important to tell the parents about a possible change in stool color, but the fluids are most important. This procedure is unlikely to cause an infection. Diarrhea is usually not a problem after this examination.

6. **Answer: C**
   RATIONALE: Tenting of skin is an indicator of severe dehydration. Soft and flat fontanels indicate mild dehydration. Pale and slightly dry mucosa indicates mild or moderate dehydration. Blood pressure of 80/42 mm Hg is a normal finding for an infant.

7. **Answer: D**
   RATIONALE: It is best to ask an open-ended question in very specific terms so that the nurse can assess for proper laxative use based on a recent history of stool patterns. Using the term daily stool patterns might be confusing to the parents. Asking the parents whether the laxatives are working may not elicit any helpful information. Asking whether they are giving him the laxatives properly would likely result in a positive response even if this is not accurate.

8. **Answer: A**
   RATIONALE: Ulcerative colitis is usually continuous through the colon while the distribution of Crohn disease is segmental. Crohn disease affects the full thickness of the intestine while ulcerative colitis is more superficial. Both conditions share age at onset of 10 to 20 years, with abdominal pain and fever in 40% to 50% of cases.

9. **Answer: D**
   RATIONALE: A hard, movable "olive-like mass" in the right upper quadrant is the hypertrophied pylorus. A sausage-shaped mass in the upper mid abdomen is the hallmark of intussusception.

Perianal fissures and skin tags are typical with Crohn disease. Abdominal pain and irritability are common with pyloric stenosis but are seen with many other conditions.

10. **Answer: A, D**
    RATIONALE: Hepatitis A virus is transmitted by contaminated food or water. Hepatitis B virus may be transmitted perinatally from mother to infant, intravenous drug use with contaminated needles, sexual contact with an infected person, and blood transfusions. The mother may have contracted the virus prior to giving birth to the child. Infection with the hepatitis B virus may result in jaundice, fever, and a rash.

11. **Answer: A, B, C**
    RATIONALE: Famotidine may cause fatigue. Omeprazole can cause headaches. Prokinetic use may result in side effects involving the central nervous system. Omeprazole use more likely will result in diarrhea, not constipation. Children with GERD should not lie down after meals.

12. **Answer: B**
    RATIONALE: Once any organic process is ruled out as a cause, constipation may initially be managed with dietary manipulation such as increasing fiber and fluids. However, behavior modification is necessary for most children. Children need to relearn to allow bowel evacuation when stool is present. Medications are used when other measures have failed. Frequent toileting may or may not be beneficial.

13. **Answer: A**
    RATIONALE: The child's presentation is consistent with cholecystitis, which necessitates surgery in most cases. The child should be kept NPO and antacids are of no benefit. Genitourinary involvement is atypical.

14. **Answer: 48**
    RATIONALE: Urine output should be calculated using weight in kilograms.
    6 kg × 1 mL/kg = 6 mL/hr
    6 mL × 8 hours = 48 mL/8-hour shift

15. **Answer: 289**
    RATIONALE: The child weighs 63.5 lb.
    63.5 lb × 1 kg/2.2 lb = 577.2727 mL
    577.2727 mL of normal saline/2 hours = 288.6364 mL
    Rounded to the nearest whole number = 289 mL/hr

CHAPTER 43

SECTION I: ASSESSING YOUR UNDERSTANDING

Activity A FILL IN THE BLANKS

1. Suppression
2. Testicular
3. Renal
4. Flow
5. Enuresis
6. 30 mL

Activity B LABELING

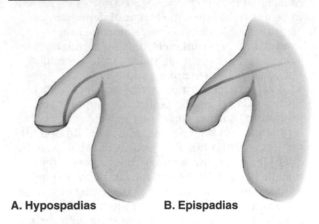

A. Hypospadias   B. Epispadias

Activity C MATCHING

Exercise 1
1. f   2. d   3. a   4. b   5. c

Exercise 2
1. c   2. d   3. b   4. a

Activity D SEQUENCING

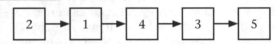

2 → 1 → 4 → 3 → 5

Activity E SHORT ANSWERS

1. After a bladder augmentation the urine may contain mucous.
2. The nurse should encourage fluids and monitor vital signs. The nurse must also be aware that child may feel burning with voiding after the procedure and urine may have a pink tinge because of the irritation of the mucous membrane as a result of the procedure.
3. Medications used in the care and treatment of end-stage renal disease may include:
   - Vitamin D/Calcium to correct hypocalcemia and hyperphosphatemia
   - Ferrous sulfate for anemia
   - Bicitra or sodium bicarbonate tablets to correct acidosis
   - Multivitamins to augment nutrition status
   - Erythropoietin injections to stimulate red blood cell growth
   - Growth hormone injections to stimulate growth in stature
4. A testicle is abnormally attached to the scrotum and twisted. It requires immediate attention because ischemia can result if the torsion is left untreated, leading to infertility. Testicular torsion may occur at any age but most commonly occurs in boys aged 12 to 18 years.
5. Normally both testes are descended at the time of birth. A watch and see approach is taken. If the testes are not descended by 6 months of age surgery is indicated.

SECTION II: APPLYING YOUR KNOWLEDGE
Activity F CASE STUDY

1. The discussion should include the following points:
Urinary tract infections (UTI) occur most often due to bacteria coming from the urethra and traveling up to the bladder. The most common organism that causes UTI is *Escherichia coli,* which is usually found in the perineal and anal region, close to the urethral opening. UTIs are very common in children, especially infants and young children and after 1 year of age are more common in females. One explanation for UTI occurring more frequently in females than in males is that the female's shorter urethra allows bacteria to have easier access to the bladder. Additionally, the female urethra is located quite close to the vagina and anus, allowing spread of bacteria such as *Escherichia coli* from those areas.

2. The discussion should include the following points:
Administer oral antibiotics as prescribed and complete the entire course of antibiotics even if Corey is feeling better and is not showing any signs or symptoms any longer. Push oral fluids, which will help flush the bacteria from the bladder. Administer antipyretics, such as acetaminophen or ibuprofen, in order to reduce fever. A heating pad or warm compress may help relieve abdomen or flank pain. If the child is afraid to urinate due to burning or stinging, encourage voiding in a warm sitz or tub bath.

3. The discussion should include the following points:
Encourage Corey and her family to follow-up as the physician has ordered for repeat urine culture after completing the course of antibiotics. Ensure Corey drinks adequate fluid to keep urine flushed through the bladder and prevent urine stasis. A decreased fluid intake can contribute to bacterial growth, as the bacteria become more concentrated. Encourage drinking of juices such as cranberry juice that will acidify the urine. If urine is alkaline, bacteria are better able to flourish. Avoid colas and caffeine which irritate the bladder. Encourage Corey to urinate frequently and avoid holding of urine to avoid urinary stasis which allows bacteria to grow. Avoid bubble baths which can contribute to vulvar and perineal irritation. Teach Corey to wipe front to back after using the restroom, to avoid contamination of the urethra with rectal material. Wearing of cotton underwear can decrease the incidence of perineal irritation. Avoid wearing of tight jeans or pants and wash the perineal area daily with soap and water.

SECTION III: PRACTICING FOR NCLEX
Activity G NCLEX-STYLE QUESTIONS

1. **Answer: C**
RATIONALE: The girl's partner should be treated, but she must strongly encourage the girl to require her partner to wear a condom every time they have sex, even after he undergoes antibiotic therapy. The other statements are accurate.

2. **Answer: C**
RATIONALE: Normally both testes will descend prior to birth. In the event this does not happen the child will be observed for the first 6 months of life. If the testicle descends without intervention further treatment will not be needed. Surgical intervention is not needed until after 6 months if the testicle has not descended.

3. **Answer: A**
RATIONALE: Epididymitis is caused by a bacterial infection. Treatment may include scrotal elevation, bed rest, and ice packs to the scrotum. Pharmacotherapy may include antibiotics, pain medications, and non-steroidal anti-inflammatory drugs (NSAIDs). Warm compresses would result in vasodilation and do little to relieve the pain and swelling of the condition. Corticosteroid therapy is not included in the plan of care for the condition. Voiding is not impacted by epididymitis. Catheterization is not indicated.

4. **Answer: D**
RATIONALE: The discharge instructions for the child who has had a circumcision will include a listing of warning signs to report. Redness or swelling of the penile shaft is not a normal finding and must be reported. Petroleum jelly is often used for the first 24 hours after the procedure but not for a period of 2 weeks. Small amounts of bleeding may be noted. This bleeding if scant in amount does not warrant reporting to the physician. Reduction of water to impact voiding is inappropriate.

5. **Answer: C**
RATIONALE: Urinalysis is ordered to reveal preliminary information about the urinary tract. The test evaluates color, pH, specific gravity, and odor of urine. Urinalysis also assesses for presence of protein, glucose, ketones, blood, leukocyte esterase, red blood cell count, white blood cell count, bacteria, crystals, and casts. Total protein, globulin, albumin, and creatinine clearance would be ordered for suspected renal failure or renal disease. Urine culture and sensitivity is used to determine the presence of bacteria and determine the best choice of antibiotic.

6. **Answer: C**
RATIONALE: Acute glomerulonephritis often follows a group A streptococcal infection. Strep A infections may manifest as an upper respiratory infection. The history of urinary tract infections, renal disorders, or hypotension is not directly associated with the onset of acute glomerulonephritis.

7. **Answer: B**
RATIONALE: The nurse should weigh the old dialysate to determine the amount of fluid removed from the child. The fluid must be weighed prior to emptying it. The nurse should weigh the new fluid prior to starting the next fill phase. Typically, the exchanges are 3 to 6 hours apart so the nurse would not immediately start the next fill phase.

8. **Answer: D**
RATIONALE: The girl cannot eat whatever she wants on dialysis days. She can eat what she wants during the few hours she is actively undergoing treatment

in the hemodialysis unit. The other statements regarding a high sodium diet and potassium intake are correct.

9. **Answer: C**
   RATIONALE: It is very important to administer in the morning, encourage large amounts of water/fluids and encourage frequent voiding during and after infusion to decrease the risk of hemorrhagic cystitis.

10. **Answer: B**
    RATIONALE: The best response would be to include the child in plans for nighttime urinary control. This gives the child a sense of hope and reminds him that there are actions he can take to help achieve dryness. Telling him that he will grow out of this does not offer solutions. Providing statistics can be helpful, but does not offer a solution. Reminding him that pull-ups look just like underwear does not address his concerns.

11. **Answer: C**
    RATIONALE: Hemolytic uremic syndrome is defined by all three particular features—hemolytic anemia, thrombocytopenia, and acute renal failure. Dirty green-colored urine, elevated erythrocyte sedimentation, and depressed serum complement level are indicative of acute glomerulonephritis. Hypertension, not hypotension, would be seen and the child would have decreased urinary output which would not cause nocturia.

12. **Answer: C**
    RATIONALE: The nurse should withhold routine medications in the morning that hemodialysis is scheduled since they would be filtered out through the dialysis process. His medications should be administered after he returns from the dialysis unit. A Tenckhoff catheter is used for peritoneal dialysis, not hemodialysis. The nurse should avoid blood pressure measurement in the extremity with the AV fistula as it may cause occlusion.

13. **Answer: D**
    RATIONALE: The nurse should always auscultate the site for presence of a bruit and palpate for presence of a thrill. The nurse should immediately notify the physician if there is an absence of a thrill. Dialysate without fibrin or cloudiness is normal and is used with peritoneal dialysis, not hemodialysis.

14. **Answer: A**
    RATIONALE: Complications of hydronephrosis include renal insufficiency, hypertension, and eventually renal failure. Hypotension, hypothermia, and tachycardia are not associated with hydronephrosis.

15. **Answer: A, C, E**
    RATIONALE: A VCUG will be performed to determine the presence of a structural defect that may be causing the hydronephrosis. Other diagnostic tests, such as a renal ultrasound or an intravenous pyelogram, may also be performed to clarify the diagnosis. A urinalysis may be performed to assess the quality and characteristics of the urine but the test will not confirm a diagnosis of hydronephrosis. A CBC may be used to assess the level of a genitourinary infection but it will not confirm the diagnosis of hydronephritis.

CHAPTER 44

SECTION I: ASSESSING YOUR UNDERSTANDING

Activity A FILL IN THE BLANKS

1. Epiphysis
2. Convex
3. Decrease
4. Involuntary
5. Hypotonia
6. Neural tube defects
7. Synovitis

Activity B LABELING

Figure A shows meningocele
Figure B shows myelomeningocele.
Figure C shows normal spine
Figure D shows spina bifida occulta

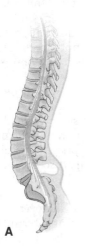
A

B

C

D

Activity C MATCHING

1. a   **2.** c   **3.** d   **4.** b   **5.** e

Activity D SHORT ANSWERS

1. The four classifications are spastic, athetoid (dyskinetic), ataxic, and mixed. Spastic is the most common form and ataxic is the rarest.
2. Nursing management of a child with myelomeningocele focuses on preventing infection, promoting bowel and urinary elimination, promoting adequate nutrition, and preventing latex allergic reaction. The nurse is also concerned with maintaining the child's skin integrity, providing education and support to the family, and recognizing complications such as hydrocephalus or increased intracranial pressure (ICP) associated with the disorder.
3. A plastic or bowing deformity involves significant bending without breaking of the bone. A buckle fracture is a compression injury; the bone "buckles" rather than breaks. A greenstick fracture is an incomplete fracture of the bone. A complete fracture occurs when the bone breaks into two separate pieces
4. Risk factors for neural tube defects include lack of prenatal care; insufficient intake of folic acid preconception and/or prenatally; previous history of a child born with a neural tube defect or a positive family history of neural tube defects; and certain drugs that antagonize folic acid absorption, such as anticonvulsants, that are taken by the mother during pregnancy.
5. There are nine types of muscular dystrophy, with Duchenne muscular dystrophy being the most common childhood type. All types of muscular dystrophy result in progressive skeletal (voluntary) muscle wasting and weakness. The disease is inherited, but there are various patterns of inheritance among the various types of muscular dystrophy.

SECTION II: APPLYING YOUR KNOWLEDGE

Activity E CASE STUDY 1

1. The discussion should include the following points:
   - Cerebral palsy (CP) is a term used to describe a range of nonspecific clinical symptoms characterized by abnormal motor pattern and postures caused by nonprogressive abnormal brain function. The cause of CP generally occurs before or during birth and is often associated with brain anoxia. Often no specific cause can be identified. Prolonged, complicated difficult birth and prematurity are risk factors for CP. CP is the most common movement disorder of childhood and is a life-long, nonprogressive condition. It is one of the most common causes of physical disability in children.
   - There is a large variation in symptoms and disability among those with CP. For some children the disability may be as mild as a slight limp and for others it may result in severe motor and neurologic impairments. However, its primary signs include motor impairment such as spasticity, muscle weakness, and ataxia. Complications of CP include mental impairment, seizures, growth problems, impaired vision or hearing, abnormal sensation or perception, and hydrocephalus. Most children can survive into adulthood but may endure substantial effects on function and quality of life.

2. The discussion should include the following points:
   - Earliest signs of cerebral palsy include abnormal muscle tone and developmental delay. Primary signs include spasticity, muscle weakness, and ataxia. Children with CP may demonstrate abnormal use of muscle groups such as scooting on their back instead of crawling or walking. Hypertonicity with increased resistance to dorsiflexion and passive hip abduction are common early signs. Sustained clonus may be present after forced dorsiflexion. Children with CP will often demonstrate prolonged standing on their toes when supported in an upright standing position.

3. The discussion should include the following points:
   - Nursing management focuses on promoting growth and development through the promotion of mobility and maintenance of optimal nutritional intake. Treatment modalities to promote mobility include physiotherapy, pharmacological management, and surgery. Physical or occupational therapy as well as medications may be used to address musculoskeletal abnormalities, facilitate range of motion, delay or prevent deformities such as contractures, provide joint stability, and to maximize activity and to encourage the use of adaptive devices. The nurse's role in relation to the various therapies is to ensure compliance with prescribed exercises, positioning, or bracing. Children with CP may experience difficulty eating and swallowing due to poor motor control of the throat, mouth, and tongue. This may lead to poor nutrition and problems with growth. The child with CP may require a longer time to feed because of the poor motor control. Special diets, such as soft or pureed, may make swallowing easier. Proper positioning during feeding is essential to facilitate swallowing and reduce the risk of aspiration. Speech or occupational therapists can assist in working on strengthening swallowing muscles as well as assisting in developing accommodations to facilitate nutritional intake. Consult a dietician to ensure adequate nutrition for children with cerebral palsy. In children with severe swallowing problems or malnutrition, a feeding tube such as a gastrostomy tube may be placed.
   - Providing support and education to the child and family is also an important nursing function. From the time of diagnosis, the family should be involved in the child's care. Refer caregivers to local resources including education services and support groups.

CASE STUDY 2

1. The discussion should include the following points:
   Drying time of the cast will vary depending on type of material used. Help the child keep the cast still and position it on pillows. If a plaster cast has been applied, "petal" the cast with moleskin or other soft material that has adhesive backing in order to prevent skin rubbing. Perform frequent neurovascular checks of the casted extremity. Assess for signs of increased pain, edema, pale or blue discoloration, skin coolness, numbness or tingling, prolonged capillary refill, and decreased pulse strength (if able to assess). Notify physician of changes in neurovascular status, persistent complaints of pain, odor, or drainage from the cast. Elevate casted extremity and apply ice if needed.

2. The discussion should include the following points:
   The child can resume increased levels of activity as the pain subsides. The right arm should be elevated above the level of the heart for the first 48 hours. Ice may be applied for 20 to 30 minutes, then off 1 hour and repeat for the first 24 to 48 hours. Check his right fingers for swelling (have him wiggle his fingers) hourly. Check the skin around the cast for irritation daily. If he reports itching inside the cast blow cool air in from a hair dryer set on the lowest setting. Never insert anything into the cast for scratching and do not use lotions or powders. Keep the cast dry. Apply a plastic bag around the cast and tape securely for bathing or showering. Do not let the child submerge the cast in a bathtub. Call the physician if the casted extremity is cool to touch; inability to move his fingers; severe pain occurs with movement of his fingers; persistent numbness or tingling; drainage or a foul smell comes from the cast; severe itching inside the cast; temperature above 101.5°F for longer than 24 hours; skin edges are red, swollen, or exhibit breakdown; or the casts gets wet, cracks, splits, or softens. Educate the family on follow-up needs and medications (including pain medication) if ordered.

SECTION III: PRACTICING FOR NCLEX

Activity F NCLEX-STYLE QUESTIONS

1. **Answer: B**
   RATIONALE: The baby will most likely wear the harness for 3 months. Telling the parents that the harness does not hurt the baby is appropriate, but stressing the importance of wearing the harness continuously is a higher priority to ensure proper care and effective treatment. Only the physician or nurse practitioner can make adjustments to the harness.

2. **Answer: A**
   RATIONALE: Asymmetry of the thigh or gluteal folds is indicative of DDH. Hip and knee joint relationship are not indicative of DDH. The lower extremities of the infant typically have some normal developmental variations due to in utero positioning.

3. **Answer: A**
   RATIONALE: It is important to be vigilant in inspecting the child's skin for rashes, redness, and irritation to uncover areas where pressure sores are likely to develop. Applying lotion is part of the routine skin care regimen. Applying lotion, gentle massage, and keeping skin dry and clean are part of the routine skin care regimen.

4. **Answer: C**
   RATIONALE: In Type II metatarsus adductus, the forefoot is flexible passively past neutral, but only to midline actively. The forefoot is flexible past neutral actively and passively in Type I. The forefoot is rigid, does not correct to midline even with passive stretching in Type III. An inverted forefoot turned slightly upward is indicative of clubfoot.

5. **Answer: B**
   RATIONALE: It is very important to teach parents to identify the signs of neurovascular compromise (pale, cool, or blue skin) and tell them to notify the physician immediately. The other statements are correct.

6. **Answer: C**
   RATIONALE: The best response for a 6-year old is to use distraction throughout the cast application. He is resisting the application of the cast, so the best approach at this point is distraction. Telling him that application will not hurt is not helpful; nor is asking the child whether he wants pain medication. It is helpful to enlist the cooperation of the child by showing the child cast materials before beginning the procedure; but if he is resisting treatment, distraction would be the best approach.

7. **Answer: C**
   RATIONALE: The nurse should emphasize that the child should not be allowed to lie on his side for 4 weeks following the surgery to ensure the bar does not shift. The parents should be aware of signs of infection; but the position must be emphasized to protect the bar. The nurse would be expected to monitor the child's vital capacity, not the parents. The prone position is acceptable.

8. **Answer: A**
   RATIONALE: The Ilizarov fixator uses wires that are thinner than ordinary pins, so simply cleansing by showering is usually sufficient to keep the pin site clean.

9. **Answer: D**
   RATIONALE: Because the mother is crying and experiencing the initial shock of the diagnosis, the nurse's primary concern is to support the mother and assure her that she is not to blame for the DDH. While education is important, the nurse should let the mother adjust to the diagnosis and assure her that the baby and her family will be supported now and throughout the treatment period.

10. **Answer: D**
    RATIONALE: Blue sclera is not diagnostic of osteogenesis imperfecta, but it is a common finding. Foot drawn up and inward (talipes varus) and sole

of foot facing backward (talipes equinus) are associated with clubfoot. Dimpled skin and hair in the lumbar region are common findings with spina bifida occulta.

11. **Answer: A, B**
RATIONALE: This child has taken a benzodiazepine. Common side effects associated with this medication are dizziness and sedation. The skeletal muscle relaxes and the spasms will diminish. Nausea and upper gastrointestinal pain are not common side effects associated with this medication.

12. **Answer: B, C, E**
RATIONALE: The parents should call the physician when the following things occur: The child has a temperature greater than 101.5°F (38.7°C) for more than 24 hours, there is drainage from the casted site, the site distal to the casted extremity is cyanotic, or severe edema is present.

13. **Answer: B, C, D, E**
RATIONALE: Slipped capital femoral epiphysis most often occurs in males between the ages of 12 and 15 years. It more commonly affects African-American boys. The femoral plate weakens and becomes less resistant to stressors during periods of growth. Boys are more frequently affected. Obese boys are more likely to develop this condition.

14. **Answer: B**
RATIONALE: The nurse needs to obtain a clear description of weakness. This open-ended question would most likely elicit specific examples of weakness and shed light on whether the boy is simply fatigued. The other questions would most likely elicit a yes or no answer rather than any specific details about his weakness or development.

15. **Answer: D**
RATIONALE: The persistence of a primitive reflex in a 9-month-old would warrant further evaluation. Symmetrical spontaneous movement and absence of the Moro and tonic neck reflex are expected in a normally developing 9-month-old child.

16. **Answer: B**
RATIONALE: Dimpling and skin discoloration in the child's lumbosacral area can be an indication of spina bifida occulta. It would be best to respond that the dimpling and discoloration is possibly a normal variation with no problems and indicate that the doctor will want to take a closer look; this response will not alarm the parent, but it also does not ignore the findings. Spina bifida is a term that is often used to generalize all neural tube disorders that affect the spinal cord. This can be confusing and a cause of concern for parents. It is probably best to avoid the use of the term initially until a diagnosis is confirmed. Nursing care would then focus on educating the family.

17. **Answer: C**
RATIONALE: Symptoms of constipation and bladder dysfunction may result due to an increasing size of the lesion. Increasing ICP and head circumference would point to hydrocephalus. Leaking cerebrospinal fluid would indicate the sac is leaking.

18. **Answer: B**
RATIONALE: It is very important to remind the parents that they must always wash hands very well with soap and water prior to catheterization to help prevent infection. The other statements are correct.

19. **Answer: C**
RATIONALE: The best response would be to remind the boy that there are many children with muscular dystrophy that could be found at the local support group. Teenagers do not like to be told that they "have" to do anything. Telling the boy that he needs to be active or simply suggesting activities does not address his concerns.

20. **Answer: A**
RATIONALE: A sign of Duchenne muscular dystrophy (DMD) is Gowers sign or the inability of the child to rise from the floor in the standard fashion because of weakness. Signs of hydrocephalus are not typically associated with DMD. Kyphosis and scoliosis occur more frequently than lordosis. A child with DMD has an enlarged appearance to their calf muscles due to pseudohypertrophy of the calves.

21. **Answer: D**
RATIONALE: The nurse can offer the child a snack and observe if she has any difficulty chewing, swallowing, or feeding herself. Inquiring about a typical day's diet opens up the conversation to discuss the quantity and quality of food the girl eats. Asking about swallowing or whether the girl feeds herself would most likely elicit a yes or no response. Checking her hydration status and respiratory system is important, but does not open a dialogue.

22. **Answer: A**
RATIONALE: The use of ticking is often a successful technique for assessing the level of paralysis in this age of child, either initially or in the recovery phase. Symmetrical flaccid weakness, ataxia, and sensory disturbances are other symptoms seen during the course of the illness.

23. **Answer: B**
RATIONALE: The central nursing priority is to prevent rupture or leaking of cerebrospinal fluid. Keeping infant in prone position will help prevent pressure on lesion. Keeping lesion free from fecal matter or urine is important as well, but the priority is to prevent rupture or leakage. The nurse should consider the lesion first when maintaining the infant's body temperature.

24. **Answer: A, C, D, E**
RATIONALE: Ditropan is used to increase the child's bladder capacity when they have a spastic bladder. The caregivers and the child should be taught about urinary catheterization techniques to allow the bladder to empty. The child and caregivers should be educated about the clinical manifestations associated with a urinary tract infection so that it can be treated promptly. Sometimes surgical interventions such as vesicostomy and the creation of a continent urinary reservoir are used to treat neurogenic bladders.

25. **Answer: A, B, D**
RATIONALE: Significant muscle wasting is associated with this diagnosis. Creatine kinase levels increase with muscle wasting. A muscle biopsy will show an absence of dystrophin. Gowers' sign will be positive. An electromyogram will indicate the problem is with the muscles, not the nerves. Genetic testing will reveal the presence of the gene associated with Duchenne muscular dystrophy.

26. **Answer: A, B, D, E**
RATIONALE: The following are clinical manifestations associated with cholinergic crisis: Sweating, bradycardia, severe muscle weakness, and increased salivation.

27. **Answer: A, B**
RATIONALE: Corticosteroids should be given with food to minimize gastric upset. Corticosteroids can mask infection. This child should avoid large crowds to prevent exposure to infectious organisms. The other parent responses are correct regarding corticosteroids and dermatomyositis.

28. **Answer: 1**
RATIONALE: The supplement has 5 µg of vitamin D in each 0.5 mL. The child is supposed to receive 10 µg each day of supplemental vitamin D.
Desired/Have × Quantity = dose
10 µg/5 µg × 0.5 mL = 1.0 mL
Ratio/proportion:
0.5 mL/5 µg = x/10 µg = 1.0 mL

29. **Correct Order: A, B, C, D**
RATIONALE: Guillain–Barré syndrome paresthesias and muscle weakness. Classically it initially affects the lower extremities and progresses in an ascending manner to upper extremities and then the facial muscles. Progression is usually complete in 2 to 4 weeks, followed by a stable period leading to the recovery phase.

CHAPTER 45

SECTION I: ASSESSING YOUR UNDERSTANDING

Activity A FILL IN THE BLANKS

1. Decreases
2. IgE
3. Hypersensitivity
4. Cradle cap
5. Androgens

Activity B MATCHING

Exercise 1

1. b   2. c   3. d   4. a   5. e

Exercise 2

1. d   2. c   3. a   4. b

Activity C SEQUENCING

2 → 5 → 3 → 4 → 1

Activity D SHORT ANSWERS

1. Dark-skinned children tend to have more pronounced cutaneous reactions compared to children with lighter skin. Hypopigmentation or hyperpigmentation in the affected area following healing of a dermatologic condition is common.
   Dark-skinned children tend to have more prominent papules, follicular response lichenification, and vesicular or bullous reaction than lighter-skinned children with the same disorder. Additionally, hypertrophic scarring and keloid formation occur more often.

2. Four criteria to describe lesions:
   - Linear refers to lesions in a line
   - Shape: The lesions are round, oval, or annular (ring around central clearing)
   - Morbilliform refers to a rosy, maculopapular rash
   - Target lesions look just like a bull's eye

3. Impetigo is a readily recognizable skin rash. Nonbullous impetigo generally follows some type of skin trauma or may arise as a secondary bacterial infection of another skin disorder, such as atopic dermatitis. Bullous impetigo demonstrates a sporadic occurrence pattern and develops on intact skin resulting from toxin production of *Staphylococcus aureus*.

4. Pressure ulcers develop from a combination of factors, including immobility or decreased activity, decreased sensory perception, increased moisture, impaired nutritional status, inadequate tissue perfusion, and the forces of friction and shear. Common sites of pressure ulcers in hospitalized children include the occipital region and toes, while children who require wheelchairs for mobility have pressure ulcers in the sacral or hip area more frequently.

5. Acne vulgaris affects 50% to 85% of adolescents between the ages of 12 and 16 years. The sebaceous gland produces sebum and is connected by a duct to the follicular canal that opens on the skin's surface. Androgenous hormones stimulate sebaceous gland proliferation and production of sebum. These hormones exhibit increased activity during the pubertal years.

SECTION II: APPLYING YOUR KNOWLEDGE

Activity E CASE STUDY

1. The skin reaction seen in atopic dermatitis is in response to specific allergens (such as food or environmental triggers). So when Eva comes into contact with the triggers it causes her body to respond and her skin starts to feel itchy. This sensation of itchiness comes first and then the rash becomes apparent. Other factors such as high or low temperatures, perspiring, contact with skin irritants (such as fragrance in soaps), scratching, or stress can also trigger the skin to flare up.

2. Management of atopic dermatitis focuses on promoting skin hydration, maintaining skin integrity, and preventing infection. Parents and

caregivers need to be instructed to avoid hot water and any skin and hair products that contain perfumes, dyes, or fragrances. Bathing the child twice a day in warm water using a mild soap for sensitive skin is encouraged. Do not rub the child dry but gently pat them and leave the child moist. Apply prescribed ointments or creams to affected areas. Apply fragrance-free moisturizers. Re-moisturize multiple times throughout the day. Avoid clothing made of synthetic fabrics or wool. Avoid triggers (often food, especially eggs, wheat, milk, and peanut, or environmental triggers such as molds, dust mites, and cat dander) known to exacerbate atopic dermatitis. Cut the child's finger nails short and keep them clean. Avoid tight clothing and heat. Use 100% cotton bed sheets and pajamas. It is very important to stop the child from scratching since this causes the rash to appear and causes trauma to the skin and secondary infection. Antihistamines given at bedtime may sedate the child enough to allow for sleep without awakening because of itching. During the waking hours, behavior modification may help to keep the child from scratching. The parents should keep a diary for 1 week to determine the pattern of scratching. Discuss specific strategies that may raise the child's awareness of scratching such as use of a hand-held clicker or counter to help identify the scratching episode for the child, thus raising awareness. Discuss the use of diversion, imagination, and play to help to detract Eva from scratching. Pressing the skin or fist clenching may replace scratching. Keep the child active and positively reinforce by praising desired behaviors.

SECTION III: PRACTICING FOR NCLEX

Activity F NCLEX-STYLE QUESTIONS

1. **Answer: C**
   RATIONALE: Airway injury from burn or smoke inhalation should be suspected if stridor is present. Cervical spine or internal injures would not point to airway injury. Burns on hands would not be indicative of airway injury.

2. **Answer: C**
   RATIONALE: Initially, the severely burned child first experiences a decrease in cardiac output with a subsequent hypermetabolic response during which cardiac output increases dramatically. During this heightened metabolic state, the child is at risk for insulin resistance and increased protein catabolism.

3. **Answer: D**
   RATIONALE: Staphylococcal scalded skin syndrome results from infection with *Staphylococcus aureus* that produces a toxin which then causes exfoliation. It is abrupt in onset and results in diffuse erythema and skin tenderness. It is most common in infancy and rare beyond 5 years of age. Bullous impetigo presents with red macules and bullous eruptions on an erythematous base. Nonbullous

impetigo presents as papules progressing to vesicles then painless pustules with a narrow erythematous border. Folliculitis presents with red raised hair follicles.

4. **Answer: C**
   RATIONALE: The nurse should emphasize that the parents should avoid hot water. The child should be bathed twice a day in warm water. The other statements are correct.

5. **Answer: A**
   RATIONALE: Tinea pedis presents with red scaling rash on soles, and between the toes. Tinea capitis presents with patches of scaling in the scalp with central hair loss and the risk of kerion development (inflamed boggy mass filled with pustules). Tinea cruris presents with erythema, scaling, maceration in the inguinal creases and inner thighs.

6. **Answer: B**
   RATIONALE: Small round red circles with scaling, symmetrically located on the girls' inner thighs point to nickel dermatitis that may occur from contact with jewelry, eyeglasses, belts, or clothing snaps. The nurse should inquire about any sleepers or clothing with metal snaps. The girl does not have a rash in her diaper area. It is unlikely that an infant in this age would have her inner thighs exposed to a highly allergenic plant. Discussing family allergy history is important, but the nurse should first inquire about any clothing with metal that could have come into contact with the girl's skin when she displays a symmetrical rash.

7. **Answer: A**
   RATIONALE: Erythema multiforme typically manifests in lesions over the hands and feet, and extensor surfaces of the extremities with spread to the trunk. Thick or flaky/greasy yellow scales are signs of seborrhea. Silvery or yellow-white scale plaques and sharply demarcated borders define psoriasis. Superficial tan or hypopigmented oval-shaped scaly lesions specially on upper back and chest and proximal arms are indicative of tinea versicolor.

8. **Answer: C**
   RATIONALE: The nurse should administer diphenhydramine as soon as possible after the sting in an attempt to minimize a reaction. The other actions are important for an insect sting, but the priority intervention is to administer diphenhydramine.

9. **Answer: B**
   RATIONALE: Second degree frostbite demonstrates blistering with erythema and edema. First degree frostbite results in superficial white plaques with surrounding erythema. In third-degree frostbite, the nurse would note hemorrhagic blisters that would progress to tissue necrosis and sloughing when the fourth degree is reached.

10. **Answer: A**
    RATIONALE: It is important to apply moisture multiply times through the day. Petroleum jelly is a recommended moisturizer that is

inexpensive and readily available. The other statements are correct.

11. Answer: A
RATIONALE: Impetigo is an infectious bacterial infection. The crusts should be removed after soaking prior to applying topical medications. Leaving the lesions open to air is not contraindicated. Children diagnosed with impetigo may attend school during treatment.

12. Answer: C
RATIONALE: Tinea pedis is commonly known as athlete's foot. It is a fungal infection. The fungi are able to readily grow in warm, moist conditions such as shower areas.

13. Answer: A, B, C
RATIONALE: The treatment of diaper rash may include topical ointments containing vitamins A and D as well as zinc.

14. Answer: A
RATIONALE: Atopic dermatitis is commonly associated allergies to food. Common culprits may include peanuts, eggs, orange juice, and wheat-containing products.

15. Answer: B, C, E
RATIONALE: When caring for the child with atopic dermatitis the focus of care will be on the prevention of infection, maintenance of skin integrity, and promotion of skin hydration.

CHAPTER 46

SECTION I: ASSESSING YOUR UNDERSTANDING

Activity A FILL IN THE BLANKS

1. Hemogram
2. Volume
3. Sepsis
4. Size
5. Limb salvage
6. Mean platelet volume (MPV)
7. Anemia
8. Leukemia

Activity B LABELING

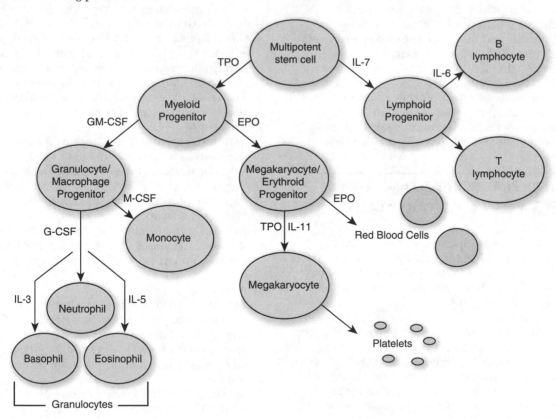

Activity C MATCHING

Exercise 1

| **1.** e | **2.** c | **3.** d | **4.** b | **5.** a |

Exercise 2

| **1.** c | **2.** b | **3.** d | **4.** e | **5.** a |

Activity D SHORT ANSWERS

1. There are a number of differences between childhood and adult cancer: Most common sites for childhood cancer are blood, lymph, brain, bone, kidney, and muscle. The most common sites for adult cancer are breast, lung, prostate, bowel, and

bladder; Environmental factors have a strong influence on the cause of adult cancers versus minimal influence on childhood cancer; and childhood cancers are typically very responsive to treatment if diagnosed early enough, whereas adult cancers tend to be less responsive to treatment.

2. The recommended action is to confirm the level with a repeat lab within 1 week, as well as educate the caregivers to decrease lead exposure. Refer the family to the local health department for investigation of the home for lead reduction with referrals for support services.

3. Color changes to the skin such as pallor, bruising, and flushing. Changes in mental status such as lethargy can also indicate a decrease in hemoglobin and decreased oxygenation of the brain.

4. Sickle cell anemia is most commonly seen in persons of African, Mediterranean, Middle Eastern, and Indian decent. In the United States, the number of infants born with sickle cell anemia is approximately 2,000, with 1 in 400 being African American.

5. Iron deficiency anemia occurs when the body does not have enough iron to produce Hgb, often related to dietary issues. Children between the ages of 6 and 20 months, and those at the age of puberty are the periods when iron deficiency anemia is most prevalent.

SECTION II: APPLYING YOUR KNOWLEDGE

Activity E CASE STUDY 1

1. The discussion should include:
   - How much milk does Jayda drink per day? (excessive cow's milk consumption, greater than 24 oz a day, leads to an increased risk for iron deficiency anemia)
   - When did Jayda start on cow's milk? (cow's milk consumption before 12 months of age leads to an increased risk for iron deficiency anemia)
   - Was Jayda formula fed? If so, what type (low iron formula can lead to iron deficiency anemia); or breast fed? If so, did she receive iron supplementation (including eating iron-fortified cereal) after 6 months of age?
   - What are Jayda's food preferences and usual eating patterns?
   - Is she on any restricted diet?
   - Is she taking any medications? (certain medications, such as antacids can interfere with iron absorption)

2. The discussion should include:
   - Oral supplements or multivitamin formulas that have iron are often dark in color as the iron is pigmented. Teaching of Jayda's parents should include to precisely measure the amount of iron to be administered and to be sure to place the liquid behind the teeth since iron in liquid form can stain the teeth. Use of straw and brushing her teeth after administration may help. Another

problem that frequently occurs is constipation from the iron. In some cases reduction of the amount of iron can resolve this problem, but stool softeners may be necessary to control painful or difficult to pass stools. Encourage parents to increase their child's fluid intake and maintain adequate consumption of fiber to assist in avoiding the development of constipation. Instruct the parents that stools may appear dark in color due to iron administration. Instruct parents to keep iron supplements and all medications in a safe place to avoid accidental overdose.
   - Providing juice enriched with vitamin C can help aid absorption of iron. Limit cow's milk intake to 24 oz per day. Limit fast food consumption and encourage iron-rich foods such as red meats, tuna, salmon, eggs, tofu, enriched grains, dried beans and peas, dried fruits, leafy green vegetables, and iron-fortified breakfast cereals (iron from red meat is the easiest for the body to absorb). Encourage parents to provide nutritious snacks and finger foods that are developmentally appropriate for Jayda. Toddlers are often picky eaters. This often becomes a means of control for the child, and parents should guard against getting involved in a power struggle with their child. Referring parents to a developmental nurse practitioner that can assist them in their approach to diet with their child may prove beneficial.
   - Encourage appropriate follow-up and review signs and symptoms of anemia.

3. The discussion should include:
   - Low socioeconomic status which can lead to a lack of adequate food supply
   - Recent immigration from a developing country
   - Culturally based food influences that lead to dietary imbalances
   - Child abuse or neglect leading to improper nutrition

CASE STUDY 2

1. The discussion should include the following:

   The child, who has a low neutrophil count (neutropenia), is at a significant risk for developing a serious infection since neutrophils are the primary infection fighting cells.

   Neutropenia precautions need to be instituted for this child. Precautions related to neutropenia generally include:

   Family and visitors must be educated regarding the need to restrict the child from contact with known infectious exposures and the importance of practicing meticulous hand hygiene. The family should also be educated on the importance of proper nutrition, hydration, and rest for the child.
   - Maintain hand hygiene prior to and following each child contact
   - Place child in private room
   - Monitor vital signs every 4 hours

- Assess for signs and symptoms of infection at least every 8 hours
- Avoid rectal suppositories, enemas or examinations, urinary catheterization, and invasive procedures
- Restrict visitors with fever, cough, or other signs/symptoms of infection
- No raw fruits or vegetables, no fresh flowers or live plants in room
- Place mask on the child when transporting outside of room
- Maintain dental care with soft toothbrush if platelet count is adequate

2. The discussion should include the following:
   Teach the family to monitor for fever at home and report temperature elevations to the oncologist immediately (Seek medical care if temperature is 38.3°C (101°F) or greater). Family and visitors must practice meticulous hygiene. The child should avoid any known ill contacts, especially persons with chickenpox. If exposed to chickenpox notify the physician immediately. He should avoid crowded areas, and should not receive live vaccines. The child's temperature should not be taken rectally nor should he be given any medication rectally. Prophylactic antibiotics should be given as ordered by the physician.

3. The discussion should include the following:
   Children desire to be normal and in order to maintain appropriate growth and development; parents need to promote this normalization. The child should attend school whenever he is well enough and his white blood cell counts are not dangerously low. Other activities that he enjoys should be promoted if medically appropriate. Encourage him to play with his friends while remembering to avoid ill contacts. Special camps are available for children with cancer and offer the child an opportunity to experience a variety of activities safely and to spend time with many other youngsters who are experiencing the same challenges.

SECTION III: PRACTICING FOR NCLEX

Activity F NCLEX-STYLE QUESTIONS

1. **Answer: C**
   RATIONALE: The parents should seek medical care immediately if the child has a temperature of 101°F (38.3°C) or greater. This is because many chemotherapeutic drugs cause bone marrow suppression; the parents must be directed to take action at the first sign of infection in order to prevent overwhelming sepsis. The appearance of earache, stiff neck, sore throat, blisters, ulcers, or rashes, or difficulty or pain when swallowing are reasons to seek medical care, but are not as grave as the risk of infection.

2. **Answer: B, C, D, E**
   RATIONALE: Observation revealing a thick, yellow discharge is typical of infectious conjunctivitis, not retinoblastoma. Headaches and hyphema, a

collection of blood in the anterior chamber of the eye, are associated with retinoblastoma as is leukocoria, "cat's eye reflex." Health history reveals associated symptoms, including strabismus.

3. **Answer: A**
   RATIONALE: The priority intervention is to monitor for increases in intracranial pressure because brain tumors may block cerebral fluid flow or cause edema in the brain. A change in the level of consciousness is just one of several subtle changes that can occur indicating a change in intracranial pressure. Lower priority interventions include providing a tour of the ICU to prepare the child and parents for after the surgery, and educating the child and parents about shunts.

4. **Answer: B**
   RATIONALE: Ewing sarcoma may result in swelling and erythema at the tumor site. Common sites are chest wall, pelvis, vertebrae, and long bone diaphyses. Dull bone pain in the proximal tibia is indicative of osteosarcoma. Persistent pain after an ankle injury is not indicative of Ewing sarcoma. An asymptomatic mass on the upper back suggests rhabdomyosarcoma.

5. **Answer: A, C, D, E**
   RATIONALE: Telling the group that Testicular cancer is one of the most difficult cancers to cure would not be part of the teaching plan. It would be more accurate and appropriate for the nurse to stress that testicular cancer is one of the most curable cancers if diagnosed early. Self-examination is an excellent way to screen for the disease. Girls should know that they can take responsibility for their own sexual health by getting a PAP smear. All the children should understand that early intercourse, sexually transmitted infections (STIs), and multiple sex partners are risk factors for reproductive cancer. Information should be provided so the teen girls can discuss the benefits of receiving the human papilloma virus vaccine since many cervical cancers are attributed to human papillomavirus.

6. **Answer: C**
   RATIONALE: Giving medications as ordered using the least invasive route is a postsurgery intervention focused on providing atraumatic care and is appropriate for this child. Since the child has a stage I tumor, it can be treated by surgical removal, and does not require chemotherapy or radiation therapy. Applying aloe vera lotion is good skin care following radiation therapy. Administering antiemetics and maintaining isolation are interventions used to treat side effects of chemotherapy.

7. **Answer: D**
   RATIONALE: Increased heart rate, murmur, and respiratory distress are symptoms of hyperleukocytosis (high white blood cell count) which is associated with leukemia. Increased heart rate and blood pressure are indicative of tumor lysis syndrome, which may occur with acute lymphoblastic leukemia, lymphoma, and neuroblastoma. Wheezing and

diminished breath sounds are signs of superior vena cava syndrome related to non-Hodgkin lymphoma or neuroblastoma. Respiratory distress and poor perfusion are symptoms of massive hepatomegaly which is caused by a neuroblastoma filling a large portion of the abdominal cavity.

8. **Answer: A**
   RATIONALE: Coupled with the mother's reports, observation of nystagmus and head tilt suggest the child may have a brain tumor. Elevated blood pressure of 120/80 mm Hg may be indicative of Wilms tumor. Fever and headaches are common symptoms of acute lymphoblastic leukemia. A cough and labored breathing points to rhabdomyosarcoma near the child's airway.

9. **Answer: B**
   RATIONALE: Along with the symptoms reported by the mother, the fact that the child has Beckwith–Wiedemann syndrome suggests that the child could have a Wilms tumor. Down syndrome would point to leukemia or brain tumor. Shwachman syndrome would suggest leukemia. A family history of neurofibromatosis is a risk factor for brain tumor, rhabdomyosarcoma, or acute myelogenous leukemia.

10. **Answer: A**
    RATIONALE: It would not be necessary for the nurse to inform the parents about postoperative care since this is not a treatment method for the disease. The treatment of choice for Hodgkin disease is chemotherapy, but radiation therapy may be necessary; however, discussing the treatment methods may be overwhelming at this time. Upon first learning the diagnosis, it is most helpful for the nurse to explain that staging refers to the spread of the disease (stages I through IV); and that A means the child is asymptomatic, while B means that symptoms are present.

11. **Answer: A, C, D, E**
    RATIONALE: Common adverse effects of chemotherapeutic drugs are immunosuppression, alopecia, hearing changes, and nausea. Another common adverse effect is microdontia, not enlarged teeth.

12. **Answer: A, B**
    RATIONALE: The child in neutropenic precautions should be placed in a private room. Prior to transportation to other areas of the hospital, the nurse should place a mask on the child before she leaves her room. The nurse should monitor the child's vital signs at least every 4 hours. The nurse should carefully assess for signs and symptoms of infection at least every 8 hours. The nurse should perform hand hygiene before and after contact with each child.

13. **Answer: B**
    RATIONALE: If neurological deficits are assessed, immediate reporting of the findings is necessary to begin treatment to prevent permanent damage.

14. **Answer: D**
    RATIONALE: A convex shape of the fingernails termed "spooning" can occur with iron deficiency anemia.

Capillary refill in less than 2 seconds, pink palms and nail beds, and absence of bruising are normal findings.

15. **Answer: A**
    RATIONALE: When the MCV is elevated, the RBCs are larger and referred to as macrocytic. The WBC count does not affect the MCV. The platelet count and Hgb are within normal ranges for a 7-year-old child.

16. **Answer: D**
    RATIONALE: If the screening test result indicates the possibility of SCA or sickle cell trait, hemoglobin (Hgb) electrophoresis is performed promptly to confirm the diagnosis. While Hgb electrophoresis is the only definitive test for diagnosis of the disease, other laboratory testing that assists in the assessment of the disease include reticulocyte count (greatly elevated), peripheral blood smears (presence of sickle-shaped cells and target cells), and erythrocyte sedimentation rate (elevated).

17. **Answer: A**
    RATIONALE: While iron from red meat is the easiest for the body to absorb, the nurse must limit fast food consumption from the drive-thru as they are also high in fat, fillers, and sodium. The other statements are correct.

18. **Answer: B**
    RATIONALE: The best response for a 7-year old is to use distraction and involve him in the infusion process in a developmentally appropriate manner. A 7-year old is old enough to assist with the dilution and mixing of the factor. Asking for help with the band-aid would be best for a younger child. Teens should be taught to administer their own factor infusions. Telling him to be brave is not helpful and does not teach.

19. **Answer: A**
    RATIONALE: The priority is to emphasize to the parents that they precisely measure the amount of iron to be administered in order to avoid overdosing. The other instructions are accurate, but the priority is to emphasize precise measurement.

20. **Answer: C**
    RATIONALE: Symmetrical swelling of the hands and feet in the infant or toddler is termed dactylitis; aseptic infarction occurs in the metacarpals and metatarsals and is often the first vaso-occlusive event seen with sickle cell disease. Symmetrical swelling of the hands and feet are not typically seen with the other conditions listed.

21. **Answer: B**
    RATIONALE: This response answers the parent's questions. In the nonsevere form, the granulocyte count remains about 500, the platelets are over 20,000, and the reticulocyte count is over 1%. The other responses do not address what the parents are asking and would block therapeutic communication.

22. **Answer: C**
    RATIONALE: Laboratory evaluation will reveal decreased hemoglobin and hematocrit, decreased reticulocyte count, microcytosis and hypochromia,

decreased serum iron and ferritin levels, and increased FEP level. The other findings do not point to iron deficiency anemia.

23. **Answer: A, C, D, E**
    RATIONALE: This girl's erythrocyte count is below normal, which indicates she is anemic. The mean corpuscular Hgb concentration is below normal which indicates that her cells are hypochromic with a diluted amount of Hgb available. The mean corpuscular volume of the erythrocytes are decreased which indicates her cells are microcytic or smaller than normal.

24. **Answer: A, C, D, E**
    RATIONALE: The caregivers should seek medical treatment promptly for any clinical manifestations associated with an infection. The child should receive prophylactic antibiotics. The child should be provided with immunization against the following organisms: *Streptococcus pneumoniae, Neisseria meningitidis,* and *Haemophilus influenzae* type B. The child should be taught techniques to reduce the transmission of infection. The child should wear his medic alert bracelet all the time.

25. **Answer: B, D**
    RATIONALE: Iron supplements should not be mixed in milk because it reduces absorption. Iron supplements may make the child constipated. All of the other options are correct.

26. **Answer: 36**
    RATIONALE: The dose should be calculated using weight in kilograms.
    21.5 kg × 5 mg/1 kg = 107.5 mg/day.
    107.5 mg/3 doses = 35.8333 mg/dose
    Rounded to the nearest whole number = 36 mg

27. **Answer: 3450**
    RATIONALE: Bands + segs/100 × WBC = ANC
    14 + 9 = 23% = 23/100 = 0.23
    0.23 × 15,000 = 3,450

28. **Answer: 0.99**
    RATIONALE: Square root of (height [cm] × weight [kg] divided by 3,600) = BSA.
    The child is 130 cm tall and weighs 27 kg: 130 × 27 = 3,510; 3,510/3,600 = 0.975; and the square root of 0.975 is 0.9874.
    The BSA would be 0.987, when rounded to the hundredths place = 0.99.

29. **Correct Order: A, B, C, D**
    RATIONALE: The bone marrow releases a stem cell. Thrombopoietin acts on the cell to help turn it into a myeloid cell. Erythropoietin acts on the cell and it turns into a megakaryocyte. The megakaryocyte becomes an erythrocyte (red blood cell).

30. **Correct Order: A, B, C, D**
    RATIONALE: During induction, the child receives oral steroids and IV vincristine. During consolidation, the child receives high doses of methotrexate and 6-mercaptopurine. During maintenance, the child receives low doses of methotrexate and 6-mercaptopurine. During central nervous system prophylaxis, the child receives intrathecal chemotherapy.

CHAPTER 47

SECTION I: ASSESSING YOUR UNDERSTANDING

Activity A FILL IN THE BLANKS

1. Self-antigens
2. Chemotaxis
3. Bone marrow
4. Butterfly
5. Peanuts
6. Maculopapular
7. T-helper

Activity B MATCHING

1. e   **2.** d   **3.** b   **4.** a   **5.** c

Activity C SEQUENCING

4 → 2 → 3 → 1

Activity D SHORT ANSWERS

1. The complement system is a series of blood proteins whose action is to augment the work of antibodies by assisting with destruction of bacteria, production of inflammation, and regulation of immune reactions.

2. The enzyme-linked immunosorbant assay (ELISA) method detects only antibodies so results may remain negative for several weeks up to 6 months (false negative). A false-positive result may occur with autoimmune disease.

3. Delayed hypersensitivity reactions are mediated by T-cells rather than antibodies. An infant's skin test response is diminished most likely due to the infant's decreased ability to produce an inflammatory response.

4. If a child acquires HIV infection "vertically" this means the disease was transmitted perinatally, either in utero or through breast milk. Transmission of the disease "horizontally" refers to transmission by nonsterile, HIV-contaminated needles or through unprotected sexual contact; less frequent is contaminated blood product transmission.

5. Avascular necrosis is an adverse effect of long-term use or high dosages of corticosteroids, causing tissue damage to a joint due to lack of blood supply to the joint. Any child receiving long-term or high-dose corticosteroids as treatment, such as a child with systemic lupus erythematosus (SLE), would be at an increased risk of developing this complication.

SECTION II: APPLYING YOUR KNOWLEDGE

Activity E CASE STUDY

1. The discussion should include the following:
   A CBC, which may show a decreased hemoglobin and hematocrit, decreased platelet count, and low white blood cell count.
   Complement levels, C3 and C4, will also be decreased.

Antinuclear antibody (ANA), though not specific to SLE, is usually positive in children with SLE.

2. The discussion should include the following:

There is currently no single laboratory test that can confirm whether a person has lupus. In addition, since many of the symptoms with lupus come and go and tend to be vague, lupus can be difficult to diagnose. The physician will look at the entire medical history along with the results from the laboratory tests to determine whether your daughter has lupus.

3. The discussion should include the following:

Education will focus on the importance of a healthy diet, regular exercise, and adequate sleep and rest. Teach the girl to apply sunscreen (minimum SPF 15) to her skin daily to prevent rashes resulting from photosensitivity. Administer NSAIDs, corticosteroids, and antimalarial agents as ordered. If the girl develops severe SLE or frequent flare-ups of symptoms she may require high-dose (pulse) corticosteroid therapy or medication with immunosuppressive drugs. Teach her to protect against cold weather by layering warm socks and wearing gloves when outdoors in the winter. If she is outside for extended periods during the winter months, educate her about the importance of inspecting her fingers and toes for discoloration. Ensure that yearly vision screening and ophthalmic examinations are performed in order to preserve visual function should any changes occur. Refer the girl and her family to support services such as the Lupus Alliance of America and the Lupus Foundation of America.

SECTION III: PRACTICING FOR NCLEX

Activity F NCLEX-STYLE QUESTIONS

1. **Answer: C**
RATIONALE: Children with Wiskott–Aldrich syndrome should not be given rectal suppositories or temperatures since these children are at a high risk for bleeding. Tub baths are not contraindicated. Pacifiers are not contraindicated in Wiskott–Aldrich but should be kept as sanitary as possible to avoid oral infections.

2. **Answer: D**
RATIONALE: Premedication with diphenhydramine or acetaminophen may be indicted in children who have never received intravenous immunoglobulin (IVIG), have not had an infusion in over 8 weeks, have had a recent bacterial infection, or have history of serious infusion-related adverse reactions. The nurse should first premedicate, and then obtain a baseline physical assessment. Once the infusion begins, the nurse should continually assess for adverse reaction.

3. **Answer: C**
RATIONALE: An epinephrine auto-injector should be jabbed into the outer thigh, as this is a larger muscle, at a 90-degree angle, not into the upper arm. The other statements are correct.

4. **Answer: D**
RATIONALE: The ELISA test will be positive in infants of HIV-infected mothers because of transplacentally received antibodies. These antibodies may persist and remain detectable up to 24 months of age, making the ELISA test less accurate in detecting true HIV infection in infants and toddlers than the polymerase chain reaction (PCR). The PCR test is positive in infected infants over the age of 1 month. The erythrocyte sedimentation rate would be ordered for an immune disorder initial workup or ongoing monitoring of autoimmune disease. Immunoglobulin electrophoresis would be ordered to test for immune deficiency and autoimmune disorders.

5. **Answer: A**
RATIONALE: Older children and adolescents with allergic reactions to fish, shellfish, and nuts usually continue to have that concern as a life-long problem. The other statements are correct.

6. **Answer: D**
RATIONALE: Alopecia and the characteristic malar rash (butterfly rash) on the face are common clinical manifestations of SLE. Rhinorrhea, wheezing, and an enlarged spleen are not hallmark manifestations of SLE. Petechiae and purpura are more commonly associated with hematological disorders, not SLE.

7. **Answer: B**
RATIONALE: The parents must understand that their child cannot consume any part of an egg in any form. The other statements are accurate.

8. **Answer: B**
RATIONALE: Lip edema, urticaria, stridor, and tachycardia are common clinical manifestations of anaphylaxis.

9. **Answer: C**
RATIONALE: The nurse should instruct children and their families to avoid foods with a known cross-reactivity to latex, such as bananas.

10. **Answer: A**
RATIONALE: Polyarticular JIA is defined by the involvement of five or more joints, frequently the small joints, and affects the body symmetrically. Pauciarticular *JIAs* is defined by the involvement of four or fewer joints. Systemic JIA presents with fever and rash in addition to join involvement at the time of diagnosis. The child with JIA is not at greater risk for anaphylaxis.

11. **Answer: B, C, D, E**
RATIONALE: The following are common signs and symptoms of anaphylaxis: tongue edema, urticaria, nausea, vomiting, and syncope. Typically, the child who has developed anaphylaxis will be tachycardic.

12. **Answer: B, C, D**
RATIONALE: IVIG should be given only intravenously and should not be given as an intramuscular injection. IVIG cannot be mixed with other medications. The nurse should closely monitor the child's vital signs during the infusion of the IVIG. The child may require an antipyretic and/or an antihistamine during infusion to help with fever and chills.

13. **Answer: B, C, E**
   RATIONALE: The following children may have a primary immunodeficiency: a child with a persistent case of oral candidiasis, a child who has been diagnosed with pneumonia at least twice during the previous year, and a child who has taken antibiotics for 2 months or longer with little effect.

14. **Answer: A, D, E**
   RATIONALE: The child diagnosed with JIA should not take the oral form of methotrexate with dairy products. The approximate time to benefit from methotrexate is typically 3 to 6 weeks. The child will need blood tests to determine renal and liver function during treatment. Children with juvenile idiopathic arthritis usually find swimming to be useful exercise for them because it helps maintain joint mobility without placing pressure on the joints. Sleep may be promoted by a warm bath at bedtime.

15. **Answer: D**
   RATIONALE: This child's symptoms are consistent with systemic lupus erythematosus (SLE), which is usually treated with corticosteroids. Antiretrovirals, IVIG, and phototherapy are of no benefit in the treatment of SLE.

CHAPTER 48

SECTION I: ASSESSING YOUR UNDERSTANDING

Activity A FILL IN THE BLANKS

1. Langerhans
2. Exophthalmos
3. Polyuria
4. Tetany
5. Kussmaul
6. Deficiency
7. Hyperthyroidism

Activity B LABELING

Areas on the body corresponding with insulin injection sites.

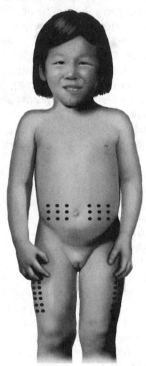
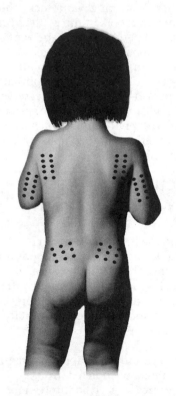

Activity C MATCHING

1. e   2. c   3. b   4. a   5. d

Activity D SEQUENCING

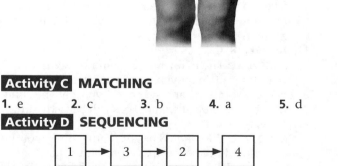

Activity E SHORT ANSWERS

1. Diet should be low in fats and concentrated carbohydrates. Lists of foods high in carbohydrates, protein, and fat should be provided. The parents need to understand the need to plan for periods of rapid growth, travel, school parties, and holidays. Referring the parents to a nutritionist with diabetes expertise will be helpful. There should be a plan for three meals and two snacks per day in order to maintain blood glucose levels. Regular exercise should be encouraged, as well as participation in age-appropriate sports. The parents should be reminded of the importance of monitoring the insulin dose, food and fluid intake, and hypoglycemic reactions when exercising.

2.

Hypothyroidism	Hyperthyroidism
Nervousness/anxiety	Tiredness/fatigue
Diarrhea	Constipation
Heat intolerance	Cold intolerance
Weight loss	Weight gain
Smooth, velvet-like skin	Dry, thick skin; edema on the face, eyes, and hands
	Decreased growth

3. Nursing implications when teaching, discussing, and caring for children with diabetes mellitus (DM) are as follows:

   a. Infants and toddlers: Attempt to achieve consistent dietary intake. Give the toddler foods to choose from. Help the toddler to find and use a word or phrase to describe feelings when hypoglycemic symptoms occur. Establish rituals/routines with home management.

   b. Preschoolers: Use simple explanations and play therapy when instructing or preparing for a procedure or situation related to the disorder.

   c. School age: Use concise and concrete terms when instructing. Allow children to proceed at their own rate. Assist the family to incorporate the testing and injections into the school day and plan for field trips. Use the school nurse's assistance and help with the school plan.

   d. Adolescents: Care can be slowly turned over to an adolescent with minor supervision from family. Watch for depression in this age group.

4. *Healthy People 2020* recommends screening all children periodically to identify early signs of overweight or obesity based on CDC guidelines. In addition, families should receive education regarding appropriate diet and exercise early during the toddler years in an attempt to prevent obesity, thus decreasing the likelihood of diabetes.

5. The nurse should instruct the family to report headaches, rapid weight gain, increased thirst or urination, or painful hip or knee joints as possible adverse reactions.

SECTION II: APPLYING YOUR KNOWLEDGE
Activity F CASE STUDY

1. The discussion should include the following:

In the past, DM type 2 occurred in adults with only a small percentage of cases seen in childhood. Since the early 1990s, the incidence has increased significantly in children. Many of these children have a relative with type 2 DM or they have other risk factors such as being overweight, African American, Hispanic American, Asian American, or Native American heritage.

Type 2 DM begins when the pancreas usually produces insulin but the body develops a resistance to insulin or no longer uses the insulin properly. As the need for insulin rises, the pancreas gradually loses its ability to produce sufficient amounts of insulin to regulate blood sugar. Eventually, insulin production decreases with the result similar to type 1 DM.

2. The discussion should include the following:

Nursing management will focus on regulating glucose control, monitoring for complications, and educating and supporting the child and family. Other important interventions involve nutritional guidelines and exercise protocols.

3. The discussion should include challenges related to educating children with diabetes:

   • Children lack the maturity to understand the long-term consequences of this serious chronic illness.

   • Children do not want to be different from their peers and having to make lifestyle changes may result in anger or depression.

   • Families may demonstrate unhealthy behaviors making it difficult for the child to initiate change because of the lack of supervision or role modeling.

   • Family dynamics are impacted because management of diabetes must occur all day, every day.

SECTION III: PRACTICING FOR NCLEX
Activity G NCLEX-STYLE QUESTIONS

1. Answer: D

   RATIONALE: Administering intravenous calcium gluconate, as ordered, will restore normal calcium and phosphate levels as well as relieve severe tetany. Ensuring patency of the IV site to prevent tissue damage due to extravasation or cardiac arrhythmias is an intervention for any child with an IV, and monitoring fluid intake and urinary calcium output are secondary interventions. Providing administration of calcium and vitamin D is an intervention for nonacute symptoms.

2. Answer: B

   RATIONALE: Pubic hair and hirsutism in a preschooler indicates congenital adrenal hyperplasia. Irregular heartbeat on auscultation and pain due to constipation on palpation may be signs of hyperparathyroidism. Hyperpigmentation of the skin suggests Addison disease.

3. Answer: A

   RATIONALE: This child may have syndrome of inappropriate antidiuretic hormone (SIADH). Priority intervention for this child is to notify the physician of the neurologic findings. Remaining interventions will be to restore fluid balance with IV sodium chloride to correct hyponatremia, set up safety precautions to prevent injury due to altered level of consciousness, and monitor fluid intake, urine volume, and specific gravity.

4. Answer: C

   RATIONALE: Monitoring blood glucose levels during this study is the priority task along with observing for signs of hypoglycemia since insulin is given during the test to stimulate release of growth hormone. Providing a wet washcloth would be more appropriate for a child who is on therapeutic fluid restriction, such as with syndrome of inappropriate antidiuretic hormone. Monitoring intake and output would not be necessary for this test but would be appropriate for a child with diabetes insipidus. While it is important to educate the family about this test, it is not the priority task.

5. **Answer: B**
   RATIONALE: Observation of an enlarged tongue along with an enlarged posterior fontanel and feeding difficulties are key findings for congenital hypothyroidism. The mother would report constipation rather than diarrhea. Auscultation would reveal bradycardia rather than tachycardia, and palpation would reveal cool, dry, and scaly skin.

6. **Answer: A**
   RATIONALE: Observation of acanthosis nigricans in addition to the obesity and amenorrhea is a further indication of polycystic ovary syndrome. Reports of blurred vision and headaches are signs and symptoms of diabetes mellitus. Increased respiratory rate on auscultation points to diabetes insipidus. Hypertrophy and weakness on palpation is typical of hypothyroidism.

7. **Answer: A**
   RATIONALE: A history of rapid weight gain and long-term corticosteroid therapy suggests this child may have Cushing disease, which could be confirmed using an adrenal suppression test. A round, child-like face is common to both Cushing and growth hormone deficiency. A high weight to height ratio and delayed dentition are findings with growth hormone deficiency.

8. **Answer: C**
   RATIONALE: The primary nursing diagnosis would be deficient fluid volume related to electrolyte imbalance. It is important to increase the child's hydration to minimize renal calculi formation. Disturbed body image related to hormone dysfunction is a diagnosis for growth hormone deficiency. Imbalanced nutrition: more than body requirements would be important for a child with diabetes mellitus. Deficient knowledge related to treatment of the disease is appropriate for hyperparathyroidism, but it is not a priority diagnosis.

9. **Answer: D**
   RATIONALE: Side effects of hypothyroidism are restlessness, inability to sleep, or irritability. These should be reported to the physician. Educating how to recognize vitamin D toxicity is necessary for a child with hypoparathyroidism. Teaching parents how to maintain fluid intake regimens is important for a child with diabetes insipidus. Teaching the child and parents to administer methimazole with meals is necessary for hyperthyroidism.

10. **Answer: A, C**
    RATIONALE: Delayed puberty in the female is indicated if she has not developed breasts by the age of 13; delayed puberty in the male is indicated if

he has had no testicular enlargement by the age of 14. In females, pubic hair should appear before the age of 14. In males, pubic hair should appear before the age of 15 and scrotal changes by the age of 14.

11. **Answer: A, B, C**
    RATIONALE: Signs and symptoms related to the development of thyroid storm include fever, diaphoresis, and tachycardia. Children with thyroid storm are typically restless and irritable.

12. **Answer: B**
    RATIONALE: Instructing child to rotate injection sites to decrease scar formation is important, but does not focus on managing glucose levels. Teaching the child and family to eat a balanced diet, encouraging the child to maintain the proper injection schedule, and promoting a higher level of exercise all focus on regulating glucose control.

13. **Answer: 393**
    RATIONALE: The dose should be calculated using weight in kilograms.
    32.727 kg × 12 μg/1 kg = 392.727 μg
    Rounded to the nearest whole number = 393 μg

14. **Answer: 0.075**
    RATIONALE: The dose should be calculated using weight in kilograms.
    26.3636 kg × 0.2 mg/1 kg = 0.5273 mg of growth hormone per week.
    0.5273 mg/week × 1 week/7 days = 0.0753 mg/day.

15. **Correct Order: A, B, C, D**
    RATIONALE: Lispro is a rapid-acting insulin. Humulin R is a short-acting insulin. Humulin N is an intermediate-acting insulin. Lantus is a long-acting insulin.

CHAPTER 49

SECTION I: ASSESSING YOUR UNDERSTANDING

Activity A FILL IN THE BLANKS

1. Alleles
2. Consanguinity
3. Phenotype
4. Heterozygous
5. Nondisjunction
6. Genome
7. Chromosome

Activity B MATCHING

1. d   2. e   3. a   4. c   5. b

Activity C SHORT ANSWERS

1. Complications of Down syndrome include cardiac defects, hearing or vision impairment, developmental delays, mental retardation, gastrointestinal disorders, recurrent infections, atlantoaxial instability, thyroid disease, and sleep apnea.

2. Building a relationship of trust, empathizing with and understanding the family's stresses and emotions, rejecting personal bias, encouraging open discussion.

3. Phenylketonuria excretions exhibit a mousy or musty order caused by a deficiency of the liver enzyme that processes phenylalanine; children with maple syrup urine disease have a maple syrup odor associated with a deficiency of the enzyme that metabolizes leucine, isoleucine, and valine; children with tyrosinemia have excretions with a rancid butter or cabbage like odor as a result of a deficiency of the enzyme that metabolizes tyrosine; and excretions have a rotting fish odor with the disorder trimethylaminuria, resulting from the body's inability to normally produce flavin (which breaks down trimethylamine).

4. Trisomy 21, also known as Down syndrome, occurs in 1 in 730 births across all maternal ages and socioeconomic levels, and 85% of trisomy 21 conceptions result in spontaneous abortion. It is the most common genetic defect that is linked with intellectual disability. The incidence is 1 in 1,000 for women younger than 30. The highest incidence of the disorder occurs in mothers who are over 35 years of age, with the likelihood of having a trisomy 21 baby is 1 in 353 at the age of 35, 1 in 85 at the age of 40, and 1 in 35 at the age of 45.

5. The infant with trisomy 13 will likely display a microcephalic head with wide sagittal suture and fontanels. Other physical features include malformed ears, small eyes, extra digits, cleft lip and palate, and severe hypotonia. Severe intellectual disability will most likely be exhibited as the child ages.

SECTION II: APPLYING YOUR KNOWLEDGE

Activity D CASE STUDY

1. The discussion should include the following:

Newborn screening is done to detect disorders before symptoms develop. Recent developments in screening techniques allow many metabolic disorders or inborn errors of metabolism to be detected early. Chloe's test results tell us that additional testing is needed to rule out a false positive or confirm the diagnosis. Most inborn errors of metabolism presenting in the neonatal period are lethal or can result in serious complications such as mental retardation if specific treatment is not initiated immediately. This is why it is so important that you came in today for additional testing.

2. The discussion should include the following:

In fatty acid oxidation disorders (such as medium-chain acyl-CoA dehydrogenase deficiency) the goal is to prevent or avoid prolonged fasts and to provide frequent feedings. Special consideration during illness is very important. If Chloe is unable to tolerate food she needs to be seen by a physician immediately; intravenous dextrose may be required. Supplementation with specific vitamins may also be important in the treatment and a dietician and the physician will work with you. Strict adherence to frequent meals is necessary to prevent complications from arising.

Nursing management will focus on education and support for the family and caregivers. Ensure they have thorough knowledge about medium-chain acyl-CoA dehydrogenase deficiency and its management. Refer the family to a dietician and other appropriate resources, including support groups. Monitor the developmental progress of Chloe and initiate therapies if concern arises.

SECTION III: PRACTICING FOR NCLEX

Activity E NCLEX-STYLE QUESTIONS

1. **Answer: B, C, E**
   RATIONALE: Numerous café-au-lait spots on the trunk of the child, a slightly larger head size due to abnormal development of the skull, and abnormal curvature of the spine (especially scoliosis) are clinical signs of this disorder. A first-degree relative rather than a second-degree relative having had neurofibromatosis is a risk factor for the disorder, and freckles in the child's axilla and groin, not the lower extremities, are symptoms of the disorder. Two or more clinical signs and symptoms of the disorder must be present for a diagnosis to be made.

2. **Answer: B, C, D, E**
   RATIONALE: Although children with Marfan syndrome have a number of physical problems, respiratory conditions are not one of them, so it would not be appropriate to arrange in home respiratory therapy. The other interventions are needed for children with Marfan syndrome, because they do have ophthalmologic, orthopedic, and cardiac problems.

3. **Answer: D**
   RATIONALE: Angelman syndrome is characterized by jerky ataxic movements, similar to a puppet's gait. Hypotonicity is a symptom of Angelman syndrome as well as Prader–Willi syndrome, and Cri du chat. Cleft palate is a symptom of velo-cardio-facial/DiGeorge syndrome.

4. **Answer: B**
   RATIONALE: The priority intervention is to assess the family's ability to learn about the disorder. The family needs time to adjust to the diagnosis and be ready to learn for teaching to be effective. Screening to determine current level of functioning, explaining the care required due to the disorder, and educating the family about available resources are interventions that can be taken once the family is ready.

5. **Answer: C**
   RATIONALE: Children with phenylketonuria will have a musty or mousy odor to their urine, as well as an eczema-like rash, irritability, and vomiting. Increased reflex action and seizures are typical of maple sugar urine disease. Signs of jaundice, diarrhea, and vomiting are typical of galactosemia. Seizures are a sign of biotinidase deficiency or maple sugar urine disease.

6. **Answer: D**
RATIONALE: The nurse would likely find records of corrective surgery for anal atresia because it is a symptom of VATER association. The nurse may observe that the child has a hearing deficit, under-developed labia, and a coloboma, along with heart disease, retarded growth and development, and choanal atresia if the child had CHARGE syndrome.

7. **Answer: A**
RATIONALE: A major anomaly is an anomaly or malformation that creates significant medical prob-lems and requires surgical or medical management. Café-au-lait spots are a major anomaly. Polydactyly, or extra digits, syndactyly, or webbed digits, and protruding ears are minor anomalies. Minor anom-alies are features that vary from those that are most commonly seen in the general population but do not cause an increase in morbidity in and of themselves.

8. **Answer: B**
RATIONALE: Galactosemia is a deficiency in the liver enzyme needed to convert galactose into glucose. This means the child will have to eliminate milk and dairy products from her diet for life. Adhering to a low phenylalanine diet is an intervention for phenylketonuria. Eating frequent meals and never fasting is an intervention for medium-chain acyl-CoA dehydrogenase deficiency. Maple sugar urine disease requires a low-protein diet and supplementation with thiamine.

9. **Answer: C**
RATIONALE: Children with Sturge–Weber syndrome will have a facial nevus, or port wine stain, most often seen on the forehead and one eye. While the child may experience seizures, retardation, and behavior problems, they are not definitive findings.

10. **Answer: C, D, E**
RATIONALE: Boys with Klinefelter syndrome may have learning disabilities, underdeveloped testes, and gynecomastia. Typically, they have long legs and short torsos and are taller than their peers.

11. **Answer: C, D, E**
RATIONALE: Babies born with trisomy 18 may have been born with a congenital cardiac defect, web-bing between digits and low-set ears. Microcephaly and the development of extra digits are not associated with trisomy 18.

12. **Answer: B**
RATIONALE: This disorder is not X-linked. Either father or mother can pass the gene along regardless of whether their mate has the gene or not. The only way that an autosomal dominant gene is not expressed is if it does not exist. If only one of the parents has the gene, then there is a 50% chance it will be passed on to the child.

13. **Answer: A, B, D**
RATIONALE: The following are risk factors for genetic disorders: oligohydramnios, paternal age over 50, a family history of genetic disorders, positive alpha-fetoprotein test, and multiple births.

14. **Answer: A, B, C**
RATIONALE: Monogenic disorders (caused by a single gene that is defective) include autosomal dominant, autosomal recessive, X-linked dominant, and X-linked recessive disorders. Mitochondrial inheritance and genomic imprinting are considered multifactorial disorders (caused by multiple gene and environmental factors).

15. **Answer: B, C, D, E**
RATIONALE: The following people should receive genetic counseling: paternal age over 50, the presence of consanguinity, parents of African descent, and those parents who have a child at home who was born blind or deaf. A mother-to-be over the age of 35 may also benefit from genetic counseling.

CHAPTER 50

SECTION I: ASSESSING YOUR UNDERSTANDING

Activity A FILL IN THE BLANKS

1. Bowel
2. 6
3. Dyslexia
4. Stocking
5. Neglect
6. Munchausen syndrome by proxy (MSbP)
7. Autism spectrum disorder (ASD)

Activity B LABELING

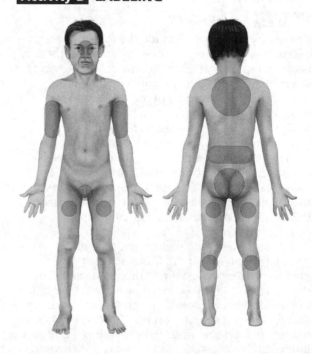

● Common nonaccidental injury sites

Activity C MATCHING

1. b   **2.** a   **3.** d   **4.** e   **5.** c

Activity D SHORT ANSWERS

1. Behavior management techniques include the following:
   - Set limits with the child, holding him responsible for his behavior
   - Do not argue, bargain, or negotiate about the limits once established
   - Provide consistent caregivers (unlicensed assistive personnel and nurses for the hospitalized child) and establish the child's daily routine
   - Use a low-pitched voice and remain calm
   - Redirect the child's attention when needed
   - Ignore inappropriate behaviors
   - Praise the child's self-control efforts and other accomplishments
   - Utilize restraints only when absolutely necessary

2. Radiographic skeletal survey or bone scan, CT scan of the head, and rectal, oral, vaginal or urethral specimens.

3. Generalized anxiety disorder (GAD) is characterized by unrealistic concerns over past behavior, future events, and personal competency. Social phobia may result in which the child or teen demonstrates a persistent fear of formal speaking, eating in front of others, using public restrooms, or speaking to authorities.

4. Obtain a health history from the adolescent and his parents separately. Assess for a history of recent changes in behavior, alterations in school, changes in peer relationships, withdrawal from previously enjoyed activities, sleep disturbances, changes in eating behaviors, and an increase in accidents or sexual promiscuity. Ask about potential stressors, conflicts with parents or peers, school concerns, dating issues, and abusive events. If possible utilize a standardized depression screening questionnaire.

   Assess for history of weight loss. Observe for apparent apathy. Inspect the entire body surface for the presence of self-inflicted injuries which may or may not be present.

   Assess for risk factors of suicide including a change in school performance, changes in sleep or appetite, disinterest in former preferred activities, expressing feeling of hopelessness, depression, thoughts of suicide, and any previous attempts at suicide.

5. The most common classifications of medication used for the management of ADHD include psycho-stimulants, nonstimulant norepinephrine reuptake inhibitors and/or alpha-agonist antihypertensive agents. The goal of treatment with medication is to help increase the child's ability to pay attention and to increase the ability to control impulsive behavior. Medications for ADHD do not cure the disorder.

SECTION II: APPLYING YOUR KNOWLEDGE

Activity E CASE STUDY

1. The discussion should include the following:
   ASD is a developmental disorder that has its onset in infancy or early childhood. Autistic behaviors may be first noted in infancy as developmental delays or between 12 months and 36 months when the child loses previously acquired skills. Children with ASD demonstrate impairments in social interactions and communication. The exact cause of autism is unknown; it is believed to be linked to genetics, brain abnormalities, altered chemistry, a virus, or toxic chemicals. The spectrum of the disorder ranges from mild to severe.

2. The discussion should include the following:
   Warning signs of autism that may be seen with infants and toddlers include no babbling and no pointing or using gestures by 12 months of age; by 16 months of age the child is not using single words and by 24 months of age is not using any two-word phrases; and the child exhibits loss of language or social skills at any age.

SECTION III: PRACTICING FOR NCLEX

Activity F NCLEX-STYLE QUESTIONS

1. **Answer: B**
   RATIONALE: An IQ of 35 to 50 is classified as moderate. An IQ of 50 to 70 is classified as mild. An IQ of 20 to 35 is classified as severe, and an IQ less than 20 is considered profound.

2. **Answer: B**
   RATIONALE: It is important to continue the usual routine of the hospitalized child, particularly of children with intellectual challenge. By asking an open-ended question about a typical day, the nurse can identify the routine activities that can potentially be duplicated in the hospital. Telling the girl she will be going home soon or asking about art supplies does not address her concerns. Asking whether she has talked to her parents is unhelpful at this time.

3. **Answer: B**
   RATIONALE: Typical FAS facial features include a low nasal bridge with short upturned nose, flattened midface, and a long filtrum with narrow upper lip. Microcephaly rather than macrocephaly is associated with FAS. Clubbing of fingers is associated with chronic hypoxia.

4. **Answer: D, E**
   RATIONALE: Children diagnosed with dyslexia and dysgraphia experience difficulty with reading, writing, spelling, and producing written words.

5. **Answer: B**
   RATIONALE: The nurse should pay particular attention to reports of a child spending hours in a repetitive activity, such as lining up cars rather than playing them. Most 3-year olds are very busy and would rather play than sit on a parent's lap. The other statements are not outside the range of normal and do not warrant further investigation.

6. **Answer: C**
   RATIONALE: The nurse should encourage the family to explore with their physician the option of one of the newer extended release or once daily ADHD medications. The other statements are not

helpful and do not address the mother's or boy's concerns.

7. **Answer: B**
RATIONALE: Sudden, rapid, stereotypical sounds are a hallmark finding with Tourette syndrome. Toe walking and unusual behaviors such as hand-flapping and spinning are indicative of autism spectrum disorder (ASD). Lack of eye contact is associated with ASD but is also noted in children without a mental health disorder.

8. **Answer: C**
RATIONALE: The nurse should emphasize the importance of rigid unchanging routines as children with ASD often act out when their routine changes. The other statements would not warrant additional referral or follow-up.

9. **Answer: A**
RATIONALE: The nurse should be aware that rapid nutritional replacement in the severely malnourished can lead to refeeding syndrome. Refeeding syndrome is characterized by cardiovascular, hematologic, and neurologic complications such as cardiac arrhythmias, confusion, and seizures. Orthostatic hypotension, hypertension, and irregular and decreased pulses are complications of anorexia but do not characterize refeeding syndrome.

10. **Answer: A**
RATIONALE: The nurse should be sure to carefully assess the mouth and oropharynx for eroded dental enamel, red gums, and inflamed throat from self-induced vomiting. The other findings are typically noted with anorexia nervosa.

11. **Answer: C**
RATIONALE: It is important to remind the parents that medications for the management of ADHD are not a cure but help to increase the child's ability to pay attention and decrease the level of impulsive behavior. The other statements are correct.

12. **Answer: A, B, C**
RATIONALE: An 18-month-old toddler should have babbled by 12 months. He should be using gestures and using single words to communicate. The use of sentences to communicate and the ability to stand on tiptoe would be expected later.

13. **Answer: B, D, E**
RATIONALE: Common side effects related to the use of psychostimulants are headaches, irritability, and abdominal pain. Children typically exhibit a decreased appetite and may have difficulty with insomnia.

14. **Answer: A, B**
RATIONALE: The parents should use a calm, low-pitched voice when communicating with her. They should ignore inappropriate behaviors. The parents should not argue or bargain with the child about set limits. They should praise the child for accomplishments and help the child see the importance of accountability for her own behavior.

15. **Answer: A, B, D**
RATIONALE: Altered sleep patterns, weight loss, and problems at school are commonly found in children with mental health disorders. There also may be alterations in friendships and changes in extracurricular activity participation.

CHAPTER 51

SECTION I: ASSESSING YOUR UNDERSTANDING

Activity A FILL IN THE BLANKS

1. Pediatric
2. "LEAN"
3. Airway
4. Pupil
5. Cyanosis
6. Jaw-thrust
7. Femoral

Activity B LABELING

A = Sinus tachycardia: normal QRS and P waves, mild beat-to-beat variability.

B = Supraventricular tachycardia (SVT): note rate above 220, abnormal P waves, no beat-to-beat variability.

C = Ventricular tachycardia: rapid and regular rhythm, wide QRS without P waves.

D = Coarse ventricular fibrillation: chaotic electrical activity.

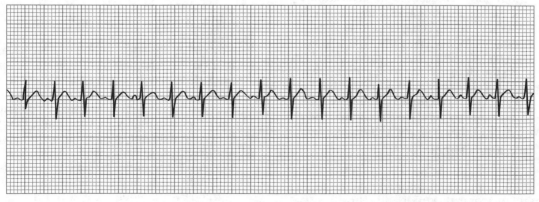

A

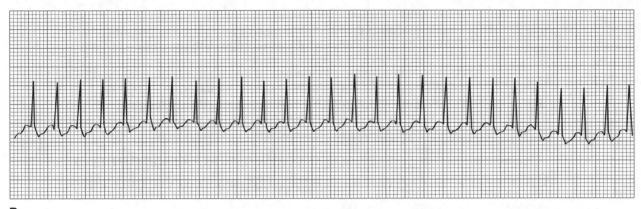

B

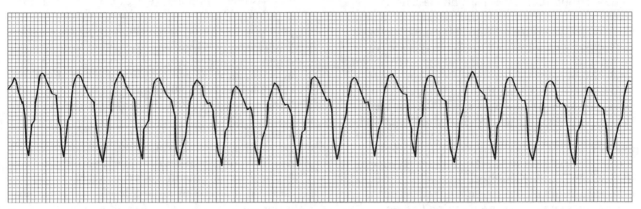

C

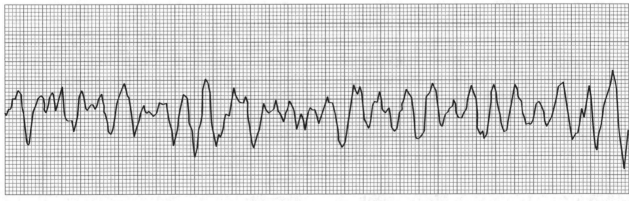

D

Activity C MATCHING

1. c   **2.** a   **3.** b   **4.** e   **5.** d

Activity D SEQUENCING

4 → 5 → 1 → 3 → 2

Activity E SHORT ANSWERS

1. Infant:
- One-person CPR: 30 compressions to two breaths; Hand placement: two fingers placed one finger breadth below the nipple line
- Two-person CPR: 15 compression to two breaths; Hand placement: two thumbs encircling the chest at the nipple line

Child:
- One-person CPR: 30 compressions to two breaths; Hand placement: heel of one hand or two hands (adult position in larger child) pressing on the sternum at the nipple line
- Two-person CPR: 15 compressions to two breaths; Hand placement: heel of one hand or two hands (adult position in larger child) pressing on the sternum at the nipple line

2.

	SVT	Sinus Tachycardia
Rate (beats/ minute)	Infants >220, children >180	Infants <220, children <180
Rhythm	Abrupt onset and termination	Beat to beat variability
P-waves	Flattened	Present and normal
QRS	Narrow (less than 0.08 seconds)	Normal
History	Usually none significant	Fever, fluid loss, hypoxia, pain, fear

3. Choose an appropriate size bag and mask using a Broselow tape or referring to the code reference sheet. Connect the bag valve mask (BVM) via the tubing to the oxygen source and turn on the oxygen. Set the flow rate at approximately 10 L/minute for infants and small children, and 15 L/minute for an adolescent who is adult-sized. Check to make sure that the oxygen is flowing through the tubing to the bag. Open the airway. Place the mask over the child's face. Use the thumb and index finger of one hand to hold the mask on the child's face, and the other hand to squeeze the resuscitator bag. Use upward pressure on the jaw angle while pressing downward on the mask below the child's mouth to keep the mouth open.

4. Cricoid pressure may be used during the ventilation portion of resuscitative efforts to prevent gastric distention, possibly leading to vomiting and aspiration, during ventilation. Pressure is used to occlude the esophagus so that air does not enter the stomach during ventilation.

5. The mnemonic is used to assist in determining a worsening respiratory status of a child who is intubated. Each letter represents possible problems that require further assessment:
   D: Displacement of the tracheal intubation tube
   O: Obstruction of the tracheal intubation tube from mucus of other sources
   P: Pneumothorax
   E: Equipment failure

SECTION II: APPLYING YOUR KNOWLEDGE

Activity F CASE STUDY

1. The discussion should include the following:
   The use of AEDs on children was not recommended by the AHA until 2005. If the child is over 1 year of age and the emergency is a sudden witnessed collapse, the AHA suggests the use of an AED; this recommendation comes from the result of studies indicating that the AED can be sensitive and specific for detecting and treating arrhythmia by defibrillation in this population.

2. The discussion should include the following:
   The chain of survival for children differs from the adult chain of survival due to the common causes of pediatric versus adult cardiopulmonary arrest. These differences affect the priority of steps during an emergency. The pediatric chain of survival begins with prevention of cardiac arrest and injuries, followed by early CPR, then early access to the emergency response system, and ends with early advanced care. The adult chain of survival begins with activation of the EMS, followed by early CPR, then early defibrillation, and ends with early access to advanced care.

SECTION III: PRACTICING FOR NCLEX

Activity G NCLEX-STYLE QUESTIONS

1. **Answer: C**
   RATIONALE: The American Heart Association (AHA) emphasizes the importance of cardiac compressions in pulseless clients with arrhythmias, making this the priority intervention in this situation. Current AHA recommendations are for defibrillation to be administered once followed by five cycles of CPR. The AHA now recommends against using multiple doses of epinephrine because they have not been shown to be helpful and may actually cause harm to the child.

2. **Answer: A**
   RATIONALE: The nurse would be suspicious of a 7-month-old climbing out of his crib, since it is not consistent with his developmental stage. Other areas of concern are if the parents have different accounts of the accident and if the injury is not consistent with the type of accident.

3. **Answer: A**
   RATIONALE: Due to the potentially devastating effects of drowning-related hypoxia on a child's brain, airway interventions must be initiated immediately. The child's airway should be suctioned to ensure patency. Other interventions such as covering the child with blankets, inserting a nasogastric tube, and assuring that the child remains still during x-ray are interventions that are appropriate once airway patency is achieved and maintained.

4. **Answer: B**
   RATIONALE: Unilateral absent breath sounds are associated with foreign body aspiration. Dullness on percussion over the lung is indicative of fluid consolidation in the lung as with pneumonia. Auscultating a low-pitched, grating breath sound suggests inflammation of the pleura. Hearing a hyperresonant sound on percussion may indicate pneumothorax or asthma.

5. **Answer: B**
   RATIONALE: An adolescent, not a 9-year old, would most likely require an oxygen flow rate of 15 L/minute for effective ventilation. A flow rate of 10 L/minute is appropriate for infants and children. All other options are valid for preparing to ventilate with a bag valve mask.

6. **Answer: C**
   RATIONALE: Decrease skin turgor is a late sign of shock. Blood pressure is not a reliable method of

evaluating for shock in children because they tend to maintain normal or slightly below normal blood pressure in compensated shock. Equal central and distal pulses are not a sign of shock. Delayed capillary refill with cool extremities are signs of shock that occur earlier than changes in skin turgor.

7. **Answer: D**
RATIONALE: Once the ABCs have been evaluated, the nurse will move on to "D" and assess for disability by palpating the anterior fontanel for signs of increased intracranial pressure. Observing skin color and perfusion is part of evaluating circulation. Palpating the abdomen for soreness and auscultating for bowel sounds would be part of the full-body examination that follows assessing for disability.

8. **Answer: B**
RATIONALE: Inserting a small, folded towel under shoulders best positions the infant's airway in the "sniff" position as is recommended by the American Heart Association (AHA) Basic Cardiac Life Support (BCLS) guidelines. The hand should never be placed under the neck to open the airway. The head tilt chin lift technique and the jaw-thrust maneuver are used with children over the age of 1 year.

9. **Answer: B**
RATIONALE: Exhaled CO_2 monitoring is recommended when a child has been intubated. It provides quick, visual assurance that the tracheal tube remains in place and that the child is being adequately ventilated. When moving the child, maintaining tube placement would be crucial. The other interventions would also be appropriate but not as essential as monitoring the child's exhaled CO_2 level. Unlike the other interventions, exhaled CO_2 monitoring can provide an early sign of a problem.

10. **Answer: C**
RATIONALE: Attaining central venous access is the priority intervention for a child in shock who is receiving respiratory support. Gaining access via the femoral route will not interfere with CPR efforts. Peripheral venous access may be unattainable in children who have significant vascular compromise. Blood samples and urinary catheter placement can wait until fluid is administered.

11. **Answer: 6**
RATIONALE: The following formula should be used to calculate the correct tracheal tube size for a child: Divide the child's age by 4 and add 4 = size in millimeters

$$(8 \text{ years old}/4) + 4 = 6 \text{ mm}$$

12. **Answer: 5,700**
RATIONALE: Cardiac output (CO) is equal to heart rate (HR) times ventricular stroke volume (SV). That is, $CO = HR \times SV$

$$76 \text{ beats per minute} \times 75 \text{ mL} = 5,700$$

13. **Answer: 25**
RATIONALE: Urine output should be calculated using weight in kilograms.

$$25.46 \text{ kg} \times 1 \text{ mL/kg} = 25.46 \text{ mL/hour}$$

The child must produce 25 mL/hour

14. **Answer: 709**
RATIONALE: Dose should be calculated using weight in kilograms.

$$35.456 \text{ kg} \times 20 \text{ mL/kg} = 709.1 \text{ mL}$$

When rounded to the nearest whole number = 709 mL

15. **Answer: 84**
RATIONALE: Use the following formula (according to Pediatric Advanced Life Support (PALS):

$$70 + (2 \text{ times the age in years})$$

The minimal systolic BP of a 7-year old is
$70 = (2 \times 7) = 84$.